The
MX Book
of
New
Sherlock
Holmes
Stories

Part XXXVI
"However Improbable . . . ."
(1897-1919)

THE MX BOOK OF NEW
SHERLOCK HOLMES
STORIES

PART XXXVI
"HOWEVER IMPROBABLE...."
(1897-1919)

SOUTHAMPTON
STREET

359

EDITED
By
David
Marcum

OFFICES

TRADITIONAL HOLMES
ADVENTURES
COMPILED FOR THE
BENEFIT OF THE
RESTORATION OF
UNDERSHAW

First edition published in 2022
© Copyright 2022

ISBN Hardback 978-1-80424-113-4
ISBN Paperback 978-1-80424-114-1
AUK ePub ISBN 978-1-80424-115-8
AUK PDF ISBN 978-1-80424-116-5

Published in the UK by
MX Publishing
335 Princess Park Manor, Royal Drive,
London, N11 3GX
www.mxpublishing.co.uk

David Marcum can be reached at:
thepapersofsherlockholmes@gmail.com

Cover design by Brian Belanger
www.belangerbooks.com and *www.redbubble.com/people/zhahadun*

Internal Illustrations by Sidney Paget

CONTENTS

Forewords

Adventures

(Continued on the next page . . . .)

(Continued on the next page . . . .)

(Continued on the next page . . . .)

**These additional Sherlock Holmes adventures
can be found in the previous volumes of**
The MX Book of New Sherlock Holmes Stories

(Continued on the next page . . . .)

PART III: 1896-1929

PART IV – 2016 Annual

(Continued on the next page . . . .)

PART V – Christmas Adventures

(Continued on the next page . . . .)

PART VI – 2017 Annual

(Continued on the next page . . . .)

PART VII – Eliminate the Impossible: 1880-1891

PART VIII – Eliminate the Impossible: 1892-1905

(Continued on the next page . . . .)

Part IX – 2018 Annual (1879-1895)

(Continued on the next page . . . .)

Part X – 2018 Annual (1896-1916)

Part XI: Some Untold Cases (1880-1891)

(Continued on the next page . . . .)

Part XII: Some Untold Cases (1894-1902)

PART XIII: 2019 Annual (1881-1890)

(Continued on the next page . . . .)

PART XIV: 2019 Annual (1891 -1897)

(Continued on the next page . . . .)

(Continued on the next page . . . .)

Part XVII – Whatever Remains . . . Must Be the Truth (1891-1898)

Part XVIII – Whatever Remains . . . Must Be the Truth (1899-1925)

(Continued on the next page . . . .)

Part XIX: 2020 Annual (1882-1890)

(Continued on the next page . . . .)

The Adventure of the Matched Set – Peter Coe Verbica
When the Prince First Dined at the Diogenes Club – Sean M. Wright
The Sweetenbury Safe Affair – Tim Gambrell

Part XX: 2020 Annual (1891-1897)
Foreword – John Lescroart
Foreword – Roger Johnson
Foreword – Lizzy Butler
Foreword – Steve Emecz
Foreword – David Marcum
The Sibling (*A Poem*) – Jacquelynn Morris
Blood and Gunpowder – Thomas A. Burns, Jr.
The Atelier of Death – Harry DeMaio
The Adventure of the Beauty Trap – Tracy Revels
A Case of Unfinished Business – Steven Philip Jones
The Case of the S.S. Bokhara – Mark Mower
The Adventure of the American Opera Singer – Deanna Baran
The Keadby Cross – David Marcum
The Adventure at Dead Man's Hole – Stephen Herczeg
The Elusive Mr. Chester – Arthur Hall
The Adventure of Old Black Duffel – Will Murray
The Blood-Spattered Bridge – Gayle Lange Puhl
The Tomorrow Man – S.F. Bennett
The Sweet Science of Bruising – Kevin P. Thornton
The Mystery of Sherlock Holmes – Christopher Todd
The Elusive Mr. Phillimore – Matthew J. Elliott
The Murders in the Maharajah's Railway Carriage – Charles Veley and Anna Elliott
The Ransomed Miracle – I.A. Watson
The Adventure of the Unkind Turn – Robert Perret
The Perplexing X'ing – Sonia Fetherston
The Case of the Short-Sighted Clown – Susan Knight

Part XXI: 2020 Annual (1898-1923)
Foreword – John Lescroart
Foreword – Roger Johnson
Foreword – Lizzy Butler
Foreword – Steve Emecz
Foreword – David Marcum
The Case of the Missing Rhyme (*A Poem*) – Joseph W. Svec III
The Problem of the St. Francis Parish Robbery – R.K. Radek
The Adventure of the Grand Vizier – Arthur Hall
The Mummy's Curse – DJ Tyrer
The Fractured Freemason of Fitzrovia – David L. Leal
The Bleeding Heart – Paula Hammond
The Secret Admirer – Jayantika Ganguly

(Continued on the next page . . . .)

Part XXII: Some More Untold Cases (1877-1887)

(Continued on the next page . . . .)

(Continued on the next page . . . .)

Part XXV: 2021 Annual (1881-1888)

(Continued on the next page . . . .)

(Continued on the next page . . . .)

Part XXVIII: More Christmas Adventures (1869-1888)

(Continued on the next page . . . .)

Part XXIX: More Christmas Adventures (1889-1896)

(Continued on the next page . . . .)

Part XXX: More Christmas Adventures (1897-1928)

(Continued on the next page . . . .)

Part XXXI 2022 Annual (1875-1887)

Part XXXII 2022 Annual (1888-1895)

(Continued on the next page . . . .)

Part XXXIII 2022 Annual (1896-1919)

(Continued on the next page . . . .)

The following contributors appear in this volume:
The MX Book of New Sherlock Holmes Stories
Part XXXVI – "However Improbable . . . ." (1897-1919)

The following contributors appear
in the companion volumes:
Part XXXIV – "However Improbable . . . ." (1878-1888)
Part XXXV – "However Improbable . . . ." (1889-1896)

Editor's Foreword:
The Dramatic Moment of Fate
by David Marcum

"Now is the dramatic moment of fate, Watson, when you hear a step upon the stair which is walking into your life, and you know not whether for good or ill."

— Sherlock Holmes
The Hound of the Baskervilles

In early 2022, we celebrated the 168th birthday of Mr. Sherlock Holmes, (born on January 6th, 1954). We're racing toward his *bicentennial*. That's a true *Good grief!* realization. (And if you think those next thirty-two years to 2054 won't fly by, you're either kidding yourself or still very young. By the time these current volumes see print, we'll almost be celebrating Holmes's *169th*!)

When I was a ten-year-old kid, discovering Mr. Holmes in the mid-1970's, the days of gaslight and hansom cabs were already long gone – but I knew some people who still remembered those days. Just imagine the changes that they lived through. My grandparents were born into the era of horse-drawn vehicles. (My dad's father and mother bought the first automobile ever driven in their small town.) They lived to see the world go from that type of existence to a man landing on the moon. Now, with our own exponential technological advances, we're also seeing changes moving at an even swifter pace. But for many, there's something deep inside that looks backward to different, supposedly simpler, times – and those are farther away with each passing year.

The Holmes Era – essentially the final third of Queen Victoria's reign and the Edwardian era, give or take a few years – conjures up definite images of dark and mysterious London streets and passages, often occluded by rolling fogs. Cabs and carriages carry finely dressed people past pedestrians who could have never afforded a cab ride in their entire lives. There was the rigid formality and ritual for those who *had*, and the scrambling, dangerous, and often short existence of those who *had not* – with all of them living jammed together in the space of just a few square miles.

London's wealthiest sector – the wealthiest sector, in fact, in the whole world – was located within just a few blocks of the City's poorest. These societal extremes must have been mightily confusing. There were

1

expected rules and behaviors that could not be violated. And while the cities pulled all of these conflicting layers tightly together, many rural areas remained just as remote as they had been for centuries. The countryside was dotted here and there with pockets of industry, extending their influence a bit more each year by way of railway tendrils – but only along profitable paths, leaving other vast tracts in isolation.

It was a time when science was revered and pursued by some – academics and gentleman amateurs – while at the same time many embraced superstition and ignorance with enthusiasm and anger by way of mediums and spiritualists. Often it was far too easy for the ignorant to proudly believe that the impossible was possible, consciously choosing to ignore science and knowledge and fact.

And in the midst of this chaos – rich and poor, knowledgeable and willfully ignorant – one clear note began to be noticed, quiet at first, almost beyond hearing, but gradually becoming stronger and more steady, resolving the various discordant tones around it. This note – possibly one could liken it to a steady air on a single Stradivarius string – brought in some small way balance to societal disparity, and light to shadowed and intentional disregard of knowledge.

This resolving influence was Sherlock Holmes.

The human mind is, by nature, drawn to the mysterious, from big questions like what happens after death, to the small, such as what's around that next curve or over that far hill. In the years when Sherlock Holmes was in practice, England was a peculiar stew of modern science and method, along with centuries of acceptance that humans were at the inevitable mercy of an overarching Fate on a grand scale, or mysterious, deadly, and immediate creatures in the shadows right outside the door. Holmes believed that answers could be found – *must be found* – or else mankind, at the bottom of things, had no course but to be blown without choice in whatever direction the fateful wind sent him.

"*No ghosts need apply,*" he famously told Watson in "The Sussex Vampire", refusing to believe in a supernatural explanation for a series of mysterious wounds. This four-word quote is often pulled out and referenced to indicate that Holmes had no use specifically for belief in *ghosts*, but to understand its wider implication, the entire quote must be recalled:

> "*But are we to give serious attention to such things? This agency stands flat-footed upon the ground, and there it must remain. The world is big enough for us. No ghosts need apply.*"

2

He refers to the *"agency"* – the team of Holmes and Watson – being *"flat-footed"*. Defined by Merriam-Webster, this means *"proceeding in a plodding or unimaginative way"* – or perhaps in a better light, *"in an open and determined manner"*.

Holmes often decries the lack of imagination shown by the Scotland Yarders – they accept the easiest explanation without attempting to see to a deeper layer, or to imagine what might actually have happened. But when Holmes himself shows imagination, it is in a *"flat-footed upon the ground"* way. No ghosts – or any impossibilities for that matter – will be considered, for to do so opens a door that cannot be shut, and the involvement of too many possibilities. If murder suspects include both the likely human candidates and the countless dead who might have involved themselves, then there is no possibility for resolution.

Holmes had no use for the impossible. Why waste time considering something that is *impossible*? Eliminate it, and one will inevitably narrow in upon the true solution, however improbable. In The Canon, he references this method a number of times:

> *"How often have I said to you that when you have eliminated the impossible whatever remains, however improbable, must be the truth?"* and also *"Eliminate all other factors, and the one which remains must be the truth."* – The Sign of Four

> *"It is an old maxim of mine that when you have excluded the impossible, whatever remains, however improbable, must be the truth."* – "The Beryl Coronet"

> *"We must fall back upon the old axiom that when all other contingencies fail, whatever remains, however improbable, must be the truth."* – "The Bruce-Partington Plans"

> *"That process . . . starts upon the supposition that when you have eliminated all which is impossible, then whatever remains, however improbable, must be the truth."* – "The Blanched Soldier"

Too often, because Sherlock Holmes is such a heroic figure, there is the temptation to place him in impossible stories, with situations ranging from absolutely incorrect, where he's living and working in the modern world instead of the correct time period, to having him face actual monsters, serving as a pop-in substitute for Van Helsing or Kolchak the Night Stalker. If a story has these impossible aspects, *then it isn't a*

Sherlock Holmes story, but rather a *simulacrum*, with a *faux* Holmes acting out all the Holmes-like parts and making the familiar motions in a situation that would never have actually been a part of Holmes's experience.

Besides the incorrect stories where Holmes is frozen and then thawed in modern times like an amusing duck-out-of-water, or the impossible situations of a modern-day character having absolutely nothing in common with Holmes but a stolen name, there are the efforts to have him battle aliens, vampires, werewolves, and ancient Lovecraftian horrors, and at some point in the story, one is dismayed to find that these turn out to be actual aliens, vampires, werewolves, and ancient Lovecraftian horrors. They might be well written by an author that one respects – but when encountering these, listen for that one clear note, quiet at first, almost beyond hearing, but gradually becoming stronger and more steady. This note has lyrics to resolve the discord:

> *"But are we to give serious attention to such things? This agency stands flat-footed upon the ground, and there it must remain. The world is big enough for us. No ghosts need apply."*

This resolving influence is Sherlock Holmes, and *No ghosts need apply.*

This series of anthologies started because the True Sherlock Holmes was being slowly worn away and diminished. There was a rise of simulacrums – modern Holmes, damaged Holmes, broken Holmes, monster-fighting Holmes. That version was creeping into the public perception of who Holmes truly was like a penumbral shadow sliding across the sun. Too often aspects of these incorrect versions were being included in what were supposed to be representations of the True Holmes, and it was feared that soon the True Holmes would be lost in the umbra.

These volumes have always had the overall basic requirement that the stories *must* present Holmes and Watson as *heroes*, and that the stories can stand alongside the original Canonical efforts that appeared in *The Strand.* It turns out that there was a need for stories like that, as many authors wanted to be part of such an effort, and many readers wanted to experience it. When I first started soliciting stories for these books in early 2015, I truly believed I'd be lucky to get a dozen for a small paperback book. As that year progressed, more and more authors heard about the project and wanted to contribute, and that small beginning led to three simultaneously published hardcover volumes with over sixty stories – Parts I, II and III –

4

the largest Holmes anthology of its type at that time. We've since surpassed it in a number of ways.

From the beginning, all author royalties have been donated to the Undershaw school for special needs children – called "Stepping Stones" back in 2015 – which is located at one of Sir Arthur Conan Doyle's former homes. As of June 2022, the books – now at 36 massive volumes (with more in preparation) and with over 750 traditional Holmes adventures from over 200 worldwide contributors – have raised over $100,000 for the school. I'm incredibly proud of this achievement, and more thankful than I can ever express for the contributing authors, and also the fans who have bought the books.

But even more important to me is the presentation of adventures reaffirming the True Sherlock Holmes.

After the first three volumes, I actually believed that there would be no more, but within weeks, contributors – both previous and new – wanted to know about being in the *next* set. It didn't take much convincing to keep going, because by then I was quite addicted to people sending me new Holmes adventures nearly every day. The various decisions had already been made regarding the books – sizes, cover style, format, *etcetera* – so it was just a matter of soliciting more stories. That was very successful – so much so that we ended up publishing two sets per year, an *Annual* in the spring, and a themed collection in the fall. These themes have included several sets of Christmas Stories and Untold Cases . . . and seemingly impossible cases that have rational solutions.

When the first set of these was announced, *Eliminate the Impossible* (Parts VII and VIII, 2017), a Sherlockian who only wants to have Holmes facing real monsters, despite Holmes's own words to the contrary, commented on social media at the time that these were "Scooby Doo" books. He was correct – these do have Scooby Doo aspects, where, at the end of the story, Holmes unmasks the supposed monster or ghost to reveal a very-human villain. (One might turn it around to say that *Scooby Doo* was Holmes-like, because in their world – at least for many years until the stories shifted and were ruined when they faced actual supernatural villains – no ghost needed to apply there either.)

There might be ambiguous aspects to the stories in these *Impossible* MX anthologies – maybe there is some unexplained side aspect that might be an actual ghostly encounter – but the solutions absolutely cannot involve real supernatural elements as the solutions – because that's a cheat.

At times, I've had to turn some stories away, as the contributors haven't understood the brief. (Having Holmes, for instance, deduce that he's a character in a fictional story might seem to be a clever idea, but it doesn't fit the scope of these books. Likewise, neither does having him do

5

battle to the death with a real vampire, only to turn and find that Watson is now a vampire too.)

Although a few contributors indicated that they couldn't come up with ideas that fit these requirements, in many other cases it has actually stimulated more clever story ideas. In 2019, the concept was repeated with *Whatever Remains . . . Must Be the Truth* (Parts XVI, XVII, and XVIII). Again, the theme inspired some really brilliant stories from our contributors.

By fall 2021, it was time for me to come up with the idea for the next themed set – because the theme had to be announced in late 2021 to give time for the stories to be submitted by the June 30th, 2022 deadline. Having used all the other pieces of Holmes's famous quote, *However Improbable* was the natural title for this collection:

> . . . *when you have eliminated the impossible whatever remains, however improbable, must be the truth.*

I'm not sure what to do about a similar-themed set a few years down the road. Quite likely I can start using pieces of Holmes's other famed quote from "The Sussex Vampire":

> *"This agency stands flat-footed upon the ground, and there it must remain. The world is big enough for us. No ghosts need apply."*

"Flat-footed Upon the Ground"? Possibly. *"The World is Big Enough for Us"*? No, that sounds too much like a James Bond title. Probably *"No Ghosts Need Apply."* Stay tuned . . . .

When announced, contributions were solicited to receive stories much like the previous sets – primarily cases that seemed supernatural but weren't. But then a fun thing happened: The contributors began to nudge and expand the requirements, opening them up a bit. I received a number of seemingly supernatural-that-aren't cases, but also new stories about seemingly impossible crimes – wherein the impossible was eliminated, leaving the improbable truth. I was thrilled, and it was – as always – great fun to see all the clever impossible situations that the contributors contrived, and how Holmes cut through the tangles to a solution. As expected (and required), he's a hero, and that's what he does.

The beauty of reading Holmes stories – and I read a *lot* of them – is that from their basic underpinnings, they can jump in any direction. The stories in these books have to fit certain givens: Holmes and Watson must act like Canonical Holmes and Watson. The dates in their lives and the history through which they move have to be acknowledged and respected. The contributors can't make any changes like killing major characters. Rather, these characters can be used, but then they have to be put back on the shelf, as good as new, for the next person. After satisfying those basic requirements, every new story is a surprise. It can be a comedy or tragedy, a romance or a technical procedural. It can be narrated by Watson or Holmes or some other person. It can be epic or small, a private affair or something that might lead to global war. It can be set in the city or the country, and in England or on the Continent, or in the United States or Tibet – as long as the time-frame fits with the other events of Our Heroes' lives.

In *The Hound of the Baskervilles*, Holmes states, *"Now is the dramatic moment of fate, Watson, when you hear a step upon the stair which is walking into your life, and you know not whether for good or ill."* I know of what he speaks. Nearly every day, I receive a new Holmes story in my email inbox, a submission for the MX Anthologies, or one of the other Holmes books that I edit. Each arrives with infinite possibility, and I can't wait to read it and see what previously unimagined adventure is about to entangle The Detective and The Doctor.

When I was a kid, first meeting Mr. Holmes, I soon realized there weren't enough stories about him. Sixty is really a drop in the bucket for The World's Greatest Detective. New stories appeared on a very irregular basis, and I wished so much for so often that I might have more of them. Now, by way of these books and the modern publishing paradigm and the incredibly gifted and generous authors who contribute to this series, my wish has come true.

I'm amazingly lucky to have the opportunity to see these stories first, fresh from the Tin Dispatch Box, and it's always a thrill when the various collections come together and can be released to the wider world. Now, with this new set – Parts XXXIV, XXXV, and XXXVI – there are more Holmes stories than there were before, and that's a very good thing. I hope you enjoy them, and with any luck, we'll be back soon with another round – because there can *never* be enough stories about the traditional Canonical Holmes, whom Watson called, *"the best and the wisest man whom I have ever known."*

"Of course, I could only stammer out my thanks."
– The unhappy John Hector McFarlane, "The Norwood Builder"

As always when one of these collections is finished, I want to thank with all my heart my incredible, patient, brilliant, kind, and beautiful wife of thirty-four years, Rebecca – every day I'm more stunned at how lucky I am than the day before! – and our amazing, funny, creative, and wonderful son, and my friend, Dan. I love you both, and you are everything to me!

With each new set of the MX anthologies, some things get easier, and there are also new challenges. For almost three years, the stresses of real life have been much greater than when this series started. Through all of this, the amazing contributors have once again pulled some amazing works from the Tin Dispatch Box. I'm more grateful than I can express to every contributor who has donated both time and royalties to this ongoing project. I also want to give special recognition to multiple contributors Josh Cerefice Arthur Hall, Tracy Revels, Dan Rowley, Tim Symonds, and Margaret Walsh. Additionally, Ian Dickerson provided not one but two "lost" scripts from the Rathbone and Bruce radio show by Leslie Charteris and Denis Green.

Back in 2015, when the MX anthologies began, I limited each contribution to one item per author, in order to spread the space around more fairly. But some authors are more prolific than that, and rather than be forced to choose between two excellent stories and let one slip away, I began to allow multiple contributions. (This also helped the authors, as their stories, if separated enough from each other chronologically, could appear in different simultaneously published volumes, thereby increasing their own bibliographies.)

I'm so glad to have gotten to know so many of you through this process. It's an undeniable fact that Sherlock Holmes authors are the *best* people!

I wish especially thank the following:

- *Nicholas Rowe* – In 1985, my deerstalker and I were on the front row for the opening-day showing of *Young Sherlock Holmes.* I was a college sophomore and skipped a class that afternoon to be there. (I'm pretty sure that this was the first Holmes film that I ever saw in a theatre.) I'd also bought the novelization, which I started reading that night – waiting until then to be surprised by the film. Although I did have some

8

reservations about a non-Canonical early meeting between Holmes and Watson in their younger days, pre-January 1st, 1881 at Barts, I found the story to be wonderful and exciting, and in particular, Young Holmes was portrayed to perfection by Nicholas Rowe.

Fast forward to 2015, when my deerstalker and I were back in a theater, this time on the opening day of *Mr. Holmes*. Over the previous couple of days I'd re-read the novel upon which it was based, Mitch Cullin's *A Slight Trick of the Mind*. That's a pretty bleak story, and while I give credence over written original versions over film adaptations, in this case I heartily recommend the latter over the former. While I was enjoying how the tone in the film had shifted from the despair of the book to hope, I was also thrilled to find that Nicholas Rowe was back as Holmes – playing a cinematic version that elderly Holmes (played by Ian McKellen) goes to see in a theatre.

I was incredibly surprised when Sherlockian author Paula Hammond put me in touch with Mr. Rowe, and truly amazed when he agreed to write a foreword. Nick, thanks so much for being part of this and your support.

- *Steve Emecz* – From my first association with MX in 2013, I saw that MX (under Steve Emecz's leadership) was *the* fast-rising superstar of the Sherlockian publishing world. Connecting with MX and Steve Emecz was personally an amazing life-changing event for me, as it has been for countless other Sherlockian authors. It has led me to write many more stories, and then to edit books, along with unexpected additional Holmes Pilgrimages to England – none of which might have happened otherwise. By way of my first email with Steve, I've had the chance to make some incredible Sherlockian friends and play in the Holmesian Sandbox in ways that I would have never dreamed possible.

Through it all, Steve has been one of the most positive and supportive people that I've ever known.

From the beginning, Steve has let me explore various Sherlockian projects and open up my own personal possibilities in ways that otherwise would have never happened. Thank you, Steve, for every opportunity!

- *Brian Belanger* –I initially became acquainted with him when he took over the duties of creating the covers for MX Books, and I found him to be a great collaborator, and wonderfully creative too. I've worked with him on many projects, with MX and Belanger Books, which he co-founded with his brother Derrick Belanger, also a good friend. Along with MX Publishing, Derrick and Brian have absolutely locked up the Sherlockian publishing field with a vast amount of amazing material. The old dinosaurs must be trembling to see every new and worthy Sherlockian project, one after another after another, that these two companies create. Luckily MX and Belanger Books work closely with one another, and I'm thrilled to be associated with both of them. Many thanks to Brian for all he does for both publishers, and for all he's done for me personally.

- *Roger Johnson* – From his immediate support at the time of the first volumes in this series to the present, I can't imagine Roger not being part of these books. His Sherlockian knowledge is exceptional, as is the work that he does to further the cause of The Master. But even more than that, both Roger and Jean Upton are simply the finest and best of people, and I'm very lucky to know both of them – even though I don't get to see them nearly as often as I'd like – in fact, it's been six years since out last meeting, at the grand opening of the Undershaw school (then called "Stepping Stones"). I look forward to getting back over to the Holmesland sooner rather than later and seeing them, but in the meantime, many thanks for being part of this.

- *Paula Hammond* – Paula has been a regular contributor to these MX anthologies in recent years, and while she wasn't able to send a new adventure for this set, she amazingly "introduced" me to Nicholas Rowe. Paula: Very much appreciated, and thanks for the support and being part of these books!

And finally, last but certainly *not* least, thanks to **Sir Arthur Conan Doyle**: Author, doctor, adventurer, and the Founder of the Sherlockian Feast. Honored, and present in spirit.

As I always note when putting together an anthology of Holmes stories, the effort has been a labor of love. These adventures are just more

10

tiny threads woven into the ongoing Great Holmes Tapestry, continuing to grow and grow, for there can *never* be enough stories about the man whom Watson described as *"the best and wisest . . . whom I have ever known."*

David Marcum
October 2nd,, 2022
143rd Anniversary of
"The Musgrave Ritual"

Questions, comments, or story submissions
may be addressed to David Marcum at

thepapersofsherlockholmes@gmail.com

Foreword
by Nicholas Rowe

I have a confession to make. In life as in fiction, one half of a couple may admit to a past affair simply in order to appease his or her conscience, when best advice might just be for the guilty party to say nothing and carry on without off-loading – Why cause unnecessary hurt? Mine will be a different breed of confession, but I am driven to make it because the secret has been with me for too long now, and I have a sense that I may be among friends here, an unofficial member of a global appreciation Society that worships with varying healthy degrees of dedication at the altar of Arthur Conan Doyle and his creation, Sherlock Holmes.

The fact is that I am a dilettante in this field, or rather an interloper. My "membership" of the club, so full of *bona fide* Sherlock Holmes devotees who have read all there is to read about the Great Detective and who may have gone so far as buying the meerschaum and donning the deerstalker, was thrust on me out of the blue when I was only just out of school. Christopher Columbus (Wait . . . I'm not THAT old . . . I'm talking about the film writer/director) had written a screenplay for Paramount Pictures that imagined Sherlock as a schoolboy, meeting John Watson for the first time, and falling in love with an eccentric inventor's niece. It had the three of them getting involved in an adventure with an Egyptian sect brought to the streets of Victorian London. It was, to all intents and purposes, my first real experience of acting in a film, throwing me in at the deep end playing a character so loved and "'owned" by millions of people . . . and I had only ever read *The Sign of Four*. My knowledge of Holmes and Watson was confined to the brilliant world created by the unbeatable Basil Rathbone (happy to argue about this) and the brilliant Nigel Bruce. At some point I got hold of a clever biography of Holmes and remember a small incident at the Reichenbach Falls . . . but that was it.

Since then I have dallied from time to time with Holmes – a little cameo in Jeffrey Hatcher's *Mr. Holmes*, enjoying Clive Merrison on the radio, watching old re-runs with Jeremy Brett as your man, and of course Benedict Cumberbatch. The eventual success of my first foray (it wasn't an instant hit in the cinema – far from it) made me understand just how robust this character was, and how much appetite there was to see ever more of him. I could have done more research – probably should have done – but (Your Honour), we were all guessing just a little, playing around with characters from a sacred future, but who were for now still in their embryonic form. We perhaps felt we could allow ourselves a little more artistic licence.

So, I have made some excuses, but have I resolved anything?

Maybe . . . As I consider the achievement of David Marcum in compiling a whole new world of Sherlock Holmes stories, hundreds of them, and the bravery and enthusiasm of the many writers who have created them, I tell myself that I just need to relax a little. I am at least in the good company of people who fly the flag for the future of Sherlock Holmes.

Nicholas Rowe
June 2022

"Why, You Are Like a Magician"
by Roger Johnson

You'll remember the incident in "The Adventure of the Beryl Coronet". Sherlock Holmes is gleaning evidence at Fairbank, the house from which the precious diadem has been stolen. When he asks the young mistress of the house, Mary Holder, whether a surreptitious nocturnal visitor is "a man with a wooden leg", her reaction is rather dramatic:

> Something like fear sprang up in the young lady's expressive black eyes. "Why, you are like a magician," said she. "How do you know that?" She smiled, but there was no answering smile in Holmes's thin, eager face.

Magicians have proved to be good detectives, of course – in fiction, at any rate. The Great Merlini solves apparently impossible crimes in long and short stories by Clayton Rawson, who was himself a notable magician. On television, there's the equally brilliant Jonathan Creek, who creates the tricks and illusions for an unappreciative egotist named Adam Klaus. Because he knows how these things work, Creek can spot the tell-tale clues that most of us miss. All thirty-two episodes were written by David Renwick, who is otherwise known for his comedies – which shows that you don't have to *be* a magician in order to *think* like a magician.

Members of the Magic Circle are forbidden to reveal their secrets except to *bona fide* students of the art. That, of course, is a restriction that can't apply to the conscientious detective story writer. Derren Brown, David Blaine, or Dynamo don't tell us how they achieve the miraculous, but Clayton Rawson and David Renwick do just that, because a real detective story must have an explanation. The all-time master of the impossible mystery was John Dickson Carr, author, under his own name or as Carter Dickson, of seventy novels and numerous short stories, all devilishly clever and nearly all compulsively readable. It's only fitting that his biography by Douglas G. Greene is called *John Dickson Carr: The Man Who Explained Miracles*.

The "impossible crime" is usually epitomised in the locked-room mystery and its variants, in which a murder or other felony is committed in a space to which no one has access. This was Carr's specialism, but he wasn't the first: Consider Poe's "The Murders in the Rue Morgue", for instance, or that grand Father Brown story "The Dagger With Wings" by

14

G.K. Chesterton. Or – and it's time we introduced Sherlock Holmes – "The Speckled Band".

The apparently impossible becomes even more disturbing in a sinister atmosphere, which is something that all these writers excelled at. There are effective weird touches, for instance, in "The Copper Beeches", "Wisteria Lodge", and "The Blanched Soldier". And this is from Conan Doyle's description of Stoke Moran manor house, the setting for "The Speckled Band":

> *The building was of grey, lichen-blotched stone, with a high central portion and two curving wings, like the claws of a crab, thrown out on each side. In one of these wings the windows were broken and blocked with wooden boards, while the roof was partly caved in, a picture of ruin.*

The supernatural is no more than hinted at in that particular story, but in Sherlock Holmes's most famous case, *The Hound of the Baskervilles*, its presence is almost expected. The same is true of "The Sussex Vampire" – with that title, it would have to be – and "The Devil's Foot". The latter case, which Holmes calls "The Cornish horror", plays out in a landscape that almost outdoes the Dartmoor of *The Hound*:

> *It was a country of rolling moors, lonely and dun-colored, with an occasional church tower to mark the site of some old-world village. In every direction upon these moors there were traces of some vanished race which had passed utterly away, and left as it sole record strange monuments of stone, irregular mounds which contained the burned ashes of the dead, and curious earthworks which hinted at prehistoric strife. The glamour and mystery of the place, with its sinister atmosphere of forgotten nations, appealed to the imagination of my friend, and he spent much of his time in long walks and solitary meditations upon the moor.*

But it's mystery that Holmes loves. Our great detective has no truck with the supernatural. That's as it should be. And that why those stories – and the stories in this book – are so satisfying!

Roger Johnson, BSI, ASH
Commissioning Editor: *The Sherlock Holmes Journal*
June 2022

An Ongoing Legacy
for Sherlock Holmes
by Steve Emecz

Undershaw
Circa 1900

The MX Book of New Sherlock Holmes Stories has grown beyond any expectations we could have imagined. We've now raised over $100,000 for Undershaw, a school for children with learning disabilities. The collection has become not only the largest Sherlock Holmes collection in the world, but one of the most respected.

We have received over twenty very positive reviews from *Publishers Weekly*, and in a recent review for someone else's book, *Publishers Weekly* referred to the MX Book in that review which demonstrates how far the collection's influence has grown.

In 2022, we launched The MX Audio Collection, an app which includes some of these stories, alongside exclusive interviews with leading writers and Sherlockians including Lee Child, Jeffrey Hatcher, Nicholas

Meyer, Nancy Springer, Bonnie MacBird, and Otto Penzler. A share of the proceeds also goes to Undershaw. You can find out all about the app here:

https://mxpublishing.com/pages/mx-app

In addition to Undershaw, we also support Happy Life Mission (a baby rescue project in Kenya), The World Food Programme (which won the Nobel Peace Prize in 2020), and *iHeart* (who support mental health in young people).

Our support for our projects is possible through the publishing of Sherlock Holmes books, which we have now been doing for over a decade.

You can find links to all our projects on our website:

https://mxpublishing.com/pages/about-us

I'm sure you will enjoy the fantastic stories in the latest volumes and look forward to many more in the future.

Steve Emecz
September 2022
Twitter: *@mxpublishing*

The Doyle Room at Undershaw
Partially funded through royalties from
The MX Book of New Sherlock Holmes Stories

A Word from Undershaw
by Emma West

Undershaw
September 9, 2016
Grand Opening of the Stepping Stones School
(Now *Undershaw*)
(Photograph courtesy of Roger Johnson)

It seems not so long ago I was writing with news from Undershaw, and here we are again with even more achievements to report. The school is now well into our new academic year with an unprecedented number of students on our roll, and we are busy firming up our place as a Centre of Excellence for SEND education, not only in our locality but further afield.

As an example of the positive culture we have at Undershaw, we received the most wonderful feedback from a work experience placement student we hosted recently. Here's what she had to say about our school from the time she spent with us:

> *Coming to Undershaw was a fantastic experience. I really appreciated the opportunity to spend time with your students, and even to take part in some drama improvisation! Your students were articulate, confident, and thoughtful. Sports Day was a real highlight for me – I felt it was inclusion at its best. The range of activities on offer, and the careful thought*

that had gone into the design of the day to ensure that every child could enjoy and achieve was inspirational.

Earlier in the summer we took our accolades to new heights when Undershaw was awarded a Gold Award by the Skills Builder Programme. This is a framework which identifies eight vital life skills, such as problem solving, leadership, and listening. When mastered, these skills ensure our students are fully equipped to take their places as economically and socially independent young adults. At Undershaw, we work tirelessly to ensure our students are immersed in every feasible aspect of their academic and character education, both of which furnish them for their rich and dynamic futures, wherever they may lie.

Undershaw is making a mark as a great seat of learning, proven this year with a fantastic set of GCSE, BTEC and Functional Skills results. We are so very proud of the results which are testament to the students' hard work, resilience, and perseverance. The way that they approached the examinations, having had their previous learning and opportunities to practise with mocks disrupted by the pandemic, is remarkable. Our students move on with a great set of qualifications and achieved the school's first ever Distinction grades, but just as important, they have developed their social and communication skills, built their confidence, and have become the most delightful group of young people. We look forward to hearing all about their next steps and their future successes.

I often say we have the best "job" in the world, as we are privileged enough to witness these remarkable students, who may not have had the best experiences in education before they came to us, find and fuel their passion under our tenure and ready themselves to spread their wings. My inbox is awash with emails from alumni telling me of their latest triumphs as they carve out their niche in the world. I will leave you with the sign-off from one alumnus who wrote to me recently and signed off with the words, *"Thanks for the confidence in me"*. That just says it all.

On behalf of all the wonderful students, committed and talented staff, and the families we support, I extend my heartfelt thanks to you all for being by our side. Undershaw would not be the school it is today without the selfless dedication of all at MX Publishing. We are honoured to have such friends in our midst.

Until next time…

Emma West
Headteacher
October 2022

"Undershaw," Hindhead, Conan Doyle's House.

Editor's *Caveats*

When these anthologies first began back in 2015, I noted that the authors were from all over the world – and thus, there would be British spelling and American spelling. As I explained then, I didn't want to take the responsibility of changing American spelling to British and vice-versa. I would undoubtedly miss something, leading to inconsistencies, or I'd change something incorrectly.

Some readers are bothered by this, made nervous and irate when encountering American spelling as written by Watson, and in stories set in England. However, here in America, the versions of The Canon that we read have long-ago has their spelling Americanized, so it isn't quite as shocking for us.

Additionally, I offer my apologies up front for any typographical errors that have slipped through. As a print-on-demand publisher, MX does not have squadrons of editors as some readers believe. The business consists of three part-time people who also have busy lives elsewhere – Steve Emecz, Sharon Emecz, and Timi Emecz – so the editing effort largely falls on the contributors. Some readers and consumers out there in the world are unhappy with this – apparently forgetting about all of those self-produced Holmes stories and volumes from decades ago (typed and Xeroxed) with awkward self-published formatting and loads of errors that are now prized as very expensive collector's items.

I'm personally mortified when errors slip through – ironically, there will probably be errors in these *caveats* – and I apologize now, but without a regiment of professional full-time editors looking over my shoulder, this is as good as it gets. Real life is more important than writing and editing – even in such a good cause as promoting the True and Traditional Canonical Holmes – and only so much time can be spent preparing these books before they're released into the wild. I hope that you can look past any errors, small or huge, and simply enjoy these stories, and appreciate the efforts of everyone involved, and the sincere desire to add to The Great Holmes Tapestry.

And in spite of any errors here, there are more Sherlock Holmes stories in the world than there were before, and that's a good thing.

David Marcum
Editor

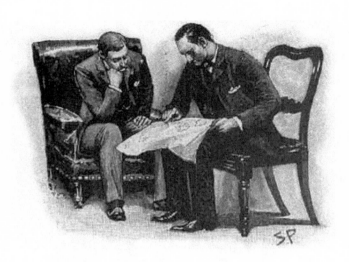

Sherlock Holmes (1854-1957) was born in Yorkshire, England, on 6 January, 1854. In the mid-1870's, he moved to 24 Montague Street, London, where he established himself as the world's first Consulting Detective. After meeting Dr. John H. Watson in early 1881, he and Watson moved to rooms at 221b Baker Street, where his reputation as the world's greatest detective grew for several decades. He was presumed to have died battling noted criminal Professor James Moriarty on 4 May, 1891, but he returned to London on 5 April, 1894, resuming his consulting practice in Baker Street. Retiring to the Sussex coast near Beachy Head in October 1903, he continued to be associated in various private and government investigations while giving the impression of being a reclusive apiarist. He was very involved in the events encompassing World War I, and to a lesser degree those of World War II. He passed away peacefully upon the cliffs above his Sussex home on his 103rd birthday, 6 January, 1957.

Dr. John Hamish Watson (1852-1929) was born in Stranraer, Scotland on 7 August, 1852. In 1878, he took his Doctor of Medicine Degree from the University of London, and later joined the army as a surgeon. Wounded at the Battle of Maiwand in Afghanistan (27 July, 1880), he returned to London late that same year. On New Year's Day, 1881, he was introduced to Sherlock Holmes in the chemical laboratory at Barts. Agreeing to share rooms with Holmes in Baker Street, Watson became invaluable to Holmes's consulting detective practice. Watson was married and widowed three times, and from the late 1880's onward, in addition to his participation in Holmes's investigations and his medical practice, he chronicled Holmes's adventures, with the assistance of his literary agent, Sir Arthur Conan Doyle, in a series of popular narratives, most of which were first published in *The Strand* magazine. Watson's later years were spent preparing a vast number of his notes of Holmes's cases for future publication. Following a final important investigation with Holmes, Watson contracted pneumonia and passed away on 24 July, 1929.

Photos of Sherlock Holmes and Dr. John H. Watson courtesy of Roger Johnson

The
MX Book
of
New

Sherlock
Holmes
Stories

Part XXXVI
"However Improbable . . . ."
(1897-1919)

The Mythological Holmes
by Alisha Shea

"It is complete nonsense," Holmes brusquely said
With a dismissive glance and a toss of his head.
"Such things don't exist in Heaven or Earth,"
He further expounded grinning with mirth.
I maintained my own council. I'd heard it before.
He couldn't countenance facts not made sure.
But I knew the truth, I'd seen myriad creatures
Usually hiding beneath human features.

I've witnessed a mighty kraken rise from its stuporous torpor,
Summoned by its latest brazen challenger.
He fixes his all-encompassing steely gaze on his opponent
Before viciously thrashing them to fragments in a frenzy of activity;
Then the leviathan promptly sinks back to the depths of the divan
With lethargy born of inexorable ennui.

I have caught a glimpse of a hidden *fae*.
His slender form swaying gently,
A rapturous smile traversing his features;
His nimble feet tripping lightly as any fairy.
The bow dancing daintily across the strings
Producing sweetly golden tones
To linger blissfully in the warm evening air.

I know I have watched a warlock alchemist hard at work,
Procuring arcane knowledge from methods of his own devising.
Hunching diligently at his battered work table
A cloud of noxious vapor billows dangerously heavenward
As he dexterous combines two clearly reactive reagents
His expression a mask of focused concentration.

Though Holmes would no doubt laugh at me and likely roll his eyes.
I still insist that all myths can be found in human guise.

34

The Adventure of the
Murderous Ghost
by Tracy J. Revels

Inspector Lestrade looked ill. The Scotland Yard detective, and Holmes's erstwhile foil, was pale as death, his face covered in a glistening sheen of sweat. He smoked as he talked, his fingers twitching so violently that he spread ash and the occasional glowing ember across our bearskin rug. I kept a cautious eye upon the untidy pile of newspapers beside my friend's chair, fearful that at any moment an errant spark might ignite them.

"It just isn't possible," Lestrade babbled, the words tumbling out without so much as a breath between sentences. "The witnesses directly contradict each other, yet all are earnest and conspicuously truthful. But if the points are impossible to be reconciled, then the entire *thing* is impossible. It can't be true – *and yet it is!*"

Sherlock Holmes, who had been watching this performance with the patient manner of a senior warden at Bedlam, rose and poured the inspector a glass of brandy. Despite the earliness of this autumn morning, Lestrade bolted back the drink. It seemed to calm his nerves, and for a few moments staunched the tirade.

"Lestrade, if you will give that medicinal draught time to take proper effect, and state your case more precisely, perhaps I can be of service to you."

"Precisely? Very well. How can a man be both dead and alive? How can he murder his lover in St. Johns Woods while his body is being embalmed in his house in Curzon Street?"

Holmes scowled. "The answer is obvious. He cannot."

"So it is impossible. Yet I am telling you that is exactly what happened. And if I don't get to the bottom of the thing, unravel this snarl, I will become the laughingstock of the Yard."

"Become?" Holmes posed. Lestrade ignored him and turned back to me.

"Have you found it yet?"

"Yes, I have it here. The story ran in the evening edition, yesterday." I folded back the second page of one of London's most salacious newspapers, one read primarily by those in search of sensational, if largely fictionalized, articles. "The headline is '*Murderous Ghost Slays Former Lover*'."

Holmes chuckled. "That will make many a schoolboy part with his pennies. Regale us, Watson"

I cleared my throat and offered up the following:

> *A dreadful slaying has been made more horrific by the discovery that the killer wasn't a flesh-and-blood villain, but a vengeful specter. At precisely three p.m. yesterday, Phillipa Conner, the maid of Miss Simone Willow, answered the door at the lady's residence near Lord's Cricket Ground. The man who waited there was well-known to the girl, as he had been a frequent caller at the residence. She admitted him to the front parlor and went to fetch her mistress. Miss Willow was surprised by the visit and hurriedly prepared herself to come down to greet him. The maid had just closed the sliding doors of the parlor and was retreating upstairs when she heard a scream and a gunshot. By the time the frightened girl gathered her wits and ran into the room, the murderer had fled through the front door, leaving Miss Willow dead upon the carpet, shot directly through the heart. The hue-and-cry were quickly raised, and the intrepid Inspector Lestrade of Scotland Yard was summoned. Our readers will recall this paragon of deduction, an unparalleled sleuth, a human bloodhound whose adventures –*

"Skip that part," Lestrade growled. I scanned down several lines to find the thread of the tale again.

> *Conner informed the inspector of the murderer's name and address – Mr. Vincent Ravel, of Curzon Street. Lestrade hastened to the residence, only to find a black wreath upon the door. He was informed by Miss Ramona Ravel, sister to the named killer, that her brother had expired at noon, and that the undertaker was even now completing his somber tasks. The inspector viewed the corpse and spoke with the individuals who had been inside the house over the course of the afternoon – Miss Ravel, Mr. Pearson Hobbs (the undertaker), and Mrs. Jennibelle Brown, the cook. All agreed that no one had entered or exited the establishment. Yet the victim's maid swears upon all holy works and her own soul that it was Mr. Ravel who fired the fatal shot. Can it be that death-dealing shades walk among us? Do wraiths seek*

36

revenge for the wrongs committed against their mortal forms?
Should mediums now be hired as detectives? If so, then –

"That's quite enough," Lestrade growled. "Now, Mr. Holmes, do you see the pickle that I am in?"

"Why in Heaven's name did you allow such a breathless and imaginative reporter to accompany you?" Holmes asked.

"Brad is the Chief Inspector's nephew," Lestrade muttered. "I thought you would have deduced it already."

Holmes smiled archly. "A favor was obvious, but for whom I was uncertain. However, let us stick to the problem at hand. Watson . . . what is this agency's rule on ghosts?"

I had to force myself to bury a chuckle. "None need apply."

"Excellent. So we may rule out the idea of a murderous phantom entirely. Lestrade, what more can you tell us about the deceased suspect, the victim, and the other individuals in this most bizarre affair?"

Lestrade finally crumpled onto our sofa and took out his notebook. "The dead man is Vincent Ravel. He was sixty-seven years old, born in London, and a retired stage magician – quite famous in his time."

"I've never heard of him," I said.

Lestrade looked snide. "That's because he was famous in Australia – unless you've been to Sydney or Melbourne, Doctor, you'd have no reason to know him. But five years ago, his wife was killed – terrible accident, something about a stagecoach – and he came back to London and moved in with his spinster sister. He became attached to Miss Willow about two years back. She is – "

"A notorious adventuress," Holmes said.

Lestrade made a face. "Must you know everything, Mr. Holmes?"

My friend waved at his bookshelf. "Forgive me, Lestrade, but I have spent the last few days updating my Index, and the lady's article is a memorable one. She was a ballerina, a *chanteuse*, and the author of a sprightly memoir about her affair with an archduke – a book which has been banned in Catholic countries. She is fluent in six languages."

"*Was*," Lestrade corrected. "She's being buried in Highgate as we speak. Only thirty years old and an exceptionally beautiful woman. Pity."

"Was Ravel's relationship known to his sister?"

Lestrade almost laughed. "You might say so – That lady had no kind words for the deceased. I quote – 'That witch killed my brother. I hope she burns in Hell!'" Lestrade shrugged. "Strong language, but it fits her. I thought at first that she might have worn a disguise and sought revenge, but that's impossible. The undertaker stated that she was in the house the entire time."

"And the cook?"

"A half-witted old lady, beside herself with grief. I tracked down the doctor who pronounced the man dead, and he confirmed that before he left the home he administered a sedative to her, which put her to sleep instantly."

"And the undertaker? You seem to not question his veracity."

Lestrade stiffened. "I'd think not. He's a relative of mine, a distant cousin, and I've known him since he was a lad. A most religious man, very respectable, just coming along in his trade. He'd know better than to lie to me!"

"Have you found the cabbie who drove the 'ghost'?" At the inspector's blank look, Holmes sighed. "I suppose you never thought a spirit would need transportation. Very well, Lestrade, I will take the case. The pertinent addresses if you please."

Our first action was to pay a call at the residence of the late Miss Simone Willow. It was a small but charming home, set back from the street and distinguished by an ornate brass gate. There was a heavy black wreath upon the door, and Holmes's polite knock went unanswered for almost five minutes. At last, the portal was opened by a young woman in deep mourning. She was petite and rather plain of face, with small spectacles upon her nose and her brown hair drawn tightly back beneath a servant's cap.

"Miss Phillipa Conner?" Holmes asked. The girl nodded nervously, but when Holmes spoke his name, her face brightened, and she eagerly took his hand.

"Oh, thank God you have come, sir! The inspector said he might send you, that you often assisted him in his cases."

Holmes raised an eyebrow. "Ah, so now I am Lestrade's assistant? Well, he is the 'professional' in such matters, and I am merely the 'talented amateur'. Do forgive us for intruding upon your grief, young lady. One need not be a detective to see how sincere and deep it is."

Miss Conner lowered her eyes. "You will want to view the parlor where it happened. Come this way, please. And you may ask me anything, for I want nothing more than to see justice served for my dear mistress."

"How long had you been in her employ?"

"Five years, sir. She rescued me from a workhouse, taught me all that I needed to know to be her maid and to manage her household."

"There are no other servants?" I asked.

"Mr. and Mrs. Floss were her cook and butler for many years, but they retired six months ago. Miss Willow said we could do things for ourselves – she thought we might be travelling very soon, and so saw no need to hire more staff." We had entered a small, oval-shaped formal parlor, a room decorated in delicate hues of pink, with chairs that seemed made by a fairy's hand. Everything in the chamber spoke of beauty and perfection, except for the single, dreadful spot of blood upon a white carpet. "The Flosses were the only other mourners at the funeral. There were a number of beautiful flowers sent to the chapel but . . . my mistress wasn't the kind of lady that men might grieve for openly, without causing misunderstandings."

Holmes's gestured for our hostess to sit. "Can you describe what occurred on the afternoon of your mistress's murder?"

"Oh, how I wish I could forget it, but I know I will see it forever, even in my dreams. The clock had just struck three when I heard a loud knock. I was very surprised to find Mr. Ravel at the door, as he hadn't visited in over a month."

"And you are certain it was him?"

"Yes – he had that strange cavalier-style hat with the big brim and the long feather. And he was wearing his purple cloak, all drawn up around his face in that dramatic way that he favored. He had marvelous ice blue eyes, and they stared at me as if daring me not to admit him."

"Did he speak?"

"No. He merely pointed at the parlor, where my Lady had so often entertained him. I ushered him in and then ran to the bedroom. My mistress had just emerged from a bath, but when I told her who was downstairs, she was most eager to dress and go down to meet him."

"Yet I was given to understand that the lady had discarded him as a companion."

The girl's face turned red. "That is a harsh word, sir. You should understand that my mistress made a vow never to fall in love or to marry, for she saw her mother abused by her father, and came to believe that marriage wasn't a sacrament, but a prison. Yet Heaven granted my Lady many favors. See – here is her picture!"

The girl leapt to the mantel and plucked down a photograph in a silver-gilt frame. The young woman it portrayed was indeed among the loveliest of mortals, with a fair face, a swan-like neck, and a great mass of artful curls slipping over the perfect curves of her bare shoulders.

"I know that the world condemns such women," the maid continued, "but why should she have refused the gifts showered upon her by admirers? Why should she have declined the jewels, carriages, journeys to spas and casinos? She was always honest with her companions – that she would dismiss any she tired of. When she found one boring or demanding, she sent him packing!" the maid added, with a lifted chin and a flash of spirit.

"So how did Mr. Ravel offend her?" Holmes asked.

The girl settled back into her chair. "I don't know, sir. My Lady said that he wasn't a rich man, but a charming one – and old enough to be her father! He was a magician, you know, and he used to perform tricks to entertain her. One time, when his sister was away, he took my mistress to his home on Curzon Street and showed her the marvelous props from his career. She told me all about the floating table, and the Oriental box in which an assistant would disappear. He even had a strange bird that performed in his act, and my Lady returned with one of its feathers. It rests there, in that vase. She said that a paper flower from Mr. Ravel was more valuable to her than the ruby pendant the Prussian archduke hung around her neck." The girl hesitated, then fumbled for a handkerchief to dry the tears which were quietly trickling down her cheeks. "Before God, Mr. Holmes, I don't know why she sent Mr. Ravel away when she seemed to honestly adore him. All I can tell you is that a little over a month ago, I heard him leave in the middle of the night, in a great rush. The next morning, my Lady wouldn't speak of him, but I could tell her face was swollen and her eyes were red."

"And he didn't return. Did she try to write to him?"

"Just once, sir, a little over a week ago. I don't know what was in the letter, but there was never any answer."

Holmes leaned forward, adopting his most parental tone. "I don't wish to alarm you, Miss Conner, but I must know if any of your late mistress's companions parted with her on less-than-amiable terms."

"There was one man who made a terrible scene at the door until the police drove him off, and a brute who was foolish enough to think he could abduct her. He carries a broken nose to this day, for my Lady knew how to defend herself. But there was another – a young man, an Oxford scholar – who was so broken-hearted when she turned him out that he threw himself into the Thames. His father is a nobleman and has made terrible threats that he would destroy my Lady."

"His name?" Holmes inquired, nodding for me to write it down. The girl went pale as she whispered one of the highest titles in the land. I knew the case immediately. It had been given out that his son had perished in a boating accident.

"I will ask just two more questions," Holmes said. "Are you aware of the contents of Miss Willow's will? And if so, who stood as her beneficiaries?"

The girl twisted her hands together. "My Lady was generous to charities for children. She was the discreet patron of an orphanage and left a hundred pounds to it. But she had no family to endow. She left a small amount – some fifty pounds – to the Flosses. The rest of it – the house, her gowns and furs, her jewels, all of it – she bequeathed to me." With this breathless admission, Miss Conner lifted tear-filled eyes to Holmes.

"Please, sir, you must find who did this . . . for otherwise, they will think that I killed her!"

"Watson, what is wrong?" Holmes asked as our cab moved through traffic. "You have been out of sorts ever since we departed from Miss Willow's dwelling."

I tightened my folded arms and glared at Holmes. "I am angry with myself."

"That, I suppose, is something of a relief, as I have seen you throw a punch and wouldn't wish to be upon the receiving end of it. But why are you infuriated?"

"Because I should have figured it out from the start." I sputtered in annoyance at his raised eyebrow. "The maid is the killer! Of course, it makes sense that she would do away with her mistress when she learned such an inheritance was within her grasp. By blaming it on a ghost, she diverts everyone's attention, including my own."

Holmes shook his head. "There is much against your theory."

"Such as?"

"How did she know Ravel had died earlier that morning?"

"A confederate, perhaps a lover, told her," I said with a shrug. "What does it matter?"

"A great deal, if we are to get to the truth," Holmes said. "Try not to be so hard on yourself, Watson."

"Did you suspect the girl?"

"Immediately," Holmes replied. "But the evidence leads elsewhere."

"Where?"

"To the Good Old Index," Holmes said as we arrived at Baker Street. "Do wait with the cab."

Before I could question, my friend had sprung from the vehicle and raced inside. Not a minute later, another hansom pulled up to the curb, and the driver went to the door of our residence. Intrigued by this development, I paid our man and followed the interloper inside. By the time I reached our rooms, I could hear a strange, croaking voice addressing Holmes.

"It was the dead who I drove, sir! I saw it in the paper and realized, 'Why, that's the chappie I squired about!' I knew he seemed odd, but I had no idea he was a ghost!"

As I entered our sitting room, our guest sprang up from the sofa. He had a wild, hunted look in his eyes, and for an instant seemed ready to throw himself through the window. Holmes quickly stepped between him and the glass.

41

"Doctor Watson, meet Mr. Herbert Lawson, a member of London's vast cab driver fraternity and an admirer of your stories. It seems that clues come to us these days! Do sit down, sir. I am most grateful that you have presented yourself. I must ask, however, why did you come to me instead of going to the police when you realized the part you played in this affair?"

The gruff man twisted his cap in his hands. "I spent five years in prison as a lad. Let's say the bobbies are no friends of mine. There . . . might also be a warrant . . . for a bit of burglary."

Holmes smiled. "I am the last to throw stones. Your name and information shall remain safe with me. Speak truthfully and I will reward you."

"I shall do my best, though there isn't much to tell. I saw the man walking down Curzon Street that afternoon, and he hailed me. He had on a strange hat and a big purple cloak. He handed up a card with the name – *Ravel* – on it, and something about a king. On the back was written the lady's address and instructions to wait for him there, then return him to Curzon Street. He passed up five pounds as well, and who was I to argue with that? He was in and out of the house in less than ten minutes, and never said a word. I thought it was a jolly good business to have such a fare!"

"It was indeed," Holmes chuckled. "Here is something for your troubles in seeking me out. There is no need for you to reveal yourself to the police."

"Oh . . . thank you, sir. God bless you and keep you free from ghosts!"

With that, the man hurried away. Holmes turned back to his book, studying it with a series of *Hmm*'s and *Ah*'s. In a minute, he slammed it shut.

"Watson," he said, with an exasperated air, as he turned back to me, "since you have been untrustworthy and allowed our chariot to depart, do have the courtesy to hail another."

"How did you know – "

"No time to explain! The cab, quickly!"

A short time later, our vehicle came to a halt before a drab building with a glass window etched with the words:

Pearson Hobbs – Undertaking and Memorials

We stepped into a long, dark chamber where mourning accoutrements – gloves, hats, black-bordered stationery, and jet beads – were displayed in a series of cases. Off to one side was a heavy desk, with two elegant chairs drawn up before it. A pale young man rose from his work at a massive ledger and took Holmes's card. Less than a minute later, we were being ushered to an interior office and greeted by the proprietor, the man who had been called to the Ravel home to prepare the body for viewing and travel.

"My cousin, the inspector, sent word that you would call, though I don't know what more I can tell you," Hobbs said. He was a tall man, thin and angular, with thick black hair and an air of piety in his calmly folded hands. His unusual, almost-golden eyes glistened behind a *pince-nez*. "I received the summons to the Ravel home at twelve-thirty, but was detained by the necessity of completing some errands and didn't arrive until after two. Miss Ravel met me and was kind enough to offer me refreshments, even though her only servant had taken to her bed, prostrated by grief. I told her it would be unnecessary. She showed me to her brother's bedroom, where his body lay, and then excused herself to her own chamber, which was on the floor above. It took approximately two hours to complete my tasks, and the entire time I was very much aware of her presence."

"How so?" Holmes asked.

"Her tears, sir – her wailing. It barely paused, all while I was working. Never have I heard such prolonged and painful sobs. They ceased only moments before the police arrived at the door. You may imagine my surprise, sir, to find that the corpse I had just washed, embalmed, and dressed was accused of having risen from his bier and done murder!"

I noticed that Holmes's gaze was resting on a photograph on the undertaker's desk, which showed a woman and a young child. "Were you familiar with the Ravel family before this tragedy?"

"To only a slight degree. Miss Ravel came to visit me two weeks ago. She told me that her brother was very ill, and not expected to last much longer. She was already grief-stricken by the thought of losing him, but she is an exceedingly practical woman, as many maiden ladies of her age are. She explained that her brother's wish was to be buried beside his wife in Australia. Therefore, his body would need to be embalmed and a special coffin selected, one heavy and well-sealed, to carry him back to his plot. She made her selections and gave me her address. Therefore, when I received her note, I came as quickly as possible."

"But you know nothing of the family beyond this?"

The undertaker shrugged. "Only that the lady's grief was very real. She had never married, and her brother had become her world since his return from the colonies."

Holmes nodded. "One final question: I have great respect for your profession's skills. Undertakers are trained to be observant, and your

43

practical knowledge rivals that of medical men." Here he turned, with a half-apologetic glance at me. "From what do you believe Mr. Ravel died?"

"Old age and exhaustion, sir. Perhaps you will find this a disappointment, but there was no sign of foul play upon his body."

Our final stop was at the home of the late Mr. Vincent Ravel. It was a slender house of three stories, identical to its neighbors along the row, and possessing neither grace nor charm. A cheap black wreath hung upon the door. An elderly, stout woman in an ill-fitted servant's mourning gown answered the bell.

"Mrs. Brown, is it not?" Holmes asked, quickly offering her his condolences, speaking of Ravel as if he had been her relation rather than her employer. The effect was instantaneous, as the woman began to sob into her starched apron.

"Oh, sir, if only you could have known him. A kindlier man never walked the earth. He was a prince, sir! Why just last month, before he grew so weak, he was pulling shillings from my ears and making the Queen of Hearts disappear from the deck, so I might find her hiding in my flour pan! To think anyone would believe such nonsense – that he could have murdered a woman while he lay on his bed, a sweet smile on his face, gone to his rest like an innocent lamb!"

"Was it his heart?" Holmes asked, as the woman lead us toward the parlor.

"Yes, I think it was – such a hard life he led, travelling all over Australia, doing his little shows at the diggings and on the trails. It wore him out, it did!"

"Jenny!" The strident tone came as we reached the opening of the room, where a clutch of women gathered around a tea set. They were an extraordinary ensemble. Two of them were dressed in male attire, complete with high collars, gaiters, and cigars clenched in their teeth, while another was clad in what could only be described as a medieval costume, a long dress with great belled sleeves and a coronet upon her loosened hair. The fourth woman rose from the group and made a rough wave at the servant. "That will be quite enough, Jenny. My friends," she said to the staring women, who all regarded us as if we weren't two gentlemen, but rather a pair of vile serpents suddenly dropped from trees, "thank you for coming to comfort me. I shall let you know about the service before we depart for Australia."

The trio exited without a further word, giving us a moment to study their hostess. Miss Ramona Ravel was a tall woman who could easily look Holmes in the eye. She had broad shoulders, long arms, and large, rough hands. Her white hair was thick and curled, but cut short, with no attempt

44

at fashion. Only her clothing, a simple black dress which was tastefully hushed, proclaimed her femininity. She nodded at Holmes.

"I know who you are, sir. Inspector Lestrade holds you in high regard and advised me that you were assisting him."

Holmes didn't correct her, an action that showed remarkable forbearance on his part.

"I don't wish to intrude upon your grief, Miss Ravel. I am sorry to have disrupted your conversation with friends."

"It doesn't matter – I was weary of them anyway, and they were more Vincent's friends than mine." She gestured us into the recently vacated chairs. "No doubt you found them odd birds? Vincent had many strange acquaintances in the theatrical and artistic worlds."

"But what of his special friend?"

Miss Ravel stiffened. "Let us not dance around the topic, sir, but speak openly. I have no sympathy for Simone Willow. In another age she might have been a famous courtesan or a concubine, but to me she was no more than a common, public woman. She lured my poor brother into her clutches when he had nothing to offer her except his soul. She toyed with him even as I begged him to honor the memory of his late wife, and that if he must find companionship again, to choose a respectable woman. But he was entranced by her. I confess she bore a striking resemblance to Adelaide, his wife, whom he adored more than life. Then one night he returned from that fiend's lair broken in body and spirit. He lost all interest in simple amusements and pleasures. He shunned even his dearest friends. He began to die, as if he were being slowly poisoned."

Holmes held up a hand. "Did your brother receive letters from Miss Willow?"

"Yes, one note, but it arrived after he had slipped into unconsciousness."

"And did you read it?"

"No, I burned it."

"So your brother had no further interaction with his mistress?"

"None."

I felt myself drawing back from this harsh, cold woman, the way I would lean away from a repulsive lizard. Holmes deftly switched the subject. "You were here all afternoon, as Mr. Hobbs performed his tasks?"

The lady exhaled loudly. "How many times must I repeat it? I never left my room. I lost all track of time, as I could do nothing but weep. Knowing that Vincent was dying, I had made all the proper preparations for the sad event – but when Hobbs came, and it was more than just a terrible dream to me, I could hold back my emotions no longer. Perhaps you cannot understand. You are a man, so your feelings are less refined."

45

She motioned to the room, which was tasteful yet bland, decorated with paintings, palms, and trinkets, yet somehow soulless. "I was always the practical one. My betrothed died of cholera when I was twenty, and I have made my own way in this world ever since. What little money I inherited from my parents I invested well, so that I could live comfortably. Vincent was the romantic fool of our family. How I hoped he would come to understand that we could spend our final years in a pleasant retirement, but no . . . he returned with all his boxes and props and memories, and he could never, in the end, let that illusion depart."

Holmes rose. I assumed the interview was over.

"May I pay my respects to your brother?" my friend asked.

Miss Ravel motioned to the staircase. "Of course. His bedroom is on the first floor. My room, which in your professional capacity you no doubt wish to see, is just above it. I have no reason to forbid you, or to follow you. I only ask that you not upset poor Jenny – she was much attached to my brother, and she was the one who found him gasping for air that awful morning. She ran and fetched the doctor, though Vincent expired just moments after the physician arrived. The doctor assured me there was nothing that he could have done to save him. Jenny was so distraught that a sedative was given to her, and she was senseless until the policeman arrived."

Effectively dismissed, we made our way up the narrow steps. I whispered to Holmes as we climbed. "What are you hoping to find?"

"The thing that is missing," he answered.

Slowly and reverently, we entered the dead man's chamber. He was laid out upon his bed, with tapers burning on either side. Vincent Ravel had once been handsome, though time had taken a cruel toll. Even the finest mortuary arts couldn't completely erase the lines on his face, or heal the sunken nature of his eyes. His hair was silver, as was his neat, pointed beard, and he was clad in evening attire, complete with white satin gloves and the distinctive purple cape that Miss Conner had described. A jaunty, cavalier-style hat was laid beside him.

As I meditated before the body, Holmes quickly scanned the room. It was filled with relics of the man's adventurous life, including several brightly painted boxes, strands of long silk ribbons, and bouquets of artificial flowers. Gaudy images were displayed on the walls, including a set of remarkable advertising posters for Vincent and Adelaide Ravel, "The King and Queen of Magic". I was struck at once by the resemblance Miss Ravel had spoken of. The stunning Mrs. Adelaide Ravel could easily have been the cousin, if not the twin, of the ravishing Miss Simone Willow. Holmes fingered a long blade mounted beneath a poster advertising a "Decapitation of John the Baptist" tableau.

"Rubber," he said with a low chuckle, running an unscathed palm along the sword. "So many wonderful secrets are here. Including that one."

He gestured toward a large metal stand. It confused me until I realized that it was an ornate perch for a bird, complete with a tin cup to hold seed and another to provide water.

"I don't understand. What do you – "

Holmes had departed. With a sigh, I followed him up another flight of stairs to Miss Ravel's chamber. It was as bland as her sibling's had been imaginative – pale cream wallpaper, a small bed on an iron frame, a vanity with only a brush, a comb, and a mirror upon it. An armoire held several rather outdated frocks. The two pictures on the wall were bucolic country scenes. There was but one bookshelf in the room. Holmes allowed his fingers to dance along the spines of its volumes.

"Have you found it?"

Holmes was now looking through the window, which opened over a tiny garden.

"I believe I have, Watson. Lestrade will be delighted when I tell him."

I blinked. "You have the murderer?"

"I do. And it is a double homicide that this individual shall be charged with. Come along."

As we reached the door, the elderly servant met us with our coats and hats. It was clear she hadn't stopped crying, and a red blemish on her face hinted that she had been slapped.

"Forgive me for asking this," Holmes said, "but when and where will the local service for Mr. Ravel be held?"

"Two days from now, sir, at St. Martin's."

"I see. I will perhaps be engaged on another case at that time, but I shall be sure to send a floral tribute. I once saw a most remarkable one, made into the shape of the deceased's favorite dog. I only wish I could find some way to honor Mr. Ravel in such a unique manner. Did he perhaps have a little Fido that he loved?"

"God bless you for your kindness, sir. He didn't have a dog, or a cat, but he adored Charlie, his lyre bird. Brought him all the way from Australia. I found Charlie the very next morning, fallen to the carpet, cold as clay. His heart was broken."

"Our first instincts are often our best ones," Holmes said as he lit his pipe. He had invited Inspector Lestrade to Baker Street for a late supper, and our friend from Scotland Yard had barely touched his food. "But the ideas our instincts generate must be tested, of course. We must collect all the facts before we become enamored of any theory, even one that seems perfectly reasonable. Yet so often the true solution to a case is the most

47

obvious one – and Lestrade, if you say, 'the ghost was the killer', I shall send you home without dessert."

"Well then, who was it?"

Holmes waved a hand like a schoolmaster. "What was your first thought?"

"That no man can be in two places at one time." The inspector bristled. "Therefore, since Ravel was dead, someone had chosen to impersonate him."

"A rational thought. And the only answer."

"But no one left that house – unless they are somehow all conspirators, and willing to lie for each other," I said.

"A possible but unlikely scenario," Holmes countered. "Lestrade was correct in his assessment of his relative's veracity. Also, the undertaker had no previous relationship with the family and no reason to be involved in committing murder. The servant is elderly and would be an unlikely double for the offended gentleman. The sister, however . . . ."

I thought about her height, her short hair, her generally mannish appearance. She would have had no difficulty donning some of her brother's clothing and, with the addition of a collared cape, a false beard, and a low-brimmed hat, she could have fooled anyone.

"But the undertaker said she was there, the entire time!" the inspector protested. "Hobbs would never lie about what he heard."

Holmes snapped his fingers. "And there you have it, Lestrade! What he *heard*. He didn't see the lady after she went upstairs, but he heard her."

"Even if she played a phonograph," I said, "the recording wouldn't have lasted long enough for her to go on her murderous errand."

"An astute observation. That is why she needed a living accomplice." Holmes rose and went to the shelf, plucking down a heavy volume of his Index. "Do you recall Miss Conner's story? What was the sole treasure Mr. Ravel bestowed upon his lover?"

I felt like daylight was breaking from behind heavy clouds. "A feather from his exotic bird!"

"A lyre bird, to be precise. See this engraving – and the match to the feather on the mantel? Native to Australia, the lyre bird is an exceptional mimic, and can be trained to replicate a wide variety of sounds, everything from the shrill whistle of a train to the bark of a dog to the excessive weeping of a distraught woman." Holmes closed the book. "I have no doubt this bird was slain the moment its usefulness was served."

"Good Lord – it's so simple! But why? Why go to such an effort to commit murder?" the astonished inspector cried.

"I would suggest, Lestrade, that you ask that question when you arrest her."

As my readers are perhaps aware, Lestrade's dash to Curzon Street was in vain. When he reached the house, he found only the dead man and the bereaved maid – Miss Ramona Ravel had vanished. Despite a report in the same tawdry newspaper which hailed Lestrade as a hero whose *"remarkable theorizing"* and *"incomparable knowledge of the natural world"* had led him to the solution of the crime, many London residents remained convinced that murderous ghosts floated among them, and the sales of magical charms – as well as attendance at séances – continued to rise.

A year later, Holmes opened a letter with a foreign stamp and postmark. He gave a cry of delight and thrust it at me. It read as follows:

Dear Mr. Holmes,

> *I didn't kill the bird.*
> *While my finger didn't shake as I pulled the trigger of the pistol and sent that wicked adventuress to face judgment, I found I couldn't bring myself to end the life of an innocent creature which my brother considered a partner in his magical acts. Charlie died a natural death, one no doubt brought on by strain and grief. The day after my brother's passing, Jenny found the poor thing dead below his perch – but my hand didn't cause his demise.*
> *I knew I had to flee when I heard you propose a floral tribute to my brother. I understood the conversation at once for what it was – confirmation of that final clue. I was listening on the landing above and, had you but looked up over your shoulder, you would have seen the horror on my face as I recalled that my brother had given that witch one of Charlie's feathers as a keepsake. A man of your abilities would certainly figure out the connection. Thus, if I were to maintain my liberty, I had to vanish immediately.*
> *Where I am now is unimportant – I am beyond the ability of you or any of your minions at Scotland Yard to capture. But I wished you to know that I respect your talents. So I will make a deduction of my own . . . you are still curious as to why I killed Simone Willow.*
> *It was simple matter of revenge – She murdered my brother. No, she didn't poison him or fatally wound him with*

49

a sword. But she humiliated him, and to a man of his nature, pride was life.

My brother, you see, was a sensualist. He loved his wife dearly, but he couldn't resist the pull to savor all of life's fleshy delights. From his twenties onward, he was an adventurer, a seducer, a rascal. More than once, he was nearly killed when an irate husband interrupted a vow-breaking tryst. Poor Adelaide knew his faults, but her love for him overcame it.

When he returned to London after her death, he claimed his romantic affairs were done, that he wished only to live a retired life. Yet when Simone Willow crossed his path, he couldn't resist her. My brother possessed no fortune, but what little he had he spent on her, and then he began to beg money from me. I refused, and we had rows over it.

One night he returned home in anguish. I suspected Vincent had begged Simone to marry him. I knew her answer would have been no, for I had read her disgusting little book and learned how her twisted mind worked. It was not until I intercepted her letter that I discovered the true cause of Vincent's rapid decline, his deep depression, his refusal to eat, and his surrender to the sicknesses that had always hovered at the threshold, ready to draw him down.

I shall be as discreet as possible: She had mocked him as a lover who had disappointed her in the most intimate of ways. He was already unwell, and this notion – that he, who had knowledge of women on four continents – would never please a lady again, broke him as assuredly as if he had been dropped from the gallows. He was already comatose by the time the apologetic letter arrived. He never had a chance to read it. Her confession of her cruel words to him on that final night burned a hole in my heart. Simone apologized for her vicious taunt. She pleaded for his return. Yet within a week, he was dead and could never answer.

I had truly not planned to do murder – but when Charlie, whom I had moved to my room, began his cries, I sprang to action, for it seemed that nature itself was calling out to me to avenge my brother. Vincent had shared many secrets of his trade with me, so I knew how to paint myself and apply a false beard. You obviously noted my strong resemblance to my brother. By writing instructions on cards, I was able to avoid speaking, for I wasn't certain I could produce a convincing

50

masculine voice. Simone Willow's maidservant was easily cowed, and the foolish vixen came eagerly to her death with open arms. It was only at the very last second that she saw through my disguise.

Her scream did her no good, for I am an excellent shot.

The High Table Hallucination
by David L. Leal

Chapter I – Telegram at Baker Street

The telegram arrived on a cold Sunday evening, as Sherlock Holmes and I sat in the glow of the warming fire and the memory of an excellent dinner. I was perusing the latest issue of *The British Medical Journal*, while Holmes was reading his latest acquisition from the Church Street corner bookstore.

Mrs. Hudson had just cleared the dishes when we heard a knock at the front door, and a minute later, she brought the missive to Holmes. My friend set aside his book, which to my surprise was *In a Glass Darkly* by Sheridan Le Fanu.

He opened the envelope, scanned the several lines of text, and languidly tossed it into the fire.

"A communication from our old friend, Hilton Soames," Holmes explained. "He is happy to hear of our impending visit to the famous university town and asks if we will stay as his guests in St. Luke's College. I will miss The Chequers and its notable port and linen, but I haven't experienced collegiate life since I went down. Is that agreeable to you?"

I replied that I would be happy to see a Camford college from the inside. Our previous visit to St. Luke's, during the affair of the Three Students, allowed only brief glimpses of the college. My own university days were at the University of London, a modern institution designed for research and teaching, not the creation of an elite. I rang for Billy and asked him to send a wire to The Chequers, cancelling our reservations.

I reflected that our visit to Camford was timely, as few clients had crossed our threshold that winter. As the Holmes's's reputation grew, some potential clients were dissuaded from requesting his assistance. He maintained his love of all that was *outré*, and he still remitted his fees for those of modest means, but fame could deter the distressed while attracting the merely curious.

While Holmes showed no signs of craving the old stimulant, I wished to see him occupied at all times. Our visit to Camford was therefore most welcome, as it signaled the resumption of his work on a topic of longstanding interest: Early English charters. His previous efforts were interrupted by the case of the three candidates for the Fortescue Scholarship. Holmes solved the case without any difficulty, and I believe he understood the course of events as soon as he surveyed Mr. Soames' rooms. Our somewhat nervous and excitable friend was grateful that the college, and indeed the entire university, was spared a painful scandal.

Nevertheless, the case wasted two valuable days, and his researches didn't advance beyond the early stages. Because he was then retained by Commodore Billingsley on the occasion of his court martial, the examination of the archives in the library was shelved, so to speak, for another time.

I also suspect that Holmes found historical research more challenging than he anticipated. A monograph that compiles facts is one thing – to understand the course of English constitutional history is quite another. His previous works contained images of tobacco ash and ears, but that isn't quite research by the standard of the new German style of scholarship that has swept Europe. Scholars are now expected to be professionals who specialize in a topic, thereby making discoveries that weren't possible in the "gentleman scholar" era. To adequately study any subject now requires many years of training. With research literatures growing by the month, there is little room for the amateur dabbler.

Three years after our previous visit, having taken this initial lay of the archival land, Holmes wished to revisit Camford with a more specific topic in mind. Rather than the entire history of English charters, he now sought to examine the charters of the great religious houses dissolved during the English Reformation. On more than one occasion he referred to the dissolution of the monasteries by Henry VIII as "that greatest of cultural crimes in English history". This research would help to better understand how power corrupts, and absolute power corrupts absolutely, as his former client Lord Acton so succinctly observed.

Chapter II – Train to Camford

After a leisurely breakfast on Monday, Holmes and I packed clothing and other necessities for a week's visit. At noon, Mrs. Hudson brought us luncheon along with a stack of letters from the recent post. One was from Hilton Soames. Holmes roughly slit the long blue envelope with a butter knife and read aloud the short note:

Dear Mr. Holmes:

As I communicated in my earlier telegram, I eagerly await your arrival. As I dared not communicate, I hope you will be able to clear up a new mystery. Some students and servants report seeing a ghost who roams the cloisters at night. They

53

have identified him as a fellow from a century ago who was murdered by a town mob after converting to Catholicism. I am not only anxious to put this superstition to rest, but to avoid inflaming religious tensions. I trust that you will be able to spare some time from your researches to help us solve this vexing matter.

Yours, etc.

I could tell from his expression that Holmes wasn't pleased by this development. I knew well that his rational mind objected all that was superstitious.

After a pause, he complained. "Our friend does have a habit of confiscating our time. I can see that we will need to sooth him again. I wonder if he invited us to lodge in the college with an eye to securing my professional services. Some people do impose on old friendships."

It was too late to decline the invitation, so we hailed a four-wheeler and were soon at King's Cross. We had a first-class compartment to ourselves, and Holmes began to read the several newspapers he purchased at the station – *The Daily Telegraph, Pall Mall Gazette, The Clarion,* and *The Manchester Guardian.*

Holmes cared little about politics and international affairs, however, and I always failed to draw him out on wars, parties, leaders, and elections. These were the preoccupations of his brother Mycroft, who lived for nothing else and lodged for many years across from the Diogenes Club in Pall Mall. My companion's focus was the agony columns, crime news, and anything else relevant to his work.

Chapter III – Arrival

Two hours later, we arrived at the familiar station of the great university town. We walked into a light rain, but Holmes instantly recognized an elderly porter, Johnson by name, who had served customers of Midlands and Humber Railroad for decades. He loaded our bags onto a cart and led the way to a growler, and we were on our way to St. Luke's.

We passed the familiar landmarks – the parish church of St. Mary, the old residence of Charles Darwin, the closed mill – and we were soon on the High Street. Holmes was in good spirits, which was unusual for him while traveling. He typically missed the comforts of our Baker Street rooms, and without his chemical apparatus, newspaper clippings, and small but comfortable bedroom, he could be a difficult companion.

On this occasion, he pointed out, with a hint of nostalgia, the locales he knew so well from student days: The botanic garden, the Exam House, the university library, the Westonian Theatre, the Fitzmolean Museum, and finally, St. Luke's. He remarked that each one contributed to his diverse body of knowledge and aided his future career. He had no practical plan in mind when he supplemented the formal and ancient curriculum with explorations of nature, past cultures, music, and out-of-the-way books. As he added this unusual lumber to his mental attic, he came to see how it gave him an advantage in criminal deduction. When his friends brought him unusual problems, he not only observed many obscure details, but was able to understand what they meant. Later, in London, he found that he could best police inspectors, who only had experience to guide them. They were lost when anything new occurred, whereas Holmes was in his element when connecting unusual dots.

Everyone he encountered was bewildered by his abilities. Even I was often lost at sea, a metaphor I once subtly emphasized with a reference to "one of Clark Russell's fine sea-stories".

As we pulled up in front of the college gate, an ancient porter slowly made his way from the lodge to the street. As he looked inside, he exclaimed, "Lord luv a duck, if it isn't Mr. Holmes!" He then hastened, "I beg your pardon, sir, for speaking as I did, but I was surprised to see you. I believe it was three years since you last visited us."

"Yes, Patterson, and I'm glad to be back" replied Holmes. "I haven't forgotten your many kindnesses during my student days. I must have been rather trying to the college servants, conducting illegal chemical experiments in my rooms at all hours, and often with the most deplorable results. I still cannot imagine how you cleaned my rooms after that explosion, I'm sure you will remember which. I am also grateful that Warden Nichols never discovered who was responsible for the dreadful noise."

"Young men will be young men," said the porter with a smile. "We are glad to see you back, sir." He observed the driver unloading our luggage and asked, "You will be staying in the college, I believe, sir?"

"Yes, we are the guests of Mr. Hilton Soames. May I introduce to you my friend, Dr. Watson?"

"It is an honour to meet you, sir. Yes, I am a devoted admirer of your stories, as are all the college servants." He looked furtively from side to side and added, "I hope you will not be offended if I tell you that we have placed a small plaque next to the door of your old rooms. It reads '*Mr. Sherlock Holmes Lived Here*'. Just a small token of our esteem, sir, and I hope we haven't taken a liberty. The fellows are never found in that staircase, which only has student rooms, so this is something of a secret, you understand."

"It is safe with me," said Holmes, and I read both embarrassment and pleasure on his face.

The porter walked back to his lodge and returned a minute later, holding a sheet of paper. "You will be in H staircase, gentlemen. You will remember it is in Surrey Quad, so just go through the main quad and turn to your right. I will have your bags sent over right away. You will remember that Mr. Soames is in D staircase, also in Surrey."

"Thank you, Peterson. I think we will call on Mr. Soames just in time for tea."

Chapter IV – Mr. Hilton Soames

His rooms were on the ground floor, and as he wasn't sporting the oak, we knocked on the inner door. He opened it himself and gave an exclamation of happy surprise. "It is very good to see you both. Too much time has passed since your last visit. Please come in – tea is about to be served. Have a seat on the couch – or would you prefer to walk past it and sit on one of those chairs?" he added with a smile.

At that moment, a college servant entered the room with a tea tray. "This is Smithson, my scout, who replaced Bannister. Smithson, this is Mr. Sherlock Holmes and Dr. Watson, who will be staying with us for a week." Smithson replied with a suitable acknowledgement, set the tray down on a table, and withdrew.

"I was sad to lose Bannister. He was a good man, a leal man. It was a shame that his loyalties were put to the test. As you know, scouts look after the fellows and their rooms, and a scout can make all the difference between a comfortable and a vexing life. Smithson is quite competent. He started working at the college as a young man and has been a scout to one fellow or another for many years."

I could tell that Holmes and Soames wanted to discuss old times, but they were too polite to introduce any topic to which I couldn't contribute. Instead, Soames began recounting the fates of the three students, who I recalled were Daulat Ras, Miles McLaren, and young Gilchrist. Their stories were so fascinating that I may relate them in a separate essay for my readers.

Holmes listened with close attention, drinking his Darjeeling tea. When Soames concluded, my friend said, "I would like to ask you about your letter, which we received today before our departure. Am I to understand that this college has a ghost?"

Soames did not immediately reply, and I could see that some of his old nervousness had returned. After a moment, he said, "It is a delicate matter, and some of the fellows are quite upset. They believe it is a foolish prank, and most unwelcome. If it became generally known that our students and servants claimed to see ghosts, our reputation would suffer a grievous blow. This testimony isn't easy to dismiss, however. The students are quite respectable young men, hardly prone to tomfooleries, and the servants are sober and reliable. I'm sure we can rely on your discretion, in any case."

"If it is a ghost, there is little I can do, as the supernatural is beyond my remit. I assume you believe the problem to be a very human one, probably with a student origin. Wait, don't tell me – you wish me to solve the mystery and bring the episode to a conclusion with as little publicity as possible and to avoid, as you yourself once put it, a hideous scandal?" He added, although with a smile, "Really, my friend, this is becoming repetitive!"

With much relief, Soames responded, "I am sure we will all be grateful for your assistance, and I do apologize that the college is continually calling upon your services. I understand that your goal is to conduct research, not to chase a ghost, but hopefully the latter will not impede the former. I, myself, am conducting research into an ancient Greek manuscript, which could be the long-rumored lost chapter of Thucydides. This is the one I dared to give the students three years ago for the Fortescue Exam. Perhaps it was unfair of me to give them such an unfamiliar text, and I may even share some of the blame for Gilchrist succumbing to his unfortunate temptation."

He continued, and with an air of complaint that was unburdened by any irony. "My work is continually delayed, however, as I have so many calls upon my time."

I sensed that Holmes was on the verge of a sarcastic response, but Soames continued to talk in his excitable manner. "I hope you both will join us for High Table during your visit. Please meet me here at six p.m., and we will attend Evensong, followed by drinks at the Senior Common Room, which an American visitor recently called our 'Faculty Lounge'. At the S.C.R., you will meet many of our fellows, and then we shall dine."

We agreed to this most pleasing prospect, took our leave, and made our way back to H staircase. Our trunks were waiting, and a scout was unpacking the contents.

We discovered the college had assigned us Smithson, so during our visit we would share the same scout as Soames. When every item had been put in its place, he inquired about our breakfast needs. We requested sausage, eggs, toast, thick cut marmalade, and coffee, and he retired.

Chapter V – Evensong

As arranged, we met Mr. Soames in his rooms at six p.m.. He was wearing his black gown and inquired about the adequacy of our accommodations. We walked down the staircase and into the quad, along a cobblestone path, and through an archway in the center of a building. We alighted into the appropriately named Chapel Quad, and the object of our destination took up an entire south side. While it didn't rival in size the chapel of King's or the cathedral of Christ Church, it was among the largest in Camford. We were soon in the baroque ante-chapel, and Holmes spent a few minutes looking at the memorial plaques on the wall. He later said that the Warden of his day, Sir Edward Nichols KBE FRCS, was so memorialized.

With his interest in polyphonic motets, Holmes was looking forward to Evensong. We entered the chapel and took a place in a stall on the immediate right, while Soames walked further down and sat in one of the fellow's stalls. The other attendees included about three-dozen students, a dozen fellows, and the college chaplain. Organ music wafted down from above, and for several minutes we were alone with our thoughts. The chapel had a rather Catholic atmosphere, and I admired the stained glass, reredos, and statues.

The chapel choir, dressed in the traditional raiment of white surplices over black robes, processed in two parallel lines from the ante-chapel and took their places in facing stalls. The service began in its familiar and timeless manner, immediately instilling a reflective mood. While I rarely attend church services, I understood why many saw this ancient office as a fitting end to the day.

As I recalled from the religious instruction in my public school, Evensong combined the ancient offices of vespers and compline. St. Luke's Chapel used the version in *The Book of Common Prayer*. It featured a service that is largely sung, accompanied by Old Testament and New Testament readings, *Psalms*, prayers, and sometimes hymns. It had the advantage, in my mind at least, of being shorter than a Sunday service.

The service began, moving from the Invitation to the *Magnificat* (setting by Thomas Tallis) and from the *Nunc dimittis* (with the new setting by Charles Villiers Stanford) to the Lord's Prayer. It concluded with a hymn.

We watched the chaplain and choir depart, followed by the fellows and students. Holmes and I walked outside to find Soames, who led us to the S.C.R.

Upon entering the room, we saw about two-dozen fellows conversing in small groups. Some held a glass of sherry, and all wore gowns.

Soames motioned toward a distinguished man in a clerical collar and gown. "That is the Reverend Hugh Spotifield, our Warden. I know what you're thinking – that he is the very picture of respectability – but I assure you that he is no caricature. Our Warden is well known for his sense of humor and passion for sports. He recently installed a 'real tennis' court alongside our cricket oval."

I knew Holmes had already intuited the sporting interests of the man from the development of his hands and other signs, but I remained silent.

The Warden walked over to our group and Soames made the introductions. The hearty reverend said, "I'm sure I speak for all the fellows when I say that the college is honoured by your visit. We are always glad to see old students, but we have few who have affected the course of European history in such unexpected ways. I dare say you have been more important to England than a brace of cabinet ministers.

"I would like to introduce you to some of our junior fellows. This is Stanley Reece, the new tutor for Greek. He won the Fortescue Scholarship two years ago – an excellent young scholar from Durham. John Montagne studies modern history, one of those newer degrees, which must have been in its infancy in your time. Jane Knight-Werck is a fellow not of our college, of course, but one of the women's colleges, St. Hildegard. Her uncle is our Dean, so we see quite a bit of her, don't we, my dear? Captain Taylor is our new ancient historian, and one of our empire builders. He served with Major-General Hunter and the 10th Sudanese at the Battle of Abu Hamed in the Sudan last year."

In an aside to Holmes, Warden Spotifield said, "Lots of opinions about that war in the college. The fellows were quite divided, so it's a subject best avoided."

As always, I was overwhelmed by so many introductions, and I doubted I could remember any name but that of Jane. I noticed that Holmes was carefully studying them, although why he should be so interested in a collection of language and history scholars I didn't know.

They asked Holmes a range of friendly questions about his work. They had apparently read all of my stories and discovered quite a few inconsistencies, which I found somewhat embarrassing.

At last, a servant entered the room and sounded a gong, and it was time for that most famous of Camford rituals, High Table. The Warden remarked, "That is Jamieson, the head servant in the hall. He is one of the men who reported seeing the ghost, so you will undoubtedly speak with him later.

"I see you are curious about the gong, Dr. Watson. Yes, we keep up the old traditions here. That gong has called fellows to High Table for over two-hundred years. I think it was part of the spoils of empire. Some of our students in those days sought commissions in East India Company regiments, and one may have brought it back – from where I know not."

On a large piece of paper near the door was a diagram of High Table, with names indicated at specific places. I saw that I was placed across from the Warden and between two scholars unknown to me. Holmes was seated at a far end, with a fellow named Roger Atkinson on his right and no one on his left.

Chapter VII – High Table

The Senior Common Room was a medium-sized space on top of the building that contained the hall. I thought we would descend to the main hall entrance and then process between the rows of candlelit undergraduate tables until we reached the High Table at the opposite end. As in most traditional college halls, the High Table was so named because it rests on a raised platform. In earlier eras, students from the aristocracy would sit at this table with the fellows, but now it was reserved for fellows and their guests, who always appreciated the invitation.

Instead, I was surprised that we exited out of the S.C.R. through a glass door and walked directly onto the roof. We had a broken view of a quad as we trooped past ancient battlements on our way to another door, which opened to a staircase. We walked down a level and entered directly onto the High Table platform. The students were in no way surprised by this unusual entrance, and once we were seated, the Warden gave the Latin grace, *Benedictus benedicat.*

The only sources of light were the few candles on the table, and the atmosphere was consequently dim. The fellows, dressed alike in black robes, were cast in shadows and could have been mistaken for medieval monks at a communal meal. I only saw clearly the fellows to my left and right. Even those across the table were somewhat indistinct.

As the meal began, I experienced the frisson that comes from partaking in a tradition that goes back centuries. I reflected that modern man discards such communal rituals at his own risk.

I glanced up and saw portraits on the walls from centuries past, each illuminated by its own candle. I imagined the old fellows looking down upon us, perhaps judgmentally. Did they find us wanting?

I was reminded of the description of the hall in *Tom Brown at Oxford*: ". . . *rather a fine old room, with a good, arched, black oak ceiling and high panelling, hung round with pictures of old swells, bishops and lords chiefly, who have endowed the college in some way, or at least have fed here in times gone by, and for whom –* 'caeterisque benefactoribus nostris' *– We daily give thanks in a long Latin grace.*"

During the early dinner courses, I saw Holmes conversing with the fellow to his right, who I later learned was Roger Atkinson, an antiquarian who specialized in Africa and the Middle East. They had quite an animated discussion during the initial courses, but I was unable to discern the topic.

By an unspoken college tradition, when the main course was served, the High Table to Holmes's left now had an occupant, a rather elderly fellow who appeared to be hard of hearing, as he was leaning precipitously toward my friend.

I will long remember that glorious evening. For almost two hours, we enjoyed excellent food, wine from one of the finest cellars in the kingdom, and a dessert I will long remember. I used ancient silverware that had served centuries of fellows, ate from plates embossed with the college arms, and drank from fine crystal. Numerous college servants walked silently around the table, bringing and removing dishes and refiling drinks.

The Warden finally stood up and intoned the departing grace, *Benedicto benedicatur*. He turned around and departed through the small door in the back wall. We all followed him and were soon back in the S.C.R. for more drinks. How these fellows got any work done, in the midst of such plenty, is a mystery worthy of Holmes.

Chapter VIII – Back in the S.C.R.

Holmes and I accepted glasses of port, which to my delight were from the renowned vintage year of 1851, and we fell into conversation with the Warden. A small group of fellows congregated around us, and Holmes recounted two recent cases. One involved a member of the House of Lords, although the more intriguing case was brought to us by one of London's many gas-lamp lighters.

Holmes introduced me to Roger Atkinson, one of his High Table neighbors. He was among the new generation of fellows with a PhD, and they had conversed about recent acquisitions by the British Museum. He had spent much time in the field and was concerned about how items of cultural value from other countries were brought back to Britain but then put into storage and forgotten. "We should either display them or return them," he said. He reminded us that Prime Minister Gladstone, a devout

Christian, had publicly criticized the removal of items from Abyssinia after Britain's punitive expedition in 1868.

This statement occasioned an awkward pause, and Atkinson changed the subject by asking Holmes, "Who was your other conversation partner – the fellow to your left. I didn't notice him at first, but you two had much to say."

Holmes replied, "I had a most interesting conversation about English constitutional history with a William Desjardin. He is a fount of knowledge, and I hope to speak to him again after I've revisited the archives. I don't see him in this room, so if someone can tell me where he lives in the college, I'll be certain to pay him a visit."

My friend has made many statements in his time that shocked the people around him, and this was among the most memorable. One fellow dropped his glass, another sputtered as he drank, and the rest stared at him incredulously.

The Warden was the first to speak, albeit hesitantly. "I think I can appreciate a joke as much as the next man, but you may be going too far. Some of these fellows have been much troubled by the ghost sightings. Come now, Mr. Holmes. With whom did you actually converse?"

Holmes was surprised by this statement. "The man introduced himself as William Desjardin, a college fellow and legal scholar. He asked about my research into early charters, and we had a very interesting conversation about the law during the English Reformation. Are you claiming he was someone else? And how does this involve your ghost trouble?"

Hilton Soames was the first to answer, although his voice quavered slightly. "As I mentioned in my letter, a ghost has been seen in the college at night. He is said to be William Desjardin, who was killed a century ago by a town mob after his conversion to Rome. There have been rumors of his continued presence in this college ever since, and some of our students and servants claim to have seen him this very year. His portrait hangs in the hall, but you probably didn't notice."

"I noticed all fourteen oil portraits in the hall," responded Holmes. "They appear to be genuine except for the smallest on the north side, which portrays a bishop. It is very striking but undoubtedly a recent forgery. Sometimes paintings of questionable provenance come to a college as gifts from benefactors or retiring fellows. It is rather awkward to question a gift, so they are often hung despite misgivings."

An astonished look appeared on the Warden's face. "You are more than living up to your reputation, Mr. Holmes. We have long suspected that painting of having a, shall we say, complex history. The painting of Mr. Desjardin is on the opposite wall. The students see it every day, so it must have been quite a shock for some to observe that face floating through a cloister. Two servants also claim to have seen the ghost this year, but these men are from the town and subject to the most incredible superstitions."

He then looked at the fellows, who had all drawn near and were listening intently. "Did any of you see the man seated to the left of Mr. Holmes? Did you see him in the S.C.R. beforehand, or did you walk with him into or out of the hall?"

Nobody replied, and Holmes said drily, "If I understand you correctly, I sat next to a ghost and carried on a conversation with him about early English charters."

"As a recent American guest would say, that's about the size of it. What can you tell us about the alleged Desjardin? What did he look like? When did you first see him? Did he leave with you? And where is he now?"

Holmes provided his usual precise details. "As you know, the only source of illumination was the candles on the table, so I couldn't clearly see him. He was thin, of medium height, soft spoken, elderly, had a full head of grey hair, and appeared to be hard of hearing. As he raised his glass, I noticed that his fingers had faint but visible ink stains, as well as the characteristic marks caused by the habitual holding of a quill. I have made a small study of occupational marks on the human hand. You may have seen my monograph on the subject.

"I didn't notice him in the S.C.R., nor was he present for the first part of dinner. I recall that he sat down just as the main course was served and we shifted our conversation partners, and he left just before the Warden said the Latin grace. I didn't see him on the walk back up to the S.C.R., although I was looking for him in order to continue our discussion."

Little more could be said at that point. None of the fellows believed that a ghost dined at High Table, yet this incident was difficult to doubt. There is something in Holmes's character that forbids contradiction. This gathering should have been a happy event, but an uneasy spirit of perturbation now pervaded the room. The fellows began to say their farewells and drift back to their college rooms or their homes in town. We were left alone with the Warden, and Holmes promised that we would visit him tomorrow to talk the matter over. We returned to H staircase, but it was some time before I could fall asleep.

Chapter IX – Investigation

The next morning, our scout Smithson brought breakfast to our room. My appetite was limited, but Holmes ate heartily. I'm not a man well attuned to spiritual matters, but I was beginning to wonder if ghosts moved among us.

"Holmes, could this college actually be haunted? The idea is impossible. It contradicts the rational spirit of the age and is incompatible with my scientific training. Yet you, the most rational of men, may have conversed with a ghost."

Holmes was by no means discomposed. "I have no definite reason to believe this William Desjardin was a ghost. He appeared human to me, and I wonder why a ghost would want to converse about English law. On the other hand, he did resemble his portrait, and there is no explanation for his appearance and disappearance. Two students, who are said to be reliable, reported seeing him recently. I am also not so dismissive of the testimony of college servants. They often see themselves as the keepers of college tradition, more so than do the fellows. They wouldn't introduce any controversy lightly."

We made our way to the Warden's lodge. Etched on a brass plate by the door was the name, "*The Rev. H. D. L. Spotifield CBE*". Holmes muttered, with a twinkle in his eye, "It's his real name, anyhow, and that is something to note."

The Warden received us with much hospitality, and we were seated in chairs that looked out onto a small garden. It would be a most attractive view in the summer. We conversed for a few minutes about the architecture of the college, but the reason for the visit wasn't far from our minds.

"I am happy you are here because nobody else can settle the matter. We will accept your judgement about whether a ghost is haunting the college. May I ask how you propose to investigate?"

I could tell that Holmes was unhappy about being involved in yet another mystery at St. Luke's. Every day, a new obstacle was thrown onto his path to the archives.

"To begin, can you tell me about the two students who claimed to have seen the ghost?"

The Warden reported that the students in question were stolid and reliable. "Reginald Farrington and Bertrand Dunleavy are from the shires, the sons of local squires. They play cricket for the college and are popular among the students. They will never win any academic prizes, no sir, but our nation needs their type. Reginald has a large family estate to run, and Bertrand will likely succeed his father as member for the district. What they learn from St. Luke's is more about manners and polish than scholarly knowledge, but you know the famous saying, *Manners maketh the man*."

"I would like to question these young men, along with the servants who reported a sighting. Also, can you arrange a group meeting with the servants who attended us at High Table?"

"Yes, that can all be done. The two students live in Chapel Quad, in B staircase. I anticipated your request, so I sent a message asking them to wait upon your visit in their rooms. As I mentioned earlier, one of the college servants who saw the ghost is Jamieson, who oversees the meals in the hall. He is on duty all day in the kitchens, and we have found him to be quite steady and trustworthy over the years. As a young man, he saw action in Afghanistan with the Royal Munsters. The other servant is Smithson, who I assigned to be your scout, so you have undoubtedly met him already. He is Soames' scout, and also for all the rooms on D staircase. Smithson has loyally served the college for many years. You can question him at any time. As you wish to meet with the hall servants as a group, the most convenient time is during the Evensong hour, as they have little to do before the S.C.R. reception begins. I will arrange a meeting today."

During our interview with the Warden, rain began to fall on this ancient town of emerald lawns, lichen-tinted courts, and towering spires. We took our leave and walked briskly across the slippery cobblestones to Chapel Quad. We trooped up the stone staircase and, seeing that the outer door was open, we knocked and entered.

Chapter X – The Two Students

The two young gentlemen rose as we entered the sitting room. We were clearly among sportsmen, as cricket equipment and team photos were the primary decorations. The mantel was filled with invitations, a testament to their popularity, but few books were evident.

"Thank you for meeting with us," said my friend. "I am Sherlock Holmes, and this is my friend and colleague, Dr. Watson. As you know, we're investigating the alleged ghost of this college, and we understand that you are the most recent student witnesses. Dr. Watson can tell you about my doubts regarding spiritualism and the spirit world, but I don't want to prejudice my investigation. I must keep an open mind, and I hope you can tell me precisely what you saw, where you saw it, and when you saw it."

The young man on our left, wearing a cricket sweater with burgundy and gold piping, was the first to respond. "We are glad to meet you, sir, I'm sure. I'm Reginald, and this is Bertrand. We have both read of your adventures, so we are pleased to be part of a case. Our encounter with the ghost took place in the main quad. It was the Tuesday of last week. We were out late at St. Dominic's, the dining club for athletes. We arrived just before the college gates closed at ten p.m. We didn't want to be fined again, so we were a little out of breath when we arrived. As we made our way to our rooms, we saw someone walking through the cloister to our left. We thought nothing of it, as people walk around the college at all hours, but Reginald saw the face and stopped in his tracks. I looked to see what was the matter, and there he was, the very likeness of his portrait in the hall."

"Did he say anything, or make any gesture?"

"No, sir, he just looked at us while walking. We lost sight of him when he reached the shadows at the end of the cloister, which was also a mystery. It took a minute to steady our nerves, but when we had a look around, he was gone. We aren't sure how he could have disappeared, as there are no staircases at that end, but I guess that would be no trouble for a ghost."

I was surprised by Holmes's next question. "When you saw him, did you sense any psychic disturbance or have any unusual spiritual feelings? In other words, was your initial impression that he was a ghost, or just a man who looked like the fellow in the portrait?"

This time, Bertrand answered. "I can't say that we sensed anything odd, sir. We were surprised. It was dark, and we had just returned from a rather jolly dinner. We aren't superstitious, but we cannot explain his presence or disappearance. We mentioned it to our moral tutor, the Reverend Jeremiah Fainsod, as we needed to pay him a visit anyway. I'm afraid he suspected our dinner had been too jolly and that we were seeing things. He must have mentioned it to the Warden, for we received a note from him this morning asking us to wait upon your visit."

"Have you reached any conclusion about whether the figure was a ghost?"

"No, sir, we have not. We're all in favor of a college ghost – just the thing to brighten up the atmosphere here, so studious and serious, don't you know? But why would any ghost want to haunt the college – and you can hardly call it a haunting. In literature, ghosts are always shrieking or seeking revenge, but this one just walks around, enjoying an evening constitutional."

With this final statement, Holmes thanked the students and we made our way to the kitchens to interview Jamieson.

Chapter XI – Smithson

On our way to see Jamieson, Holmes decided to take a detour and interview Smithson. We found him in a fellow's room on the first floor of the staircase, dusting a collection of fragile figurines, including a rather antique porcelain portrayal of the infant Samuel at prayer.

Holmes apologized for interrupting his work but requested a few minutes of his time to discuss the ghost. Smithson was in no way surprised, and immediately began his tale.

"It was like this, sir. My dooties keep me in the college from breakfast to dinner. I bring the gentlemen breakfast and luncheon, although one or two do not eat it, and then I see to whatever needs to be done. Sometimes a fellow prefers to eat luncheon or dinner in his room instead of in hall, and if so, I serve him. In between meals, I see to anything the fellows require – sending clothes out for mending, for example, or seeing to a chair that needs repair. There is always something to occupy me hours.

"One early evening, after the sun had set, I had just brought dinner to Mr. Richardson's rooms when I looked out of the long, low, latticed window and saw a figure just outside. He wore a fellow's robe, but he moved furtive-like, almost suspicious. I can't explain exactly, but it drew my attention. He looked up into the window, and core blimey if it wasn't the old man in the portrait! I must have exclaimed, because Mr. Richardson asked what was the matter. I explained, and he came over to have a look. The mysterious figure was gone by then, and although we both walked around the quad, there was no trace of him."

Holmes asked, "How would you describe him?"

"Well, sir, I could see his grey hair reflecting in the moonlight, and he was clearly an old man, but I can recall no other detail."

Holmes asked other questions about his appearance and movements, but no useful information could be obtained. Holmes thanked the man for his answers, and we resumed our quest for the kitchens.

Chapter XII – Jamieson

The kitchens were in the basement under the hall. They were enormous and vaulted, likely constructed in the late Middle Ages. Perhaps they were originally part of the Dominican monastery that stood on this land before the college was founded.

We found Jamieson sitting at a large table, surreptitiously reading a copy of *The Manchester Guardian*.

"We aren't allowed to read during slack times" he explained. "They say we must always be alert and on duty, so we hide the newspaper under this ledger. When the coast is clear, we raise the ledger and read for a while."

"My sympathies are entirely with you," said Holmes. "We only wish to ask you about the ghost you reported seeing several weeks ago.

"Yes, sir. It was quite a thrill to see a living, breathing ghost, if you get my meaning, Mr. Holmes."

He looked around for a moment, and then lowered his voice as one who is discussing a state secret. "I wouldn't say this to anyone except yourselves, but our Warden is much in favor of the ghost. He is a religious man and believes in a spiritual world that is beyond our ken. He doesn't like to hear mockery about the ghost, which he sees as relatin' to these Darwinian doubts about anything religious. He worries you will decide against the ghost, which will enliven the scoffers.

"The day I last saw the ghost was the previous month, on St. Scholastica Day. I was on duty during High Table, and I then attended the fellows in the S.C.R. I live in the college, which is old fashioned, but I stick to the old ways. Living in town isn't for me, sir."

"As I walked to K staircase, where my room is on the top, I spotted a figure making his way along a cloister toward the lodge. Then the sky cleared and I saw his face in the moonlight. He was an elderly man, not a student, of medium build, and with thick grey hair. I had the shock of a lifetime to realize he was the spitting image of the man in the portrait. Never, even when I was with the Munsters in Afghanistan, was I ever as frightened. I'm afraid of no man, sir, but I wasn't expecting a ghost at night."

He continued, "There is a long tradition of ghosts at this college, including the spirit of this particular man. Stories are passed down across the years, and I can tell you that many students and servants have seen him. I've served this college for four decades, and there has always been ghost talk. Some fellows may also have seen him, but they would never admit it. I dare say they would find it against their dignity."

When our interview concluded, we left the kitchens and made our way to the porter's lodge. We noticed a troop of boy scouts passing into the college. In response to our questioning glances, Patterson explained. "The Warden is a strong supporter of the scouting movement. He is allowing the scouts to camp overnight on our playing field, provided they attend chapel first. The Warden will conduct the service himself. I worry that one of these boys will prove irreverent, claim to see a ghost, or engage in some type of prank." Patterson sighed at the thought of his Warden needlessly upset.

Holmes asked him if a ghost had ever been seen from the lodge, and he replied in the negative. "I have long heard stories of ghosts in this college, but I have never seen one. I'm not saying that I doubt they exist. The servants, and some of the students, are convinced we are haunted. If anyone can solve this case it is you, sir, with your reputation for seeing further than other men – if I'm not taking a liberty by saying so."

68

Additional questioning revealed no more information, so we took our leave.

Chapter XIII – The Hall Servants

The next step in our investigation was to question the hall servants. As promised, they were assembled an hour before the S.C.R. reception. Holmes had a remarkable ability to put humble witnesses at their ease, and while they initially responded to his questions with quick "Yes" and "No" answers, they soon began to talk more freely.

The results were disappointing, however. None of the men remembered any detail about the elderly fellow sitting next to Holmes. The evening was just another dinner with fellows and their guests, and aside from differences in age, one academic looked much like the other. We were led to understand, in so many words, that relations between fellows and servants were formal and distant. The servants saw the fellows more as an amorphous group than as a set of distinct individuals, which paralleled how the fellows saw the servants. The servants could swear to the presence of few individual fellows on that night. They recalled the Warden, of course, as well as two fellows who were known for frequently complaining about the wine, and the college's famous guest, Mr. Sherlock Holmes, but nobody else. They even claimed they didn't remember seeing me.

They all, however, believed a ghost was haunting the college. More than that, they were excited about it, as if it added a bit of mystery to the atmosphere. They were all from the town, and of course imbibed from a young age the traditional English superstition concerning ghosts.

After realizing that further questions would be fruitless, we thanked them for their time and walked back to our rooms. We were tired and not eager for further conversation, but my friend was in a contemplative mood, so we attended Evensong but skipped the subsequent S.C.R. and High Table. Instead, we walked to The Chequers for a meal that made up in heartiness for what it lacked in formality.

Chapter XIV – Detour in the Archives

Holmes insisted on devoting the next day to his archival research in the library. He departed in the morning and spent the daylight hours among the dusty records. It was almost time for luncheon when Mr. Soames appeared in my rooms, and if ever a man was distressed, it was he.

"I heard that Mr. Holmes has abandoned us, that he was seen in the archives. Does he not have a solution to our mystery? I don't understand how he can treat this matter so lightly. Is the mystery too great? Have his considerable powers finally met their match? Does he not understand the position of the college if the rumors aren't addressed?"

I endeavored to sooth him, pointing out that Holmes was present in Camford to conduct long-overdue researches. His last visit was interrupted by the mystery of the Fortescue exam, and now it was a ghost interfering with his work. "Rest assured that he hasn't forgotten your problem. I think you will find him refreshed now that he has turned his mind to a different problem. You have read my accounts, and you must know that appearances can be deceiving. When Holmes at his most taciturn, he is often closing in on the solution." I could see the dismay on his face, so I urged him to occupy himself in some scholarly matter until Holmes returned.

To distract myself, I walked down to the Greens and watched the St. Luke's cricket team take on the Trinity eleven. It was a stirring match, with St. Luke's batting second and winning by only an over. Two young players received their "caps" for playing in their first collegiate match. I thought back to my own school days, filled with rugby instead of cricket.

Holmes returned in the late afternoon, but he refused to say a word about the case. He had brought with him a small package, which he set on the writing table. We later joined Soames at the S.C.R. before dinner. He was still agitated, and his impatient questions were accompanied by excited gesticulations. Holmes would only respond that we would all meet for breakfast and discuss the matter further. Soames was in a dreadful fidget, but Holmes wouldn't be drawn further.

He did seek to question the fellows who sat closest to the alleged ghost. Roger Atkinson had been on Holmes's right, but he claimed to have noticed nothing about the mystery figure. His first conversation at High Table was with Holmes, and he then became engaged in a discussion with the fellow to *his* right, who was many years his senior and had little sympathy with his opinions about antiquities.

The person across the table from Holmes, who sat several seats to my right, was Miss Knight-Werck from St. Hildegard. She admitted spotting the figure about halfway through the meal, and she registered at the time how unusual it was for a fellow to join High Table so late. She denied that she had paid him any attention. He was just one of many indistinct fellows in the penumbras of a traditional High Table, although she vaguely recalled his grey hair.

When we returned to our rooms after High Table, Holmes sat in a chair by the coal fireplace, lost in thought. I was tired and went to sleep early, but I knew that my friend would have a restless night, smoking and pacing until he solved the mystery.

Chapter XV – Revelation

When I awoke, Holmes was already dressed and smoking his before-breakfast pipe, filled with the plugs and dottles from the previous day. He was in an affable mood, stating, "Welcome to the land of the living. Did you encounter any ghosts in your sleep?"

By his jocularity, I took it that he had reached some conclusions about the college mystery. His only further statement was that breakfast with our neglected friend, Hilton Soames, was in order. We were soon in those familiar rooms, and I wondered if another dramatic revelation awaited us.

"I hope you have solved the mystery!" said our friend with considerable agitation. "You must understand the position of this college if you cannot. We will be the laughing stock of Camford – indeed of the kingdom!"

"Calm yourself, I beg of you" responded Holmes, as he set the mysterious box on the desk. "I can assure you that I have given this episode my full attention, although it wasn't a difficult puzzle to solve. Before I say more, I will admit that I'm not sure why you are so determined to excise its ghost. Many institutions benefit from a resident ghost, and what better place to haunt than your ancient buildings? Nevertheless, I will explain all.

"Before I begin, can you ask the two students, as well as Jamieson and Smithson, to join us? They saw the ghost, so they deserve to hear my conclusions. The Warden should also be present."

Soames was surprised at this request, but he rang his bell and sent messages to all five. After about fifteen minutes, the party was assembled. The students sat in chairs along the wall while the servants stood near the door. Mr. Soames sat at his desk with the Warden seated nearby, and I stood near the window. We all looked up at Holmes, who was pacing near the bedroom door.

"As you may know, my dictum is, 'No ghosts need apply.' A haunting spirit is more appropriate to the fiction of Mr. Le Fenu than the accounts of Dr. Watson. I therefore worked from an assumption that the ghost was of human origin."

"I also heard that the ghost was doing no harm, merely ambling through the cloisters on fine evenings. I would be rather inclined to join him than chase him away. I then asked why this ghost, who was identified as Desjardin, would choose to make earthly appearances rather than enjoy his reward for martyrdom in the afterlife? I couldn't think of an answer."

"If the ghost wasn't real, then who was playing his rôle, and why? Those in the college most open to the idea of a real ghost were the servants. The fellows were embarrassed by it, believing it harmed the dignity of the

71

college. While the Warden looked with favor on the idea of a ghost, I couldn't imagine him dressing up as one. The two students were charmed by the idea of a ghost, but their description of the encounter was matter-of-fact. They weren't partisans of the ghost party, but neutral witnesses to an event they couldn't explain.

"I asked myself: How did the rumor of a ghost persist for so many decades? The most likely answer is that it was perpetuated by the servants."

"When I saw the troop of scouts yesterday, I mused how the word 'scout' has several meanings in English. The boy scouts led me to wonder about the college scouts who loyally serve the fellows for generation after generation. Could an inherited memory exist among them? Could the scout of William Desjardin, for example, have decided to perpetuate his remembrance through rumors of his ghost haunting the college? A ghost sighting would easy to claim, and difficult to disprove. Did he confide this secret to his replacement, and so on?"

"Watson has written about my flair for the dramatic, and I hope you will forgive me for this demonstration." He reached inside the box and pulled out some sort of hat. To my surprise, it was a grey wig, and he walked over and placed it on the head of a surprised Smithson, crying, "Gentlemen, I give you your ghost!"

Chapter XVI – Explanation

The room was silent for some time. Then we heard the voice of Smithson, who said, "I will not lie to the great Sherlock Holmes. It was me who dressed as the martyred fellow and walked around the quad. I had to be careful about choosing the right moments, as otherwise I might be apprehended, which would do my position in the college no good.

"Yet I deny that I meant to spread false rumors about a ghost. I am sure that such a ghost exists, and I tell you I have seen him. The arrival of Sherlock Holmes in the college was a providential opportunity to prove it. If the famous detective wasn't only a witness to a ghost, but actually conversed friendly-like with him, then nobody could deny it. The ghost would have to be acknowledged by even the most skeptical fellow. Dr. Watson might have written one of his famous stories about it, and then the English-speaking world would know of our ghost."

Holmes replied, "You must tell me how you engineered the appearance of the ghost at dinner."

"It was very easy, sir. Nobody notices a servant. You can walk around all day, and none of the fellows will remember it. I arrived at dinner near the halfway point, carrying with me a small bundle, consisting of a

72

fellow's robe, a wig, and a small tin of makeup. I could tell the hall servants didn't pay me any attention, as scouts often appear in that building to pick up meals for their fellows.

"Just before the main course was to be served, the point at which the fellows were about to switch their conversations, I walked onto the High Table platform. The unusual design of the hall made this easy to do, as you can see, because of the door that leads right onto it. As I predicted, the fellows paid no notice, too busy conversing with each other. I walked to the end of the table, right behind Mr. Holmes, and bent down as if to tie my shoe. I quickly slipped on the robe, put on the wig, and applied a small amount of aging makeup, just like the fellow at the shop showed me. In the dim candlelight, I would have been a stranger to my own mother."

"If you were the mystery fellow, how did you manage to carry on a conversation about English Charters?"

"Well, sir, I knew about your interest in charters from your previous visit to the college with Dr. Watson. The servants are a curious bunch, sir, and we had soon learned all about the reason for your visit and how the affair of the Fortescue scholarship derailed your researches. I found an encyclopedia and memorized a few facts."

Holmes replied, "But you were quite knowledgeable about the subject."

"You know how it is, sir. If you listen to another man, he thinks you are a great conversationalist. I tried to look intelligent, nodded regularly, and asked a few questions based on what you were saying. We servants are all used to hearing the fellows talk, and I am good at impersonations. When I went into service, me old mum used to say that what the college gained, the stage lost."

"But the marks on your hands were the imprints of a writer from a century ago."

Smithson could barely suppress a smile. "We read your monograph on human hands, sir. You sent a copy to the college library three years ago, and we studied it. To get the effect of a writer's hand from a century ago, I taped a quill tightly to my fingers the night before and didn't remove it until before High Table began. I also rubbed a little ink on my fingers. The indents and stains weren't very distinct in the candlelight, but I made sure to raise my glass in a way that would bring them to your attention."

Holmes cut in, saying, "You say 'we'. Were other people involved in this plot?"

"I can only tell you my secrets, sir. It wouldn't be right to involve those who would prefer to be unknown."

"How did you manage to elude the two students who said you disappeared into the shadows of a cloister?"

"That was easy, sir. I have keys to the many doors in the quads, some of which open to staircases and others into storage rooms. It is no difficulty to unlock one and hide until the coast is clear."

Holmes pondered these answers. Finally, he asked, "But why did you do it?"

"To honor the blessed memory of Mr. Desjardin, that is God's own truth. The fellows never think about us servants. To most, we are anonymous and interchangeable. But the good Desjardin did notice because of his love for all people, regardless of their station in life. He was more than kind to his scout – Harold was his name. He cared about Harold's life and his soul, did Mr. Desjardin.

"When he was killed by that mob, Harold swore that his memory would live on, but how? He thought of the idea of seeing his ghost. As all you scholars know, there is a long tradition of seeing ghosts in England, quite popular among the people. Harold waited a couple years, and then announced his vision to the other servants. The rumor spread, and the tradition was passed down to a younger scout, and so on, all the way to me. However, I actually saw the ghost, so I wonder if maybe the story was garbled – that the ghost of Mr. Desjardin was really seen by Harold. Well, a century has passed, so who can tell. You may think me a fraud, Mr. Holmes, but I maintain that I was only enhancing, if you will, the truth."

The Warden was the next to speak. "Thank you for this confession, Smithson. You have served the college for many years, and we cannot doubt that your motives were honorable. Your ghost has done no real harm, and while some of the fellows have been put out, they are a dry lot and could use a bit of goosing."

"Smithson and Jamieson, you may go, and please don't discuss this with anyone until we have decided how to act."

To the students, the Warden said, "And that goes to you both. I know it will be a temptation to discuss this with your friends, but I believe I can rely upon your sense of honour."

Chapter XVII – Resolution

The students and servants departed, and a visibly relieved Hilton Soames exclaimed, "That puts to rest the ghost story! Thank you, Mr. Holmes, for clearing up this superstition. The fellows will be glad to hear it."

The Warden didn't share his excitement. "I'm not sure we can conclude that no ghost exists. This fraud doesn't disprove a century of sightings."

Mr. Soames was about to remonstrate, but Holmes interjected. "I quite agree, Warden. I also confess that I found your ghost charming, and it may well be that the memory of 'the good Desjardin' is one to keep green."

"One wrinkle is what I discovered yesterday in the archives," Holmes continued. "The true story about Desjardin is more complicated than the college believes. He was killed in town, yes, but it involved a dispute over a local woman. I doubt there was any dishonor in his actions. In those days, fellows were forbidden to marry, but many had relationships that were in every way conducted with affection and discretion. However, a jealous rival incited a mob to attack the good reverend over religious differences, and he died. He was a martyr both to religion and to love but the college would rather remember the former and forget the latter.

"If the story of Smithson's impersonation comes out, it will draw unwelcome attention to the college. The press can hardly be expected to ignore a story involving myself and a ghost in Camford. They will write about the recent deceptions and the tradition passed down from scout to scout. An enterprising journalist will eventually visit the archives and learn the full story of Desjardin. The sensationalistic press will claim he wasn't a religious martyr as much as a quarreling paramour.

"My suggestion is that we leave this as we found it – a local mystery of interest to only ourselves. We will say nothing of recent events and let people think what they will. It will not improve my reputation, but I will maintain a profound silence on the matter."

Our friend Soames was about to further object, but the Warden brought the episode to a conclusion. "I agree, Mr. Holmes. There is no good to be done by revealing this impersonation or Desjardin's understandable human weakness. As you said, the ghost has done no harm, so let the scoffers scoff and the believers believe. St. Luke's will be a more colorful place because of it. And as I recall, our college's ancient Latin name is *Collegium Sancti Lucae et Spiriti Sancti* – "The College of St. Luke and the Holy Ghost".

The Checkmate Murder
by Josh Cerefice

"A good move, Watson," said my friend, tapping a fingertip against his lips as he considered his response. Then, after several silent moments of careful deliberation, his cold, grey eyes brightened with understanding. "But you've left your king undefended." Inevitably, Holmes moved his bishop across the board in a swift, diagonal motion. "That's mate, I believe."

I studied the pieces and hoped he had made a miscalculation. Unsurprisingly, and much to my disappointment, he had not. "Well played," I said graciously. Then, chastising myself for my mistake, added, "But how did I not see your bishop?"

"You were too focused on attacking my rook and neglected to defend your most important piece. A skilled strategist, however, knows that defence is sometimes the best form of attack."

"I'll beat you one of these days," I said gamely, though he had dispatched me with ease. "It's only a matter of time."

Holmes chuckled, clearly amused by my bravado. "What you lack in talent, you certainly make up for in tenacity."

"Err . . . Thank you . . . ."

"If it's any consolation, I have a significant advantage over you."

"You do?"

"Indubitably. Chess is a game of problems and solutions. Your opponent presents a problem, and you must find the solution. That, too, is the fundamental principle upon which my career as a consulting detective is predicated. Instead of killing kings, however, I catch criminals."

"Well, that makes me feel somewhat better about my defeat," I said, even though Holmes's victory had brought my intellectual inferiority into sharp relief.

Putting our game aside, Holmes and I spent the next few minutes in sociable silence, during which I decided to peruse the morning columns. "How's the investigation going?" I asked eventually, placing my paper down beside me. I was alluding to a particularly confounding case in which my friend had found himself newly engaged. "Is Oswald Trent really one-hundred-and-sixty-nine years old?"

He shook his head. "That would have violated the very laws of nature itself," he said simply. "As I suspected from the beginning, it was all an elaborate hoax designed to extort money from the crowds of credulous people who bought tickets to marvel at the miracle of 'The Immortal Man', a sobriquet wholly unbefitting of a person who was, it transpires, no older than seventy-three."

"Freak shows are ghastly things, anyway," I said. "People shouldn't be treated like museum exhibits. It's immoral."

"The eye regards with curiosity that which the mind struggles to comprehend."

This sage sentiment marked the end of our conversation for, but a moment later, there was the familiar sound of footsteps upon the stairs outside, followed in short order by the appearance of Mrs. Hudson, whose head protruded from the gap in the half-open door like a puppet peeking through the curtain in a Punch-and-Judy Show.

"A gentleman's here to see you," she announced before withdrawing. Then, from behind the door there emerged a tall, stylishly suited man in his early thirties with a sharp jaw and thin lips on which a well-manicured moustache was precariously perched. Despite his impeccable appearance, however, there was a melancholic look in his eyes which told of the tragedy that had recently befallen him.

"It's good to see you again, Mr. Quinn," said Holmes, with a sympathetic smile. "I just wish it were under more felicitous circumstances."

Our well-dressed guest wasn't unfamiliar to us, for we had met him a few evenings earlier at a private chess match hosted by his father, Augustus Quinn who, as well as being an acquaintance of Holmes's brother – from whom we acquired the tickets – also happened to be one of the two participants in the contest. It was a thoroughly enthralling game, and the great champion had been prevailing by a narrow margin when he suddenly clutched his chest and collapsed to the floor as everyone in the audience looked on in impotent shock. Being the only doctor present, I attempted to resuscitate him, but sadly, my efforts were in vain.

"Watching your father the other evening has inspired me to start playing again," Holmes said, and gestured at the chess board sitting on the table in front of us. "He possessed an extraordinary mind."

"That's very kind of you, Mr. Holmes," he said, and removed his top hat to reveal a crown of brown, combed-back hair glistening with wax. "I'm sorry for calling unannounced," he added, fidgeting with the rim of his hat, "but the matter I have come here to discuss with you couldn't wait a moment longer."

My friend gave an insouciant shrug. "Unexpected visitors are something to which we've grown increasingly accustomed over the years. But where are my manners?" He waved to the vacant chair opposite him. "Please make yourself comfortable."

Our aggrieved guest lowered himself into a seat. "I still can't quite believe he's gone," he said, shaking his head sorrowfully. "It doesn't seem real somehow."

"Losing a loved one never does," I said, thinking of the grief that had engulfed me when my beloved Mary had passed. "The pain never goes away, but in time, you'll learn to live with it."

Mr. Quinn sighed. "I'm afraid I can't do that until I find out who killed him."

Indeed, when I had endeavoured to revive the man's father, I had noticed the distinct odour of bitter almonds emanating from his mouth – a perfume, I knew, which was peculiar to the poisonous substance, sodium cyanide.

"Have you read the coroner's report yet?" Holmes asked.

Mr. Quinn nodded. "As Doctor Watson suspected at the time, my father had in fact suffered a fatal cardiac arrest brought on by acute cyanide poisoning."

I shook my head ruefully. "From the moment he started rubbing his chest, I thought something was awry. If only I had acted sooner, he might still be alive today."

"You mustn't blame yourself," my friend said consolingly, and Mr. Quinn agreed. Then Holmes faced our guest and asked, "Has Scotland Yard made any progress with the investigation?"

"Inspector Parker has the matter in hand. But with your assistance, Mr. Holmes, I'd be more confident of a favourable outcome."

"I would have helped you sooner had I not been attending to an urgent ministerial matter concerning the 3rd Marquess of Salisbury. However, as that problem has now been resolved, I am at your service."

Our visitor gave a grateful bow of the head. "I'm indebted, Mr. Holmes."

"We should begin by asking ourselves the most salient question," Holmes said. "Namely, who has a credible motive to murder your father?"

"There's my parasite of a stepmother," he said contemptuously. "The only reason she married him was because of his money. She's young enough to be his daughter, for Heaven's sake!" he added, getting hot under the collar. "If she truly cared for him, she would have been beside herself with panic. But she just . . . stood there."

Vividly, I recalled the gasps of horror from those in the audience when the man's father had been twisting in pain on the floor. Mrs. Quinn, however, had looked on with an expression of cool impassivity, seemingly unruffled by the disaster developing before her.

Holmes said, "And does she stand to inherit anything from your father's legacy?"

"The will hasn't been read yet, but I already know she'll be the sole beneficiary. She'd been trying to persuade him to change it from the moment they cut the wedding cake," he bemoaned, "and he eventually succumbed to her persistence – not to mention her feminine charms. When it came to women, my father was weak."

"Well, she certainly had a good reason for sending him to Highgate Cemetery," I remarked.

Holmes turned his attention back to the method of murder. "Cyanide is a fast-acting poison capable of killing within minutes, perhaps even quicker if the victim already had a cardiac condition, which I believe your father did. The match began at nine o'clock," he continued, "and your father went into cardiac arrest at around a quarter-past-eleven. Due to the toxin's fast-acting nature, that means the poisoner must have administered it *during* the game. It couldn't have been done before the match, as your father would scarcely have had time to make his first move before feeling its deadly effects."

"But Mrs. Quinn was sitting beside me throughout the entire match," I pointed out, "and she didn't move from her seat the whole time."

Holmes highlighted another problem with his own theory. "The room was also packed with dozens of spectators, so she couldn't have gone near her husband, as someone would have seen her."

I threw up my arms in resignation. "It's impossible, then. There's no way she could have done it."

"Not impossible," my friend said, wagging a finger. "Just highly improbable."

Despite our doubts, Mr. Quinn was steadfast in his suspicions. "She did it," he said adamantly. "I don't know how, but she killed him."

"Don't allow your hostility towards the woman to shape your judgement," Holmes advised. "Feelings often blind us to the truth. Facts, on the other hand, illuminate it."

Our visitor looked affronted. "You don't believe me, do you?"

"What I presently believe is immaterial, Mr. Quinn," Holmes said firmly. "I'm simply suggesting that we adopt an objective approach rather than yielding to our emotions. After all, your stepmother may not have been the only person to benefit from your father's death."

This seemed to appease the man. "I apologize for my curt tone," he said, blanching slightly. "I'm still feeling rather raw."

Holmes gave a nonchalant wave. "It's only natural for you to want answers. In your position, I'd want the same." Holmes rose to his feet, and our guest took this as his cue to do the same. "Leave it with me, Mr. Quinn. I will ensure your father's killer is brought to justice."

"I'm much obliged, Mr. Holmes. In the meantime, should you need to reach me, you can find me at 31 Hanover Square."

"I will inform you of any details as they surface." He smiled courteously. "For now, though, good afternoon to you, Mr. Quinn."

After our client left, Holmes turned to me, his eyes ablaze with the same boyish excitement they always possessed whenever he was about to embark upon a new case. "Come, Watson!" he said, and threw his frock coat over his narrow shoulders. "It's time to play our opening gambit."

After visiting the coroner's office to read the report for ourselves, which verified everything our client had told us, we went to the Yard and spoke to Superintendent Taylor – who gratefully accepted our assistance with the police investigation – before taking a hansom to the home of Augustus Quinn.

When we had travelled there a few days earlier, the darkness of dusk had precluded me from having a proper view of my surroundings through the cab window. Now though, in the brilliant midday sunshine, the elegant grandeur of Belgravia, with its verdant garden squares, luxury townhouses, and fashionable restaurants, became even more evident. So too did the presence of its well-to-do inhabitants, who perambulated along the cobbled pavements in their top hats and tailcoats, untroubled by the travails of life.

Though part of me couldn't help but be impressed by the magnificent architecture and immaculately dressed residents, another part was repulsed by the excessive affluence on display. It felt unjust to me, immoral perhaps, that such a place could exist when only a few miles away in Whitechapel, people were living in desperate poverty, many of them doomed to a life of vagrancy and having to resort to beggary or theft – or much worse – just to put food in their mouths. I expressed as much to Holmes when our cab came rattling to a halt outside the home of the late Augustus Quinn, a large, terraced townhouse in Grosvenor Crescent with a mansard slated roof, white stucco façade, and Doric porch.

The door was opened by Tillman the butler, a pale, gaunt man of mature years who seemed to permanently have his hands clasped behind his back. "Mr. Holmes . . . Doctor Watson," he stammered, blinking at us from beneath tufts of black eyebrows. "I must say, I didn't expect to see you here again. To what do I owe the pleasure?"

"Good afternoon," Holmes replied with a polite bow. "We're here at the behest of Sebastian Quinn, who has asked us to investigate his father's death." There was a momentary pause. "Is the lady of the house around?"

Tillman nodded. "Last time I checked, Mrs. Quinn was in the lounge."

"May we speak with her?" Sensing the man's uncertainty, Holmes added airily, "It's only a formality . . . a couple of questions, that's all."

Tillman retreated into the hall before reappearing moments later. "Mrs. Quinn has agreed to see you," he said, waving us into an immodestly decorated entrance hall.

"Before we see her," Holmes said to the old man, "I should like to revisit the ballroom. If it's all right with you, of course."

Tillman gave a stiff bow. "Very well," he acquiesced. "This way." And so saying, he escorted us through a series of lavish hallways until we found ourselves in a large, well-lit ballroom with a black-and-white tiled floor and set of French windows looking out onto a lawn of freshly-mown grass.

"Mrs. Quinn hasn't set foot in here since the match," said our guide. "She just can't face it at the moment."

"I presume, then, that nothing has been disturbed in that time?"

He spread his arms expansively. "As you can see, everything is exactly how it was left."

Holmes nodded approvingly. "That's fortuitous," he said as we drifted over to the centre of the room, where rows of chairs, previously occupied by spectators, encircled a small table with a chess board on top, its pieces scattered strategically over its surface and organised in lines on either side of the table. "Since this is now the location of a crime," Holmes murmured to me, "its preservation will prove advantageous to our cause."

"It's a beautiful chess set," I said by-the-by. "It looks very expensive."

"It's a Staunton," the butler said, overhearing him. "Mr. Quinn was something of a collector of them. This one, I believe, cost over a hundred pounds and was purchased last year from a local carpenter who made all the pieces by hand."

"What does *N.C.* stand for?" I asked upon noticing the initials that were engraved in elegant calligraphy along the edge of the board.

"That would be the craftsman who carved it, Mr. Norman Colby."

"Hmm . . . that's strange," my friend said.

"What is?" I asked.

"There are only thirty-one pieces here. The white queen is missing." Then, his eyes alighted upon something glistening on the floor near the leg of the table. "And what do we have here?" He bent down and picked up the object, holding it in his palm. "A gold earring," he said. "A rather curious place to find one, don't you think?"

As I considered the import of all this, Holmes reached into his jacket pocket and pulled out his large magnifying glass, with which he began to inspect the board and table. From what I could tell, he appeared to be

81

examining a small pile of fine, white powder on the right-hand side of the table, where the missing piece should have been standing. Then, lowering his lens and stooping further, he pressed his nose against the buffed wood, sniffing as he did so, before rising to his full height and pocketing his ocular accoutrement.

"It looks like cigar ash," I said.

He shook his head. "The white, powdery appearance and distinct smell of bitter almonds is unmistakably that of sodium cyanide," he corrected me.

Next, he picked up a half-empty glass of water on the side of the table where Mr. Quinn had been sitting and afforded it the same adenoidal scrutiny. "There is also residue of the same substance on the rim of this glass."

"Which means that the poison was dissolved in the water," I deduced quite simply.

Tillman suddenly looked uncomfortable. "But I poured it myself," he said. "It was clean from the tap."

Holmes asked, "You put the glass of water here on the table before the match began, I presume?"

He nodded. "Mr. Quinn often had a dry throat during games, especially when he was nervous."

"And from what you can recall, did you leave the glass unattended at any point during the evening?"

"No, I didn't. I'm certain of it."

"How, then, was the poisoner able to contaminate the glass?" I wondered. "Unless he or she did so during the game, which is impossible."

"But that's the only logical explanation," my friend asserted. "You may remember that Mr. Quinn took several sips of water during the first hour of the game, so if someone had tampered with the drink before the match, which our good man here affirms wasn't the case, the poison would have killed him within that window of time. Only when he had taken another draught later in the match did he suffer a heart attack just minutes later. Thus, the cyanide must have only been in the glass later in the game, and not at the beginning."

"But it was on this table the entire time, and everyone in the audience was over there," I said, indicating the empty chairs that stood several feet from our position. "There's no way anyone could possibly have interfered with the water during the game."

Holmes stroked his lip. "It's certainly an intriguing puzzle," he said, and turned to the butler. "I think I'm done in here for the moment."

Upon this pronouncement, Tillman led the way out of the ballroom and conducted us to the lounge. A luxuriously furnished room that bore all the hallmarks of refined taste and immodest wealth, its most notable features were a bronze chandelier and marble fireplace, above which there hung a large oil painting of the late chess champion. The artist, I thought, had depicted the man's mane of frizzy white hair and penetrating blue gaze with unnerving exactitude.

In the middle of the room, a strikingly attractive woman in her early thirties lay curled up upon a chaise lounge, a book on her lap and a glass of red wine in her hand. So absorbed was she in its pages, in fact, that she didn't appear to be aware of our presence until Tillman announced our arrival, which caused her to sit up and put her drink down on the table in front of her.

"Mr. Sherlock Holmes and Doctor Watson," the butler announced.

"Thank you, Tillman," she said, dismissing him with a wave. Then, she invited us to take a seat, and, with a smile that never reached her eyes, said, "It's good to see you again, gentlemen. I believe we met briefly at the chess match, didn't we?"

For someone who was supposed to be grieving for the death of her husband, Alexandra Quinn, I thought, struck a rather serene figure. Her husband hadn't long thrown off his mortal coil and there she was, indulging in potations and recreations as if nothing had happened. Her appearance, too, was wholly incongruous with her grim circumstances. Instead of a plain black dress she wore a pretty white gown, and her face, which ought to have been hidden behind a veil, was covered in rouge and lipstick. Far from being a woman in woe, she looked more like a wife-to-be.

"I suppose you're here about my husband, Mr. Holmes?"

Holmes nodded gravely. "Your stepson has hired me to investigate his murder."

She wasn't surprised, and I concluded that she was already aware of the coroner's findings. "Well, I hope you have more success than the police," she said. "They don't appear to have learned anything so far."

"I will do my best, Mrs. Quinn."

"I'm very grateful. The sooner this dreadful business ends, the better. It's been quite a trial, to say the least."

"Yes, I can see that," Holmes said, throwing an ironic glance at her wine glass. "To lose a husband is bad enough, but for it to happen in such a manner . . . it doesn't bear thinking about."

She looked incredulous. "I just don't understand who would do such a wicked thing."

"That's what I intend to find out," he said stoutly. "Speaking of which, I hope you don't mind if I ask a few questions. I realize the timing couldn't be worse . . ."

83

"No, no, not at all. You can ask as many questions as you like if it helps you to find my husband's killer."

With her consent gained, Holmes commenced his enquiries. "Did your husband have any enemies?" he asked. "Anyone who may have wished him harm?"

She paused, contemplating the question. "I wouldn't go so far as to call him an enemy," she said eventually, "but I know Sebastian won't be mourning his passing, that's for sure."

"But your stepson was the one who hired me," Holmes said. "Why would he ask me to investigate his father's murder if he didn't care for the man?"

"I wish I knew the answer," she said, equally mystified. "The pair of them have been estranged ever since Augustus – God rest his soul – cut him out of the will."

"Speaking of which, I understand you are to be the sole beneficiary." I looked at Holmes, who, like an archaeologist deciphering ancient hieroglyphs, was reading the woman's face for any inscriptions of guilt written therein. The flicker of an eye, the curl of a lip, the wrinkle of a brow – none of them would escape his studied gaze.

"That's correct, yes," she said with an inscrutable countenance. "He knew Sebastian would only have squandered it on girls and gambling." She shook her head disapprovingly. "It's about time my wastrel of a stepson learned to live under his own steam rather than relying upon his father. It'll do the boy good."

"Did your stepson know that his father intended to disinherit him?"

"Oh, yes! He told him in no uncertain terms that unless he reformed his reckless ways, he wouldn't be getting his hands on a single shilling."

"And you believe this had driven a wedge between them?"

Mrs. Quinn nodded. "The other night was the first time they've been in the same room together for months," she said, picking up her drink and taking another sip. "Sebastian blamed me for it all, of course, and accused me of manipulating his father for my own personal gain."

"And did you?" Holmes asked bluntly.

She gave my friend a withering stare. "I won't even grace that question with an answer," she said, clearly affronted, "and quite frankly, I'm insulted you felt the need to ask it. Tillman!"

The butler appeared seconds later at the door. "Yes, Madam?"

"Show these gentlemen out, will you?"

Holmes held out a placatory palm, recognizing his mistake. "Forgive the impertinence, Mrs. Quinn. I meant nothing by it."

"Good day to you, gentlemen," she said in a voice as cold as a winter's breeze.

84

"I assure you, Mrs. Quinn – "

"I said good day!"

"Mrs. Quinn was positively rude," I said to Holmes as we rolled out of Belgravia and into Pimlico. "The instant you questioned her rectitude, her comportment changed immediately."

"It's still too early to say whether her indignation was indicative of innocence or guilt," my friend replied.

"She didn't exactly look like a woman in mourning, though, did she?"

"That's true," Holmes agreed. "Mrs. Quinn seemed quite content to eschew almost every convention of bereavement – particularly as far as her attire was concerned. Nevertheless, as I've said time and time again, we shouldn't leap to conclusions before we have all the necessary data. She may be a rapacious bloodsucker, but it doesn't necessarily follow that she's willing to spill blood to get what she wants."

"And what about our client?" I asked. "Surely he has to be a suspect now as well?"

"Indubitably," Holmes concurred. "Being disinherited by his father would have cut deeply, and must have felt like a betrayal of the worst kind. Given the enmity that has arisen between father and son as a result, it isn't beyond the realms of possibility that the son would wish to carry out a reprisal for the ignominy he suffered. Patricide may seem extreme, but we have known children to murder their fathers for less."

"There's also a chance he's hired your services in an effort to frame his stepmother," I suggested. "If she ends up in Newgate, that may make it easier for him to contest the will."

"That's another credible hypothesis, but I certainly won't be wrongfully accusing anyone of murder. As you well know, I never err in my judgement."

"Like his stepmother, though, our client was seated in the audience the entire time," I reminded him, "and the glass of water was on the table beside Mr. Quinn. Unless they are imbued with powers of invisibility," I said, thinking about H.G. Wells' *The Invisible Man*, a novel I had recently been reading, "I cannot fathom how either of them could have contaminated the drink without someone seeing them. It doesn't make a jot of sense."

It was at that point that I stole a glance out of the cab window and saw the towering spire of St. Gabriel's Church rising above the trees and townhouses of St. George's Square. "Where are we going?" I asked, wondering why we weren't returning to Baker Street.

"To speak to somebody else who may have had reason to murder Mr. Quinn."

85

"You're referring to his opponent?" I surmised.

Holmes nodded. "Let's not forget that Mr. Wentworth sat just three feet away from the victim when he was killed."

"It's still highly improbable," I gainsaid. "Unless he possesses a magician's sleight of hand, how could he have contaminated his opponent's water without him or anyone else noticing?"

"It's a valid question."

"Incidentally, how did you find out where the fellow lives?"

"That was rather serendipitous," he said. "After the match, I saw him climb into a passing hansom and overheard him giving his address to the cabbie just as he was closing the door. Ah! Here we are!" Our cab had come trundling to a halt outside 11 Lupus Street, a stylish Georgian townhouse not entirely dissimilar to the one from which we had just been evicted.

I rang the doorbell and we were greeted an instant later by a bespectacled butler with receding grey hair and a salt-and-pepper beard, who informed us that his master had just gone to the Savile Club. Thanking him, we hailed another cab and journeyed north toward Mayfair, arriving at 107 Piccadilly approximately ten minutes later.

After paying our fare, we made our way inside the imposing two-storied building – which was owned, I had heard, by our former Prime Minister, Lord Rosebery – and spent the next half-hour scouring every red-carpeted hallway of the place in search of the celebrated chess maestro. I was almost ready to give up the hunt when we eventually found the man in one of the club's plush parlours, sitting in a tanned-leather armchair with a newspaper on his knee and a cigar clutched between his teeth.

Roland Wentworth was a stout, ruddy-faced man of middle years with large jowls and an even larger opinion of himself. I had briefly spoken to him a few nights earlier before his match with Mr. Quinn, and, in truth, I found the man to be a pompous braggard who, during our conversation, had boasted ceaselessly about his record of incredible victories and the impressive trophy collection he had amassed throughout his career. He was also, by all accounts, a man of little integrity who, according to the papers, had been embroiled in a match-fixing scandal the previous year. What other desperate measures, I asked myself, would such an unprincipled man be prepared to take to win a game of chess?

"Ah, Mr. Holmes, Dr. Watson!" he said. "Now this *is* a pleasant surprise." He waved a chubby hand to the two chairs opposite him. "Join me, why don't you?"

My friend smiled graciously. "That's good of you."

After we were both seated, the chess master pointed his cigar at the board sitting on the table in front of us. "Do either of you gentlemen play?"

"Now and again," I said, "though Holmes is far better than I am."

"How about a game then? I'll go easy on you, I promise."

"Oh, I don't think that'll be necessary," Holmes said, setting the pieces up. "You can be white."

Wentworth raised an eyebrow. "You follow the example of the late Mr. Quinn, I see. He too, preferred playing as black."

After his opponent had taken his turn, Holmes made his first move. "Congratulations on your victory the other night," he said. "You played superbly."

He took one of Holmes's pawns. "It's the only way I know how to play."

I found the man's vanity to be downright vexing, and I considered reminding him that he had only won by default because his competitor had died. Though I was keen to bring him down a peg or two, I decided to restrain myself, knowing it would only prove to him that he was riling me, something from which a man like him, I imagined, would derive immense pleasure.

"I suppose you've heard that Mr. Quinn was poisoned?" asked my friend, getting immediately to the heart of the matter.

"A dreadful business," Wentworth said, blowing languidly on his cigar. "Do you have any idea who it was?"

"We have our suspicions, but it's too early to say at this stage of the investigation."

"And I suppose I'm on your list of suspects?" Looking unconcerned, he moved his bishop into a defensive position.

Holmes seized the opportunity to mount an attack. "Your bitter rivalry with Mr. Quinn was well publicized. According to the gossip columns, you and he had been at loggerheads for years."

"I'm not going to pretend I liked the fellow," Wentworth countered, developing his rook, "nor that I'm sad about his death, but I assure you that I had nothing to do with his murder."

Holmes employed a new gambit. "By all accounts, you felt as though you were living in his shadow, forever eclipsed by the blinding light of his success – not to mention his greater celebrity. That must have been maddening for a man as proud as you, I dare say."

Wentworth snickered. "Please spare me the *faux* alienism, Mr. Holmes," he said, bringing his knight into the fray. "Why should I feel threatened by someone who was my intellectual inferior?"

Holmes chose to play an even more aggressive ploy. "You never actually beat him, though, did you?"

87

"Your strategy is far too obvious, my dear fellow. You focus too much on attack and leave yourself vulnerable." Wentworth moved his queen into a dangerous position. "That's check."

Holmes narrowly escaped the trap. "Incidentally, you and Mr. Quinn put a substantial wager on the match, didn't you? How much was it again? Three-thousand pounds, I believe?"

"If you're suggesting that I killed him for the prize money, then evidently you haven't seen my house," he said haughtily. "I'm far from a penurious man, Mr. Holmes."

I was about to tell him that we had just come from there, but I didn't want to interrupt the game at such a critical juncture.

"I wasn't suggesting anything," replied Holmes, taking Wentworth's queen. "I was merely curious."

"Hmm . . . an interesting move, one taken directly out of Mr. Quinn's playbook, no less."

Holmes shrugged. "I model myself on the best."

"Then I think you need a new role-model." He advanced toward Holmes's king, before declaring nonchalantly, "That's checkmate."

Holmes, to his credit, was generous in defeat. "Well played," he said, proffering a hand. "I have no shame in losing to a player of such prodigious skill."

"You are a competent player yourself, Mr. Holmes . . . for an amateur."

Holmes ignored the gibe and gave a superficial smile. "Well, thank you for the game, Mr. Wentworth." He stood up. "We won't disturb your recreation any further."

"Good luck finding your killer, Mr. Holmes," he said casually, as though he were talking about the latest horseracing results. Then, as we were walking away, I thought I heard him say, "It looks like you'll need it."

In the days that followed our interview with Mr. Wentworth, little was mentioned of the murdered chess master. I knew, however, that Holmes, who had a propensity for being maddeningly discreet about the progress of investigations while they were ongoing, was working diligently in the background to bring the case to a satisfactory conclusion.

On several occasions during this period, my friend would venture out alone and return hours later, often in twilight, with a renewed spring in his step. Sometimes, I would even find him playing chess by himself. Was this another of his experiments? I wondered bemusedly. Or had he completely taken leave of his senses?

Then, early one morning, I came downstairs to find a fresh-faced officer sitting in my chair, talking animatedly to Holmes. Upon seeing me enter the room, the young fellow sprang to his feet. "You must be Dr. Watson!" he said, removing his cap and shaking my hand with such enthusiasm that I thought it was going to fall off my arm. "I'm Inspector Parker. It's an honour to meet you." He bowed his head reverently. "I've read all your stories in *The Strand*, and I find them to be utterly captivating. Did John Clay really commit grand larceny by inventing a league of red-headed gentlemen?"

"Yes, he did," I verified. "I can't deny that it was a cunning scheme."

"And it's true that Dr. Grimesby Roylott tried to kill his stepdaughter with an Indian swamp adder?"

I nodded. "A more heinous villain I have never met."

"The creativity of the criminal mind knows no bounds," said Holmes. "It's a pity such people don't use it for the betterment of society."

I turned to Holmes, eager to learn why the inspector was in our sitting room. "You've solved the case, then?"

He nodded. "It was an intriguing little problem, one that presented quite a unique set of challenges."

I gestured to the young officer. "And based on the inspector's presence here, I assume you have collected enough evidence for an arrest to be made?"

"You are very perceptive this morning," he teased.

Then, I dared to ask the most significant question of them all. "So who killed Augustus Quinn?"

For a hopeful moment, I thought he was going to give me a name then and there, but he was as enigmatic as ever. "Patience. All will be revealed soon enough."

Though I had grown accustomed to it over the years, and even, perhaps, learned to tolerate it to some degree, I nonetheless found my friend's taciturnity to be a trifle infuriating, particularly when there appeared to be no good reason for it. However, I cannot deny that I have taken great pleasure in hearing, through letters I have received from some of my most devoted readers, that such narrative abeyance is to the advantage, rather than the detriment, of my chronicles.

"We should get going," the inspector said, glancing at the mantel clock. "The superintendent wants a full report by lunch time."

I was still wearing my dressing gown, so I quickly went up to my room to get changed, hastily completed my ablutions, and wolfed down my breakfast, before following Holmes and Inspector Parker into the street, where we waved for a growler and instructed the cabbie to take us to Grosvenor Crescent.

We arrived at the home of Augustus Quinn twenty minutes later – the mid-morning traffic meant we had to take a less direct route through Westminster – and were once again welcomed at the door by Tillman the butler.

"Has there recently been an infestation of mice in your scullery?" Holmes asked the old man as he led us through the hallway.

"Certainly not," Tillman said, apparently just as perplexed by the peculiar question as I. "Our scullery maid is nothing less than meticulous in her duties."

Before long, we found ourselves in the drawing room. There, sitting together in uncomfortable silence on crimson leather armchairs, were all three of the principal suspects: The cold and curt Mrs. Quinn and her dandyish and dashing stepson, who were exchanging a few choice words that I don't care to repeat, and the pompous and portly Mr. Wentworth, who, with his legs comfortably crossed, looked like a man not in the least bit concerned about the predicament in which he presently found himself.

"Thank you all for coming," began Inspector Parker, clearing his throat. "As you're all aware, it has been established that Augustus Quinn was poisoned during a chess match that took place in this very house." He scanned the room, clearly delighting in the theatre of it all. "And the perpetrator of that heinous crime is sitting here amongst us."

Parker stepped aside and invited my friend to speak. "Thank you, Inspector," Holmes said, turning his attention to Mr. Wentworth. "It's quite apparent that you were envious of Mr. Quinn's greater celebrity and threatened by his superior intellect. It's also true that you couldn't abide losing, especially to your greatest adversary, and would attempt to prevent such a scenario coming to pass by any means necessary, whether fair or foul." I presumed Holmes was alluding to the match-fixing scandal in which Mr. Wentworth had become entangled the preceding year. "You would do anything to win – but would you kill for it?"

The chess player sucked on his cigar. "As I have already told you, Mr. Holmes, I had nothing to do with the man's death," he said lethargically.

Next, Holmes addressed our client. "According to your stepmother, your father disinherited you, knowing that you were too reckless to be trusted with his fortune. Since then, your relationship with him became fractious, and the two of you had, for all intents and purposes, become estranged. Feeling humiliated by what you saw as a betrayal, would you seek bloody retribution?"

Sebastian Quinn was curt. "Mr. Holmes, might I remind you who is paying for your services?"

Lastly, my friend turned to the beautiful widow. "Then there's you, Mrs. Quinn. Your stepson here suspected you right from the start, claiming you only married his father for his vast wealth, which you now stand to inherit. Thus, materially at least, you had the most to gain from your husband's death."

"I don't appreciate your insinuations, Mr. Holmes," she said icily. "I hope I won't have to ask Tillman to show you out again."

"Oh, that won't be necessary, Mrs. Quinn. You'll be the only one being escorted out of here today . . . with a pair of handcuffs around your wrists."

"I beg your pardon!"

"My suspicions were first aroused by your clothes, Mrs. Quinn," he said, indicating her elegant white dress. "Evidently, you hadn't been grieving for your husband. Furthermore, though you claimed his death had caused you dismay, you showed no outward signs of that being the case. On the contrary, you seemed quite content sipping your wine and reading your book. Your whole demeanour, in fact, was entirely inconsistent with a state of widowhood."

"That doesn't prove a thing," she contested.

"No, you are quite right." He put a hand in his pocket and pulled out a white chess piece. "But this does."

"Isn't that the missing white queen?" I asked, recalling how, when he had inspected the chess board a few days ago, he had counted only thirty-one pieces.

He nodded. "To be precise, it's a replica of the piece Mrs. Quinn used to murder her husband."

The widow barked an incredulous laugh. "And how do you propose I did that? It's just a chess piece."

"Ah! But as you well know, Mrs. Quinn, it's no ordinary chess piece, is it?" He pulled at the crown, which slid smoothly off. "This detachable top allowed the cyanide powder to be poured into the hollow centre." He turned it over and drew our attention to a tiny hole in its base. "And this is where the poison would have escaped."

Something occurred to me. "That's why you discovered traces of it on the table, where Wentworth's queen had sat after Quinn took it out of the game."

"Exactly."

"But why didn't we find any on the board as well?"

"The hole in the base was small. Therefore, the cyanide could only escape slowly. Wentworth moved his queen frequently throughout the match, so it seldom remained on the same square for long. That meant there was scarcely time for the particles to accumulate on the squares occupied by the queen. When the piece was taken out of play by Quinn, however, it sat in the same spot on the table for the remainder of the match, near Quinn's right hand. That's why the powder began to gather there."

"Wouldn't the players have seen it, though? Or smelled it like I did?"

"That which had collected on the board was so minimal that neither man was likely to notice it, especially as they were so absorbed in the game. And even if they had, they probably would have just mistaken it for cigar ash. If you recall," he said, throwing a glance toward Wentworth, "Quinn's opponent was smoking throughout the game. What's more, not everyone can smell its odour of bitter almond."

"That makes sense," I said, though I was still baffled about something. "How, though, did Quinn come to ingest it?"

"Ah! Now that is the crucial question!" he said, raising a finger. "Wentworth had lost his queen, you may recall that Quinn began to play his moves more quickly, keen to capitalize upon the advantageous position in which he now found himself. To better focus his mind at this crucial stage in the match, he picked up his opponent's fallen queen – which was now on his side of the table – and began turning it over in his hand. As he was fidgeting with the piece, the poison would have continued to slowly trickle out of its base, now directly onto his fingertips. The powder has a fine texture, so he would barely have felt anything. Besides which, as I've said, his attention was firmly fixed on the match.

"Then, in a moment of intense concentration, he rested his fingers on the bottom of his mouth, like this – " He mimicked the action. " – causing the poison to pass from his fingers to his lips. According to Tillman, Quinn often got a dry throat during matches due to his nerves, so he was inclined to lick his lips. In this case, that harmless habit proved to be fatal."

"So that's why there were traces of cyanide on the rim of his glass," I said, realization dawning upon me. "Any residual powder from his lips would have deposited itself there when he next took a sip of water."

"Quite."

"And though Quinn consumed a relatively small quantity of cyanide, his pre-existing heart condition would have dramatically increased the chances of a cardiac arrest."

"An accurate diagnosis," said my friend. "All those years of medical experience haven't been for nought, after all."

I smiled at the glib remark. "And your solitary games of chess the last couple of evenings . . . you were reconstructing the match, weren't you?"

He nodded. "It helped me to better picture the sequence of events in my mind."

"But I don't understand . . . if the cyanide powder was in the white queen, wouldn't Wentworth also have fallen victim to its deadly effects?"

"No, because he only touched the top of the queen when he was moving it around the board. Not once, however, did he finger the bottom of the piece."

In spite of Holmes's allegations, Mrs. Quinn refused to capitulate. "Unless I possess powers of clairvoyance, how could I possibly know my husband would do all of those things you've just mentioned?"

"You couldn't know for sure," Holmes conceded, "but you were fully aware of your husband's idiosyncrasies, which allowed you to foresee, to a certain extent, how he would behave. No doubt in previous matches, you had seen him clutching pieces in his hand as he contemplated his next move. And many people press their fingers to their lips when they are in a state of profound cogitation – I often do it myself. These predictable behaviours meant there was a high probability of your plan succeeding."

"And I just happened to know that he'd play as black and take his opponent's queen out of play, did I?"

My friend turned his attention to Wentworth, who appeared vaguely amused by the familial drama unfolding around him. "During our game the other day," he said to the corpulent man, "you mentioned that your arch-rival preferred to play as black and suggested he had a proclivity for capturing his opponents' queens."

He addressed Mrs. Quinn again. "Having watched your husband play countless times before, you knew there was a very good chance he would do both of those things." He added, "And even if it had gone awry on this occasion, you simply would have waited until your husband's next match and made sure your plan met with more success on that occasion. Failing that, a woman of your cunning, as unfettered by morality as you, could easily conceive of other methods of murder, no doubt equally as fiendish as this one."

Parker nodded his head, apparently satisfied with my friend's explanation. "And presumably, she must have destroyed the counterfeit queen later that evening when everyone had gone."

"Highly probable, given that it was the single most incriminating piece of evidence."

"But if I hadn't smelled the cyanide on Quinn's body," I said, "everyone would have just assumed he had succumbed to his cardiac problems. Also, because it dissipates rapidly in the blood, the poison is almost impossible to detect in autopsies."

"Mrs. Quinn doubtless considered all of this and had intended the whole thing to look like a tragic misadventure," Holmes said. "But that plan went awry when you discovered evidence of foul play. Notwithstanding, she was still impervious to blame as she was sat in the audience the entire time. As such, she had the perfect alibi." He faced Mrs.

93

Quinn. "Despite its shortcomings, it was quite an ingenious plan, I'll admit that."

The widow went on the counterattack. "As entertaining as this farrago of fantasy is, Mr. Holmes, there's no way you can possibly connect me to my husband's murder."

"On the contrary, Mrs. Quinn," Holmes said, digging a hand into his breast pocket, from which he produced a single gold earring. "I discovered this in the ballroom, lying on the floor underneath the chess table. I will wager that its mate is upstairs on your dressing table right now." He pocketed the piece of jewellery. "The right earring must have come loose and fallen to the floor when you were removing the chess piece."

She shrugged. "It still doesn't prove that I poisoned my husband, though, does it?"

"Not conclusively, but the missing earring placed you at the site of the murder and went a good way towards confirming my original suspicions of you. Next, all I had to do was verify my hypothesis by ascertaining where you had acquired the counterfeit queen."

"This should be amusing!"

Holmes, however, was unruffled by her jibe. "The other day," he explained, "your butler informed me that your late husband was an avid collector of Staunton chess sets. Last year, he had commissioned a local carpenter by the name of Norman Colby to design the very one used during the match several days ago. When I suspected that the white queen was the murder weapon, I visited Mr. Colby's workshop in Halkin Street. There, I met the man's son, Benjamin Colby, who informed me that his father had since put down his hammer and chisel, and bequeathed the business to him.

"Despite this minor inconvenience, he was willing to provide me with his father's address in Ayrton Road, where I spoke to the retired carpenter. Mr. Colby intimated to me that you had called at his shop last month and asked him to make a white queen identical to the one in my pocket. I convinced him to make another – which I've just showed to you – and it worked just as I theorized," he explained. "When Mr. Colby questioned your peculiar request, you said you planned to make use of the item as a decorative saltshaker and were purchasing it as a present for your husband's forthcoming birthday." He stared accusingly at Mrs. Quinn, whose face was sculpted into an expression of stony inscrutability. "As it turns out, though, you used it for an altogether more nefarious purpose, didn't you?"

I still had one more question. "But where did she obtain the sodium cyanide?"

94

"A crucial question, Watson, and one to which I found the answer only yesterday," he replied. "When I suspected that Mrs. Quinn was guilty, I asked the Baker Street Irregulars to follow her around town and report back to me with any evidence that could be used against her at the forthcoming inquest. During their reconnaissance, they learned that Marylebone is a favourite stomping ground of hers and that she likes to go shopping there on a regular basis. Equipped with this knowledge, I decided to visit several chemists in the area, knowing there was a high probability I would soon hit upon the one which had sold Mrs. Quinn the poison. At first, my search was to no avail, and I was considering heading home, when I walked through the door of *John Bell and Croyden* in Wigmore Street.

"The apothecary there remembered Mrs. Quinn calling in at his shop last month to purchase a bottle of sodium cyanide. When he asked what it was for, she made up some hogwash about having an infestation of mice in the scullery, knowing that the toxin is also an effective rodenticide. However, according to Tillman, there have been no mice scurrying around the scullery of late." He faced Mrs. Quinn, his lips curling into a wry smile. "You played a clever game. But I'm afraid that this is checkmate!"

"It seems that I underestimated you, Mr. Holmes," she drawled. "Apparently, not all men are as easy to fool as my late husband."

I looked at her stepson and noticed that his hands were gripping the arms of his chair more tightly than before. Mercifully, before the situation escalated, Inspector Parker approached the guilty woman and declared, in as commanding a voice as he could muster, "I'm placing you under arrest for the murder of Augustus Quinn. If you'd like to accompany me to the station, please."

After the prisoner had been escorted off the premises, Mr. Wentworth, who appeared entirely uninterested in the whole matter, left without uttering a single word, while our client, for his part, thanked us profusely for our help in sending his conniving stepmother to the gaol and assured my friend that he bore him no ill will for calling his innocence into question.

"It would have been remiss of me had I failed to consider every possibility," Holmes explained. "It's the prerogative of any competent detective."

"I understand, Mr. Holmes." He hung his head in dismay. "I just wish my father was still here."

"I realize it's little comfort to you, but at least now you finally have the knowledge you sought," I said. "Justice has been served."

"And for giving me that, you have my eternal gratitude." He shook our hands. "Thank you once again, gentlemen, and farewell."

"It never ceases to amaze me what people will do for money," I said later that evening in the sitting room.

"Avarice can cause people to do terrible things," he said sagaciously. "Need I remind you of the case of Miss Violet Smith and her covetous captors?"

"How can I forget it?"

"Incidentally," he said, "this may not be the first time Alexandra Quinn has committed murder for pecuniary advantage. During the week, in between my visits to the carpenters and chemists, I went to Brooks's in St. James's Street and spoke to Langdale Pike, hoping to learn more about the woman."

"You *have* been busy!"

"Indeed. Rumour has it that she was married twice before, firstly to a merchant banker and subsequently to a wealthy industrialist, both of whom died due to some sort of calamity. The banker, a Eugene Morris, was found in a vault, buried under a pile of gold bullion, while the factory owner, Harold Godwin, was dismembered by one of his own machines. In both instances, the woman we knew as Mrs. Quinn inherited all her husbands' fortunes."

"Her stepson was right about her all along," I said, shaking my head in disgust. "She was nothing but a parasite feeding off wealthy men."

"According to Pike, those who knew of her evil deeds called her 'The White Widow'. Like that deadly species of arachnid, Mrs. Quinn lured her mates into her web before killing them. Instead of feasting on their flesh, however, she dined on their riches."

"And she was a widow who preferred to wear white," I said needlessly.

Holmes was tickled by this superfluous comment. "Yes, Watson. That too! When you eventually commit this narrative to the page, I suppose you'll insist on giving it a fanciful title like you usually do," he said wryly. 'The Widow's Web', or something of that ilk, I imagine."

I pondered for a moment. "No," I said after a while. "I prefer 'The Checkmate Murder'."

96

When Spaghetti was Served at the Diogenes Club
by John Farrell

It was the first, and only, time that spaghetti was served in the dining room of the Diogenes Club. Spaghetti was not something that suited the peculiar sensibilities of the Diogenes Club's rather unusual membership.

Most of all, there was the noise involved in eating the Italian specialty. Silence was the principal driving force of the Diogenes, and that silence was cherished in the club's dining room as nowhere else. Waiters were given dinner orders in writing. Each diner had every sort of condiment, salt cellar, and pepper mill available individually so no one need ever ask for anything from a fellow member. Even the click of knife and fork on China and the gurgle of wine poured into crystal were carefully minimized lest a member come to the attention of the Committee to be admonished for creating a scene.

There were a few members, the more adventurous, who enjoyed their brief encounter with Italian cooking, but many of the others made it clear that such an honor would not again be welcome. Roast beef, they felt, was good enough for honest English gentleman, and the peasant foods of southern climes were not a suitable replacement. And so, even when served to a group of generally elderly and conservative gentlemen as a special honor, spaghetti was not a success.

That spaghetti appeared even once at the Diogenes was the inadvertent fault of Mr. Mycroft Holmes. It was not his intent to either challenge or educate the pallets of his fellow members. Indeed, if the truth be told, he would have rather avoided the whole matter.

Still, when the King of Italy insisted on offering his hospitality and the services of his personal chef to the club for an evening's gustatorial pleasure, it was difficult for the club to reject the proposal without offending His Majesty. It must be said that the wines provided from the Royal cellars, the liqueurs, the delicious soup, shrimp caught in the Mediterranean and brought on ice to London, and beefsteak in the Florentine style all proved extraordinary. The spaghetti, however, was a failure. The relevant facts follow.

Mr. Mycroft Holmes much preferred to conduct official business – Her Majesty's business – in the comfortable office that his Queen had

97

provided for those matters on a quiet floor of the Foreign Office. His life was such that he preferred to keep his affairs each in their proper place. The office was for matters of government, the Diogenes Club his personal refuge. But when the Foreign Secretary asked that he speak with the secretary to the Italian Ambassador, Count Cipriano Livorno, in a non-official manner and at a place where privacy was certain and press comment could be avoided, he realized that the request was one of great political importance, and he agreed to meet the ambassador in the Stranger's Room at his club, the only place where conversation was allowed, if only barely tolerated within its confines.

The Foreign Secretary was also a member of the Diogenes, a membership he owed to Mr. Mycroft Holmes's good offices. He knew there were several members of the Diogenes who were wont to consider current British foreign policy to be rather too liberal, especially that cautious friendship with France, which these members remembered only as the home of that upstart, Napoleon the First. With such a reactionary membership, it was felt the Count should appear *incognito*. He arrived on a Tuesday in November, a wet and gray day on which pedestrians hurried on their way, shivering under their ineffectual umbrellas.

From his comfortable seat in the Stranger's Room, Mycroft Holmes had been watching the passing scene. Presently, an elegantly dressed gentleman came into view, wearing a shiny black silk top hat and Van Dyke beard. He stepped from a hansom under the club's *porte cochere*. Mycroft Holmes, without moving from his chair, signaled to his favorite waiter to bring two double Scotches to his table.

The gentleman who entered the room was a study in understated elegance. His frock coat was of conventional cut, but of a cloth of great beauty. His boots, tiny and pointed, were as sharp as his beard and matched his slicked-back hair in their glossy blackness.

The Count, operating under the *nom-de-guerre* of Signore Cipriano, was hardly five feet tall and moved with a quick, bird-like gait that showed a crisp intelligence and a careful awareness of his surroundings. In the sometime-violent world of Italian royal politics, that awareness had more than once avoided a serious and violent moment of crisis.

Count Livorno knew Mycroft Holmes at sight. His corpulent figure, dark, intelligent eyes, and broad, bland face hid an encyclopedic knowledge of British foreign affairs and, in his ten years as secretary to the Italian Ambassador in London, the diplomat had come to trust Mycroft Holmes's judgment in political matters. He had also heard of Sherlock Holmes – as who hadn't in London? – but never before had he had the ill-fortune to be confronted with a matter that required that gentleman's knowledge of crime.

98

Signore Cipriano, the Count's alter ego, had been created by an over-eager member of the Italian Embassy staff, and the Count had been warned to maintain the secret of his identity with vigor, so as he stepped across the Stranger's Room, he rather more loudly than was quite necessary called out to Mycroft Holmes.

"Ah, Mr. Holmes. I am Signore Cipriano. It is so good of you to see me. The directors of the company that employs me need advice on British export law and you were recommended to us as an expert. It is kind of you to see me here in your club."

Truth be told, Mycroft Holmes was nonplussed by Count Livorno's effusive greeting, but his diplomatic training was more than enough for the crisis. Ignoring the raised eyebrows of several members, he used a flipper-like hand to guide his guest to a comfortable armchair and as the Count sat down, he leaned over him and whispered into his ear, "No need to overplay your character, my dear Count Livorno. Here in the Diogenes, no one will notice you at all. It is a part of the inherent courtesy of the club that we make a point of never noticing each other, except when unavoidably necessary."

"Ah, you will excuse me, I am sure," the Count said in a much quieter voice, and in a much less exaggerated manner, "but our recent tragedy and, perhaps, undue caution on the part of my Embassy colleagues, has made me more than a bit sensitive."

"Your feelings are understandable, of course," Mycroft Holmes replied. "I understand that you are here to consult me about the death of a young man in your office?"

From Mycroft Holmes's manner, if not his words, it was clear that he knew much more about the matter than he admitted.

"Do, first, have a sip of that Scotch. I have it on authority from a medical friend of my brother's that whisky is a nerve tonic, and this is one of the best twelve-year-old single malts anywhere, available only to the Royal Family and, by the Prince of Wales' graciousness, to our cellar."

The Count raised his glass, toasted in gesture to his host, and sipped some of the golden liquid, holding it briefly on his tongue before swallowing. He uttered a little sigh before speaking.

"In Italy we have some of the finest wines, and some of the most ancient of vineyards but, if I may say so, there is nothing we produce, not even our finest brandies or our herbal liqueurs, which are as complex and rewarding as the whiskies of the British Isles. I trust you will hold that opinion as a diplomatic secret."

"Your secret I will keep. I am afraid the reputation of the whisky is already broadcast. Come, though, and tell me of your problem. It must be a serious one indeed to require the precautions you have undertaken to protect it."

"It is no less than murder that I come to ask you about," the Count said in an emotional whisper. "At the least, I believe it is murder, though I cannot explain how the murder was committed, cannot find a motive for it, and my colleagues, while they are as shocked as I am at the event, do not believe it to be anything more than an accidental death."

"Pray give me all the details, Count Livorno, even the most trivial, and I will do my best to give you an answer." Sitting back in his armchair, his large fist closed around the crystal tumbler, Mycroft Holmes looked at the ceiling and prepared to listen.

"You must first understand how our Embassy functions to realize the terrible impact this event has had on all of us there," Count Livorno said in a voice strained with anguish. "Italy has been in a political furor for years, with attacks on government officials only one of many problems afflicting our nation, which is both one of the oldest in Europe, dating from our Roman history, and one of the newest, reunited within living memory. While our government has, from time to time, recalled the current Italian ambassador and replaced him with someone more representative of the then-current faction, our staff here in London has remained largely unchanged, like a family. It is felt this is safer, since we can be certain of the long-term loyalties of those who have served for many years.

"Still," said the Italian nobleman, pausing for a healthy sip of the whisky, "we do require new staff members from time to time, and they are chosen carefully, based not only on educational success, but family ties and reputation as well. I know this seems old-fashioned, but in Italy, family is an important consideration, and even those appointed to junior positions are certain to belong to at least the cadet branches of important families that have a long history of loyalty to the Royal Family.

"Such a one was Giovanni Martinelli, who came to us just three months ago. Although he was young – twenty-seven years old, I believe – his good looks and bright smile made him seem several years younger, which certainly did him no harm with the older women who act as typewriters and translators on our staff. Martinelli came of a fine family. His mother's father lost his life in the revolution that put King Victore Emmanuelle on the throne, and his father had fought with the rebels as well.

"Further, his academic accomplishments were remarkable. He had studied Latin and Greek in his church-school, and at University showed an even greater facility for languages. He spoke perfect French, and six different Italian dialects. This is an important factor in success in our young and still loosely unified nation. This is not to mention how, in one year at Oxford, he acquired a command of accent-less English. It was considered a notable achievement.

"He was certainly marked to go far in our service. His good looks and considerable personal charm – never a disadvantage in the diplomatic world – together with his linguistic skills, would certainly have been matched by knowledge gained by experience, and soon enough would have raised him to an important rank. In three months, he'd already attracted the favorable notice of the Ambassador, who sent a letter to Martinelli's father praising his son. He was slated for a career of great service to his country. Yet now he is dead, and no one can offer a reasonable explanation for that death."

"Allow me," Mycroft Holmes said, "to interrupt your very admirable narrative. No doubt you would benefit from another whisky, which I will order for you." He did so with a hand-signal to the waiter across the room. "Pray continue."

"Thank you, sir," replied the Count. "It is true that this matter has been one of great emotional distress for all of us, and especially for me, because I must admit I found in young Martinelli many of the attributes I might have looked for in a son, if I had one. His mysterious death shocked me as much as anyone in the Embassy. The fact that it remains unexplained is even more deeply troubling."

"Tell me the details of his death, then, and let us see what we can conclude. There are few human mysteries that will not yield to human ratiocination, and those others must be left to the Church authorities for their consideration."

The Count crossed himself. "Indeed, Mr. Holmes, you are right, and I hope this is not one of those. We shall see. It was only last week that this happened. Today is Tuesday, and it was just a week ago, in the afternoon, that we noticed that Giovanni Martinelli was not himself."

"How so?"

"The young man in question was usually a picture of perfect physical health," Count Cipriano said. "He enjoyed rowing in the park, horseback riding, and football. He had even played your English Rugby and found it entertaining. Martinelli had a healthy appetite and especially enjoyed the bitter Italian liqueur called Campari, which he drank with relish every afternoon at our office during what we like to call our 'teatime' – though we Italians have doubts about the health-giving properties of that beverage and usually prefer wine or an aperitif in the afternoon.

"Last Tuesday at luncheon, the young man ate nothing, saying that he had no appetite whatsoever and plead that his stomach was slightly upset. Nor did he drink anything more than a little water that afternoon. He complained of a headache and slight dizziness as well. I suggested he visit

101

a physician, but he said again it was just a mild stomach upset and I thought no more of it.

"The very next day, Wednesday last, he came to the office at his usual early time, though we all could clearly see that he did not feel well. We urged him to go home or seek medical assistance, but the young often feel they are immortal, and in truth dyspepsia is not a fatal illness. Again he ate little at lunch, and seemed ill at ease throughout what would have been an otherwise convivial meal.

"He returned to his office and there complained to a colleague about a severe headache and worse – dizziness. Shortly thereafter he experienced convulsions and collapsed, barely breathing. We called in the local physician who handles Embassy cases, but there was apparently nothing he could do. He applied various stimulants, including volatile salts, but Martinelli never regained consciousness, and his heart beat and breathing weakened and then stopped entirely."

"There would be no autopsy or coroner's inquest required, I quite understand, since the death occurred in what is technically Italian soil," Mycroft Holmes said. "Nonetheless, the physician must have had some idea what caused the death?'

"He had no idea whatsoever, save for the conventional. He said there were no indications of poisoning by any of the well-known means, and the symptoms – dizziness and a weakness of the heart – might well be the explanation. But I knew this was a vigorous young man in the peak of condition, and I do not believe that he had a weak heart.

"The Ambassador would prefer to ignore the matter, and has refused to do more than send a telegram of regret to Martinelli's family and to the young noblewoman to whom he was betrothed. I am before you without official brief, but I feel this young man deserved better of his country, and I was able to ask a favor of one of your ministers, who was glad to accommodate me. Thus, I am here to consult you privately."

"You will pardon my frankness, then, Count, when I say that you have left at least one important fact out of your otherwise detailed account of the affair."

"And that is?" the Count said with a little asperity.

"While I feel that your concern for this afflicted young man is genuine, I must wonder whether there is a more political reason for your concern. Bluntly, did Giovanni Martinelli have access to any important Embassy secrets?"

"Mr. Holmes!" said the Count, rising.

"My dear Count," said Mycroft Holmes in a voice of soothing condolence, "I do not wish to know your government's secrets, if indeed there are any we do not already know. I am acting here purely in a capacity

102

of criminal investigator, and I must inquire as to whether there is a motive for Martinelli's death. Did he know anything that that might have compromised him or your legation? Is there a motive that might indicate that his death was anything but a natural one?"

"Martinelli, despite his family contacts and his linguistic abilities, was still merely a junior clerk in our office," the Count said. "He could not have known anything more about our government's affairs than the day-to-day calendar of activities. He would not have been privy to diplomatic communiques, had no access to diplomatic cyphers, and did not involve himself in any more serious activities in the office. It would have been some months before he was trusted with those *mattes* in any way."

"That is all perfectly clear, then," said Mycroft Holmes. "Allow me, then, one more question, and I think that I shall be able to advise you of what you will find it necessary to do."

"And that question is?" said the Count, sitting forward in his seat in eagerness.

"You looked at Giovanni Martinelli after his death?"

"Yes, I did. It was a sad sight, Mr. Holmes."

"Then no doubt you noticed that his skin, the whites of his eyes, and especially his gums were bright yellow?"

The Count sat back in his chair in amazement. "How could you have possibly known that?" he asked in incredulity. "It is almost as though you were there!"

"It does not matter how I know it, but only that I do. You wish my advice?"

"Most certainly."

"It is very urgent. You must return to your Embassy at once and cancel or delay your king's upcoming visit to Queen Victoria."

"That cannot be done. As you yourself know, we have spent more than a year arranging for King Umberto's arrival. He will not admit to anyone stopping his visit at this late date."

"Nonetheless, it must be done," said Mycroft Holmes. "If your ambassador cannot manage affairs, then I personally will make sure the visit is canceled. It is that urgent. Surely King Umberto might find himself indisposed for a few days. Perhaps an unannounced visit to a European spa might be arranged. I can tell you that this matter of urgency can be taken under advisement and solved in a few days. But you must delay His Majesty's arrival."

"Mr. Holmes, I came to you for your advice and I must be willing to take it," the Count said. "I will go at once and do my best to delay His Majesty, with the assurance that if I cannot, you will be able to arrange that feat."

103

"Like me, Count, you have a lifetime of service to your country, and you know, as I do, that in the final accounting, it is not the kings and queens, who are detached from day-to-day matters, nor the ministers serving short terms, who have the power to affect daily decisions. I am sure that you can persuade your king that a brief rest for his health is in his best interest, and while he rests, I am sure I can explain the death of your young clerk."

The Count left in haste to carry out his mission, and Mycroft Holmes signaled to the club's commissionaire for a telegram form. On it he wrote:

Sherlock Holmes
221b Baker Street
London, W1

Brother: Clerk in Italian Embassy died last Wednesday, two weeks before arrival of Italian King on State visit. Stop. Clerk had bright yellow skin, eyes, and gums. Stop. You will know what to do. Stop.

Mycroft

It was just one week later, on a day of glorious sunshine and warm breezes, that the ill-disguised Signore Cipriano visited Mycroft Holmes for a second time in the Stranger's Room of The Diogenes. This time the elegant little man knew not to introduce himself so publicly, and he settled into the armchair that Mycroft Holmes indicated, accepted his whisky, and waited for his host to begin the conversation.

"First, if I may, allow me to offer a toast to the health of King Umberto," Mycroft said with a rare smile. "I understand he was feeling under the weather last week and had to postpone his visit here."

"You most of all know his health was affected," Count Cipriano said.

"And because I know that, I can safely say that I am sure he will recover his full health immediately."

"That I will gladly toast," said the Count with more enthusiasm than he had shown hitherto. "Does this mean that you know what happened to Giovanni Martinelli?"

"Oh, I knew that from the end of our last interview," Mycroft Holmes said off-handedly. "It merely took this long to find and catch those responsible."

"But that is fantastic, almost unbelievable, Signore Holmes," the Count said. "You know only what I know of the incident, yet you were able to discern something I did not."

104

"While it was true that I knew no more of the incident than you – indeed a good deal less – I possess a more specialized knowledge and was able to act immediately on it."

"Please do not keep me in suspense, sir. I must know what you have discovered."

"Well, it has been said of the Holmes family that we have a penchant for the dramatic, which I believe is more evident in my brother than myself. Nonetheless, I think the story will be better told in an orderly fashion than in pieces. Here, to begin, is the counterfoil of the wire I sent to my brother as you left last Wednesday. I think you will find it of some interest."

Count Cipriano grabbed the piece of paper eagerly from Mycroft Holmes's hand but, after reading it through twice, seemed no more illuminated than before.

"What does it mean, Mr. Holmes?" he asked with a little exasperation in his voice. "I can see nothing in it that explains anything."

"Before we go into details, perhaps you should read this telegram I received a few hours ago, immediately after which I sent for you." He handed the Count a telegram he first removed from his billfold:

Brother:

You will no doubt be interested to read that Friend Lestrade has added to his laurels by capturing anarchist bomb ring in Eastside house this morning. Stop.

Sherlock

"There are more details here in this afternoon's earliest edition of *The Daily Mail*, which you may not have seen."

Count Cipriano Livorno took the newspaper from Mycroft Holmes. It had been folded so that one small story was at the center:

Scotland Yard has just announced that an anarchist bomb-building ring has been captured in an otherwise unremarkable house in suburban London. The arrests were supervised by the well-known Scotland Yard Detective Inspector G. Lestrade, the man who on many occasions has been able to use his vast experience to solve cases beyond the ken of the city's various private detectives, including Mr. Sherlock Holmes.

Mr. Lestrade bravely led a group of twenty constables in surrounding the house in question, where they arrested six men.

105

Of apparently Sicilian origin, they were using the house to manufacture explosives and bombs to be used in undoubtedly dastardly plans. More will be known after further investigation but, in the meanwhile, the people of London can breathe easier knowing that Scotland Yard's Inspector Lestrade is still at work.

"I must admit that I am as confused as ever," the Count shook his head. "I notice that this 'G. Lestrade' must be the man to whom your brother refers. Did you anticipate his plans, or know of them when I consulted you? You should have told me then and I might have been able to forestall His Majesty's feigned illness."

"Calm yourself, my dear Count. Until today, I knew nothing of Lestrade's activities – nor my brother's, for that matter. I am not a man of action, as you may have perceived. I prefer to sit and contemplate while others do the more strenuous work. I did not know that Lestrade would conduct this morning's raid, nor that it would lead to the capture of six men and an explosives laboratory. But I had deduced the existence of the laboratory, the bombs, and the plot against the life of King Umberto before you left here last week."

"How could you have known all that on such scanty information? Surely there was nothing of a plot in what I told you."

"On the contrary, there was in your story everything I needed to know, once I added to your narrative certain data which I happened to have in mind – indeed, information which you also know. To that knowledge, I added a few quickly-reached conclusions."

"Information I knew already?" the Count said with astonishment.

"Certainly," said Mycroft Holmes placidly. "You knew your King Umberto was planning a to Great Britain and would arrive in a few days' time. I knew it, as I had played a part in making the detailed arrangements for the visit. Most everyone in London knew of it, for that matter, from newspaper accounts. You failed to connect Giovanni Martinelli's death with the impending royal visit."

"I still don't see the connection."

"Nonetheless, there is one. The suspicious death of an Italian Embassy official, no matter how junior, less than a fortnight before the visit of the king, seemed to be a coincidence that was remarkably suggestive."

"Now that you speak it, I recognize the fact. But I must admit that I was too grieved to think of that at the time. Does that mean that Martinelli was involved with the plotters?"

"It might have. At that time, I was still collecting evidence and merely stored away the fact for further consideration. It was suspicious, but I

106

needed further information, and when you described the details of the young man's death, I was certain of the fact. Your astonishment when I described the color of the dead man's skin, eyes, and gums confirmed my hypothesis, and I knew at once there was a serious threat to King Umberto's safety."

"How could you possibly know that?" asked the Count. "And I admit that hard to believe that Giovanni was part of the plot."

"It will be better if we take matters one at a time. Let me first relieve your mind about your clerk. I can conclusively state that he was a victim of the conspiracy, not a member of it. Although I held him suspect at first, as soon as you made certain the circumstances of his death, his innocence was obvious. He had clearly died of some sort of poisoning, as you also suspected.

"It is highly unlikely that a conspirator would kill himself before a plot had come to fruition. Nor would his fellow conspirators allow him to die in your office in great pain since, if he knew anything incriminating, he might blurt it out. No, it was clearly a case of murder, though I doubt we will be able to prove that these bomb-makers were his murderers, at least not in a court of law."

"But the threat to His Majesty?"

"That was inherent in the details of Martinelli's death. It was clear there was a bomb plot involved."

"But he died of poisoning, not from an explosion!" the still perplexed diplomat cried out.

"Exactly. The poison was the key to the bomb plot. We are far from the days of your own Lucretia Borgia, Count Livorno, and I feel sure," Mycroft Holmes continued with a raised eyebrow, "poison is not much a part of current Italian diplomacy.

"One of many subjects to which I have given special attention is the effects and symptoms of poison, and your description of Martinelli's illness and death was suggestive. Combined with my supposition that his death had something to do with King Umberto's visit, I asked you about young Martinelli's yellow pallor and hit the mark."

"You knew, then, what killed Martinelli?"

"Yes. Signore Martinelli was killed by the ingestion, over several days, of a fatal dose of picric acid."

"Picric acid?"

"Certainly you have heard of it?"

"As you discerned, Signore Holmes, I am not a very good chemist."

"Nor, if I may add, do you interest yourself in military matters."

"No, that has never been one of my duties."

"If it had been, you would have certainly heard of picric acid, for it is the high explosive of choice for artillery shells in our murderous modern world. Your government, that of Her Imperial Majesty, the Germans, the French, and others, have devised special formulas for picric acid to use in their high explosives. I understand there have been experimental attempts to use dynamite as a military explosive, but that explosive has proven too unstable so far."

"Yet surely these men who were arrested were not military men?"

"Certainly not. The picric acid that is used for military purposes is stabilized and is specially manufactured. But picric acid itself is easily manufactured by a skilled chemist, and the yellow crystalline acid is what is called a percussive explosive. It can be set off with a fuse or, if the fuse fails, throwing the container or a bomb full of the acid onto hard ground can set it off. Anarchists find it the most practical explosive available – much more powerful than black powder. It is easily manufactured, and stable so long as the crystals are kept under water.

"Picric acid also has medicinal uses, especially in dilute solutions applied to serious burns. It can cause poisoning if too much is applied, and can be fatal if ingested. But its rather bitter flavor makes that a rare occurrence. Your young friend liked bitter aperitifs, so it wasn't at all difficult to slip a fatal dose of only a few grains of picric acid into several drinks. The symptoms you mentioned – inability to eat, dizziness, headache – are all typical of picric acid poisoning, which cannot be detected after death – save for the yellow skin of the victim."

"How you guessed all of this is incredible."

"No guessing was involved, I assure you," said Mycroft Holmes. "Once I suspected there was picric acid in the case, it was obvious that a plot against someone's life was in the offing. King Umberto was the obvious – indeed the *only* target associated with both anarchist plotting and the Italian Embassy.

"The telegram I sent to brother Sherlock explained everything he needed to know, and I relied on his taking action. He has all the family energy. I have none."

"But Signore Holmes," the Count asked, "I still do not see how your Inspector Lestrade was able to find the plotters with such ease."

"Ah, Lestrade. He is not a man of cleverness, but like a hound, once given a scent, he is inexorable. My brother, as he has so often in the past, gave the old hound the scent. I talked to him briefly this morning: He has a telephone, but uses it only grudgingly.

"It was, as he said, an elementary investigation. I knew from the facts which you provided had that young Martinelli had most certainly died from picric acid poisoning, and that picric acid was an anarchist tool.

"Sherlock saw as much immediately from my telegram. He was able, with little difficulty, to find where Martinelli spent his evenings, and was able to trace his friends, if we may call them that, since it was they who poisoned him. They extracted the information they needed from the young man and then, since their plot was near fruition, coldly eliminated him to remove a potential witness."

"But surely Martinelli wasn't in on their plot?"

"Well, not exactly. He knew nothing of their plans and seems to have given them no secrets. The king's travel agenda was common knowledge within the Italian diplomatic corps, and Martinelli's single indiscretion served to confirm those plans. Once the plotters were sure of the final dates, they no longer needed Martinelli, who might inadvertently give them away, and so they disposed of him. It was their choice of picric acid as a poison that gave me and my brother the one clue we needed."

"But how did your brother go from poison and a plot against our King to Inspector Lestrade's raid on the conspirators this morning?"

"He night never hear me admit it, but Sherlock is a master of disguise. He went to the cafe where Martinelli was a regular customer and overheard a good deal, though nothing incriminating. I should like to have seen him disguised as an Italian workingman. I knew he had enough of the language to get by, of course, but I'm sure I would be amused at his choice of clothing.

"In quick order, Sherlock was able to identify several men who were – to his mind – suspicious, and he followed one of them home. My brother finds such a matter simplicity itself. The man he followed went to a detached suburban villa which seemed, to all except a trained observer, as innocent a dwelling as you might find anywhere in London."

"What, then, gave it away?"

"I will tell you what my brother told me: 'It was the dead pigeons.'"

"Dead pigeons?"

"Yes, dead pigeons. You see, in making picric acid, deadly fumes are produced that have to be removed from the laboratory by special ventilation. The plotters apparently vented their fumes through one of the chimneys in the house, and the pigeons who spend their nights near the warm chimney pots were overcome by fumes.

"You will have noticed that you never see dead pigeons in London, despite the large flocks in our public squares. Pigeons, when ill, hide and are rarely found dead. When Brother Sherlock found four dead pigeons, all within a few feet of the house's chimney, he knew that picric acid fumes had hilled them.

"Lestrade, who is always willing to take my brother's advice when he can gain credit from it, quickly assembled a large force of constables and quietly surrounded the house. Early this morning, when all in the house were fast asleep, he sprang his trap, arresting seven men, and found considerable explosives already made into bombs, plus the equipment and chemicals for making more. Lestrade will, as always, be commended for his acumen in the newspapers, and neither my brother nor I will not be mentioned."

"And Martinelli's murderer will be punished," the Count said firmly.

"Possibly, possibly not," Mycroft Holmes replied. "Certainly, the plot to kill your king has been destroyed, and Martinelli's murderers caught. The Crown will likely turn the plotters over to your government for prosecution in conspiring to kill King Umberto. The plotters are, from my brother's account, fanatical and unlikely to incriminate one another. With little prodding, I dare say Her Majesty's government will also turn over the particulars regarding the case of the murdered young Martinelli for you to prove."

The Count nodded. "I believe that is what will occur. I regret the loss of our young friend but I am glad their plans regarding His Majesty have failed. I am sure that he will want to reward you and your brother for your singular services in this painful matter."

For Sherlock Holmes that reward proved to be a discreet but heavy gold ring with the royal crest on it, an elegant piece which the detective often wore.

For Mycroft Holmes and the Diogenes Club, it was a fine dinner prepared by the king's personal chef – a dinner enjoyed by some members and decidedly not enjoyed by others.

The experiment was not repeated.

Holmes Run
by Amanda J.A. Knight

Prologue

As the narrow alleyway loomed before her, Mary glanced nervously behind. Not entirely certain why she felt ill at ease, she watched as the tall, slim man followed closely. Several times in the past Mary had been aware of him watching her, though always from a distance. This was the first time he had made an approach. His expensive frock coat and top hat were not an uncommon sight in these quarters, and a genial smile spread broadly beneath his rather prominent nose. Despite this feature, he wasn't unattractive, his angular face being well-proportioned and showing a strong character. Pausing, Mary smiled in return. Maybe she would earn enough for a bed tonight after all.

Upon reaching her side, he lifted up one hand and softly stroked her cheek. "How much?" he asked quietly, still smiling gently. She relaxed a little and moved in closer to him.

"Four-pence." She turned her head to one side and smiled in what she hoped was a coquettish manner. Although this was a little more than usual, she prayed he wouldn't quibble, for she was weary and all she really wanted was a glass of gin and a proper bed for the night.

"Very reasonable," he laughed.

She sighed inwardly. She would sleep indoors after all.

He stepped in behind her, placing his arms around her waist, squeezing gently with one hand while the other stroked her side. She continued to smile at the thought of a glass in her hand, though still with a feeling of apprehension she could neither explain nor deny.

Suddenly his arms moved up and she saw the flash of steel. Her own smile turned to a scream that was cut short as his iron grip upon her mouth gagged her. He pressed closer still, crushing her feeble body against his surprisingly powerful one, and the knife flashed before her frightened eyes. She felt the bite of steel on her neck.

He was in no hurry, slowly finishing his grotesque business. Having stood behind the girl whilst making the fatal cut, he ensured next to no blood had spattered on his person. Only one part of him told, and as he looked dispassionately down at the dark wetness covering his hands, he knew this was taken care of easily enough. After wiping away most signs of his deed from both hands and blade on a piece of cloth torn from her petticoat, he tossed this causally aside. The darkness was also his friend, he thought to himself. No one would scrutinise him too closely. He returned down the alley from whence he had come.

Aggie was wandering aimlessly in search of tuppence herself, so she observed with interest the man who emerged into view from an alleyway just ahead. About to try her luck, her face fell in disappointment as she recognised him, knowing there would be no point. Ignoring her greeting, he continued on his way. A little miffed at this insult, Aggie reached the mouth of the alleyway and, as she glanced down it, the sight that confronted her almost made her gag. She turned hurriedly to see where he had gone, but there was no sign. He had vanished. It didn't matter. She knew who he was. She found it hard to believe her eyes, but she had seen him close to. There could be no mistake.

Chapter I

"Holmes, what do you make of this fellow?" Watson had been gazing out of the window for the past half-hour. Bored with his reading, he had instead occupied himself with watching the passers-by on this pleasant autumn afternoon in Baker Street. "He seems to me to be a very curious fellow."

Holmes had been long-engrossed in a particularly smelly chemical experiment, which had just reached a critical moment. Ignoring the doctor and not taking his eyes from the glass tube in his hand, he poured the contents very carefully into the beaker held suspended in a wire frame above the Bunsen burner.

"Holmes?" queried the doctor once more, turning to look at his unresponsive companion.

"Not now, Watson," said Holmes in annoyance. There was a loud rap on the door. Holmes almost dropped the glass. He had been just about to pour another element into the beaker and if he didn't concentrate, he could very easily blow up half the house.

With considerable irritation, he carefully placed the glass tube in its holder. Sighing, he looked up as Watson answered the door.

Mrs. Hudson held out the missive. "Just now delivered, Doctor, for Mr. Holmes, by a most peculiar gentlemen," she remarked crinkling up her nose and frowning as she spoke as a rather repugnant odour wafted in the air. She turned to hand the envelope to Holmes who was staring at her with ill-concealed impatience. As quickly as her brow had furrowed it now cleared and she asked brightly, "Would you or the Doctor care for some coffee, Mr. Holmes?" Before Watson could open his mouth to say he thought that would be an excellent idea, Holmes uttered, "Mrs. Hudson, I am at a most delicate moment in my experiment and would be grateful if everyone would please be quiet." The last was spoken with rising exasperation. There had been so many little annoyances that day, mostly caused by Watson trying not to disturb him and failing miserably, but some by the landlady herself banging about downstairs in the kitchen, no doubt preparing their next meal of which he had no desire to partake. She hadn't endeared herself to Holmes this day. Although his temper was by now quite short, the doctor and Mrs. Hudson were oblivious as to any reason for his foul mood.

"Humph," Mrs. Hudson raised her eyebrows. Then frowning once more, she handed the note to Watson instead and then retreated back to the sanity of her kitchen, closing the door quietly behind her as she left.

"Really, Holmes, I think you were a little too rude. Mrs. Hudson does put up with some rather appalling habits from the pair of us," Watson was loath to point out that it was in reality his friend who possessed the appalling habits, not he. He thought it prudent to share the blame. "Not to mention an almost continuous range of revolting smells," he continued, now it was his turn to wrinkle his nose at this latest assault to his senses. "I doubt we would find someone else so understanding if she were to throw us out."

"I deduce you have been reading those appalling American romances again," sighed Holmes, resigning himself to the fact that he wasn't to be permitted to conclude his experiment this day.

Turning off the gas to the Bunsen burner, he stood and strolled over to where his friend stood, outstretching his hand. "Let me see what's so important that I'm not allowed to complete my research." With one swift motion he snatched the envelope from Watson's hand and moved to the mantel. He examined it minutely before slicing it open along the top with his jack knife. He then subjected the contents to the same close, if brief, scrutiny. A puzzled frown creasing his forehead.

"What is it?" Watson could clearly see his friend was disturbed by what he saw.

"It is a very short message."

"But what does it say?"

Holmes lowered the sheet of paper, letting his hand fall to his side. "It says," he stated dispassionately, "in letters snipped from *The Times* by the use of nail scissors, and affixed with deliberate precision to unremarkable stationery using a common gum, '*your time has come*'. That is all. There are no smudges or tell-tale bits of fluff or any other erroneous deposits. Most intriguing. I would hazard that whomever sent this wore cotton cloves when compiling it." Holmes sat down in his armchair by the fire. Still frowning, he dug deep into his dressing gown pocket and

113

produced his cherry-wood pipe. Smiling as if greeting a long lost friend, he began to fill it methodically with shag from the Persian slipper.

"But Holmes," continued Watson most agitated, "this is a threat."

"It is undoubtedly a threat, my dear fellow, but of its exact nature I know not. Nor have I any clue from whom it originates. The envelope and letter itself give me nothing. Whomever is behind this knows my method. He or she has been careful to leave no clues, though it is clear that this person has at least had a basic education." Holmes's perplexed expression deepened. "No doubt we shall not be kept in suspense for too long a time."

"Does the postmark tell you nothing?" asked Watson.

Holmes smiled. "No postmark. It was after all hand delivered."

"I saw the fellow through this very window. Don't you recall I mentioned a very odd looking person to you just before Mrs. Hudson brought up the note?"

Showing signs of amusement, Holmes asked, "Describe him to me."

Watson's face creased in concentration. "Well . . . I confess it's difficult to remember him now. I just recall how odd he seemed – almost unreal. His face was strangely white and smooth. You might say ghostly."

"You fascinate me, Watson. However, as you can give me nothing more than a smooth face and a ghostly aura, that narrows it down." This sarcasm wasn't lost on the Good Doctor.

"He was dark, I can tell you that."

"Anything else?"

"He was wearing a black frock coat and trousers." Watson's face fell as he realised he couldn't remember any great detail.

"Nothing more?"

"Oh . . . he was tall – as tall as you yourself."

"Indeed."

"Perhaps you could ask Mrs. Hudson. She saw him and at close quarters."

"Perhaps I shall," commented Holmes with no real conviction. "I think, however, that our man will have gone to great lengths to be unrecognisable, or he's simply a messenger with no knowledge of the contents of the letter."

Holmes looked up and smiled at Watson's troubled expression. "Don't take on so. This is hardly the first time a protagonist has troubled to inform me of their intention to do mischief."

"No, but you usually know from whence that trouble comes. How can you protect yourself when you have no idea in what way danger will present itself?"

"Ah, Watson, danger is part of my trade." He smiled reassuringly at his companion.

114

There was only one case in which he was engaged at present, and he had barely begun his enquiries. Today's experiments were related to an older problem that had already been concluded satisfactorily, but in which the chemical reaction had continued to elude him. He had wished to resolve this before he threw himself fully into any new enquiry. He had hoped that the salient point would soon fall into place. Annoyingly, this had so far failed to occur.

Still, this new threat might hold some promise of a more stimulating adventure, though he must not neglect his new client any further. With this in mind, Holmes turned to address Watson, bringing him into his confidence. However before he could make an utterance, the downstairs bell rang loudly once more.

Holmes and Watson's eyes met – Holmes's in curiosity and Watson's showing a little anxiety. As the front door was being opened by Mrs. Hudson, a four-wheeler could be heard pulling up outside. Holmes stirred himself and went to peer out of the window. "It's a police van," he said thoughtfully. "Interesting,"

Further comment was interrupted by footsteps on the stairs, followed by a strong and forceful knock on their chamber door. Watson obliged and in strode Inspector Lestrade. He wasn't smiling.

"Doctor Watson," he nodded a greeting. "Mr. Holmes." The inspector turned his black and beady eyes towards the detective.

"What's this, Lestrade?" asked Holmes as his sharp eyes moved from Lestrade to the three very large constables just stepping through the door at the Scotland Yarder's back. All wore ominous expressions.

"It is my solemn duty – " breathed Lestrade in a half-strangled voice. Then, having gathered himself, he continued firmly. "It is my solemn duty to ask you, Mr. Holmes, to make an account of your movements of around two o'clock this very morning." Lestrade had trouble holding Holmes's eyes with his own. They kept darting down, seeking refuge in his notebook.

"Are you serious?" Holmes almost laughed. Almost . . . He could see by Lestrade's face that this was no joke.

"I'm deadly serious, Mr. Holmes." Lestrade now looked the detective full in the eyes. He had his duty to perform and no matter how ludicrous the matter might seem, he must do his duty.

"Well, I'm rather afraid that I cannot." Holmes looked a little disturbed.

"Why not?" asked the inspector.

Holmes and Watson exchanged a brief glance.

"Watson here will have to confirm that I left the house at about seven o'clock last evening and didn't return until five this morning." Holmes again glanced at his friend. "Although Watson is probably unaware of the time I returned."

Watson looked uncomfortable. He wanted desperately to put Lestrade's mind at ease. The inspector was obviously here in an official capacity and not to consult Holmes, as was usual. Rather, it was clear he meant to accuse him of something, farcical as that might be. Watson had no idea where or what Holmes had been up to, but that was nothing unusual. "That is true, Inspector," said Watson, glancing worriedly between the two men.

"That is indeed a great pity, Mr. Holmes," sighed Lestrade. "I was hoping we could have cleared this whole mess up straight away, but now . . . ." He glanced furtively between Holmes, Watson, and his three constables. "I even brought the witness here in the hope that we could settle the matter without recourse to the station."

"Inspector Lestrade, why don't you sit down and tell me what has happened to arouse such agitation." Holmes, exuding charm from every pore, was now becoming genuinely alarmed at the turn events were taking, but wouldn't dare to show it. Lestrade evidently had something of a very serious nature on his mind.

"I won't sit, thank you, but I would like to bring in the woman concerned. If you have no objections?"

"Woman concerned with what, Lestrade?" asked Holmes in exasperation. "You still haven't told me what this is about."

"The woman was witness to a particularly violent murder." Lestrade's words hung heavy.

"And you suspect me." Holmes voice was a mixture of incredulity and resignation.

"Really, Inspector, you must be joking." Watson was far beyond incredulous – he was downright angry.

"I assure you gentlemen," said Lestrade raising his hand along with his voice, "I'm not jumping to any conclusions, but the woman has identified you, Mr. Holmes."

"Come, Lestrade," said Holmes, "surely you can't believe this witness. Someone must have paid her a great deal to become involved in such a dangerous game."

"She swears it was you and was prepared to come here and say so. What's more, she insisted on doing just that. I don't think she believed we would take her seriously. She is quite adamant, and says she has no reason to lie about it. She says she knows you and couldn't have believed it of you if she hadn't of seen it with her own eyes."

"By all means, Lestrade, bring her up." Holmes stole a glance at a very worried Watson and smiled reassuringly.

116

Watson's eyes opened in astonishment as the woman in question was brought into the room. She was quite clearly a woman of the street. How could the police possibly take her word over that of Sherlock Holmes?

As she entered the room, her eyes brushed lightly over the doctor and settled quickly onto Holmes's agile face.

"That's 'im all right." She stared accusingly and angrily at Holmes in quite obvious recognition.

To his amazement, Holmes knew her too. He had spoken with her often in the course of his enquiries over many years. Although he didn't trust any woman completely, he felt sure that she wouldn't betray him lightly.

"Hello, Aggie," said Holmes in a kind voice. "Haven't seen you for a few months. How've you been keeping?"

"Haven't seen me eh? Well, I saw you right enough last night."

"Not me, Aggie."

"D'you think I don't know you when I sees you?" She was angry and confused. She had always liked him. He had always played fair with her and a select few of the girls – the ones who could be trusted to keep their mouths shut. He didn't use them as some might, and always paid over the odds for any information they might give him. But she knew what she had seen, and nothing could change that.

"I assure you, Aggie," Holmes voice grew in intensity, "that whomever you saw may well have resembled me, but was most definitely not."

"He didn't resemble you – he *was* you!" Aggie was shaking with genuine rage, and even Holmes couldn't doubt her sincerity.

"I'm sorry, Aggie, I really am, but it wasn't me you saw." Holmes spoke quietly but firmly.

Before the interview could degenerate any further, Lestrade interrupted, "All right, Aggie, you've made your point." Turning to one of the constables, he added, "Take her down to the carriage, will you, McPherson?"

The constable nodded and escorted a very angry Aggie, still issuing accusations as she was led out of the room.

"What do you say to that, Mr. Holmes? She seems genuine enough to me."

"I'm very much afraid you are right." Holmes glanced at Watson, whose frown threatened to disfigure him permanently.

"Well, we now know what form the danger takes."

"Holmes," blurted Watson, "of course! Lestrade – here, you must look at this." Watson dashed to where Holmes had allowed the letter to fall to the floor. "This just arrived." Upon picking it up he thrust it at Lestrade, who took it, curious to see.

"What have we here?" He read it and then frowned at the pair from Baker Street. "Means nothing. I dare say you get all kinds of threats in the space of a month. There's nothing to say it has anything to do with this business."

"Oh, come now, Lestrade," protested Watson. "This is surely too much of a coincidence, even for you." Watson was allowing his anger to speak.

Under these difficult circumstances, Lestrade tried not to let the insult colour his treatment of the situation, but it did nothing to improve his humour. Holmes remained strangely silent throughout this exchange.

"Coincidence or no," continued Lestrade, "I have no choice in the matter." Turning back to Holmes with determination, Lestrade continued. "I must warn you, Mr. Holmes, that anything you say may be taken down . . . ." The inspector coughed, embarrassed. "Well, I'm sure you know how it goes, Mr. Holmes." The Scotland Yard detective straightened himself up to his full height, which was significantly less than Holmes, and continued in his most official voice. "You will accompany me to the station, on suspicion of the murder of one Mary Jacobs of Spitalfields."

"Jenkins – " Lestrade motioned to one of the constables, who produced a pair of black iron handcuffs.

"Surely that isn't necessary," pleaded the doctor. He couldn't believe what was happening.

"I'm very much afraid that in this case, it most definitely is. The Commissioner was most insistent. He also insisted that I bring with me three of the largest constables we have at the station. It is felt that extra precautions should be taken when dealing with Mr. Sherlock Holmes." Lestrade eyed Holmes ruefully before signalling Jenkins to fasten the handcuffs. "As an added precaution, you'd best handcuff him to yourself as well." Lestrade eyed the large constable significantly. He reasoned even Holmes might find it a bit difficult to drag Jenkins about the place.

Jenkins fastened one side of the handcuffs to his own left wrist, and as he leaned forward to close the darbies over Holmes's right wrist, Holmes suddenly pushed him violently away and leapt over the settee and into his bedroom, slamming the door and tearing out onto the landing through the second door. He just managed to scuttle out of the reach of Dobson, the other constable present who had had the wit to realise Holmes had only one means of escape. The man caught Holmes's sleeve, but couldn't get a firm grip as Holmes slid down the bannister to the landing, and then down the next set of steps. He positively flew out of the front doors onto the street, pushing over the startled form of Constable

McPherson, who was just re-entering the house, leaving him sprawled on the pavement in his wake. In a flash Holmes had raced up the road, dodging between cabs and barrows, with now three constables on his heels. The three soon returned, looking rather forlorn, Dobson still carrying Holmes dressing gown. "We lost him in the crowd," wheezed Dobson breathlessly. His face flushed from more than mere physical excursion.

Watson stood on the steps of 221b in utter bewilderment and grief. Mrs. Hudson stood close behind, sharing his amazed confusion.

Chapter II

Holmes was breathless as he threw himself down the alleyway. People had stood and watched, startled, as he had forced his way through the crowd in his flight from the police. Most, however, showed merely a mild curiosity as he had bent back to the task at hand. None had tried to hinder him. Running through the streets in his shirtsleeves would present a problem, however. It would be difficult to remain inconspicuous when one indeed stood out like a sore thumb. He had dodged and weaved and generally managed to throw off the constables, but he couldn't now afford to draw attention to himself. Slowing his pace he glanced behind him. No one in sight. He paused to catch his breath. Having run for some little time, he was now quite close to one of his many hiding places.

Cautiously Holmes approached a run-down two-story building in one of the lesser streets off the Edgware Road. Glancing about, making certain no one was observing him, he slipped silently through the door and up the stairs to the first floor. With a quick and insightful gaze he took in the room in an instant. Nothing had been touched since he had last been there. Going to a small cupboard, he retrieved a rather disreputable brown coat and shouldered hurriedly into it, removing his collar and tie, also changing into scruffy trousers and boots. In the past it had proved very useful to maintain a room so close to home, and it was certainly true today. However, it wouldn't do to stay too long in the event he had been observed. He would move on to one of his other strongholds in this minimal, if shabby, disguise. He held a very squalid abode in one of the vilest alleyways in the whole of London, right near the centre of the action, as it were. Roughing up his hair and placing a dilapidated cloth cap on his head, he slipped silently down the stairs and out.

Chapter III

"Are you telling me, Lestrade – " The Commissioner of Police regarded the inspector with undisguised disgust, his voice a smouldering volcano. " – that you had this man Holmes in his own rooms and you let him escape?" This last was spoken as if the volcano were erupting.

Lestrade stood dejected, staring at the floor. What could he say? Holmes had done it again – made him look a complete fool, though this was more serious than usual and he was intensely aware of it.

"This isn't the first time you have disappointed me, Inspector." The Commissioner's voice was cold. "I am taking you off the case. Be grateful I'm not relieving you of duty as well. Now get out of my sight." He lowered his eyes to his desk and gave no further indication to Lestrade that he even existed.

By the time Lestrade had reached his office, he was shaking with indignation. Curse that reprobate Holmes – he was in deep trouble this time. Both of them were. It was strange, he thought, how his fortunes seemed to be irrevocably tied to Sherlock Holmes. Lestrade was holding on to his job by a mere thread and Holmes was on the run for murder.

Trying to calm down and consider the position further, he couldn't bring himself to believe that Sherlock Holmes would commit murder. Irritating and infuriating as he was, he was at heart, Lestrade believed, a good man. Still, the evidence was there and he had made a run for it at the first opportunity. Surely he wouldn't have done that if he were innocent.

Not much point in worrying about it now, as he was off the case. He had several thefts to follow up and numerous assaults required his attention. Frustrated as he was, he would have to get on with these and leave the problem of Holmes to some other poor fool.

Secretly, he was almost glad to have been removed from the case. It meant that someone else could bear the brunt of Holmes's games and the inevitable humiliation that went with them.

Chapter IV

Watson sat fretting by the fire. It had been three days since Holmes had so dramatically fled. Watson couldn't understand why Holmes had run. Certainly he was innocent. Therefore, would it not have been better to go to the police station and sort it out? Holmes, however, wasn't one to do things in the conventional manner. Watson had to concede that if anyone could untangle this mess quickly it was Holmes himself – not something he could accomplish languishing in some prison cell. Still, Watson was supremely worried for his friend.

120

Holmes stalked the streets of Spitalfields with deliberation, his three-day beard growth making his appearance even more disreputable than his ragged clothes. Accordingly, he could move about with relative safety amongst the teeming thousands of this most squalid part of London. He hadn't bathed any part of himself for the last three days. Consequently his face itched annoyingly and there was definitely the beginnings of a rather offensive smell about his person. However, this was infinitely preferable to being hanged.

He spent his time speaking to a great many prostitutes and numerous others who weren't familiar with his face, but none had had anything useful to say. He decided against an elaborate disguise for now, as he was sufficiently protected by grime and hair. This would prove easier to maintain over a prolonged period, and he had no doubt that this would take some time.

It was close to ten o'clock on a very chilly evening when he approached a young girl leaning against the wall of a cobbler's shop. In a husky voice he asked, "All right then, lass?" She turned her cheeky pale green eyes towards him. Smiling, she said, "I'm all right, my lad. I could make you all right an' all." She was no more than twenty he judged, as she winked playfully at him, and surprisingly healthy. He scrutinised her with a casual glance, deducing she hadn't been long on the game. Recently from Ireland, most probably a farmer's daughter, fallen on hard times. Bringing his attention back to more pressing matters, he came up close to her.

Under these circumstances, he was forced to spend a prolonged time with the street girls, studiously avoiding those who already knew him, and if he wished to remain inconspicuous, he couldn't continuously mingle without at least the appearance of making use of their services, so he went with her to her hovel. She was one of the fortunate few who had lodgings. Most had to make do with an alleyway or park.

"How much?" asked Holmes as they entered her tiny though presentable room. She might now be a prostitute, but she clearly had her own set of standards to keep.

"Depends what you want," she said, laughing.

"Well," continued Holmes, "I'm in no particular hurry." His smile was as charming as he could manage in these trying conditions.

She cast a penetrating eye over him. He seemed agreeable enough in a roguish sort of way and she had already decided she liked him. He wasn't brutish in his manner as were many of her clientele, and she was still not fully accustomed to some of the worst that men demanded of her. She tried to face her misfortune with a smile on her face as often as not.

121

"For you, my sweet, a shilling for the night." She moved over to the bed and sat down, looking expectantly at him.

Holmes looked at the floor for a moment and then casually strolled over to the only chair in the room, an old straight-backed wooden carver. Seating himself, he cocked his head to one side and smiling ruefully said, "You know, now that that's settled, there's no hurry. I don't know about you, but I could do with some grub, and a drink wouldn't go astray."

This could be a half-decent night, she thought to herself, if he's willing to pay for food and drink as well. She'd had hardly more than a scrap of bread for two days. It wasn't often that a mark wanted more than a very brief satisfaction and to be on his way, but this one seemed a little lonely – wanting company more than anything else, most like. "How 'bout I pop out and get us a couple of bottles of stout and some fish and chips," said the girl, holding out her hand expectantly.

Holmes laughed lightly and delved into his pocket, producing a few coins. Stopping shy of placing them in her hand he looked at her slyly. "Now you wouldn't be thinking of leaving me here while you go off and enjoy yourself would you?"

She laughed herself and patted him playfully on the cheek saying, "Oh now, go on with you. I wouldn't do that to you. I like you." Smiling sweetly, she took his money. "Besides, you know where I live. I won't be long," she threw over her shoulder as she closed the door. She had no problem with leaving him alone in her room. She had nothing worth stealing.

Holmes stood from his chair and strolled about the tiny room, inspecting her possessions, such as they were. There was a small wardrobe with one well-worn dress and a faded threadbare shawl, as well as a small number of equally threadbare undergarments. In the drawer of a dilapidated table beside the single bed was a comb with two teeth missing, a few hairpins, half a pencil, a bottle opener, and a battered picture of an older man. The man in this picture was standing beside a plough and, although handsome, his features were rather care-worn. Her father, Holmes had gathered by the remarkable resemblance between them. There were no other personal possessions at all in the room. Not a book or letter, nothing for him to gain any insight into her circumstances or character. These few pitiful things constituted her worldly goods.

Sighing, he sat back down to await her return. Perhaps he would do better to look for someone else. It was clear that she hadn't been long in London. This he had deduced from her relatively good state of health and her cheery disposition. Her spirit hadn't yet been crushed by the ceaseless grinding poverty, nor was her brain sodden by too much gin, but he knew that in time this would be her fate and the thought saddened him. He chastised himself. This was no time for sentimentality. It was hardly an unusual story for women with no money or support. He must concentrate on the matter in hand. She probably had no useful information to give him. Still, he was here now and she might know something. Besides, he was weary of talking to so many unfortunates with little or no gain. This one at least seemed to have a sense of humour.

Ten minutes after he had retaken his seat she returned, wearing a bright and gleeful expression. Closing the door on the chill of the night, she set down two stoneware bottles of stout on the side table and produced a package of fish and chips wrapped in newspaper. Sitting on the bed she looked at him, inviting him to sit next to her and share the meal. "Thank Heaven, I just caught old Jacoby before he shut up shop." Smiling, she handed Holmes one of the bottles as he approached the bed. Holmes took it gratefully. He hadn't realised just how thirsty he really was.

She winked at him. "There you go. I hope you like Guinness, for I'll drink nothing else."

Holmes took a long draft of his and, sighing, said, "Hits the spot just fine." Sitting next to her on the bed, he turned his attention to the food. This looked exceptionally greasy, but he was hungry. He'd eaten next to nothing since fleeing 221b.

The time passed surprisingly pleasantly. Kathleen, as he was soon aquatinted was her name, proved to have a dry sense of humour accompanied by a quick wit – something Holmes wasn't accustomed to appreciating in a woman. In spite of his predicament, he found he quite liked the girl and began to feel sorry for her circumstances once more. She seemed more than happy to take his money for nothing more than talking.

Truth be known, she was more than glad of it. It had been a long day, and the chance to relax and enjoy the evening with a full stomach and good company was a luxury she had almost forgotten.

"Do you do this often?" she asked, teasing him.

"Do what?"

"Pay – simply to sit and talk."

Holmes smiled. "As it happens, yes I do." He leaned back against the wall at the opposite end of the bed. "Though not usually for the entire night. However, on this occasion, I have nowhere else to be."

She smiled at him and they talked on casual matters for some time. It wasn't until the wee hours of the morning that Holmes, after placing Kathleen at her ease, brought the conversation around to his desired outcome.

"So tell me," said Holmes casually, "how came you to London?" Kathleen was lying back on the bed, her arms folded behind her head, a gentle smile playing on her lips. The smile faded at Holmes question.

"I thought I might have more luck here than at home." She sat up on the bed and looked off into the distance, her eyes suddenly sad. "'Twas not to be," she sighed.

"You came alone from Edenderry, with no one here to help you?" There was genuine concern in his voice.

"No. My Da had died, and there was no one else. I knew it would be hard in Dublin and worse in Belfast, so I thought I might be able to make my way in London, but with no references, no one would take me on – not even washing dishes, let alone a governess or companion. So with no money left to get home and no real home to go to, I ended up here." She looked suddenly at Holmes a little suspiciously. "How'd you know I come from Edenderry?"

Holmes smiled. How often had he been asked such a question. Skirting round the issue, he said, "Ah, your accent I'm afraid." She wasn't convinced. Edenderry wasn't exactly the hub of Ireland. It wasn't far from Dublin, but not so close either.

"I'd a thought one Irishman would sound much like another to an Englishman." She was looking hard at him now. "Ireland isn't so small. I could'a come from anywhere."

"Well, I've been there, you see," Holmes lied, trying to reassure her. "That's how I could tell."

"Oh aye, to Edenderry?" she said, still not convinced.

"How long have you been here?" persisted Holmes, trying to move on without losing his foothold on the conversation. It would be wearying to have to start again.

"'Bout three months." She lay back down on the bed. It really didn't matter to her how he knew where she came from.

"Had much trouble?"

She laughed. "Nothing but."

A sardonic smile touched the corners of Holmes's mouth. "Not the safest of professions, I expect. Someone as young and appealing as yourself might attract a bit more trouble than most." He must take care, for she was no fool, and, although she might be tired, she could easily become suspicious of his motives.

"Aye, well, there is always a risk. Poor ol' Mary copped it just the other night, not three streets from here." Kathleen shrugged. "Still, she isn't the first and she'll not be the last, but he was a brute, I'll tell you that. Practically cut her poor head off, so they say."

Holmes tried not to show his interest. "You knew this Mary then?" he asked mildly.

"We used to talk a bit now and then. She was one of the few who would talk to me. I'm not with anyone, you see. A couple of the fellers

124

that run the other girls have . . . Well, let's just say I'm more careful now. Not keen on competition round here, you know, 'specially from a Mick." At that she laughed. Holmes smiled at her. Somehow she managed to retain a cheerful outlook in spite of all that life had dealt her. Holmes doubted *he* would be as cheerful in her place. Still, he had enough trouble of his own to worry about.

Kathleen became serious, "They say it was that detective feller, Sherlock Holmes, that did it."

Holmes raised an eyebrow.

"Word on the street is that old Aggie saw him, and the other girls say she would know." Kathleen looked intently at Holmes. "Some of the girls say they know him too. They have plans for him. I think I'd like to help them," she added emphatically.

Holmes coughed, half-choking on his beer, and nearly dropping the bottle. "Do you really think that would be wise?" he managed to say, while wiping the spilled drink from his trousers. "After all, if the man is as vicious as you say, he would surely be dangerous to approach. Besides, he may well be innocent."

"Innocent, huh? Whose side are you on anyway? Well, you are a man, after all," she said, as if that was something to be ashamed of.

"I assure you," said Holmes gravely, "I don't condone murder, particularly of a woman. Any woman."

"Anyway," continued Kathleen with passion, "Aggie says it was him and I'll take her word. As for being dangerous – if enough of us girls get hold of him, we'll finish him." Suddenly, a forced smile appeared. "So now, let's talk no more about it."

Chapter V

Aggie Pinkerton was still a very agitated woman. She had witnessed Sherlock Holmes do a runner from right under the police's nose and she wouldn't be surprised if they had let him get away. They all stick together in the end, and who was she? A nobody.

An inspector of police had been 'round to speak to her yesterday. A new one. Seemed the other one had been given the chop. Placed on other duties, this one said. He wanted her to go over the whole thing once more and took down copious notes, but she didn't hold much hope of him doing anything about it either. Just giving a good show, that's all. Aggie had been around for a good many years and she knew the score right enough.

She was standing on Greenfield Road, not far from Commercial Road, waiting with several other girls. It had been a slow night, only a half-dozen gents in the offing.

125

About four in the morning a carriage pulled up – a big four-wheeler with the blinds drawn. It pulled up close by.

Good, she thought, someone with money. The door opened, but the occupant remained in shadow, without hesitation she stepped up into the carriage. Before she could scream the door had slammed shut, the man's hand pressed hard on her mouth. It was him – *My God!* She tried to scream, but no sound came out as the four-wheeler pulled away. No one on the street was any the wiser that anything was amiss.

Inspector Cruft was new to the area. He'd been brought in by Commissioner Parkhurst himself. It seemed the commissioner wanted a fresh face and a different approach to this case. Cruft knew of Sherlock Holmes by reputation – most policemen did – but he had never met the man, nor did he credit all that he had heard about him. No one could be that good. He'd only been here two days, and already he had found that people either admired or loathed Holmes, but no one seemed to like him very much, with the exception of that fellow Watson and his landlady. And apparently there was a brother about somewhere.

Cruft knew he would get nothing useful out of Watson. All the man had done was protest in the strongest possible terms that Holmes was innocent, and that this was all some ghastly mistake. Not very enlightening.

Cruft had to consider the possibility that Doctor Watson was an accessory, either before or after the fact, but to be honest it didn't seem likely. The landlady – Cruft referred to his notes – a Mrs. Hudson, had insisted that Doctor Watson hadn't left the house all evening. When asked how she could be certain of that, she'd replied, "Why, I know when either of my gentlemen leaves or arrives home," while looking at Cruft as if he were some sort of imbecile for thinking otherwise. She continued when it became clear that Cruft wanted more of an answer. "I'm a light sleeper and my room is close to the front of the house, so I can hear when any visitor arrives and let them in for Mister Holmes. If it's very late and I've already gone to bed, then either Doctor Watson or Mister Holmes himself lets them in – but I always hear," she said adamantly. "And I'm telling you the doctor never set foot outside this house." She stared defiantly at this upstart of an inspector who dared to accuse the only two men in London – indeed in all the world, she believed – who could *never* have committed any such crime. The very idea was preposterous.

Having made no progress at 221b Baker Street, Cruft had decided an interview with the only witness was in order. He'd had no difficulty in finding Aggie, as most cities follow the same lines when it came to brothels and streetwalkers. He found her to be just as adamant that it was

126

without doubt the famous detective that she had seen leaving only moments before she found Mary. "Her throat was horrible cut and the blood still flowin'. She been done in that very minute. It 'ad to be 'im." Her eyes were blazing and Cruft believed her. She had no reason to lie as far as he could tell and if true, then it would be a feather in his cap if he caught this rogue, make no mistake, but he mustn't get ahead of himself.

It would be no easy thing to trace Holmes, who apparently knew every dodge in the book and then some, and Cruft was new to London. The commissioner had assured him that anything he wanted was his. Any personnel or equipment, he had only to ask. "We can't have this fellow running rings around the Force, you know," the Commissioner had said on greeting Cruft. "It looks very bad. I trust that you will not disappoint me, Cruft." This wasn't a question and Cruft knew he had better get it right or he'd be back in the sticks again before one could say "On the beat". It was only because of his recent success in solving the Bronson murders that he was here at all, and he was well aware how short memories could be. It was the latest failure that people always remembered, not the second latest success.

PC Holloway, a slightly overweight man and fond of a drink or two, though not surly with it, was making his rounds down Philpot Street. It was four-thirty a.m., and he was close to going off shift. "An' not a moment too soon," he thought warmly. He'd endured a bad head cold for the last week, and night duty was doing nothing to alleviate the problem. Still, there was one place he'd best make a quick check before heading back to the station. Upon reaching the corner of Walden Street he paused, sneezing loudly and profusely. God, a hot-toddy and a good morning's sleep was what he longed for right now. Pulling a large handkerchief from his pocket, he proceeded to blow his rather bulbous nose with gusto and then continued to stroll on. Always worth a look down here for any nefarious activity. He noticed something huddled against the wall. Some dosser no doubt. Still, he'd best go and see, even if his heart really wasn't in it. As he approached the bundle in the street, PC Holloway stiffened suddenly. Even on this moonless night he could see, in the light of his bulls-eye, the pool of something dark and liquid making an irregular line towards the gutter.

Cautiously, Holloway moved up close and examined the bundle, turning the body over onto its back. "My Gord, it's ol' Aggie!" Holloway had on many occasions taken Aggie in charge for various misdemeanours. He knew her well, as he did most of the girls who walked the streets of his beat. But who would want to do such a thing to old Aggie? Been around donkey's, she had. Then Holloway remembered the business with

127

Sherlock Holmes and how it was Aggie had put the finger on him. "Bloody *Hell*!" he thought. "This'll put the cat amongst the proverbials well and truly." PC Holloway straightened up and, pulling his whistle from his pocket, blew for all he was worth.

Holmes returned to his bolt hole in an extreme state of exhaustion. It had been more than three days since he'd had any real sleep, and if he didn't put his head down soon he would be good for nothing. Kathleen had been a surprisingly charming companion for the evening and not entirely without use. However, he would have to search further and speak to a good many more of her sisters of the street if he was to come up with anything he could use in pursuance of this case. Someone had gone to a great deal of trouble to implicate him in murder, and although there were more than enough people who would dearly love to take revenge upon him, he could think of none who would do it in this way. A simple knife in the ribs would amply suit the needs of most. No, this had to be more than revenge, and with the passing of the late and unlamented Professor James Moriarty, he would have to look elsewhere for a suspect.

Chapter VI

Cruft arrived at the mortuary within ten minutes of receiving the message that his chief witness had been murdered. He looked down upon her contorted face, twisted in the agony of her death. Her throat was cut from ear to ear, and her head was almost severed from her body. "Who found her?" demanded Cruft of the constable standing by the door.

"PC Holloway, sir, on his regular rounds . . . Sir?"

"Yes, what is it," said Cruft irritably.

"Well, sir, I was just wondering – it couldn't be old Jack back in business could it?"

"What?" exclaimed the inspector, furious. "Don't you go starting stupid rumours, Constable. The last thing we need is a major panic. This is *not* the work of Jack the Ripper. These women had their throats horribly cut yes, but that's all. Nothing to suggest Jack is back. And if you say that name again, I'll have your hide! Is that clear?"

"Yes, sir!" The constable snapped to attention.

"Right. I want every whore in the whole of the East End questioned. Someone must have seen something. I also want to speak personally to Holloway. See to it." Cruft waved his hand for the constable to leave. This was very bad. He had barely begun his investigation and already he'd lost his chief witness. "Bloody Hell!" Cruft swore softly as he turned his back on the body and walked slowly around the room deep in thought.

128

Holmes awoke after only three hours feeling more wretched than when he'd fallen asleep. Dragging himself slowly from his cot, he dropped into a chair by the now-cold fire. Staring at the ashes, he pondered what to do next. He must think. Exhibiting just enough energy, Holmes retrieved his pipe and tobacco and leaned back in deep contemplation. Upon further reflection, his expedition of last night had been less-than-exceptional and he needed discover the identity of the killer soon. He could escape capture for some time, he felt sure, but in the end he didn't wish to spend the remainder of his life evading the police – not what he had envisioned for the rest of his career.

It was perplexing. His antagonist was an elusive fellow, and possibly not alone in his actions. Holmes considered further. He was almost certain this was a conspiracy, and not the work of a single agent. Yet who was behind it? Who could he have annoyed enough of late to warrant such a drastic step? Over the last several days he had spoken to many tens of people, but none had disclosed anything useful – only their opinions of what they would like to do to Sherlock Holmes if they were ever to see him. He had to smile at that. Kathleen had been the last of a long line, and at least she had been a young woman of some intelligence. But it was all to no avail. He was no closer to discovering the murderer or the reason for his own implication in the matter.

Holmes turned his thoughts to another possibility. His latest case might possibly be the link he sought, though for the life of him he couldn't see how. But then he had only just been engaged on the matter. It might well prove to be of a significant nature, but as yet he hadn't proceeded very far, and further pursuance of the affair now seemed less than likely. His client by now must be aware of his new circumstance and in no way optimistic of a satisfying result. This person had come to him only the day before Mary Jacobs' murder and, although he had set one or two things in motion, his enquires had now been unceremoniously cut short. Perhaps this was no mere coincidence. Still, at this time he could make no serious assumptions or conjectures. Though he could see no real connection, he felt that at least it was a place to start. After all, as far as prostitutes were concerned, he was getting nowhere fast.

Having resolved on a course of action, Holmes stirred himself and, though exhausted, would leave his refuge to seek out one Major-General Rutledge. Holmes's client, Colonel Guthrie, had come to him in the strictest confidence. Holmes had had every intention of including Watson in the investigation. However, that eventuality had been rather abruptly forestalled.

129

Colonel Guthrie was extremely worried about suspicions he held regarding the Major-General, and though he wouldn't dream of questioning a superior officer in the normal state of affairs, certain things had come to his attention which had disturbed him greatly and which he couldn't ignore. Thus he had engaged Holmes discreetly to investigate and to hopefully prove his fears "groundless", as he had put it.

"It is no easy thing to come here and speak to an outsider about the most intimate details of the regiment," Guthrie had stated, "but as a loyal servant of Her Majesty, I couldn't ignore the matter."

Holmes had found Guthrie to be a slightly pompous man, but an honest and loyal soldier. His fears related to the illegal supply of weapons to the enemies of the Empire through the legitimate route of his regiment. Many more weapons had been processed through the regiment than could be reasonably accounted for, and they were authorised by the Major-General himself.

Guthrie wouldn't have been aware of this but for the fact that the Quartermaster had suddenly been taken ill and Colonel Guthrie had supervised the latest shipments to India and South Africa himself. He couldn't account for the truly astronomical amount of rifles and ammunition being sent over along with a disproportionate amount of explosives, and with no real paper work to accompany them. Guthrie had pointed out to Holmes that although things were prone to unrest in both regions, the present situations couldn't justify such large shipments of weapons, and he couldn't go to the Major-General himself for obvious reasons. Therefore, he felt it his duty to make some discreet enquires of his own.

Holmes had agreed to investigate, but had only begun the very night before his attempted arrest. This was either an amazing coincidence, or Rutledge was extremely well informed. Perhaps Colonel Guthrie hadn't been as discreet as he believed. "This is inconceivable!" exclaimed Holmes to an empty room. "How could the Major-General have arranged things so quickly? The short answer is, he couldn't. Therefore he has nothing to do with my present predicament, or – " He paused thoughtfully. " – he has some very powerful friends." Then he laughed. "Get a grip on yourself," he admonished silently, knocking out his pipe and immediately refilling it.

Point One (he thought): It would be risky to get the weapons from the usual suppliers, for the large amounts might be questioned.

Point Two: The Quartermaster must be involved.

Point Three: If this was related to his own predicament, how had things been arranged so quickly? And how had they known of Holmes's involvement at all – ? Perhaps hearing of the Quartermaster's illness was enough to alert the Major-General. Suspecting Guthrie might now be aware of such a large shipment of weapons and taking no chances, perhaps they'd had him followed. Hmm, a possibility. He must check on Guthrie, for if his speculations where correct, then the Colonel could be in grave danger.

Where did this leave him? He had no idea . . . .

Sighing, Holmes dragged himself out of his chair. After dressing quickly, he slipped out of the door, down the stairs, and into the street. Keeping his hat pulled down low, he moved about in the cool of the early morning, heading for the docks. As he passed a paperboy, he saw the headline: "*Noble soldier found dead.*"

Could it be? Holmes bought a paper and headed to one of the dockland pubs so he could peruse it in comfort.

As he read he became more confident that he was on the right track, though he was saddened by what he read. Not only did it confirm that he was in serious trouble, it also meant he had failed his client miserably.

The noble soldier found dead was none other than Colonel Guthrie.

The Colonel had been found shot in the head, apparently an accident while cleaning his revolver. How terribly convenient, thought Holmes.

Holmes headed immediately for the Colonel's house. Mingling with the numerous other sightseers, he watched as Inspector Gregson bumbled about, no doubt missing all the significant clues – although Gregson wasn't as bad as some.

Holmes found his present situation frustrating in the extreme. Obviously, he couldn't allow himself to be seen, and from where he stood in the crowd, he couldn't get a close-enough look at the location of the crime. He had to satisfy himself with a close inspection of the surrounding area. This revealed some slight evidence. There had quite clearly been a four-wheeler there within the last twenty-four hours, as it hadn't rained within that time. The tracks still showed clearly in the mud a few doors down from the fatal house, though he had to concede that it might be unrelated. He must get into the house and examine it for himself.

Three a.m. the following morning found Holmes forcing the kitchen window of the late Colonel's residence. He had observed the servants retire at around ten o'clock, and had waited until all was still and quiet.

After only a little exertion with his knife, he was lifting the window cautiously and climbing in, careful to make no sound.

Lighting his bulls-eye lantern and with its shutters half-closed, he made a circuit of his surroundings, listening for any sign that his entrance had been detected before moving deeper into the house. Cautiously he opened the kitchen door and crept out into the hallway. The low light was just adequate to make his way towards the front of the house, glancing briefly into several rooms before finding the one he sought. The study was large and well-furnished, with a Turkish rug adorning the floor, while a brown leather chesterfield sofa was situated about ten feet from the fireplace with two matching armchairs on either side of it, forming a semicircle. There was a locked glass cabinet containing several revolvers, two rifles, and a shotgun. One hook was empty – the space left by the fatal weapon no doubt, removed by the police for examination.

Curtailing his frustration at not being able to examine this himself, he moved to one of the armchairs by the fireplace. A generous dark stain was clearly visible on the back of the chair and on the carpet behind. He studied these with considerable interest. The splattering of blood indicated to him that the weapon had been fired from an elevated position, not as one would expect from lower down. If the wound had been caused by accidental discharge of the weapon while cleaning it, one would expect to find a spattering of blood above the level of the shoulders – nearly all was below. This plainly suggested to Holmes that the weapon had been fired from above the victim's head – a very strange accident indeed, even if "accident" had been meant as code for suicide. In either case, *not* at all likely.

Chapter VII

Watson paced the sitting room of 221b in a great distress. He had heard nothing from Holmes since he'd fled some days before, and he was growing frantic as to what to do. He decided to take matters into his own hands. He would go down to the East End of London himself. He couldn't bear to wait any longer and feel completely useless.

Hailing a cab, he directed the man to take him to Spitalfields, and once on his way had to concede that as to what he would actually do or hope to achieve . . . well . . . he had no idea. Even with no real plan in his mind, he felt a strange sense of relief that he was at least doing something, no matter how pointless.

As night drew near, he became aware that there were a great many more women on the streets than he'd anticipated. Their purpose all too clear to him, he did his best to avoid them, but his presence was so conspicuous that they naturally believed he was there for only one reason. It grew very tiresome having to discourage so many unsolicited advances.

He would find himself wandering, retracing his footsteps from Whitechapel to Spitalfields on regular occasions – looking for Holmes or he didn't know what. On one such occasion, a young street Arab accosted him for some change and then ran off, a few penny's richer. It wasn't until he reached the comfort of his chair by the fire in Baker Street that he discovered the note in his pocket.

It was clearly in Holmes's hand and set out a very explicate set of instructions as to how to proceed to a particular place and time – one of the less salubrious areas of London. The next evening, Watson left 221b and, after letting two cabs pass, he hailed the next, swapping cabs several times and coming, by the most circular route after walking for the last ten minutes of his journey, to the corner of Philchurch and Ellen Streets in Whitechapel. It was a moonless night and the street lighting was less-than-adequate. He was confident, however, that no one had followed him. He shuffled nervously, his feet in the cold night air as he awaited the appointed time. After more than half-an-hour passed, he was beginning to wonder if Holmes would come . . . .

"Watson." Holmes stepped out of the shadows and approached his friend, casting a shrewd eye about him. "I'm very glad you came. I'm also pleased to observe you weren't followed." He smiled, extending his arm to shake Watson by the hand.

"I followed your instructions to the letter." Watson took Holmes's hand enthusiastically.

Holmes raised an eyebrow. "I'm so very glad to see you, and rest assured, no one will know we have met. You will not be compromised."

"Surely you must know I care nothing for that."

Still smiling, Holmes approached closer. "I know, but all the same, how are you, my dear fellow? I hope the police aren't making your life too unbearable. I imagine Lestrade must have been extremely vexed by my escape." He gave a little chuckle. "Still, I could hardly leave it to them to sort out, or I'd have been hanged before the day was over if some of his fellow officers had anything to do with it."

Watson's face became clouded, "Lestrade is off the case," said he, trying to contain his joy at finding his friend apparently safe and well.

"Indeed, I know," responded Holmes in a more serious tone, "I'm sorry for that, but it couldn't be helped." Holmes was becoming uneasy glancing around. "Tell me, how *are* things with you?"

"I have been harassed by that new oaf, Cruft. He insists that I must know your whereabouts and that I'm shielding you. Well, of course if I did know. I most certainly wouldn't tell *him*."

Holmes smiled at Watson indignant outrage and was grateful he had such a friend, but he couldn't involve Watson in this . . . it was far too dangerous. "Listen to me, Watson. You must not under any circumstances come looking for me again as you did last night. It isn't safe." He held up his hand to forestall Watson's protest. "Please – you can serve me best by

133

staying home and keeping Mrs. Hudson safe. I have my fears for you both if you are seen to interfere. I'm sure they'll be watching you very closely. They'll know you're about the area. This is why I asked you to take such elaborate precautions tonight."

With extreme reluctance, Watson agreed to return home and not to search for Holmes again – but only after Holmes had agreed to send word whenever he could.

Holmes watched as his friend left to head back to Baker Street, and as he turned to begin his own dreary journey to his own hovel, he spotted someone. Excitement thrilled through him. He raced after the spectre of *himself* as fast as his could. As he reached the corner around which the imposter had turned, he observed him walking swiftly a couple-of-hundred feet further on. Moving as rapidly as was possible, he closed the gap. The man stopped, turned, saw Holmes and smiled, and then he jumped up into a four-wheeler that had obviously been waiting for him. Holmes couldn't catch him now. He raced back to the street from which he'd seen the man emerge and found a crowd gathering.

Another murder, he was certain. He could scarce credit it. The man looked so completely like himself . . . he wouldn't have thought it possible, but he now knew that unless he found some way to catch this man and show the two of them standing side-by-side, no one would believe him innocent – possibly not even Watson or his own brother.

This was getting out of hand. Then a thought occurred to him: This latest atrocity might have been staged for Watson's benefit. That was a terrifying prospect – one that had only narrowly been foiled for now. It only strengthened his resolve that he mustn't involve he dear friend at any cost.

Chapter VIII

Holmes hurried directly to his room. Slumping in the chair by the fireplace, he had much to contemplate. After stoking a blazing fire, for he was truly chilled to the bone, he pulled his pipe from his coat pocket and stuffed it carelessly with tobacco. Leaning forward and lighting the pipe without conscious thought, he stared at the glowing coals in the grate, contemplating what to do next. This fiend was truly his *doppelgänger*. Where had he come from? Why had he not been seen before now? And who was behind this? If he didn't discover these facts soon, then he knew he was doomed. Nearly every man's hand was turned against him. He knew that even though Watson was willing, he could be of no real aid to him. No, he would do nothing that may endanger the life of his friend.

134

What of his brother? Surely Mycroft could help? He dared not approach him. It was certain that he too would be closely watched.

Watson climbed the stairs to the sitting room with renewed hope, and even though his encounter with Holmes hadn't gone entirely according to plan, at least he knew his friend was alive and well, for the time being. Holmes had nonetheless looked tired and drawn, his eyes bloodshot, wearing filthy and torn clothes, and sporting many days growth of beard – not at all his usual dapper and spotless self. This alone was enough to give Watson concern.

Major-General Rutledge opened the letter, read it, smiled, and then threw it on the fire. Things were going well, although not entirely as he'd hoped. That bumbling fool at Scotland Yard had allowed Holmes to escape his grasp. The Commissioner must really buck up his staff – but no matter. He had further ensured that when Holmes was eventually tracked down, he would surely hang. Another murder with several witnesses had been arranged . . . Good. It would not be long now.

Holmes had been wandering the streets for hours. Suddenly feeling too weary to take another step, he looked up at the door in front of him and found himself outside Kathleen's room. He hadn't consciously come here, but now that he was, he found he was in desperate need of company. He couldn't recall ever feeling so downcast in his life. He had been alone many times before, but not quite like this. He dare not risk involving Watson, and although seeing his friend had cheered him briefly – now he'd never felt quite so unnerved. It was very late – or should he say early? Dawn wasn't far off. Kathleen might well be engaged as it were, but he knocked on her door regardless. No response. After a slight pause he knocked again. This time he could hear someone stirring within, and it wasn't long before the door opened a crack and Kathleen's face peered out, sleep in her eyes, and looking foggy and confused.

"Who is it?"

"I'm sorry to wake you, I shouldn't have disturbed you."

"Oh, it's you." She looked at him quizzically. "What d'you want?"

Holmes stared down, not answering.

She looked around the square and then back at him. "You'd better come in."

Without a word Holmes stepped into her room and stood quietly as she closed the door behind him.

Being more awake now she asked in a more firm voice. "What is it that you want? I don't get much time to sleep, you know, so this had better be good." She was obviously annoyed at being awakened.

Still at a loss for words or as to what he was actually doing there, Holmes continued to think of a reasonable explanation.

"Has something happened to you? Is someone after you? Come on now, lad, I haven't got all night, you know." She sat down heavily on the bed, looking up at him. "Tell me what you want. You look awful."

Holmes laughed at that. "I bet I do." So saying he slumped into the chair. "I'm sorry for waking you, and I confess I don't really know what I'm doing here, I simply had nowhere else to go." A very small self-conscious laugh escaped his lips as he looked up at her. "Please forgive me. I'll take up no more of your time." As he rose to leave, Kathleen rose also. "Wait a moment. You don't think that after waking me at this ungodly hour, I'm just going to let you walk out of here like that do you?" She smiled at him. "Come on, now. Sit down and tell me what's troubling you."

Holmes looked at her quizzically. Could he trust her, or would she run screaming for the nearest constable?

"What is your impression of the sort of man I am?" he asked quietly.

"What?" she asked perplexed.

"What sort of fellow do you take me for?"

Pausing to consider, she replied, "I don't really know you. A little sad and lonely, I suppose. Why?"

"Would you take me for a murderer?"

"Mother of God, what sort of question is that? And at this time of the night!" She was trying to laugh, but not really succeeding.

"An honest one."

"Are you trying to tell me you've killed someone?"

"No. I'm trying to ask you if you think I *could* kill someone."

"Hell, I don't know. Like I said, I don't really know you. I *think* I like you, but with questions like this, I might change my mind."

Holmes laughed mirthlessly. "Yes, you may well indeed. Do I frighten you?"

"You're beginning to."

"I apologise, that wasn't my intention."

"What is it? What's troubling you?"

Holmes sighed and made a decision. "Would it surprise you to learn that I'm wanted for murder? A murder I didn't commit, I might add."

She looked at him with wide eyes now, looking nervously about the room.

136

"I have frightened you and I'm sorry. I'll leave now, if you wish.,"
He made no move to do so.

"No," she said cautiously. "Just tell me what you're talking about."

He looked her squarely in the eyes. "My name is Sherlock Holmes."

With this she leapt to her feet and stared wildly at him. Suddenly she rushed for the door. He made no move to stop her, but spoke quietly.

"Please, don't call for the police, I must talk to someone, and for some strange reason I cannot fathom, I feel that you might believe me.'

Slowly she withdrew her hand from the doorknob and looked at his slumped form, head bowed. He looked more like a lost dog than a killer.

"What do you want from me?" Her voice was a little frightened.

Looking up at her once more, "I don't really know. I need someone to listen, and to believe me." He laughed mirthlessly. "I find I need a friend." He sighed, his eyes pleading, "The whole thing is so incredible that I can scarce believe it myself." He looked so lost that, despite her own misgivings, she almost felt sorry for him. Indeed, he had never tried to molest her in any way. It was almost as if he were waiting to see what fate would decide for him.

Slowly she returned to sit on the bed and looked intently at him. One thing she knew: She was no coward, and come what may, she would have the truth for Mary's sake. "All right, I'll listen before I make any decision."

"Thank you." Holmes proceeded to tell her all he knew of the case involving Guthrie and of his own implication in the women's murders. Her eyes grew wider and wider as his story drew to a close.

"Well," she said, pondering, "you really are in a pickle, aren't you?"

"But do you believe me?" His eyes betrayed his anxiety.

She didn't speak for some time, merely looked at him in perplexity. He remained still, giving her the time she required. Finally she spoke. "I think I do. Though I can't for the life of me think of a good reason."

Holmes visibly relaxed and, taking his pipe from his pocket, asked, "Would you object if I smoke? It always helps me to think."

Chapter IX

With considerable trepidation, Kathleen alighted from the cab and approached the address with which she had been supplied. Holmes had given her money for new clothes and for the cab. "For one thing," he had said, "you deserve some decent clothing, and for another it wouldn't do to draw attention to yourself in that part of town. Also – " Here Holmes chuckled. " – we must consider my poor brother's reputation." He had seemed very pleased with himself when she had returned with her new acquisitions and, after leaving her room for a few moments while she changed into them, he beamed at her saying, "Very fine. Not too ostentatious, but very fine indeed." She had to smile at his chivalry, considering they both knew what she did for a living. Still, he had treated her with the respect due to a lady – treatment she had almost forgotten.

Reaching up, she knocked loudly three times and, with little delay, the door was opened by a large and imperious landlady who eyed her with apparent distaste. Kathleen became self-conscious despite herself. She felt that this woman could see right through her fine clothes and knew without doubt what she had been doing for the past few months to put bread in her mouth. Kathleen knew in her heart this wasn't true, that this woman couldn't possible know anything about her circumstances, but she felt it just the same. Not that Kathleen had been given a choice, but this ogre made her feel, with one withering glance, that she was nothing but dirt. Plucking up her courage, she addressed this paragon.

"I am here to speak with Mr. Mycroft Holmes." It was a statement, not a request.

Again eyeing Kathleen with disdain, the woman motioned her to come inside and wait in the hall while she went to fetch her tenant. Kathleen was now of the opinion that this woman would eye even the Duchess of York with distaste.

"Mr. Mycroft says you may go up. First floor, second door on the right."

"Thank you," said Kathleen with as much grace as she could muster and began to climb the stairs. Before reaching the top, a giant of a man came out onto the landing and looked her up and down. His gaze was penetrating thought not judgmental. His form was the antithesis of his sibling, yet in his eyes she could see his younger brother. Mycroft sighed and motioned her to enter, directing her to a comfortable armchair by the fire.

"You come from my brother, I perceive."

Kathleen was dumbfounded. She hadn't so much as uttered a sound in his presence and yet –

"Come my girl, it isn't such a wild assumption on my part. My brother has a well-known taste for the dramatic and he also frequents the lowest parts of London with regrettable regularity. No slur to you intended. However, it is plain to see that you are recently from Ireland, and that due to unforeseen circumstances you must now sustain life and limb by prostituting yourself for money. Although I happen to know my brother doesn't indulge in that particular vice, I'm also aware that his northern roots have imbued him with a rather socialistic ideal towards the teaming masses, of which even he is unaware. Nevertheless he seldom passes an opportunity, however unknowingly, to demonstrate this point of view to

138

me – although in this instance things are a little more complicated, are they not?" Mycroft finished this diatribe by settling back in his own armchair and lighting an enormous cigar.

Kathleen was barely able to follow half of what this giant was saying, but she swallowed hard and said what she had come here to say. "It is true, I do come from your brother. I believe him innocent, and he asked if I would consent to deliver this letter to you." So saying, Kathleen retrieved a sealed envelope from within her garments and handed it to Mycroft.

Taking the letter from her, he examined it closely before opening it.

"He said I should wait to hear your response."

Mycroft nodded and proceeded to read the contents of the envelope.

> *First, I must ask that you not trace my whereabouts through this young lady –* (Straight to the point as always, thought Mycroft, with no little affection.) *– even though we both know this would be child's play to you. Kathleen is now my only confidante. I need you as I have never needed you before. If you cannot find it in your heart to believe me innocent of these crimes, then I am surely lost. Whoever is behind this has found someone of remarkable resemblance to me. I need you to look into this and go to the places that I can no longer go. Watson is willing, but I fear he doesn't possess the necessary credentials, and I wouldn't risk his life any further than it is already.*
>
> *I need you to speak to the people concerned, or at least make enquires in your indefatigable style. Below, you will find a list of all the principals of which I'm aware, I must trust to you to find the missing pieces. I'm by no means certain that this case is indeed the reason for my present predicament, but I have no other leads at present. All I can do is trust that you will have greater luck than I. As you can imagine, my resources are severely limited at present. I cannot be seen by anyone who knows me, which has cut off my usual sources of information rather effectively.*
>
> *I thank you, Mycroft, in advance.*
>
> *Your grateful brother,*
> *Sherlock*

The tone of the letter was something that Mycroft wouldn't have expected from his younger brother. *Desperate* was the only word to describe it. Sherlock had always been fiercely proud yet practical, and though this wasn't the first time his younger sibling had asked for his help,

139

it was the first time he had begged anything from anyone to the best of his knowledge.

Mycroft studied his visitor from under hooded eyelids. "You have seen Sherlock recently. Tell me, in what state would you say is his mind? And tell me why *you* believe his story and not the evidence of other people's eyes?"

This man's scrutiny was almost more than Kathleen could bare. Mycroft Holmes's eyes were in some ways more intense than those of his brother – a feature she had noted when first she had met both men. Now knowing Sherlock Holmes as she did, having spent several days and nights with the man, she felt she would trust him with her life – which was just as well, for that was exactly what she was doing. He had stayed with her since his unannounced arrival and not once had he tried to take advantage of the situation or to molest her in any way, and he had always been the perfect gentleman. Perhaps this had persuaded her more than anything, but she could no more see him killing anyone in cold blood than she could herself.

"I can give you no solid evidence, Mr. Holmes, only my belief in his innocence. Do you think I could come here on his behalf if I truly thought he had murdered my sisters, so to speak?"

"Women have been known to stick by their man in such circumstances."

"He isn't my 'man'!" said Kathleen indignantly. "He has never taken advantage. You mustn't think – !"

Mycroft chuckled. "No, no, my dear, I know my brother too well. You must excuse me. A dubious sense of humour runs in our family. Now, you may tell my brother – " Before Mycroft could complete his sentence, there was a knock at the door.

"Very sorry to disturb you again sir, but there is an Inspector Cruft here to see you. I told him you were engaged, sir, but I don't think he believed me."

Kathleen started at this news, but Mycroft held up a reassuring hand, and she settled back into her seat. "It's perfectly all right, Mrs. Ross. Please show him in."

Cruft entered abruptly and stopped short as he saw Kathleen. "I'm sorry if I've called at an inconvenient moment, but I'm afraid it can't wait."

"I am in no way inconvenienced," said Mycroft genially.

"I need to speak to you about your brother." Cruft glanced at Kathleen significantly. He knew not who she was and didn't wish an audience.

140

"Allow me to introduce my cousin, Kathleen. Inspector, you may speak freely in front of her. She is fully acquainted with my brother's predicament."

Cruft eyed her more closely, "I see. Well, we have just received information of another murder, only this time there were several witnesses." Cruft waited dramatically to see the reaction. Mycroft, however, remained disappointingly calm.

"I see," was all he would say, in a non-committal tone.

"Yes," continued Cruft, looking deep into Mycroft's eyes. He was acutely aware that Mycroft hadn't offered him a seat. "Therefore, I have come to you. The Doctor is unwilling, and probably incapable, of tracking down Sherlock Holmes. However, you on the other hand must know his habits, his – "

"Inspector," interrupted Mycroft, "I find it rather insensitive of you ask me to help you find my own brother and send him to the gallows. Certainly less than compassionate on your part, to say the least." Mycroft rose slowly from his chair. Kathleen sat perfectly still, hoping to remain unnoticed. Mycroft glanced at her, then turned his attention fully on Cruft. "I will in no way hinder you, Inspector, but it is a little unreasonable, I think, for you to come here and ask me to deliver my brother into your hands. Now if you will excuse me, I have pressing business elsewhere." It was plain that this interview was now at an end.

Kathleen took this opportunity to leave as rapidly as dignity would allow. "Yes, I too must be off. Thank you for your time . . . Cousin." With this she swept from the room, and it was all she could do to walk calmly down the stairs and not run out of the house as if the Devil himself were after her. Mycroft would have wished that she had remained, but he couldn't convey this to her without raising Cruft's suspicions even further. She had plainly been rattled by his presence, and it might only make matters worse to try to make her stay. Reluctantly he must let her go and allow things to take their course.

Cruft felt a sudden urge to follow this woman. He couldn't say why exactly – just instinct, and he knew he had good instincts – so he would deal with Mycroft Holmes another time. "Very well, Mr. Holmes. I can understand your reluctance. I will no doubt be seeing you again." And with that he left hastily to catch up with his quarry.

Mycroft observed Cruft through the window as he ran after the unsuspecting Kathleen. This could prove inconvenient, but there was little he could do to prevent it. His brother must take his chances as best he could. Mycroft found the whole business perplexing. It required a great deal of thought before he could decide on a course of action.

141

Naturally, he believed his brother to be innocent. Wrongful hangings, however, did occur with all too common regularity.

Chapter X

Kathleen made her way as quickly as she could and, hailing the first cab that came her way, she instructed the driver to take her straight home. She was completely unaware that Cruft had also immediately procured a cab and was right behind her.

Pressing herself nervously back into the cushions, Kathleen was uncertain what to tell Sherlock Holmes when she reached him. His brother had been about to convey a message, but hadn't time to do so. The cabbie opened the flap in the roof and yelled down, "Almost there miss. Are you sure you want this neighbourhood? It's no place for a lady."

Kathleen laughed. "I'll be fine, thank you. Just drop me here if you would." The two-wheeler pulled over to the curb and Kathleen climbed out. As she reached into her pocket to retrieve the money Holmes had given her, her eye was drawn to a cab pulling up a little distance away on the other side of the road. She wasn't at all sure why this particular cab caught her eye, but suddenly she became cautious. Trying to appear uninterested she kept a close eye on the other cab as she paid off her own. No one stepped down from the second vehicle and this made her nervous. "Thank you, driver," she said affably.

"My pleasure, Miss."

"Would you do me a great favour?"

"If I can, Miss."

"When you leave, would you turn your cab around and go back the same way you came." The cab driver looked puzzled but readily agreed.

"Sure thing, Miss. Makes no difference to me." So saying, he lightly flicked his whip and turned the head of his horse around. Kathleen watched and waited until the other cab was obscured. Immediately she darted down the nearest alley and ran as fast as her legs would carry her. Coming to another even narrower alley she turned swiftly again and kept running. After several more turns she slowed and chanced a look behind her. She could see no one. Leaning against the brick wall, she tried to regain her breath. She had no real reason to suppose that the other cab had anything to do with her, but she felt it in her bones. Why had no one alighted from it, and why had it stopped so close to hers? She must get home and ask Holmes what he thought of it.

Cruft swore. He had been annoyed when the cab had pulled in front of his view, but now he was livid. She had vanished. Little minx. Must

142

have spotted him. This made him even more convinced he was on the right track. But how to find her? Obviously Mycroft Holmes knew more than he was saying, and now this so called "cousin" had given him the slip. Still, he was reasonably certain she hadn't spotted him before she left the cab, so at least he was in the right area.

Kathleen burst through the door, quickly slamming it shut behind her. Leaning back against it, her breath came in quick shallow bursts.

"What on earth is the matter?" asked Holmes, rising swiftly from the bed where he had been so rudely awakened.

"I was followed."

Holmes rushed to the window.

"It's all right, I think. I believe I lost him."

"Who?"

"I don't know. Could have been that policeman – a feller called Cruft. Seems he's the new copper in charge."

"How would he come to be following you?" asked Holmes, glancing anxiously through the window.

"He came to see your brother while I was there."

As Holmes listened to Kathleen's tale, he continually checked the alley through the window.

"I swear I didn't know he was following me until I saw the cab stopping behind mine."

"Very careless of him."

"You think it *was* him then?"

"It would seem the logical conclusion."

"What do we do now?"

"*We* shall do nothing, *I* shall smoke."

Kathleen lay sleeping and Holmes watched her, without really looking, as he was so deep in thought. It was clear that these people had planned for all contingencies, and keeping watch on Watson would have been an obvious necessity. Once he started walking the streets of the East End, they had hatched a plan to convince him of Holmes's guilt. This much was clear. Happily, Holmes had intercepted Watson before this had occurred and spoiled their efforts, though it had been by luck and not judgement on his part, he had to concede. Indeed, Holmes himself had followed his friend on several occasions, eventually deciding to slip him the note with the aid of one of the many street Arabs, though not one of his Irregulars. It had been good fortune that this had coincided with these murderers plans to fool his friend and no doubt try to convince even

143

Watson of his guilt. It had to be said that Watson would have made a damning witness against him, if successful.

Holmes conceded he must consider the unpleasant thought that even *he* himself was being watched.

He made a decision. Rising quietly from the chair, he slipped silently out the door.

Major-General Rutledge smiled as he sent the telegram. It was time to stir the pot. Things were moving too slowly. Holmes mustn't be left at large for much longer. He had foiled his master stroke in connection with the stoic Watson . . . Ah, well, no matter.

There was, however, still a slight chance that he could interfere with business and that couldn't be allowed.

The police were showing a deplorable lack of ingenuity in tracking down their quarry, so now it had become necessary to give them a little push in the right direction.

Cruft had kept the surveillance low-key around the area where the woman had gone to ground. He didn't want to frighten his game away. Only two officers, apart from himself, were on the lookout and in civvies. So far no joy, but he would keep at it. He hadn't solved the Bronson murders by giving up at the first obstacle.

"There's a telegram for you, sir," said Constable Osborne, having just returned from headquarters. He wasn't comfortable when dealing with his superior officers. He preferred walking his beat, where he knew what he was about. Now he was forced to deal with Inspector Cruft on a daily basis, and he didn't like it – or the man, for that matter. He'd been given special duty on account of his detailed knowledge of the streets. "Just my luck," he thought.

"Don't call me 'Sir', you fool," said Cruft in an angry whisper.

"Sorry, sir – I mean . . . sorry."

"Just give me the telegram, idiot." They were seated in a quiet corner of The Hare and Hounds, one of the many pubs in Spitalfields. Osborne thought this was a pointless charade as most knew him by sight, whether in plainclothes or not.

"Well, well, well," said Cruft, upon reading the telegram.

"Anything useful, si – . . . Anything useful?"

Glaring at Osborne, Cruft replied, "It just might be. Come on."

Mycroft was extremely annoyed. He didn't appreciate having his routine disturbed. However, since his brother's life was at stake, he would grudgingly make an exception and divert from his usual paths, if only

144

briefly. Having once hailed a cab, he'd made his way to the Ministry of Defence.

Now seated back at his desk, Mycroft pondered the events of the previous evening – what his brother might call, a six-pipe problem.

Mycroft's secretary walked in loaded with papers for his master's perusal.

"Alfred," said Mycroft in a calm but deliberate voice. "Send for Edward."

Without so much as a pause in his placing the papers on the desk in front of his superior, Alfred replied, "Right away, sir."

Alfred had been quietly wondering how long it would be before Mr. Mycroft would send for Mr. Edward.

Chapter XI

Cruft was growing increasingly impatient in direct relation to how cold he felt. The telegram had said to be at Gouch Street by ten p.m. and it was now closer to eleven, and still nothing. No one had come near him, not even the prostitutes. He wasn't aware of the fact that they could all pick him as a copper from a good thirty yards away. Then, just as he was thinking the message must have been a hoax, he saw him. He had seen a photograph of Sherlock Holmes at the station and this was the man himself. No doubt about it. He was just crossing from a street a little way ahead and Cruft was after him like a shot, keeping in the shadows. He would follow his quarry for a while. He had only Osborne with him and couldn't risk Holmes escaping down one of the many alleys and paths. Best to follow him to his lair. He signalled for Osborne to join him.

Holmes seemed in no great hurry, and indeed he wasn't particularly clandestine in his movements, just walking down the street calm as you please.

Cruft and Osborne kept close, but not so close as to be seen. Finally their quarry stopped at one corner commonly used by the unfortunates and waited.

It wasn't long before one of the ladies in question appeared and they spoke briefly.

"Shouldn't we take him now, Guv?" asked Osborne, concerned.

"No."

"But sir – !"

"I said not yet."

"But he might kill her!" protested the young man.

"We wait," asserted Cruft. "I'll take the responsibility, you needn't worry."

"It isn't me I'm worried about."

"Shut up and watch."

Osborne continued watching, sullenly. He really didn't like Cruft. He wasn't a Londoner and it seemed clear he didn't care what happened to any of its citizens. Osborne was no saint, but even if they were only prossies, he didn't think the girls were dirt. They had a hard enough life already, and he felt they deserved what little protection he could offer them – which was next to nothing, he had to admit, but Cruft was just using this girl and quite obviously didn't care whether she lived or died.

Several minutes passed with Holmes and the woman talking quietly. She seemed a little the worse for drink and tended to sway ever so slightly. Finally they seemed to reach an agreement and they walked off together.

"Come on!" whispered Cruft. They followed at a discreet distance until the two presently slipped down an alley.

Osborne was all for rushing them, but Cruft held him back.

"Slowly, Constable. Don't want to frighten him away." Maybe I should send this young fool off for reinforcements, thought Cruft. No time.

"But he might be – "

"Slowly, I said. If he gets wind of us, he'll be off like a rabbit."

As they slowly approached the corner, they could hear a muffled scream. As one they both bolted forward and rounded the corner at a run.

"Oh my God!" whispered Osborne.

"Damn!" swore Cruft.

"Hey!" shouted the constable as he rushed forward.

The villain didn't even look towards them as he ran off at a tremendous speed. Cruft gave chase, but Osborne stopped to look down in horror at the wreckage on the ground before him.

Soon Cruft returned, swearing loudly. "He got away. God, that man can run. And where the hell were you? What the devil are you doing here when you should have been helping me to catch him?"

"She's dead." Osborne's voice was numb, "and it's our fault." He glared at Cruft.

"Don't be a fool!" answered Cruft, in even greater annoyance.

"We could have stopped this." Osborne pointed bitterly at the corpse.

"Could we? Perhaps, but now we know beyond doubt that we are hunting the right man."

"Is that all you care about?"

"At this moment, yes. And I'd watch your tongue if I was you, laddie, I don't much care for your tone. Now get every man we can spare, and even if they can't be spared, get them down here anyway. I want him taken tonight, and I don't care how you find him. Clear?"

146

Osborne had to fight hard to control his anger. "What about her? We can't just leave her here?"

"Of course not, you fool. I'll stay with her until you return." And in a slightly kinder tone he added, "Now get going.'

"No, Lestrade, don't." Holmes grabbed the policeman before he could join in the chase.

"Good God, it's you! But I just saw you over there not a second past with a knife in that poor girl's throat."

"Not me, Lestrade. How can I be there and here?"

"But I could have sworn it was you!"

"That is precisely the point."

"My God . . . But then who is it?"

"That's a very good question."

"But how the devil . . . ?"

"You saw – they took a calculated risk and have made a fatal mistake. Now we must take advantage of it."

"Well, at least you're in the clear now."

"No, we must keep that to ourselves for the present."

"But – "

"No one must know. No one – do you understand? Especially not your superiors."

"But why on earth not? I can tell everyone for certain it wasn't you, only someone who looks like you. I saw it with my own eyes."

"Yes, but you wouldn't have believed it if you hadn't seen with your own eyes. How can you expect anyone to believe us without solid evidence – such as the killer and me looking identical and standing side by side. They will hang me in an instant and be glad of it, and they'll send you off to pasture – or worse, lock you up in Bedlam."

Lestrade looked grim.

"You know," Holmes continued, "if I was that fellow, I would be very worried. Once they get rid of me, I'm sure he'll be the next to go. Too dangerous to have him around. Still, I would dearly love to know who the devil he is, and how he comes to look so much like me."

"You aren't joking, but what now?"

"Continue on as normal, I shall be in touch." Before he could rush off, Lestrade grabbed his arm.

"But what are *you* doing here?"

"I might ask you the same question,' said Holmes in an amused voice.

"I've been following Cruft for the last few days. One of my men, Osborne – that's him over there – he came to me with some concerns over

147

the new inspector. He didn't know what to do, so I've been keeping an eye on him. And you?"

"Well . . ." said Holmes dryly. "I've been watching you watching him." He smiled at Lestrade's open mouth.

"You've been . . . ?"

"I thought it might be in my best interest to keep an eye on you both. I was right. We have now all seen the real killer, only you and I know it isn't me. A quite remarkable resemblance, don't you think?"

"Uncanny."

"There is one thing you could do for me if you would."

"Name it."

"Would you tell my brother Mycroft what you have seen? And you might tell Watson. I know they will both be concerned – just to put their minds at rest. They have shown great loyalty and faith in me, but they must have their misgivings. It would be only natural. You must be very careful not to be seen. These men are dangerous and powerful."

"I shall be careful, and it will be my pleasure to tell them both."

"Thank you. Now off you go. I shall be in touch."

"Just one thing, Mr. Holmes – How will I know if it's really you?"

"Ah," Holmes thought for a moment and then with a brief though very cheeky smile. "I shall precede any message with the word 'Norwood', and end with the word 'builder'."

Lestrade harrumphed and rolled his eyes. Then smiling good-naturedly, he added, "Good luck, Mr. Holmes."

"Thank you, Lestrade."

Chapter XII

Holmes returned stealthily to Kathleen's room. She was waiting anxiously.

"What has happened? Where have you been? Are you all right?"

"One question at a time please," laughed Holmes. "It has been a fruitful evening."

"I woke up and found you gone. I didn't know what to think. I didn't know if you were coming back." Her voice was thick with worry. Holmes was touched by her genuine concern.

"I am sorry, it wasn't my intention to worry you. All is becoming clearer, though unfortunately there has been another murder. But I was fortunate enough to meet with Inspector Lestrade and he now knows the truth."

"Then you are saved."

"No, I'm afraid not. Not by a long chalk."

148

"But why not? If he knows the truth . . . ."

"It is still very complicated and I can prove nothing. Lestrade is out of favour at the moment, and the man who is in still firmly believes I'm the guilty party. Now more than ever as he believes he has just seen me actually commit murder."

"What?" bellowed Kathleen.

"Yes, I saw the fellow myself this time, but was too late to intervene. I was following Lestrade who was following Inspector Cruft, and to be truthful, Lestrade had very nearly lost his counterpart. It was a piece of good fortune that we were present at all. I'm afraid the lag in time cost another life. Still, I hope it will be the last murder. They have accomplished what they wished. Cruft is convinced of my guilt beyond doubt. I can see no need for them to kill again."

"Maybe they enjoy it."

Holmes brooded. "You may be right. I hope for the sake of others that you're wrong."

"What will you do now?"

"I shall smoke."

"Smoke?"

"Yes," he said calmly. "Smoke."

"Heaven's above, you have most of the police out looking for you and all you can do is smoke."

"It helps me to think," he said, distractedly. He wasn't consciously listening to her anymore. His mind wandered over the whole landscape of the problem – sifting and weighing each part to find its proper place.

Cruft looked grimly after the black coach as it carried the body of the latest victim away. "Damn!" he swore once again. He knew Osborne would be trouble, and that he blamed him for the death even more than he did the killer. Damn young puppy, he thought. Besides, if he had given chase with me, as he should have done, we would more than likely have the brute in charge by now. He swore again under his breath as Osborne approached.

"All the men are in position, and they've been given your instructions . . . sir." The last was spoken with as much insolence as could be put into a single word.

"Look Osborne, it really couldn't be avoided – "

"Really, sir? It couldn't? Well, if we had taken him immediately, it could."

"Listen, Osborne, if we had caught the blighter, we would have a watertight case. He would go straight to the gallows, no question."

"Well, we didn't, did we?"

149

"And who's fault was that?" erupted Cruft

"It wasn't my fault he got away," replied Osborne petulantly.

"Oh really. And who was it that was standing around slack-jawed the whole time I was chasing him, by myself?"

"I'd just seen a woman's throat cut."

"Just how long have you been on the beat, Constable? Because of your inaction, the culprit got away."

Before Cruft could say anymore, three constables approached. "'Scuse me, sir. Should we start now, or – ?"

"Of course you should start now, you fools. Get a move on. He can't be far away." Cruft's career could be hanging in the balance and these idiots were waiting to be told how to conduct a simple search. "Move!" he bellowed at them. They ran off as much to escape his wrath as to carry out his orders.

Systematically they worked their way outwards in a spiral from where the last murder had taken place, knocking on doors and breaking down those that didn't open. It would be a long and noisy night.

Kathleen awoke to increasing sounds of distress from the streets outside. There was a loud banging and shouting coming from all around. She started up in bed.

"What's happening? Is it a riot?" She found Holmes looking anxiously out of her small window. "What in God's name is happening?" she exclaimed.

"They're breaking down the doors – looking for me no doubt."

"Glory! Can they do that?"

"They *are* doing it."

"What shall we do?"

"You will stay here. Say nothing. They have no reason to suspect you."

"But that man Cruft – he knows me."

"It's unlikely to be the man himself who comes knocking on this particular door. You will be infinitely safer if I leave now. Remember, say nothing. I must go." Kathleen rushed to the door after he had slipped through, but he was already out of sight.

For once Holmes wasn't quite correct. The police had no reason to suspect her, but her neighbours apparently resented her for some reason – Well, she was Irish, after all. Could be one of those bombers. Evan an Irish spy. They were all too pleased to blather about the man who had been staying with her lately, a man who could no longer be found. Kathleen was taken into custody, as much to protect her person from an increasingly

150

angry mob as for being a suspect. The crowd had been unceremoniously turfed out of their beds and someone was going to pay.

Kathleen was taken away on a wave of hysteria right into the loving arms of Inspector Cruft.

Chapter XIII

"Well, now, my girl. Mr. Mycroft Holmes cousin, isn't it?" His voice filled with sarcasm and his smile wasn't a humorous one. Kathleen sat still, ramrod straight and scared stiff. She already hated this man, with his smug face and his all-too-clear attitude towards her. What should she say? She didn't know, so she would follow Holmes's instructions and say nothing.

"Well, come on. I don't have all day. We both know you are no relation to Mr. Holmes. Come on girl, you are in quite enough trouble already."

"I don't know where my cousin is and, even if I did, I wouldn't tell you," she said, afraid but defiant. She didn't know why she was continuing with this quite obvious deception. Perhaps it was because she liked the two brothers, or perhaps it was a reminder of a better life. If she were their cousin, then it would be highly unlikely she would be a common prostitute.

Cruft wasn't having any of it. "No, my girl, we both know you're no relation, and don't think either one of them will lift a finger to help you now. You were just a convenience to them."

Kathleen's face fell a little. He might be right. She was in deep trouble with no one in the world to turn to. No . . . she couldn't believe it of Sherlock Holmes. He wasn't like that. He wouldn't betray her . . . *Would he?*

"Where is he? You have no reason to keep quiet. He left you to our mercy."

"I don't know what you're talking about."

"All right . . . ." Cruft paused for a moment to calm himself. "Who was the man staying with you? Why did he leave in such a hurry, hmmm?"

"Who says he did? Anyway, he was just a friend who needed a place to stay for a little while, that's all."

Cruft slammed his fist down on the bench. "Don't treat me like a fool, girl! You better start telling me the truth, or things will become most unpleasant for you.

Osborne, who had accompanied his superior to interview the girl in her cell, was growing increasingly worried by Cruft's attitude.

"Steady, Guv'. She isn't likely to protect the man who's been killing others just like her, is she?" He wouldn't normally dare to speak so to a

151

superior in such a fashion, but Cruft really made him angry, and as far as he was concerned the girl was harmless. He even felt a little sorry for her.

Cruft turned angrily on his subordinate. "Mind yourself, Constable." His voice was menacing. Osborne clamped his mouth shut tight. He wasn't that brave . . . or stupid.

Before Cruft could start again on the girl, another constable entered the cell.

"Sir, there is someone here to see you."

"I'm busy."

"I'm sorry, sir. He says it can't wait." The constables' eyes darted nervously between Cruft and Osborne. "He's from the Ministry," he finished, as if that should explain everything.

"The Ministry? What Ministry? What the blazes does he want here? I'm in the middle of a murder inquiry."

"I don't know sir, but the Super wants you to come right away."

"Bloody Hell! All right." He turned on Kathleen. "You think very carefully about what you're going to say when I get back." He then stormed out, leaving Osborne to look apologetically at Kathleen. Then he too left, followed by the young constable. As the door closed behind them, Kathleen sank back onto the bunk, feeling very alone and frightened.

After leaving the police station, Edward returned to Mycroft's office. When he entered, Mycroft merely raised a questioning eyebrow.

"The girl has been released," said Edward in his deep calm voice.

"And my brother?"

"Still at large."

"Very well."

Edward silently closed the door behind him as he left. He needed no further instructions.

Mycroft smiled to himself. His little brother may have his band of street Arabs, but he had Edward – there wasn't another fellow like him. Quiet, efficient, and stealthy. Ex-Grenadier Guards.

Indeed, Mycroft himself was no slouch when it came to informants. He had eyes and ears everywhere. He wouldn't leave Sherlock Holmes languishing in prison at the tender mercies of Cruft. Wouldn't be cricket.

Chapter XIV

Kathleen made her way towards her room, though what she would find there she shuddered to imagine. Her so-called neighbours had been all too glad to see the back of her and had probably thrown what few

152

possessions she had into the street – what they hadn't kept for themselves that is.

As she approached her digs, she saw candlelight flickering on the blind. She'd had just about enough for one day, and as she thrust open the door, ready to give whoever it was a mouthful, she stopped short . . . .

"Mr. Holmes! What in Heaven's name are you doing here?"

"Come, my dear, I'll take you somewhere safe." Sherlock Holmes would say no more in answer to her questions, but being so happy to see him she left with him gladly – even if he was acting a little strangely. It appeared he'd also found time for a wash and a shave . . .

Perhaps this meant that things were looking up at last. She gathered her few paltry things – it seems the police had sealed her room to prevent any pilfering – and left with him.

Holmes had managed to out-manoeuvre the Wooden-tops without too much difficulty, but he couldn't go on running forever. He decided that it was time to pay a call on the Major-General. Two o'clock in the morning should suite nicely.

All was still and quiet. Nothing stirred as he silently slipped the window up. Cautiously climbing in and settling gently to the floor, he paused, straining to hear any sound. All was silence. Having entered through the pantry, he made his way first to the living room via the kitchen, then on into several rooms before he found the study. Closing the door silently behind him, he began his search.

Suddenly the door burst open, and he found himself looking down the barrel of a gun.

"Ah, Mr. Holmes, I've been expecting you. What took you so long?" The man who stood before him bore an extremely smug smile across his – in Holmes opinion – very punchable face.

"It was a calculated risk," stated Holmes impassively.

"One that you have lost."

"Have I?"

"Oh yes. I myself have many options, but as I see it, *you* have only one."

"Really? And what might that be?"

"Simply this: Unless you wish to be personally responsible for yet another woman's death, you will hand yourself over to the police, and what's more," the man's face became even more worthy of being hit with every passing moment, "you will make no statement or try to defend yourself in any way."

"Is that so?" Holmes almost laughed out loud. "You expect me to surrender myself for hanging for the sake of some unknown woman?"

153

"Certainly I do, and she is by no means an unknown woman." The gloating was really beginning to become very aggravating. "A rather pretty young Irish prostitute, not yet made old and ugly by her profession. At least she is pretty at the moment. How long she will remain that way depends entirely on you." His voice was threatening. "You will go quietly to the gallows, or she shall go before you." His voice grew lighter again. "You have made the one mistake you have always avoided in the past: You have allowed personal feeling to cloud your judgement, and what is worse, you have let your enemy see your weakness. How quaint . . . how foolish." As Rutledge's smile increased so did Holmes's annoyance, mostly at himself.

"I see," said Holmes trying to sound casual. "Why not just shoot me now and hand over a corpse to the police? No one will argue the point with you."

"Well . . . I could do that I suppose, but where is the fun in that? Also, why should I come into the matter at all? It will be so much more satisfying to watch your humiliation, your total surrender to *my* will . . . not to mention the grand finale of watching you hang." It took all of Holmes self-control not to leap on the man and smash his face in, if only to wipe that accursed grin from it. "I shall enjoy that special treat."

"I'm sure," replied Holmes dryly, showing none of his internal turmoil. At least, he hoped so.

"Well?"

"How do I know that you have her or that you will keep your word and leave her be?"

"I have no interest in the girl. My only problem is you. Once you are dead, she will be quite safe . . . Well, from me anyway."

Holmes was visibly disturbed, his brow furrowed and he lowered his gaze to the floor in deep thought.

"If you are thinking that you can reach her first and whisk her away to safety, then you are already too late." He raised his hand and pressed the bell on the wall. Within moments, an exact replica of Holmes walked in. The man smiled broadly at Holmes, visibly amused by Sherlock's obvious astonishment.

"Bring her." The other man bowed and left the room.

Holmes was stunned by the resemblance. This close up he would have expected to see some differences, but it was like looking at himself in the mirror. A few minutes passed before the man returned escorting Kathleen. She appeared unharmed and apparently unconcerned until she saw a second Sherlock Holmes standing before her, looking as scruffy and unkempt as she remembered. She realised immediately her predicament.

154

However, before she could move, the impostor grabbed her roughly and held her tight.

"Now, Mr. Holmes, you will do as you are told or you know what will happen. She will be released unharmed if you do as instructed."

Holmes sighed inwardly. Unless he was prepared to sacrifice the girl, he had little choice. Even without considering her, he was still in a pretty sticky position. All he could do was hope that Mycroft and Lestrade would be able to help in time.

He knew this man wouldn't release her. She had seen his face, but if he didn't do as directed immediately, then this fiend would kill her in very short order. No, he would have to go along with it for the time being and trust to his brother.

"All will be well, Kathleen," said Holmes in a calming voice. "They will not harm you." He glared at his mirror image to say that they had better not. He felt she would be safe enough for now – at least until *he* was hanged.

He turned to face his antagonist. "Very well, it appears you have won. Well played. I shall surrender myself."

"No," breathed Kathleen.

"Don't fret, Kathleen, I will be perfectly alright." Holmes smiled in what he hoped was a reassuring manner.

"Oh yes, Mr. Holmes, all will be well once they have stretched your neck."

"Send for the police now. Then there can be no doubt."

"Come, Mr. Holmes, really. As I have already said, I see no need for my name to ever appear in this matter, nor do I see the need to run the risk of anyone seeing our friend here. But I'm sure none of these things were ever your intention." He looked menacingly at Kathleen.

"All right, Rutledge. Leave her be. You can't blame a man for trying. I'll go quietly. I give you my word. Now release her."

"Charming as the ideal of honour is, she will not be released until you are swinging. Do I make myself perfectly clear?"

Holmes looked deep into this man's eyes, they were cold, hard and maniacal. There was no doubt in his mind that he would kill Kathleen if he didn't comply. Just at this moment, he could see no alternative.

"Very well." Holmes turned without a second look at anyone and headed out the door. He would present himself at the nearest police station. That was the only clue he could leave his brother at the present.

Chapter XV

"I believe you have been looking for me." Holmes smiled.

155

"For *you*, sir?" An elderly Sergeant looked up from his paperwork, a little annoyed at the interruption. "And just why would we be looking for you?"

"My name is Sherlock Holmes."

"*Blimey.*"

Holmes found himself being whisked hurriedly away to Scotland Yard. Here he got his first close up look at the new man. Cruft had quite clearly come up through the ranks – never an easy journey – and it showed on his uncompromising face.

"What I want to know is why the great Sherlock Holmes simply walked into a police station and gave himself up?" Cruft leaned in over the table and glared at Holmes, who sat with hands cuffed behind him. They were taking no chances this time.

"That is a very interesting question, and one I feel you should ask," stated Holmes, the very briefest of smiles appearing on his lips.

"Don't try to be funny with me, Mister. I don't have a sense of humour."

"I wasn't joking."

"Really."

"No. I absolutely believe you should ask yourself that very question."

"Why did you kill those women?"

"I didn't."

"You didn't."

"No."

"I saw you."

"You didn't see me."

"Oh really. Just someone who happen to look like you I suppose."

"Funny you should say that – "

"Are you going to give me a straight answer or not?"

Holmes sat silent.

"I see. Osbourne, take him down to the cells and explain why he should cooperate."

"My pleasure, sir."

The door to Holmes's cell closed behind them quietly. It was all too clear what was coming.

"I saw you kill her,' said Osborne with passion. "I know they'll hang you, but I want to give you a little something from me before you go."

In a straight fight Holmes knew he could take this young fellow without difficulty. The handcuffs, however, were a complication. Given the circumstances, it seemed prudent to take his punishment without

156

complaint. After all, the constable would only return later with some of his friends if he went away unsatisfied on this occasion.

The young man was strong and enthusiastic, though inexperienced. Consequently, his blows weren't as punishing as they might have been. Still, it wasn't pleasant, and it was with great relief Holmes heard a friendly voice.

"What the hell do you think you're doing?" Lestrade bellowed.

"Only what he deserves."

"As a matter of fact, he doesn't. Even so, this is no way to treat a prisoner – especially an innocent one."

"Innocent?"

"Yes, you cloth-head – *Innocent!* Croft has the wrong one!"

"Wrong one . . . what? No sir, I saw him . . . ."

"You saw someone else. I was there."

"No, sir – "

"Don't argue with me, boy. Just get out. Wait – take off those handcuffs."

"Sir?"

"*Now!*"

"Yes, sir!" Osbourne grudgingly removed the darbies from Holmes wrists in none-too-gentle a fashion by roughly turning him over on the floor and kneeling on his back as he did so.

"Osborne, don't give me anymore reason to put you on report." Lestrade was smouldering. Recognising that he may have just gone too far. The constable stood up and, with one last angry look at the private consulting detective, he departed.

"I'm sorry, Mr. Holmes." Lestrade helped him off the floor and onto the bunk. "Are you all right?"

"I've had better days. I'm glad you arrived when you did. I could withstand his fists with no great difficulty. Nevertheless, his size elevens were beginning to tell."

"Young fool!" complained Lestrade.

"Don't be too hard on him, Inspector. From his point of view, I can understand his attitude, though I don't condone his actions. What brings you to this timely intervention?"

"I was on my way to see Watson when I heard that you had walked into a police station and presented yourself. What on earth possessed you?"

"They have the girl."

"What girl? Who have her? What the devil are you talking about?"

"She helped me when no one else could. She believed me when no one else would." He bowed his head. "I can't let her die for me."

157

"Good God! Tell me – what can I do to help?

"There is nothing you can do Lestrade. It's . . . complicated. Mycroft will – by now I hope – have accumulated a great deal of information. I shall tell you all I know and you must convey it to him, but as for the girl, leave that to my brother, there's a good fellow. He has the right sort of connections."

"But I'm the police!" stressed Lestrade.

"Yes, precisely my point."

"Just tell me what you want," said Lestrade, a little sullenly.

As briefly he could, Holmes explained all that had occurred up to that point. "And perhaps," he continued, "to add to that, you could point out to Cruft that it's impossible to grow two weeks' of bristle, shave it off, and then regrow it in less than two days, hmm?"

"What do you mean?"

"Oh please, Lestrade – you did notice that the man we saw killing that unfortunate woman was clean-shaven? I, as you can see, I have a good fortnights' growth. It isn't a fake beard, as can be easily proven."

"Do you think that will be enough to convince him?"

"I don't know. For a rational man perhaps, but just how rational is he? Will he see the truth, or what he wants to see?"

"There *is* a lot of pressure from above," scowled Lestrade, "as I have good reason to know."

"Yes. Cruft doesn't seem to have noticed this discrepancy yet – or if he has, he isn't going to let a little thing like the impossible stand in his way of a conviction."

"I'll make him see," determined Lestrade.

"You can try, but if it's all the same to you, I would rather not stake my life on the outcome. You will go to my brother soon?"

"Immediately after I have spoken to Cruft."

Holmes reached out and placed his hand on Lestrade's shoulder. "Thank you, Inspector, for all your help."

Lestrade looked touched. "Yes, well, hmm . . . Can't have innocent men being hanged." Trying not to show his embarrassment, he left Holmes alone with his thoughts.

Things didn't go well with Cruft. Holmes was right – the man wasn't going to let a little thing like logic get in his way. It was now even more imperative that he see Mycroft Holmes as soon as possible. Watson would have to wait still further to hear news of his friend.

Chapter XVI

Edward crept silently through the house. Three of his men were stationed outside. However, they would be of no use to him alone in here. He had already dispatched the only sentinel patrolling outside as he'd approached the rear door. His instructions were clear: Remove the girl to safety, engaging as few as possible to that end. Take no other action. Although there had been no time for the usual surveillance, he was confident that the girl hadn't been moved, and he could make an educated guess as to which part of the house she was being kept. The hall clock struck the half-hour chime after three in the morning as he silently climbed the stairs to the second story. He knew he had found the room he sought, for not only was there a guard outside the door, but that guard was napping in his chair – the usual overconfidence of those who feel superior to others, he smiled inwardly.

They obviously saw this girl as no threat and deemed that Sherlock Holmes had been neutralised. They didn't appreciate Mycroft Holmes's power or determination when his family was threatened.

Edward silently climbed the last stair and swiftly circled behind the gently snoring man. Without hesitation he gave him a precision blow to the back of the head, catching the man as he fell to ensure no sound was heard. Opening the door just as silently, he found his quarry sitting by the window, staring vacantly out at the darkness. He was in the room and had closed the door before she had become aware of him.

"Please don't make any sound if you value your life," he urged quietly. "I'm here to take you to safety." Not one to mince words, he strode over to the window and gently pulled her up by her arm, placing a finger to her lips as he did so.

"There is no time to waste," he reassured her. "I come from Mr. Holmes."

"You come from Mr. Holmes?"

"Yes."

"Which one?"

"Does it matter? I need you to be silent, agile, and obedient. Can you manage that?" This was all stated in an unemotional and matter of fact voice.

Kathleen looked at him in no little astonishment.

"Both our lives depend on it," he continued softly.

Kathleen nodded

"Excellent. Follow me."

Still frightened and apprehensive, Kathleen nevertheless obediently stood and followed, for what else could she do. If he spoke the truth, then she was saved. If not, then she knew that there was nothing she could do anyway.

She looked down apprehensively at the unconscious body of her guard as they passed out of her prison door. As silently as he had entered, Edward retraced his steps with the girl in tow. As they made their way towards the exit as quietly as was humanly possible, Edward suddenly held up his hand in a warning gesture. Kathleen froze on the spot. She could hear someone coming up the staircase. Edward ushered her into the shadows and took up a place in a doorway near the top of the stairs. Kathleen held her breath. She could barely bring herself to look, but was strangely transfixed.

As the man came into view at the top of the stairs, he must have spotted her, as he made a sudden move towards her. He didn't notice Mycroft's man come up from behind and strike a savage blow that sent him down, unconscious, to join his fellows. As the man fell, Edward covered his mouth with one hand and caught him with the other, gently lowering him in one fluid motion. To her credit, Kathleen made no sound nor shied away. She stayed close and did as she was told. She couldn't help a glance at this second very still form on the floor as they passed. She was grateful this man was obviously her friend and not her foe, for she now knew she would otherwise have been doomed.

Without further incident they were soon safely in the street. The instant they set foot out of the house, a four-wheeler approached from the other side of the road and its door was flung open. Edward ushered his prize in and they were away. All of this had taken less than ten minutes. He looked back in time to see the Horse Guards storm the house.

Mr. Mycroft Holmes sat in his most comfortable chair, pondering. The entire rescue operation should take less than twenty minutes, and if all went smoothly the rest would be in custody within another half-an-hour after that.

Because of Colonel Guthrie's wisdom in seeking out his brother and then paying the ultimate price, Mycroft now had the tools he needed to push into areas where he wouldn't normally have been able to penetrate. He had been able to put together the trail that would convict Major-General Rutledge and the Quartermaster, and if they were quick about it, those in India and Africa also. It would take time for news of the arrest of Rutledge to reach those parts, and with luck they could round up the entire outfit. With still a little more luck, they would find the real murderer in the house – or possibly in the grounds – perhaps literally.

Mycroft steepled his fingers together, lost in his thoughts, not realising just how much he resembled his younger sibling in that moment.

160

Chapter XVII

"Lestrade has told me what he saw. It's hard to believe, yet less difficult than believing you are a murderer. Of course, I never would have accepted such a thing."

"Thank you, Watson." Holmes smiled a little, thinking of how close it had come to that actually being tested. He then abruptly returned to the more familiar unemotional expression to which Watson was so accustomed.

Watson sat on the bunk next to Holmes. Lestrade had taken him down personally to see his friend. If Cruft found them there, then all Hell would break loose, but Lestrade was reaching the point where he didn't care anymore. The man was being obstructive and vindictive, and frankly he just didn't like him. Still, he knew which side his superiors would come down on. "I'm sorry to hurry you, gentlemen, but I need to get the Doctor out of here before Cruft finds us.

"Too late." The man himself now stood by the door. "Just what the blazes is going on here?" Before the inspector could open his mouth, Cruft continued. "Never mind trying to explain, Lestrade. I don't want to hear it. Just get out and take your friend with you."

Watson was about to protest, but both Holmes and Lestrade motioned that he should do as he was told. Before either could reach the door, however, Osbourne arrived carrying a basin, soap, and a razor, closely followed by two burly officers.

"Just what is going on here?" This time it was Lestrade making indignant demands.

"None of your business."

"You can't change the truth by trying to pretend it isn't there! There are witnesses to this and to Holmes's innocence. Remember, I was there that night – "

"We only have your word for that," interjected Cruft, rudely.

"You little – ! I have told you what really happened, yet here you are prepared to pervert justice because it doesn't agree with your version of events." Lestrade could barely contain his rage. "Frankly, I've had just about had enough of you." Holmes and Watson looked at each other, but otherwise did nothing to interfere.

"Get out, Lestrade, before I have you thrown out!" Their raised voices could now be heard quite clearly halfway through the building.

"You touch his beard and I'll see *you* in prison, Cruft, and that's a promise! You know deep down you've got the wrong man and you can't admit it." Lestrade was in his stride now. Weeks of frustration bubbled out of him. "It proves what we've been trying to tell you: Holmes didn't kill

161

those women, another man did. One who looks just like him, but didn't think to grow a beard when he carried out those murders. Don't you see your playing right into their hands?" Holmes was touched by Lestrade's loyalty.

"I won't tell you again, Lestrade: *Get out!*"

"No, Cruft. You touch one hair and I'll have *you!*" Things looked set to get physical when –

"Gentlemen!" they all turned as one to see the Commissioner of Police standing just outside the doorway.

"Sir – ?"

"You can't let this – !"

"*Quiet!*" The Commissioner didn't like having to raise his voice. However, sometimes there was just no other way.

Silence fell as he looked sternly from one to the other. He noted that Sherlock Holmes stood calmly and quietly – perhaps even a little expectantly. Was that a touch of hope in his eyes. Watson looked worried and Cruft and Lestrade both looked fit to burst.

"I have just been paid a visit by the Minister of Defence, no less. I won't bore you with the details," the Commissioner said with no little sarcasm, though he himself hadn't been bored. He had been torn off a strip by the Minister and wasn't about to let that be known about the place. "It seems that Mr. Sherlock Holmes is indeed innocent of all charges. The guilty party has been found – dead as it happens."

"That's convenient," interrupted Cruft.

The Commissioner continued as if he hadn't spoken, though he gave Cruft a distasteful look. "However, those who are left alive are being delivered here forthwith, to be charged with not only murder but treason." He looked gravely at Cruft. "I hope you have a very good explanation for what's going on here, Inspector. I will see you in my office in fifteen minutes."

Cruft, red in the face, turned on his heels and stalked out of sight.

Before there could be an outburst from anyone, the Commissioner rounded on Lestrade. "I want you back in charge, Lestrade. Release Mr. Holmes and go and interview your prisoners as soon as they arrive. Is that clear?"

A stunned Lestrade could only manage to blurt out, "Yes sir!" before the Commissioner nodded then turned and left with a much dignity as he could muster.

A further stunned silence followed for some moments until Watson burst forth, "Thank God!" Grasping Holmes by the hand, he shook it furiously. "Let's get out of this place."

"Yes, Mr. Holmes," joined in Lestrade. "Congratulations. I'll have you out of here in an instant."

"I can honestly say I'm more than a little relieved. It would appear my brother has surpassed himself."

"Let's get you home. After a good meal and a hot bath, you won't know yourself." Watson ushered Holmes out of the cell as if he were dealing with one of his patients.

Chapter XVIII

"My dear little brother, how are you faring after your ordeal?" Mycroft sank down gratefully into the sofa at 221b. After Watson had supplied Mycroft with brandy and a cigar, he too sat heavily in his armchair by the fire, looking expectantly at his friend.

Sherlock Holmes, savouring his cigar, smiled appreciatively at his sibling. "Thanks to you, I am alive and well. If not for you, I cannot but feel the shadow of the gallows over me."

"Think nothing of it." Mycroft smiled wryly.

"Tell me, Mycroft: How goes your investigation? Will you reach a successful outcome in all areas, do you suppose?"

"Some aspects will remain unresolved, I fear. As you now know, Rutledge died whilst resisting arrest, and so did several of his accomplices, including your *doppelgänger*. Unfortunately, this makes identifying him problematic. We may never know exactly where this man came from."

"An intriguing mystery to be sure. Is there something you aren't telling me? Is there some dark secret in the family that has been kept from me?" Holmes eyes twinkled with mischief.

"There is nothing to my knowledge about any long lost-relative," Mycroft replied in a completely unflappable manner, "certainly no one who would be able to account for our murderous friend. Most likely he came from somewhere in India or Africa. Hence, we had never laid eyes on him before now"

"It may well remain a mystery then."

"I fear so."

Watson interjected. "I've heard that from time to time nature does throw up these little surprises. The Major-General may have simply taken advantage of one such – had him up his sleeve as it were . . . just in case he was ever needed. I mean, if you are criminally inclined, having your very own Sherlock Holmes waiting in the wings could be very useful. And so it proved."

"As you say," concluded Mycroft. "Still, we will never know for certain."

A ring of the downstairs bell penetrated the air, and then the unmistakable sounds of Lestrade greeting Mrs. Hudson echoed up from below. Sherlock Holmes rose swiftly and bellowed, "Come up and join us in brandy and cigars, Inspector."

"I'll be right there," came the enthusiastic reply.

After making himself comfortable, Lestrade announced, "I've just heard that Cruft has been sent packing back where he came from, and if you ask me, he's lucky not to be charged."

"Perhaps the Commissioner couldn't abide any more upheavals," interjected Mycroft. "Let us not forget that he knew Major-General Rutledge personally."

"Yes," said Watson dubiously. "Are we certain he had nothing to do with the gun running or the murders?

"Quite sure," replied Mycroft. "No one was more mortified to find out the truth. It took hard evidence to convince him such as documents in his friend's own hand and so on. I think the shame will encourage an early retirement."

They all fell silent as they each contemplated their own thoughts on the affair.

Sherlock Holmes broke the silence. "Mycroft, I must also thank you for taking care of that other matter."

"What other matter?" enquired Watson.

"Finding a suitable place for Miss Curran," interjected Mycroft. "A charming family I know in Scotland, with two delightful children in need of a governess. She should do well for herself. A brave and intelligent female, Sherlock." He looked significantly at his brother.

"Yes," he agreed stony faced, but would say no more.

Mycroft laughed, knowing he would get no further response from his brother. Sherlock would never admit to any sentimental feelings.

Sherlock Holmes knocked softly on the door. After a short time it opened, revealing a radiant Kathleen.

"Mr. Holmes!" she cried with delight. "I'm so glad to see you! Are all right?"

"Yes, I am, and in no small part thanks to you." He smiled with genuine pleasure at seeing her again. "You look very well yourself. I see my brother was able to find you some adequate lodgings."

"I can't thank you both enough." She cast her eyes down shyly. "I don't think I could have faced . . . well, you know."

"Don't think about that, Kathleen," Holmes couldn't bear the thought of her having to go back on the street either. "I understand the position my brother has found you as a governess is with a good family."

"Yes," she smiled enthusiastically, but before she could begin a tirade of gratitude Holmes interrupted.

"It is no more than your due. You saved my life, after all. In any event, it was through no fault of your own that circumstances forced you into that plight. Indeed, you deserve much better than *we* can offer you, but it is better than the alternative, at least." There was a brief awkward moment of silence.

"Have a long and happy life, Kathleen. May things turn out greener and brighter for you in the future." As he turned to leave, she reached out and touched his sleeve.

"I enjoyed our time together, even when I was scared. I . . . I . . . well I hope things go well for you also, Mr. Sherlock Holmes."

"Goodbye, Kathleen."

"Goodbye."

Holmes turned and walked away without looking back. Kathleen gazed after him for some time. She had grown fond of him in the short time that she'd known him, but she knew he wasn't the sort of man to show it if he had felt anything for her. Their worlds were too far apart, and she wasn't certain she would care to live in his world anyway. No, she was very happy with the way things had transpired. She was going to a good job and security. If the Holmes brothers said the Harris family were good people, then she was confident this would be true.

At the end of the street Holmes turned and looked back at Kathleen's lodging house. A wistful smile played momentarily on his lips. He turned away and breathed in deeply the London air, filled with the smells and sounds of more than five-million people, all jostling together in the great city. Very soon he knew there would be a new puzzle that would require his unique skills to solve. He smiled happily as he walked briskly towards Baker Street . . . .

NOTES

1. Horse Guards: The Queen's personal guard.
2. Fish and chips as we know it today was well underway in London by the late 1800's, being recognisable as early as 1860. *www.niagara.co.uk/fish_and_chips*
3. The first record of Guinness being drunk in London is 1794
4. The Major-General was a close friend to the Commissioner, but the Commissioner was not consciously involved – though he was most likely the Major-General's source of inside information.

The Adventure of the
Murderous Gentleman
by Arthur Hall

During the years of my long association with my friend Mr. Sherlock Holmes, it was inevitable that we should meet individuals of strange, perhaps improbable, character. After a while it became almost normal to encounter, as I assisted him in some of his most unusual and bizarre cases, men who would stop at nothing to achieve their aims, whether the means to do so was by robbery, murder, or other heinous acts. Apart from these, there was still another variety of criminal, though thankfully less common than the usual – I refer to those who kill their fellows for pleasure, to whom profit from their actions is a secondary attraction. Regarding these, one instance springs instantly to mind and, since my friend has recently permitted it, I will now set it onto paper so that the public will at last be aware of what took place.

I recall that the affair began one fine early summer morning when Holmes and I returned to our Baker Street lodgings after an invigorating walk in Hyde Park. We entered the premises to be immediately confronted by Mrs. Hudson, our landlady, who informed us that a client had called during our absence and now awaited us in our sitting room.

Holmes preceded me on the stairs and we entered to find a clean-shaven gentleman of about fifty years of age, looking most unhappy as he sat stiffly in the basket chair. At the sight of us, he immediately rose to his feet.

"Mr. Holmes, Doctor Watson." He approached, extending his hand. "I have read of you both in the dailies. I do hope that I have acted correctly in coming here."

"That," my friend replied, "depends on your reason for seeking a consultation. Pray resume your seat and tell us what it is that's causing your evident distress."

"I hadn't realized that it was so obvious."

"I have seen despair written on many faces during my career as a consulting detective, and have long learned to recognise it. Hopefully we may be able to remedy your situation. Shall I call for tea?"

"Thank you, no. Your landlady has already made that kind offer."

"Then let us proceed. Let me assure you that you can rely on our absolute discretion, and request that you endeavour to omit not even the smallest detail."

When we were settled, our client put his head in his hands briefly, again demonstrating his troubled state of mind. After a moment he looked at us with grieving eyes that seemed to me to contain also a hint of outrage, or anger.

"My name is Mr. Chesney Lifford," he began. "You have probably already deduced from my accent that I'm from the north of the country. After selling the tannery which had been in my family for generations, I moved to the capital six months ago. Shortly after, I met a woman at a garden party. She was in her early twenties and appeared to find me interesting. Old fool that I am, I grew to care for her and we married not long after. Now I see that the only attraction on her part was financial."

"That is a familiar story," I commented, "and I'm truly sorry to hear that such an experience has befallen you."

Holmes's expression was now one of disinterest. "Are you certain, Mr. Lifford, that you are seeking solace or assistance in the right place? I don't see how, as no crime has been committed, that we can be of help."

"Please, there is more." Our client shook his head hopelessly. "I was struggling to accept that my wife had never loved me, and resolved yesterday morning to take a long walk to clear my mind of some of the anxiety that I felt. On returning home to Marylebone, I encountered a fellow of extraordinary proportions awaiting me outside my house. I knew that Jeanette, my wife, would have left on her unexplained daily absence, and so the caller had received no attention. I enquired as to the reason for his visit, and he replied that it was a matter of life and death. Although I had no inkling of his meaning, my curiosity was aroused and I invited him in. When we were seated in my drawing room and I had poured port for both of us, I asked him to explain. It is his reply, delivered in such a calm and matter-of-fact manner, that shook me to the very core. Even now, I cannot countenance it."

We leaned forward in our chairs, so that none of our client's painfully whispered words should escape us.

"Pray elaborate," Holmes said.

Mr. Lifford hesitated, clearly collecting himself with difficulty. "This man introduced himself as Mr. Harland Guild. He told me, quite without embarrassment, that his business was removing obstacles from the lives of those affected by circumstance. I found this puzzling, and as to what such a person would want with me I couldn't imagine, but he quickly enlightened me. He claimed that my wife had hired him to, as he put it, 'dispose' of me. They had come to an agreement where she would pay him

168

the sum of one-hundred pounds, upon inheriting my estate. My first thought was that this was some sort of jest, but his expression, particularly his eyes, assured me otherwise. Also, although he displayed the manners of a gentleman, there was something insensitive about his speech. I was horrified and dumbfounded."

"If this was the case," I remarked, "then surely this man was working against himself by warning you of his intentions."

"Oh no, sir, the very opposite. You see, he went on to explain that his visit was to offer me a proposition. It was that, for twice the sum my wife had offered, he would turn his attentions to her and leave me in safety."

"He was willing to make your wife the victim, even though she had hired him?" Holmes queried with some astonishment.

"That is what he suggested. He explained that there is no personal element in his work, which he undertakes for his own pleasure and profit."

"The notion is outrageous, from beginning to end," I retorted.

"This man has come to my notice before, although he has never crossed my path." Holmes recalled. "Scotland Yard has yet to prove anything against him. Several unexplained murders that could be laid at his door come to mind."

"Something that he mentioned might explain the difficulties of the official force," Mr. Lifford suggested. "He assured me that my wife's demise would in no way reflect upon me, since he took pride in ensuring that each death had the appearance of an accident."

"Have you, in fact, notified Scotland Yard of these circumstances?"

"I have not. What could they do that they haven't already done, since no crime has been committed?"

Holmes nodded. "Indeed, I could well imagine Lestrade or Gregson using those very words in response to your assertions."

"How did you answer Mr. Guild's proposition?" I asked our client.

"I was so taken aback by his audacity and the nature of his suggestion that I found myself speechless. After a few minutes, however, though still dismayed, I asked him to leave my house at once. He appeared oblivious to my disgust and anger, asking me if I was certain that my decision was the correct one. I fear that I was less-than-polite to him then, but he merely replied that we would meet again."

As he often did, Holmes lapsed into a thoughtful silence. After a few moments our client began to look uncomfortable, but I reassured him with a gesture. A heavy cart of some sort rumbled along Baker Street, the sound reaching us through the half-open window as my friend opened his eyes and addressed Mr. Lifford.

"I will look into your case," he said. "Kindly furnish Doctor Watson with any further details that you consider to be helpful. I sympathise with you regarding your marital difficulties, but with those we cannot be of assistance. The problem of Mr. Guild, however, is quite another matter."

I retrieved my notebook and committed to paper all that Mr. Lifford was able to add. As I completed my task, Holmes again addressed our client.

"It is of paramount importance that you now follow my instructions exactly. Watson and I will accompany you to your home, where you will gather enough clothing and personal items to sustain you for a sea voyage of several weeks. From there, we will hire a carriage to convey us to Victoria Dock, where a journey will be arranged for you at one of the shipping offices. No, do not raise objections, Mr. Lifford, but keep in mind that you are being pursued by one who is a merciless and experienced killer. By removing yourself from the capital, you are ensuring your safety and also simplifying my investigation. As a further precaution, it may be as well to adopt a different name for the duration of your stay in the country of your destination."

"Very well, Mr. Holmes. I am in your hands."

"Excellent." Holmes got to his feet and we retrieved our hats and coats. "Let us depart at once."

Transportation was secured immediately, and we left Baker Street with my friend alert at all times for observers or pursuers. We proceeded as Holmes had suggested, until we finally bade Mr. Lifford farewell as he boarded the *S.S. Saturnalia* bound for Copenhagen.

"Hopefully," Holmes said then, "Mr. Lifford is now beyond the reach of Mr. Guild until he returns, by which time I have every expectation that this affair will be concluded. But for now, Watson, we will return to Baker Street, since I perceive that you are already displaying a need of sustenance."

It didn't surprise me that he was silent throughout our meal, for it was his custom to consider deeply the implications of a forthcoming case. Mrs. Hudson had cleared away everything but the coffee cups before he spoke again.

"I'll endeavour to gather enough evidence to present to Scotland Yard. It would be as well I think, to place Mr. Guild in Newgate for the rest of his life, even if he escapes the hangman."

"Undoubtedly. Did you not say that you'd encountered this man before now?"

"Not directly. I'll tell you that tale at a later date." He removed his napkin and rose. "This afternoon I must devote to discovering more about him and perhaps making a few arrangements. No, I'll not require your company, Watson, but I would be obliged if you would mention to Mrs. Hudson that I may be late for dinner."

With that he put on his hat and coat and left abruptly. As always on such occasions, I felt somewhat put out at being excluded, but I told myself that by now I should have recognised his actions as one of his eccentricities. I made myself comfortable in my armchair with the mid-day edition of *The London Post* and several accumulated medical journals near at hand.

As it happened, Holmes returned not long after our usual mealtime. We sat down at the table at once, I brimming with curiosity, and our landlady served a sizeable portion of roast goose. He ate with more enthusiasm than was usual for him, but his expression told me that his thoughts were far away. When we had adjourned to our armchairs, I could contain myself no longer.

"How did you fare this afternoon? As you have no look of despondency about you, I feel safe in assuming that you achieved some success."

He reached for the Persian slipper and began to fill his old briar. "I think it safe to say that my immediate preparations are complete. On leaving here I sought out the Irregulars and bestowed upon them the task of spreading throughout London that a certain Mr. Verdon Dean, of Hackney, has need of the services of someone skilled in the removal of, shall we say, persons who represent an inconvenience to others, and requested that they act as go-betweens. After that, I arranged for temporary accommodation in rooms in Hackney and Limehouse. If we're fortunate, we may hear something this evening or tomorrow morning – but we must be patient." His expression changed and he suddenly sat up straight. "But I'm assuming that you wish to be involved. Forgive me for not asking your permission to include you."

I smiled. "As always, I am with you."

We were well into an evening of reading and lively discussion when the doorbell rang. Holmes put down his glass of port and listened intently as our landlady answered.

"I heard no carriage arrive, so it's unlikely to be a new client," he concluded, "and by the tone of Mrs. Hudson's voice, I suspect that our caller is a messenger from the Irregulars. I'm surprised at the speed of their accomplishment, and of the quickness of Mr. Guild's response."

"As Mr. Lifford is now unavailable to him, perhaps he's in need of work."

"Perhaps. I'll go to save the young man from some of the scolding that he is certainly enduring."

171

With that he leapt from his chair and descended the stairs quickly. I reflected that the gang of street Arabs to which the messenger belonged had been invaluable to Holmes over the years. He often mentioned that their presence went unnoticed in the streets of the capital, enabling them to see and hear much that was barred to others. I heard our landlady's high-pitched voice cease abruptly, discontinuing her unfavourable appraisal of our caller as my friend dismissed her kindly. From then on the conversation was conducted in hushed sentences until the lad departed and the door closed.

"It went well," Holmes told me as he resumed his seat. "Mr. Harland Guild is apparently well-known as a kill-man for hire among the London underworld. Wiggins sent that young fellow Jonah to tell me that our adversary is available, and I've replied that Mr. Verdon Dean will meet him at the Hackney address tomorrow morning at ten. Suitably disguised, we will present ourselves as Dean and his partner in a building enterprise."

The following morning, our appearances were indeed altered considerably. By the time we procured a hansom outside our lodgings, Holmes now had grey hair and a drooping grey moustache, while my face was reddened and my acquired beard black and full. It was without surprise that I had seen that our reflections bore no resemblance to our usual selves, for I had witnessed my friend's skill with theatrical makeup on many previous occasions.

We arrived at a rather nondescript street in Hackney, well before the appointed time. The house that Holmes led me to was old but well preserved, and had apparently been the home of someone quite wealthy until recently. After we had settled ourselves in a well-decorated living room, occupying stiff-backed chairs around a polished oval table, he proceeded to reiterate his instructions regarding the part I was to play. This continued for a while, but was suddenly interrupted by a discreet knocking of the street door.

"If you would be so good, Watson."

I made my way along the short corridor and opened the front door. A man of enormous size, his morning suit immaculate, stood smiling before me. I noted his innocent expression and that he used a perfumed oil on his unruly dark hair.

"Mr. Verdon Dean?" He enquired in a pleasant and educated voice. "I received a message that you wished me to call. I am Mr. Harland Guild."

"And I am Mr. Dean's partner in our venture," I replied. "My name is Fergus Greystone. Mr. Dean awaits us within."

We joined Holmes and polite introductions were made, although there was no shaking of hands, before we seated ourselves. After a few minutes of pleasant but pointless general discussion, during which our

172

visitor did indeed display the manners of a gentleman, he paused to favour us with a charming smile.

"So, gentlemen, you are presumably aware of my profession or you wouldn't have summoned me. You have but to state your difficulty for me to devise a way to remove it."

"The matter concerns a miser called Mr. Benjamin Kyte," Holmes said in a hesitant voice that was quite unlike his own. "We have offered him a fair price for his hovel in Limehouse but he refuses to sell. Mr. Greystone and myself have purchased every other habitation in Calders Row to fulfil a contract to demolish and renew the entire thoroughfare, but with the present state of things we cannot proceed. There is a considerable sum involved in this, and we stand to lose much by the delay."

"So I would imagine. Have you ascertained that the removal of this man would leave the way clear for the progress of your venture?"

"We have made enquiries and come to an arrangement with the beneficiaries of Mr. Kyte's will," said I. "He doesn't seem to be well thought of, even among his own people."

Mr. Guild nodded. "I have encountered many such. For a consideration of one-hundred-and-fifty pounds, I have no doubt that this problem could be solved quite soon."

"Very well," Holmes agreed, "but there must be no question of any connection to Mr. Greystone or myself."

"Good Heavens, sir!" Mr. Guild's smile had become furtive, and I fancied that I saw a strange light in his eyes. "I am no amateur. My skill is considerable, and I believe that a list of my successes over at least the past ten years would surprise you. You need have no concerns on that score."

"But how to avoid the attentions of Scotland Yard? I understand that some of their detectives are most proficient where murder is involved."

"We aren't speaking of murder, but of accidents. When a body is found that has obviously suffered an accident, there is no investigation because there is no crime. The fact that I am walking the streets of London as a free man after so long testifies to this, does it not?"

Holmes and I glanced at each other, our faces carefully expressionless.

"When could such an event be arranged to take place?" I asked.

Our visitor shrugged his massive shoulders. "As soon as you would like. You have only to instruct me and, of course, to furnish my fee."

"Tomorrow, perhaps?" I suggested.

"There are various other arrangements that I must make," said Holmes, "but they should be completed by then."

"As you wish. At what time of day would be most convenient to you?"

173

"Let us say eleven o'clock"

"Then you have only to supply me with the details and the money, and you can consider our arrangement fulfilled after precisely that time."

Holmes produced a wad of banknotes and counted off the specified sum. I gave Mr. Guild a slip of paper, written in a much-disguised hand, bearing the address of his victim. We rose to our feet as one.

"Should it have crossed your minds that I might abscond with your money, on that also you need have no concern. Such a dishonest act would cause my reputation irreparable damage in certain quarters, and could even bring about my ruination. That is your guarantee, gentlemen. You may depend upon me."

Holmes gave a little bow of acknowledgement. "Goodbye then, Mr. Guild."

"There is more to discover, I think, about Mr. Guild," Holmes remarked after we had returned to Baker Street and resumed our normal appearances. "I shall endeavour to learn more of the man this afternoon." He saw that I rubbed my irritated face. "Oh, I am sorry about that beard, Watson. You have my word that no further disguise will be necessary for you during the remainder of this affair. What did you make of our gentleman murderer?"

"His movements puzzled me," I remembered. "One shoulder was held lower than the other, and he walked with a pronounced limp, but not consistently. I'm not skilled in the new science of curing disturbed minds, but I would say that he suffers also from some sort of mental derangement. His indifference, delight even, at the prospect of destroying his fellow-man strongly indicates this. His boasts of many victims I find horrifying. In addition, I noticed strange purplish marks in the corners of his eyes and at the tips of his ears."

"Bravo!" Holmes leaned forward in his chair. "Your powers of observation increase still. It is those marks that have today put to rest a question that has been in my mind for a long time. I haven't forgotten that I promised to tell you of my previous knowledge of Mr. Guild." He glanced towards the clock that ticked away on the mantelpiece. "I believe that there is just sufficient time before luncheon."

"You mentioned that you hadn't actually met the fellow," I reminded him.

"Indeed, but you will recall Barker, the private agent who has been of some assistance on occasion. Some years ago he related to me an account which, on hearing Mr. Lifford's description of Mr. Guild, I remembered at once. The tale concerns the one and only time that I have

174

ever had the slightest doubt in my belief of the invalidity of the supernatural."

"Pray elaborate. I am intrigued."

After a moment, Holmes continued. "At that time, the killings of a number of wealthy and notable individuals were the talk of London. Scotland Yard was close to arresting a suspect whose description matched that of Mr. Guild closely, although his name was different. Suddenly the man was reported to have died. It was thought to have been because of a failing heart, and this was confirmed after an examination by a police doctor and another eminent practitioner.

The corpse was set aside for a short while to await any who might claim it, but before long it was found to have disappeared. Until now I agreed with the popular supposition that body-snatchers were responsible, although for a short time murders carried out in an identical fashion continued. What troubled me therefore, was the widespread inability to explain how this man could have risen from the dead to continue his crimes, when he had been twice certified as deceased. Naturally, there were rumours of witchcraft and the voodoo cults of Africa and the Colonies and I confess, in the absence of a rational explanation, of allowing myself to doubt my conviction that these and all other supernatural practices are little more than fairy stories."

"Mr. Guild, apparently, didn't take the trouble to disguise his crimes as accidents in those days."

"No, indeed. As far as I am aware, nothing more was heard from him until he approached Mr. Lifford. Of course, there could be any number of other instances as yet undiscovered."

"What then of today? You implied that the spots on Mr. Guild's ears and near his eyes were significant."

Holmes nodded. "Since those times I have, as you know, conducted much research on a variety of subjects that could conceivably assist my work. Quite recently I read an account by an explorer who had witnessed a remarkable demonstration by a shaman in the jungles of South America. The man was feared among his tribe for his ability to induce apparent death to his chosen subjects, followed by their resurrection some time afterwards. The connection here, Watson, is that, if the traveller is to believed, the resurrected men and women, without exception, were permanently marked by purplish blotches such as we have seen today."

"So you believe that the drug, or whatever it may have been, used by the shaman was known to Mr. Guild some years previously?"

"I'm satisfied that it was, although how he came by it we may never discover. I was somewhat relieved to have my disbelief in all things mystical vindicated."

Before I could reply further, Mrs. Hudson served our meal. After we had eaten, and with an apology, Holmes left before I could finish my coffee. He had assured me that he would return in time for dinner, so I resolved to visit several of my patients.

Unexpectedly, my return was delayed. I was eventually able to cause an elderly lady, a patient of long-standing, to understand that the spreading paralysis that she was convinced afflicted her was nothing more than a touch of rheumatism.

Mrs. Hudson was about to serve dinner, a well-filled chicken pie, shortly after my arrival at our lodgings. Holmes faced me across the table with an expression that told me at once that his afternoon had turned out to his satisfaction. As I awaited my dessert, he having refused any, I politely interrupted his discourse on the new science of fingerprinting to enquire as to his success.

"Later, Watson. I see that Mrs. Hudson has put a light to the fire during our absence, which is as well since it had become a little chilly in here. When you've finished your meal, we will repair to our armchairs and indulge ourselves in a glass of brandy. I'll then tell you the essence of what has transpired since luncheon."

When we had taken our seats and Mrs. Hudson had cleared away our plates, Holmes poured from the crystal decanter.

"There is more to Mr. Guild than I had suspected," he began after we'd taken our first sips of the harsh spirit. "On leaving Baker Street, my first destination was a haunt of one of my informers who has spent much of his life on the fringes of the criminal underworld. There I learned much more about our adversary, including the reason for the cessation of his killings from shortly after his 'death' to his approach to Mr. Lifford. You were quite correct in your assumption that his mental state is abnormal, since he is known to have spent some months in an asylum during his younger years. He was apparently able to obtain his release through the bribery of an unworldly but well-meaning uncle. From childhood, Mr. Guild was always of unusually large stature with the temper of an enraged wolf. As he grew he became adept at hiding his true disposition, and took on the veneer of charm that we have seen. Afterwards I consulted several other of my scouts around the capital but, apart from confirmation, discovered nothing more."

"I formed the impression that you had more to tell," I ventured.

"Indeed I have, but it will be more appropriate to disclose it to you in Limehouse tomorrow morning. I visited the house earlier to effect some minor but essential alterations, before dispatching a telegram to an old friend of some years ago. I expect his answer this evening."

176

I knew from long experience that to press him for further information would be futile. Therefore, when he abruptly began to discuss the latest headline emblazoned across the late edition of *The Standard*, I restrained my curiosity with difficulty. The clock showed almost nine-thirty when the doorbell rang. Holmes had left the room before the chimes died away.

Moments later he returned holding a yellow envelope that he had already torn open.

"Is it good news?" I enquired.

"Indeed." A satisfied smile crossed his face. "We can now proceed with confidence. The trap is set."

"Excellent. Tell me, does Mr. Benjamin Kyte fully understand the risk to his safety?"

"Oh he does, Watson, he does."

"But who is he?"

A slow smile crossed his face. "Who else but myself?"

I felt an immediate sense of disgust as the hansom set us down in Calders Row. The terraced houses that lined both sides of the thoroughfare were, without exception, a depressing sight. The doors and window-frames had been starved of paint for many-a-year and the curtains, where any were in evidence, hung in filthy tatters. Birds, I noticed, had nested in some of the chimney-pots and on the roofs where slates had been displaced, while most walls bore cavities where mortar had long since crumbled away.

Holmes had become an aged grey man with a rasping voice and grim countenance, and I marvelled again at his skill at disguise. His thin form was bent and he hobbled uncertainly as we approached the house and he produced a key that opened the door with difficulty, the hinges protesting loudly.

"Welcome to the home of Mr. Benjamin Kyte, Watson," he laughed. "The state of the place is disgusting, but I am supposed to be a miser. I give you my word that we will leave at the earliest moment possible."

We entered a dark and dismal room, heavy with dust and containing nothing but the remains of some furniture. The floor was tiled unevenly, and the windows, one at each end, were smeared to the extent that the light was much affected.

"Holmes, how could you – "

"It was necessary, I assure you." He guided me through the shadows. "Take great care while ascending these stairs. They are criminally dangerous and should have been replaced years ago. Keep to the left, against the wall."

177

We proceeded slowly, and I swear that I felt the entire staircase move beneath us. It was with some relief that I reached the top behind Holmes, who seemed unaffected by the risk to life and limb that we had undoubtedly taken. He opened the door confronting us, but neglected to close it after we had entered. I saw that the room contained nothing but an old table and chairs with a made-up bed against one wall. All appeared considerably cleaner than below, but the light was equally subdued.

"The door to the right, at the far end of the room, leads to a rear entrance," he explained as we stood near the doorway. "It is reached by means of a dark alley that runs behind the building. The door to our left, behind the table and chairs, conceals a large cupboard. I have removed the shelves and provided you with a seat and a spy-hole, so that you can bear witness to the proceedings for the sake of Scotland Yard."

"Holmes, you're exposing yourself to the greatest danger. That man is an experienced killer possessing tremendous strength. I know well your skill at defending yourself, but his extraordinary size is against you. His hands are almost twice the size of yours."

"Indeed, but I have a defence that I haven't disclosed to you." He took something from his pocket. "Here is a police whistle. I want you to use it loudly, the instant Mr. Guild makes any attempt to assault me."

I took it, in disbelief at this ineffectual proposal. "But this won't be heard outside the building, and in any case the street is empty. I've brought my service revolver, and you have my word that I will not hesitate to use it should you be attacked."

"As I undoubtedly will be, since this man has a curious pride in his profession. Promise me, Watson, that you will resort to your firearm only if the action I have recommended proves ineffective."

Reluctantly, I complied.

During the moment of silence that followed I heard movement elsewhere in the house. At first I imagined it to be the sort of sound that is usual in an aged structure, but when it was repeated I turned to Holmes.

"We aren't alone here."

He nodded. "Pay it no attention. Everything is arranged."

"You mentioned, I believe, that there is more about all this that you wish me to know."

"Indeed there is," he inclined his head, "but I hear a heavy rapping on the front door. I will tell you afterwards, but by then much will have become evident to you."

At that he gestured that I should take my place in the cupboard, which I did immediately. I closed the door and sat upon the stool to look through the spy-hole. It gave an adequate view at precisely the correct height, and I had seen that it wasn't visible from outside. In the silence of this place I heard Holmes descending. I could make out his polite greeting of the visitor, and recognised the voice of Mr. Guild. Except for Holmes's caution on the stairs, no more of what was said reached me until they entered the room and sat at the table. Through the spy-hole I could see that Mr. Guild was dressed as immaculately as before but in more sober apparel.

Mr. Guild placed his hat beside him on the table. "As I indicated just now, Mr. Kyte, I am employed by the Northern and Cities Bank. We are currently enjoying a surplus in available funds as a result of several maturing investments, and are seeking to lend a proportion in such ways that will create maximum benefit to the recipients. It has come to our notice that your residence, although most charming, is in need of some repair – "

"This has been so for years," Holmes interrupted in a trembling voice, "but I fear that my meagre finances wouldn't support such a venture. For that reason, I have taken to using this room only. It isn't ideal, but one becomes accustomed to one's limitations. A man must cut his cloth according to his pocket."

"That is my point exactly. I have here some explanatory notes that will reveal to you the most attractive rates of interest that would be applicable to a loan from us that would enable you to restore your home to its former glory. Pray read them now, and tell me of your conclusion."

Holmes fumbled in his waistcoat pocket and produced a set of *pince-nez*, which he held to his face. He lowered his head until it was almost touching the table, in order that he could begin his inspection. With his attention diverted, he couldn't see the danger. Mr. Guild had poised a giant hand behind his neck, ready to deliver a blow with the force of a sledgehammer. As I watched, a cruel expression, that of a wild beast, came into his face, and his eyes shone with a curious indifference. That Holmes was seconds away from death I had no doubt, and my first instinct was to reach for my service weapon. Then I remembered my promise to him and blew the whistle he had given me with all my might, my heart sinking with the futility of the gesture. The shrill sound was loud in the enclosed space and I had no faith in it, but then the door at the far end of the room, that which Holmes had explained as leading to a rear entrance, was flung open and I was astounded by what was revealed.

A spotted feline beast, like the leopards I had seen on the Asian continent, slowly entered the room. It stood hesitant, as if taking stock of the situation or choosing its prey. Its soulless eyes were fixed on Holmes and Mr. Guild, as it lowered its body as if to spring.

Such was the shock that I experienced that my attention had been distracted from both men. Now I saw to my astonishment that Holmes

179

displayed no fear but had become perfectly still. Mr. Guild also had ceased in his intention, staring at the animal with bulging eyes and his mouth open in a silent scream. His arm dropped and he placed a hand on the table to force himself to his feet, his glance fixed as if hypnotised. For a moment he stood statue-still, before giving voice to a hideous cry of terror and dashing abruptly through the open door.

The cat followed him with its eyes, and then lay down to lick its paws. A tremendous crash which shook the building told me that Mr. Guild had forgotten the instability of the staircase to his cost. A cloud of dust entered the room, to be curtailed immediately as Holmes rose and closed the door. I got to my feet and emerged from the cupboard, at the same moment that a man who was vaguely familiar to me appeared behind the animal. He was red-faced, with a mop of black hair and a long, untrimmed moustache. Other than the certainty that this wasn't our first meeting, I could recall nothing of him.

Holmes produced a cloth and wiped make-up from his face. The newcomer attached a leash to a collar around the neck of the beast, stroked its head affectionately, and spoke soothingly in a thickly-accented whisper.

"Good girl, Mabel. Just lie there for a minute or two." He then addressed me. "Don't be afraid, sir. I've had her since she was a cub. She's never attacked a living soul."

Nevertheless, I ventured no nearer until Holmes made the introduction.

"Watson, you may recall Mr. Zamil, who we met during that affair in Warwickshire involving Lady Heminworth."

The memory came flooding back. "The circus master! Of course."

We shook hands.

"I am retired from the ring now, sir, but I couldn't leave behind some of my pets." Mr. Zamil smiled proudly. "The circus goes on forever, but I am settled happily in Surrey."

"Allow me to wish you a long and contented respite."

He bowed in acknowledgement and turned to Holmes.

My friend, who had stood with his back to the door, gave him a bulging envelope.

"As agreed, Mr. Zamil. You will recall my assurance that you have committed no crime. Today you have served justice well, but I suggest that you don't delay in forgetting the incident."

"It shall be as you say, sir. I ask no questions. Goodbye, gentlemen." With that he left us, the feline trotting before him. It occurred to me to wonder how he proposed to return to his home.

As soon as we heard the outer door close, we emerged onto the landing. Dust swirled before us, but it had begun to settle. After a short while we could see that a sizeable portion of the balustrading was missing, and much of the staircase had become a gaping hole. Below, on the tiled floor of the living room, lay the body of Mr. Guild in a spreading pool of blood. I flinched as I saw that his fall had impaled him upon one of the broken stair-posts, but Holmes was unaffected by the scene.

"It could be thought of as fitting, I think, that his death should appear as accidental," he said as we returned to the room. "Nevertheless, I shall have to see Lestrade a little later, with some sort of explanation."

"You had indicated that our intention was to gain evidence against Mr. Guild, and then inform Scotland Yard."

"Indeed, but I have observed before now that such situations often find their own conclusions."

"I would be grateful if you would explain the outcome of all this to me."

He scrubbed at his face, removing the last of his disguise. "Oh, it is all quite simple. During my foray of yesterday, I was able to discover more of Mr. Guild than I have so far disclosed to you. To begin with, the interval between shortly after his supposed demise and his approach to Mr. Lifford is explained by a visit to India. Whether this was to avoid further pursuit by the official force here, I have no means of knowing. From what I've determined, he continued his criminal career there with great enthusiasm, murdering quite a few individuals without paying the price. Another thing that is certain is that he once during that period he ventured into a forest at night and was attacked by a tiger."

"A terrible experience," I remarked. "I'm surprised that he survived."

"Probably he wouldn't have done, but for the intervention of a party of villagers who beat the beast off with sticks. You may have noticed the scars on his hands and neck that testify how close he came to death, as does his peculiar way of carrying himself. He eventually recovered, but the incident caused him to develop *ailurophobia* which, as you may know, is a morbid fear of felines.

Every man has his Achilles Heel, and on becoming aware of these facts I knew that, despite our adversary's physical advantages, I now had a way to defeat him. I was at a loss to find a way to gain the temporary use of a big cat – surely no zoo or similar establishment would allow it – and then Mr. Zamil came to mind. He had no tiger, as I had hoped, but his pet cheetah filled the role admirably. His answer to my telegram assured me that the beast had been his pet from birth and had no history of attack. This having been said, Watson, I confess to sharing your anxiety during its presence and your relief at its departure."

181

I heard him out, appalled. "But there was so much that could have altered the result of your plan. What if Mr. Guild had responded differently?"

"From the description that I received, I was fairly certain of my ground. Had things turned out otherwise, I had a firearm concealed upon me. But my best line of defence was yourself and your readiness to intervene on my behalf." He glanced around quickly. "There's nothing more to be done here. We can leave by the rear entrance, and then I suppose we must call at Scotland Yard on our way back to Baker Street. But afterwards, I would be delighted if you would join me in sampling a rare cognac. It was a present from a grateful client and I have yet to open it."

The Puzzle Master
by William Todd

Whenever Sherlock Holmes returns from a day out, I am frequently amazed at what the man brings back from his ambles. There are times he is like a stray dog showing up at the heels of a potential master, wishing to please him with a stick or a random bit of paper clutched within its jaws, tail wagging diligently for acclamation. In my friend's case, the stick might be a cryptic cipher given to him by Lestrade that only he can break – the random bit of paper, a letter from some far-flung nobility wishing to untie themselves from problematic marriages. Imagine my surprise when Sherlock Holmes returned one pleasant April evening with a dead man.

Holmes and I had been invited to the Diogenes Club by his brother, Mycroft. I declined the offer, for, in my opinion, the place has a stodgy gloom, absent of any conversation in all but The Stranger's Room. I elected instead to stay in and read up on some long-neglected medical journals. Holmes, however, never passing up a chance to match wits with Mycroft, or just bathe in the club's misanthropy, hastened a cab as soon as the invitation was received.

It was half-past-seven as I sat down to a cold ham sandwich and tea that Mrs. Hudson had prepared while I continued pouring over my journals when a breathless Holmes plunged through the door of our flat. He was ashen-faced, yet held a certain glint in his eye. "Watson, your services are needed in the cab outside. Please grab your medical bag, *post haste!*"

With that exclamation, he disappeared from the room, bounding back down the stairs.

I quickly grabbed my bag and was on the heels of my friend, taking the steps two at a time.

I rushed out the front door of our flat, my bag at the ready. Holmes had managed, with no slight difficulty, to retrieve a lethargic gentleman from the hansom parked at the kerb. As soon as he had barely put both feet upon the walkway, the man collapsed to the ground.

I rushed to his side and performed a quick assessment. He was thickly built but not obese, perhaps approaching forty years, clean-shaven, with thick black hair streaked with grey at the temples. He was dressed for dinner out, and his homburg still lay upon the hansom seat.

"Sir? Sir!" I shouted as I shook the man with no response. I then hastily felt for a pulse with a similar negative result. Lifting the man's eyelids, I next examined him for signs of life. There were none.

I sighed. "This man needs more than me now," said I to Holmes. A slight odour suddenly wafted up from the man's clothing. "What is that I smell? Wet hay?"

My friend helped me hastily regain my feet. "What would you say was his cause of death?" he then asked in a tone that told me I was being put to a test.

I looked the man over, checking his wrists, his hands, and fingernails, his neck under his collar – any outward clue that might help me with my diagnosis. Once complete, I said, "Based on a cursory examination, without the aid of a *post mortem* or patient history, I would suggest his grey colour and *petechiae*, those little hemorrhages in the whites of his eyes – there, along with blue nailbeds – reveal death came by anoxia. His lungs stopped working properly, and he was starved of oxygen. That is typical in strangulation, which I don't suspect here. There are no marks on his neck. I've seen similar symptoms in mine deaths, but that is obviously out of the question in the middle of London, so I would suggest this man suffered from a severe cardiac defect that prevented the proper exchange of oxygen in his lungs. The man suffocated to death from a heart deficiency. That would be my assessment."

"Capital, Watson, but you have focused on the distant fence and have knocked over the nearer. Your horse has been disqualified. He was poisoned, my good man. Or more precisely: *Gassed*. That scent of wet hay you so observantly noticed is the telltale sign of phosgene exposure. I thought you were on the right path when you brought up the odour, but was disappointed when you just as quickly dismissed it."

"It seems I was looking for a more natural death," I replied curtly.

"Had you first inquired about the circumstances in which I came to be in the same cab as this gentleman, your examination might have taken a different course. That, my dear Watson, was the fence you missed."

"Are you certain it was phosgene exposure killed the man?"

"I would not have said so had I not been," he quipped. "You know I have studied poisons extensively, which included toxic gases. He had the indicative signs in the cab."

"Why did you bring him here and not to a hospital? Surely, they could have given better care than I?"

Holmes scoffed at the statement. "You know I trust your judgment in these matters over what passes for medical expertise in some of our illustrious medical institutions."

"Your predilections should have played no role in trying to save this poor man's life," I remonstrated.

"There are times," my friend went on dismissively, "that one needs to take a rather long view of things. I knew instinctively that he was not long for this world, yet I heartily concur that there is still a moral obligation in attempting to save a life. That is one reason why I brought him to you."

"*One* reason," I repeated. "What, I wonder, is the other?"

His lips quickly stretched into a half-grin, which then just as rapidly disappeared. It was one of those little quirks I have come to realize over the many years of our friendship that he employs when he is privy to information to which others are not. "Had I followed your sentiment," he explained, "and taken him to hospital, *and* he died in their care, which I knew was a foregone conclusion, this man's death would have been passed off to lesser-equipped intellects. He might have never gotten the justice he deserved. Pray have faith in me, Watson. Once I explain how I came to be in the same cab as this man, you might give me absolution for my sin."

Holmes pounced to the cab driver and handed him a coin. "Please pull off to the side and wait. I'm sure the authorities will have some questions. Here is an extra sovereign for your troubles."

The driver tipped his hat and did as Holmes had asked.

He then turned back to me. "I've already employed one of the little foot soldiers in my street brigade to send word to Lestrade. Another is off looking for a constable as we speak to come stay with the body until Lestrade arrives. Let me convey what I know, and I'm sure you will be an interested listener."

I took off my lounging jacket and placed it over the deceased because, although I couldn't stomach the indignity of the poor man lying dead on the walkway as lookers-on began to gather round, I also wanted to prevent any phosgene fumes from affecting anyone else.

"Go dress for the weather," Holmes said, "and I shall hail another cab. And grab your service revolver. It may be needed before the night is over."

"Shouldn't we wait for Lestrade?" I asked. "We cannot leave a dead man just lying on the walkway outside our home."

At that very moment, a constable rounded the corner with one of Holmes's bedraggled little Irregulars waving his hand diligently for the officer to follow.

"See, Watson!" Holmes exclaimed. "Reinforcements have arrived. Good boy, George – an extra shilling for your trouble!"

As Holmes explained to the constable the situation as it currently stood, I returned to our flat and put on an overcoat, replaced my medical bag with my service revolver, grabbed my bowler, and rejoined Holmes on the street below.

The constable was now sentried over the body, waving back the gathering crowd.

Holmes had hailed a hansom and then waved an anxious hand for me to follow him in. Once seated, he shouted to the driver, "Hotel Rider, as fast as you can!"

As the horse hooves clapped to life I asked, "So how did you come by this man?"

"It was a most curious bit of luck, or I should have missed him altogether. I was winding my way home after leaving the Diogenes Club," he started with his eyes closed contemplatively. "I am not usually one for indecision, as you well know, but I couldn't resolve whether to return by foot or by cab. Had I decided cab, I would have hailed one outside the club, and this man's death would have been relegated to a few paragraphs buried in *The Times*. As it was, while in this malaise, I began to walk. A few streets over, I passed a man, that very man lying dead at our stoop, He had just exited Boodle's and struggled up against a light post just outside, as if inebriated." Holmes opened his eyes and engaged me directly. "However, something about his appearance didn't sit right with me. He seemed too alert. His face didn't have that slovenly, half-lidded appearance one has when one drinks to excess. As I recall, he struggled for breath. Nevertheless, paying no mind to what I initially thought was a man having had too much wine with his dinner, I let him air himself out and kept up my pace, deciding the brisk air felt good on the lungs after being cloistered all day."

I cut Holmes off. "Shouldn't we then be going back to the location of the crime? Boodle's?"

Interrupting my friend's train of thought was typically taboo, and his usual rejoinder to that affront was a swift and complete reproach. However, Holmes had been absent of any meaningful work for some time. His visit with Mycroft had been an adequate distraction. Nonetheless, Holmes needed something tangible to engage his overactive mind. It might be upsetting to some who don't know my friend as I do that he can take what one might wrongly assume is delight over death. However, death is natural to all, yet not all death is natural, and Holmes's singular mission is that, where he can, justice be levied for those whose death is at another's hand. Realizing this, I posed the question, and Holmes, content with having something substantial with which to finally occupy his mind, let my discretion pass unobjected.

"Going to Boodle's," he replied vapidly, "is precisely what Lestrade will do. Then we shall be stepping on each other's toes. And you deceive yourself, Watson, thinking that we aren't actually starting at the genesis of this little mystery."

"But – " I started but was quickly cut off.

186

"The man was staying in a hotel. It is then logical to deduce his hotel room is the proper foundation from which to start an investigation. His room at the Rider might give us clues as to why he was murdered. That, in turn, will help us determine by whose hand he was murdered. Lestrade will no doubt find some *de minimis* to keep him occupied for a time at Boodle's. I have no doubt our paths will cross the closer we get to concluding this little affair."

"I see," said I.

He then cleared his throat, "Now, please, no further interruptions until my narrative is complete."

I waved him on silently to continue.

"*So*," he continued with sarcastic emphasis, "a few streets farther along in my sojourn, who should pass me by in a hansom, slumped forward, head between his knees, but our now deceased gentleman – yet then he was still alive, if only barely. I waved the cab to a stop and asked the driver where his fare had instructed him to go. He said the Rider, but I quickly redirected him here. Unfortunately, the man succumbed quicker than I had anticipated." He slapped his knee angrily. "Oh, Watson, had I paid more attention to my instincts when I first passed him, we might not be starting out with such a handicap. I can only blame it on the amiable weather. If London had more of it, I might not have treated this evening as such a luxury. At any rate, my good fellow, his quickly deteriorating state meant that a hospital would have been a fool's errand, as well."

I nodded my agreement, and Holmes noticed me reflexively patting my coat pocket, feeling for the revolver. He said soberly, "I'm glad you are with me, Watson. A man lies dead on our doorstep. The next death may come just as easily by pistol than poison, so it is imperative that we set ourselves up on an equal playing field."

Our cab dropped us off at the Rider, whose welcoming red awning stretched to the street from the entrance of the elegant Georgian building.

A choking wave of carriages approached us from the west as several of the theaters let out simultaneously. The street and walkway suddenly became riddled with traffic.

"We made it just in time," Holmes remarked as he paid the driver. "A moment later, and we would have been swept away by the Gaiety and Adelphi dinner crowds."

We left the cabman to his fate and rushed into the building.

As we quick-stepped up to the front desk, I asked, "Do we have the name of the deceased? A physical description alone will hardly be enough to narrow down whose room it is we need to inspect."

"My dear Watson, could I be so careless?" Holmes replied. "I posed two questions to the man before he lost consciousness for good. My first

187

query was his name."

We were obliged by a smartly dressed man at the front counter, hands clasped in front of him expectantly. He smiled a welcome at us as we approached, yet its authenticity seemed lacking, and his eyes held only an ersatz interest in us. Although his demeanour seemed somewhat deficient, his appearance was nothing if not immaculate. The only blemish I could see was a large bandage on the top of the man's right hand. Otherwise, all his lines were perfect, from his apparel to his clean-shaven jaw, to his poker-straight nose. Even his sandy mane was impeccable, with not a strand of hair out of place.

"Can I help you gentlemen?" he asked when we stopped before him. His tone held the barest remnant of an accent, perhaps Italian, but I must confess it was so negligible as to be almost impossible to ascertain with any degree of certainty.

"I am Sherlock Holmes," my friend stated. "This is my colleague, Dr. Watson. We are here on official business. Can you please give us access to the room of one Barnaby Thomesson?"

At this point in Holmes's remarkable career, he was known almost universally in London. And those who knew the name Sherlock Holmes also knew that on many cases, he worked at least tangentially with Scotland Yard.

"Absolutely, Mr. Holmes," the man replied with an eagerness often afforded the great detective by those who appreciated the medium in which he worked. He opened the thick guest ledger with one fail swoop and began fingering down the list of names on that page as Holmes watched with keen interest.

"I remember the man," the clerk said when his finger finally stopped.

"With the size of the hotel and its many patrons?" my friend pressed with a wave of his long arm at the numerous people milling about the lobby.

The clerk smiled sheepishly. "My powers of recollection aren't nearly as refined as yours, Mr. Holmes. First, we aren't nearly as full as you might think." Nodding to the people in the lobby, he continued, "Business is actually rather slow at the moment. These guests represent probably half of who is here. I didn't register all of them, but I did register Mr. Thomesson two days ago, which is why I remembered him."

"Did he have any companions or was he alone?"

The man hesitated, then replied, "It was only Mr. Thomesson . . . and his son."

Holmes shot me a grave look then asked, "And how old would you say his son is?"

"I would guess about ten years old – a bit odd-looking and quiet," the

188

man replied. "I do hope it isn't a serious matter."

"No, no," Holmes lied. "Just a small trifle that needs clearing up. I'm sure that all will be remedied with a quick look in his room, and they shall return in short order. Did you happen to see Mr. Thomesson leave?"

"I did. He walked right by me no more than three hours ago."

"*He*, not *they*?"

"No, Mr. Holmes. The man was alone."

"Have you seen the boy at any other time since they arrived?" my friend pressed.

The man hesitated again.

With an inpatient slap of the counter, Holmes entreated, "Sir, this is vital! Did you see the boy at any other time?"

"I haven't seen the boy at all since they arrived."

"Thank you," Holmes replied with a forced, contrite smile.

"My apologies," the clerk said meekly.

"None needed," said Holmes as he held out his hand. "The key?"

The clerk nervously handed the key to my friend. "Room 211. Top of the stairs, turn right, and it's the first room on the left."

"Thank you," Holmes said, snatching the key. "Should anyone from Scotland Yard arrive, please direct them to us."

The man nodded. "As you wish, Mr. Holmes."

"Come, Watson!"

With that, we hurried across the lobby.

"A man lying dead outside our flat," Holmes said as we made the stairs, "and a young boy who hasn't been seen for two days. I don't like the direction this is going."

As we began our ascent up the grand stairway, I endeavored to get clarification on something. "You mentioned asking Mr. Thomesson two questions," said I. "What was the second?"

"I asked who killed him."

With that, we bounded up the remaining stairs to the second floor.

All the way up the stairs I expected some sort of elucidation from my friend, but it didn't come. It wasn't until we were inside the man's room that I pressed, "Well, are you not going to tell me what his response was?"

Holmes put a long finger to his lips and surveyed the dark, quiet room with a critical eye as I closed the door behind us.

"Please turn on the light, if you would."

I switched on the electric light next to me and endeavoured to get my question answered, "Holmes!" I pressed again.

"I only said I *asked* two questions. I didn't say he gave two answers. Apologies for my aloofness. I leave the inscrutable for Lestrade."

"Well, that, at least, is a response."

189

We looked around the small room, each with a determined eye. Most of the furniture was laid out in line against the back wall. On the right was an unmade bed with a small nightstand by its side. Next to that was a writing desk that fronted a courtyard-facing window, and a large wardrobe was last in line on the left. The most curious thing, however, was on the floor before us: Ten completed jigsaw puzzles placed in two rows of five. There was barely enough room to place a foot between them. *

Holmes considered the puzzles as I carefully made my way to the nightstand without disturbing them.

"I had held out hope that the boy was holed up in the room, waiting for his father to return," I said. "I won't lie, I am a bit deflated seeing the room empty."

"Considering what we could have found, I count a missing child as good news," my friend rebutted. "Apparently our missing boy loves puzzles," he then replied, a thoughtful finger tapping his lips. "A forest of bluebells, two farms, a duck, two ships, two fairytale castles, and two assorted meadows."

I picked up a silver-framed picture from the nightstand. It was of a boy at the seaside. His thin strands of light hair were tousled in a breeze. "This is curious. Why would Thomesson have a picture, I presume of his son, on his nightstand when his son was with him?"

"Curious, indeed," Holmes replied, leaving the puzzles and joining me at the bedside.

There was something about the child's features that interested me, and I relayed this to my friend. "See here," I said, pointing to the photograph. "The boy's ears sit lower on his head. The slightly protruding lower jaw, the high forehead, the stout body style, the almond-shaped eyes. I have seen more pronounced features on others with this affliction, surely, yet I'm certain this boy has a defect known as Mongolism." *

"Bravo, Watson!" Holmes exclaimed. "An area I dare say you possess more acumen than I."

"My knowledge is limited. I have only seen a few people with the condition because unfortunately, most children with the deformity end up in asylums. I did, however, sit in on a lecture given by Dr. Down several years ago at the Medical Society of London. He identified the condition."

A grim shadow passed across my friend's features. "It seems we now have to add abduction to this murder inquiry. There are too many things that at present don't make sense, but the boy must now be our priority. Hallo, what is this?" He picked up what looked like a receipt sitting atop a pile of loose papers on the writing desk.

Waving the paper, he said, "It appears these puzzles were just purchased this morning from a toy shop not far from here. Well, Watson, you are the resident expert on the condition. Would the boy be capable of doing these himself in such a short time, or would he have needed the assistance of his father?"

I thought for a moment, doing my best to recall some of the details of the lecture, then I replied in earnest, "It's certainly within the scope of the defect that the boy could have done the puzzles himself, but typically they cannot without help. Most possess minimal intelligence and lack fine motor skills. However, I remember Dr. Down recalling one of his patients memorizing *The Decline and Fall of the Roman Empire* and could recite it verbatim both forward and backward."

"Remarkable," Holmes said, impressed.

"I also seem to recall an American doctor, some time ago – I forget his name now – having a slave with a similar affliction who, when asked how many seconds there were in the age of a man who was seventy years, seventeen days, and twelve hours old, gave the correct answer after only a moment's reflection, and the answer, as I recall it, was something akin to ten digits long. Others, I have heard, can play a concerto on piano by listening to it but one time."

My friend slapped me on my shoulder and replied, "See, you are too liberal with the adulations you shower upon me when I but state the obvious."

"*'Idiot savant'*, I believe is the term Down coined, referring to those afflicted with low intelligence, yet having some profound gift. I never liked the term myself."

Looking at the puzzles once more, Holmes said, "What is missing are the puzzle boxes. They should be right here, yet they aren't."

His resolute eyes darted around the room momentarily. Then he bounded to the bed, swiping his long arms into the shadows underneath. With some effort, he recovered all ten puzzle boxes. "If Mr. Thomesson helped his son put the puzzles together, what would the purpose be of hiding the boxes," he thought aloud. "Yet . . . ."

He clapped his hands together triumphantly after a moment of reflection. "If your memory holds true, then I believe it is possible his son has this gift. I would then equally surmise Thomesson let his son see the pictures of the boxes once then hid them under the bed and let him put the puzzles together from memory. I might even go a step further and say his father dumped all the pieces on the floor, mixed them up, and let the boy reassemble them from the mass of pieces jumbled together. What say you, Watson?"

"That is certainly a possibility, even a probability – if the boy is a *savant.*"

"Well, it seems our missing boy has a penchant for puzzles. That is

191

very telling."

"What does that tell you?" I queried.

"Let us see if there is anything else the room has to offer. Clay, Watson! I need clay to make my bricks. When I have built up enough of the structure, I'm sure even you shall see it!"

Holmes examined the wardrobe while I rifled through the loose papers on the writing desk.

"Mr. Thomesson has only packed enough changes of clothes for three days," he said. "I don't see any changes of clothes whatsoever for his son."

"So the boy has been wearing the same clothes for the last two days?"

"Or the valise containing his clothes was taken away along with the boy, which denotes a certain premeditation to the abduction. If the boy was taken in haste, his change of clothing would not be paramount on the blackguard's mind."

I continued my perusal of the writing desk and picked up a loosely folded piece of paper next to the ink well. Opening it, I exclaimed, "Ah, come look at this! It's a telegram he was apparently going to send to his wife. It's addressed to Mrs. Isadora Thomesson of Number Five, Cherry Court, Waltham Abbey."

"Enlighten me of its contents."

"It says:

> *My dearest Isadora, I am sorry for all the sadness I have caused. I thought I had found a way to make things right, but my transgressions only seem to grow. Despite assurances, I fear the worst for little Charley. I have one more opportunity to set things right.*

"What do you make of it?" I asked.

"I would wager we could get some of these blanks filled in by Mrs. Isadora Thomesson in Waltham Abbey. Come. We need to get to Kings Cross Station. I believe we can make it before Mrs. Thomesson puts her head to pillow."

As we ran from the room, Holmes said, "I hope you are well-reposed. I fear we are in for a very long night."

Once in Waltham Abbey, we quickly procured a cab to the Thomesson home, a small thatched cottage surrounded by a chest-high stone wall at the end of the high street. It was after ten, but a light still shone in a first-floor window.

Holmes paid the driver and asked him to wait.

A young woman with soft features and long, dark hair answered the

192

door and looked from one to the other of us with an expectant countenance. "Please tell me you have found her," she implored.

"Found who?" Holmes asked.

"Why, my sister. Isn't that why you are here at such an hour?"

"Then you are not Isadora Thomesson?" I asked.

"No, I am her sister, Esme." At this, the young woman's eyes glistened over with tears.

Holmes asked, "Is there a problem, Miss – ?"

"Fisher," the woman finished with a sob. "Isadora went out for her afternoon walk two days ago and has never returned. I notified the constabulary but have heard no developments. I thought perhaps you were here with news."

"We're here with news, but not pertaining to your sister," my friend explained. "May we come in?"

"Who are you again?"

Holmes bowed slightly. "My apologies. I am Sherlock Holmes, and this is my colleague, Dr. Watson."

"Ah, the detective and his chronicler. I have read some of your accounts. Please come in."

She led us into a small parlor. She sat in one of a pair of armless chairs in front of the crackling hearth. I sat in the other while Holmes stood between us. The place had a homey, lived-in feel. Photographs lined the mantel. A crystal decanter and some spirits sat on a side table near a window and a settee with unfinished needlework was placed haphazardly upon the cushions – no doubt that was the work in which she was engaged when our knock came at her door. A side table next to the settee had a folded newspaper and various scraps of paper strewn about it.

"So what brings you here, if not my missing sister?"

"I'm afraid that I have more unpleasant news to bear, Miss Fisher. Your brother in-law, Mr. Thomesson, has been murdered."

The woman's chest heaved. "And – and Charley? He had his stepson, Charley, with him."

"The boy is missing."

Her breath caught in her throat. She seemed on the verge of faint but with a mighty inner strength fought off the urge.

"My Heavens, what black cloud has settled over our family?" she lamented as she wiped away a stream of tears from her reddened cheeks.

Holmes began to slowly walk around the room, taking it in in quick glances. "Miss Fisher, do you know why Mr. Thomesson procured a room at the Rider Hotel for him and his son?"

"Barnaby – Mr. Thomesson – often spent days on end at various hotels to accommodate the sometimes long hours he would work, especially of late. It was easier to stay in London than taking a train home, only to turn around and leave again with only a few hours' rest. He adored Charley, and he hated being away for long periods, so he would sometimes take Charley along. Charley has – "

"Mongolism, yes. We have seen his photograph in the hotel room."

The young woman's brow furrowed. "That's odd. Why would he take a photograph when he had Charley with him?"

"An echoed sentiment," I replied.

"I do apologize, Miss Fisher," Holmes responded with an air of frustration, "but I need pertinent information. Time is of the essence. In what business was Mr. Thomesson employed?"

"Of course. He was very secretive about his employment, but he works – worked – at the Royal Arsenal in Woolwich. He wasn't in the habit of talking about his work while in my company, so I don't know much. However, I had overheard whispers between Barnaby and Isadora on a few occasions. It was about his involvement with the assembly and implementation of a new distribution device for poison gasses. It was developed with the utmost secrecy. Apparently, there are several machine shops around London employed to make one particular part of the machine, and each location has the plans and prints for just that particular part. All the components are then couriered to and assembled at Woolwich."

"What exactly was Mr. Thomesson's role in that process?"

"I believe he made sure that all the parts for each device were present, and then he sent them off somewhere else on the premises to be assembled."

"He didn't assemble them himself?"

"No, sir, he did not."

"You seem to know more than you let on, Miss Fisher."

"I am easily forgotten here, Mr. Holmes, and much is said when they think me absent, yet I'm just in the next room."

Scrutinizing some photographs on the mantel, Holmes plucked one, a picture housed in a grand, gold-filigreed frame, and showed it to Miss Fisher. "This is Mrs. Thomesson?" he asked.

"It is," she replied.

"Recent?"

"No more than a month."

Holmes handed it to me to inspect. It was of a woman with similarly dark, flowing hair, but sterner features than her sister. She was wearing a beautiful, laced dress and standing behind a seated Charley with her hands on his shoulders. She had penetrating eyes which seemed devoid of emotion. Charley, conversely, was wearing a grand smile.

194

I returned the picture, and Holmes gave it one more studious glance before returning it to its perch.

"You mentioned that Charley is a stepson," Holmes went on.

"Yes. A past indiscretion when my sister was younger and knew less of the world than she imagined. She began associating with a group who harboured dark ideas and fell in love with one of its members, Hugo Richtor. That indiscretion left her in a family way, and before she even had the baby, the snake disappeared, and she was left to raise Charley alone. Then she met Barnaby. He absolutely loved Isadora and Charley. He adopted Charley when they married."

"And recently?" my friend queried. "Has anything changed?"

"No, sir, nothing."

"Come now – nothing?"

"I don't follow. If you wish to ask a particular question, I shall give an honest answer."

"I know for example that Mr. Thomesson was a betting man – horses in particular – and he has lost a considerably sum, yet he bestows what wages he makes upon his wife. He is now in considerable debt, and no doubt it was this debt that led him down this perfidious path."

"All you say is true, but how did you know?"

"The paper on that side table is folded to the horse racing section. There is at least one betting slip next to it, which has been crumpled. He lost his bet. Your lodgings are adequate but not elaborate, yet Mrs. Thomesson is wearing a dress with the hallmarks of a Worth, which would come at a considerable cost. The photograph of her in that dress happens to be the only one in a gold frame. Not to mention the suit Mr. Thomesson was wearing was well-worn, and his shoes had been re-soled – *Ergo*, he lavishes upon his wife to the detriment of the rest of the family."

The woman nodded. "For the better part of a year, Barnaby had his work, Isadora had her walks, and I had Charley. My entire day is taken with the boy, which is all I need in this world. He gives me a sense of purpose that I would not otherwise have. His favorite game is 'Ring-a-Ring-a-Rosey'. I sing it as we twirl around – Charley only speaks a few words himself, you know – then we both plop onto our bottoms together. His laugh is like the sun." She giggled at the thought, and new tears streamed down her flushed cheeks.

"Miss Fisher, if you please!" Holmes chided. "Fine though they may be, children's games get me no closer to finding the boy or his abductor and your brother-in-law's murderer."

"My apologies, Mr. Holmes, but Charley is the light of my world, and any thought of him only brings fond thoughts. More to the point, however: About five months ago, Isadora began to fall into a deep despair."

"Was this about the time she had taken to her afternoon walks?"

"I believe so."

"Continue."

"At first, Barnaby began bringing her little trinkets from London, and she began to come out of it. But soon she started asking for more and more expensive things. Barnaby would do anything for her but, unfortunately, her extravagance began to outpace his earnings. He turned to betting on horses in hopes of a windfall."

"Was betting on horses his idea?" my friend asked.

"Come to think of it, I believe it was at Isadora's insistence. Unfortunately, gambling is not an endeavour suited to Barnaby – he was horrible at it. He ended up borrowing money on what he was told was a sure bet. It wasn't. Soon, he was underwater with the wrong people. That is where we stand presently. I hope this is a help to you, Mr. Holmes."

He smiled. "Yes. Much help, indeed. Now, back to the boy. From what I have gathered, he is very adept at puzzles."

"Oh, yes, Mr. Holmes, but how – "

"Puzzles in the hotel room," my friend replied before she could finish her thought.

"Yes, Charley can put the most incongruent puzzles together in minutes. Barnaby would purchase multiple puzzles and jumble them together on the floor and Charley could put them all together so quickly. It is rather astounding that a young boy who has a twenty-word vocabulary can be so clever with puzzles."

"Just as we suspected."

"And you have been helping care for Charley?" I asked.

"From his birth. He can be a bit of a handful, Charley can. Isadora tried but, well, she doesn't seem to have the patience needed to take care of a boy with his difficulties. She had entertained the thought of putting him away, but Barnaby would have none of it."

"Charley is very lucky to have you," I replied. "This environment is much better suited than an asylum."

Holmes quickly motioned me to my feet. "Thank you for your time, Miss Fisher. There is still much to be done if we are to return the boy home safe and sound."

She rose and shook our hands. "I shall say a prayer for your success, for Charley's sake."

"Thank you, Madam. I shall not turn away whatever assistance Providence wishes to bestow."

As we made the front door, Miss Fisher asked, "Do you – do you think the same fate as Barnaby has befallen my sister?"

"It is a distinct possibility, Miss Fisher, I will not lie. But do not give

196

up hope."

On our way back to the station, I asked, "So what is our next move? A dead man, a missing boy, and now a missing mother."

"There is only one of two outcomes for Mrs. Thomesson: She is either part of this dark plot, or she is dead. For what it's worth, my wager is the latter. We will know her fate when we arrive at out next destination."

"And where would that be?"

"The Surrey Docks."

"The Docks? That is so utterly out of place in this affair that I have to assume you know who is behind all this, and the Docks is where we will find him."

"You are correct. Although I don't know all the particular actors in this drama, I do know its author. That is precisely my reason for heading to the Docks."

"Well, are you going to enlighten me?"

Holmes smiled. "In due time, Watson. You wouldn't want me to spoil your enjoyment of a three-act play by telling you how it ends after only the second act, would you?"

Holmes sent a telegram to Lestrade at Scotland Yard from the train station with the hope that he would receive it in time to meet us at the docks. It was well after midnight when we finally made it there ourselves, but there was no sign of Lestrade or any of his footmen with a message.

As we alighted from the cab in the cloistering fog that often overcomes the banks of the Thames, Holmes said, "I had hoped Lestrade and his men would have preceded us. They do little to help in the investigative process, but they are like dogs with a bone with the act of apprehension."

Suddenly, there were more hoof claps upon the cobblestone in the distance and drawing near.

"I had entertained the thought of filling you in on what we are up against while waiting out Lestrade, but elucidations will have to come after the fact. Come, Watson, let us make ourselves scarce until we know who our company is."

"Could it not be Lestrade?"

"With so little fanfare? I doubt it."

I followed Holmes down the walkway, and we quickly disappeared in the gloom of the foggy night.

A hansom stopped under a gas lamp at the entrance to the wharf, and a man and boy descended.

I whispered to Holmes, "That man looks familiar."

Holmes replied under his breath, "He should. He gave us the key to the hotel room. He is the boy's father."

197

"But – "

"Later, Watson, we must keep them in our sights."

Once the man and boy were on the wharf, Holmes and I followed far enough behind and in enough shadow to prevent us from being seen or heard.

They turned right and disappeared down a quay between two steamers.

We hurried ahead to catch a glimpse of their destination, but the quay was dark and empty. Holmes craned his neck up at the names of the ships, barely discernable by a nearby gas lamp. After inspecting each, he motioned me to follow him.

"How do you know it was this ship they boarded?" I whispered.

"The other ship is Canadian, and this ship is Danish," Holmes replied in a secretive hush.

"I don't follow."

"All in good time, my dear fellow. All in good time."

From the corner of my eye, I saw something in the darkness above us move. Holmes saw it as well. He put a finger to his lips. The shadowed man and boy were on the ship's deck, walking from bow to stern. The man said something to the boy. It was unintelligible but the tone was heated. At that point, the poor boy started sobbing.

There was a gangplank thirty feet down the quay hidden in the shadows. This we ascended as the two made for the stern of the ship.

Once we were onboard and hidden down in the shadows, Holmes whispered, "I fear your service revolver will more than likely be needed. I daresay these blackguards will not be keen on giving up the boy without force."

I pulled the revolver from my coat.

"I want you to stay behind me in the shadows where they cannot see you, but close enough to take direction from me should I see the need to give it. Understood?"

"Yes. What will your course of action be?"

There isn't a desultory bone in the man's body, so it took me by surprise when he replied, "I don't know, Watson, but this ship cannot leave England with that boy on board."

He crept down the deck with me twenty feet behind. All the above-deck cabins were dark, so we made our way to the stern of the ship unimpeded.

I stopped when Holmes stopped at the back of the aft cabins.

Here, the boy could be heard sobbing from somewhere nearby.

Holmes dared to steal a glance around the corner then motioned me closer.

198

Once I halved the distance between us, Holmes suddenly stepped out from the shadows. "You would do well to let the boy go," he said.

"What the – ?" the man clamoured.

I couldn't see him, but by the tone of his voice, he was taken aback by my friend's sudden appearance.

I squatted onto my hands and knees and dared to watch the events unfold by peeking from around the lower corner. The man was cast in a pool of wan light that emanated from a lantern placed at the entrance to a stairwell that led somewhere below deck.

After a momentary pause to collect himself, the man went on despondently, "It isn't surprising that you knew where to find me. I am quite at a loss, however, how you came to figure it out so quickly."

"Let the boy go," Holmes repeated with more vigour.

"Or what?" the man almost dared, his accent – German – now demonstrably thicker. "You will come snatch him from my hand? Tell you what, Herr Holmes – why don't you come and take him from me. I'll cut him from ear to ear before two steps are even taken." With that, he produced a peasant knife from his back pocket, waving it in front of Charley's face.

"You bluff. You would be killing the only person who has the capabilities of putting the gas dispenser together with the components you've dedicated so much time and money to appropriate. I think not."

"Well, if the choice is between him or me . . . ." With that, he put the blade closer to the boy's neck.

Holmes held out a calming hand, "There is no need for that."

"Are you not the least bit interested in why I even want the boy?" the man asked.

"We are aware of his unique abilities."

"Ah, yes, *we*," he said as he looked beyond Holmes into the darkness where I had hoped I couldn't be seen. "You seem to be alone. Where is your famous associate? I didn't think you went anywhere without him."

"He stayed behind at Waltham Abbey to attend to Miss Fisher, Mrs. Thomesson's younger sister. She was quite overcome with grief at Charley's disappearance."

"Ah, yes, Esme. I heard that she had taken a fancy in his nurturing. Frankly, I could never see Isadora in that role. She didn't have the patience for maternal endeavours."

"I have no doubt her disappearance was at your hands. Tell me, where will we find her body?"

The man laughed coldly. "I have no idea to what you are referring, I'm sure. But I will say this: She was never a very good swimmer."

At this, Holmes took a few tentative steps forward. He was now directly between myself and the man and Charley.

"So how did you know where to find me?" he asked.

"A process by which you can scarcely understand, so there is no need to waste our energies there. Let us keep the conversation on your son."

"That too is a waste of energies," the man replied insouciantly. "And frankly, this conversation is beginning to bore me. I am going to take the boy below deck, and we shall depart to Denmark at first light, where we will then catch a train to Germany. There, we will disappear. The climax of this wonderful plan you shall then read on the front page of any paper you pick up in roughly one month's time. If you have any notion to try and stop me, the boy dies, and in the process, you shall die as well."

"You seem confident in your abilities. Leave the boy there. Come, test it on me. I will even allow you the benefit of keeping the knife."

Holmes was trying to separate the man from the boy.

The man laughed, "I don't do the heavy work, Herr Holmes. I have others for that undertaking. One shout and I can have a half-dozen brothers up here and have you cornered before you ever make it to the gangplank, and in the morning, the authorities will find your bloated carcass bobbing in the Thames. However, if you just turn and walk away, you and the boy shall both live. You see, the reality is I would very much prefer you alive. I want you to see for yourself what devastation my brotherhood can bring about with such a small metal box! I believe even you shall be impressed."

"How can I trust that you will be true to your word and let the boy live?" Holmes asked.

The man returned an iniquitous grin. "That's the thing – you can't!"

I knew that Charley wouldn't make it to the end of this affair alive. Once the boy was finished with the task set before him, they would discard him like an unwanted scrap of rubbish. If I knew Charley's fate, Holmes certainly knew it as well.

"You have a choice to make, Herr Holmes: Certainty versus uncertainty. The boy is certain to die if you try to stop me. However, there is at least a chance that I am being truthful and will give the boy up unharmed once we are through with him. Which will it be?" At this, he motioned with his hands as if they were a great scale weighing the boy's worth.

I will not lie, I was beginning to lose my patience with our inaction in the matter. However, my impatience was tempered by knowing that the great mind of Sherlock Holmes was already devising a way out of this, even if I didn't know the particulars.

"I know you have all the components to make at least one of the devices. You don't need the boy. Surely, you and your henchmen should have enough intelligence between you to put one together without his

200

involvement."

"Not without the plans. Have you seen the components? Just how many pieces there are? No, time is of the essence if we are to accomplish our objectives, and Charley gives us the best chance – the only chance – to have a working dispenser in the timeframe needed. Besides, this will give little Charley a sense of accomplishment. That is important for a child with his condition, is it not?"

The man then patted Charley roughly upon his head, making the boy wince, and the action turned his sobbing into an uncontrollable cry.

"Stop crying!" the man then hissed. "Stop, or shall give you something to cry about!"

"That isn't necessary," replied Holmes, arms outstretched pleadingly. My friend took another step toward the man.

"That is far enough unless you want this boy's blood on your hands."

"You would murder your own son?"

"He is no more my son than stepped-in dung is a part of my shoe."

The crying continued.

"Stop, I said! Stop now!"

As the man persisted his heated Hessian invective, Holmes put up yet another calming hand, imploring serenity, while he surreptitiously brought his other hand round behind him and motioned me forward. Wishing not to be seen, I remained crouched on all fours where the shadows were deeper and slowly crawled my way around the corner, making certain to keep Holmes directly between myself and the blackguard, only twenty feet separating us.

Holmes interrupted the man's fit of anger. "I don't wish for the boy to get hurt. I shall do as you wish. I shall leave and hope you will be true to your word. But I fear the boy's crying will be too trying for nerves already frayed to their breaking points. While talking to Miss Fisher – Esme. I believe you know her – she mentioned a nursery rhyme the boy likes. If you will allow me, maybe reciting it with Charley will calm him down. Then I shall acquiesce and leave."

"And a guaranteed free passage to open waters. If we run into any problems, the boy dies."

"Understood. I will keep quiet. Now, that nursery rhyme?"

The man gave Holmes a strange look. I must confess that I too might have been wearing that same expression, for I never in my wildest dreams would have imagined hearing Holmes recite a nursery rhyme.

Holmes then engaged the boy. "Charley?" he offered in a hyperbolically cheerful tone. "Charley, I am a friend of your Aunt Esme."

"Esme, yes," Charley replied through sobs. "Yes, yes! Esme!" His speech was deliberate and thick but understandable.

"Esme said you like to play *'Ring-a-ring-a-rosey'*?"

"Yes, yes! Rosey!"

"Would you like to play?"

At this, Charley immediately stopped crying and clapped his hands. "Yes, yes! Rosey!" he repeated.

"Do you know how it goes?" Holmes asked.

"You, you!" Charley said, pointing an animated finger at my friend.

"All right, Charley, do it with me. We have to do it together. Ready?" Charley shook his head excitedly.

"Ring-a-ring-a-rosey – " Holmes started off slowly, deliberately. He began to turn in a circle where he stood, and Charley mimicked him.

" *– Pocket full of posies* – "

Sherlock Holmes and I had been friends for nearly two decades at this point, and we had been in more than our fair share of scrapes where lives were at stake. Over those years, there had developed by necessity an unspoken language between us that we had honed whose tacit utterances and subsequent actions had saved many lives, ours included. He was now facing me in this slow, deliberate twirl, and the look in his eyes spoke my directive as he slowly completed his circuit.

" *– A tishoo a tishoo* – "

I knew what needed to be done.

" *– We all fall down!*"

With that, both Holmes and Charley, who was now laughing, collapsed together onto the deck.

And at that very moment, with one quick, stealthy motion, I stood, pointing my revolver at the man.

A single shot rang out.

The man lay motionless on the deck with a bloody hole in his chest, and Charley, hands cupped over his ears, was crying once again.

Holmes ran over to the boy with me at his heels. He scooped up Charley in his long arms as I ran to the gravely wounded man.

"You will have to forgo your Hippocratic Oath, Watson, and leave this man, or I fear we may all end up suffering the same fate."

At that instant, we heard a commotion coming from the open doorway. The "brothers" the man spoke of were coming up from below deck to search out the genesis of the gunshot.

We both ran as quickly as our legs could take us.

We made the bow of the ship, almost tumbled headlong down the gangplank, and planted our feet on solid ground in what seemed like a painfully slow crawl but in reality was probably mere seconds. From there, we raced back to the dock entrance where multiple lantern lights now vacillated through thick tendrils of fog.

202

When we finally made the dock entrance, a mob of constables met us, lanterns and pistols at the ready.

Holmes put Charley down and patted him on the head as he searched out the inspector.

"Your timing couldn't be more predictable, Lestrade," he said as Lestrade pushed his way around several men.

"My apologies, Mr. Holmes. We have a new night dispatch officer who didn't follow protocol. I didn't get your telegram until I returned to the Yard, instead of having a constable sent out to me with your message."

"You will find out soon enough," Holmes went on, "that deadly force had to be used, or we would have lost our new friend, Charley, here."

"Which rotter got it?" Lestrade asked.

"Hugo Richtor, the boy's father and the mastermind of today's events."

"Thomesson wasn't the boy's father?" Lestrade offered back, perplexed. "So this Richtor fellow murdered Thomesson to get at his boy?"

Holmes gave a vehement shake of his head. "No, no, Lestrade. You are making incorrect assumptions based on irrelevant data."

"Then tell me what is relevant."

"I shall, Inspector, but first you need to send your men around to the Danish ship *Josephine*, the third ship down the quay on the right, or they shall all jump ship and you will have little to show for your work."

Lestrade sent all but four constables to round up the crew of the *Josephine* while the remaining stayed behind should any slip through the cracks.

"I would have liked to take Richtor alive," my friend went on. "However, his ambivalence towards the boy's life made it impossible."

He then turned to me. "I am sorry, Watson, that I christened you the judge, jury, and executioner for Mr. Richtor."

"No doubt you saved The Crown some money," Lestrade remarked.

I replied steadfastly, "If it came down to the man or the boy, I would not hesitate to do it again."

Lestrade said, "In your telegram, you mentioned the missing Thomesson woman, as well."

"Yes, I fear she has met her end – at least Richtor intimated as much. I would send men up to Waltham Abbey and search out any millponds or estate lakes in the area. No doubt you'll find her body in due course."

"How the devil did she get tangled up with a thug like that?"

"It seems a dubious past had caught up with her. An unfavourable union with Hugo Richtor in her youth produced Charley. As so often happens, the man fled, leaving her to raise the child alone. Providence,

203

however, would favor her with Barnaby Thomesson. Yet her old ways came to the fore, and she fell back in with her troubled past. Either by fate or by deliberation, when she agreed to meet Hugo Richtor after all these years, her fate was sealed – a fate that almost befell her entire family, as well."

"Well, who the devil is this Hugo Richtor?"

"One of a myriad of henchmen belonging to the *Einzeln Freikorps*."

"*Einzeln Freikorps*?" He then asked with a wrinkled brow. "What the devil is that?"

"You might know it by its more popular English translation, the *I.F.C.* – the *Individual Freedom Corps*."

Lestrade's eyes widened, "You managed to nip members of the *I.F.C.*? That's only one of the nastiest anarchist groups on the continent. Their numbers are relatively small, but they have big ideas and are a right nasty bunch. They are wanted for bombings in Antwerp, Paris, and Munich."

"And if this bold scheme had succeeded, it would have been quite a little feather in their cap. I believe they intended to murder the consulates from several countries during a meeting to be held next month in Berlin. But fortunately, Inspector Lestrade and Scotland Yard have thwarted another enemy of Her Majesty's Realm."

"There are bits to this little affair that I'm not quite seeing through yet," Lestrade admitted.

"Yes, there are a few threads I still need to knit together myself, which will require a call to my brother, Mycroft. Clarification must wait, however. I fear that little Charley, here, needs to reclaim the comfort of his home and his aunt."

The boy gave a great yawn and rubbed his reddened eyes.

"I'll have Jeffries take him back to Waltham Abbey."

At this, the bear of a man, Jeffries, like Moses parting the Red Sea, appeared from the fog, got down on one knee, and smiled at the boy. "Charley, is it?" he said in a tone more soothing than his appearance.

Charley shook his head, *Yes*.

"How 'bout I take you back home? Would you like that?"

"Yes," Charley said, twisting his fingers nervously. "Esme, please. Yes."

"Is there anything I need to know?" Jeffries asked as he regained his considerable height. "Any special needs he might have for the trip back home?"

I said, "Other than a limited vocabulary, I think he should be fine. Keep outside stimuli to a minimum."

Jeffries nodded.

"You wouldn't happen to have a puzzle hidden in that considerable bulk would you?" Holmes added cheekily.

"I'm afraid not, Mr. Holmes."

"That's too bad. The boy so loves puzzles."

Handing the boy off to Jefferies, Holmes then turned his attention back to Lestrade. "If you can see yourself to it, come round to our rooms, say around nine this morning? By then I should be able to enlighten all who have an interest in this little affair. I shall ask Mrs. Hudson to have our breakfast ready then."

"Nothing heavy for me, thank you," Lestrade replied. "Maybe just tea and a scone."

"That last sentiment was meant for the other person occupying the flat for whom Mrs. Hudson routinely cooks."

I laughed.

"But I shall ask our landlady if she would be so kind as to put out some additional fare for our guests as well," Holmes said with a grin.

Jeffries departed with Charley, and Lestrade was left with the rounding up and arresting of the *I.F.C.* confederates, while Holmes and I fetched a cab to our digs in Baker Street.

Holmes was already up when I appeared from my room around eight, was sitting in an armchair next to the window, dressed in his grey lounging coat, smoke wafting above his head from his pipe as he casually read *The Times*.

"Nice of you to join me," he said without looking up.

Yawing and pouring myself a cup of tea from a setting Mrs. Hudson had already put out, I replied, "I don't know how you do it. I'm still tired, and you look as fresh as a daisy."

"Years of practice. Don't forget, while you were keeping hours attuned to your married life and medical practice, I was still rigorously denying my body the sleep a normal human being needs. I pummeled it into submission some time ago."

"I take it you've already spoken to Mycroft?"

"I rang him up this morning, and now I have a more complete picture of this horrid, little affair."

Remembering the events of the night before, I couldn't help but let out a subdued chortle.

"What's so funny?" Holmes asked.

"Just the thought of you reciting a nursery rhyme. It wasn't something I thought I'd ever hear you utter. I didn't even know your vast knowledge included Mother Goose."

"Contrary to popular belief, I did have a childhood."

"So you played '*Ring-a-Ring-a- Rosey*'?"

"Of course not. I watched others play it while I collected fungi for my herbarium."

The bell rang downstairs.

"Ah, that would be Lestrade, now, come for his breakfast!"

A moment later, the inspector came in, alone.

"Ah, Lestrade. You're early. No Jeffries? He has been your Watson of late. You rarely go anywhere without him in tow. I fear Mrs. Hudson has made too much food."

Taking off his overcoat, Lestrade replied, "No, I left him at the Yard to do paperwork." He took a seat and poured himself a cup of tea. "Well, I am as ready as three hours of sleep will afford me, Mr. Holmes. Tell me what you know of this mess."

"Yes," I said, taking my seat near the hearth, "I am dying to know myself, as I have been in the dark from the beginning."

Holmes relinquished the paper, leaned back satisfactorily in his chair, and engaged us more directly. "On what points do you need enlightened? Once this little narrative is complete, I'm sure you will see things as clearly as I do."

I began while Lestrade looked over the fare set out before him, "I may be starting a bit in the middle, but I would like to know how you knew it was this Hugo Richtor we were after and, just as perplexing, how to find him."

"I had already worked out the organization behind this little mystery, but I didn't know the henchmen involved. It was the photograph on the mantel that furnished the answer. I handed it to you, Watson. Didn't you see it?"

"I confess, I did not."

"So what gave it away?" Lestrade pressed.

"It began at the Rider Hotel. I had noticed the clerk at the front counter had a bandage on his hand. Surely you saw that, Watson."

"I did. No doubt it covered an injury."

"It did not. It was the only blemish on the man, so my eyes couldn't help but be drawn to it. It covered what looked to be a tattoo. It was almost completely covered, but not all. What I could make out was that of a snake."

"What could a partial tattoo possibly tell you?" Lestrade asked as he picked out a scone.

Holmes gave the inspector a sympathetic smile. "It can tell you much if you would just learn to be more observant."

"That's what we have you for," he replied.

Holmes went on. "Well, if you insist on the particulars, then I shall oblige. The ledger, roughly four inches thick, was closed when I asked for Mr. Thomesson's room number. When the man opened it to look up the room number, he opened it up precisely to the page he needed – and before you ask, there was no page marker in the ledger. A four-inch-thick ledger has approximately five-hundred actual sheets to write on – front and back – based on the page thickness for a standard thousand-page ledger. Besides the first and last page, the ledger will show you two pages at once when opened, so for a thousand-page ledger, he would have a one-in-five-hundred chance of opening the ledger to the exact page he needed, yet he did that very thing. Would you bet on a horse who had a one-in-five-hundred chance of winning the race?"

"Point taken," Lestrade mumbled back as he bit into his scone.

"All this told me the man was already intimate with Mr. Thomesson's details. Since Richtor required him to stay at the hotel where he was employed, he never actually needed to check the room number. His ledger search was only a farce for our benefit."

"That still does not get us on the *Josephine*," I pressed.

Holmes waved me off. "Patience, Watson. We have hot tea and scones and nowhere to be. Let me expound, my dear fellow."

I motioned for him to continue.

"My next clue happened to be in the photograph of Mrs. Thomesson and the boy. I could see plain as day a tattoo on the top of her right hand – the same tattoo that Richtor had tried to hide under the bandage on his hand – snake coiled around an eagle. It is the symbol for the *IFC*. Every member has it."

"So you knew that Mrs. Thomesson was an anarchist?" Lestrade asked.

"In her youth, yes. And as Miss Fisher relayed to us – that was when she met Hugo Richtor, and their relationship produced Charley. She obviously still had sympathies which led to this current travesty."

"So that gets us to Waltham Abbey. How do we get to the *Josephine* from there?" I asked.

"I'd had dealings with this organization in the past, which is how I recognized their inked calling card. I put away a low-level scoundrel who did a very bad job trying to steal a diamond necklace to hock it for money when the *I.F.C.* was first trying to get a foothold on English soil a decade ago. Their way in and out of the country unnoticed was by becoming crew or stowing away on ships bringing in timber from Scandinavia. *That* is how I knew to go to the Surrey Docks and the *Josephine*."

"That is all well and good," Lestrade replied. "That gets us abduction for this Richtor fellow, but that doesn't get me to the murder of Mr. Thomesson."

207

"I am afraid you will not be able to pin that on the *I.F.C.* However, a breach of the Official Secrets Act should do nicely in its place. And if you are able to find the body of Mrs. Thomesson – well, that would be icing on the cake. Either way, your prisoners will all see the gallows."

"Whatever do you mean, I won't be able to pin the murder on them?" Lestrade shot back. "By your own admission, Thomesson's son was abducted, and he was poisoned."

"Gassed," Holmes clarified.

"Fine, *gassed,*" replied Lestrade, flourishing the emphasis by stuffing the last of his scone in his mouth.

"Surely, it is clear to you, Watson."

"I must admit," I replied, "that the situation is still rather opaque to me."

Holmes snapped his fingers. "My apologies, Lestrade," he exclaimed, rising from his seat, hurrying over to his frock coat pocket, and retrieving a folded piece of paper. Handing it to the inspector, he said, "I completely forgot to give you this letter, which we found in Thomesson's hotel room."

Lestrade read it, and then put it in his own pocket for safe keeping. "What does it mean? What's this *one last thing* Thomesson was going to attempt?" He let out a heavy sigh, "Please, I am a simple man and a tired man. I go from point *A* to point *Z* in a very straight line. Can you please start at the beginning?" This he said, casting an accusatory eye in my direction. "And go in a straight line from dead Thomesson to me drinking tea and eating scones in your flat."

A smile tugged at Holmes's lips. Then he began. "It is, or at least should be, quite obvious that Barnaby Thomesson was privy to knowledge that only a few possess. You are aware of his occupation, Lestrade?"

"I am aware."

"The knowledge Barnaby Thomesson possessed working at the Royal Arsenal would be worth a king's ransom to certain powers on the Continent."

"Yes, I thought of that," I replied. "But Thomesson only had access to the individual parts, not the prints to actually build the device. That was done elsewhere at the facility."

"Yes, but it goes without saying that it wouldn't be that difficult for Thomesson to find out where the devices were being assembled, working at the Arsenal himself. Once that hurdle had been cleared, he could easily get his hands on a copy of the prints and plans."

"What you are saying, then, is that the *I.F.C.* wanted to get their hands on the plans of that device," Lestrade said.

"Or a facsimile thereof," replied Holmes cryptically.

"What good would the assembly prints do if the *I.F.C.* didn't have

208

the parts to assemble?" Lestrade asked as he eyed another scone.

"What makes you think they didn't have the parts?"

I replied, "Well, since all the different components were made in different places, wouldn't that make it nearly impossible for any entity to get their hands on *all* of the components needed for the construction of the device?"

Holmes sighed. "Watson, you place the data you receive into boxes, then stuff them into your brain like a cluttered attic. Then, when you need to retrieve that data, you must open each box to find out its contents instead of having everything out in the open where you can see your entire inventory at once."

"Is that not what ninety-nine percent of humanity does?"

"Yes, and that is why ninety-nine percent of humanity doesn't do what I do. Until you learn to set out everything before you and examine the bigger picture, you will fail to see what I see."

"I am happy to be in the same boat as the other ninety-nine percent of humanity," I replied, "so forgive me if I just wait until you give me the answer."

Holmes laughed at my jest, "Yes, Watson, I shall give you that, but you at least try, which is more than I can say for that other ninety-nine percent. No offense, Lestrade."

"None taken," the inspector replied unperturbed, sipping his tea.

"Please fill us in on what is obvious to you but not so obvious yet to me," I replied.

Holmes went on, "Thomesson had gotten his hands on the assembly prints for this new gas dispersal device, only briefly, but that was all he needed. And as you so eloquently put, it would be of no use if they didn't already have all the components to assemble at least one. I'm certain they already had the components and only needed the plans to assemble the device."

Here, Lestrade spoke up. "Yet the Royal Arsenal wouldn't be so clumsy as to let an assembly print or individual components go missing. They must keep strict tabs on everything entering and leaving the facility."

"You're correct, Lestrade, but probably not at each of the manufacturing facilities. It would be nothing for one piece out of several hundred made to come up missing. I believe there was someone on the inside at each of these facilities who was in charge of absconding with one of these components. Once the piece was pilfered, it and the employee who took it disappeared."

Lestrade pulled out a notebook and scribbled in it. "I shall be making inquiries as to where these facilities are located and who has left their employment over the last few weeks. With any luck, we shall nab a few more *I.F.C.* members for our trouble."

I decided at this point to sit back and listen as Lestrade took over the questioning.

"But surely the assembly print would be nary impossible to take out of the Royal Arsenal," he said. "They must have a known amount of copies and keep them under lock and key when not in use. If one came up missing, then an alarm would be sounded. All the ports would close, and no one would be permitted to leave the whole of England until that print was found."

"*If* the print was missing," Holmes replied.

"How could they know how to assemble the device without the assembly print?" he asked.

"Mr. Thomesson had the wherewithal to not only find out where each component was made and pass along the information, but he also had a secret weapon that passed under everyone's noses. That secret weapon is how he smuggled the plans out of the Royal Arsenal."

"I'm not following," he said.

"Charley," Holmes replied with a flourish. "Miss Fisher said Thomesson often took Charley to work with him. No one would suspect someone with Charley's affliction of suspicious activity. He could pass any defense unsuspected with Thomesson leading him."

"The boy with Mongolism? That boy?"

"Lestrade, Charley is also a *savant*. He has an amazing memory and can put the most complex puzzles together."

"Yes, I believe I've heard of them," he said after some contemplation. "They can perform outlandish math equations and the like, but can't button their trousers – that sort of thing."

"That is one way of putting it," said I, holding back a more acerbic response.

Holmes went on, "If the boy got but one look at those plans, it would be nothing for him to assemble the device from memory, just like the puzzles."

"So they kidnapped the boy for their own evil means. I must confess, I did not see it. You continue to astound me, Mr. Holmes."

"Everything was there for you to assemble."

"But I didn't have the plans," Lestrade responded in kind.

"Nor I, my good man, yet I was able to construct the puzzle, nonetheless."

"Yes, well I am sure you and the boy would be grand entertainment at parties," the inspector retorted.

After scribbling some more notes in his pad, he asked, "So all this time we've talked about the husband but not the wife. Where does she fit into this?"

"Miss Fisher had mentioned that Mrs. Thomesson had been in the habit of going on long walks in the afternoon while her husband was away at work. Shortly after the walks started, the wife started to intimate to her husband that she had become bored with their simple life and wished to have some of the finer things, the overture to which the husband responded by giving his wife what she wanted. It took very little time for her extravagances to usurp his earnings. According to Miss Fisher, he then tried borrowing money and betting on horses in hopes of a windfall. She didn't know from whom the money was borrowed, but I have no doubt the lender was the *I.F.C.*, set up by his wife. Thomesson proved ill-equipped for gambling and lost it all. With no way to pay back what he owed, I believe the wife then convinced him of this scheme with Charley, which had been the actual plan all along."

"So the wife and this Richtor fellow concocted this whole thing to use Thomesson and Charley to get not only the parts of the device, but also the plans to assemble it?"

"I'm quite certain that Mrs. Thomesson was meeting with Hugo Richtor on those afternoon walks. It was during these meetings that the seeds of this undertaking were planted. When Richtor had no more use for her, he killed her."

"I have men up there now searching the millponds and lakes. We should find her in due course."

"I'll leave that in your capable hands."

"So, in the end," Lestrade asked, "who was guilty of poisoning – that is, *gassing* – Thomesson?"

"Barnaby Thomesson," Holmes revealed dispassionately.

"I am not following," Lestrade said. "Are you saying he took his own life?"

"Not intentionally, no," Holmes said. "With some assurances on my part to disseminate this information to you and you only, Lestrade, in my conversation with Mycroft this morning, he revealed that at the Arsenal there is a sealed room with a working prototype of the device. It is used for, shall we say, testing its efficacy. The door to the room was found forced open. Thomesson must have known about this room. That *last attempt* Thomesson was referring to was an attempt at getting that working prototype and giving it to the *I.F.C.* in exchange for Charley. What he didn't know is that the device was welded to a table, which was, in turn, welded to the floor. It proved impossible to get the device out of the room. His guilty conscience for giving the boy up proved to be his downfall for, in that attempt, he accidentally exposed himself to a low level, yet still lethal, amount of phosgene. In high enough concentrations, it kills within

211

minutes. In lower concentrations, it can take hours or even up to a day before the onset of death."

"Incredible," Lestrade said.

"I believe, failing this last attempt, he went to Boodle's to partake in a bit of self-pity, began to feel the effects of the phosgene, stumbled outside, where I first encountered him, and he succumbed to the gas before I could acquire Watson's services. The rest you know, and here we are."

Yawning, Lestrade said, "See, that wasn't so hard. We could have been done by now if we had just started at *A* and gone through to *Z*."

"Yes," I offered. "However, that would have been the difference between you eating one scone or the three you've had since arriving."

Lestrade looked at his plate where the scones were now missing and to each of us. "Sorry."

Holmes laughed. "So long as we have been of service."

Getting up from his seat, Lestrade replied, "You most certainly have. I will not lie – you may get a medal out of this."

"Resolving the matter is its own reward. Any outlay of precious metals should go to the boy."

"Speaking of which," I then pondered, "what do you think will become of Charley and Miss Fisher?"

Refilling his tea, Holmes replied, "With his ability at puzzle solving, there may be a career for him as a consulting detective when I retire to Sussex and my bees. Until then, he has a most capable custodian in Miss Fisher. Of that I am certain."

NOTE

*   *Mongolism* is a Victorian term for *Down Syndrome*, which wasn't coined until the 1970's.

The Curse of Kisin
by Liese Sherwood-Fabre

The telegram arrived as we were finishing our dinner. I had already planned a stroll in the cool spring evening and considered the intrusion more than slightly annoying. My friend Sherlock Holmes was in high spirits, having recently completed the case of the singing blackbird, and had agreed to accompany me on my evening walk. Any time I could persuade him to take from his usual melancholy pursuits I considered a victory. Of course, the telegram from Scotland Yard requesting his assistance raised his spirits even more.

"What do you know about the Mayan civilization, Watson?" he asked and handed me the telegram.

"Central American, I believe," I said as I skimmed the missive requesting his assistance at the Explorations Club where a death had recently occurred. "Why do you ask? I see no reference to them here."

He stepped to a bookshelf and pulled out one of his scrapbooks. "Lestrade doesn't have to. The address says it all. The club has recently gained quite a bit of notoriety following the publicity of their most prominent member, Sir James Brandon-Smythe."

"I recall reading about him," I said, rubbing my chin. "He received his knighthood for having discovered a temple, I believe."

"A temple of the god Kisin, the Lord of the Underworld." He flipped through the pages of his scrapbook and stabbed his finger on one item. "Here it is: '*Sir James Brandon-Smythe Displays Grisly Sacrifices Returned from Mayan Temple.*' Apparently, he discovered some well-preserved mummified remains in the structure's foundation."

I read the article over his shoulder, studying the illustration that accompanied the piece. "Amazing that those items survived the climate there. He says it was due to their having been sealed in some sort of vault."

"The Mayans must have had advanced knowledge of preservation techniques," he said with a nod. "I should like to examine the pieces more closely. Imagine being able to maintain specimens . . . ." After a brief reflection on this idea, he slapped the book shut and dropped it on the nearest chair. "Perhaps I shall request a small sample for some chemical analysis."

Lestrade was waiting for us at the entrance to the Explorations Club near Pall Mal. It was a rather unassuming building for the gathering place of some of the most prestigious and daring adventurers of our day – just a

213

simple white stone building with a large wooden door. Inside, however, it became apparent this was no common club. The hallway was filled with maps, game trophies, and glass cases of ancient and native artifacts conveyed from faraway places. Ordinarily such a display would have piqued my friend's interest but, on this occasion, Holmes followed Lestrade with a deep intensity to the broken door frame halfway down the main hall where the dead man had been found.

"The man's name is Joseph York, Sir James' assistant," Lestrade said, stepping aside to let Holmes peer into the room. "They had to break in to get at the poor chap." The inspector consulted a small notebook before continuing. "The butler discovered the man had locked himself in, but Sir James demanded they break down the door. It's some sort of laboratory the club provided to store and examine the things he brought back from Central America. Between him, the doorman Davidson, and the butler Winston, they were able to force open the door. Found him just like he is."

"And the men who broke in?" Holmes asked. He still stood in the doorway, his gaze moving around, most likely taking in every detail.

"My men are guarding them in the library. I assumed you'd want to interview them yourself. Sir James warned everyone not to touch anything in case whatever killed York could still be lethal. Said something about the 'Curse of Kisin'."

I stepped to the door to get my own view of the scene. The room appeared to be some sort of laboratory with several black-topped tables arranged in rows where specimens could be spread out. Only one was in use now. A series of thin papers covered in drawings were spread across its surface. Lining three walls were a number of cabinets displaying ancient Central American artifacts – arrows, pottery, and even a few shrunken heads. One cabinet to the far right of the tables stood open. On a chest-high shelf, a clay pot lay on its side. A cluster of five short arrows protruded from the pot's open mouth, and a liquid dripped from it to the floor. Sir James' assistant, however, was not visible.

Holmes pulled a pair of leather gloves from his pocket. "I think I'll have a look about the room and the victim now. I would suggest you use your gloves as well – until we know what is leaking from that pot."

He headed toward the open cabinet but stopped and disappeared behind a table in front of it. "I'd appreciate your medical opinion here, Watson."

"That's where Mr. York is," Lestrade whispered to me. "He's lying on the floor in front of that table."

The dead man lay on his side, his back to the door as if in repose. I knelt next to him and lifted one arm. It flopped back to the ground with a dull *thump*. "I need to see his face to check for *rigor*."

With as much care as we could, we turned the man onto his back. When we did so, the cause of death became very apparent. An arrow, similar to the ones still in the overturned pot, protruded from his chest. After peering at the man's features, I said, "Stiffness will indicate how long since death. I see no signs of *rigor*, suggesting this happened very recently."

"Is that all you observe?" Holmes asked.

I picked up his hand. "No *rigor* here, either. His palms aren't calloused, and his nails are more groomed than mine. Researching ancient Mayan cultures doesn't appear to be a very dirty job."

He appeared not to have heard me because he pointed to a red spot on the man's collar. "What do you make of this?"

"There's a nick just above it on his neck. May have cut himself shaving this morning and bled a little on the collar. Odd. As well-groomed as he is, I would have expected him to change it. He must not have noticed it."

Before I finished this comment, Holmes had already turned to an examination of the man's clothing. In the right jacket pocket, he found a key. He studied it and the broken door, then stored it in his own waistcoat. Rocking back on his heels, he took in the man from head to toe and then stood, moving to the cabinet.

He focused his attention first on the overturned pot. "There's some sort of primitive spring inside. It appears that the assistant may have disturbed the pot, and it ejected an arrow into his chest. Additional analysis is needed, but I would guess it is tipped with curare."

Curare.

I shook my head. Not the first time we had stumbled upon its use. When investigating a report of a vampire in Sussex, Holmes had uncovered an attempt to murder a child with the substance. While not successful in that case, the Mayan trap appeared more effective.

"If it is curare, then the time of death is earlier than I originally suspected. Unfortunately, the drug slows the onset of *rigor*," I said.

"I'm not sure how that bit of information would enlighten us," he mumbled, now surveying the cabinet's contents from a few feet in front of its open doors.

I pulled my chin back at the slight his words carried and couldn't keep all my indignation from my voice. "It would have helped to more clearly define when the accident happened."

"Perhaps," was another muttered response as he turned from the cabinet and made his way to the table with the thin papers.

I joined him there, curious to see what they held.

Up close, I saw they were a sort of rubbings like those done of old gravestones to copy the original names and dates, only these were stylized figures – more blockish in nature than any carvings I'd seen.

"Fascinating," Holmes whispered. He removed his glove and ran a finger below the images copied there. "I believe these lie at the heart of Sir James' discoveries. Not only do they prove the site was a temple to Kisin, but also chronicle how the Mayans built their temples. He concluded the civilization had domesticated horses and other beasts of burden and used them to drag the large stone blocks to the site."

"What are those?" I asked, pointing to a stack of large glass plates next to the tracings.

My friend picked up one and held it before a lamp. "They appear to be copies of the temple drawings. These can be projected onto a wall for presentation to an audience." He spun about to address Lestrade, who was still in the doorway. "I should now like to speak to those in the library."

Two police officers guarded the room but stepped aside as we approached.

"Has anyone entered or left this room since they were dispatched here?" the inspector asked one.

The man stood as if at attention. "No, sir. They haven't even made much noise. It seems the scene froze their tongues."

"Let's hope they'll thaw a little for us," Holmes said.

As expected for a club dedicated to exploration, the library housed a great number of books on the room's four walls, but also included display cases like those in the hallway. Several globes topped different tables scattered about the room, and the wall space not lined in books held framed maps instead of the paintings or portraits common to such rooms. Wing-backed leather chairs were arranged in clusters around the tables to foster conversations between members, although at present, the three men seated in chairs near the fireplace didn't seem in a very sociable mood. Their pale faces suggested they were still in a form of shock, despite the time that had lapsed since discovering Mr. York.

Even though I lacked Holmes's powers of perception, I could identify the butler Winston and the doorman Davidson from their uniforms. I concluded that the third, dressed in a well-made but ill-fitting suit, was Sir James. He had apparently lost a lot of weight recently.

They turned toward us when we entered, and after my friend had studied their rounded stares, he asked, "Which one of you was the last to see York alive?"

216

Sir James raised his hand. "I was. I planned to make a presentation to the club tomorrow and had York assisting in my preparations. He'd copied some of the temple drawings on glass so that I could project them onto a wall, and was going to gather some of the objects for a display."

"When exactly did you see him?"

"About three o'clock." He shook his head and made a sort of *tsk-tsk* sound. "I told him to be careful with the items. They had to be handled delicately because the Mayans were known to set traps to keep thieves from stealing temple treasures. One of the workers at the temple site tripped something which severed his head from his body. The natives call it the 'Curse of Kisin'."

"He did warn us to be careful when we broke in," the doorman said. "Said there might be traps."

Holmes turned to the man. "We'll get back to that point. I want to understand the sequence of events first." Returning his attention to the knight, he asked, "You say you left him at three o'clock. Did anyone see you leave?"

The other two exchanged glances before the butler, Winston, said, "We both did, sir. I was down the hall and heard Sir James take his leave of Mr. York. When he stepped into the hallway, he asked me to inform Davidson he would need a cab and said he was going to the kitchen to arrange that dinner be brought to Mr. York at six o'clock. I told him it was quite irregular to allow a non-member the use of the club's amenities, especially meals, without a member present."

As if aware of how the dispute might appear to others, Sir James responded to the accusation before Holmes could frame his next question. "I assured Winston the club's board had provided a special status to York for his assistance in my preparations, and that I would return around that time anyway. He left to order the cab, and I followed."

"And where did you go for those few hours?"

"I met with some of the sponsors of my original trip. They wanted an update on the research I will be presenting here at the club."

"And you returned – ?

The knight glanced at the clock ticking over the mantel. "It's been about two hours now. So, a quarter-past-six."

The butler nodded. "Sir James sought me out to ask if I had served Mr. York his dinner. I explained that he hadn't responded to my knock and that the door was locked."

"That's when he came to the entrance and asked me if Mr. York had left," said Davidson. "I assured him that I hadn't seen Mr. York since his arrival this morning."

"All this was highly irregular for York," added Sir James. "He's a very meticulous person. That was one reason I had him copying the tracings onto the glass."

His remark made me recall the image of his well-groomed nails.

Sir James continued, "I requested Davidson accompany us and assist in gaining access to the room."

"And there is no other key?" Holmes asked.

"That particular room was never locked in the past," said Winston. "We had only the one, which I passed to Sir James when he was given the room for cataloging his discoveries."

"We would regularly lock the room from the inside to avoid just the type of accident that befell York," said the explorer with another shake of his head. "I couldn't be responsible for someone else falling to Kisin's curse."

"And so you three broke down the door." Holmes puckered his lips before asking, "Did all of you go into the room?"

"When the door gave way," offered Davidson, "we somewhat fell in. We didn't see Mr. York at first, him being on the floor and behind the table and all. Sir James sent us to count the tracings. Said there should be twenty. He was afraid someone had tried to steal 'em."

Holmes listened, gaze down as if in thought. At this bit of information, he directed his attention to Davidson. "Who noticed Mr. York first, then?"

"Well," the doorman said, drawing out the vowel a bit. "We went to the table, but before we could count 'em, Sir James gave a little yell, saying York's been hurt."

"We started toward him, but he pointed to the pot with the arrows and told us to get out of the room because there might be poison in the air or it might let another arrow fly," said Winston.

"And all of you left at the same time?"

The three nodded, and Davidson added, "I went outside and flagged down a passing officer. Told him what happened, and he said to stay away from the room, and here we've been since Inspector Lestrade and the other officers came."

My friend paused, hands behind his back. He sucked a bit of air through puckered lips as if he were about to light his pipe, although he had none in his mouth, a clear sign he was deep in thought. What was it that puzzled him? The events seemed clear to me. York had opened the cabinet to retrieve something and hit the pot by accident, springing the arrow that pierced his chest. The poison brought on a slow death as his whole body paralyzed, suffocating him. The thought of the poor man's drawn-out demise sent a shiver down my spine. I'd read of experiments with the poison. The victim remained conscious, fully aware of events with no loss of feeling, but unable to move. He might have been revived with the proper assistance, but with no one there and unable to call for help, he became the only witness to his own death.

My thoughts returned to the present when Holmes addressed Sir James. "I wonder if you would allow me to take a sample of the substance in the pot for analysis?"

The man's eyes rounded. "Do you think it safe? One scratch – "

"Yes," Holmes said slowly and continued more to himself than to anyone in the room. "One scratch . . . ."

He spun on his heel and spoke to me over his shoulder. "Come with me, Watson. I may have need of your assistance. And Winston – " The man stiffened, as if to attention. "Please be so kind as to supply me with a small flask or two to collect the sample."

I hesitated when we reached the broken doorframe, with the small glass bottles that the butler had passed me in my hands. "Are you sure it's safe?"

"Perfectly. Curare is only dangerous when administered under the skin. The South and Central American tribes use it for hunting, paralyzing their prey to kill it. They then consume the meat with no harmful effects, despite the drug in the animal's system. If we don't disturb any of the other items, there should be no issue."

As he spoke, Holmes made his way to the open cabinet. He studied the scene for a second time before requesting one of the flasks. "This pot's been moved. The dust on this self has been disturbed."

"Probably when York was getting something for the presentation."

"But what?" he asked, scanning the objects on that and the other shelves. "Once I collect these samples, we can return to Baker Street."

As we turned to leave the room, I gave York one last glance. Now on his back, his arms to his sides, he could almost have been asleep, except for the arrow rising from his blood-stained shirt. I dropped my eyes out of respect for the hapless victim of the ancient curse.

Before returning to our flat, Holmes stopped at the telegraph office to send off a few messages. He didn't share to whom they were addressed, or on what business. Once back in our residence, he moved to the chemistry equipment occupying one corner and spoke little except to request I inform Mrs. Hudson that any responses to his telegrams be brought to him immediately.

After completing this assignment, I retired to my bedroom.

He was still at it in the morning when I came to breakfast. My first action was to open the windows and let in some fresh air. "What have you been burning? It smells like . . . ." I paused, unable to find the words to describe the terrible stench. "I may eat my breakfast in my room to keep from tasting whatever you've been incinerating."

"Ah, Watson," my friend said as he turned in my direction. He held a flask in one hand and was swirling the dark, murky liquid about in it. "You've arrived just in time. I've finished my analysis of the substance in the pot. In case of any doubt, I have definitively determined that it was curare. However, not potent enough to kill a man. Observe the bird on the table."

"Good Heavens!" I said with a gasp. "You've killed Mrs. Hudson's canary!"

"Not killed, merely paralyzed." He glanced at his watch. "Another minute or two and he will rouse himself. If this formula won't kill a canary, it certainly wouldn't harm a man of thirteen stone. The replies to my telegrams arrived during the night as well. I have almost all I need to draw my conclusions."

As if on cue, the bird blinked its eyes, signaling a return of its faculties, but Holmes paid it no heed. Obviously deep in thought, he stared out the window. When he turned back, he seemed reanimated. "I need to go out for a consultation. I'll be back in a bit."

"But breakfast – ?"

"No need for food at present. Dulls the mind. But, please, enjoy yours. I will, however, ask you to have Mrs. Hudson prepare some coffee for when I return. In about – " He checked his watch. " – two hours should do it. Then we shall be heading back to the Explorations Club."

My friend returned in almost two hours to the minute. He was as animated as any hound before the hunt. He downed a cup of coffee from the pot Mrs. Hudson had provided, rubbed his hands together, and gave a self-satisfied smile. "I have it all now. Come along, Watson. They will be waiting for us at the club."

This announcement caused me to pause in the doorway. When Holmes had noted we would be returning to the club, I'd assumed he wished to review the room a second time. I called down the stairway, where he waited for me by the entrance. "They? Who is this 'they' waiting for us?"

"Why Lestrade and the three men who found Sir James's assistant. I already sent out the telegrams, requesting they be at the club at a quarter-to. We must not keep them waiting."

While I would have liked to ask him just what he'd discovered, he was much too agitated and preoccupied to find my questions anything but an annoyance, so I kept my peace, knowing that all would be answered shortly.

220

Once again, we found ourselves once again in the library with Sir James, Winston, and Davidson. Inspector Lestrade and two of his officers awaited our arrival as well.

The loss of his assistant had deeply affected Sir James. Not only did he wear a black mourning armband, but he also seemed even more shrunken than he had the day before, as if grief had depleted him.

"I see you all received my invitations, and I thank you for responding. First, let me state that based on my investigation, I have concluded Mr. York was murdered."

The inspector drew in his breath. "Now see here, Mr. Holmes, you can't be making accusations like that without – "

"But I can, Lestrade. I have proof this was no accident. It was *made* to appear like one. We can be certain of the following: York opened the cabinet, disturbed a pot filled with curare-tipped arrows set to impale anyone lifting the lid, and was hit by an arrow. Sailors refer to this as a 'booby trap', although Sir James calls it the 'Curse of Kisin,' a myth meant to discourage intruders from desecrating the temple."

The inspector broke in again. "What makes you think it wasn't this curse?"

"Because of the anomalies – of which there were many." He ticked them off on his fingers. "First, what was he retrieving from the cabinet? The only intact pot was the one with the arrows. All others were shards, and pieces of pots. Furthermore, the pot with the arrows had been recently moved toward the cabinet's edge. Nothing else had been disturbed in the cabinet. He had nothing in his hands, nor did anything else show signs of being moved or fallen. Even more intriguing was the scratch on his neck. Initially, like Watson, I thought he had simply nicked himself shaving, but it was too fresh for that. Furthermore, the curare in the pot was too weak to kill a grown man. My analysis and a telegram from one expert confirmed that the poison comes in different potencies, and this one would have paralyzed him, but not killed him. It wasn't even strong enough to kill a small bird."

The image of Mrs. Hudson's canary flitted through my brain, and then came the realization that poor York had lain on the floor while someone . . . .

"Good Lord," I said. "The murderer stabbed him with the arrow? Into the heart?"

"Exactly, Watson. An injection of the poison directly into his heart accomplished what the scratch wouldn't. Having ensured his demise, the murderer arranged the scene to make it appear like an accident and left."

Winston glanced around at those in the room. "Who did that? You think one of us? I had no reason to harm the man. Besides, he'd locked

221

himself in. You found the key in his pocket. And I heard Sir James conversing with him before he left."

My friend spun about to face him. "Did you? Hear a true conversation between Sir James and York? Or did it just *appear* that Sir James was talking to someone?"

The butler paused, apparently recalling the events of the previous evening. He drew in a sharp breath. "You're right. Sir James said at the door he would arrange dinner for him, but I don't remember York replying."

At this pronouncement, the knight rose to his feet. "Now see here, I'll not listen to any more of these baseless accusations! The man York made a grave error by opening the cabinet and disturbing the pot."

He moved as if to leave, swaying slightly on his feet, but the two officers who had accompanied Lestrade stepped in front of the library door, effectively blocking the only exit. Holmes placed himself between the man and the officers and continued reciting his conclusions.

"You, sir, are the one who made the grave error. You set the pot on the edge of the cabinet shelf and instructed York to open the door to retrieve something from the cabinet. When he did so, the pot tipped over and released the arrow. It, however, almost completely missed the man, only scratching his neck. Enough to paralyze him, but not enough to kill him. You had to do this yourself."

"I want no more of this – this fairy tale," he said and took a step toward the door.

With his next step, he swayed again, appearing unable to keep his equilibrium. Despite his stated desire to leave, he collapsed into the nearest chair. I made a move toward him, but the knight waved me off. "I don't need your help."

Lestrade frowned. "I do have one question of my own, Mr. Holmes. What about the key?"

"After discussing the dinner arrangements with Winston, Sir James sent him to request a cab. He merely locked the door behind him before leaving the building. When he and the others broke in the door, he sent the others to count the tracings. While the two men were busy with this task, he slipped the key into York's pocket before the others saw the murdered man."

"Fiction, I tell you," Sir James said, his face now turning a deep vermillion. "What possible reason would I have to harm the man – let alone murder him?"

"That is what puzzled me at the beginning. Not the *how* – I quickly deduced the sequence of events – but the *why*. The motive. Why murder an assistant who had never set foot outside of England, or London for that

222

matter? If you wish to accuse someone of fairy tales, Sir James, I would look no further than yourself. All this poppycock about a Mayan curse. If such misfortune derived from the temple's desecration, you, sir, are the main desecrator, and would be lying on the floor.

"No, the motive lay elsewhere. About five feet elsewhere. I sent a telegram last night to the country's foremost expert on South American flora and fauna, as well as the authorities, to learn more about the death of the worker you described. This morning I compared your tracings with similar temple carvings on display at the British Museum. I determined three facts: There were no horses – or most species of cattle (the bison being the exception, of course) – in the Americas until the arrival of the Europeans. That the deceased worker was the victim of yellow fever. And apart from the aforementioned animals, Sir James' tracings bear a remarkable resemblance to those in the British Museum. I confirmed the meticulous Mr. York had visited the Museum and must have come to the same conclusions about the temple carvings. He must have presented this information to Sir James. The man had just been knighted because of his discoveries. He couldn't risk the scandal the truth would have caused."

Sir James leaped from his seat, glanced around the room as if seeking a place to run, and literally crumpled to the floor, his legs unable to support him. The seven of us rushed forward to carry him to the nearest couch, although all of us weren't needed to do so. When I took his wrist to check his pulse, I found him to be only skin and bones.

I revived him with ammonia and brandy provided by Winston. A pale bit of color returned to the man's cheeks.

Once more aware of his surroundings, he muttered so softly, I had to bend forward to hear him. "What have I done? Poor York. I killed him. And for what?" He turned his head and focused on my friend, his voice a bit stronger. "You're right, of course, Mr. Holmes. I shouldn't have tried to fool you. Better to have accepted the shame than to take a man's life. I – I simply couldn't return with nothing to show for my work or to the trip's backers. Two years tramping through the jungle. The Curse of Kisin!" He sneered at the name. "Yellow fever was my curse. It killed the worker outright. In my case, it caused a lingering illness that will be my death one day soon. I spent weeks shaking and sweating in a native's hut. When I recovered enough to leave, I bargained with those in his village for the trinkets you see in those cabinets."

I glanced at Holmes and Lestrade and shook my head. The shock of the exposure of his deceit and his weakened condition had taken its toll. The man was likely to be an invalid for the rest of his life, if he survived at all. "This man needs more medical attention than I can give him here. He should be taken to hospital immediately."

As the ambulance carrying Sir James disappeared around the corner, Holmes turned to Lestrade. "It is, of course, up to you whether to arrest the man or not, but I believe he is not long for this world. He will most likely not survive to be tried."

"Doesn't seem right, though," said the inspector as he tugged on his waistcoat, "not punishing him for taking another's life."

"I would say his punishment will come swiftly enough. Both he and his assistant have fallen to the curse of this Mayan god."

The Case of the
Blood-Stained Leek
by Margaret Walsh

It was a chill, grey, morning in the February of 1901 when my good friend, Sherlock Holmes, and I were summoned to the Diogenes Club to meet with Holmes's older brother, Mycroft. As I have mentioned in previous tales, Mycroft worked for, and in some respects actually *was*, the British Government. It was obvious that the meeting was of some importance and much secrecy. At that time of day, Mycroft should have been in his office at Whitehall.

The weather reflected the mood of the city, which was in mourning, our dear Queen Victoria having quietly passed away in late January. Though she had spent much of her later life voluntarily immured at Osborne House on the Isle of Wight, we all felt her passing keenly, along with that of the age to which she had given her name. Time would tell if the new Edwardian age of her son would be as glorious for Britain as hers was. The mood of the city was still sombre, however, with the Queen's funeral having only occurred just two weeks previously.

The usher who led us to the Stranger's Room wore a black armband around his right bicep. That was the only outward sign of mourning in the place, however. *Regina mortua est; vivat rex*, as the saying goes.

Mycroft was waiting for us, along with a well-dressed man, whom I recognized, with some shock, as the current Prime Minister, Robert Arthur Talbot Gascoyne-Cecil, 3rd Marquess of Salisbury. I realized that whatever was to come was of such importance that neither man could be seen to visit the other openly.

"Gentlemen," Mycroft said gravely, "Thank you for coming. We have a situation in which we need your expertise, Sherlock."

"And what would that be?"

"Murder, Sherlock. Bloody murder."

"You have policemen for that. There must be something usual about this murder for you and the Prime Minister to request our involvement."

I saw that the Prime Minister looked sideways at me. Holmes saw it too, as he said, "And I mean *our* involvement. Watson is invaluable when investigating such cases as Mycroft brings to my attention."

Gascoyne-Cecil inclined his head. "I stand corrected, Mr. Holmes. His Majesty's government will be forever in debt to both of you if you can salvage the situation."

Holmes nodded briskly. "But first we must know exactly what the situation is."

Mycroft waved us to seats. "The situation is as follows: You are aware that the coronation is scheduled for August next year?"

"The papers have been filled with little else," Holmes replied.

"There is also the need to have Prince George officially invested as Prince of Wales, and to that end the government sent a man to Abergavenny to scout out a suitable location for the investiture to take place."

I frowned. "Why Abergavenny? Doesn't the investiture of the Prince of Wales usually take place in Carnarvon?"

"It does, Dr. Watson," the Prime Minister agreed, "but His Majesty felt that the place was somewhat contentious, with it being the location that spurred the English conquest of Wales in the thirteenth century. His Majesty felt that somewhere like Abergavenny, still within the borders of Wales, but with less obvious associations, would be more suitable. Our new monarch is first, and foremost, a peacemaker."

Personally, I felt that our new monarch was first and foremost a rakehell. He was conjectured to have had at least fifty mistresses, most notable amongst them being the actress Lily Langtry, and Daisy Greville, Countess of Warwick.

The Prime Minster continued, "The Palace dispatched a young secretary, Mr. Michael Wakelin, to Abergavenny to check for a suitable site for the investiture. Three days ago, Mr. Wakelin's body was found hanging from the rafters of the Drill Hall in Baker Street, which is the headquarters of the 4th Volunteer Battalion of the South Wales Borders."

"Suicide?" I asked.

"Unlikely, Doctor," Mycroft said. "There are circumstances that suggest otherwise."

"And those are?" Holmes asked.

"When the body was discovered the next morning, the item which caught the eye of the attending police officer was a leek which had been dipped in blood and placed in Wakelin's breast pocket."

"A leek dipped in blood?" I blinked in bemusement.

"Yes."

"An odd *accoutrement,* to be sure," Holmes observed. "And one that obviously has some significance to you both."

"It has," Mycroft agreed. "The emblem of the blood-stained leek is very familiar to the Prime Minister and to myself, though usually it is depicted clutched in the paw of a lion. It is the badge of the Byddin Rhyddid Cymru, or Welsh Freedom Army. They wish for a Wales free from English dominion, and espouse the methods used by the Fenian group Clan na Gael to attempt to gain what they want."

"In other words," Holmes said softly, "terror, mayhem, and death."

"Exactly."

"And you believe that Wakelin was murdered by them to send a message to The Crown and the Government?" I asked.

The Prime Minister looked at me, "It would be a strange man indeed, Dr. Watson, that let himself into a building in which he had no business being – "

" – Nor had a key – " Mycroft inserted.

" – in order to commit suicide," Gascoyne-Cecil continued. "And furthermore, why would he do so with bloody leek in his pocket?"

"All very good points," Holmes said. "Very well, Mycroft, I believe that Watson and I can take a trip to Abergavenny and take a little look at your problem for you."

"Naturally, you will be discreet, Mr. Holmes?"

"Of course, Prime Minister. I would never deliberately embarrass The Crown, nor the Government. I'm sure my brother has already assured you of that fact."

"He has. I am just afraid of the consequences if this gets out."

"Then we will do our outmost to ensure that it does not."

"And I give you my assurances," I added, "that I will not write about it for publication."

"You have both set my mind at rest. I look forward to your resolution of this problem. A good day to you both." The Prime Minister then departed, leaving us alone with Mycroft, who handed us an envelope. "This contains train tickets to Abergavenny. I've arranged with the local police for you both to be accommodated at a local hotel."

Holmes took the envelope, tucking it carefully into his pocket. "My thanks. You will hear from us when we have solved the case."

We then took our leave. Once outside, I asked, "You are sure we can solve it?"

"Every crime has the seeds of its solution within it. This case is no different to any other, except for the rank of those who have engaged us."

The very next morning we took a Great Western Railway locomotive from Paddington Station. Mycroft had generously provided us with first-class tickets, so we had a comfortable ride. The time passed quickly. Holmes was deep in his thoughts, and I took pleasure in watching the world outside the windows of the train.

We were met at Abergavenny Station by a well-dressed man in his thirties, with dark curly hair and soulful brown eyes. He introduced himself to us as Inspector Rhodri Evans, the police officer in charge of the investigation.

He shook Holmes's hand vigorously. "I am pleased to make your acquaintance, Mr. Holmes. And yours as well, Dr. Watson," he added, shaking my hand. "It is a relief to me to have someone with your knowledge and abilities here. This case is well beyond my experience. Drunken fights over women I can handle, but something like this, with the political aspects – No, it isn't something that I feel confident about handling."

This relieved my mind a great deal. Going into a police case – or rather, being thrust into a police case – can be tricky. Quite often the officers in charge resent us being there. To know that we were welcome would make things go much more smoothly.

Inspector Evans took us to the police station, which happened to be situated in Baker Street. I found it amusing that we had left Baker Street for another Baker Street. Holmes just shook his head. "I'm sure, my dear Watson, that you will find a Baker Street or Road in just about every town and city in the British Isles, being named as they are for the profession that was conducted here in the medieval period and perhaps earlier."

The police station and the Drill Hall both sat on an odd little triangle of land formed by Baker Street, Frogmore Street, and Lewis's Lane. The station sat in the corner of Baker Street and Lewis's Lane. The Drill Hall, though officially known as the Baker Street Drill Hall, had its entrance off Lewis's Lane. One could quite literally throw a stone from one building to the other.

We left our luggage in the care of the station sergeant and accompanied Inspector Evans across the road to the hall. "Because of the location of both the station and the hall, the commander of the battalion that uses the hall leaves a key at the station in case of trouble. It makes more sense than having to fetch him if there is trouble."

"Who found the body?" Holmes asked.

"I did. A young lad who works for the butcher in Baker Street was coming down Lewis's Lane on his way to work, from his home in Lion Street. He noticed that the door was ajar, so he came into the station to tell us, before heading on to his work."

"A civic minded young gentleman," Holmes observed.

"Young Aled is the son of one of my colleagues," Evans replied. "He may not have had any desire to join the police, but he is right-minded, all the same."

Evans unlocked the door and let us into the building. "With the exception of the removal of the dead man, the hall is as we found it." He gestured to a beam high above us. "I found the body dangling from that. And before you ask, there was no sign of how he got up there. Not ladder, nor a chair. Not that he could have reached the beam with a chair. As it was, we had to borrow a ladder from my cousin Monty, who is a window cleaner, to be able to get Wakelin down."

"Was there any sign of forced entry?" Holmes asked, as he looked around the hall.

"None. The lock was either expertly picked, or they had a key."

Holmes went over to the door and withdrew his magnifying lens from his pocket.

"They?" I asked.

"It has to be more than one man, Dr. Watson. It took two of my men to manoeuvre the ladder into place to get the corpse down. Someone would have to be guarding Wakelin."

"Unless it was set up in advance," Holmes replied from his position at the door. He straightened up. "The murderer or murderers used a key to get in. There is no sign that the lock has been picked. Lock picking leaves behind very distinct scratches. I'm assuming the body has already been sent back to London?"

"Yes, Mr. Holmes, but we have detailed photographs, as well as the *post mortem* report, waiting for you at the station."

"Excellent, Inspector. Shall we go? We have learned all there is to learn from the hall."

"I am afraid that there wasn't much to learn," Inspector Evans said apologetically.

"On the contrary," my friend replied. "I've found this place to be remarkably interesting."

"What is interesting about it?" I asked as we followed Inspector Evans across the road. "There was nothing to see."

"And that, my dear Watson, was what was so interesting."

I shook my head. I knew by now that I would never follow just how my friend's incredible mind worked. All I had seen was a clean and empty hall. Holmes had, once again, obviously observed something that had bearing on the case.

Back in the police station, Inspector Evans settled us in his own office with the documents and, most welcome of all, a pot of tea and a plate of sandwiches.

Holmes read the police report and I read the *post mortem*. I had only glanced through a few paragraphs before I stopped and waved the report. "Holmes, look at this!" He raised his eyes and took it, reading aloud: "'*The*

229

neck was cleanly snapped between the third and fourth cervical vertebrae. This may or may not have been the cause of death, as the larynx was completely crushed which also would have resulted in death.'"

"He most definitely didn't hang himself," I said. "There is no sign of a bruise caused by a submental knot under the chin. Nor is there any sign of any bilateral fracture traversing the *pars interarticularis* of the second cervical vertebrae with the associated traumatic subluxation, or dislocation, of the third cervical vertebrae."

"Otherwise known as the 'Hangman's Fracture'," Holmes said. "Someone put their hands around the poor chap's throat and squeezed and shook him until his neck snapped." He handed me several photographs. "Look at the bruising pattern."

One was a close-up of the neck. My friend was correct: The bruising was clearly not from a rope. In fact, there was a little skin abrasion, but no sign of blood from the scrapes, showing that the rope had been applied after death. The second photograph caught my eye. It was a head and chest view of the corpse, still clad, and with the rope around the neck, before the *post mortem* was performed. I noticed a dark stain on the man's shirt. It wasn't blood, because I could see the blood-stained leek we had been told about peeking out the pocket on the opposite side of the shirt from the stain.

"Is there anything in the police report about that stain?" I asked.

Holmes smiled slightly. "Well spotted, Watson. According to the Good Inspector's report, the stain was still wet and smelled strongly of beer." He tapped the photograph. "There is something else."

I looked again and frowned as I realized what my friend was drawing my attention to. "The rope is a perfectly tied hangman's knot."

"And in the correct position," Holmes said.

"Which doesn't tie up with the evidence of the body," I said.

"Exactly." Holmes fairly beamed at me. "Interesting, is it not?"

"Inspector Evans did the right thing in notifying London," I said. "He has sound instincts."

"In some respects," Holmes replied. "In others, not so much."

"What do you mean?"

Holmes handed me a bundle of paper. "These were attached to the police report. They are statements from the owner of the Baker's Arms Hotel where Wakelin was staying, and those of the owner's wife and daughter."

"Is there something wrong with them?"

"All three of them were singing exactly the same song, and it certainly wasn't 'Men of Harlech'."

"Meaning?"

"Yes, Wakelin stayed with them. No, they didn't see him talk to anyone. No, he didn't drink in the bar."

"He had beer on his shirt!"

"Inspector Evans never asked them about the beer. In short, the Good Inspector asked very few relevant questions. He didn't even ask if they knew who had keys to the hall."

"Perhaps he already knew the answer to that question."

"Be that as it may, the question should still have been asked and the answer recorded. It is a valid and important question. A corpse is found in a building. One of the first things asked should be, 'Who had access to the building?'."

"This isn't Scotland Yard," I reminded him.

He looked at the police report with some disgust. "More's the pity. I cannot imagine Lestrade or Gregson, or even Jones, not asking so basic a question."

I leafed through the reports. "Evans only questioned the publican and his family? No regulars?"

"Apparently Mr. Pumphrey, mine host, couldn't remember who was in the bar that night. Neither could his wife and daughter."

"But that doesn't make sense. Yes, Abergavenny is a town, not a small village, but he would have regulars."

"Exactly. In fact, he would more likely notice who *wasn't* present than who was."

"So the publican knows something?"

"There is a very high probability that he does. At the very least, he suspects someone."

"Could he be afraid of the Byddin Rhyddid Cymru?" I was sure that I had mangled the name, but Holmes understood to whom I was referring.

"It's possible. Heaven knows such groups rule the local population with fear in other countries."

Inspector Evans came into the office. "Have you finished with the reports?"

"We have," Holmes replied. "They were most informative." Evans missed the sarcasm in Holmes's voice completely.

"Excellent," the inspector said. "We need to find somewhere for you gentlemen to stay. There is no shortage of good hotels around here."

"My friend and I would quite like to stay at the Baker's Arms, Inspector, if that is at all possible," Holmes said.

"I am sure that can be arranged," Evans replied.

As he turned to leave, Holmes called after him. "Inspector, do you happen to know who has keys to the drill hall?"

231

"I do. The Commander of the 4ᵗʰ Volunteer Battalion, the South Wales Borders has a key, as does his immediate subordinate. There is a key kept here, and the cleaning lady also has a key."

"I see. Who, may I ask, is the cleaning lady?"

"Marge Pumphrey, the wife of Dylan Pumphrey – "

"The publican of the Baker's Arms," Holmes finished. "Thank you, Inspector Evans, that is most interesting. Oh, and I would like to examine Mr. Wakelin's personal effects."

"We left them in storage at the hotel. I shall have them delivered to your room there."

"Left them at the hotel," I muttered in Holmes's ear. "What on earth – ?"

"As you intimated before, Watson, we aren't in London anymore. Obviously, they do things differently here. Not necessarily better, but definitely different."

We gathered our luggage from where we had left it and followed Inspector Evans up the street to the Baker's Arms. The hotel was old – a fifteenth-century coaching inn that was painted white, with mullioned windows and a roof of good Welsh slate.

We received a somewhat subdued welcome from Mr. Dylan Pumphrey, but he readily found us two rooms on the second floor and delivered Wakelin's belongings to Holmes's room under the watchful eye of Inspector Evans.

Evans then took his leave of us, saying that he would see us in the morning. There was a chair in front of the window in Holmes's room that looked out onto Baker Street below. From that position, I watched Holmes rummage through Wakelin's meagre belongings. There were three shirts of reasonable quality, a much-patched and darned nightshirt, several undershirts and drawers, and four pairs of newish black socks. After a while, I grew bored. "Do Waklein's belongings tell you anything?"

"Very little, except that he was a miserly man who didn't care to spend money if he could avoid it."

"How do you work that out from a few clothes?"

"Clothes can be very informative, my friend." He beckoned me over.

Curiosity aroused, I got to my feet and joined him where he had Wakelin's valise open on the bed. "You note that the under-things are mostly cheap. This could be a sign of a man down on his luck except for two things: One is the quality of the suit he was wearing, and also that of his shirts and socks. Socks wear out as frequently as underclothes do, but Wakelin wasn't buying cheap socks. These, unless I miss my guess, are made from the finest Australian merino wool."

"So why the cheap underclothes but expensive socks?" I admit I was now quite curious.

"Elementary. The trouser leg will ride up on occasion, as you well know, displaying the socks to those passing by. Wakelin was obviously a man who valued his image. He couldn't be seen to be wearing cheap socks with an expensive suit. And judging from what we saw in the photographs, the suit was good quality tweed and most likely made in Savile Row – not by the very best of the Savile Row tailors, such as Gieves and Hawkes, but certainly by one of their lesser competitors."

"But what if he was short of money?"

Holmes shook his head. "The police report detailed the items found on the body. Didn't you read that part?"

"I didn't get a chance."

"Well, if you had read it, you would have seen that found on the body was a wallet containing £3 10s 7d – a large amount of cash for a man to be carrying. As a secretary at Buckingham Palace, Wakelin would have been well paid." Holmes proceeded to shove everything back into the valise. "Come, Watson, I think it's time that we made the acquaintance of our fellow guests and the regulars."

"And how shall we do that?"

"Time for a few drinks in the bar." Holmes smiled at me slyly. "You know what I always say: There is no place like a public house for gathering information."

"Gathering gossip, you mean," I said with a smile of my own.

Holmes waved a hand from side to side. "Information or gossip – it's six-of-one and half-a-dozen of the other, as the old saying goes. Are you coming?" He walked out of the room, leaving me to follow.

The bar in the Baker's Arms was busy and loud, but the noise dropped to a low almost-suspicious hum when Holmes and I entered the room. I felt that we were being watched with hostility, but Holmes ignored it and sailed up to the bar where Dylan Pumphrey was serving. "Beer for myself and my friend, Mr. Pumphrey, and a round of beer for everyone as well."

"Are you sure, sir?" Pumphrey asked somewhat hesitantly.

"Of course," Holmes replied.

Pumphrey drew beers for both of us and then signalled to everyone else to line up to get theirs. I noticed that Holmes's casual announcement had immediately melted whatever hostility there had been in the room.

Holmes brought a pint glass to me, sipped his own, and gazed benevolently around the room. Men kept coming up to thank him for his generosity. Holmes would smile and murmur a few words about not liking

233

to be a stranger. He got more than a few hearty claps on the back. A large, beefy lad did so hard enough that he almost fell over.

"Sorry about that, sir," another man said as he grabbed my friend's shoulder to steady him. "Robert doesn't know his own strength, sometimes."

"Robert?" I asked.

"Robert Priddy," came the reply. "Works on a farm just outside the town. With my own eyes, I have seen him right a fallen sheep all by himself."

"Right a fallen sheep?"

The man chuckled. "You city men! The weight of the sheep's own fleece can cause them to fall and roll on their backs. If they aren't set back up on their feet, the sheer weight of their fleece will lead to death by suffocation." He held out his hand to me to shake, "Hugh Jones, local farm hand."

"Please to meet you, Mr. Jones. I am Dr. John Watson, and this is Mr. Sherlock Holmes."

"A pleasure to make your acquaintance, gentlemen. Now I must be off." Mr. Jones wandered away to join the group of which Robert Priddy was a part.

Another man stepped into his place. "Mr. Holmes," he murmured, "Dr. Watson. It is a sad thing that brings you to Abergavenny."

"It is, indeed, Mr. – ?"

"My name is Gareth Scurlock. I have some advice for you."

"And that would be?"

"Don't look to Byddin Rhyddid Cymru for the culprit."

"Why not?" Holmes asked softly.

"There is no benefit to be had in killing the messenger, Mr. Holmes, rather than the man who sent him." Scurlock raised his glass to us, his lips curving in a sardonic smile. "Thank you for the beer." His eyes flicked briefly towards the bar where Mr. Pumphrey and his daughter were serving. "Use your much vaunted powers of observation, Mr. Holmes." With that Gareth Scurlock turned and walked away from us.

Holmes led me to the bar. "Mr. Pumphrey, can I trouble you for a moment?"

"What is it, Mr. Holmes?" The publican seemed wary.

"I briefly made the acquaintance of Hugh Jones. Do you think his group would mind if my friend and I joined them?"

Pumphrey looked across at the group. "Well, Hugh Jones is bright enough. But I doubt Robert Priddy would be able to hold a conversation with you. His only interests are sheep, beer, rugby and . . . Well, sheep, beer, and rugby." I noticed that his daughter gave him a hard look, placing her hands on her hips as she did so. The movement caused her sleeves to slide up, revealing, just for a moment, a ring of bruises on her left wrist.

"My good friend Watson used to play rugby." Holmes nudged me sharply.

"Oh, yes. I played for Blackheath in my younger days."

Pumphrey gave a nervous chuckle. "Then no doubt Rob would like to talk with you."

"And the other gentlemen?" Holmes asked.

"That's Monty Evans. He's Inspector Evan's cousin."

"Inspector Evans mentioned him. Said he was a window cleaner."

"That he is. The other chap is Charlie Calcraft Price. He works for Monty."

"Calcraft is an unusual name," Holmes said.

Pumphrey looked like he had swallowed a lemon. "It's something of a nickname, sir. I don't know where he got it. Anyway, I'm not sure he would want to chat with you gentlemen. He doesn't much care for the English – even if they do buy him beer."

"Well, then," said Holmes, "we will not disturb them. My friend and I will take a brief walk and then retire for the night. Good night, Mr. Pumphrey, Miss Pumphrey." He nodded to them both and guided me out of the hotel and into the street.

"Where are we going?"

"Just a short walk along the street to the police station. I need to use their telephone."

"Who do you want to call?"

"Mycroft. I need to let him know that the case is solved."

I stopped dead in the street, staring at him with my mouth agape. Holmes continued to walk on, leaving me to stumble after him.

Holmes was on the telephone to Mycroft for only a few minutes. He replaced the receiver, thanked the sergeant on duty, left a message for Inspector Evans, and led me back out into the street. "Mycroft was most pleased. Someone will be here on the first train tomorrow to take the killer into custody. Come, it is time we both got some sleep."

We returned to the Baker's Arms and made our way up to our rooms.

The next morning was a fine and clear one. After a tasty breakfast of bacon with coddled eggs and mushrooms, we walked to the Abergavenny station where we met up with Inspector Rhodri Evans, to await the arrival of the morning train.

It arrived dead on time, and I think that Holmes, as well as I, were surprised to see Mycroft himself disembark. He was accompanied by

Inspector Lestrade of Scotland Yard, as well as several other more junior detectives, and a well-dressed man of middle-years who was introduced to us as Mr. Horace Padgett, Wakelin's immediate superior at the Palace.

Holmes looked at his brother with raised eyebrows. "I'm surprised to see you here."

Mycroft's face showed his distaste at both having to travel and the breaking of his normal routine. "The Prime Minister insisted upon it, as did His Majesty. It is, after all, a matter of national security."

"Well, it shouldn't take too long, and we'll have you back to London in time for supper."

"For that, Sherlock, I would be most grateful."

Lestrade had moved to stand beside me, and I introduced him to Inspector Evans.

Holmes turned to Lestrade. "It is good to see you again. What did my brother have to do to drag you away on an excursion to Wales?"

"Not much, Mr. Holmes," Lestrade laughed. "Your cases are always interesting, so I am always pleased to be involved. Where do we have to go to apprehend our felon?"

"Inspector Evans here will show us the way."

"I will?" Evans looked nonplussed.

"Yes, to the farm where Robert Priddy works."

"But Priddy isn't a member of Byddin Rhyddid Cymru," Evans protested. "I would stake my pension on it."

"I would tend to agree. The man doesn't have the subtlety required for membership in such an organization," Holmes said. "But Byddin Rhyddin Cymru did not murder Michael Wakelin."

"They did not?" I asked.

"No. I shall explain later. Come, gentlemen – we have a murderer to arrest."

When Robert Priddy saw us, he tried to run. Though he was a big man, he wasn't especially fleet of foot. One of Lestrade's junior officers brought him down in a flying tackle that would have made him desirable to any rugby team in the land. The other detectives piled on and soon had Priddy handcuffed. The man was blubbering. "I didn't mean to! It was an accident!"

"Was it?" Evans asked softly, looking at Holmes.

Holmes shook his head. "That's for a jury to decide, but I have no doubt that the charge will be that of murder, for you cannot grab a man around the throat and not expect him to die."

We returned to the police station, where Evans had Priddy locked up in a cell until he could be transported to London. "The Palace is insisting on a trial at the Old Bailey. It must be shown that murdering employees of

The Crown will not be tolerated," Mycroft said as he settled himself into a chair that Evans had hastily provided.

"Indeed," Horace Padgett added. "And His Majesty will be most impressed with the speed that you have solved this case, Mr. Holmes."

"It turned out to be quite simple in the end," my friend replied.

"Simple to you," I said, "but for the life of me, I cannot see how you came to realize that Robert Priddy was the murderer."

"I would quite like to know that as well," said Inspector Evans. "Along with all the details, such as how the body came to be hanging from the rafters of the Drill Hall."

"It was obvious from the beginning that Wakelin hadn't been hanged, despite the rope around his neck. From the *post mortem* report, it was clear that Wakelin hadn't died from hanging, but most likely from someone breaking his neck with their hands. The man's larynx was crushed, as well as his neck being broken in the wrong place."

Evans frowned. "But the rope was tied in a hangman's knot."

"It was."

"But – "

Holmes held up a finger. "I will clear that up in a moment. The *post mortem* report, the police report, and the photographs gave a clear picture of a conspiracy to make the death look like a hanging. And if they did that, then why not make it look like someone else was to blame?"

"The blood-stained leek?" Mycroft asked.

"A red-herring," Holmes replied. "All became clear last night in the bar of the Baker's Arms."

"It did?" I asked. I shook my head. "I saw nothing to indicate that."

"As I've said before, my dear Watson, you see, but you do not observe. There were more than enough clues to put it all together."

"Please do so, Mr. Holmes," Padgett said, leaning forward eagerly. "This is most interesting."

"In the first instance, a member, possibly the leader of Byddin Rhyddid Cymru, told me that they weren't responsible for the killing. It was intimated that they would have waited and struck at Prince George or his father."

I spluttered. "Who? What? I don't remember that!"

"Gareth Scurlock, who came up to us. Remember his words, Watson: *There is no benefit to be had in killing the messenger, Mr. Holmes, rather than the man who sent him.*"

"Good Lord!" Padgett looked aghast. "Can you arrest this man?"

Lestrade shook his head. "No. He has done nothing wrong. He made no obvious threat. It would never get to court."

"I tend to agree," Mycroft said. "Please continue, Sherlock."

"After that, it was simply a matter of observation. Young Alys Pumphrey had bruises on her left wrist, such as would be left if someone grabbed it and applied pressure."

"You mean Wakelin attacked the girl?" said Mycroft.

"I don't think he got a chance beyond grabbing her by the wrist. Her sweetheart saw what was happening and lost his temper. Grabbing Wakelin by the throat, killing him either inadvertently or by design. That he grabbed him violently is shown by the beer stain on Wakelin's shirt. He obviously had his glass in his other hand at the time."

"The lass and Priddy. But – " I was out of my depth.

"Last night, I asked Dylan Pumphrey about Priddy and those he was drinking with. Pumphrey told us that Priddy was only interested in sheep, beer, and rugby. But he almost added something else, before correcting himself."

A memory struck me – of Alys Pumphrey, hands on her hips, glaring at her father. "Of course. He was going to say Alys's name as the fourth thing that Priddy was interested in, but realized that it could give him away."

"Exactly. After that, it wasn't hard to work out exactly who had assisted in hanging Wakelin's body up to be found."

"He had assistance?" Mycroft asked.

"He did. Robert Priddy isn't the most intelligent of men, but he does have loyal friends."

"Who and how?" Lestrade asked.

Holmes looked at Inspector Evans. "I am sorry to say that your cousin may be involved."

"May be?" Evans asked softly.

"It isn't certain. His assistant certainly is. It may just be Charlie Price and Dylan Pumphrey that were involved in the deception."

"Why them?" I asked.

"Dylan Pumphrey is obvious. His wife cleans the Drill Hall and therefore he has access to her key. And also to the kitchen, where it was easy enough to obtain a leek and blood from whatever meat was set aside for the next day's meals."

"And Charlie Price?" Evans asked.

"Mr. Price has an interesting nickname, according to Dylan Pumphrey. He referred to Price as Charlie 'Calcraft' Price."

Lestrade gave a short laugh. "William Calcraft, Britain's longest serving hangman. He carried out somewhere between four-hundred-thirty and four-hundred-fifty executions, including the double hanging of Frederick Deeming and his wife, Maria. That particular little show drew a crowd of between thirty-thousand and fifty-thousand spectators."

"So Price has been a hangman?" I asked.

"Or simply an apprentice, or even just an assistant. Whatever his position, he would have learned how to tie a hangman's knot."

"You will give evidence at the trial, Sherlock?"

"Of course."

"And the others," Padgett asked. "Can they be charged with anything?"

"At the very most, it would be obstructing the course of justice," Lestrade said. "Possibly interfering with a corpse."

"It certainly wasn't malicious," Holmes said. "Their only thoughts were to protect Robert Priddy and, by extension, Alys Pumphrey."

Mycroft rubbed chin, deep in thought. After a moment he said, "We will only charge Priddy. But we will ensure that the Pumphreys and Price are all brought to London as witnesses. Do make sure that photographs are taken of the bruises on Miss Pumphrey's wrist. As to Prince George's investiture as Prince of Wales . . . ." He looked at Padgett, his eyebrows raised.

"I think we will be recommending to His Majesty that His Royal Highness be quietly invested in London. Let us not poke the beehive with a stick," Padgett replied.

"Excellent!" Holmes rubbed his hands together. "Now, if we can get our luggage from the Baker's Arms, we can all get back to London by this evening." He looked across at Inspector Evans with a slight twinkle in his eye. "It seems you really didn't need me after all."

"I wouldn't say that, Mr. Holmes," Evans replied. "You did solve the crime when I could not."

"Do you remember what you said when you met Watson and me at the station?"

Inspector Evans frowned, then shook his head.

"You said, 'Drunken fights over women I can handle'. And that, Inspector, is exactly what this turned out to be."

The Bookseller's Donkey
by Hal Glatzer

"There he is again."

"Who?"

No case had come to Sherlock Holmes for four days, and he was bored. Once, he would have fought *ennui* with cocaine. Fortunately, during the two decades I'd known him, he'd come to understand the pernicious effects, and had largely weaned himself from it. But boredom continued to plague him, for by the turn of the century, there was simply less work to be had.

Many police departments around the world had adopted methods of detection quite like those he'd pioneered, and were therefore less often baffled. As well there were more detectives to hire, and more and larger private enquiry agencies, to whom people in trouble could turn for help.

Those four days of inactivity had severely frustrated Holmes, so at my suggestion, he agreed to use the spare time for a critically important task: Updating his commonplace books. Much of his extraordinary knowledge of crime depended upon the *aides-memoire* in these volumes. While Holmes was augmenting his scrapbooks with fresh newspaper clippings and a tall jar of mucilage, I was looking out the window into Baker Street.

I pointed. "It's that itinerant bookseller with the donkey. He came along Baker Street last month. Shall we go down and see what he's offering?"

"Go yourself, Watson. You're more the constant reader than I. And my fingers are rather sticky just now."

It was a warm day for October. Indeed, the autumn of 1901 had been unseasonably warm, so I didn't need a topcoat as I stepped out of doors and crossed the street.

Dealing in books is a venerable business in London. There is at least one bookshop in every neighborhood, and many of them also have their own press and bindery. On any given day one can browse stalls full of books around the corner from the British Library.

This fellow, however, didn't have a stall – nor a shop, nor or even a pushcart. Instead, he (or someone) had constructed leather panniers that hung right and left over the donkey's flanks. Each of them held three wooden shelves, with buckled straps across their fronts to keep the books from tumbling out when the donkey walked. Where a saddle would have been, across the top, was a leather-sided box in which volumes too large for the shelves were carried flat. Upon halting in the street, the man picked up those tall ones and set them spine-out, using the sides of the box for bookends.

Many pedestrians paused to stare, point, or snicker, but I was the only one to step off the sidewalk and browse the wares displayed in his four-legged equine book-rack.

The vendor was a man of seventy at least, and by their bindings his books looked to be at least as old, or older. Likely aged, too, was the donkey. The fellow gave his beast a pat on the neck, bade him stand still, and fed him a couple of purple carrots, green tops and all.

I'm embarrassed to say that, a month earlier when I first beheld the fellow through the window, I couldn't fathom why anyone would load up a donkey with a hundredweight of books and ply the streets like a tinker. I had even joked to Holmes that, if I were that man, I would drum up business in the manner of "Molly Malone", crying, "Volumes and pamphlets, alive-alive-oh!"

But now that he'd come nigh our door again, I regretted my flippancy, and, close-up, I realized how pathetic was his condition. The black suit would have been costly when new, but had frayed at the cuffs and lapels. Stringy white hair came down to his shoulders. His eyelids drooped behind small steel-rimmed spectacles, but he also squinted, suggesting that a lens-grinder had not kept pace as his vision declined.

The donkey, too, was getting on in years. His muzzle had gone all white, and there were bald spots in the hair of his brown-and-black hide. By his prominent ribs and withers, I could tell he was undernourished.

> *I have been here before. I know by the smell of the greengrocer at one end of the road, and the flower vendor at the other.*
>
> *That time before, few masters and mistresses came to us. My load was not lightened. And Master Himself, so sad was he that he walked right past the greengrocer and brought me no mangelwurzels. All the way home, his head drooped. And he did not brush me down with his usual vigor before latching me into my stall to sleep.*

I felt I had to buy something – anything – to help the old man survive. Still, I was taken aback when he asked a guinea for a six-volume set of Fielding's *Tom Jones*.

"They are from the very first edition ever printed, in 1749," he explained. "If you buy the set today, and hold fast to them, and keep them

241

in good shape, you'll have had a right good bargain off me, for the set will be worth more than a hundred some day."

A modern edition of the novel in a single volume can be had for little as half-a-crown: 2/6 at second hand, and even less if dog-eared or tattered. But more out of pity than from taking a flutter on their rising a hundredfold in value, I said, "All right."

As he slid my sovereign and shilling into a leather pouch at his waist, he said, "Might I interest you in something more by Fielding? I have another first-edition." He stepped around the donkey and pulled a thin volume – a bound pamphlet with a stiff, discoloured cover – from the pannier on the other side. "Here is his essay from 1752, on '*The Interposition of Providence in the Detection and Punishment of Murder*',"

"Well, well. I've never heard of it, but I happen to know someone who might be interested. I shall make him a present of it."

"Will you give three-and-six for it?"

To make both men happy, I did so.

"Here's something for you, Holmes," I said as I closed the door behind me, and placed the little book beside his unpasted clippings.

He grinned – which he rarely does – and wiped the mucilage off his hands with a tea-towel. "I read this essay years ago, of course, but I haven't seen a first-edition since my university days. Thank you, Watson. What's that stack of books you set down beside the hall-tree?"

"*Tom Jones* – and likewise a 'first'."

"Quite the antiquarian, that fellow!"

"From what I observed . . . Well, it seems likely that he isn't an established bookseller with a clever gimmick. Rather, I deduce he is a scholar, or perhaps a former professor who, out of dire necessity, is selling his own books – books he's collected over a lifetime."

"Else he would not risk letting a donkey haul his treasures through the city, where they might tumble into the street. But what's *this*?"

With his long fingers, he tugged out a bit of paper that had been stuck between the last page and back cover of the pamphlet. "Not foolscap, nor stationery. Wrapping-paper, most likely from – " He took a sniff of it. " – a confectioner, though it's been in ordure recently. Torn to size, not cut. The text . . . well, likely not written by your erstwhile academic." He held it up to show me well-formed letters, written with a thick lead pencil:

I'm sorry. I didn't mean to kill her.

* * * * *

242

*Because I am patient, I have time to ponder great
mysteries. How do the masters and mistresses rule the cycle
of light and dark? They can make light shine even when all
around is darkness. From where did they get this power? I
believe they obtained it in trade for two of their limbs.*

*They cannot stand or walk on all four. By rearing up on
their hind limbs so much, their forelimbs have shrunk to
slender sticks that end, not in sturdy hooves, but in fine and
delicate tendrils. Why would they want such useless
appendages, so unsuited to running, if they had not obtained
something valuable in return? And surely that must be the
power to make light. There is still much about them that I do
not understand – that I may never understand.*

"I'm intrigued, Watson. Is the fellow still about?"

I looked out the window. "Packing up."

"Let us hurry down."

"Ah," said the old man as we approached. "Come for more? Please browse my shelves again. I'll open the straps."

"This Fielding pamphlet," said Holmes, brandishing it. "Have you had it long?"

He stopped fiddling with the pannier and squinted. "A magistrate are you? As Fielding himself was? A solicitor or barrister perhaps?"

"No. A consulting detective."

"Ah! That's why your friend said you'd like to have it. Are you, sir, also a detective?"

"I'm a doctor, but I – "

"How long have you had this pamphlet?" Holmes cut in.

"Many years. It seemed a good companion to the *Tom Jones*. Which is why I offered it to – "

"Do you not examine your books before you take them out for sale?"

"I handle so many books every day, sir, I scarce have time to do more than stack and un-stack them."

"There was a bit of cheap paper stuck inside."

"Oh? A book-mark? Please accept my apology. Or . . . did you want me to refund your – ?"

"No, no," said I. "We were merely wondering how the book came into your possession."

"I bought it in the Sixties, in Paris. Funny you should call my attention to it today, though. It must have fallen last Saturday, when I unloaded the pannier. I didn't realize it had gone until this morning, when I found it on the stable floor beside Bottom."

243

"What is 'Bottom'?"

He stroked the donkey's mane. "This is Bottom."

I couldn't suppress a grin. "So, Bottom wrote this note?"

"Oh, no. Donkeys are very intelligent, but reading and writing are beyond their ken. They . . . oh, you are chaffing me!"

Holmes wasn't smiling. "How then, did . . . Bottom come to be in possession of the book?"

"I've no idea. And you must not think that he 'possessed' it, as you or I might. No. I found it in his stall then. I dusted it off and returned it to the – "

"Did the discovery not strike you as odd?"

"It did, indeed, but I was grateful for its re-appearance. Occasionally a book or two does slip out when I take the straps off. No one in the stable would likely have read it – nor left it behind. The landlord is away all this week and next, and his boy is nearly illiterate. Now, sir, I should be on my way."

"A moment longer, if you please. Where is your stable?"

"Doughty Mews."

Holmes closed his eyes for a moment, undoubtedly searching in his memory (or visualizing his still-unmounted clippings) for news of recent homicides in that vicinity. "Have there been any . . . untoward incidents in the neighborhood, lately? The sudden death of a woman, perhaps?"

"No." But then, with a tilt of his head he added, "Not what you'd call a woman."

"I beg your pardon."

"A mare: Tillie. She was found dead, day before yesterday. Sunday morning. She had the stall next-but-one to Bottom. He may have seen what happened. I sent the stable boy to fetch a constable, but when the fellow came, he merely laughed, and wouldn't give a listen!"

"You expected Bottom to talk?"

"No, no. It was I to whom he refused to listen. I would have told him that Tillie was a sturdy mare, very healthy, and near-time to getting a foal."

"She was pregnant?"

"Yes, Doctor. It was distressing to find her dead. Queer too, if you ask me."

"How so?"

"There was a gash in her neck, and blood in the straw beneath her. As I say, Bottom was nearby. If anyone saw who slit Tillie's throat, it would be he."

Whenever water comes down from the sky, Master Himself does not work, so neither do I. But when the air is dry, and the light comes to awaken us, Master Himself slings the cowhide panniers over my back and loads them up with delicate little things that flutter like leaves when they fall down. They must be valuable, these things, for when one does tumble into my stall, his mouth makes a loud, angry noise. And he will take it up gently, smooth its leaves, and make it to lodge again on my back. Sometimes he forgets to pick one up, but after another cycle of dark and light he will usually do so.

He ties the panniers down with cowhide straps under my belly and around my hind end. He slips the bit into my mouth, behind my back teeth, and makes a familiar sound. It means he is sorry for having to do that.

Then we set off on our way out of the stable and into the noisy streets. They are greasy with manure and strewn with rubbish. Once or twice in the light of the sun, Master Himself will touch tendril limbs with other masters and mistresses, and then give them a few of the leafy things. Each time he takes some of that weight off my back, I slide my nose up against him in gratitude, and he strokes my muzzle.

"Perhaps my friend and I can be of help," said I. "This is Mr. Sherlock Holmes. He's quite an expert in the art of detection, and extremely knowledgeable on the subject of murder."

Holmes shrugged. "Investigating the death of a horse, even ostensibly its murder, isn't really in my line. But I have no pressing engagement, and there is a bizarre aspect to this situation that has caught my interest. We cannot invite . . . both of you up to our sitting room, of course. However, I should like to hear more of your story."

"There is a tea shop in the next street," said I. "You may tether the beast outside and keep watch on your books through the front window."

The bookseller nodded agreement and finished securing his books. Leading the donkey by leather reins, he stopped briefly at the greengrocer's and then followed us up Baker Street and around the corner.

Master Himself made many mouth-sounds with a new master. Then another master arrived, and they all made mouth-sounds together. But Master Himself did not take me straight home. He walked me into the next street with these two masters, hung a bag of mangelwurzels over my muzzle, and tied my reins to a ring in the curbstone.

He and the two masters then disappeared behind a strange kind of wall. I could see them through it, but also the

245

reflection of the sun behind me. And – dimly – I could also see a creature with four limbs like mine, long ears like mine, and striped withers like mine. I could see he was a jack, like me, and he was wearing a feedbag just as I was. I pondered this for as long as it took me to eat, and finally concluded that the creature I was looking at must be me, myself!

The old man consumed two cress sandwiches and three cups of tea. He pointed to my pencil and notebook, and said, "Are you also a journalist, Doctor?"

"An author, actually. But I often assist my friend here by taking notes. Watson's my name. What is yours, sir?"

"Horace Beamer Stillwell."

Holmes indicated the man's cravat, with its academic emblem. "The beast, we may assume, did not read literature alongside you at Oxford."

He smiled. "No sir. Bottom would have read animal husbandry."

I grinned at his witty reply, but said, "Could the horse have caught her neck on something sharp or pointed? A splinter? A nail?"

"Oh, no! Someone who keeps animals –even the cruelest of keepers – would never leave such a dangerous thing sticking out in a stall!"

"You believe she was murdered, and that your donkey might know who killed her. Were you serious?"

"Oh yes, Dr. Watson. Murder was done. Her throat was cut."

"She was found Sunday morning?"

"Yes. She died on Saturday night."

"Please go on."

"Sunday morning, Tillie was lying on her side, in the straw. She had a wound in her neck, a pool of blood beneath it, and a farrier's hoof-knife lying beside her that had blood on it."

"You said you summoned a constable."

"Sent the stable boy to fetch one, yes. He came back with the copper who patrols Doughty Street and John Street, and the near end of Guilford Street. Gordon's his name. He looked inside and laughed, and said, 'Don't you be wasting my time, old man! There's no law against killing a horse. You don't want a policeman. You want a knacker!'"

I touched his shoulder. "I'm sorry, Mr. Stillwell. Had you owned the horse a long time?"

"Owned her? Oh, no, Dr. Watson. I could never afford to keep a horse! What a donkey eats in a week a horse will eat in just a couple of days."

"To whom did Tillie belong?"

"To the landlord."

246

"Where did he ride her? There are no bridal paths in that part of London."

Stillwell grinned. "Oh, Tillie wasn't for riding, Mr. Holmes. Nor for hauling. She was for getting mules."

"Eh?" Holmes made a little squint.

"Mules are quite valuable," said Stillwell. "They're almost as strong as horses, but they're smaller, and need less food. The landlord's main business is raising and selling mules."

"So he keeps mules for breeding as well?"

I suppressed a chuckle. On subjects that Holmes considers irrelevant to crime and detection, his knowledge is quite skimpy. "A mule," I told him, "is the offspring of a male donkey and a female horse."

"And mules are hybrids," Stillwell put in. "The mating of two different species may produce live, healthy offspring, but almost always, hybrid creatures are sterile, and cannot reproduce themselves." He shot me a glance, as if to say, *Your friend is obviously well-educated. How does he not know this?*

Holmes shrugged, in lieu of thanking us for enlightening him. "Tillie was carrying a foal, and the sire was . . . Bottom?"

"Yes. Over the past twelve years, they'd gotten ten mules together."

"And you said Bottom did not raise an alarum. Did he not make a great noise in the night?"

"He may have done. Perhaps he did. Perhaps Sarabande did also."

"Sarabande? Another horse?"

"No, sir. Sarabande is a gennet."

"A 'jenny'?"

"A female donkey," said I. "A male's a jack."

"Bottom and Sarabande have been stablemates, oh, some twenty years now. They've gotten little donkeys together, too. Five at least. If they were people, I'd say they ought to have married by now! You seem to know about donkeys, Doctor. Have you owned one?"

"No, but when I was an Army doctor in Afghanistan, a dozen donkeys were attached to our troop to carry food and ammunition. I was assigned one, for taking medical supplies to the field-hospitals. All of the donkeys were stabled together, though."

"They would be, of course," said Stillwell. "Donkeys like company. They're rather sociable – 'club-able,' you might say. They get along all right with horses, too, as long as the horses aren't too skittish."

"Was Tillie skittish?"

"Yes, when she was pregnant or . . . receptive to being mated with."

Holmes nodded. (That much, at least, he understood.)

247

Sarabande is always happy when I come home to her.
Every time I return from work, she lays her neck alongside
mine, touches my nose with hers, and bites me gently on my
flanks. That always gets me excited, but she would kick me
hard if I tried to act on that excitement when she isn't ready.
And she is not ready now. More cycles of light and dark will
have to pass. I am patient. I can wait.

"Think on Saturday night again, Mr. Stillwell. Did you hear Tillie or the donkeys cry out?"

"My lodging is at the other end of Doughty Mews, where it meets John's Mews. If Bottom or Sarabande brayed vigorously, I was too far away to hear it."

"Bottom is yours, then. What about Sarabande?"

"She and Tillie belong to our landlord."

"Why does he keep Sarabande? To raise donkeys?"

"Partly, yes. But she works, too. There's a fellow called Thompkins who lives in the bed-sit next to mine. He rents Sarabande on sunny days, puts a folded blanket on her back, and takes her to Russell Square, where mothers and nursemaids from the surrounding houses bring their children. The little tykes are sat upon her, and led in a circle along the park perimeter. The charge is a thruppenny bit for five minutes – sixpence for ten. And Thompkins has a friend with a camera. For half-a-crown, he takes the child's picture astride the donkey and sells the photographs to their families."

"I see." Holmes closed his eyes for a moment, then said, "Do you rent your lodgings from the same landlord that owns the stable?"

"Rent it? Certainly. I have neither property nor income: Naught a year but what I earn from dealing in books. It pays for my bed-sit and board, for Bottom's stall, and for his feed. But I must also rent the tack room in the stable – where they used to keep bridles and saddles – as a storeroom for my books. In exchange for that, I tutor the landlord's son, the stable boy. He'd never been taught to read before, and is slow to learn his letters."

"That's the boy you sent to fetch the constable?"

"Yes."

"Did *he* hear anything out of the ordinary that night?"

"I don't know." He poured more tea for himself. "Perhaps I am wasting your time, you and Dr. Watson . . . ."

I touched his shoulder. "We do want to help."

He brightened. "Would it be possible for you to come with Bottom and me, and see poor Tillie for yourselves?"

"Has she not been removed to a knacker's?"

248

"The boy told me the knacker is unable to come until tomorrow."

"Have you completed your rounds for the day? Sold enough books that you can return to the stable without further commerce?"

"Yes – thanks to Dr. Watson's guinea."

"Take Bottom back there. We will follow in an hour or so, to examine the scene before it is disturbed any further."

> *Master Himself is good to me. He treats me kindly. So I believe I should try to help him when I can. Most masters who work in the streets, as he does, do not have a servant as loyal as I. Those masters have to carry wares on their own backs, or in boxes with wheels, which they must push or pull by themselves.*
>
> *And they cry their wares in the streets. They cry to offer dead creatures from the sea, which I suppose masters are somehow able to eat. Some cry for sharp strips of metal, which they hold against a round stone that makes them sing with an awful screech. Others cry to offer brushes and brooms. I do know what those things are. Master Himself strokes me with a brush when we come home from work, and the young master in the stable wipes the straw from our stalls with a broom.*

A century ago, men in London stopped their noses with perfumed handkerchiefs to distract their brains from the overwhelming reek of equine manure. Nowadays we are fortunate that, although the city may have hundreds of thousands of horses, it also has men with shovels, and barrels on wheels, to clean the streets. Doughty Mews, however, was evidently not on any of the street sweepers' routes, for when we alighted from the hansom there, we were nearly overwhelmed by the cloying stink.

Stillwell had likely arrived shortly before us. He was in the stable at the far end of the mews. Holmes and I helped him unload the books from the panniers and carry them into the erstwhile tack room, where crude shelves imitated the "stacks" of a library. The floorboards were uneven, and there were no lanterns hung. Unloading his books by himself, every evening, he might not notice if a few were to fall.

He led Bottom into a stall next to that of another donkey – Sarabande, no doubt – who had been watching. Over the low wall between their stalls, she bumped Bottom a couple of times with her head and nipped at his flanks with her teeth. As he did not flinch, I supposed it must be the donkey version of a wife's kiss. Then she turned to stare at Holmes and me.

The slain horse lay in the stall beyond hers. The stench wasn't yet intolerable – as if the place needed a greater olfactory insult! But flies had been at her for two days, and didn't quit when Holmes pushed the stall door open. He used his stick to brush straw from a little spot on which to kneel beside a farrier's curved hoof-knife that was crusted with mud it had scraped from the horse's old shoes, but it also bore dried blood.

"Fortunately," said he, "no one has removed it." He gently wrapped it into a handkerchief and handed it up to me. Then he examined the wound through his lens. Without looking up, he called, "Is anything missing?"

"There is nothing here worth stealing," said Stillwell.

"Where was the Fielding pamphlet when you found it this morning?" He pointed. "Just there, beside the tack room door."

Holmes examined where Stillwell had indicated. "Has any other animal in this neighborhood been attacked recently?"

"No, sir. I'd have seen!"

That came from a youthful voice behind me. A young man was leaning against the stable door.

"This is Tim," said the bookseller. "The landlord's son."

He had dark hair and the beginnings of a wispy beard.

"Tim," said Holmes, "did you come in here Sunday morning?"

"I come in every morning, sir."

"When you came, did you see anything that wasn't right? Anything that wasn't usual."

"Tillie was dead, sir."

"Do you remember the night before that morning? Saturday night?"

"I sleep at night."

"Did you hear any noises in the night-time? Noises coming from the stable? A strange noise?"

"Yes, sir."

"A cry of pain, perhaps?"

"It was more like laughing sir."

"Did anyone enter the stable that night?"

"No, sir."

"On Sunday morning, when you saw Tillie was dead, what did you do? Did you raise an alarum?"

"My Da's away."

"You would have knocked up your father, of course."

"Yes, sir. So I knocked up Mr. Stillwell."

"When you returned here with him, were Bottom and Sarabande in their stalls?"

"Yes, sir."

"Watson – show him the knife. Tim – have you ever seen this knife before?"

He leaned close in. "Yes, sir."

250

"Do you know whose knife this is?"

"The farrier, sir."

"Has he been here recently?"

"Saturday. He scraped away mud from Tillie's shoes."

"Were you aware that Tillie was carrying a foal?"

"Oh yes, sir. She was due to get her last mule next month."

"Her 'last'?"

"Getting too old, she was. Da's gone to buy a young mare."

"Do you know Constable . . . Gordon, is it?"

"Yes, sir."

"Please go and fetch him."

Stillwell nodded approval. Tim scampered out and ran down the mews.

Master Himself does not cry his wares, so I do not know the names of the feathery things I bear on my back. But since he does not cry their names, I sometimes try to do so, hoping to get other masters to pay attention to him. I imitate the masters who cry their wares by making a loud noise from my throat. But it does not work as I intend. Masters in the street ignore me when I do this. And some – the youngest, typically – imitate my cry. They walk up to me and yell right at my snout. I think they are making themselves amused, but I am but a servant, and they are masters. Masters are entitled to mock me, if they choose. I can only hope they will not also choose to hurt me.

The boy soon returned with a uniformed constable, who immediately addressed Stillwell with, "What is it now, old man? Another dead horse?" But noticing Holmes and me, and how well we were attired, he doffed his helmet and said, "Excuse me, gentlemen. Do you require assistance from the police?"

"Yes," said Holmes. "We are investigating the death of the horse."

"Oh. Surety agents, are you? I'm surprised the landlord paid to insure the nag. She was no Derby winner."

"We are pursuing a different line of enquiry."

"What for? The mare is dead! And there's more important things to 'enquire' about in this neighborhood."

Holmes's mouth twitched. "Crimes?"

"Well, one kind of crime, anyway."

"Do tell!"

"Burglary. There's been a raft of it lately, around Russell Square. The inspector's charged us coppers to keep our eyes out for suspicious characters what might be, as we say, 'casing' houses for valuable things to steal."

Holmes stepped closer. "That is very interesting, Constable. Tell me: How many burglaries have been made there in . . . how long has it been?"

"Seven burglaries during the past four months."

"What's been taken?"

"What does this have to do with a dead horse?"

"Leave that to me. What did they take?"

"Funny old stuff."

"Antiques?"

"I guess you could call them antiques. Fancy dishes. Little statues. Oh, and clocks – cuckoo clocks. Folks around here collect things like that."

"Are you working on those burglary cases?"

"Me? No. I'm just a constable-on-patrol. But I hear all about it in the station house. You'll want to talk with my inspector about the burglaries."

"His name?"

"Bradstreet."

"Excellent! I know him well. Thank you, Constable Gordon. You have done a commendable job. There is one thing more, if you don't mind. You must have seen Mr. Stillwell here take his donkey out with a load of books."

"Oh, sure! Almost every day."

"Do you ever see the fellow who takes the *other* donkey out? What was his name, again?"

"Charlie Thompkins," said Stillwell.

"I see him here in the mews, and when he leads Sarabande into Guilford Street. But I don't know where he goes after he's passed out of my patrol beat."

"Thank you. You have been of great assistance." Holmes gave my elbow a tug, said, "We must be on our way," and then, to Stillwell said, "You will hear from me."

I have spent much of the present time in the light thinking about horses. I had made their acquaintance long ago, on the farm where I was born, and long before Tillie came in to our stable.

She is the only mare whose foals I have ever sired. But I would not want to be stabled any closer to her than I am. She stands taller than I do, and greatly outweighs me. When I am led into her stall to sire a foal, I must be vigilant, for she is quick to kick out. If I were distracted, and she were displeased, or were merely in a foul mood, she could kick me hard. Iron has been nailed into her hooves. A kick from one of her hind limbs could easily shatter one of my own limbs or, striking my body, make me hurt deep inside.

I do think I know what makes Tillie so mean. After our foals are weaned, they are led away and we see them no more. It may well be that Tillie wishes she could care for her foals for more cycles of warm and cold days, until they have grown bigger. Perhaps she would simply like them to stay near enough for her to enjoy their scent.

Sarabande and I have gotten foals of our own. I do not know another way to express this, but we have gotten as many foals as there are tendrils on the foreleg of a master, whereas Tillie and I have gotten as many foals as there are tendrils on both of a master's forelegs together. After they are weaned, they too are led away. It is possible that Sarabande feels sad at the loss, as Tillie does. But if so, she does not express it. Horses are quick to show unhappiness or distress or discomfort. We donkeys keep such feelings to ourselves.

That makes me wonder if perhaps Sarabande is jealous. She may resent it that I do not sire foals exclusively with her. So I am on my on my guard, always, against a kick from Sarabande, too. Of course, she is my true mate, and has great affection for me. She shows this by nipping gently at my flanks with her front teeth, and then nuzzling her head against my neck. Is there any truer proof?

But still . . . all those foals out of Tillie . . . .

The next morning, Holmes emerged from his room and slipped out the door while I was having toast and tea. I busied myself writing a narrative from notes I'd made on a case from five years before, and had composed about one-third of the account, when Holmes returned, calling, "Dress yourself for a stroll in the park, Watson. But casually. We go, not to be seen in our finery, but to observe others in theirs."

We took a hansom to Russell Square. At mid-day, most of the benches were occupied by nursemaids and "nannies" in sober attire who sat rocking perambulators, back and forth, to lull the babies within to sleep. Older children scampered about, occasionally hiding behind some bushes, but never really out of sight of their minders.

Holmes and I stood in the shadow of a tall plane tree. I was about to ask what advance, if any, his morning excursion might have brought to the case, when he held up his hand and bade me to look east.

A man leading a donkey by a rope emerged from Guilford Street, and rounded the corner into Russell Square.

Holmes whispered, "Sarabande."

"Yes."

The man was in his twenties, clean-shaven, and neatly coiffed. But his gait was unsteady, requiring the use of a stick. "That would be Mr. Stillwell's neighbor, Charlie Thompkins."

"No doubt. What can you tell me about him, Doctor? About his limp, I mean."

"Oh. Well, it isn't congenital. See? He's switching hands with the stick – he's probably never needed one before. I'd say he's had an injury. And . . . he could very well have been kicked by the donkey."

"I believe you're right. Thank you, Watson."

A clutch of six children who'd been rolling hoops saw them enter the greensward and rushed over, each claiming a bit of the donkey to pet or tickle. Sarabande did not resist. She seemed to enjoy the attention. Probably she'd been led here almost every day throughout the warm months.

The fellow folded a blanket and laid it across Sarabande's back as a boy brandishing a thruppenny bit pushed his playmates aside. He gave it to the fellow, who then hoisted him onto Sarabande, drew a watch from a pocket in his corduroy trousers, and led the donkey and her young rider along the Square's perimeter. The rest of the children and three of their nursemaids followed behind, some of the youngest dropping to all-fours in imitation of the donkey's gait.

About halfway around the greensward, the lad's five minutes were up and a girl in a blue dirndl replaced him. Her ride took longer – evidently sixpence-worth.

> *I hesitate to say this, but I do believe that Sarabande did not like Tillie, that she has always resented my time with Tillie, siring foals, and that she would prefer that I sire foals only out of her!*
>
> *And based on that insight, I am drawn to deduce what I am loath to declare: That it may well have been Sarabande is somehow responsible for Tillie's death.*

"Halloo, Charlie! Halloo, boys and girls!" cried a fellow of about the same age as the donkey man, just after the next child had begun a turn

254

astride. He was a bit taller than Thompkins, with dark hair down to his shoulders, and he sported the kind of waxed moustache and goatee one associates with as-yet-unknown artists and composers of the French or Bohemian type. After smiling and waving to the children, he walked to a sunny spot and began unpacking the little satchel he'd been carrying.

"The photographer," said Holmes, quietly.

"I shouldn't think so. Where's his tripod stand? And what's that he's pulled out of his bag? It isn't a camera."

I'd expected to see bellows, a wooden frame with metal fittings, a brass-bound lens, and a black cloth hood to shade the ground glass while viewing the image. What the man unpacked, however, was merely a black box: A little cube barely six inches on a side.

"I went this morning," said Holmes, "to talk with a fellow in Great Portland Street who is up-to-date on the latest technologies of the photographic arts. I asked about posing a child atop a donkey, a subject unlikely to remain stock-still during the exposure. 'How would someone take such a photograph?' I asked.

"He told me that traditional equipment wouldn't do, and showed me a new kind of camera that would be ideal, and easier to transport, as well. It was one of *those* – " he pointed. "It's called a 'Brownie', for being so small, like a pixie or fairy glimpsed in a garden. They are manufactured by the Eastman Kodak Company in the United States, and are sold and serviced here in England by a subsidiary called the Kodak Works in Harrow."

"But how can such a little thing take photographs?"

"In a revolutionary manner. There are no glass plates inside. Each image is captured singly, with the press of a button, and stored on a coil of translucent celluloid film, thinner and more flexible than a celluloid collar. The film is removed from the camera and mailed to Harrow, where the images are developed and printed on paper, and mailed back to the photographer along with a fresh coil of film. One merely presses a button, and the Kodak Works does the rest."

I had often considered how useful photography would be to Holmes's work – and as an *aide-memoire* for me, along with my notes, when writing about his exploits – but I had never taken it up. The equipment would fill an entire wardrobe, and the processing would require making a room totally dark – a room with running water, at that! If I could carry a Brownie camera, however, and exert no more effort than pressing a button . . . Well, that might do very nicely!

Therefore, I paid close attention as the hirsute fellow began to take his photographs. At the start of each ride, he motioned for the child and donkey to be still. But then he walked along during the ride, frequently glancing down at the Brownie and touching it with one finger – presumably pressing the button. After taking each exposure, he turned a small crank, which likely advanced the film coiled within.

After about ten minutes Holmes gave a little shrug, meaning he'd seen enough, and we walked out of the Square.

Two cycles of dark and light time have passed since Sarabande last gave me her welcoming nuzzle-and-nip. That was when Master Himself was joined by the two masters from the street of the greengrocer and florist. When they came into my stall, and Sarabande's, and Tillie's, they scratched about in the straw. We do not like to have our familiar arrangements changed like that. But later, after those masters had gone, Master Himself gave us a fresh salt lick.

I am worried that Sarabande has lost her affection for me. What could have caused it? I did not tell her of my worry – that maybe, out of jealousy, she had caused Tillie to die. But could she have somehow known I was thinking this? Gennets do seem to have a way of knowing things, without needing to ask jacks to explain them.

Which makes me wonder whether that might be so among other creatures. Even mistresses might have this ability! Could they know things about which they do not need to ask masters?

"Mr. Holmes! What brings you and Dr. Watson to see me?"

"We have been looking into the slaughter of a horse."

Inspector Bradstreet leaned back in his chair and laughed. "Constable Gordon told me two men had been called in to investigate the dead mare in Doughty Lane. I didn't know it was you. Pardon me for saying this, but isn't it a wild-goose chase?"

I volunteered, "A wild-*horse* chase!" and we all laughed.

"Tell me, Bradstreet: Have you any solid leads regarding the string of burglaries in Russell Square?"

He had known Holmes almost as long as I had – long enough to follow willingly in whatever direction Holmes might turn. "Truthfully, no. Most cases like these, we talk to a few 'fences' that deal in stolen goods. There's enough of 'em who'll impeach their rivals after a little persuasion, if you know what I mean. But none of 'em's heard tell of a thievery ring in this part of town."

256

"Could there be a few otherwise respectable dealers in antiquities," I suggested, "who turn a blind eye? Say, if a piece is rare enough, they might not inquire after its provenance."

"You mean: Not ask who owned it? We've thought of that too, Doctor. But what's been stolen isn't gold or jewelry or silverware. And not really 'antiques' either. Clocks, fancy serving dishes, little bronze statues . . . none of 'em made more than ten, twenty years ago. How much could a professional thief get from a fence for something that? Not enough to risk going to prison for burglary! That's what has us stumped."

Holmes's eyes were closed, and he had clasped his fingers together in a tent before his face. "We may be looking at a new kind of theft," he said at last. "One in which the thief doesn't go blindly into a home and gather up a bag of things in hopes of getting a few quid. Imagine, rather, a burglar who enters knowing in advance what is there, and takes only such items for which he already has a customer."

"I know what you're saying, Mr. Holmes. We've had cases like that. But they've all been inside jobs, where a confederate in the house – a servant or a poor relation – will hire a thief to steal something he thinks he's owed."

"But how likely is it," I asked, "that this largely middle-class neighborhood should abound with so many larcenous servants or disenchanted heirs? It doesn't seem realistic."

"I agree, Doctor. That's our dilemma."

Holmes looked up. "I have an idea that could resolve the dilemma. And with your help, Bradstreet, I would like to pursue it."

"What do you want me to do?"

"May I assume that your constables have already gone around the Square, asking at each home if they have been burgled, or if they have seen or heard suspicious activity?"

"Of course."

"Have they, by any chance, asked if there are children in the household, young ones who are taken out to play in the Square?"

"What for?"

"Humor me, Bradstreet. Poll the houses again, if you haven't already done so, and let me know if there is a correlation between children's homes and burgled homes."

"It has never profited me to ignore your advice, Mr. Holmes. If that's what you want to know, I'll have my men find it out."

"And I should also like to see a complete list of the items that have been stolen."

Just as the sun was setting, a constable brought Bradstreet's list to us in Baker Street, along with a short note to the effect that all of the burgled houses were homes to small children.

Holmes wrote a reply immediately, which I read before he called down for a street urchin – one of his so-called "Irregulars" – to take to Bradstreet personally: *"Please introduce Watson and me to a family in a house which has not yet been burgled. I shall set a trap."*

> *Sarabande gave me to understand that, in the green trees-and-leaves place where she is taken for work, she saw the same two masters who had come to our stable with Master Himself. Sarabande is strong enough to bear masters far larger than the little ones, but these two did not show any interest in having her bear them.*
>
> *Rather, they stood in the shade of a tree and watched the two masters with whom she is already familiar: Her own master, who leads her to the green place, and another master who appears when they are in the green place, and who walks abreast of her while she is carrying the little masters, holding a black object in his tendrils.*

Bradstreet, Holmes, and I appeared at the door of No. 21 Russell Square on Thursday afternoon, with two accomplices.

Theodore Bailey was the smallest of Holmes's Irregulars. He was much older than the children who play in the Square – fourteen or perhaps fifteen. (He truly did not know.) But he stood only a little over four feet and was pudgy in the face, as if he still had "baby fat". Holmes had him dressed that afternoon in a youngster's sailor-suit, to help him pass for a boy of ten.

Aleida Rijn was a female enquiry agent in her forties, a native of Holland, with whom Holmes had occasionally worked on international cases. Slender, but with what I could see were muscular arms, her long blonde hair was wrapped up in a conservative bun. And she wore the kind of severe, inexpensive skirt and shirtwaist typical of a governess.

Bradstreet introduced us to the householders. Mr. and Mrs. Harald Armstrong were prosperous *bourgeoisie* who owned a number of millinery shops. Their home was comfortably furnished but not at all ostentatious. They showed us into their front room, which had tall windows on the Square that let in plenty of sunlight.

On the low table before the sofa, the Armstrongs had set out a copy of *The Memoirs of Sherlock Holmes*. I was pleased to see the eight-year-old book was officially licensed, and not a "pirate" edition. But its

258

prominent display surely meant I would be asked, later, to autograph it with a personalized dedication.

"This is so very exciting," declared Mrs. Armstrong as we took seats.

Holmes let her banter about the warm weather for a minute or so, but finally said, "As Inspector Bradstreet has informed you, he has a plan to capture the burglars who have been plaguing your neighbors." (Holmes always prefers to give policemen credit for what he himself has done.)

"And this is the plan: Dr. Watson shall assume the persona of the man of this house, with Theodore pretending to be his son. It is our intention to have Miss Rijn take the lad into the Square this afternoon, pay the donkey-man for rides, and ask the accompanying photographer to take his picture. She will give this house as the boy's address, and a day or so later, we expect the photographer to bring his pictures here and offer them for sale. Dr. Watson will invite him in, buy some pictures, and engage the fellow in conversation, during which he will ensure that he notices various *objets d'art* on display. We believe that the man will photograph them surreptitiously with a tiny camera.

"Inspector Bradstreet's review of the police reports suggests that, within a day or two of a householder purchasing pictures, a burglar will enter the home to steal one or more of these objects. It is the inspector's contention that the photographer is acting on behalf of collectors – men who are obsessed, beyond reason, with augmenting or completing their collections. When presented with photographs of objects they collect, their obsession is so great that they will buy them without regard for the illegality of their acquisition."

"Most of the pieces that have been stolen," said Bradstreet, "are either Spode 'stoneware' dishes that mimic Chinese porcelain – cast-bronze reproductions in miniature of ancient Greek and Roman statuary, or cuckoo clocks from the Biedermeier workshop in the Black Forest of Germany.

"With your consent, we would like to bring such pieces to this house and set them out here in this room when Dr. Watson admits the photographer. Thereafter, and for as long as it takes, Miss Rijn, and Theodore, and a few other youngsters in the pay of Mr. Holmes, will keep watch on the house, day and night, ready to alert my constables when the burglars arrive and attempt to break in.

"We are certain that, upon being confronted, the thieves will impeach the photographer, and that he, in turn, will impeach the collectors for whom he has been the procurer. This way, we will round up the entire ring, and recover all or most of the stolen objects as well."

"That is a marvelous plan, Inspector!" said Mrs. Armstrong. "Dr. Watson, we have read your accounts of Mr. Holmes's exploits, and my

259

husband and I will regard it as a great privilege to help you catch these miscreants. Our daughter is too old to participate, or we would volunteer to join in this charade ourselves. When the adventure is concluded, you must all be our guests at a dinner party in your honor – mustn't they, Mr. Armstrong?"

"Indeed, my dear. We – "

"Dr. Watson," she went on, "before you go, I wonder . . . would you kindly autograph . . . ?"

Once our business was concluded, we stepped outside. Thompkins and Sarabande would be arriving soon, so Aleida began to lead Theodore across the street, taking him by the hand. Initially he resisted, but quickly remembered the role he was to play, and skipped along as she led him into Russell Square.

> *I was born and spent the first few cold and warm cycles of my life on a farm that grew much of what I was fed, and which also fed creatures who were raised to be eaten. When masters slew them, they did it by drawing shiny metal things across the creature's throat. That, in turn, released a great quantity of red water. Losing all or most of a creature's red water caused it to die.*
>
> *From that, I deduce that what was inside those slaughtered creatures is much like what was inside Tillie, and hence much like what is inside Sarabande – and me. If that is so, then I conclude that Tillie died because a shiny strip of metal punctured the hide over her neck, releasing her red water, which made a puddle beneath her when she fell over.*
>
> *And that causes me to remember that the farrier had come during that light time. He used a shiny strip of metal to scrape mud from Tillie's hooves. He has done this many times before, and some of those times, he forgets to take it with him when he goes away. So it may well have lain in Tillie's stall during the dark time that followed.*
>
> *I was wrong. Sarabande could not have killed Tillie. If it was the shiny metal thing that cut open the mare's throat, then how could Sarabande have taken it up and wielded it?*
>
> *Like all of our kind, there are no tendrils at the ends of our forelimbs. Neither are our hooves cloven, like the creatures whom masters raise up to be eaten. And regarding those creatures: I have never seen them open and close the aperture in their hooves in such a way that would enable them*

to take hold of things. Like ours, their hooves are hard, best for walking and running and standing upon.

So there must be another explanation. I try to remember when Tillie was slain, but I know only that I was asleep. And when I sleep, I prefer to stand with my face toward the wall of the stable. That is the only time I find the sense of being confined more pleasurable than that of being in the open air. There is something reassuring in closing myself off from everything outside of my stall. Perhaps I am, somehow, remembering dark times in my past, dark times during my youth, when I could sleep snuggled up to my dam . . . .

But memory is of no use here. Being asleep that night, I did not – could not – see what happened to Tillie. I cannot pretend that I did. I must reason only from what I know to be true, and must not let myself imagine things of whose veracity I cannot be certain.

"Come in, sir, come in! You are welcome!" I bellowed to the photographer. "Little Theodore has been so excited all week! He is at school just now, of course, but he is quite anxious to see your pictures. I fancy that we will commission frames, and set out the pictures where all our family and visitors may admire them! Tea has just been brought. Will you have some? Marvelous. Please sit here – " I indicated a settee that faced into the room. From its vantage point, he would easily notice the ornate Biedermeier cuckoo clock on the wall and the bronze casts of famous sculptures on the mantelpiece: *The Discus Thrower* and *The Winged Nike of Samothrace.*

"Do you like beautiful things? We do! Let me show you something. It's right here . . . no, wait. It must be in the next room. Excuse me a moment." I trotted through the door into the hall, staying out of his sight, but positioned where an angled mirror had been set to give a glimpse into the front room.

Sure enough, seeing how much light was there, he drew out his Brownie, took a couple of pictures, and then slipped it back into his bag just as I returned with a large ceramic plate. "Ever seen one of these? It's from Spode! Such lovely thing, isn't it?"

"Beautiful indeed," said he. "But now you must look at my photographs."

"Of course. How silly of me! It is the reason for your visit, isn't it? And I'm sure you must have other children's homes to visit, on your agenda for today. Let me see the pictures. How much are they?"

261

He produced six, each in a pasteboard folder. "They are priced at one pound each. But you may have all six for five pounds. I know, I know – you expected to obtain just one for your home, but surely there are aunts and uncles – cousins too, maybe – who would appreciate a gift of the lad's photo? He will never again be this young, you know. These photographs will always remind you of his youth – a precious memory. And Christmas, after all, isn't many weeks away . . . ."

"You are absolutely right, young man! I shall forthwith purchase all six. My wife and I will take them this very evening to my brother's house and give him his choice of photographs to keep. Thank you!"

> *I have noticed that, since Tillie was killed, the master who takes Sarabande to the green leaves-and-tree place moves in quite a different manner. Whereas he used to put one hind limb in front of the other with equal energy, he now favors one hind limb and drags the other behind him. He also, with one forelimb, clutches himself in the middle of his girth, and with the other grasps a short branch of a tree, employing it as if it were an extra limb. He has never walked this way before.*
>
> *So I deduce that he is in pain. Tillie was always short-tempered, but even more fearful and quicker to kick out when she was heavy with a foal. It seems to me that, when Sarabande's master brought her home, he may have gotten too close to Tillie's hindquarters – too close for her comfort, that is – and that she may have struck him with a hind hoof.*
>
> *In my life, I have seen how quickly masters can be brought to a state of anger. I have seen how easily some of them can lash out in a rage after even the slightest provocation. A kick from Tillie would have been unimaginably painful. He must have sought to revenge himself upon Tillie. So perhaps, he seized the metal strip with his tendrils, and with it cut her throat.*
>
> *I do not think he intended that Tillie should die. But die she did.*

"Charlie Thompkins?"

"Yeah. But it ain't me you want. The fella with the camera doesn't live here."

"We don't want 'the fella with the camera'. We want the fella who was kicked by a horse last Saturday night."

"And I'm a doctor. Do you need medical attention?"

262

"I already got some pills called 'herro-eeen'. I don't need whatever nostrum you're flogging."

"Do you recognize this knife?"

"Who in blazes are you? And how'd – "

"My name is Holmes. The doctor and I have read your note. We know what you did to Tillie."

He let out a great sigh and leaned back against the stable wall. But the pain of his injury forced him to scuttle down and sit on the floor. "I figured somebody'd find out, sooner or later."

"How did it happen?"

"I'd been out drinking and had just put Sarabande to bed when I saw a little book on the floor. Something old Stillwell must've dropped, sure. There was something about murder in the title, and that caught my attention. So I picked it up and started to read. I got distracted and didn't realize where I was walking. So I got too close to Tillie's hindquarters, and she let fly with a shod hoof." He clutched his hip and grimaced, much as we'd seen him do in Russell Square.

"Struck me right *here*. Look, I'm real good with Sarabande, but I never much liked Tillie. She was too skittish. And I guess she never liked me, either, what with all the time I spend with Sarabande, and none with her. So, there I was, down on the floor, curled up in pain, cursing her to Hades . . . .

"That's when I saw the hoof-knife. The farrier must have forgotten to take it home. I wasn't thinking straight. I was angry, I was in pain, I was out of my mind, like an inmate of Bedlam. I grabbed the knife, stood up, took hold of Tillie by the neck, and . . . .

"Right after, I realized what I'd done. And I wished I hadn't. But I couldn't bring her back. I sat down again, tore a bit of paper off a sweet that one of the kiddies had given me for a tip, and wrote an apology. I didn't know what to do with it, but I figured Stillwell would find it if I tucked it into his little murder book."

"Why didn't you admit all this straight away to Tillie's owner?"

"For one thing, he's in the country right now. But he's my landlord! If I told him what I'd done, I'd be lucky if all he did was evict me. More likely, he'd slap me with a lawsuit!"

"Surely you've earned a few extra quid, lately – "

"Well, I – "

"A share of the spoils, no doubt, from 'the fella with the camera'."

"How'd you – ?"

"Go on with your story."

He took a moment realigning himself to get slightly more comfortable. "Look. I didn't know about the thievery until that very night.

He always gave me a shilling or two, at the end of a day. But Saturday he told me what he'd really been doing – not just taking pictures, I mean – and how it made him some real money. He took me to the local pub, bought me a lot of drinks, and put a fiver in my hand! I haven't seen five quid, all at one time, in – I don't know – *years*! With all those drinks, I was pretty wobbly when I put Sarabande into her stall. Next day, I didn't even remember what I'd done, until I saw the blood on my jacket. That sobered me up, and I realized I was in trouble. A fiver's good to have. But it's nowhere near what a magistrate would have me dunned for, for killing my landlord's mare!"

"True enough. And he will surely, sooner or later, realize that no one but you could have cut Tillie's throat."

"You guys gonna 'peach me?"

I shrugged. "You haven't actually broken a law, so there's no action the police can take against you."

"I will accept your word that the photographer was taking advantage of you," Holmes said, "and that you did not go into the stable intending to kill Tillie. And writing the note shows that you regretted immediately what you'd done. But – and clearly you agree – you owe the landlord compensation for depriving him of his property. Fortunately for you, Tillie was too old to bear any more foals after this one. It is mainly the loss of a new mule for which you're responsible. So let me advise you, Mr. Thompkins, to write a letter of apology to the landlord and enclose the fiver. You may also consider showing his son, Tim, how to take over your work with Sarabande in Russell Square. Then you should go far away from Doughty Mews and hope that the landlord doesn't hire a detective to locate you."

"We have them!" declared Bradstreet as he strode through the door into our sitting room. A week had passed, and so had the warm weather. The final days of October were appropriately chilly again. He accepted the basket chair by the fire, sipped the brandy we proffered, and drew deeply on a cigar. "Got them all, to a man!" he crowed.

Holmes smiled "Amateurs, as I suspected?"

"Yes, indeed. None of 'em had been in trouble with the police before, which is why we couldn't find a fence to give us a lead. The burglars 'peached the photographer, and he 'peached his customers. The householders got back everything that was stolen. I can't thank you enough, Mr. Holmes. You too, Doctor. Please convey my thanks to the lad, and to the lady agent as well."

"You may do so yourself, at the Armstrongs' table, Tuesday next," said Holmes.

264

"Sure. But will you not attend?"

"I will claim to be away, on a fresh case, for I cannot abide being fawned over. Mrs. Armstrong, whatever her virtues, is inclined to gush with enthusiasm. Moreover, I suspect that it will not be a small gathering. Rather, she will invite a horde from the neighborhood to rejoice in the victory, and celebrate their albeit tiny role in our success. No, thank you. Such affairs are not at all to my taste."

"I happen to know that they took up a collection and handed you a nice reward."

"Oh, but I gave that away immediately. I tipped a bit extra above their pay to Miss Rijn and Theodore. But the rest of it went to Horace Stillwell, the itinerant bookseller. I had been so bored, so desperate for a case to work on, that even an *equine* murder mystery was better than nothing. And without that, of course, the burglary case would never have come to my attention.

"Stillwell thanked me profusely. He will use the money to improve his condition – to rent a flat with room for his books that he will no longer need to sell off."

"Now Bottom can retire from the bookselling business, too," I added. "He'll have no need to work any longer."

Holmes took a puff from his cigarette, reflected a moment, and then said, "With no work to do, he will quickly get bored. Watson, show Bradstreet Bottom's report on the case."

I took an envelope from my desk and passed it to the inspector. "This came by post yesterday. Read the letter inside. It's an amateur detective's account of the horse's murder, and he identifies the man who killed her."

Bradstreet withdrew the pages and squinted at the neat handwriting. "'*I have been here before*'," he read aloud. "'*I know by the smell . . . .*' What on earth – ?"

"Keep reading."

He finished it in silence, and finally said, "A four-legged detective!"

"A very good detective, for an amateur!"

"Do you expect me to believe that this was written by a donkey?"

"His logic is impeccable. And his conclusion," said Holmes, "does fit the facts."

"He says here it was the man who walks the donkey around Russell Square – that he's the one that slit the horse's throat."

"And I think he is right. I concur with his deduction."

"Maybe, Mr. Holmes, but there's no way to prove it. The man has disappeared. He left his bed-sit a week ago, still owing rent, and hasn't come back. I get that. He must've been worried his pal with the camera was going to implicate him."

265

"That is the most likely explanation for his disappearance, yes. But do you not think that Bottom, the donkey, deserves some credit here for sound detective work?"

"I agree with Holmes," said I. "Bottom formed a hypothesis, tested it – formed a new hypothesis after the first couldn't be proven, and eventually – "

"Hey, hey, you two! Stop pulling my leg! It was you, Doctor. You wrote this!"

"I did not!"

"Then who did?"

"The author is an elderly gentleman who was once a distinguished scholar. I looked him up in the academic registries. He studied and later taught at Oxford. And he was, for a time, the university's leading authority on Aesop and the beast fables – you know: The ant and the grasshopper, the tortoise and the hare – all those old folk tales about animals who can talk . . . ."

The Adventure of the
Black Perambulator
by Tracy J. Revels

Over the course of his many years as London's greatest consulting detective, my friend Mr. Sherlock Holmes welcomed humanity's spectrum into our rooms at Baker Street. Morning might find Holmes speaking with a baroness who perched grandly upon our divan, and at noon that same sofa might be occupied by a fishwife, a costermonger, or a schoolboy. Old and young, of all social ranks, brought their problems to him. Some paid in him handsome amounts. Others could offer only their heartfelt thanks. My friend had no prejudices, and the good fortune that came from solving the conundrums of the rich and well-connected allowed him time and energy to devote to the poor and friendless. It was with an individual of this latter category that one of Holmes's most unusual cases began, on a crisp autumn afternoon.

Jethro Jones was a tall man with a craggy face and a thick, unkempt black beard. He was dressed in a pea coat and a sailor's cap, with heavy brogans on his feet, and he carried various nautical aromas about his person. I could only imagine Mrs. Hudson's displeasure when she escorted him up the stairs.

"Forgive me, sir, I'm not accustomed to being in gentleman's houses," he said. "And I wouldn't dare to call upon you except – my heart is broken, sir. It's bad enough to lose sweet Jenny, though at least I could bury her and mourn her. But to lose my babes as well, and have the policemen tell me there is no hope for them – that they've been thrown away like rubbish. No, sir, I cannot sleep at night thinking of it. If there is any hope, any chance of finding them, why I will part with every farthing I earn from now until Doomsday. If you can make it right – bring them back to me – I will be your willing servant forever."

Holmes waved aside the dramatic offer. He insisted that Jones be seated, and that Mrs. Hudson bring up some coffee and biscuits for him. How Holmes deduced it, I don't know, but clearly the man was famished, and tore into the food.

"You are good to me, sir."

Holmes settled into his armchair, leaning forward, his bright eyes leaping about, studying his guest. "I knew why you came the moment you spoke your name," he said. "I have followed your case in the news, and I

267

must agree with you – the conclusion the official forces came to was most unsatisfactory."

"Then there is hope?" he asked.

"Perhaps, though we must take every element upon its face. Let me have your story, as I suspect the sensationalistic reporters have blotched the truth."

Jones sighed and swallowed the last of his coffee. "They turned me into a monster, Mr. Holmes. They claimed I killed sweet Jenny – with all they wrote, I should be sitting in a jail cell, and no doubt would be if my best mate hadn't been with me every minute of that dreadful day and could swear that I hadn't left his side. But – no, you want it all in order, I suppose, and I will try to tell it to you that way.

"I'm a simple man, sir, and a rough one. I was born in Whitechapel, though to honest folk. My father died when I was just a lad. Had he lived, perhaps he could have applied the rod of correction, for when I was eight, I fell in with a bad gang and did many a foul deed – picked pockets, broke windows, snatched handbags – for a wicked old man who paid us a pittance for our loot. Mother tried to keep me in school, but I ran away at every chance. When I was fifteen, I decided to go to sea, and was taken on a vessel in the India trade. For almost ten years, I was as good a sailor as any captain could want, and then I came down with the enteric fever while we were in Calcutta. I don't suppose I have to tell you what a bout of that does to a man?"

I cleared my throat. "I have had some experience – I too acquired it, while serving in India."

Jones nodded sadly. "Then you know you are never the same. Oh, your strength and flesh may return, but never do you feel as you did before you had it. I recovered aboard my boat, though I could no longer work as I had, and once I even dropped down senseless from the rigging. I was done with the sea, a nearly broken man of less than thirty years.

"But there was one stroke of luck – my captain gave my name to Sterling Shippers, and I was hired to supervise the loading and unloading of their cargo on the docks. It was a good job that suited me well. I was often awake at all hours, keeping watch over the goods. A lively little pub next to our offices, The Blue Mermaid, made it bearable. It was there that I met Maggie and Jenny. They were both the nieces of the publican, orphaned girls who had grown up on the docks. They were as different as night and day, those two – Jenny was fair-haired and pale. Maggie had raven tresses that fell to her waist, and the warm brown skin of a gypsy. Jenny was prim and proper, but Maggie was wild and free with her favors, always winking at me over the plump round shoulder which her tattered dress left bare. Like so many before me, I couldn't resist her. I hardly knew

268

how it happened, but suddenly Maggie was living in my rooms, acting as if we were husband and wife."

The man's face turned red. He twisted his big hands together, and his eyes dropped to his boots.

"It shames me, sirs, to tell you this."

"You aren't the first man to have such an arrangement with a woman," Holmes said, his voice gentle. "How long was she your lover?"

"Almost a year, sir. During that time, I was reconciled to my mother, and not a moment too soon, for she was dying of cancer. I begged her forgiveness – I had been a poor son to her. She held my hand, and with her last breath she pleaded with me to be a better man, to turn my heart to God, to be more sober, to marry, and have children. I promised her I would, and as the angels carried her soul away, I saw my path clear. I sent Maggie packing. I joined the church. I will not claim to have earned a Blue Ribbon, but I stopped my heavy drinking – no more than a pint for me in the evening. Yet things remained undone to keep my oath to my poor mama.

"I was at The Blue Mermaid when it came to me, as clear and bright as if a heavenly choir was singing in my ears: Sweet Jenny, so spotless – she would be the perfect bride. I set my cap to woo her, and to knock aside all the rivals for her hand. It took some doing, but in six months, she was willing to let me slip a ring upon her dainty finger and escort her down the aisle."

Holmes raised a hand. "How did Maggie react?"

"Well, Maggie was an alley cat – she hissed a bit when I first began to step out with Jenny, but she came around quickly enough, for she had a half-dozen sailors and rough fellows on her line. She even served as bridesmaid at our wedding. But then . . . ." Jones's face darkened. He gave his head a quick shake. "No, I shouldn't speak about the incident, as we never knew – "

"Out with it," Holmes demanded. The big man meekly obeyed, and I had the distinct impression that he was grateful to be ordered to reveal an unsettling event.

"Maggie brought Jenny a cake, just before Jenny was delivered of the twins. I put it on the table, while we went upstairs to show Maggie the nursey. When we came back down, I found our cat eating the cake, so I threw it out. The next morning, our cat was dead on the hearth – but he was an old thing, and perhaps it was merely his time. Still, I told Maggie not to bring more treats to our house, saying our doctor had forbidden Jenny to eat any sweets.

"Just a few days later, Jenny gave birth to our twins, Eddie and Eliza. You never saw such beautiful babies, sir. Perfect in every way, except," he gave a fond father's laugh, "Eddie had a birthmark on his bottom, a

269

stain in the shape of a heart. We said he must have been kissed by Cupid, and surely one day he would be the most handsome boy in London. But then . . . ."

Jones sniffed. He pulled out a large handkerchief. Holmes rose and seized a pile of newspapers, tossing pages aside until he found the sheet he wanted.

"Allow me to summarize from the reports," Holmes said, "and correct me where they err. On the morning of the first of October, you bid your wife goodbye and left her in the care of Mrs. O'Grady, an elderly lady whom you had hired to assist with the care of the twins. It was the last time you saw your wife alive."

Jones nodded miserably.

"Around one that afternoon, your wife announced her intentions to pay a social call on Maggie, her cousin. She donned a pale blue walking dress and placed the twins in a sizeable black perambulator."

"It was special one – a pal had made it for us, extra-large."

Holmes paused for a moment, as if mulling over a sudden idea. Then he shook his head briskly and returned to the paper.

"Your wife arrived at Miss Maggie Sullivan's house at one-thirty – this fact was verified both by the hostess and a Mrs. Salazar, who resides across the street."

"A nosey old widow woman," Jones muttered. "She does nothing all day but sit at her window and watch the thoroughfare."

"Yet it is helpful to have her testimony," Holmes said, "as she established both the time of your wife's arrival and her departure at just before three in the afternoon." He frowned at the paper. "'*I saw Mrs. Jones depart in her pretty blue dress. She gave me a wave and went west toward the docks. I presumed she was going to join her husband.*'" Holmes glanced at his client. "But your spouse had no such plans."

"Indeed not. Jenny knew the office was no place for her or the babes. She might have gone to the park for some air, but she never came to my door."

"And she wasn't seen again?"

"Not by any who knew or remembered her. I had some late business to handle and didn't come home until seven. Mrs. O'Grady was in a frightful state, for Jenny had promised to be back no later than five. I ran door to door, I called out the lads who work with me. We searched high and low all that night, and in the morning, I took my fears to the police. They searched too. How could a woman with two small babies just . . . disappear? And then . . . they implied that perhaps I . . . ."

Jones dropped his face into his hands and began to audibly sob. Holmes brought him water, and stood for a time in silent support, his lean hand resting on the man's burly shoulder.

"Forgive me, sir," Jones said.

"You have lost your world," Holmes replied. "It would be strange if you didn't grieve. I will describe the details of what followed as briefly as I can. Your wife's body was found late on the second evening, below a bush in tiny park near the Grand Surrey Canal. The coroner's verdict was that she had died from a blow to the head. She was found clad only in her undergarments, her shift, stays, stockings, and her boots. Yet there was no indication that she had been . . . abused by any man. The bloodstained perambulator was found nearby. The children are still missing."

Jones scrubbed his big hand over his face. "The police have told me there is no hope, that they were murdered and cast into the canal."

Holmes crossed the floor, flipped his coattails out, and leaned forward with his elbows upon his knees. "I am not certain that I agree with their conclusions. Forgive me, Mr. Jones, but I must ask you some pointed questions."

The man lifted his head. "You have hope?"

"Hope is a weak thing," Holmes said. "Let us see if we can give it strength. Did your wife have any jewelry on her person?"

Jones shook his head. "Only her silver wedding ring, which was still on her finger. "

"Did she carry a purse with her?"

"No. Mrs. O'Grady said that she found it on the table just after Jenny left. There was nothing in it besides a house key and hatpin."

"What of her hat?"

"She wore a small straw hat with a spray of silk cornflowers. It was found about ten paces from where she lay."

Holmes nodded. "Just a few more questions. What was the nature of the relationship between your wife and Mrs. O'Grady?"

"Most friendly – the dear old woman is like a second mother to us both."

"Had your wife any other close friends whom she might have visited on an impulse?"

"No. I cannot imagine that she would have taken the babes to someone else's home with no notice. Jenny was still recovering. She was tired most of the time. I had urged her not to call upon Maggie. Had I been at home, I would have prevented it.

"Ah . . . and why would you have done so?"

The man's face turned red in spots. "Sir – I don't wish to cast aspersions, but – I feared that Maggie might be jealous of Jenny. After

271

Jenny announced she was with child, there was something like a wild animal that came into Maggie's eyes. Oh, she claimed she was happy. She made quite a fuss when Jenny was brought to bed. She even came to the baptism. But just last week, she said that she never thought I would be a father. 'You aren't meant for it, Jeddy,' she said, and then she laughed in a cruel way. 'No, you aren't made to be a family man, not you.' That was when I told Jenny she should never be alone with her."

"Yet your wife didn't listen."

"She knew I had lived a wicked life with Maggie, but Jenny was sweet and kind and could never see the badness in anyone. Maggie had sent a note over the day before, begging for her company, wanting to see the babes. My wife felt an obligation, I suppose. She and Maggie grew up together in that pub. They had shared a room for many years, and they were as close as sisters. And when Maggie was bright and gay, she was good company."

"A final question," Holmes said. "Was there any person who would profit by your wife's death?"

Jones's face clouded. "Not to my knowledge. We had a small insurance policy on my life, but not on hers. And my sweet Jenny had no enemies, only people that loved her. The crowd at her funeral overflowed the church."

After this statement, Holmes dismissed his client with great gentleness, urging him to go back to his home and resume his life as best he could. He promised Jones he would do all that he could to help him. Holmes then closed the door and went to the window, not speaking again until he could see Jones walking down the street.

"What do you make of it, Watson?" he asked.

"A simple enough case," I said.

"Indeed? How so?"

"The lady visited her cousin, and then – for some reason known only to the female of the sex – decided to take her babies to visit their father at his workplace. On the way, she was set upon by a lustful criminal who killed her and her infants."

"Yet there was no sign of assault, beyond the wound which killed her." Holmes turned, folding his arms. "And where was her frock? What fiend, committing such a crime in a public place, would take time to undress his victim? Your theory presents some difficulties."

"Perhaps he wanted the clothing as some perverse trophy," I countered. "Or he left her clothed and some other criminal came along and took off her garments to sell."

"A rather bold way to earn perhaps a shilling or two – stealing clothes from a corpse on a footpath. And one wonders why this imagined beast didn't seize the hat and boots as well – items much easier to sell, and perhaps worth more than the presumably torn and damaged frock." Holmes hummed a bit, continuing to gaze through the window. "Would you fancy a trip down toward the docks? I think a few interviews are in order."

I was naturally glad to accompany my friend, and soon we were tucked into a hansom cab, mufflers around our necks, plunging deep into the dark heart of London, where ships from all countries of the world made port. The houses grew smaller and sadder, the businesses shabbier. A yellow miasma rose as we turned a final corner to the street where Miss Maggie Sullivan lived. Its dankness was oppressive, and I felt sorrow for the vast host of men and women who, by misfortune of birth or breeding, were forced to make their living in this undesirable sector. A fresh young matron in soft blue dress, pushing twin babes, must have seemed like an angel to all she passed.

"Stop here, cabbie," Holmes called. "Now, let us get a grasp of our surroundings," Holmes said as the hansom rattled away. "That house, with the crumbling red bricks, is where Miss Sullivan dwells. According to the papers, she occupies the rooms on the ground floor, and lets the rest to sailors and longshoremen. Just across, in the narrow house with the green shutters, is Mrs. Salazar, who verified Miss Sullivan's testimony as to when Mrs. Jones came and went. Let us pay her our regards to this witness first."

Holmes knocked and was met by a slovenly maid who told him that Mrs. Salazar was out doing the marketing. A shining sovereign convinced the woman that we were reporters who had come to interview her mistress about Mrs. Jones's murder. The maid led us up to a sitting room with a window.

"Did you also see the lady coming or going with her large baby carriage?" Holmes asked, taking a notebook from his pocket and scribbling eagerly. The red-faced woman puffed up a bit.

"Tah, I wish them other reporters or the bobbies what came banging on our door had cared as much as you, sir. No one asked, 'Now Becky, has you seen anything?' Well, sir, I saw them leaving. I was just coming in from the market, and I saw them across the street. Mrs. Jones was having a time of it, she was."

"What do you mean?" I asked.

"Oh, only that the pram was so heavy. She was having to push hard to go up the hill, and what with her hair all down in her face like that, I don't know how she saw where she was going."

"She was pushing a pair of twins in the carriage," I said. "I would think that would take some effort."

273

"Yes, but – they were just wee things, I heard, and she was pushing like she had a load of coal. Maybe the buggy wheels needed oiling. Anyways, I saw her, just as the fog closed in, and I thought how nice it was she still had all her pretty yellow hair. Mine went gray when my boy was born."

Holmes's pencil few over the paper. "So the afternoon was foggy?"

"Not so one couldn't see, but so's you wouldn't know someone unless you knows 'em – if that makes sense."

Holmes snapped the book closed. "It most certainly does." He motioned to a comfortable chair at the window and a pair of heavy spectacles on a table beside it. "Does Mrs. Salazar wear glasses all the time?"

The maid shook her head. "Too vain, that one. She won't go out with them on her face, or even wear them if she has company. Says menfolk don't like the looks of women in them. As if *she* will ever find another husband! Can't see a thing in the house, even with them peepers on, most of the time. I'm surprised she hasn't fallen into the Thames, blind as she is without her spectacles."

Holmes had picked up an embroidery hoop that rested beside the glasses. It was set with a sampler cloth. He chuckled as he put it down.

"I fear Mrs. Salazar will cause us to miss our deadline! Perhaps we had best check with the other neighbor instead."

"You mean Dark Maggie?" the maid asked. "Good luck with that sir! And mind you watch out – there's a dozen or more men what boards there. Rough sorts, they is. They won't take kindly to two reporters nosing about the place."

Holmes thanked her for the warning. Traffic had thickened on the street, and we paused, waiting for a safe moment to cross.

"Did you note the sampler, Watson?"

"Good Heavens, what does a bit of sewing have to do with this?"

"Only that the lady possesses a single pair of glasses and they are obviously not bifocals, but instead set to improve her distance viewing. Her embroidery suffers as a consequence – *Himo Sweat Ham* is the result."

"Are you implying that she didn't see Mrs. Jones exit the home?"

"She saw a lady with yellow hair and a blue dress pushing a large perambulator exit the building – the same individual who was spotted by the maid-servant. What an astute observation about the nature of our London fogs. Those who demean the innate intelligence of the laboring classes do so at their peril."

With that announcement, Holmes clasped my elbow and towed me across the street. He halted on the doorstep of the lodging house.

"Now you must take the lead. Once I have introduced us and gained our subject's confidence, you must use all your wiles to keep her busy while I confirm a few of my pet theories. You understand? Excellent." Holmes rapped loudly with his cane before I could object that I most certainly didn't comprehend what his game might be. The lady of the house opened the door without hesitation, though the instant alteration of her features – from expectation to disgust – did not go unnoticed.

"You lot. What are you, reporters? Haven't I told my tale often enough?"

Holmes removed his hat and spoke in his most ingratiating tones. "Forgive our intrusions, Madam, but we fear that public hasn't heard the true side of your story. I cannot imagine how difficult it must be, to have suffered the loss of a lady so dear to you, within hours of spending a pleasant afternoon in her company. If we might trouble you for just a few minutes of your time?"

"What's it worth?" she sneered.

"A guinea, for a mere quarter-hour?"

Reluctantly, the woman nodded and led us to the rear of the dwelling. It was a dark, ugly place, with peeling wallpaper and warped floorboards. The rank smell of old pipes and unwashed flesh nearly caused me to lose my breath. Holmes, meanwhile, trotted behind our guide as lightly as if waltzing through a springtime garden. He peppered her with questions: Where she had been born? How long she had lived in London? She snapped back answers, indicating that we should be seated inside her kitchen, on two rather fragile-looking cane-backed chairs. Holmes abruptly sneezed and, in a rush, put his handkerchief to his nose. I was alarmed to see the white linen suddenly spotted red.

"Blast – another nosebleed! Madam, if I might trouble you for directions to a washroom?"

She grunted and gestured skyward. "On the second floor. Mind you, keep it neat for my gents' use."

Holmes bowed himself out. Left alone, I tried to use my friend's tricks of close observation on the lady.

Clearly she had once been a woman of some beauty. There remained a brightness to her eyes and a sharpness of chin that indicated former pride, and her figure was still striking, even in a common brown housedress and apron. But her expression was one of wariness, and when she spoke, I noted the yellowing of her teeth, and that two were missing in her lower jaw, just where a smoker would hold a pipe. Her hair was cut short, with no attempt at a style, and she wore threadbare carpet slippers on her feet. Her hands were large, red, and calloused, as one might expect to find on a woman who made her living cleaning and feeding others.

275

"So?" She caught me staring at her. "What do you want to know?"

I pulled out my notebook. "My colleagues said you were a friend of the deceased. How long had you known her?"

"Since we were girls. We were cousins, both orphaned and taken in by our uncle."

"And how would you describe Mrs. Jones?"

"Blonde, small, pretty."

I waved a hand. "I do not mean in a physical sense. I mean – what was her soul like?"

Miss Sullivan snorted. "Just what kind of journal do you write for? Some of that church tripe? Oh, I suppose you'd say she was an angel, never missed a Sunday service. But angels don't steal men, do they?"

I shrugged to indicate that I didn't follow her thoughts. She banged her fist on the table.

"I should have been Mrs. Jethro Jones, not her! He loved me first, and if he'd had a family with me, then . . . Oh, I get tired of hearing what a heavenly creature Jenny was. If you'd known her as I did, since she was in short skirts, you'd see she was a schemer. Could play a long game, that Jenny. Wait and pray and hope and then look at a man with those great doe eyes! Pshh!" This last word was accompanied by a harsh expectoration into a spittoon. "If they knew her as I did, they'd not mourn for her so much."

"But if not for her, then for her children. Those two innocent little babies!"

"Aye, but who says they are dead?"

"They must be! The pram was found bloody."

The lady's eyes suddenly narrowed. "Where is your friend?"

"He will be back in a moment."

"He's been gone too long. I don't like strangers in my house." She stomped to the door and shouted at the top of her lungs. A few moments later, a heavyset man staggered into the doorway, pulling up his braces and rubbing his eyes, clearly just awakened from a deep and perhaps drunken slumber.

"What do you want, Maggie?"

"There's a man upstairs, in the washroom. Bring him down here, by the neck if you have to."

The huge fellow frowned, still rubbing at his face. "All right, but . . . Ah, why'd you cut your hair off, Maggie? You was so pretty in it!"

"Hang my hair!" she screeched. "Drag that man down here!"

"Watson!" a voice hissed. I turned to see Holmes at the kitchen window, signaling for me to retreat through the rear door even as our hostess and her henchman went stomping up the stairs. I bolted with

276

alacrity, and together we made our escape through a narrow, untended garden. Holmes gave a happy laugh once we were two streets away from the scene.

"We must be thankful for drainpipes," Holmes said. "I knew when I heard her caterwaul that the game was up. But see what I have found."

He pulled a bag from beneath his coat and opened it. Inside was a glistening pile of golden hair.

"A wig," Holmes said, "which explains Miss Maggie's new and rather unbecoming coiffure – her long locks had to be trimmed to don this aspect of the disguise. Also, I discovered a most interesting bottle. Is this familiar to you?"

I examined the small, dark container. Though some of the label had been peeled away enough remained to make the contents clear.

"*Godfrey's Cordial*. Holmes, this is laudanum and syrup!"

"Given to soothe fussy babies to sleep. Sadly, the dose is frequently misjudged, and the slumber becomes eternal. Obviously, the Jones children are dead."

It was a shattering pronouncement. I stopped in my tracks, and Holmes turned a few steps later, frowning at me. I shook my head.

"No. They are still alive!"

"Watson, the evidence is clear. Maggie Sullivan, in a fit of murderous jealously, lured her victim to her home and murdered her with a blow to the head, perhaps delivered by one of those sturdy iron skillets that dangle about her fireplace. She then removed the woman's distinctive clothes and donned them herself, over her own attire. She put on the wig and hat, knowing this would be enough to fool the nosey but poorly sighted neighbor. She placed her victim's body in the oversized perambulator, covered it up, and made her way to the footpath. It is a lonely, out of the way place, and there she hurriedly dumped her victim's corpse.

"Perhaps she intended to redress her victim and found the process too onerous – dressing a dead body is quite a bit of labor, as any undertaker will tell you. She left the hat and the perambulator at the scene, but carried the dress further away, placing it in a rubbish bin, where it is yet to be found. She then returned home and did away with the children – it is the only answer. Hers is a busy house, and no matter how gracious she might be with her favors, she couldn't count on every inmate of the dwelling to ignore two infants being hidden on the property. Most likely, when we alert the police, they will find the bodies beneath the kitchen floorboards, or buried in the garden, or secreted in the odorous pool beneath the outhouse."

"Holmes, no," I said, my voice strained and painful. "The children are still alive."

My friend favored me with a dubious look. I repeated the murderess's words to me. There had been something in them, a unique quality, one that I felt certain hinted at the truth.

"Her wicked heart was broken by him having children by another woman. Perhaps she had truly longed to be a mother – and, no matter her original intentions, she found she couldn't kill two infants. The bottle suggests that they were drugged, but it doesn't mean they were murdered," I argued.

"She couldn't keep two infants a secret in that house. She would have to – "

"Farm them out," I said.

Holmes stared at me. His eyes grew wide, then his hand slapped to my shoulder. "Watson, you scintillate! Let us hurry to Baker Street. Perhaps there is still time to save them!"

The next day was spent in a fury of planning and scheming. Holmes wrote messages, dispatched his Irregulars, and poured through the back issues of the newspapers that cluttered our rooms. As luck would have it, the following morning I was called to an old patient's home, and when I stepped out to return to Baker Street, I was waylaid by one of Holmes's urchin boys, who passed me a note, tipped his hat, and scampered off into the crowd. The message directed me to another address, one I had never been to before. It was a cheerful and prosperous-looking dwelling in Westminster, and Holmes met me at the door.

"Is this one of your secret lairs?" I asked. For several years, I had known that Holmes maintained various lodgings and bolt holes. It looked remarkably well-furnished for such an affair.

Holmes chuckled. "It is the residence of someone familiar to you, a heroine from one of your more sensational tales. Come into the parlor, where the lady of the house waits."

We stepped through an archway, and I was delighted to see that my hostess was none other than the former Miss Violet Smith, now Mrs. Cyril Morton. Though a few years had passed since we rescued her from villainous abductors, she remained lovely and fresh, as regal and boldly poised as she had been when riding upon her bicycle.

"It is just the two of us, Cyril and I," she said in response to my question. "Mother passed away last year. Of course, I was hoping for a family of my own, but Cyril feels he must be more established in his new business and – "

"There is no time for chatter," Holmes rudely interrupted. "You're late, Watson, and our prey should even now be arriving." He directed me toward the back of the parlor. "I am now Mr. Morton, and this is my lovely

278

wife, Violet – we long for the children Heaven doesn't see fit to bless us with. Your role should be easy enough to play, I think."

I nodded. I was to be the family physician, called in for this very special occasion.

The doorbell jangled. Holmes hurried off to answer it. Mrs. Morton cast her lovely gaze upon me and gave my hand a conspiratorial squeeze before settling into her assigned chair.

"How good to see you again, Doctor Watson! Oh, I do hope I don't disappoint Mr. Holmes – I mean, 'my husband'!"

Voices echoed in the hallway. It was amazing how Holmes could, with just a slight alteration in his tone and accent, become a completely different person. His voice became higher, more strident, and harried, as he welcomed a "Mrs. Dowdy" into the home. I fought not to smile, for my bachelor friend was utterly convincing as a henpecked spouse attempting to reassert his authority on a domestic situation.

A moment later, Holmes ushered a stout, red-faced woman into the room. She was overdressed in a heavy coat, with a fluffy boa around her neck and a wide-brimmed hat decorated with artificial doves and purple silk roses. She was huffing and puffing from the effort of carrying a large basket on each arm. To any outside observer, she was nothing more than a pretentious matron doing her own shopping, but Holmes had identified her as the premiere specimen of that class of dubious females known as 'baby farmers' – women who, for significant fees, found homes for unwanted infants. While some of these professionals were a blessing to unfortunate mothers, many more were cruel, neglectful, or even murderous – especially if the funds for the child's care weren't forthcoming.

"You are certain the children are healthy?" Holmes asked, with the brusqueness of a man conducting an important business negotiation.

"Oh yes, Mr. Morton. Nearly four months old and fit as two little fiddles." She placed the baskets on the floor at Mrs. Morton's feet. The lady gave a cry of delight as Mrs. Dowdy drew off some towels, revealing the sleeping faces of two infants.

"They are perfect!"

"Now, dearest, don't get your hopes up," Holmes warned. "Allow the doctor to inspect them. Start with the lad, please," he continued, motioning toward the child wrapped in a warm red cloth. "You must be frank with us," Holmes said to his guest. "What are the circumstances that brought them to your nursing establishment? I will not raise the children of drunkards or thieves."

"Cyril!" Mrs. Morton cried, her face turning pink with embarrassment.

279

"Dearest, we have discussed this," Holmes snapped, whirling back to the baby farmer. "What is their origin, Mrs. Dowdy? You come highly recommended, but I need the entire story."

"These are the children of a respectable family, sir, but theirs is a very sad story. Their mother, poor thing, died giving birth to them. Their father is a ship's carpenter, a hard-working and honest man. He did the best he could, but the poor mites were wanting a maternal touch, and his ship was to go to sea in less than a week, so what could he do? He brought them to me and bid me see if I could find a loving couple to take them. Most people, of course, aren't in the market for two babies at once! It seemed a blessing from above when I received your kind note."

"I do so want twins!" Mrs. Morton said, her voice soaked with a woman's maternal longing. She had taken the girl from the basket and the baby was cooing in her arms. Meanwhile, I had removed the male child's clothing, under the guise of a quick physical. I nodded to Holmes.

"He is perfect," I said. Holmes smiled, understanding that I'd confirmed the presence of the birthmark.

"Thank you, Doctor. Ah – well, hello, Inspector Lestrade," he added, as pocket door behind me slid open. "Here is the murderer you are looking for."

Mrs. Dowdy turned ghostly white, her hands flying to her face as the inspector moved to arrest her.

"What! No – no, I am an honest woman! I've committed no crime!"

"Perhaps, but you are lying about the origin of these children," Holmes said coolly. "Tell us how you acquired them."

She shuddered free of Lestrade's grasp and slammed her back into the wall, nearly knocking free a pair of pictures. "Saints preserve me, I have told you the truth! A man brought them to me – he said his name was John Benter. He came with the woman who had helped nurse the children – I don't recall her name. Please, sir, how was I to know? Are they stolen or kidnapped or – "

"Describe the woman who came to your house," Lestrade barked. "What did she look like?"

"A small, proud piece of work. Her black hair was cut short, she smoked a pipe – she said perhaps later she would come back to me with a husband, and take the children to raise, if no one else had."

"And the man?" Lestrade demanded.

"Oh, a big fellow, with yellow curls. How was I to know it was a bad business?"

Holmes turned to the inspector, holding out a card. "Do take Mrs. Dowdy to this address. If she recognizes the lady, she is telling the truth, and may go free. And Lestrade, you should probably take a few constables with you in case this 'Mr. Benter' or any of his housemates decide to defend the lady's honor."

Lestrade nodded. "And it is truly the missing twins?"

I had settled beside Mrs. Morton and was bouncing the fine little lad upon my knee. "It is most definitely the Jones children."

A few minutes later, after the official forces and their sobbing prisoner had exited, a pale-faced young man with a handlebar mustache poked his head around the door.

"Is the coast clear?" the real Mr. Cyril Morton asked. His wife eagerly recounted the adventure in their living room. Holmes knelt beside the lady, allowing the baby girl to grasp his finger.

"What a strange start in life these two have had. It does me good to think how overjoyed their father will be when we deliver them to him."

"And he will have you to thank," Mrs. Morton said.

"Oh no," Holmes gently corrected. "He will need to thank the Good Doctor, whose understanding of human nature surpassed my own. He heard the suggestion in Maggie Sullivan's voice that they might yet live. And Watson certainly has a better grasp on the practice of baby farming than I do – it came to him immediately as a solution to our murderess's problem. I cannot swear that it would have occurred to me that the children might still be within our grasp to rescue. Well, shall we collect our babes in arms and return them to their home?"

Mrs. Morton sighed as she placed the little girl back in her respective basket. The couple walked with us to the door and, as we stepped into the cab, I noticed that the lady was caressing her husband's arm. Unaware of my scrutiny, she suddenly lifted on her toes to kiss his cheek.

"If you will permit me another deduction?" I asked.

Holmes chuckled. "And what is that?"

"Before a year is done, I suspect their household will have grown by at least one more Morton!"

The Adventure of the Surrey Inn
by Leslie Charteris and Denis Green

Sherlock Holmes and The Saint
An Introduction by Ian Dickerson

Everyone has a story to tell about how they first met Sherlock Holmes. For me it was a Penguin paperback reprint my brother introduced me to in my pre-teen years. I read it, and went on to read all the original stories, but it didn't appeal to me in the way it appealed to others. This is probably because I discovered the adventures of The Saint long before I discovered Sherlock Holmes.

The Saint, for those readers who may need a little more education, was also known as Simon Templar and was a modern day Robin Hood who first appeared in 1928. Not unlike Holmes, he has appeared in books, films, TV shows, and comics. He was created by Leslie Charteris, a young man born in Singapore to a Chinese father and an English mother, who was just twenty years old when he wrote that first Saint adventure. He'd always wanted to be a writer – his first piece was published when he was just nine years of age – and he followed that Saint story, his third novel, with two further books, neither of which featured Simon Templar.

However, there's a notable similarity between the heroes of his early novels, and Charteris, recognising this, and being somewhat fed up of creating variations on the same theme, returned to writing adventures for The Saint. Short stories for a weekly magazine, *The Thriller*, and a change of publisher to the mainstream Hodder & Stoughton, helped him on his way to becoming a best-seller and something of a pop culture sensation in Great Britain.

But he was ambitious. Always fond of the USA, he started to spend more time over there, and it was the 1935 novel – and fifteenth Saint book – *The Saint in New York*, that made him a transatlantic success. He spent some time in Hollywood, writing for the movies and keeping an eye on The Saint films that were then in production at RKO studios. Whilst there, he struck up what would become a lifelong friendship with Denis Green, a British actor and writer, and his new wife, Mary.

Fast forward a couple of years . . . . Leslie was on the west coast of the States, still writing Saint stories to pay the bills, writing the occasional non-Saint piece for magazines, and getting increasingly frustrated with RKO who, he felt, weren't doing him, or his creation, justice. Denis Green, meanwhile, had established himself as a stage actor, and had embarked on a promising radio career both in front of and behind the microphone.

Charteris was also interested in radio. He had a belief that his creation could be adapted for every medium and was determined to try and prove it. In 1940, he commissioned a pilot programme to show how The Saint would work on radio, casting his friend Denis Green as Simon Templar. Unfortunately, it didn't sell, but just three years later, he tried again, commissioning a number of writers – including Green – to create or adapt Saint adventures for radio.

They also didn't sell, and after struggling to find a network or sponsor for The Saint on the radio, he handed the problem over to established radio show packager and producer, James L. Saphier. Charteris was able to solve one problem, however: At the behest of advertising agency Young & Rubicam, who represented the show's sponsors, Petri Wine, Denis Green had been sounded out about writing for *The New Adventures of Sherlock Holmes*, a weekly radio series that was then broadcasting on the Mutual Network.

Green confessed to his friend that, while he could write good radio dialogue, he simply hadn't a clue about plotting. He was, as his wife would later recall, a reluctant writer: "He didn't really like to write. He would wait until the last minute. He would put it off as long as possible by scrubbing the kitchen stove or wash the bathroom – anything before he sat down at the typewriter. I had a very clean house." Charteris offered a solution: They would go into partnership, with him creating the stories and Green writing the dialogue.

But there was another problem: *The New Adventures of Sherlock Holmes* aired on one of the radio networks that Leslie hoped might be interested in the adventures of The Saint, and it would not look good, he thought, for him to be involved with a rival production. Leslie adopted the pseudonym of *Bruce Taylor*, (as you will see at the end of the following script,) taking inspiration taking inspiration from the surname of the show's producer Glenhall Taylor and that of Rathbone's co-star, Nigel Bruce.

The Taylor/Green partnership was initiated with "The Strange Case of the Aluminum Crutch", which aired on July 24th, 1944, and would ultimately run until the following March, with *Bruce Taylor*'s final contribution to the Holmes Canon being "The Secret of Stonehenge", which aired on March 19th, 1945 – thirty-five episodes in all.

Bruce Taylor's short radio career came to an end in short because Charteris shifted his focus elsewhere. Thanks to Saphier, The Saint found a home on the NBC airwaves, and aside from the constant demand for literary Saint adventures, he was exploring the possibilities of launching a Saint magazine. He was replaced by noted writer and critic Anthony Boucher, who would establish a very successful writing partnership with Denis Green.

Fast forward quite a few more years – to 1988 to be precise: A young chap called Dickerson, a long standing member of *The Saint Club*, discovers a new TV series of The Saint is going into production. Suitably inspired, he writes to the then-secretary of the Club, suggesting that it was time the world was reminded of The Saint, and The Saint Club in particular. Unbeknownst to him, the secretary passes his letter on to Leslie Charteris himself. The teenaged Dickerson and the aging author struck up a friendship which involved, amongst other things, many fine lunches, followed by lazy chats over various libations. Some of those conversations featured the words "Sherlock" and "Holmes".

It was when Leslie died, in 1993, that I really got to know his widow, Audrey. We often spoke at length about many things, and from time to time discussed Leslie and the Holmes scripts, as well as her own career as an actress.

When she died in 2014, Leslie's family asked me to go through their flat in Dublin. Pretty much the first thing I found was a stack of radio scripts, many of which had been written by *Bruce Taylor* and Denis Green.

I was, needless to say, rather delighted. More so when his family gave me permission to get them into print. Back in the 1940's, no one foresaw an afterlife for shows such as this, and no recordings exist of this particular Sherlock Holmes adventure. So here you have the only documentation around of Charteris and Green's "The Mystery of the Surrey Inn" . . . .

Ian Dickerson

The Adventure of the Surrey Inn

Originally Broadcast on February 19ᵗʰ, 1945

CHARACTERS
- Sherlock Holmes
- Dr. John H. Watson
- Mrs. Hunter
- Sergeant Gribble
- Doctor Brice
- Bill Hagney
- Sam Wilton
- Announcer (Bruce Campbell)

SOUND EFFECTS
- Door open and close
- Door unlocked
- Knocking on door
- Rattling of heavy door bolt
- Window banging open
- Footsteps
- Footsteps running down stairs
- Footsteps on pavement
- Approaching
- Scuffling of feet
- Stamping of feet
- Thumping and thudding
- Dull thudding noise
- Match being struck
- Vase crashing in fireplace
- Lamp crashing to floor
- Tinkle of broken glass
- Fabric being wrenched
- Whoosh of wind
- Clink of bagful of coins

CAMPBELL: This episode from the life of Sherlock Holmes will be transmitted to our men and women overseas by shortwave, and through the worldwide facilities of the Armed Forces Radio Network. *Petri Wine brings you –*

MUSIC: THEME (FADE ON CUE)

CAMPBELL: Basil Rathbone and Nigel Bruce in *The New Adventures of Sherlock Holmes*!

MUSIC: THEME (FULL FINISH)

CAMPBELL: The Petri family – the family that took time to bring you good wine – invites you to listen to Doctor Watson tell us about another exciting adventure he shared with his old friend, that master detective, Sherlock Holmes. Now, I'm not a detective myself, but one problem I can solve what to have for dinner when you're short on meat points. Try an old-fashioned chicken dinner. You don't have to get a broiler or fryer or roasting chicken. Get a stewing hen and try chicken fricassee with dumplings. Yes, and serve it with glasses of well-chilled Petri California Sauterne. *Mmm mmm!* That chilled Petri Sauterne will make your good chicken and dumplings taste like something out of this world. Just the sight of that Petri Sauterne on the table – with its clear, golden, sunshiny color – makes your meal look like a banquet. And when you taste that good Petri Sauterne – well, you'll get to know one of the most delicate, intriguing flavors that ever touched your palate. And that's on the level. Try that Petri Sauterne with chicken tomorrow. Or say – it's great with fish, too. You can take my word for it – with food, nothing can take the place of that good Petri Wine!

MUSIC: *SCOTCH POEM*

CAMPBELL: And now let's join Doctor Watson as he sits waiting for us in the study of his northern Californian ranch house. Good evening, Doctor.

WATSON: Evening Mr. Campbell. Slip your coat off and join me over here by the fire . . . That's it.

CAMPBELL: What was the large book you were reading as I came in, Doctor? Are you just getting around to *Gone With the Wind*?

WATSON: (CHUCKLING) No, it's an even longer book than that – it's an *Encyclopedia Britannica*. I was just refreshing my memory as to the exact meaning of a word that figures very prominently in tonight's story.

286

CAMPBELL: And the word is – ?

WATSON: *Poltergeist.*

CAMPBELL: I'm certain glad you have an encyclopedia there, Doctor. Just what is a *"poltergeist"*?

WATSON: Settle yourself in your usual chair and help yourself to a fill of tobacco, and I'll tell you. (READING) "'Poltergeist' *is derived from the German words meaning* 'chattering spirit'. *It's a name applied to certain phenomena, such as rapping, knocking, unexplained movements of furniture, breaking of crockery, and the like, long associated with supernatural forces. Much of this activity has proved to be fraudulent, although some cases have remained without satisfactory natural solution.*" Does that answer your question, Mr. Campbell?

CAMPBELL: Very thoroughly, thank you Doctor. And how did you and Sherlock Holmes happen to become involved with a *poltergeist*?

WATSON: Our attention was first directed towards the matter by reading in the newspaper of strange happenings in the little village of Westcott, about thirty miles from London. Shops had been mysteriously tampered with – goods scattered all over the place during the night – though nothing had been stolen. Finally, this apparently evil spirit turned its powers on The Red Lion, the village inn. Bottles were opened and spilled. Furniture was moved in the night. Fires, of unknown origin, broke out.

CAMPBELL: And I suppose Sherlock Holmes got tired of reading about these things and decided to go down there and investigate for himself?

WATSON: Not exactly. You see, it turned out that the owner of The Red Lion, a Mrs. Hunter, was the widow of a retired cab driver who had piloted Holmes and me on many of our excursions. The poor woman, frightened out of her wits by what was happening at her inn, sent Holmes a telegram imploring him to help her. Needless to remark, a very few hours later, we were seated in the back parlor of The Red Lion, listening to (FADING) the garrulous landlady herself . . . .

287

MRS. HUNTER: (ABOUT FIFTY. COCKNEY. EFFUSIVE.) An' that's the way it's been, Mr. 'Olmes – me furniture movin' 'isself about in the night, me liquor bottles being opened and spilled, and no one can find out who's doing it.

WATSON: Mrs. Hunter, have the local police investigated this matter thoroughly?

MRS. HUNTER: Of course they 'ave, Doctor Watson. Sergeant Gribble's almost living 'ere – and drinking me out of 'ouse and 'ome at the same time – but 'e can't find out nothing. Then yesterday, this Doctor Brice comes down 'ere from London and says 'e's going to solve it for me. But if you ask me, 'e's about as much use as a pain under the 'eart.

HOLMES: Who is this Doctor Brice?

MRS. HUNTER: Some scientific gent – says he comes from The Society of Super . . . Super . . . nature-something.

HOLMES: The Society for Supernatural Research?

MRS. HUNTER: That's it, Mr. 'Olmes. 'E's staying 'ere.

HOLMES: I should like to meet him, Mrs. Hunter.

MRS. HUNTER: You will. 'E's going to have his supper 'ere tonight.

SOUND EFFECT: DOOR OPENS

MRS. HUNTER: (*SOTTO VOCE*) 'Ullo – here comes Sergeant Gribble. (RAISING HER VOICE) Evenin', Sergeant. Anything new?

GRIBBLE: (FADING IN. POMPOUS VILLAGE CONSTABLE) There is not, Missus Hunter, but I'd like a pint of old and bitter, if you don't' mind.

MRS. HUNTER: Nothing new about that. Sergeant, these gentlemen are Mr. Sherlock Holmes and Doctor Watson.

AD LIB HOW DO YOU DO'S

288

GRIBBLE: Mr. Sherlock Holmes, eh? I suppose you're going to show us country police how you do things up in London?

HOLMES: Not at all, Sergeant. I've just come down here to see if I can be of any assistance to Mrs. Hunter.

GRIBBLE: You could have saved yourself the journey, Mr. Holmes. I've been on this case since these 'ere things started happening – and I've found nothing. No clues, no fingerprints, nothing stolen, no footprints.

WATSON: Then how do you account for what's been going on?

GRIBBLE: I can't account for it. And I've handled some pretty tricky cases in my day. Did you ever hear of the Guildford bicycle robbery, Mr. Holmes?

HOLMES: I . . . er . . . I don't think so.

GRIBBLE: I solved that.

HOLMES: Congratulations, Sergeant.

GRIBBLE: And I solved the dog-poisonings over on the Dorking Road – and got myself promoted to sergeant by doing it. But this case has me beat and I don't mind admitting it.

MRS. HUNTER: 'Ere's your beer.

GRIBBLE: Thank you kindly, Missus. And here's your good health.

MRS. HUNTER: Never mind my good 'ealth. That'll be seven-pence.

HOLMES: Put it on my bill, please, Mrs. Hunter.

GRIBBLE: Much obliged to you, Mr. Holmes. (EXPANSIVELY) Yes, gentlemen, if you want my advice, I'd say you're wasting your time. There's only one explanation to what's going on down here – and that's a ghost.

MRS. HUNTER: Arthur Grimble! You ought to be ashamed of yourself. You know as well as I do there aren't such things.

GRIBBLE: You talk to that Doctor Brice that's staying here and you'll know there are. Why he was telling me just now –

SOUND EFFECT: DOOR OPENS

GRIBBLE: Oh – here he is now.

MRS. HUNTER: Evening, Doctor Brice. Ready for your supper?

BRICE: (FADING IN – SCHOLARLY, PRECISE, MIDDLE-AGED) Thank you. I prefer to wait for half-an-hour. However, I should like a glass if sherry, if you please.

MRS. HUNTER: Yes, sir. Oh, this is Mr. Sherlock Holmes and Doctor Watson.

AD LIB HOW DO YOU DO'S

BRICE: I'm very proud to meet you, gentlemen. I've read many of your stories, Doctor Watson. Interesting. Very interesting. I hope, Gribble, that Mr. Holmes has been giving you a few pointers as to how to handle the case.

GRIBBLE: No, sir. I've just been telling him that I haven't been able to find a single clue.

BRICE: And yet I have found several. Odd, isn't it?

WATSON: Oh, really, sir? I should very much like to know what you've discovered.

HOLMES: And so should I. We only arrived down here half-an-hour ago, you know.

BRICE: I'm afraid my clues wouldn't interest you, Mr. Holmes. I deal in the spiritual world, and you in the material. I am glad that you are down here, though. It will be interesting to see which of us solves the case first.

HOLMES: That sounds like a challenge, Dr. Brice.

290

BRICE: A friendly challenge, yes.

WATSON: May I ask whether you subscribe to this *poltergeist* theory, sir?

BRICE: It's a very possible solution. There are such forces. I have personally investigated more than half-a-dozen *poltergeist* manifestations – though only one of them was genuine, I'm afraid.

HOLMES: And naturally you're hoping that this will prove to be another authentic case.

BRICE: Naturally.

GRIBBLE: Seems to me, Doctor Brice, that you run a lot of risks dabbling in that ghost stuff.

BRICE: Rubbish, Sergeant. If you understand what you're doing, there are not risks to it. You see, gentlemen, a *poltergeist* is comparatively harmless. It's simply a mischievous spirit that plays pranks. There are two theories: One that they are simply rather childish ghosts who choose that method of self-expressions, and the other theory is that they are elementals who draw their force from medio-mystic people – usually children.

MRS. HUNTER: (FADING IN) Here's your sherry, Doctor Brice.

BRICE: Thank you, Mrs. Hunter.

HOLMES: Your theories are very interesting, sir, but being a confirmed materialist myself, I should like a few facts. Mrs. Hunter: How long have you owned this inn?

MRS. HUNTER: Just over four years, Mr. Holmes.

HOLMES: And who owned it before you?

MRS. HUNTER: A man by the name of Jack Slocum. 'E was murdered right 'ere in The Red Lion, you know.

HOLMES: No, I didn't know. Were you here at that time, Sergeant Gribble?

291

GRIBBLE: Aye, Mr. Holmes. I've handled the case.

WATSON: Was the murderer ever caught?

GRIBBLE: No, he wasn't, sir. It was a strange business. Old Jack Slocum was a terrible miser. He lived here with his daughter, Florence – she's married to Bill Hagney, what runs the china shop next door.

WATSON: Is that the same shop that was wrecked the other night?

GRIBBLE: Aye, sir.

HOLMES: And the murdered man's daughter it married to its owner, eh? Go on, Sergeant. What were the circumstances of the murder?

GRIBBLE: The neighbours were wakened in the middle of the night by someone banging on the front door of the inn. Jack stuck his head out of the window and hollered that it was too late to take any one in – but he was finally persuaded to come down and open the door. Half-an-hour later there was a terrible screaming and yelling, and when the neighbours busted in, they found Jack Slocum with his head bashed in, and no signs of who'd done it.

HOLMES: Where was his daughter at the time?

GRIBBLE: She was in London, Mr. Holmes. He was all alone.

MRS. HUNTER: Mr. 'Olmes, I don't want to be rude . . . but isn't it more important to find out what's going on *now* than to solve a five-year old murder?

HOLMES: The recent happenings may be very closely related to Mr. Slocum's murder, Mrs. Hunter.

BRICE: I entirely agree with you, Mr. Holmes, although I think we deduce differently from the same facts.

SOUND EFFECT: DOOR OPENS

MRS. HUNTER: 'Ere's Bill Hagney now. (RAISING HER VOICE) 'Ullo, Bill.

HAGNEY: (FADING IN – MIDDLE-AGED, ACIDULATED) Evening. Gribble – you're the law in this village. Do I have to let photographers from the London papers into my shop? Flo's gone to bed with heartburn, she's so upset.

GRIBBLE: It can't hurt you – havin' your photograph took, Bill. And it's great publicity for the shop.

HAGNEY: I don't want publicity.

HOLMES: Mr. Hagney, we were just discussing your father-in-law's murder.

HAGNEY: Who are you?

WATSON: You're speaking to Mr. Sherlock Holmes – of London.

MRS. HUNTER: 'E's down 'ere to 'elp me find out what's going on in the village.

HAGNEY: Well, that's different. What d'you want to know?

HOLMES: Your father-in-law was reputed to be a miser, wasn't he?

HAGNEY: Yes. What of it?

HOLMES: After his murder, was any hidden wealth of his ever found?

HAGNEY: No, and if you want my opinion, he never did have much money. At the time he was done in, they said he'd been killed for his savings that he hid in here. But that was five years ago, and nobody's found any trace of his ever owning anything except this inn.

HOLMES: Your shop is next door to here, isn't it?

HAGNEY: That's right, sir.

HOLMES: Sergeant Gribble – one other shop was wrecked, I understand.

GRIBBLE: Yes, Mr. Holmes. The tailor's next door – the shop on the other side of the Red Lion, run by Sam Wilton.

HOLMES: So that the visitations of this alleged *poltergeist* have occurred in this inn, and in the two shops on each side of it.

GRIBBLE: That's right, Mr. Holmes.

HOLMES: Hmm. Extremely localized – even for a . . . a mischievous spirit.

WATSON: What are you driving at, Holmes?

HOLMES: I'm driving at nothing, old chap. I suggest that we have some supper, and then I think it might be profitable for the two of us to take a little walk.

MUSIC: BRIDGE

WATSON: Holmes, it's confoundedly chilly out here. I don't see what you expect to find out just by standing across the street and *looking* at the inn.

HOLMES: Nevertheless, I have found out a great deal, old chap.

WATSON: What, for instance?

HOLMES: You'll notice that the architecture of the inn is almost indistinguishable from that of the shops adjoining it on each side. Except for the doors, and the inn sign, they might be part of the same building.

WATSON: That's true.

HOLMES: And you'll remember that I commented earlier on the fact that the activities of this supposed *poltergeist* seemed to be remarkably localized. Don't those two facts suggest something to you?

WATSON: Can't say they do.

HOLMES: Dear me, Watson, you're being very obtuse this evening. Let me give you one further clue: D'you notice that an annex – obviously recently built – and the other side of the annex adjoins Mr. Hagney's china shop? Come now – what do you deduce from that?

294

WATSON: I see what you're driving at, Holmes: The *poltergeist* is confused by the inn, the two shops, and the new annex all looking alike, and it's not certain on which building it wants to focus its attention.

HOLMES: That's a reasonable deduction – though I don't think it's the right one.

SOUND EFFECT: FOOTSTEPS

HOLMES: Come on, I notice that the lights are on in Sam Wilton's tailor shop. I suggest we have a chat with him.

WATSON: Seems pretty late at night for him to be in his shop.

SOUND EFFECT: KNOCKING ON DOOR

HOLMES: I don't know. Your village tailor is a hardworking fellow.

SOUND EFFECT: APPROACHING FOOTSTEPS

WATSON: Here he comes.

SOUND EFFECT: DOOR UNLOCKED AND OPENED

WILTON: (OFF A LITTLE – HEARTY, JOVIAL, ABOUT THIRTY-FIVE) Who is it?

HOLMES: My name is Sherlock Holmes, and this is Doctor Watson. We're staying at the inn next door. I wonder if we might come in and have a chat with you?

SOUND EFFECT: FOOTSTEPS. DOOR CLOSE

WILTON: Always glad of a bit of company. Come in the back room. I've got a fire in there.

HOLMES: Before we do that, Mr. Wilton, I wonder if you'd mind describing just how you found your shop after it had been ransacked.

WATSON: My friend's very interested in finding out what's at the back of all this business.

WILTON: So am I, gentlemen. So am I. Well, all I can tell you is that three mornings ago, I came here to find my shop turned upside down. The furniture was all in a heap in one corner. Bolts of material had been taken down from the shelves, unwound, and strewn all over the place.

WATSON: But nothing was stolen, was it?

WILTON: No, it wasn't.

HOLMES: I notice that you have shelves around the four walls. Were the bolts of material taken from all of them indiscriminately?

WILTON: Funny you should ask that, sir. No, they weren't. They were only taken from the shelves against that wall.

HOLMES: Exactly. The wall adjoining the inn, you will notice, Watson.

WATSON: By George! Yes, Holmes.

HOLMES: Mr. Wilton, you've undoubtedly heard the story in the village that these visitations have been caused by a . . . a *supernatural power*?

WILTON: Yes sir, but I don't hold any truck with that sort of nonsense. Somebody came in here and wrecked my shop – and I've got a good idea who it was.

HOLMES: Who?

WILTON: This is in confidence, you understand.

HOLMES: Of course.

WILTON: I think Bill Hagney's behind all this. He's the fellow that runs the china shop on the other side of the inn.

WATSON: But his own shop was visited – and all his crockery smashed.

WILTON: Done it himself, if you ask me, so that no one would suspect him. He carries insurance on breakages – it would have cost him nothing.

HOLMES: May I ask why you suspect him?

WILTON: He and I have been rowing ever since I came back here. You see, he married Florence Slocum after her dad got himself murdered, and I'd always planned to marry Florrie myself. So when she chucked me over to marry Bill, I joined the Army. Served nearly five years in – and when I come back here, I find Florrie miserable. It's my opinion he only married her because he thought her old man had hidden some money away in the inn – and when he didn't find it, he took it out on poor Florrie.

HOLMES: Very interesting, Mr. Wilton. I'm much obliged to you.

WILTON: Won't you come and sit by the fire, sir? It's not late.

HOLMES: My friend will probably join you. I have to make a telephone call.

WATSON: Really? Who to, Holmes?

SOUND EFFECT: FOOTSTEPS

HOLMES: (FADING) Scotland Yard. I'll see you at the inn.

SOUND EFFECT: DOOR OPEN AND CLOSE

WILTON: You can stay a few minutes, can't you, sir? It's nice to have company.

WATSON: Well, just long enough to smoke a pipe. By the way, you were saying you were in the Army?

WILTON: That's right, sir. Served in the Boer War.

WATSON: Did you now? I was an Army man myself, y'know.

WILTON: Were you, sir?

WATSON: (EXPANSIVELY) I was attached to the Fifth Northumberland Fusiliers – during the Afghan War. Got badly wounded at the Battle of Maiwand. It's a rather interesting story. In fact, if it hadn't been for my orderly – a fellow named Murray – I should have . . . .

MUSIC: UP STRONG, DROWNING DIALOGUE. BRIDGE

SOUND EFFECT: DOOR OPENING

HOLMES: (OFF) Hello, Watson. You've been a long time.

WATSON: I stayed a little longer than I expected, Holmes. That fellow Wilton gets a little long-winded when he starts describing his experiences.

HOLMES: (KNOWINGLY) Army experiences, I suppose?

WATSON: Yes. Oh, by the way – Sergeant Gribble came into the shop just now. There's been another disturbance in the village tonight. The blacksmith's forge was broken into and had sacks of flour upset all over the place.

HOLMES: Yes, I heard about it. Doctor Brice told me.

WATSON: Rather disproves your theory about the actions of the *poltergeist* being localized. The smithy's shop is at the other end of the village.

HOLMES: I know. I've already been there.

WATSON: You have? What did you find out?

HOLMES: Nothing very much.

WATSON: 'Pon my soul, Holmes, you're being more than usually cryptic this evening.

HOLMES: Am I, old chap? Never mind. When Scotland Yard returns my telephone call, I think I can give you the complete answer to the mystery. As it is, you should be able to fit a few of the pieces together yourself.

298

WATSON: I've been thinking over what you said about the similarity of this building, and the ones on each side of it, but I still can't see the significance of the fact.

HOLMES: Let me help you, Watson. Leaving out the supernatural theories, let us suppose someone comes back to this inn after a number of years. Let us also suppose that he was never very familiar with its architecture. He finds himself confused as to exactly which building he is searching for. So what does he do? He –

SOUND EFFECT: VASE CRASHING IN THE FIREPLACE

WATSON: Good Lord, Holmes! That vase on the mantelpiece – I saw it literally jump off! It's the *poltergeist*!

HOLMES: Rubbish. It's a –

SOUND EFFECD: LAMP CRASHING TO THE FLOOR. TINKLE OF BROKEN GLASS

WATSON: There goes the lamp! Look out, Holmes! The burning oil! It's setting fire to the curtains.

SOUND EFFECT: SCUFFLE OF FEET. FABRIC BEING WRENCHED

HOLMES: Stamp on it, old chap!

SOUND EFFECT: STAMPING OF FEET

HOLMES: That's it! Light the candle, Watson.

SOUND EFFECT: MATCH BEING STRUCK

WATSON: (AFTER A MOMENT) There you are . . . Holmes, I don't like this.

HOLMES: Nor do I. In fact, I think it's high time we –

SOUND EFFECT: WINDOW BANGING OPEN. WHOOSH OF WIND

WATSON: There goes the window – and there goes the candle, confound it!

HOLMES: This joke has gone far enough. We're old-enough hands not to be frightened by schoolboy tricks. Come on, Watson!

SOUND EFFECT: DOOR OPEN

WATSON: Where are we going?

HOLMES: Out into the street.

MRS. HUNTER: (OFF) What's going on? What's all the noise about?

HOLMES: (CALLING) It's all right, Mrs. Hunter. Stay in your room. We'll be back in a moment.

SOUND EFFECT: FOOTSTEPS RUNNING DOWN STAIRS. SUDDEN GURGLING CRY OF MAN (OFF). FOOTSTEPS STOP

WATSON: (BREATHLESSLY) Great Heavens, Holmes! Did you hear that?

HOLMES: Of course I did. Help me unbolt this door.

SOUND EFFECT: RATTLING OF DOOR BOLT. DOOR OPENING VIOLENTLY

HOLMES: Come on!

SOUND EFFECT: RUNNING FOOTSTEPS ON LEVEL

WATSON: It sounded as if – (SUDDENLY) Look here, Holmes – here under the street lamp!

SOUND EFFECT: FOOTSTEPS STOP

WATSON: (AFTER A PAUSE) Poor devil . . . a knife between his shoulders.

HOLMES: Turn him over, Watson.

300

WATSON: It's Bill Hagney – the owner of the china shop next door!

HOLMES: Exactly. I'm afraid we must refer to him as the *late* owner of the china shop next door.

<u>MUSIC: UP STRONG TO MIDDLE CURTAIN</u>

CAMPBELL: We'll hear the rest of Doctor Watson's story in just a few seconds. Time for me to make a fast suggestion: Namely, if you're thinking of having beef or lamb stew – or maybe pot roast for dinner soon . . . Well, then you might think about having Petri California Burgundy too, because that Petri Burgundy makes *everything* you eat taste better! Petri Burgundy is a hearty red wine . . . the old-fashioned kind of red wine with a luscious flavor that comes right from the heart of plump, hand-picked grapes. Petri Wine is so good you don't want to keep it all to yourself. Serve it the next time you have friends over for dinner. You'll make a real impression. And incidentally, serve that Petri Burgundy proudly – You can, because the name *Petri* is the proudest name in the history of American Wines.

<u>MUSIC: *SCOTCH POEM*</u>

CAMPBELL: And now back to tonight's new Sherlock Holmes adventure. The great detective and his old friend, Dr. Watson, are in the tiny village of Westcott, where they are investigating some very unusual occurrences, supposedly caused by supernatural forces. Shortly after their arrival, one of the village storekeepers has been found murdered, and as we rejoin our story, it is one o'clock in the morning and the murder is being discussed (FADING) in the back parlour of the local inn . . . .

MRS. HUNTER: (TEARFULLY) It's a dreadful thing, Mr. 'Olmes. Any of us might be murdered in our beds, you know.

HOLMES: Mrs. Hunter, I can promise you that before very long, this mystery will be solved. Dr. Brice, as the champion of the supernatural elements in this case – may I ask if you still believe that this might be the work of a *poltergeist*?

BRICE: It is not impossible – but I should like to examine the body before giving an opinion.

WATSON: Sergeant Gribble's taken it over to the morgue. I imagine you could arrange to view it before the inquest in the morning.

MRS. HUNTER: Mr. 'Olmes, why do you suppose poor Bill 'Agney was murdered?

HOLMES: Because he saw too much.

BRICE: I don't follow you, Mr. Holmes.

HOLMES: My own theory, Doctor Brice, is that Hagney caught the murderer red-handed as he was attempting to convince Doctor Watson and myself that there is a *poltergeist* in operation – and so he had to die.

SOUND EFFECT: DOOR OPEN

MRS. HUNTER: Sam Wilton! You look as white as a ghost!

WILTON: (OFF EXCITEDLY) I just heard about Hagney! Has someone broken the news to Florrie?

MRS. HUNTER: Yes – the clergyman. He's with her now.

WILTON: I must go to her. (FADING) I must go to her at once!

SOUND EFFECT: DOOR CLOSE

WATSON: (*SOTTO VOCE*) Holmes, you know that man had a very good motive for killing Hagney.

HOLMES: From what I hear, I think a lot of people had good motive for killing him. However, as soon as the morning post gets here, I can tell you who the murderer is.

BRICE: How, Mr. Holmes?

HOLMES: I telephoned Scotland Yard tonight. I wanted to know of anyone who might have been forcibly held out of circulation for about five years – say, from almost immediately after the innkeeper was murdered until just a week or so ago.

302

WATSON: But Holmes, that would surely cover a lot of people!

BRICE: Just what I was going to say.

HOLMES: It's surprising. The coincidence in dates narrows it down considerably. Actually, Scotland Yard could give me only one candidate – a man who broke into a bank five miles from here the morning after the murder. He was caught and sent to prison and was only released ten days ago. They're sending me his photograph. When I get that – the case will be solved. Meanwhile, I suggest we all go to bed and try and get some sleep, for tomorrow should prove to be a very interesting day.

MUSIC: BRIDGE

WATSON: (SLEEPILY) Holmes, I thought you said it would be a good idea if we all got some sleep. Here it is three o'clock in the morning, and you're still sitting there, puffing at that blasted pipe.

HOLMES: I'm waiting, old chap.

WATSON: Waiting? For what?

HOLMES: I baited a trap tonight. I'm waiting for it to spring.

WATSON: You mean we don't have to wait until morning?

HOLMES: I shall be amazed if we do.

WATSON: (REPROACHFULLY) You know, Holmes, I do wish you'd let me into your confidence a little bit more. You're always so confoundedly mysterious. What trap have you baited, and who's going to spring it?

HOLMES: (CHUCKLING) Don't be angry with me. I don't mean to keep you in the dark. Anyway, I should have thought the pattern of this case was obvious to you by now.

WATSON: I may be stupid, but it isn't – and I wish you'd explain it to me.

HOLMES: Very well. The man who was with the innkeeper five years ago was probably lucky enough to find out where the miser kept his money. He then killed him, but he was clumsy enough, or unlucky enough, to allow an uproar which aroused the neighbourhood.

WATSON: So that he had to escape because of the commotion before he was able to get the many.

HOLMES: Exactly. The next morning, by one of those extraordinary quirks, he was arrested for an entirely different crime and sent to prison for five years. He was released ten days ago. So what is his first move?

WATSON: He comes back here to see if the money is still in its hiding place.

HOLMES: Precisely – and finds the architectural changes in the inn. Now remember, he was a stranger here five years ago – so what is his reaction?

WATSON: (EXCITEDLY) I see it now! He gets confused and ransacks not only the inn, but the shops on each side of it!

HOLMES: Bravo, Watson! You're doing splendidly. As soon as the *poltergeist* theory was brought up, he saw it as an excellent cloak to mask his real activities. I must have worried him a bit when I remarked how localized the activities of the *poltergeist* were – because he went out of his way to create a spurious diversion at the blacksmith's at the other end of the village. This was a clumsy attempt to put me off the scent – just as tonight's little display of falling lamps and vases was a clumsy attempt to frighten us.

WATSON: But how was that engineered?

HOLMES: Crudely enough. Black thread had been tied to each of the objects – and led out through the window. A tug from outside and the desired effect was obtained. You can still see the broken thread attached to the lamp. Unfortunately for Mr. Hagney, he caught the murderer as he stood outside our window juggling with the twine – and so he was killed before he could tell the secret.

WATSON: But I still don't understand what you mean when you say you baited a trap tonight.

HOLMES: That should be obvious, Watson. I said that in the morning I would have a photograph of the murderer, didn't I? What effect d'you suppose that will have on him?

WATSON: He'll try and find the hidden money tonight – and escape with it before the morning.

HOLMES: Exactly. And I have a feeling that he won't be too subtle in trying to find the money. That's why I'm waiting to have the trap sprung.

WATSON: (SUDDENLY) By George, Holmes – I have it!

HOLMES: You have what?

WATSON: I know who did it!

HOLMES: Splendid! Tell me.

WATSON: It's Sam Wilton, the tailor! He said he'd been in the Army for five years, but of course he'd been in prison. And his killing of Bill Hagney tonight is easily understandable. He was jealous of him for marrying the innkeeper's daughter, Florence, and when you combine that with –

SOUND EFFECT: DULL THUDDING NOISE (OFF)

HOLMES: Shh!

SOUND EFFECT: THUMPING (UP)

HOLMES: (EXCITEDLY) The trap is sprung! Watson, d'you think you're still young enough to climb down the ivy vine outside our window?

WATSON: Of course I am. But why go out that way?

HOLMES: I'll tell you in a minute. In the meantime – *Come on!*

305

SOUND EFFECT: WINDOW BEING OPENED. GRUNTS OF
EXERTION AS THEY CLIMB DOWN IVY. THUDDING (UP)

WATSON: (AFTER AN APPRECIABLE PAUSE – BREATHLESSLY)
What is that noise, Holmes?

HOLMES: Unless I'm much mistaken, it's someone using an axe. Our
murderer feels he's in such imminent danger that he's no longer being
subtle about finding the missing treasure.

SOUND EFFECT: FOOTSTEPS ON PAVEMENT

WATSON: It's coming from that front room there.

HOLMES: Exactly. I think we'll post ourselves outside the window.

SOUND EFFECT: THUDDING (UP)

WATSON: (*SOTTO VOCE*) But Holmes . . . . Why did we come outside?
We could have trapped him from inside the house.

HOLMES: Oh, no. Undoubtedly he has the door locked on the inside of
the room where he is now working. He assumes that when we hear
the noise he's making, we'll try and break down the door from the
inside – which would be quite a lengthy proceeding. In the interim,
he no doubt hopes to find the money and make his escape through
this window.

SOUND EFFECT: THUDDING SUDDENLY CEASES

WATSON: Holmes – Look! The light's gone out. Someone's coming!

HOLMES: Shh!

SOUND EFFECT: WINDOW BEING OPENED. SOUNDS OF
EXERTION

HOLMES: Doctor Brice!

BRICE: Sherlock Holmes! What the – ?

HOLMES: Grab him, Watson!

306

WATSON: I've got him!

HOLMES: And I see *he's* got the money. I'll take the liberty of looking after that for you, Doctor Brice.

SOUND EFFECT: CLINK OF BAGFUL OF COINS

HOLMES: Thank you.

BRICE: You can't prove anything!

HOLMES: On the contrary, you have convicted yourself, Doctor Brice – or shall I call you *Charles Melton*? Scotland Yard seems to know you better under that name.

WATSON: Holmes – you knew what he'd done all the time!

HOLMES: Not all the time. Only after I'd talked to Scotland Yard and found that the description of Melton coincided with that of the supposed Doctor Brice.

WATSON: Then why didn't you have him arrested straight away?

HOLMES: And prevent him showing his hand *and* finding the money for us? Dear me, no.

BRICE: You're a clever man, Mr. Holmes.

HOLMES: I wish I could return the compliment. And now, let's take a walk over to see Sergeant Gribble.

WATSON: I suppose you'll let him have the credit – as usual?

HOLMES: Of course. You will remember that the worthy sergeant told us that his solution of the Dorking dog-poisoning case caused him to be promoted to sergeant?

WATSON: Yes. (CHUCKLING) And if he gets the credit for solving this case, he should become –

HOLMES: At the very least, Watson, he should be *Inspector Gribble.*

MUSIC: UP STRONG TO CURTAIN

CAMPBELL: Well, Doctor, for a while there, you had me believing in ghosts. I was pretty-well convinced that a *poltergeist* had wrecked the inn and china shop.

WATSON: Come, come, now, Mr. Campbell – you really didn't think that, did you?

CAMPBELL: Well, didn't *you?*

WATSON: (EMBARASSED) *Ahem* . . . For a few seconds, perhaps. Just a few seconds. (LAUGHS) I guess we just weren't cut out to be detectives, were we? (LAUGHS)

CAMPBELL: I guess not. The only case I ever solved was the mysterious disappearance of some Petri Wine.

WATSON: Oh? How did the wine disappear?

CAMPBELL: My father-in-law drank it. (LAUGHS) And I don't blame him . . . because that Petri Wine is really swell! That's because the Petri family took *time* to make good wine. Why, they've been making wine for generations – ever since they started the Petri business back in the eighteen-hundreds. And since the Petri business has always been family-owned, the Petri family has been able to hand down from father to son, from father to son, all they've ever learned about the fine art of turning luscious hand-picked grapes into fragrant, delicious wine. And believe me . . . in all these years, they've certainly piled up plenty of knowledge and skill and experience. You get the full benefit of this in every drop of Petri Wine. That's why – no matter whether you want a wine to serve before your dinner, or at any time, you can't go wrong with a Petri Wine . . . because Petri took time to bring you good wine! And now, Doctor Watson, how's about a clue as to next week's story?

WATSON: Next week, Mr. Campbell, I have something very exciting for you: A story that begins with my traveling halfway across Europe in

308

search of a missing lady – and ends with Holmes and myself attending a most – *er* – unorthodox funeral.

MUSIC: *SCOTCH POEM*

CAMPBELL: Tonight's Sherlock Holmes adventure is written by Denis Green and Bruce Taylor, and is based on an incident in the Sir Arthur Conan Doyle story, "The Adventure of the Three Gables" *[sic]*. Mr. Rathbone appears through the courtesy of Metro-Goldwyn-Mayer, and Mr. Bruce through the courtesy of Universal Pictures, where they are now starring in the Sherlock Holmes series.

MUSIC: THEME (UP AND DOWN UNDER)

CAMPBELL: The Petri Wine Company of San Francisco, California invites you to tune in again next week, same time, same station.

MUSIC: HIT JINGLE

SINGERS: *Oh, the Petri family took the time, to bring you such good wine, so when you eat and when you cook, Remember Petri Wine!*

CAMPBELL: To make good food taste better, remember –

SINGERS: *Pet – Pet – Petri . . . Wine.*

CAMPBELL: This is Bob Campbell saying goodnight for the Petri family. *Sherlock Holmes* comes to you from the Don Lee studios in Hollywood. This is Mutual!

The Adventure of the Traveller in Time
by Arthur Hall

It has become well-known that the exploits of my friend Mr. Sherlock Holmes sometimes followed a path that was far from conventional. Indeed, the sensational press would often place undue emphasis on what was thought of as the fantastic or bizarre aspects of our adventures together. True, he preferred cases of an unusual nature, but often these were not perceived as such before the investigation had begun. More often still, their odd nature was eventually revealed as quite ordinary, as he invariably predicted from the outset. Regarding this, I recall the singular situation of Mr. Murray Firth.

Holmes and I had enjoyed a fine dinner of roasted chicken and our landlady, Mrs. Hudson, had scarcely cleared away our plates when the harsh ring of the doorbell intruded upon our peaceful silence. We stood together at the window looking down on Baker Street, watching the light fade at the end of a warm summer's day, when he indicated someone approaching our door.

"I fear that our intended evening of perusing the day's journals isn't to be, Watson. I knew it from the moment I saw that young man cross Baker Street with such an air of determination."

This caused me little surprise. This situation had been repeated many times over the years.

"His business here must be urgent, or at least he must have convinced Mrs. Hudson that it is," I said as we moved into the centre of the room a moment later, "for she has admitted him with little hesitation."

A quick knock on our sitting room door was followed by her entrance. She stood aside and announced our visitor before withdrawing: "Mr. Murray Firth, to see Mr. Holmes on an important matter."

A dark and rather sharp-featured man of average height entered the room. I noted the prominent streak of prematurely white hair that lay awkwardly across his forehead.

"Thank you, Mrs. Hudson," my friend replied before introducing me and turning to Mr. Firth. "Will you take tea, sir? Or something stronger, perhaps?"

"Not just now, thank you, Mr. Holmes. I am anxious to seek your help, for I have witnessed a murder."

I noticed Holmes slightly raised eyebrows as he showed our visitor to the basket chair. "Then pray be seated and tell us of the matter. Omit no detail, I beg of you." He saw our visitor's quick glance in my direction. "You can depend Doctor Watson's discretion upon as you would my own. He has proved invaluable in many of my investigations."

"Of that I have no doubt," Mr. Firth agreed, placing his hat on a side-table as he sat. "I am here to consult you because I have read in the newspapers that you have often succeeded where the official force has failed, and I am becoming desperate."

"I have been of some small assistance to Scotland Yard on occasion," Holmes replied modestly as we all three settled ourselves. "Have you then sought their help already?"

"Indeed, I have. The murder I spoke of occurred two days ago, and I was informed today that no progress has been made. Clearly, both they and I need your help."

"Two days isn't long when conducting the investigation of a serious crime."

"But Mr. Holmes," our client leaned forward in his chair, "I know the murderer, for I saw him commit the crime! He threatened to kill me also, an instant after he shot my wife."

After we had expressed our condolences, I asked. "Are you aware of the reason for his actions?"

"He was stealing from my house, burgling in the dead of night. As I said, this man is known to me. His name is Caleb Marchant. I once refused to employ him because of his dishonest reputation, and this may have been an act of revenge."

"Quite possibly," Holmes agreed. "I had already realised that you hold an official, or at least a clerical position, in your place of work."

Mr. Firth gave him a curious glance. "But how did you determine that, sir?"

"Your hands show none of the indications of manual labour, and there is a small ink stain on the cuff or your right sleeve."

He held up his arm for his own inspection. "By Jove, but you're right. I hold the position of general manager at Hinsley and Cormack, a well-known shipping office near the Isle of Dogs. It's part of my duty to assess employment applications, and to dismiss workers when that proves necessary."

Holmes nodded. "As I'm able to understand thus far, your wife and yourself were disturbed in the early hours two days ago and were confronted by this man Marchant. I assume he realised that you recognised him."

"I have no doubt of it. Having been disturbed by noise, my wife and I stood outside our bedroom door as he ascended the stairs. We then found ourselves face to face with him. He raised his pistol, fired, and fled, leaving my wife bleeding profusely from a chest wound. It was obvious that nothing could be done for her, but I ran into the street and prevailed upon a passing constable to summon assistance. By means of his whistle he called another officer, who was sent for a doctor."

"I presume someone from Scotland Yard called upon you later?"

"Indeed. An Inspector Hopkins undertook the investigation, but I heard nothing until I visited there this afternoon, to be told that Marchant has so far proven to be elusive."

"Hopkins is a good man. His enquiry will be thorough."

"I have no reason to disbelieve that, except that progress is so slow. I feel that I owe it to my Jenny to seek all available help to ensure that her murderer is apprehended without delay."

"A most understandable attitude," I commented.

"Where do you reside, sir?" Holmes asked Mr. Firth then.

"In Paddington, not far from the station."

My friend spent a few moments in thought. "Very well. I will add my efforts to those of the official force. If you will inform Doctor Watson as to your address and any details that you feel may be useful to us, we will detain you no longer. I feel sure that I'm safe in saying that you will hear from us shortly."

I then retrieved my notebook and wrote down all that Mr. Firth dictated. When this was concluded, he picked up his hat and bade us a rather hurried goodnight.

"Poor fellow," I remarked as we heard the door close and the decreasing sound of his footsteps in the street, "to have his wife snatched away in such a fashion."

Holmes leaned back in his chair. "I felt he showed little compassion."

"Surely people express grief in different ways."

"Perhaps, but one thing about him troubles me."

"And what is that?"

"Did you not notice? During our conversation, not once did he meet our eyes."

The following morning, Holmes confided that he had the begun his enquiry.

"I couldn't recall immediately why the name of Caleb Marchant seemed familiar to me," he remarked as he finished his coffee, "but I have since remembered."

312

"If he featured in one of your previous cases, I cannot say that the affair comes to mind."

"That isn't surprising, for you weren't involved." He got to his feet and looked down at me. "In any case, it wasn't an enquiry, but rather something that Wiggins once mentioned. It seems that, some years ago, someone of that name joined the Irregulars for a short while but left under a cloud. Apparently, he stole from some of the others."

"And has failed to see the error of his ways since?"

"As Mr. Firth has informed us. I'm about to discover more of Mr. Marchant, and I know that you must be about your medical duties within the hour, so I will not detain you. I would be obliged however, if you would inform Mrs. Hudson that it's unlikely that I'll return in time for lunch."

"Certainly," I replied as he took up his hat and coat. Moments later he was gone, and I heard the door slam below.

As it happened, the patients awaiting my attention were fewer than usual, and their ailments mostly superficial. When I had dealt with them, I was able to return to Baker Street in time for the midday meal and found that Holmes was, as he had predicted, still absent.

My appetite was such that I ate the curried fowl that Mrs. Hudson provided with relish. When my meal was concluded, I settled into my usual armchair to review some notes I had made concerning the condition of a patient who had recently returned from South Africa. I had hardly finished adding marginal comments to the first three pages when I heard our front door close and Holmes's familiar tread upon the stairs. Moments later, he burst into the room, immediately divesting himself of his hat and coat.

"Halloa, Watson! You have, I perceive, experienced a light morning's work."

"You seem in a pleasant mood," I said thankfully, "but I cannot see how you deduced that my patients were fewer than is usual."

He smiled as he slumped into his armchair. "It is simplicity itself. The handkerchief which you have carelessly left sticking out of your jacket pocket is stained slightly with curry, the remaining aroma of which was evident to me on arrival. You were therefore back here in time for luncheon, which means that your work is over for the day, since lately you have rarely seen patients in the afternoon."

"Of course," I acknowledged, feeling annoyed that I hadn't seen through such ridiculously simple logic at once.

"As for my disposition," he continued, "your observation is correct. I spoke to Hopkins and sought out Wiggins with some difficulty, and learned that Caleb Marchant was indeed known to him and his friends for a short time, before absconding with a few shillings that they had earned and were keeping aside for food. I also discovered that his uncle is a retired professor of physics at one of our minor universities."

I put down the papers that I had been reading. "You have done well. I take it, then, that you will visit this professor soon. Tomorrow, perhaps?"

"Yes, and I would be delighted to have you accompany me. But for now, I would be grateful if you summon Mrs. Hudson. A pot of strong coffee will, I think, be sufficient to sustain me until dinner."

The next morning, Holmes dealt with his breakfast quickly, consuming half a pot of coffee before I had finished my toast. His enthusiasm to proceed with his enquiries was evident. He could barely hide his impatience as I concluded my meal.

"Very well," I said as I pushed away my cup. "I am at your disposal. I take it that you know more about this professor than you have already disclosed?"

He rose and moved to the window. "Wiggins was aware only of the man's name, which is Professor Lucas Torrance, and of the scant details that I mentioned yesterday. Since then, I've learned from *Who's Who* and other sources that he resides in Notting Hill, lives alone, and has acquired a reputation for eccentricity during the few years preceding his retirement." He glanced at me quickly. "If you would be so good as to retrieve our hats and coats, I see that a hansom stands almost opposite awaiting a fare."

Professor Torrance lived in a rather neglected house in a quiet street. As we alighted from our conveyance, I noticed that every building here was similar, being of three storeys and boasting pillars on each side of the front door in a style reminiscent of a Greek temple. As we drew closer, it became evident that the peeling paint of the window frames and the tarnished dragon's head knocker were indeed suggestive of an owner whose attention was concentrated elsewhere. Holmes rapped upon the door with his stick.

For a moment there was no response. He was about to repeat his action when a dull sound from within reached our ears. The door swung open to reveal a small man wearing a top hat, whose expression was bewildered as he peered first at Holmes and then at myself.

"Yes, gentlemen?" he asked.

"Good morning," Holmes began. "Have I the pleasure of addressing Professor Lucas Torrance?"

"Indeed, you have sir," came the reply. "Are we acquainted?"

"Not until this moment. My name is Sherlock Holmes, and this is my friend and associate, Doctor John Watson. I am by profession a consulting

314

detective, and would be most grateful for a minute or two of your time to speak of your nephew, Mr. Caleb Marchant."

"Caleb," he repeated. "My brother's boy, God rest dear Clement's soul. The young fellow visits me occasionally and I give him money because he never has any. He seems always to have fallen on hard times."

"Have you seen him recently?" I enquired.

"Why, yes," he said vaguely. "Was it yesterday – or the day before? I really can't remember. He pleaded with me for sanctuary because some rough types were pursuing him, he said."

"Were you able to assist him?" Holmes asked.

"Oh, yes. I hid him where no one can ever find him. He will return when he is ready, but until then he is safe."

Seeing our lack of understanding, his expression brightened. He stood back for us to enter.

"Come in, gentlemen," he said, "and I will make the situation clear to you."

We removed our hats and he led us away from the hallway and through a room beyond. Near the kitchen, a wide wooden door was set into the wall, and the professor drew the bolts and turned to us. "I must apologise for the untidiness that you see around you. I keep no servants, you see. What I am about to reveal to you represents the pinnacle of my career in physics. I can confidently state that you will not have encountered its like before now."

Holmes and I looked at each other, somewhat perplexed. We followed Professor Torrance down a flight of steps into a dark cellar. From a ledge, he picked up an oil lamp and lit it with a vesta, carrying it around the perimeter of the room to light others. When he set it down the cellar was well illuminated, and he stood proudly before the strange machine before us. Holmes and I regarded the tangle of pipes and wires that surrounded the heavy iron seat with dismay, for we could see no indication as to their purpose. I noted that an assortment of dials were affixed near a steering device, and that the entire arrangement was set upon a rigid frame that enclosed it. It had the appearance of some sort of bizarre vehicle resembling carriages that could function without the need of a horse. Was it a conveyance such as this then, that his nephew had used to escape his lawful punishment?

To my surprise I noticed that the professor had taken on a wild look, his eyes ablaze. His voice was full of eager enthusiasm, and strands of over-long grey hair stood out from beneath the brim of his hat.

"Do you not see?" he asked excitedly. "Caleb is safe now, until he chooses to return."

"He has undertaken a journey in a vehicle such as this," I suggested.

315

"More than that. You see before you my original concept. My nephew travelled in a later example, a much advanced design."

"I confess to being confounded," Holmes admitted. "Pray explain the purpose of your invention."

Professor Torrance adopted the pose and air of a lecturer and favoured us with a benevolent smile.

"You may recall a publication, a few years ago, by Mr. Herbert George Wells. It described a journey into another time." He looked at us critically. "Another *time* you understand, not another *place*."

He saw our lack of comprehension and paused, possibly to allow us to accustom ourselves to the notion.

"Time, you see, is a sort of distance that can be traversed like any other. One has only to discover the means of transportation to be able to journey back and forth within it. When I read Mr. Wells work, I was fascinated by the concept and wondered why I had never thought of it myself."

"But this surely cannot be," said Holmes. "This is a contradiction of all we know of physics."

"Not quite, Mr. Holmes. It is a contradiction to all we *believed we knew* of physics. But I have struck out in a new direction. I examined Mr. Well's theory, or proposition if you will, and wondered if it could become reality. I have invested many hours of thoughtful study, and still more time into building this vehicle, and it has conveyed me to both the past and the future. I have witnessed the building of the Egyptian pyramids and seen a time to come when machines have replaced the carriages that transport us." I saw that he was absorbed in his narrative, as he continued. "When Caleb returns, when he deems that our time is again safe for him, I will commit his experience to paper as I have my own. Then I will announce my triumph to the world."

"You have no way of knowing when your nephew intends to return, or where he has gone?"

"None," he confirmed. "I saw him last where you are standing now. As I said, we are speaking of a journey in *time*, not *space*. He has left here, yet he has not. Only the time has changed."

"How will *he* come to know when it is safe for him to return?"

The professor appeared mildly puzzled and paused to think. "I would expect him to make several returns, before continuing his journey until he arrives at the day or week when the threat has receded."

"Fascinating," Holmes remarked, "and most enlightening. Our thanks to you, Professor, for your explanation. Clearly, we will not be able to interview Mr. Marchant until his journey is completed."

"I will certainly mention your enquiry to him at that time."

316

We reached the top of the steps and the professor showed us out. At the end of the street, I looked back to see him waving his handkerchief in farewell.

"Is it possible," I asked my friend, "that there is something in his assertion? Could this be a new path for science to explore?"

"Ha!" Holmes laughed mirthlessly. "The professor has based his every premise on a work of fiction. Imagine if it were possible, and we journeyed back to yesterday, or a week ago. Would we then meet ourselves as we were then? No, the entire proposition is quite absurd."

"I formed the impression that he is unstable,"

"He appears to be obsessed by his fantasy, but it would do no harm to learn a little more. I noticed an opened letter from the Royal Society on his kitchen table, and membership of that organisation would suggest that he is, or *was*, a brilliant scholar. I think that we will endeavour to establish the extent of his credibility. First however, we will enjoy a scant luncheon at a coffee house I know of, which is around the next corner."

After bread and cheese and a pot of strong coffee, we prevailed upon a passing hansom for the journey to Kensington.

"Not long ago I was able to perform a small service for Professor Sven Vorgstrom, a Swedish émigré with a reputation much like that of our friend Professor Torrance," Holmes confided. "He also is a member of the Royal Society and may well be able to inform us as to the truth of the disappearance of the nephew of his fellow physicist. We will see what can be learned from him."

The driver brought the hansom to a halt outside a house of grey stone. As Holmes paid our fare, I saw that a plump and bearded man busied himself digging up weeds in the long front garden. As our conveyance left, we entered by way of the low gate and approached him.

He put down his spade as he regarded us curiously, breathing heavily from his efforts before recognition dawned.

"Mr. Holmes!" he cried. "It is good to see you!"

Holmes introduced me to Professor Vorgstrom and we shook hands. From his lack of Swedish accent, I concluded that he had lived among us for some years.

"We will go into the house," he said then, "for a glass of port together."

"My thanks to you, but we are pressed for time," Holmes responded. "We will not keep you long. I would like to ask you questions concerning a colleague at the Royal Society."

Professor Vorgstrom's expression became more serious. "Very well. Who is the man of whom you wish to enquire?"

317

"Professor Lucas Torrance."

He nodded. "Old Torrance. A sad case."

"Why do you describe him as such?" I enquired.

"Because his is a life that has been wasted. A few years ago, he was known to be a brilliant man. His essays, particularly *Physics From a New Perspective*, were considered to be standard works of reference. None of us at The Society understood the cause of the sudden change in him when he began to expound the most outrageous and quite impossible theories. Also, he took on a vague demeanour, and it became difficult to communicate with him."

"Perhaps the onset of brain fever?" Holmes suggested.

"That was the opinion of some of the members, until it was discovered that Torrance had conducted experiments on himself with various types of drugs. Consequently, he became victim to hallucinations which he believed to be actual experiences. His behaviour became such that many were relieved when he ceased to attend our meetings."

"We visited him earlier, in order to determine the whereabouts of his nephew, only to be told that the young man had set off on a journey by means of an invention of the Professor's. That explanation was, at the very least, improbable."

Professor Vorgstrom laughed shortly. "His machine for travelling across centuries? He lectured us on that long and often. I believe that he read a paper or a book by some fellow who wrote such a tale. No, Mr. Holmes, anything that Torrance confided to you regarding that contraption you can safely attribute to his drugged state. As for the nephew, he could be anywhere."

"Is it likely that he could be concealed within the Professor's premises?" I asked.

"Most unlikely I would say, Doctor, for Torrance reveres solitude. I hear that the young fellow is a criminal of sorts in any case, so he is almost certainly hiding from the authorities elsewhere."

"I had concluded as much," Holmes said. "Our thanks to you, Professor, for confirming my suppositions."

After Holmes and the Professor spent a short time in reminiscence, we left. It was as we walked at a fast pace towards the main thoroughfare in search of a cab that I asked him, "To where are we hurrying? I recall that you mentioned to Professor Vorgstrom that time is short."

"I wish to speak to Hopkins regarding this missing nephew," he answered as I raised my stick and brought a passing hansom to a halt. "Hopefully, we'll catch him at his desk."

As it happened, the inspector appeared to be in the midst of his duties for the day, as we sat opposite him in the sparse confines of his office. He

318

was dressed, as I had always seen him, in quiet tweeds and his expression was sombre. He sat ramrod-straight in his chair.

"Gentlemen, how can I assist you?" he began. "I must apologise if I appear in any way inhospitable. A complicated case of several weeks has at last come to its conclusion, and I have yet to catch up on much lost sleep."

"Not at all, Hopkins," said my friend. "It was obvious to me that you are excessively weary, from the moment we entered the room. We will endeavour therefore to delay you for as little time as possible. I wish to enquire as to the progress of the Yard's search for one Caleb Marchant."

The inspector nodded. "I regret to say that there has been very little, Mr. Holmes. As you may know, he lives on the streets and has been variously a beggar, a burglar, and now, it seems likely, a murderer. Mr. Murray Firth, whose wife was Marchant's victim, has made the same enquiry but, apart from reassuring him that every constable is on the watch, I was unable to assist him."

"Mr. Firth is my current client. He is determined to employ every resource available to him to ensure Marchant's early capture. Tell me, Inspector, has the murder weapon been found?"

Hopkins delayed his answer to listen to a skirmish in the corridor. I formed the impression that a violent prisoner was resisting as he was escorted to the cells. A door slammed, and we heard no more.

"A constable found it in the gutter, near Mr. Firth's residence." The inspector took a firearm from a desk drawer and slid it across to Holmes.

My friend picked it up carefully. "This is known as an 'M-1879 Tranter Revolver', I believe." He turned it over in his hand and worked the action. "A little stiff, I think, but otherwise in serviceable condition. I take it that it has been confirmed that the bullet from Mrs. Firth's body is of the type fired from this weapon."

"We do know our business here at the Yard, Mr. Holmes." Inspector Hopkins smiled faintly. "I was present when our man made the comparison. Beforehand, I allowed there was a slim chance that this revolver had nothing to do with the murder, although we don't find such things in the street every day, but this is the weapon all right."

"Of course." Holmes and I rose together. "My thanks to you for indulging me. Should Caleb Marchant be found, I would be grateful to be notified."

The inspector got to his feet. "Certainly, Mr. Holmes. I assume you will be good enough to let me know of any of your own discoveries pertaining to this business?"

"You may depend upon it." Holmes retrieved his hat and we shook hands with the official detective before leaving.

319

We returned to Baker Street and took a glass of brandy together before Mrs. Hudson served an excellent dinner. Holmes seemed preoccupied and ate absently, and I was therefore prepared for an evening of little conversation. This wasn't to be, however, for we had been settled in our armchairs no more than a half-hour after the dinner things had been cleared away when the doorbell disturbed our peace. A moment later we listened as Mrs. Hudson answered before preceding someone on the stairs.

Holmes lowered his newspaper. "A lady. The tread is too light to be that of a man."

The door opened to admit Mrs. Hudson, who announced a rather shabby young woman whose expression was one of irritation.

"Mrs. Margot Dearing, to see Mr. Holmes."

We rose as one.

Holmes said thank you as the door closed.

Our visitor wore a shawl, which she kept close to her body, and a tiny hat from which dark hair stuck out untidily. She glanced expectantly – first at me and then at Holmes.

"Which of you gentlemen is Mr. Sherlock Holmes?" she asked in a haughty voice.

"I am he," my friend answered. "Allow me to introduce my friend and colleague, Doctor John Watson. I perceive from your manner that you are here because of some action that we have taken, or that you believe we have taken. Pray settle yourself in the basket chair and I will call for tea before we discuss the matter."

"That will not be necessary," she replied coldly. "I'm here to explain something to you, and for nothing more. I have come directly from Scotland Yard, where Inspector Hopkins mentioned that you, as well as the official force, are seeking my brother."

"You, then, are the sister of Mr. Caleb Marchant?"

"I am, and I can tell you positively that he didn't murder Mrs. Firth. It isn't in him to kill. I have never known him to show violence to man nor beast."

"I understand your concern," Holmes allowed, "but even those closest to us sometimes act unexpectedly."

She frowned, glaring at him with angry eyes. "You would hesitate to say that, sir, if you had any knowledge of my brother. Our parents left when we were hardly more than infants, compelling us to survive alone on the streets of London. I was fortunate in that I was given employment as the maid of a former acquaintance of my mother who had married well, and even more so with my own marriage. Caleb remained as unsettled as he had always been, a beggar at first, then a burglar. A thief, yes, but he has never taken a life. I cannot imagine that he would do so, especially since the accident that befell him."

"We knew nothing of this," I said before Holmes could reply. "Kindly elaborate."

"I cannot see how that would solve anything."

"Perhaps not, but it may be significant."

"Sometimes," Holmes assured her, "the smallest details alter the way things eventually turn out."

Mrs. Dearing regarded us with ill-concealed hostility. "You may have learned this from Scotland Yard already, but I will tell it to you as Caleb told me. Not long ago, he was in the house of someone he followed from a tavern. He knew from what he had overheard that the man was rich, so he returned to Marylebone the following evening and watched the place until the man went out. Caleb got in easily enough – he is good at his trade by now – and had a good search. He found nothing so he went upstairs, and it was then that he heard the man return. He slid up a window and decided that he had a fair chance of escape if he dropped to the ground. He was clinging to the sill when the window slipped and came down on his fingers, smashing them. He said he screamed like a banshee as he hit the ground and was hardly able to run. But run he did, with his fingers bleeding all over the place."

"Most unfortunate. I assume he sought the attention of a physician?"

She shook her head. "How was that possible? He couldn't pay. He had to grin and bear it until he healed. By the time he did the Firth house, he was starving. He wanted money for food, and he thought it fitting that the man who refused him a job should be the one he stole it from. But I tell you again, gentlemen: Caleb is as much in the dark about who killed that lady as you are, or Scotland Yard."

"Mrs. Dearing," Holmes regarded her sympathetically. "Naturally, you're convinced of your brother's innocence. The facts, as far as I am aware, do not support this. Nevertheless, if you will disclose his hiding place to us, or impress upon him to surrender himself to Scotland Yard, I give you my word that I will make every effort to examine all details of his case. If he is indeed without guilt in the matter of Mrs. Firth's murder, you may be assured that I will discover the truth of it."

Her eyes searched our faces. It was evident that she was undergoing an internal struggle as the life of her brother hung in the balance. In moments, her expression cleared. She had made her decision.

"No, I can take no such risk. Thank you for your offer of assistance, Mr. Holmes, but I cannot put Caleb's life to chance."

321

Holmes made to speak again, but in an instant she had risen, turned away, and left the room. We heard her descend the stairs rapidly before the door slammed.

"What do you make of that?" Holmes asked.

"The young lady is overwrought, understandably. Her concern for her brother's life is great and will cause her to ignore the evidence, no matter how conclusive it may become."

"Quite so, but as you say, that is understandable. I'm surprised, however, that Hopkins is apparently unaware of Caleb Marchant's misfortune."

"You believe that he would be unable to carry out a burglary such as that at the Firth house while suffering such injury to his hands?"

"That is possible, but we don't know how much he had healed, nor if he had healed well at the time of that incident. No, something more occurs to me, an idea which may be vindicated when he is captured. Tomorrow I'll again see if my informants can assist us."

We resumed our seats, and he would discuss the case no further. After he had divulged to me his theories concerning two unsolved robberies that were featured prominently in the newspapers, we retired.

The following morning was ablaze with sunshine, and I determined that Holmes and I should first enjoy a beneficial walk in Hyde Park or the Regents Park. To my surprise he readily agreed, and we had put on our hats and coats and taken up our sticks with that intent when the sound of the doorbell caused us to pause.

"Let us continue," I said hopefully. "It may be the postman, or a tradesman to see Mrs. Hudson."

He paused, shaking his head with his hand on the doorknob. "It's Hopkins. His tones are quite distinctive."

We divested ourselves of our hats and coats and stood waiting. The inspector ascended the stairs quickly and unaccompanied, and Holmes opened the door.

"Good morning, Hopkins. I take it that you have something to tell us concerning Mr. Caleb Marchant."

The representative of the official force entered the room and closed the door behind him.

"Indeed. I'm on my way to another enquiry, but as I had to pass nearby I thought it best to call rather than send a message."

Holmes nodded. "Has he been found?"

"He has, Mr. Holmes. He was fished out of the Thames in the early hours of this morning."

"That is regrettable. Did he display signs of injury?"

"It seems he was clubbed from behind, for the back of his skull is shattered."

"Was there damage to his hands?"

Inspector Hopkins looked at my friend sharply. "Some half-healed and severely bruised contusions. But how did you know?"

"I have my methods."

"You have, sir, I know. I have the greatest respect for them, but I don't see – "

"Here is something else." Holmes paused for an instant, as a heavy cart passed in the street below. "I believe that the murderer of Mrs. Firth is still at large."

"That is possible. It had appeared at first that Marchant was responsible also for another murder that we discovered last night, but we now know that he was already deceased."

"Who was the victim, Inspector?" I enquired.

"Professor Lucas Torrance, who we have since found to be Marchant's uncle."

Holmes didn't appear surprised at this.

"Where was he found?" he asked.

"In the cellar of his house. A constable was nearby on his beat when he saw a figure run from a distant building. He thought nothing of it until he neared Professor Torrance's home, when he saw that the front door hung open. He entered and called out and, hearing no answer, suspected that something was amiss. After venturing into the ground floor rooms, the constable decided to inspect the cellar where he knew the professor often worked. He discovered that the professor had apparently hung himself after destroying a strange machine which had no apparent purpose."

"But it's more likely, is it not, that the fleeing figure was responsible for the death since, I take it, whoever it was that fled made no report of his discovery of a body?"

"It is indeed, Mr. Holmes, since the professor fought his assailant. A clutch of human hair was found in his grasp."

"Was there, by any chance, a note?"

"There was," agreed the inspector. "A crumpled scrap of paper, on which was written: '*Now he will never be found. Caleb is lost forever.*' The handwriting was a scrawl, indicating that the writer was in a state of excitement. I could make nothing of that, since this could indicate that the professor knew he was about to murdered or, as we are intended to deduce, that he was about to die by his own hand."

"Excellent, Hopkins. Tell us, pray, what was the colour of the hair in the hand of the deceased?"

Inspector Hopkins paused for an instant. Then I fancy that he remembered other occasions when Holmes's apparently trivial questions had proved to be of the first importance.

"Black, mostly, but there were white strands also."

"That is most interesting. My thanks to you. You can be assured that I will share any further discoveries regarding this matter with you promptly."

"I would be grateful, Mr. Holmes. It would appear that Marchant and Professor Torrance died by the same hand, since an examination has revealed that Marchant died first, and the two murders are obviously connected."

Holmes nodded. "Quite so."

Shortly afterwards, we returned to our chairs after seeing our visitor to the door. Holmes appeared thoughtful, his hawk-like expression one of preoccupation.

"Have you any appointments this morning?" he enquired suddenly.

"I have none. I am quite ready to accompany you."

He considered for a moment. "Not now. You will be of more use to me if you remain here to receive any further information that Scotland Yard decides to disclose to us. I expect to return in time for lunch."

"But what new enquiries are you pursuing?"

He reached for his hat and coat. "I need to verify one or two points, which I expect to confirm without difficulty. Therefore, hold yourself ready to see the end of this business as I complete my case this afternoon."

Before I could answer, he was gone. After a while I prevailed upon our landlady for tea. I couldn't settle to read as I awaited Holmes's return.

He was as good as his word. The aroma of roast chicken was in the air, indicating that our meal was imminent, when I heard our front door close and his tread upon the stairs.

I rose and went to greet him. "Well, have you acquired the means to conclude this affair?"

"I believe that I have." He hung up his hat and coat and we sat down at the table. "When we've done justice to Mrs. Hudson's meal, we'll set about setting matters right."

I ate with relish but Holmes, as always when the end of a case was in sight, was impatient to be away.

He rose suddenly and stood beside me. "Have you finished your stewed apple? I think we'll forego coffee until later."

I had hardly put down my spoon before he had once more retrieved his hat and coat and was eagerly thrusting mine towards me. When we were both ready, I asked him, "We are bound for Scotland Yard, I presume. Surely you will wish to share this morning's discoveries with Inspector Hopkins."

"Not at all." He ushered me down the stairs and into the street, where a cab presented itself immediately.

When we had settled ourselves he gave the driver our destination. "Paddington, if you please."

"We are to visit our client, then?"

"Indeed. I suspect he may have received some medical attention."

"How could you know that?"

"I do not, but I strongly suspect it. The accuracy, or otherwise, of my supposition will be apparent as soon as we see Mr. Firth."

He said little else but gazed at the passing scene for the rest of the journey. At length, we reached a street of terraced houses that appeared poorly maintained. As we alighted, I heard the unmistakable sound of an express arriving at the nearby station.

The hansom departed and we approached the door of our client's residence. Holmes had hardly rapped upon it with his stick when Mr. Firth answered. As the bandage around his head became evident, a quick smile of satisfaction crossed Holmes's face.

"You have met with an accident?" I enquired after we had exchanged greetings and been admitted.

"Yes," our client said with a sheepish grin. "I ventured upstairs to the attic, forgetting how low the ceiling is there."

"Most unfortunate."

Mr. Firth nodded. "But let us go into my study. My maid is busy in the sitting room, but here we will not be disturbed."

We entered a room that struck me as surprisingly large for such a small house, with bookshelves along one wall and a large desk and chairs near the window.

Our client bade us sit before settling himself behind the desk.

"I image that you have come to report your progress," he said as his eyes flitted from me to Holmes. "Have you managed to find the murderer of my wife?"

"Most certainly," Holmes answered. "I am in no doubt of it."

A look that could have been relief or a curious triumph appeared on Mr. Firth's face. "Caleb Marchant is now in the hands of Scotland Yard, then?"

"Caleb Marchant is dead, as you are aware."

"How could I have come to know this? I have heard nothing from the official force, and you are my first visitors today."

"You know because you killed him. His body was retrieved from the Thames."

Our client was suddenly very still, and a range of expressions passed across his features. When he spoke, it was in carefully controlled tones.

"I am surprised that you would jest about this, Mr. Holmes."

"Indeed, I would not. Since Inspector Hopkins informed me of the murder of Professor Torrance, your guilt was obvious. Beneath the bandage that is tied around your head is a patch of bare scalp, for the professor seems to have been surprisingly defensive. The white streak among the black strands of hair clutched in his dead hand identified you at once, as it did when you were described to me by the gunsmith from whom you purchased the weapon with which you murdered your wife. The circumstances must have appeared to you as ideal when you discovered Marchant in your house, but doubtless you intended to kill Mrs. Firth when a future opportunity presented itself."

"This is outrageous! Why would I kill this Professor Torrance, and why would I kill my wife? We had a comfortable life together."

Holmes nodded. "I don't disbelieve that you did since, as I have discovered, her inherited money supplemented your income considerably. But that was before you employed Miss Daphne Grice at Hinsly and Cormack, and began to woo her. I interviewed her earlier and learned that she was completely unaware of your marital status, and that she expected to accompany you to France within the month. I fear that our conversation caused the lady great distress."

"She is a factory girl. They are often given to wild imaginary romances."

"Perhaps so," Holmes continued, "but your attentions were observed by others at the factory. As for Professor Torrance, you somehow discovered him to be Marchant's confidante, and I believe that he explained to you the imagined purpose of his machine. You then killed him to ensure his silence because Marchant told him of the burglary and could easily have concluded that it was you who killed your wife.

"You then destroyed the professor's invention, thereby trying to leave the implication that Marchant was lost in time. You assumed that any who believed the professor's theory would accept this, and you were determined to allow for all possibilities. You then sought out Marchant and, finding him clubbed him to death . . . ."

Here my friend paused, watching Mr. Firth carefully. "There is yet another indication that exonerates Marchant from your wife's death. I've established that the revolver which killed her has a stiff action and isn't discharged easily. Marchant's fingers are severely damaged and are unlikely to have proven equal to the task."

"You weave a pretty pattern, Mr. Holmes, but why would I have consulted you if all this were true?"

"I have little doubt that you intended to reinforce the impression that you are an innocent and grieving husband. Having caused me to begin an investigation, as well as the official force, it would appear that you have made all possible efforts to bring about the capture of your wife's murderer. Don't delude yourself that this notion was original, sir, for I assure you that it has been attempted before now."

"But never successfully," I added.

Our client's countenance was now furtive. His eyes held the expression of a hunted fox. I noticed, as Holmes would have already, that his hand was slowly reaching for a desk drawer. He withdrew a heavy calibre revolver and made to point it at my friend, only to lower it to the desktop as he saw that my service weapon was already in my hand.

Holmes consulted his pocket watch. "Inspector Hopkins will be here shortly," he announced. "I thought it wise to advise him earlier by telegraph."

"Everything is arranged then," Mr. Firth acknowledged. "That is clever, Mr. Holmes, and I see that your reputation is well deserved. Yet you are a foolish man who failed to recognise my desperation. Were it not for the quick action of your companion, I would surely have done for you both before making my escape. You have robbed me of Miss Grice, but I wouldn't have faced the hangman."

Holmes faced him squarely. "Foolish, you say? I should tell you that, on leaving here, Watson and I will enjoy a pleasant walk in the Regents Park. We will then procure a hansom to deliver us to our lodgings where we will consume an excellent dinner. Meanwhile you will be taken to Scotland Yard, to await trial and subsequent execution. Who would you say is foolish, Mr. Firth?"

The Adventure of the
Restless Dead
by Craig Janacek

It was a gloomy February day in 1903 when I called upon my friend, Mr. Sherlock Holmes, to inquire about his health, which of late had been strained by his great achievements in several arduous cases, the details of which I shall someday relate. I also was concerned that my recent departure from Baker Street after many years of our sharing the suite of rooms at 221b might disrupt his typical habits and bring about a relapse of his foul humours and worse vices. My fears were partially confirmed on the morning of my visit, for I found his manner rather brusque.

After some worrying of him, however, I finally got him to relate his recent experience in Bedfordshire involving Sir James Saunders. After hearing the *dénouement*, I encouraged him to write down the experience himself. Even if his version would likely prove to be a rather dry account of rigid facts and figures, rather than something more in line with popular taste, I believed it would be an interesting exercise to study his direct views regarding an investigation.

"You are exceedingly pertinacious today, Watson," said he, with a sigh. "What do you want from me?"

"I thought you might want to hear about an interesting case sent to me by a friend."

"No, thank you."

"Come now, Holmes!" I protested. "Surely I have brought you some peculiar problems in the past? Jack Oswald, [1] Colonel Warburton, Victor Hatherley, the Cunninghams, Percy Phelps, and Robert Ferguson, to name a few."

"Yes, yes, you are a stormy petrel. Very well, what is it this time?"

"During my school-days at Winchester, [2] I had been closely allied with a lad named Jim Treadwell, who was of much the same age as myself and in the same class. He was a very adventurous boy, and we took to calling him 'Puck'. He carried away every trophy which the school had to offer, finishing his sporting exploits by eventually winning a cricket championship at Oxford. After that, he became an explorer of sorts, travelling all about the globe on various scientific expeditions. Eventually, he decided to settle down near the Sussex coast. This afternoon, I received a letter from him, which has some features of note. Shall I read it to you?"

"If you must."

Ignoring his foul mood, I pressed on and read aloud:

Knucker House,
Dolchurch, West Sussex [3]

My Dear Watson,

I have very much enjoyed reading of your adventures with your friend, Mr. Holmes. He seems to have a remarkable talent for unravelling the most mysterious crimes of an earthly nature, though I wonder how he would get on when faced with a truly supernatural mystery? I daresay that our local parish church has been the site of some bizarre happenstances of late, which can only be explained by forces from the other side of the veil.

The mayor even asked the well-known psychic detective Mr. Henry Fowler of Dunkel Street to come down and investigate the crypt. Mr. Dunkel declared that there was no possible rational explanation for the phenomena, and it was, therefore, conclusively proven to be a superlative example of ghostly contact. Should you and Mr. Holmes wish to come down for a few days and have a look about, my place has a pair of Spartan, but comfortable, spare rooms.

Your friend,
James "Puck" Treadwell

Holmes's grey eyes peered at me from beneath his furrowed brow. "Did you say, 'psychic detective'?"

"Yes, that is correct."

"And what, pray tell, is that?"

"I suppose it is someone who investigates hauntings and other psychic disturbances."

"A waste of time," said Holmes, shaking his head. "Unless they intend to debunk such manifestations as frauds. However, in this case, it appears that the credulous Mr. Fowler was easily convinced that a mystical force was at work."

"Well, anything sufficiently remarkable might be indistinguishable from the supernatural to a mind that isn't capable of understanding how it occurs. In fact, Holmes, some might consider you to be a sort of psychic detective."

"What do you mean?" he exclaimed, his brow furrowed.

"Upon each occasion when you discern someone's thoughts without explaining the links in the chain of your deductions, it seems like wizardry. In fact, I distinctly recall that you have yourself been accused of having powers of magic by the likes of Miss Mary Holder and Mrs. Ferguson."

Holmes shook his head. "I suppose that is true. But I can hardly be expected to go traipsing about the English countryside demystifying each and every local legend. I would scarcely have time to investigate genuine crimes. In fact, this very afternoon, the particulars of a poisoning case were sent to me from New Zealand, and yesterday I received a great packet of documents relating to a disputed will from Bristol."

"Trivial and uninteresting matters," said I, with a dismissive wave of my hand. "You could solve those without leaving your armchair. But you aren't your brother. I know you, Holmes. You would much rather get down on your hands and knees and examine the clues of something particularly *outré*. I assure you that Puck Treadwell isn't some naïve fool. He is as widely travelled as a certain Mr. Sigerson of my acquaintance, and not likely to be persuaded by a few odd noises. If he is sufficiently perplexed by the happenstances in the local church, I can guarantee that it shall prove to be something of interest."

I will admit that my invocation of the name Sigerson was a shameless attempt to summon a crumb of remorse in the breast of my friend – who once allowed me to believe that he was dead for a span of three long years. Fortunately, Holmes – despite his professed lack of human emotions – wasn't completely immune to such manipulations. I could see his resolve wavering and pressed my attack home.

"We could even stop in and see your friend Reginald Musgrave. Isn't Hurlstone down in those parts? I have always wished to see for myself how exactly you marched off the steps of the old ritual."

"No, it is further east," said he with a small shake of his head. [4]

But it was plain that his decision had been made, and I promptly went round to the nearest telegraph office, where I sent a wire to Puck Treadwell telling him to expect us after luncheon the next day. The following morn found us situated in the corner seats of a first-class carriage of the Brighton line from Victoria. We passed through Surrey's North Downs and the remains of the ancient Weald upon our way to the coast. Holmes's mood was somewhat less disagreeable, and he spent the journey telling me of his plans to write a monograph upon the subject of watch-chain ornaments.

"They will tell you where a settler made his money," he told me. "A New Zealand squatter will not wear a gold *mohur*, [5] nor an engineer on an

Indian railway a Maori stone. You will notice, Watson, that many a client will bring his past history – national, social, and medical – into the consulting room as he walks in, and it only takes some modicum of effort to use one's senses accurately and constantly in order to elucidate these details."

He proceeded to set some of these thoughts down in his pocket notebook, and was sufficiently engaged upon this task that, for once, I was confident that he could hardly follow the path of my thoughts. As the train sped southwards, various station signs came and went, and my memories turned to past cases linked to that corner of our fair island – from the terrible deaths at Stoke Moran near Leatherhead, to the fantastic death of Elias Openshaw near Horsham, to the bloody happenstances at Lamberley. I wondered if – now that I had again attained a state of complete happiness – I would ever again face such remarkable cases at Holmes's side?

My melancholy musings were interrupted by our arrival at the village of Dolchurch, which lay about half-a-mile from the sea on the left, or east, bank of the River Arun. From the station, a trap took us the rest of the way to my friend's estate.

Having expected the appearance of our train, Puck Treadwell met us at the gate to his property and warmly welcomed us in. Although many years had passed since our schooldays, I could still see in him the boy with whom I had once gotten into many a desperate scrape – or at least as dangerous as such predicaments once seemed to callow youths. He was a long, slab-sided man, with loose and powerful limbs, flaxen hair, and a deep and hearty voice. Only the long lines of his face gave testament to the many years that he had spent wandering the earth in search of new horizons and fresh adventures.

Leading us inside, Puck hung our hats and coats by the door and showed us to his office. There was no trace of luxury or aestheticism to be found in my friend's study. From the open window, we could inhale the invigorating breezes which came in straight off the Channel. His solid mahogany writing desk seemed more useful than ornamental, his well-filled bookshelves – where history and poetry fought for supremacy – were of the plainest and most serviceable type, and the walls were hung with a series of De Neuville's battle-pieces. [6] As we settled into a trio of comfortable armchairs, he told us the story of the polar bear's skull, which he had brought back from his cruise amongst the icebergs, and the wooden war-club that was a memento of a trip through the Tasman Sea.

"I am so pleased that you came, Mr. Holmes," said he. "If anyone can come to the truth of the matter, I am certain that it is you."

"Pray start at the beginning, Mr. Treadwell."

"I will tell you what I know. As John may recall, I grew up in these parts. When I was a child, I thought that the place was called Dolchurch because – on a foggy night – the walls of the local parish church appear to weep water in a most dolorous fashion. I learned afterwards that, instead, the founder of the great family who were once lords of all these parts was descended from a bishop of the region of Dol in Brittany.

"Beneath All Saint's – which you understand is a most ancient church, with some parts of it dating back to the days before the first William – is a vault constructed by the local leading family, called Fitzdale. [7] This vault is a very fine one, made of great blocks of Portland stone, completely sunk into the earth under the church, for the site is on an exposed hill, and the builders likely didn't wish for an above-ground crypt to be subject to the lashings of the terrific storms which sweep over these parts in the winter. The entrance is down a set of steps inside the church and is covered with a large slab of marble as heavy as a resurrection stone. [8] I have been within the vault once, and I reckon that the dimensions are about twelve-feet by six-and-a-half. So Cyclopean is the masonry, and so remote the site of our little village, that one could imagine that an inmate of the vault should be almost as secure as a pharaoh of Egypt in the heart of his pyramid. [9] In my opinion, a contractor and a gang of skilled workmen would be needed to effect an additional entrance into so solid a construction."

"But someone has done so?" asked Holmes.

"That is the very question, Mr. Holmes. You see, the last of the Fitzdales – a young woman named Eleanor – died over half-a-century ago. After she was laid to rest, to the best of the parson's knowledge, the crypt hasn't been opened since – until five months ago. The recent troubles began when Mrs. Dorcas Puttock, a widow of the village, was walking by the churchyard one night. She heard sounds emanating from the empty church. Being a tough old lady, with little fear of death, she went up the gravel walk to the locked church door and investigated further. She confirmed that the sounds could have only been coming from deep below the building – namely the aforementioned crypt."

"What sort of sounds were heard?" asked Holmes.

"She described them as scraping and booming noises."

"Could they have been some fancy of her mind?" I suggested.

Puck shook his head. "If you were to speak to her, John, I am certain that you would agree that the stolid Mrs. Puttock hardly suffers from an overactive imagination."

"Very good," said Holmes, with a nod. "What happened next?"

"Well, as you might envision, Mr. Holmes, the village was convulsed by this news. What could possibly be making such noises? After much

332

consideration, the mayor, Mr. Alan French, made the decision to open the vault and see what was happening inside. When they did so, the horrified workmen found that a coffin – which once belonged to an infant of the family – was standing on its head in the corner. It was supposed that some mischievous and sacrilegious wretch had been guilty of a senseless outrage.

"After the coffin was rearranged, the great marble slab was once again placed into position. Furthermore, the mayor hired a commissionaire named Christopher Ashdown to remain each night in the south transept. Ashdown is an old colour sergeant of the Bill Browns [10] who fought in the Sudan, and he is completely impassive. Ashdown was permitted a spirit-lamp [11] to make coffee and ensure that he remained awake to guard against any tomb-robbers. Worried that this was insufficient protection, the parson also convinced Mayor French to allow him the funds required to string the church with electric lights, making it nigh impossible for any prospective villains to hide in the shadows. An engineer from the famous Westminster firm of Morton and Kennedy installed the lighting system."

By Holmes's smile, I could tell that he was becoming interested in my friend's tale. "But the spectral forces didn't seem to mind the harsh light of science, did they, Mr. Treadwell? For those precautions proved to be inadequate and the noises continued?"

"That is correct, Mr. Holmes. All seemed quiet after that for a while, and a month or two elapsed before the vault again was heard to make its booming noises. Ashdown swore up and down that he hadn't once closed his eyes, and that no one had entered the church or gone near the stairs leading down to the crypt. The following morning, the crypt again was opened at the order of the mayor. The confusion inside was even more horrible than upon the prior occasion, with coffins littered across one another. The affair was rapidly becoming a scandal and the talk of the whole village. There were those who put it down as vandalism, and others who ascribed it to ghosts. Constable Truefitt looked all about the space, but could find nothing to explain how someone might have gotten in. Once again, the vault was closed, and once again, two months later, it was opened after more noises were heard.

"This time, a great crowd had gathered 'round to witness the massive slab being pulled aside. In the short interval, everything had again been disarranged, the coffins being abominably mishandled. A wooden coffin was broken – though some of this may have been due to natural decay – while the leaden coffins were scattered about at all angles.

"After that episode, the parson brought down Mr. Fowler from London to look over the place. Following a careful inspection of the crypt, Fowler held a séance to commune with the spirits of those whose remains occupied the disturbed space. He finally declared that one of the Fitzdales was lingering, earth-bound, because they appeared to be worried over some worldly matter that had been left unresolved at the time of their death. Furthermore, Fowler noted that this was hardly the first such example of moving coffins. He said that there was a curious case of a vault at Stanton in Suffolk, where several leaden coffins were found by the astonished clergymen to be displaced. The coffins were repositioned as before, when again – after another member of the family had died – they were a second time found shifted. And two years after that, they were found not only off the biers, but one coffin so heavy as to require eight men to raise it was found on the fourth step that led into the vault. [12] Similarly, Mr. Fowler noted that coffins were twice found in disarray in the Gretford family vault near Stamford at the turn of the prior century. Fowler recommended a ceremony be performed to dispel the restless spirit, collected his fee, and departed from Dolchurch."

"A waste of time," said Holmes, shaking his head.

"You are correct, Mr. Holmes. Though, as you can imagine, in desperation, Mr. Sharpe, the parson, carried out this suggestion with great haste. This task complete, once again the leaden caskets were reverently collected, the damaged wooden coffin was tied up, and the vault secured. But hardly a fortnight had passed when the sounds returned. This time, so great was the public agitation that it attracted the attention of the Lord-Lieutenant of West Sussex, the Duke of Petworth. With his staff and aides-de-camp, the duke attended the next ceremony of vault opening. Unfortunately, things were as bad as ever. The wooden coffin was intact, but the others were scattered about in all directions. The duke was so interested in this phenomenon that he ordered the whole structure searched and sounded by his trusted men, but they could find no evidence of a hidden approach or underground passage.

"In short, it was an insoluble mystery. The coffins were rearranged and the floor carefully sanded, so that the footsteps of any subsequent intruders would be revealed. The door was cemented up – something that had been done upon each occasion – and this time, the Lord-Lieutenant affixed his own particular seal to the grout."

"It seems that the British Government has officially entered the lists against the Powers of Darkness," said Holmes, with a wry smile.

Treadwell shook his head. "Laugh if you wish, Mr. Holmes, but the Powers of Darkness seem to be winning. Not two nights ago, the sounds returned. The mayor is at his wits end."

"If you have ruled out grave robbers, I fail to see the concern," said Holmes. "This ghost – should it exist – doesn't appear to be harming anyone still capable of sentiment. You said yourself that the last of the Fitzdales have died out."

"It isn't that simple, Mr. Holmes. Despite the parson's best efforts to calm the villagers, there are still murmurings down at The Five Bells public house that Old Nick is stalking the fields. People will hardly go out at night anymore, and even during the day, most would rather walk ten miles round than go near the church. Strangers in town are viewed with the darkest suspicion, as if they might be some revenant walking the streets. This was once a happy place, but now it seems as if a grim spell had been laid upon us."

"That is terrible!" I exclaimed. "We will do whatever we can to help."

"Thank you, John," said Puck Treadwell. "What do you think, Mr. Holmes? Do we have a poltergeist in our village?"

Holmes stood up from his chair and moved over to the window. "The sea isn't far off. I can smell the salt on the air. Furthermore, it has been a most wet winter. Therefore, the most obvious explanation for your moving coffins is that the crypt is regularly flooded with water. A lot of the old churches suffer from such things. In fact, I hear that the cathedral in Winchester is in grave danger of utter collapse due to regular flooding. [13] The water floats the coffins to new positions, and when the tide recedes, they are left at ungainly angles."

"That's right!" I interjected. "As I understand it, this very thing has been witnessed in the East Fleet Church in Dorset." [14]

Treadwell shook his head. "That may well be, Mr. Holmes, but this is something altogether different. All Saint's is built upon a hill. Even the buried vault could hardly have been touched by the highest of waters. Furthermore, when it has been opened – typically not a day past the manifestation of the sounds – the chapel is found to be bone-dry. How many subterranean chambers do you know of that don't hold on to a damp for a long time?"

Holmes nodded slowly. "That is a fair point, Mr. Treadwell, though I am rather loath to admit the possibility of a supernatural force."

"What of a tunnel?" I added. "Someone might be digging under the church."

"To what end, John?" asked Puck.

"I can hardly say. Buried treasure? Or smugglers perhaps?"

"You have been reading too many romance novels," said Holmes, with a dismissive wave of his hand. "John Clay's attempt upon the French gold was a bold one to be certain, but hardly an escapade that you happen upon every day. And the days of the great struggle between the Moon-cursers and the Excise Men have long since passed."

"I concur, Mr. Holmes," added Puck. "That was one of the mayor's first thoughts, but there have been absolutely no signs of any digging or passages."

"These sounds have been going on for half-a-year or so?" asked Holmes.

"Yes, about five months."

"And did anything noteworthy precede the commencement of this apparition?"

"Not that I recall. Why do you ask?"

"It seems to me, Mr. Treadwell, that the crypt and its occupants have been there for many years. If the last person to be buried within was laid to rest more than half-a-decade ago, why have the noises suddenly started now?"

Puck seemed at a loss. "Why, I can hardly say. If this is a ghost, surely it isn't bound by our earthly laws of logic. What seems like years to you and me may be but minutes as a ghost perceives the passage of time."

"And do you believe supernatural forces to be at play, Mr. Treadwell?"

My old school chum paused and considered this question. "When I cast my thoughts back upon my own life, Mr. Holmes, in search of things which seem particularly strange, it isn't the material events that I most clearly perceive. I have had the good fortune to have led a fairly adventurous life, and to have visited strange parts of the world under interesting conditions. I have seen something of two wars. Some might say that I have practised the most dramatic profession in the world, for I have set foot upon six continents, and travelled from the Arctic wastes of North Greenland and Spitsbergen to the jungles of West Africa and the Brazils. My thoughts can conjure up many a recollection of storm and danger, of whales and bears and sharks and snakes, and all those things used to interest me as a schoolboy. And yet, whatever I could say upon such subjects, someone else has said already with more authority and experience.

"It is rather when I look closely into the intimate workings of my own mind and spirit – the queer intuitions, the strange happenings, the inexplicable things which come suddenly to the surface and are glimpsed rather than seen, the incredible coincidences, the stories which should end one way but either end the other or else have no definite finish at all, tailing off into oblivion with ragged fringes of mystery behind them instead of the neat little knot of the tidy-minded romancer – it is these, I say, which seem to be really stranger than any fiction. [15] So if you are asking whether I believe that there is something out there larger and more unknowable than this crude world around us? Then the answer is yes. As for the happenstances under All Saint's – well, that is why I have asked you down here, Mr. Holmes. If you cannot explain them, then I am prepared to accept that something is reaching out from beyond the veil to touch our simple perceptions."

"I should very much like to have a look at the vault myself," said Holmes. "The members of the county constabulary – while generally fine fellows all – are often out of their depths when faced with more bizarre occurrences."

"I was hoping that you would say that," said Treadwell, warmly. "Shall we go over now?"

"Lead the way."

We traversed some ways along the village road, where houses in various stages of construction and decay straggled over a half-a-mile. From most of these humbled abodes, smoke curled up from the chimneys and the odour of wood fire emanated. As Puck had described, the old stone walls of the church stood upon a little hill some ways from the banks of the river. I noted that the tombstones in the churchyard appeared to lie in well-drained soil. We passed through the lychgate and – as we climbed the path to the door – tapping sounds emanating from the rear of the church attracted out attention. Holmes indicated his desire to investigate their origin before entering the building.

Therefore, we went round the corner, where we found a wooden structure snuggled up against one of the walls of the tower. The situation of this shed was such that it was obscured from the main road, while simultaneously being warmed by the rays of the afternoon sun. Just outside the door to the shed, a man – the sexton, by his appearance – was hard at work in the task of lettering a marble tombstone. Around him, several other such stones were littered.

"Hello, Mr. Marshall," said Puck warmly. "I have some visitors come to look into the matter of the crypt. This is Mr. Holmes and Dr. Watson."

The man looked up at this greeting, though his ferret-like face didn't seem pleased to see us. "You are too late."

"What do you mean?" asked Puck.

"A plan has already been made that will solve the problem once-and-for-all."

"What plan?" asked my friend.

"You will have to see the parson, Mr. Treadwell," said the sexton, with a shake of his black-haired head. "He has all of the details."

Nothing more was forthcoming from Mr. Marshall, so Puck led us back around to the front and through the church's wooden doors. The minster was a goodly-sized one for a place such as Dolchurch, and a stone screen across the middle divided it into two parts. I reckoned that the village must have once sustained a larger populace, for I estimated that its current occupants could have all fitted into the chancel. Our entrance attracted the attention of a man engaged in some work over by the altar, which he left off to come and greet us. He was dressed in rusty black, with a very broad brimmed top-hat and a loose white necktie.

"Ah, Mr. Treadwell," said the man, whom I presumed to be the parson, Mr. Sharpe. "What can I do for you?" His voice had a sharp crackle, and his manner a quick intensity that commanded attention.

Puck introduced us and the purpose of our visit. As he listened, Mr. Sharpe nodded intently.

"Very good," said the parson. "We are most happy to have you down, Mr. Holmes. I have heard of you, of course. I never thought our little trouble worth your time, or I would have engaged your services rather than those of Mr. Fowler. What do you wish to know?"

"You have been in Dolchurch long?"

"No, not at all. In fact, I have only recently returned to the home country. After I was ordained, I was sent out to one of the West Indian colonies – Saint Lucia. About seven months ago, I was recalled after the death of the former parson of Dolchurch, and given responsibility for this parish."

"Tell me about your church."

Sharpe smiled like any enthusiast asked about his passion. "This is an ancient place, Mr. Holmes. The Saxon Earl Osbeorn founded it as a priory, and the bones of our very own St. Eadmund lie somewhere in the church – though the precise location sadly has been lost to the grains of time. After the Conquest, it was re-dedicated by the Earl of Sussex, but dissolved in the early 1400's, long before old Henry started thinking about grabbing everything of value from the great abbeys and priories. The oldest parts of it – the chancel and nave – are Saxon. There is some transitional Norman in the arcade, while the tower and side chapels are early Perpendicular. In short, the entirety of the medieval era can be found herein.

"Prior to the recent disturbances, our most famous artifact can hardly be termed a religious relic. You can see over here," said he, pointing to a spot on the wall behind the font, "what appears to be an ordinary gravestone. This is the so-called 'butcher's block'. It belongs to a local lad who reputedly killed the water dragon called the 'Knucker'. You should know all about him, Mr. Treadwell."

"That's right," interjected my friend. "It is an ancient legend of these parts. In fact, on the grounds of my estate is the 'Knucker Hole' – a bottomless pool that never freezes. It once was believed that its waters were warmed by the breath of the Knucker, which would come forth to consume local livestock and even the occasional villager. The old King of

338

Sussex offered his daughter's hand in marriage to whomever would rid the land of this terrible beast. After a cunning struggle, a village lad was successful in his task. However, after a brief celebration, he succumbed to the toxic effects of contact with the Knucker's blood."

"You can see in the carving the faint marks of the knight's sword over the herringbone patterns of the dragon's ribs," continued Mr. Sharpe, taking up the tale.

"Fascinating," said Holmes. "Though I am more interested in your crypt."

"Ah, yes, certainly," said the parson. "It is a most remarkable example of the forces that can touch us from the great beyond. It is hardly unique, of course. From my recent studies, I have learned that there was another such case in the Livonian village of Ahrensburg in the Baltic in 1844. [16] Horses tethered near the vault became frantic, and loud crashes were heard to emanate from within a family crypt. When the vault was opened for a burial, several coffins were found scattered about – even resting one atop another. Only three weren't disturbed – these contained the body of an old woman said to have been very devout, and the bodies of two young children. The villagers logically inferred that demonic forces were responsible, since the coffins of the devout and the pure were untouched."

"Logically," said Holmes dryly.

"Scoff if you wish, Mr. Holmes," said the parson. "However, such popular excitement ensued that a commission was appointed to investigate. The coffins were restored to order. The pavement was torn up to make certain there was no secret access to the vault. The vault's floor and steps were covered with fine ash to reveal footprints of intruders, and guards were posted around the clock. After three days, the family vault was reopened. According to the accounts that I read, all coffins but the three were scattered about in even greater confusion. The ash was undisturbed. Many coffins had been set on end, so that the heads of their corpses faced downward. The lid of one coffin had even been forced open, and a shrivelled right arm poked out.

"It finally came out that this last individual had committed suicide by cutting his throat with a razor. The blood-stained tool allegedly was found clutched in his right hand. As you are aware, according to traditional observances, suicides aren't to be buried on hallowed ground. The family apparently had conducted a normal burial, hoping to hush up the tragedy. Subsequently, they buried each coffin separately, and there have been no further disturbances according to the official report by the investigating commission."

"And what is your conclusion?" asked Holmes.

"There is a theory," said the parson, "that a young life cut short in a sudden and unnatural fashion may leave – as it were – a store of unused vitality which may be put to strange uses."

"And you believe that something similar is happening in your crypt?"

"I do, indeed! You see, Mr. Holmes, it seems that many years ago, in the early eighteenth century, Dolchurch was the home of two brothers called Fitzdale, scions of the local clan. They had reputedly amassed considerable wealth through smuggling. They had a house ideally situated somewhere along the Arun. Its cellar opened into a cave, up into which the water came at full tide. They had hoarded their money in partnership, but one of them, Walter, announced his intention of getting married, which involved him drawing his share of the treasure. Soon afterwards, Walter disappeared, and it was rumoured that he had gone to sea upon a long voyage. As I heard the tale, the other brother – William – went mad thereafter, and the affair was never cleared up in his lifetime. It still is whispered that William killed his brother Walter rather than allow him to divide the treasure. One can certainly imagine that in so fratricidal a case, there would be a particular intensity of emotion on the part of both of the brothers, which could leave a psychic residue." [17]

"That is one theory," said Holmes.

"What other would you propose?"

"Human intervention."

Mr. Sharpe smiled indulgently. "Well, I for one can hardly imagine how you might explain what is happening here as the work of a living creature. And I am afraid that your opportunity to do so may be rather limited."

"What do you mean?"

"After the sounds were heard again two nights ago by Mr. Ashdown, I have convinced the mayor that a more drastic intervention is required."

"Such as?" asked Puck.

"They are planning to open the crypt and re-inter its occupants in the churchyard," said Holmes.

The parson's eyebrows rose sharply. "How did you know that?"

"While conversing with the sexton, I noted that he was engaged in the task of carving a score of tombstones. Unless this village has recently been the victim of a terrible plague, only such a plan could explain the sudden need for so many markers."

"Ha!" laughed Mr. Sharpe. "You are most observant, Mr. Holmes. Yes, you are correct. Such a stratagem solved the problem at Ahrensburg, and I wager that it will suffice here as well. Unfortunately, by-and-large, the coffin-plates and inscriptions upon most of the mortuary chests have faded, such that we cannot determine with certainty the remnants of the murderous William. Therefore, we have resolved to move them all out to the churchyard. While perhaps unfair to the earthly remains of the godlier of the Fitzdale family – as it somewhat goes against their final wishes – there are sadly none of that clan left alive to protest this course of action. And, of course, they will still rest in hallowed ground."

"When will this transfer take place?" asked Holmes.

"Tomorrow morning."

"And is this plan common knowledge?"

The parson smiled. "Dolchurch isn't a large place, Mr. Holmes. You know what they say about two men keeping a secret. I am certain that within roughly five minutes of my conversation with the mayor, everyone in The Five Bells had heard the news."

"Very good," said Holmes. "If some earthly villain is planning another attempt upon the crypt, it must take place tonight."

"I suppose so. And if a restless spirit from beyond the grave intends to manifest itself, I also trust that this will be its final occasion."

Holmes turned to my friend Puck. "I am afraid, Mr. Treadwell," said Holmes, his grey eyes gleaming with dancing light reflected from the stained glass, "that Watson and I shall be forced to decline your offer of a comfortable bed in your guest rooms. A rougher berth awaits us tonight."

"What do you mean, Mr. Holmes?"

"We shall join Mr. Ashdown in his watch. I should very much like to hear these sounds for myself."

Puck nodded – as if this proclamation was the most reasonable thing he had ever heard – and volunteered to go back to his house for our cases, in addition to some blankets and tiffin boxes to sustain us through the night. For his part, Mr. Sharpe waited with us until the commissionaire arrived. He instructed Mr. Ashdown that Holmes and I would also be bunking down in the church.

As advertised, the commissionaire was a rather taciturn old soldier and seemed unconcerned by the news of his additional companions. "The whole village can bunk down in here, if they wish," said he, with a shrug. "It is no skin off my back."

"I should think, Mr. Ashdown, that you might welcome the companionship," said Holmes. "Surely the noises from the crypt must be rather unnerving?"

The commissionaire smiled grimly. "I served with the Bill Browns for two decades, sir. Before I was invalided out, I was with Kitchener at Omdurman. I have seen the horrors that the living inflict upon each other. I have no fear of those who have passed on to the other side."

"Very good, Sergeant. We would be honoured to spend the night in your company."

After Puck delivered our blankets and meals and Mr. Sharpe had departed, the commissionaire lit his spirit-lamp and began boiling some coffee for all of us to share. Meanwhile, Holmes led me about the church, peering into each of its various nooks and crannies. We finally came to a corner of the north transept, where a steep stair descended into the crypt. Striking a match, Holmes illuminated this passage for sufficient time to take in the massive capstone at the bottom. As described by Puck, the stone was cemented into place and sealed with the saltire and rose of the Lord-Lieutenant. Holmes rapped on the stone and then shook out the flame. Wordlessly, he climbed the stairs back up to the church proper.

As we reached the top, I mentioned an idea. "I had a thought of what might be producing the noises."

"Oh?" said Holmes, his eyebrows raising with interest. "Pray tell."

"Well, if you have a coffin that has lain undisturbed for a couple of hundred or so years, most corpses will decompose into dry human remains," I explained. "However, some of us turn into so-called 'coffin liquor'. Apparently, sealed lead coffins are especially prone to this sort of thing, and the contents can burst out violently when the seal is broken. Such an explosion could produce a loud noise."

"An interesting theory. However, if that was the case," said he, with a shake of his head, "when they opened the crypt, they would have found the place covered in liquefied Fitzdales. No, I am afraid that there must be some other explanation."

Mr. Ashdown had the coffee ready for us and handed out two cups. "There is no need for a match, sir. I can turn on the electrical lights if you wish. They illuminate the whole place something fierce."

"You don't use the lights yourself, Mr. Ashdown?" I inquired.

The old man shrugged. "I don't mind the dark, sir. The noises in the crypt come either way, and you might say that the modern lights make it worse."

"How so?" asked Holmes.

"Well, sir, they flicker right before the sounds commence."

"Oh?" Holmes appeared most interested in this new revelation.

"Yes, sir. I mentioned it to Mr. Sharpe, and he thought it consistent with what folks know about ghostly spirits. They don't seem to like such modern contraptions and interfere somehow with their function."

"Yes, I suppose they might," said Holmes, absently, as he considered this piece of evidence.

Our conversation concluded and meals consumed, we settled in for our vigil, which proved to be a long and bitter one. In absolute silence we sat amongst the pews, waiting for the resonances of the restless dead. Because of the recent happenstances at the church, the villagers avoided it at night, so even the typical sounds of those belated souls passing to their homes from the public house were absent. An absolute stillness fell upon us, interrupted only by the chimes from the tower above us, which tolled out the progression of the hours. Outside, a fine rain began to fall, and it pattered on the slate roof.

And then, at about half-past three o'clock – at the darkest hour which proceeds the dawn – the most horrible noise rose up from the stones beneath our feet. It was the sound of something scraping across a floor, followed by a booming rattle. After a moment, it stopped, only to start up again a minute later. This rough pattern continued until we had counted four such sounds, and then it stopped.

I glanced over at Holmes in absolute horror, and was surprised to find his entire face aglow with excitement.

"By Jove!" he cried. "What was that?"

We shook off our utter astonishment and raced back down the stairs. But the great stone still barred our way into the crypt and the seal showed no signs of tampering.

Mr. Ashdown had followed us and called down from the landing. "It's no use, sirs. The whole place is sealed as tight as a drum."

Holmes slowly nodded his agreement. "Then we shall just have to wait until the morning. I must admit that I am now most curious to have a look inside."

After confirming with Sergeant Ashdown that the noises, once heard, never returned on that night, I snatched a few hours of poor sleep upon one of the benches. Holmes – per his usual habit of going without rest until he had turned over an unsolved problem in his mind – spent the night generating a massive cloud of tobacco smoke from his briar pipe.

"Awake?" he asked, when a troublesome ray from the rising sun shone a beam directly upon my eyes and roused me from my slumber.

"Yes. Unfortunately."

"Well, I expect the parson and the villagers shall be here soon. The task of opening the crypt, emptying out all of its residents, and reinterring them in the yard will surely take up a good portion of the day."

Holmes soon was proven correct. By the time the eighth bell had rung, a large crowd had gathered inside the church. This included Mayor Alan French and Constable Anthony Truefitt, to whom we were promptly introduced by the parson. Puck – bless his soul – had brought over some warm rolls and butter, which I gladly consumed while the workmen began their task of breaking the concrete seal.

Over the noise of the hammering, Holmes spoke up. "If I may make a suggestion, Mayor French?"

343

"Certainly, Mr. Holmes," said the mayor, plainly pleased to have such a famous guest in his town.

"Watson and I are impartial agents here. Let us enter alone and inspect the crypt before anyone else goes in."

The man considered this request for a moment. "I see no reason not, Mr. Holmes. Take as much time as you need. The dead are in no hurry."

When the stone door was finally pulled aside, the workmen made way for the two of us to enter. Each of us held a pocket lantern in one hand and, as I raised mine, I could immediately see that the piles of coffins – some of lead, some of stone, and some of rough pine – were in complete disarray. Furthermore, another phenomenon was immediately obvious.

"Holmes!" I cried. "There are no tracks in the sand!"

He nodded grimly at this observation and then took a step forward into the melancholy and dismal place. The ancient walls of rough-hewn stone extended up to a low-arched and groined roof. The dim yellow light of our lanterns barely illuminated the far end of the crypt, which was lost in the shadows. Even without the terrible indignity inflicted upon their final rest, the mournful scene was sufficient to give me pause. I regarded the verdigris patina obscuring the names inscribed upon the coffin-plates, though some were faintly adorned with the ruddy bars of the ancient family whose last members had passed beyond the gate of Death.

"Ah, this is most interesting," said Holmes, indicating a peculiarly-shaped coffin of cast iron. It strongly resembled an Egyptian sarcophagus, if only the Egyptians had thought to sculpt arms holding a cross and affix glass window plates into the vessels for their dead.

"What is that thing?" I asked.

"I have never seen one before, but read about them in regards to a case of potential murder that transpired in the American state of Rhode Island. Their unique airtight construction makes them secure against both odours and grave robbers. These Fisk coffins were all the rage in America about a half-century ago, much like our own fascination with safety coffins at the turn of the last century, or the current custom of using coffins made from crushed oyster shells in Formosa." [18]

I peered into the glass window. "The glass is cracked, but still intact. She was once a young woman."

"Miss Eleanor Fitzdale, born 1824, died 1845, according to the label," said Holmes. "Now then, let us sound the floors and walls to ascertain whether some subterranean passage or entrance is still concealed."

Holmes applied all his energies to this task, but when examined the walls proved to be perfectly secure. No fracture was visible, and the sides, together with the roof and flooring, presented a structure so solid as if formed from entire slabs of stone. In short, we found the crypt to be

344

perfectly firm and solid – only the faintest of cracks were even apparent in the walls.

"Well, Mr. Holmes?" called the mayor, after what the man must have considered a sufficient span of time.

"You may send the men down, Mayor French," replied Holmes.

"What do you make of it?" I asked.

In lieu of an answer, he merely shook his head and bent down to scoop up a handful of the sand from the floor. Uncertain of what to think, I followed him back up the steps.

"Mr. Treadwell," said Holmes, to my friend, "would you be so kind to run down to the local chemist and beg the use of his medium scales for an hour?"

Mystified by this peculiar request, but trusting that Holmes had some subtle plan in mind, Puck nodded and dashed out of the church. Meanwhile, Holmes tracked down Sergeant Ashdown and commandeered the use of his spirit-lamp.

While the rest of the community was engaged in the task of carrying the coffins up from the crypt and out to the churchyard, Puck, Ashdown, and I gathered about to watch Holmes as he engaged in his enigmatic task. First, he placed the sand from the crypt into one of the commissionaire's coffee cups. He then set this on the scale and noted its weight. He then held the cup over the flame of the spirit-lamp for a span of some ten minutes. When complete, he moved the cup back onto the scales and shook his head.

"It seems that you are correct, Mr. Treadwell," said Holmes. "We cannot explain the movement of the coffins by the forces of water. This cup of sand weighs the same before and after heating, proving that there was indeed no moisture to evaporate. It would be against the very laws of nature for sufficient water to be present to raise the coffins at three o'clock and vanish entirely by six hours later."

"Then what moved them, Holmes? You agreed that there are no additional entrances to the crypt."

He shook his head. "We have eliminated the impossible. Therefore, we must now consider the exceptionally improbable."

"Such as the presence of forces from beyond the grave?" asked Puck.

"Perhaps," said Holmes, inscrutably. "Now then, let us pay our respects to the vanished Fitzdales."

He led us outside and into the churchyard, where a crowd of onlookers had gathered to witness the members of that clan reinterred on the north-western slope of the hill. There, a series of nearly thirty holes had been dug, each with a stone resting nearby, ready to be placed to forever mark the final spot upon this earth for its future occupant. When the army of workmen had situated one of the coffins from the crypt into each of the graves, the parson turned to address the crowd. Mr. Sharpe's elegy was simple and direct, intended to satisfy the minds of the poor villagers that the haunting of the church was a thing of the past. But for Holmes, it seemed to do the opposite, for midway through, I noted him convulsed in silent merriment.

"Holmes!" I whispered, furiously, "have some respect!"

He composed himself, but I could see a strange merriment gleaming in his eyes throughout the remainder of the sermon.

When the service was complete, Puck turned to us with a shake of his head. "Well, that should be the end of it. Let us hope that the ghost is now well and truly settled."

"I think it safe to guarantee, Mr. Treadwell," said Holmes, "that we shall hear no more sounds from the ghosts of Dolchurch."

I was rendered speechless by this statement, so it was Puck who recovered first. "Then you are convinced, Mr. Holmes, that the restless dead were responsible for the noises?"

"No," said he, shaking his head. "I am afraid not. If you would be so kind as to ask Constable Truefitt, Mayor French, Parson Sharpe, and Sexton Marshall to step over to the tower, I believe that I may be able to explain what has transpired here."

Puck and I did as he asked and, after some convincing, these gentlemen were gathered. We found Holmes pacing about the path in front of the sexton's shed.

"Now then, gentlemen," said he, "I have a simple question for you that I believe explains everything. You all attended the ceremony just now where the Fitzdales were once again set to rest, did you not? How many fresh graves were dug in the yard?"

I considered this. "Twenty-seven. There were three rows of nine."

"Capital! You were most observant today, despite your lack of rest last night. That is correct."

"I fail to see what this has to do with the ghost, Mr. Holmes?" said the mayor, somewhat crossly.

"The answer to that, my dear Mayor French, is the little problem of the number of coffins found in the crypt. You see, when Watson and I entered the crypt this morning, I counted not twenty-seven coffins, but instead twenty-eight."

Puck frowned in confusion. "Are you certain?"

"Quite so!"

"Where, pray tell, Holmes, is the missing coffin?" I asked.

"It can be found in the shed behind me. During the confusion of the emptying of the crypt this morning, Mr. Sharpe and Mr. Marshall here

346

diverted one coffin into to the sexton's shed. They planned to open it tonight and then dispose of the contents in some expeditious fashion. Probably by sinking them offshore."

"But why?" cried the mayor, aghast.

"Because the wayward coffin belongs to Mr. William Fitzdale. And the parson believes that it holds the clue to the location of the lost treasure of the Fitzdale brothers."

All eyes turned to Mr. Sharpe. The parson swallowed and then laughed nervously. "Ha! That is most amusing, Mr. Holmes."

"I assure you that I am quite serious, sir. It was really too bold of you to tell me about William Fitzdale's treasure. Your plan was a brilliant one, and then you grew overconfident. If you hadn't set me upon that line of thinking, you might have gotten away with it."

"I still do not understand, Mr. Holmes," said Puck.

"Let me start at the beginning, Mr. Treadwell," said Holmes, laying out his case like a schoolmaster before a room of attentive boys. "About seven months ago, Mr. Sharpe came to Dolchurch from his prior situation in the West Indies. Before that time, the occupants of the Fitzdale crypt slumbered peacefully. After a little while, however, the parson hears the tale of the smuggler brothers Walter and William – likely related to him by Mr. Marshall. After doing some research, Mr. Sharpe concludes that if any clue remains of their treasure's location, it must have been buried with William Fitzdale. Sharpe recruits the sexton to help him open the crypt in secret. However, five months ago, when they finally effect an entrance, they discover that the inscriptions are almost impossible to read. They are initially unable to tell which coffin belongs to William. To take a closer look, they start shifting the coffins about. However, this noise echoes up the stairs and – unfortunately for them – attracts the unwanted attention of Mrs. Puttock. She tries to get into the church, but they have locked the doors. Nevertheless, worried that she might return with the constable that night, Sharpe and Marshall hurriedly re-seal the crypt, forgetting to move all of the coffins back into place. The following morn, when – at the insistent urging of Mrs. Puttock – the mayor and constable order the opening of the crypt to investigate the possibility of tomb robbers, they find a wayward occupant. Immediately, word goes round the village of the restless dead, undoubtedly spread by Mr. Sharpe himself."

"Why would he do that?" I asked.

"I imagine that the parson thought it would both divert attention from the possibility of tomb-robbers and keep people away from the place, thereby allowing him and his partner another opportunity to open the crypt and search for William's coffin. As he told us, Mr. Sharpe came to Dolchurch from St. Lucia in the Windward Islands. There, someone as well-studied as he would surely have heard the legend of the Chase vault upon neighbouring Barbados."

"Which is?" asked Puck.

"I read an account that described how, several decades ago, a vault on that island experienced an event exceptionally similar to the supposed moving coffins of the Fitzdales. Unfortunately for Mr. Sharpe's plan, the mayor then hires Mr. Ashdown to guard the church at night. Finding that the commissionaire is both reliable and incorruptible, the parson realizes that he must conceive of another plan. They play up the story of the restless dead even more by asking Mr. Fowler to come down from London. When the so-called 'psychic detective' credulously confirms a supernatural explanation, the stage is set."

"For what?" I inquired.

"For Mr. Sharpe's masterpiece." Holmes turned to the parson. "I have rarely encountered such a brilliant stroke of villainy, Mr. Sharpe, though you must admit that all of your poor luck with Mrs. Puttock and Mr. Ashdown was counterbalanced by your fortunate discovery of Miss Eleanor Fitzdale's peculiar conveyance to the great beyond."

"What do you mean, Holmes?"

"Mr. Sharpe's plan couldn't have worked if all of the Fitzdale coffins were made of wood, stone or lead – but the cast-iron of the Fisk case was the perfect accomplice."

"To what end?" cried Puck. "Why create such noises in the first place?"

"Why, to carry out their feat of thimblerig," said Holmes. [19] "Mr. Sharpe realized that if he could generate enough of a disturbance in the crypt, he could then convince Mayor French to again open the crypt and allow him to re-bury the dead in the churchyard. During such an event, there would be so many coffins in transit, that it would be simplicity itself for the parson and sexton to surreptitiously re-route the one belonging to William Fitzdale into the shed here."

"But how did he get the coffins to move?" I asked, still puzzled. "Once re-sealed, there was no way into that crypt."

"I concur that there was no way for a physical body to enter. But Mr. Sharpe is a most clever man. He employed a force that could reach out through solid walls. And he got Mr. French to pay for it."

"What!" cried the mayor. "That is impossible!"

"I am sorry to report that it is true, sir," said Holmes, shaking his head. "The one part of Mr. Sharpe's plan that I couldn't – at first – work out, was the need for the new electrical lighting in the church."

"That's true," said Puck. "Surely such a thing would make it harder to obscure their plan?"

"Do you know, Mr. Treadwell, that shortly after Watson and I first met, he made a list of my perceived limits?" said Holmes, with a small smile. "However, Watson failed to note my particular interest in physics, which is almost as profound as my knowledge of chemistry. If I recall correctly, Mr. Sturgeon of Lancashire was the first to conceive of the idea employed herein, though the American Henry perfected it. You see, gentlemen, you first take a horseshoe piece of iron, such as any local smith could easily make, and wind copper wires about it. You then pass an electrical current through it, thereby creating what has been termed an 'electro-magnet'. With enough turns of the wire, the device can become extraordinarily powerful." [20]

"The iron coffin!" I cried.

"Precisely. Lead and stone will not be attracted by a magnet, but iron is another matter entirely. As he had the final word regarding where each coffin was replaced after the vault was open, the parson was able to ensure that the Fisk coffin of Miss Eleanor Fitzdale was situated in a spot where it could be dragged by the magnet's attraction. Some of the other wooden coffins were situated near it, so that they too would be shifted when it was pulled across the floor. After convincing the mayor to let him install electrical lights, Mr. Sharpe carefully ensured that only half of the wire was strung. The remainder later used by him and Mr. Marshall to construct their giant magnet. Upon each occasion, they needed only make their way here into the churchyard, turn on and off the electricity to the magnet – thereby causing the interior lights to flicker – and create the noises under the church. The eminently-reliable Mr. Ashdown would serve as the perfect witness that no one else was in the church at the time of such terrible noises."

"So you inspected the shed after I went to bed?" I asked.

Holmes shook his head. "No, I haven't yet been inside."

"Then how do you know for certain that you will find an electro-magnet inside? You must have confirmed this theory?"

"I had no such need. As I said, I had already eliminated the impossible. This is all that remains. Furthermore, if I were chasing the fox into the wrong hole, proverbially-speaking, Mr. Sharpe would now be smiling in *faux* outrage at such an unfounded accusation. Instead, he displays the typical pale face and sweaty brow of the guilty man whose scheme has just been revealed."

But it was the sexton who broke first. "It was all his idea!" cried Mr. Marshall. "I just went along, because my job was on the line."

Mr. Sharpe glared at the man furiously, but held his tongue. He straightened his back and turned to the mayor. "We have done nothing wrong, sir! We only wished to restore Dolchurch minster to a place of pride by uncovering the treasure."

"If that was your true aim, there would have no need for such mummery," said Holmes, with a shake of his head. "It is true, Mr. Sharpe, that desecration of graves is only a misdemeanour in common law and not a felony. You might have gotten off with a small fine and a brief imprisonment. However, I am afraid that if there are any effects of the dead within the coffin, such as jewellery or even clothes, then the constable can hold both you and Mr. Marshall liable to a felony charge. At the very least, you will be unfrocked, Mr. Sharpe. I expect that your name will go down in the annals of your ecclesiastical order as a singularly dark one."

However, Holmes's prophecy would not come completely true. There was certainly a large iron horseshoe wound with copper wire in the shed, just as he said there would be. But Mr. Sharpe's role in the hoax would ultimately go unpunished, for it soon became apparent that the parson was onto something. After Mayor French ordered a legal unsealing of the coffin of William Fitzdale, we found within it a golden locket. This contained a yellowed scrap of folded paper scribbled with Biblical verses related to Egypt. The paper read:

> *And Joseph took an oath of the children of Israel, saying, God will surely visit you, and ye shall carry up my bones from hence.*
> *So Joseph died, being an hundred-and-ten years old: and they embalmed him, and he was put in a coffin in Egypt.*
>
> *Else, if thou refuse to let my people go, behold, tomorrow will I bring the locusts into thy coast.*
>
> *Then was fulfilled that which was spoken by Jeremy the prophet, saying,*
> *In Rama was there a voice heard, lamentation, and weeping, and great mourning, Rachel weeping for her children, and would not be comforted, because they are not.*
> *But when Herod was dead, behold, an angel of the Lord appeareth in a dream to Joseph in Egypt.*
>
> *And when he had thus spoken, he shewed them his hands and his feet.'*

350

From this meagre clue, Holmes swiftly deduced that these obscure passages must have concealed a cipher leading to the location William's treasure. As the author of a monograph, justly famous in some circles, analysing one-hundred-and-sixty separate ciphers, it took Holmes a matter of minutes to determine that the verses described a series of numbers corresponding to latitude and longitude. [21]

A great excitement followed this pronouncement. Once a Bible was located and the numbers worked out, we retreated to Puck's house. There, a quick perusal of Puck's atlas informed us that this location was situated somewhere in Dorset. Puck and I were ready to set out forthwith with our shovels in hand. However, I could tell from the furrowed line of his brow over his stormy grey eyes that Holmes was unsatisfied by some possibly-askew element in his chain of deductions. He requested that we tamper our eagerness for a moment to give him time to re-consider his calculations. He clamped his pipe between his teeth and began to emit vast clouds of a particularly noxious smoke. This went on for some time, until he suddenly began to chuckle.

"What is it?" I asked.

"You have often chided me, Watson, on the limits of my knowledge. At times, I have purposely avoided cluttering my brain-attic with the acquisition of anything which did not immediately bear upon my object of understanding criminal behaviour. And yet, increasingly I have found that an acquaintance with the workings of history to be rather a boon to my investigations. In this case, I believe that we have forgotten one most pertinent fact."

"What is that, Mr. Holmes?" asked Puck.

"I just recalled that the Greenwich Line had not yet been established in the days of William and Walter. Instead, east and west were determined from the Richelieu Arc." [22]

This epiphany was greeted with great enthusiasm by Puck. "You are a genius, Mr. Holmes!" he cried.

A slight flush of colour upon his pale cheeks was sufficient demonstration that my friend, despite his many protestations to the contrary, still harboured a secret keenness for admiration of his talents. The subsequent re-calculations of the clue's longitude soon led us to an abandoned house on the northern outskirts of town near the river. There, a hasty excavation of the cellar revealed a considerable stash of silver and gold coins from the days of Queens Mary and Anne. [23]

After this find, Holmes lost interest in the case and indicated that it was time for the two of us to return to London. Shortly thereafter, I received a letter from Puck Treadwell relating what had transpired down in Dolchurch after our departure.

Knucker House,
Dolchurch, West Sussex

My Dear Watson,

Mr. Holmes might not have been concerned to wait around and discover what transpired with the treasure of William Fitzdale, but I wager that you shall be most curious.

The Crown determined that the gold had been hidden with animus revocandi, *and as such belonged to the discoverers.* [24] *We have decided to disperse it amongst the villagers, after a modest amount is used to construct a little museum devoted to the history of the chess matches between the Contrabanders and the Revenue men. When it is finished, I hope that you will come down and see it. Furthermore, the excess wire from Mr. Sharpe's electro-magnet has already been restrung, such that Dolchurch is now the first place on the southern shore with a complete set of electrical streetlamps. I expect that we shall have to construct an annex to the old inn to house the influx of tourists!*

As for Mr. Sharpe, well, the church decided to turn a blind eye to his wayward actions, since no harm had befallen the living. He has been re-posted to the West Indies, with strict orders to spend the entirely of his time tending to his flock. Though, in truth, once the gold bug has bitten a man, it is a hard thing to give up. I would hardly be surprised to hear someday that he has come to ruin pursuing the location of some lost buccaneer treasure.

As for me, I have found that the most remarkable experiences in a man's life are those in which he feels the most, and this adventure with you and Mr. Holmes surely ranks with the best of them. I find it a wondrous coincidence that our schoolboy acquaintance and your serendipitous lunch with Stamford were the first steps on a path that led to Mr. Holmes coming down here and dispelling our extraordinary mystery. I believe that it is within the compass of these vital things that one perceives strange forces to be moving and is conscious of vague and wonderful compulsions and directions which are, I think, the innermost facts of life.

I know that Mr. Holmes will disagree, but personally, I am always mindful of the latent powers of the human spirit, and of the direct intervention into human life of outside forces

352

*which mould and modify our actions. They are usually too
subtle for direct definition, but occasionally they become so
crude that one cannot overlook them.*

*But here again we are drifting into regions which are
stranger than fiction. I need not tell you, Watson – who has
spent so many years in Mr. Holmes's company – that the
unknown and the marvellous press upon us from all sides.
They loom above us and around us in undefined and
fluctuating shapes, some dark, some shimmering, but all
warning us of the limitations of what we call "matter", and of
the need for an open heart and mind if we are to keep in touch
with the true inner facts of life.*

*Your friend,
Puck Treadwell*

After reading this, I went round to Baker Street, where I found
Holmes sitting in his armchair, meditatively smoking his black clay pipe.
He waved me to my old seat across from him, and I related the contents of
Puck's letter to him.

"I cannot agree with Mr. Treadwell," said Holmes, shaking his head
when I had finished. "And yet, I am indebted to him for bringing to my
attention the Dolchurch case. It was a singular opportunity to demonstrate
to you how – as I once wrote – a logician might infer the possibility of a
Niagara from a drop of water. It has been many years since I first jotted
down my 'Book of Life', and I am now wondering if I should follow it
with a *magnum opus* upon the practical aspects of my deductive
techniques. Thanks to our time in Dolchurch, it has occurred to me that the
Sussex Coast might be a conducive spot for such an undertaking. A place
with a view of the Channel would be an idyllic locale for such a
magnificent task."

"You would take a little holiday cottage, such as the one we once used
near Poldhu Bay?"

"Yes, perhaps," said he, enigmatically.

And then our talked turned to other matters. Of cases solved and
villains vanquished. And adventures both mundane and wondrous – much
like life itself.

NOTES

1. The case of Jack Oswald has been published as the non-Canonical novel *The Gate of Gold* (2017).
2. Watson does not name his school in the Canonical adventures. William S. Baring-Gould has identified it as Wellington College, Hampshire, while other scholars prefer Winchester College.
3. There is no place called Dolchurch in West Sussex, but this literary editor has tentatively identified it as the village of Lyminster, which has an eleventh-century parish church of St. Mary Magdalene. Although unusual, several smaller Norman churches had crypts.
4. The Elizabethan mansion known as Danny House, near the village of Pyecombe, has been tentatively identified by Sherlockian scholars as the manor house of Hurlstone. It is about twenty miles northwest of Lyminster.
5. A *mohur* is a gold coin formerly minted in British India.
6. Alphonse De Neuville (1835-1885) was a French student of Delacroix. His paintings were primarily battle scenes. According to a writer from the *World* (London) magazine – who interviewed Arthur Conan Doyle on 3 August, 1892 – the Tennison Road, Norwood home of Watson's first literary editor also had a hall lined with a series of De Neuville's battle-pieces.
7. Many parts of the story of the Dolchurch vault corresponds with the legend of the Chase Vault of Oistins, Barbados, which has been famous for its moving coffins since 1833. The story was recounted by Sir Arthur Conan Doyle in Chapter V ("The Law of the Ghost") of *The Edge of the Unknown* (1930).
8. A "resurrection stone" was a stone of immense weight that was temporarily hired out to lay over fresh graves to prevent the occupants from being stolen by so-called "resurrection men".
9. Perhaps a bad example, considering that the Egyptian pyramids at Giza were all looted in ancient times!
10. The "Bill Browns" is the regimental nickname for the Grenadier Guards, also known as the First Foot Guards.
11. A spirit-lamp is an alcohol burner, typically made from aluminum or glass. It was used to produce an open flame, like a natural-gas Bunsen burner.
12. The curious vault at Stanton was reported in the September 1815 edition of the *European Magazine*. The scholar F.A. Paley recorded the case of the Gretford vault in an 1867 letter to The Folk-Lore Society.
13. By 1905, it was clear that water from the nearby River Itchen was undermining the walls of the great Perpendicular Gothic cathedral of Winchester. After several failed attempts to pump water from the ground, the heroic diver William Walker (1869-1918) shored it up by laying concrete and bricks in water up to twenty feet in depth. Even now, the cathedral crypt floods every winter.
14. As recounted by J. Meade Falkner in his novel *Moonfleet* (1898).

15. Many of Mr. Treadwell's thoughts here and later align with those expressed by Sir Arthur Conan Doyle in an article entitled "Stranger Than Fiction" (27 November, 1915) published in *Collier's*.

16. Livonia is a historical region on the eastern shores of the Baltic Sea. The story related by Mr. Sharpe appears to correlate with that of the Buxhowden crypt on the Island of Oesel, now called Saaremaa. From 1721 to 1917, it was part of the Russian Empire, but is now the largest island in modern Estonia. The capital is Kuressaare, formerly called Ahrensburg.

17. A version of this tale was later utilized by Sir Arthur Conan Doyle in Chapter II ("The Shadows on the Screen") of *The Edge of the Unknown* (1930).

18. Almond Fisk patented his metallic burial case in 1848, and they were manufactured in Providence, Rhode Island until 1888, when demand for them petered out. The practice of using coffins made of crushed oyster shells was common in Formosa, now called Taiwan, during the eighteenth and nineteenth centuries.

19. Now called simply the "shell-game", the thimblerig confidence trick has been known in England since at least 1670 and was very popular in the nineteenth century.

20. William Sturgeon invented the electromagnet in 1824 by wrapping eighteen turns of bare copper wire around a horseshoe-shaped piece of varnished iron. Sturgeon's initial version was quite weak. However, the basic principle was greatly improved and popularized by Joseph Henry beginning in 1830. One of Henry's magnets was eventually able to support over two-thousand pounds.

21. The workings of the code are as follows: The first grouping is from Genesis Book 50, Verses 25 and 26 (summing to 51), with the next from Exodus Book 10, Verse 4. This gives us a latitude of 50°51'10.4" North. The third grouping is from the Matthew Book 2, Verses 17-19 (summing to 54), with the next from Luke Book 24, Verse 40. This gives us a longitude of 2°54'24.40" West.

22. The Greenwich Prime Meridian was established in 1851 and not universally adopted (except by France) until 1884. Prior to that, the widely-used Paris meridian arc established by Cardinal Richelieu and Louis XIII.

23. Mary II ruled from 1689-1694, while her sister Anne ruled from 1702-1707.

24. "*Animus revocandi*" is a term in English common law referring to objects hidden with an "intent to recover", as distinct from objects lost or abandoned, which devolved upon The Crown.

The *Vodou* Drum
by David Marcum

Chapter I – The Curse

I folded my stethoscope and stood upright, looking down at the man in the basket chair. "I'm not telling you anything that you don't already know."

He nodded and looked rather embarrassed. "You are correct, Doctor. I'm afraid that I'm not the best patient."

"Do you take your prescribed medication?"

"I do, but my current condition isn't simply due to my heart. It's become worse, for I must admit: I am living in fear." He lowered his gaze. "Terror, actually. I'm normally not one to seek help, but I don't know what else to do."

"Hopefully we can be of assistance," said Alton Peake, the noted consulting spiritualist – invited as I had been to Baker Street in order to hear the visitor's curious story. Peake was a good-natured and sympathetic man, and his presence would certainly go a long way as a calming influence.

I glanced over at Sherlock Holmes, seated in his favorite chair near the chemical table, with one of the windows overlooking Baker Street behind him. The afternoon light limned his outline, leaving his face in shadow except for the sharp expression of his eyes. He had watched with great interest as Mr. Clayton Enderby had paused almost as soon as he'd begun to relate his story, asking for a moment while his heart calmed itself.

As I'd risen from my own chair and begun to examine him, grateful that I had brought my medical bag with me, I had a chance to evaluate the famed author. I had read all of his books, insightful tales blending the harsh truths of everyday life with notable characters and mysterious happenings, all presented in a way so as to pull the reader ever-forward. Some critics had compared him to a modern Mr. Dickens, and there was always talk in some quarters that Enderby should be recruited to write a continuation and conclusion of Dickens' unfinished final novel, *The Mystery of Edwin Druid.* I hoped that someday he'd be convinced to undertake the endeavor.

Enderby was a solid fellow in his mid-fifties, just a few years older than Holmes, Peake, and me. His hair was cut short, as was his beard, and though both had once been dark, there were now sprinkled with white threads. He wore square bifocals, and there were squint-lines rising vertically over the bridge of his nose. I knew that he'd begun his working career as a government employee before shifting to finance. All the while, he'd been writing during his spare time, and when finally he'd been bold enough to share one of his works with a friend, the enthusiastic encouragement he'd received had been enough to prompt him to submit it for publication. After that, one book followed another, with his novels becoming something of a vast tapestry – the main character in one story appearing as a background character in the next, while similarly someone of only passing interest in this year's book would soon become a fascinating featured protagonist, showing how everyone is interconnected, and everyone's life is a fascinating story in some sense.

From all that I'd heard, Clayton Enderby was a well-respected, intelligent, and jovial individual, popular and confident in all aspects of his life. While he was a successful author, he'd continued with his modest regular employment, regularly turning out new works composed in his spare time. It was hard to reconcile that successful and steady image with the frightened man who had chosen that afternoon to visit Sherlock Holmes, full of apologies for immediately collapsing back into his chair in fear and pain.

After receiving a note from Holmes that morning, I'd rearranged my schedule to attend this appointment. I'd planned to stop by that afternoon in any case to see how Holmes was recovering, as he'd recently been in a scuffle while retrieving some documents related to the fiasco connected with Joseph Chamberlain's resignation as Colonial Secretary, ostensibly due to trade policy disagreements with the Prime Minister, but actually because of far grimmer issues. A number of other Cabinet ministers had ended up resigning as well, and the uncertainty was making the Government nervous. Holmes's brother, Mycroft, from his curious position at the center of the Government's web, had sniffed out the real reason – a nasty bit of blackmail.

Sherlock Holmes never had any use for blackmailers, and Mycroft less so. Together the two of them had set about correcting the course of the Ship of State as best they could, but their plans hadn't taken into account the fact that politicians cannot be trusted to follow directions or take matters on faith that appropriate steps were being taken, and when two of them decided to make their own separate arrangements with the blackmailer, cracks appeared in the Holmes Brothers' plan. Only by swift action, and with the unexpected assistance by a formerly discredited Freemason, was Sherlock Holmes able to avert a far greater crisis – although he would carry the aches and bruises of his encounter with the blackmailing brute, Vickers Natterson, for several more weeks.

357

I was initially unaware of that investigation, as my practice in Queen Anne Street, where I'd been for nearly a year following my remarriage, took up much more time than I would have liked – although my wife was pleased enough with my new success. Too often, I found that patients invented reasons to visit – a false cough isn't difficult to spot – so that they could say they'd met Dr. Watson, the friend of the famed detective. (Some even spent their time looking around, as if they expected to see Holmes dramatically burst into the consulting room, seeking my assistance.) It was a far different sort of practice than those which I'd maintained years before in Kensington and Paddington – seeing patients and making rounds. Now I spent most of my time indoors, and I felt more like one of the "celebrity" doctors I'd secretly despised for so long as they built their practices in Harley and Devonshire Streets, becoming some sort of personality cult for the upper class rather than actually practicing medicine.

Still, I was actually able to act as a physician more often than not, seeing people with real illnesses who needed my real help. And I did enjoy when my wife and I often walked the few hundred feet or so east to the Langham for afternoon tea –even though it wasn't as often as I would have liked. I also found time to drop by Baker Street to visit with my old friend and join him regularly on his investigations. He reciprocated by visiting Queen Anne Street to recruit me when he needed assistance – sometimes vexing my typically tolerant wife.

I had managed to get out and go on rounds that morning, and had been in Bickenhall Street after eating a quick lunch and then visiting my last patient. I arrived as planned at 221b just before one o'clock. Using my old key, I let myself in as I often did, greeted Mrs. Hudson, and climbed upstairs to the sitting room, where Holmes was sitting in his chair and discussing a pair of photographs – one of a man ostensibly dead since the 1860's, and the other of what seemed to be the same fellow from just a week before – with Peake. I knew the details of that curious inquiry, and Holmes was stating while nodding my way, "Politicians are never to be trusted, Peake – but there's no need to belabor that point to you, after what we saw during the affair of the lighthouse and the *Phalacrocoracidae* – " when the doorbell rang.

In the years that I'd either lived in or visited those rooms, I'd had the chance to listen to thousands of individuals ascend from the hallway below, first a rise of nine steps, turning at the landing, and then eight more to the space outside the sitting room door. Some visitors bounded up, while others climbed steadily. Others paused – sometimes on the landing to catch his or her breath while looking out the window at the plane tree in the rear yard, and occasionally elsewhere along the climb. Some tarried on nearly every step, which was useful when deducing that they were in poor

358

physical condition, but not so helpful when listening for an indicative limp, or a telling squeaky shoe, or a left foot with an inward twist.

We had no more than introduced ourselves and settled in to hear Enderby's story than he expressed the need to pause for a moment, leading to my examination. Now complete, I replaced my stethoscope in my bag and remarked, "I trust that your regular physician is aware of these symptoms, and that you're receiving proper treatment?"

He nodded. "I've had the symptoms for several months. My doctor has prescribed nitroglycerin."

"And do you take it as directed?" I asked.

He lowered his head. "When I can. Sometimes I'm rather busy and lose track of things . . . ."

"Mr. Enderby," I said, with all the stern physician *gravitas* that I could muster. "tachycardia and atrial fibrillation cannot be ignored. Untreated, they can lead to apoplexy, and you wouldn't want your gifts snuffed so needlessly."

He nodded, and then added, "But it's only become worse in the last few days, Doctor. Since I've fallen under the curse. Before then, the condition was so insignificant that I barely paid attention to it."

I had my doubts whether a curse, as he believed, could only recently cause the racing and lurching heartbeat that I'd just heard, but before I could query him further about his medical history and what might have caused such a dramatic presentation, Holmes – the man with whom Clayton Enderby had journeyed to consult – took over the conversation.

"You mentioned in your note that you were the victim of a curse, and now you suggest that it's affecting your health. I must inform you that I have no patience for supernatural explanations, but in deference to your reputation, and that you might not be as gullible as such a belief would imply, I've asked our friend, Alton Peake, to join us."

He nodded toward Peake, seated to the side on the settee. "Mr. Peake is a noted investigator of this type of thing," Holmes continued, "and, while we don't always see eye to eye, he has specialized knowledge which could be of great use."

"Holmes mentioned your belief in a Haitian *vodou* curse," explained Peake. "I'll admit that's something that I've had less experience with than some of our homegrown manifestations, but I have read a great deal. There was the Liveson affair of '79, when the family of eight was found dead in their sitting room in Camberwell, all staring in terror at a small doll lying on the table, an effigy of the father, pierced through the heart with a pin." He glanced at Holmes. "You'll recall that we disagreed on that one – I speculated that it did have an effect, functioning as something of a substitute golem for the victim, while you showed that the married daughter was responsible, but in the end, I was still proven – "

Enderby shook his head and interrupted. "I'm afraid that I haven't heard of that one, Mr. Peake. And after my youthful visit to Haiti, I've done quite a bit of research, and know of these *vodou* dolls, although I never saw one for myself. No, my curse has taken the form of a drum – the same rhythm I heard so many years ago."

Peake sat back. "I know something of these drums. Fascinating."

"This curse," interrupted Holmes, resuming control of the conversation. "Why do you believe such a thing is occurring?"

"I have no idea. I traveled to Haiti when I was nineteen – thirty-nine years ago – and I heard the drums then, on one terrible night. Since then, I've lived my life here in relative normalcy and only studied Haiti occasionally, as having been there, I found that it interested me. I know a bit more about the country than when I went, but I'm no expert. Over the years, I've occasionally recalled the drums – after all, it's an interesting anecdote to tell people that I've heard *vodou* drums – but I have no idea why they recently began sounding outside my own home."

"When?" asked Holmes, leaning forward and reaching for his pipe.

"Six days ago. It was at night, actually, as one would expect. I live in a small home with a bit of ground around it, in Hampstead. The house is on Hampstead Lane, situated in the southern portion of Bishop's Wood. My writing has provided me with extra income, allowing us to purchase the property over ten years ago. We're quiet people, my wife and I, and it's just the two of us – our son is grown and gone – and we have no servants. Our routine is quiet as well. I return home from my work each night, we eat the meal prepared by my wife, and then we adjourn to the study, where I write while my wife occupies herself nearby with her book, or sewing, or whatever other interest she has at the moment.

"It was just such a night last Thursday – six days ago, as I said. It was getting late, near the time when we go to bed, that it began – softly at first, no louder than the sounds of the traffic that we now hear through the windows. I wouldn't have given it any thought at all, except we're well back from the road, and typically we near no noises at all, except for those of nature – wind, birds, thunder, and rain. We were quite fortunate to find such a little sanctuary so near London, but now after nearly a week of the drums, I realize just how remote we are – only a hundred yards from the road or our nearest neighbors, yet if we're in danger, it might as well be a hundred miles.

"It was actually my wife who noticed it first, thinking that something was rattling in the wind – a loose gutter, perhaps – although there was no wind to speak of that night. We tarried for a moment as I also heard it, and

360

it was a moment longer before I realized that I knew what it was – a peculiar and regularly repeated syncopation that I hadn't heard in nearly forty years – a Haitian *vodou* drum.

"The rhythm is unmistakable – " And here he paused to tap out an odd and rather unnerving beat upon his chair arm, the thumps lurching and then hurried, and not following the typical expected regularity of those we know and absorb in our Western music. The pattern would at times seem disjointed and irregular, but then it would begin anew, and one could see that there was a plan to it, a meaning that eluded understanding. In spite of our setting – a warm sitting room in the heart of London in autumn 1903 – I felt the hairs raise on my neck, as if the beat itself could somehow summon the attention of a creature or some other entity that had ignored us until now, but upon the repetition of the rhythm, it had *heard* . . . and it was coming.

I glanced at Peake, who was leaning forward with great interest, and he was trying to mimic the pattern with a finger upon his leg. Holmes, meanwhile, had his eyes shut, clearly committing the sequence to memory.

"Was it just the one drum – with one tonality," he asked, "or were there multiple drums of different sizes, so that the beats almost had a musical quality, playing different notes?"

"Just the one," answered Enderby, finally ceasing the skin-crawling thumping. I could only wonder if the sound had travelled down the chair and into the floor, and thus through the ceiling of Mrs. Hudson's parlour just below. I wondered if she, not knowing what the patterns represented, had felt the same unease that had just gripped me.

"I have read," added the client, "of different types of *vodou* drumming – with multiple drums, as you describe, and also of faster rhythms with increasing speed, wherein those listening are prompted into some sort of ecstatic frenzy. But this was the steady beat I've demonstrated, not much faster than a resting heartbeat."

In fact, I thought, it resembled something of the man's lurching tachycardia that I had just heard through my stethoscope.

"And this was the beat you heard as a young man in Haiti?" asked Peake.

"It was. It once played incessantly throughout one long terrible night, worming its way into our minds, and thus I when I heard it again last week, I recognized it instantly."

"You said it remained steady in tempo," asked Holmes, rising and reaching for his violin. "Did it increase in volume?"

Enderby simply shook his head, watching curiously as Holmes raised the violin and began to pluck the E-string, accurately reproducing the rhythm the older man had just demonstrated. Somehow, this was even more unsettling – as if the pattern had been given a voice. He then shifted to the higher A, D, and G strings, repeating the pizzicato upon each until I felt my teeth clenching. Then, suddenly having satisfied himself, Holmes stopped, replaced the violin against the mantel, and reseated himself.

"You went outside to investigate?" he asked.

Enderby nodded. "I was unnerved, and concerned about someone trespassing upon my property, so I told my wife to wait and went rushing outside without further thought – and without arming myself. I went through the back door, as the rear of the property was where the drums seemed to originate, and it's also the most wooded part, adjoining the larger forest to the northwest.

"The drums were louder outside, and coming from the trees that grow beyond the house. I had no light with me, and as my eyes adjusted, I only saw various shades of darkness. But as I stepped in that direction, the drumming ceased. I went back inside, retrieved a lantern and a heavy stick, and returned to the woods, entering by one of the walking paths that cut through there. I looked around for several minutes, seeing and hearing nothing, and suddenly I thought that perhaps that this had been some sort of method to decoy me away from the house, where I'd left my wife alone and defenseless. Abandoning my search, I fled back to the building and up the steps, only to find her, frightened, and no intruders. I returned to lock the back door, and that's when I saw the note, left lying on the outside steps. I had missed it during my initial race to get back inside."

He reached into a pocket and pulled out a folded page, which he handed to Holmes.

I could see that it was a quarto-sized sheet, yellowed with age. "This has been dampened at some point," said Holmes. "It has old stains and ripples. Is this the way you found it?"

Enderby nodded. "It was also folded that way."

Holmes opened it and examined front and back. "'*Leave your Haiti journal on the step – Tell not that story.*'" He read it aloud and then looked up. "Written with a thick pencil in block letters, straight across the page – no rises or dips – and well-spaced. What is this journal?" He reached across to hand the note to me, and when I'd looked it over, I passed it along to Peake.

"When I went to Haiti, I kept a journal – it was encouraged, and I was glad that I did it, as it's my memento of the trip, full of daily descriptions of the events and people, as well as sketches of scenes that I observed."

"'*Tell not that story –* ' Is it your intent to write a book about your Haitian adventure?

"It is – I'm in the preliminary planning stages – outlining and researching and so on. This reference in the warning is another mysterious

362

feature of this whole business. I've kept the knowledge of the next book to myself – even my wife never knows what I'm writing about until I've finished – so I don't know how this intruder knew my plans."

"And did you leave the journal on the steps?"

"I did not. The idea of capitulating to the demands never even crossed my mind."

"Demands? You've said that the drums have played each night. Have you also received additional sheets?"

"I have. I'd hoped that this was a one-time thing, so I wasn't prepared when the drums began again on the second night. My lantern and stick were still by the back door, however, so I went out, only this time to find a note on the steps before I descended." He reached into another pocket and pulled a small folded sheaf of papers. "These are all of the rest of them."

Holmes also looked at these before commenting, "Same paper and pencil, and the exact same message. There are no threats, and no escalation of urgency. Why did you keep the first separate?"

"I've read of your methods. I suppose I thought that it might have some different significance – as if he wrote it, thinking that one warning would be enough, and then he was forced to write more, and the repetition would show some clue that he took time to avoid in the first."

"Unfortunately, he was remarkably consistent – each is equivalent to the first. But that also indicates that it's the same person, and the chore of writing new notes isn't being passed from one person to another. Did you go forth to examine the woods?"

"I did, and the drumming ceased when I reached the tree line. The next day, I asked my only close neighbor if he had heard the sound, and he replied negatively, but gave me a queer look, as if I was losing part of my mind – so I haven't asked him again.

"It was much the same on the next nights. On the third, I watched from the back window near the door to see who left a note, but no one approached. Later, when the drumming started, I found the note on the path to the woods. On the fourth, I left the lantern outside, far enough back from the house that it illuminated both the steps and the path. When the drums started, I rushed out to the woods, and it stopped, and I found no note – until this morning, when I discovered it on the front steps, on the opposite side of the house. On the fifth night, I wanted to wait outside in the darkness, to see if I could sense anyone moving about as he approached the house, but my wife begged me to stay indoors. I must add that she is becoming more and more terrified as this affair progresses, as she vaguely understands the nature of the drums and their connection to my Haitian voyage. I relented and stayed inside, and this morning I required that she go to visit her sister in Hornsey until the matter is resolved.

"Then, as I had the house to myself, I waited outside, as I'd intended for the night before. But my efforts were wasted. The drums began and I moved about in the darkness looking and listening for any signs of someone going by me to the house. But I heard nothing, and after a few minutes, the drums stopped. I lit my lantern, explored the woods without any success, and returned to the house. The most recent note was lying by the back door, the same as the first had been. It was then, Mr. Holmes, that I decided to seek your help. My wife can't remain at her sister's forever, and I have no intention of relinquishing my journal. I am acquainted with the Hendons of Thornton Heath, and know what you were able to do for their unfortunate daughter. It was with this in mind that I sought your time."

"The journal?" asked Holmes. "Is it still at your house?"

"It is. Perhaps I should have taken it with me to-and-from my employment, but I feared that I might be waylaid – for whomever wants it seems quite intent on getting it, and a violent attack probably isn't beyond the realms of possibility. But I've hidden it quite well at home – no one will find it very easily."

"Good. It's not long after midday, so we have time to make plans before this evening's performance – and there will almost certainly be one. It's unlikely that after six days your persecutor will stop for the seventh."

At this point, Peake cleared his throat. "I'm sure that we'll resolve this matter tonight – Holmes is very good at what he does, and the fellow behind this will certainly be caught – but I would be interested in hearing about your Haitian voyage, and how you first came to hear these drums so long ago."

Enderby nodded, and looked toward Holmes, as if to seek permission. My friend nodded. Having traveled quite a bit myself, and having once passed through that part of the world in my youth, I was quite interested as well, and I felt that we needed to know the historical background to understand what was occurring now at the lonely house in Hampstead.

I stood and asked if anyone wanted something to drink. After serving each of us with something from the sideboard, we settled in to hear Enderby's tale. Alton Peake sat forward the entire time, alert and fascinated at hearing of a visit to another land and culture. At times I think Holmes became impatient, but he listened intently nonetheless throughout to pick out the relevant threads as the author wove his tapestry.

364

"For you to understand the drums," Enderby explained, "and why this current experience makes so little sense to me, I must tell you how I journeyed to Haiti, and my naïve perspective as a young man. In 1863, I was but eighteen years old, and in my first year of University. Like so many, I attended because it was expected, but I had no true idea of what I wanted to do with my life. I had read a great deal, but felt that I'd seen very little of the world. It was then that I learned of an opportunity to serve as a missionary to Haiti on a short-term basis. It seemed like the perfect way to expand my horizons.

"I was raised in one of the churches belonging to the Baptist Union of Great Britain, and I continued to attend while in school. I had been vaguely aware that my church had a strong sense of mission, donating to the less-fortunate in other countries, and even sending members overseas. When it was discussed that the next trip being planned was a return to Haiti, where they had been twice before, I was suddenly interested and set about seeing if I could volunteer.

"I was only doing it because of the promise of adventure, but I believe the members of the church felt that I'd been called to life-long religious service. I wasn't truly aware of that at the time, but in hindsight, I'm sure that's the only reason why I was allowed to go. On two previous occasions, a group of eight men had taken a substantial portion of their time and sailed to Haiti to do God's work. The entire idea of the church's support of Haiti, and of sending men there to provide physical and financial assistance, had come about because a career-long Haitian missionary, Jack Hedford, had come to England and spoken to our church, along with a number of others, seeking support.

"At first my participation was discouraged, but I stuck to my guns, and they relented, making arrangements for nine of us to make the journey this time instead of eight. Throughout the winter, we met in their homes every few weeks, getting to know one another, and planning for the trip. It was strange in a way – I was not much more than a boy, and the youngest of these other men were in their forties, with the oldest over seventy. One of them, Mr. Birch, had been a former teacher of mine, and it was odd now be interacting with him as an adult. In truth, I felt like I was playing a role, trying to be an adult when I often felt like a child inside, but I've learned that many feel the same way throughout their entire lives.

"Curiously, my parents were unexpectedly supportive of the trip. Perhaps they also mistakenly believed that I wanted to be a missionary, but I suspect that my father admired my desire to see the world and wished a bit that he could have gone too. They, along with my sister, were both there at the dock to see us off in the spring of '64, along with the wives and families of the other eight men. I had just turned nineteen a few weeks earlier, but I was old enough to appreciate that I was actually setting off on a great adventure – an opportunity that many would never have.

"If you sailed anywhere in the 1860's, then you recall just how unpleasant it was. The journeys were long and dangerous. With today's steamships, able to steadily make the crossing to America in little more than a week, the age of the great sailing ships is already a memory, only to be experienced vicariously in novels. But it's something that I'll never forget, and I'm proud to say that I tolerated the voyage well enough. Some of the other eight men suffered. Able Welsh, the oldest of us, was seasick the entire time. I truly feared that he might die, and I'd never seen a man with purely blue lips before. Another of the men, Lawson Roberts, was a doctor, and he spent a great deal of time helping Old Welsh pull through.

"We finally docked in Virginia – and recall, this was in the middle of the American Civil War. The harbor was filled with the Confederate traitors' warships, but we were only there long enough to shift our meagre belongings to another vessel that had been arranged to meet us. We then sailed south along the coast, and it was early in hurricane season, but fortunately we had clear weather. I stood day after day watching to the west, occasionally catching glimpses of the American coastline. The air became warmer and more tropical, and one of the sailors told me that within a few days we'd be docking in Port-au-Prince. When we finally saw it, however, I was still amazed, watching our destination grow larger and larger on the horizon.

"The next day or so was a blur. We were met at the docks by the missionary, Jack Hedford, who helped us get our supplies loaded onto wagons. By the time we were finished, it was evening, and we still had ten miles to travel north along the bay to where we'd sleep for the night. As we traveled, I couldn't see anything in the dark, but the smells were overpowering, and both terrible and wonderful at the same time – damp jungle odors overlain with rot, and a constant smokiness that settled in my raw throat. We finally came to an inn, lit only by a couple of dim lanterns, and we gratefully tumbled into our waiting beds, assured by Jack that he'd guard our supplies through the night.

"The next morning, I walked down to the dock, wondering just what I'd gotten myself into. There was a small wooden boat, no more than fifteen or twenty feet in length, already piled with our supplies – including our heavy wooden crates of construction tools. There was no true mast. Instead, where one should have stood was a great upright tree-limb, tacked into place with supporting boards. With the supplies, three or four sailors, the nine of us from England, and Jack Hedford, it seemed that the boat was dangerously overloaded – and yet a number of other locals standing on the dock tried to climb aboard as well until Jack chased them away. Finally, with great but unexpressed trepidation on my part, we untied the ropes and set sail for La Gonave, just a hazy bump on the horizon.

"The excitement quickly overcame any uneasiness that I might have felt. We were nothing more than a cork bobbing on the vast sea, riding unimaginably blue waves up and over that were taller than our little boat. I had wisely placed myself on the stern, so that as we rocked from side-to-side to climb and drop along the waves, my motion was considerably less than the others – many of whom became quite seasick before we were done.

"After several long hours, we docked at Anse-à-Galets, a little village on La Gonave, situated around a tiny bay that was more tidal flat than deep water. We jumped into the task unloading the boat and shifting our cargo to wagons. The we climbed aboard, fitting in as best we could around the boxes, for the final push into the interior of the island, leaving the sea behind as we began a hot and tedious climb along barren and sandy hills, switching back and forth along 'roads' that were little more than eroded pathways. Often we had to climb down and push, as the slope and weight were more than the little donkeys pulling the wagons could overcome. Finally by late afternoon, we reached our remote destination: Petite Source, a tiny village of only three buildings – if one could call them that – resting at the foot of one of the larger mountains on the island, Morne Petite Source. This, then, would be our home for the next few months, and where we would build a church.

"It wasn't long after our arrival that I felt guilty, as it seemed that our presence was already a sore drain upon their resources, and more than whatever value we could provide to them by our labors. The main building was a four-room house made of wattle and daub, wherein a wooden lattice is constructed – the wattle – to form the walls. This is then daubed with a sticky material usually made of some combination of wet soil, clay, sand, animal dung, and straw. The building had been set aside for our use. I was later to learn that the family that lived there had moved out to give us the space, and that they had bartered dearly for the new sheet-metal roof which reflected brightly every day in the hot Haitian sun. A couple of other wattle buildings were on either side, and these had doors with shiny padlocks on the rough doors. It was here that the village kept their valuables – namely, their meagre supplies of grain, doled out each day for making bread. Close behind the main building was a cistern, and the narrow door on top had a lock on it as well.

"Jack Hedford introduced us to the four people with whom we would have the most dealings over the next months – I say four, but in reality, one of them proved to be rather sadly insignificant. He was a small man, the owner of the main house vacated for our stay, and the theoretical leader of the village. He looked to be ancient, but I was later to learn that he was just in his mid-forties, his figure wasted away by a lifetime of hard work and terrible conditions. He stepped forward and shook each of our hands with a very grave and sincere welcome, speaking some words in the Haitian Creole that conveyed welcome, even if their exact meaning was unknown.

"We next met his wife, a big stout woman in a white shirt, gray skirt, and blue kerchief on her head. We would come to learn that she, in truth, was the matriarch who ran the village and the immediate surrounding countryside. I never learned her name, unfortunately, but I've never forgotten her. She was grim, as one would expect in that life, but it wasn't long before she betrayed flashes of humor.

"Next was their daughter, Marulla, a beautiful girl of twenty-five or so, as I later found through my limited conversations with her. She had moved to Port-au-Prince several years before to work and obtain money for her family, but during the course of our stay, she'd returned to Petite Source to help do any extra work that we might generate, such as assisting in the preparation of meals, and dealing with our laundry.

"Finally, standing to one side, was a tall and lanky young man, also brought over from the capital by Jack Hedford to act as a translator – as Marulla's English was quite limited. His name was Daniel – pronounced *Dan-yell*, in the French way – and he was twenty-one. Over the weeks that we were there, I made friends with him as best as I could, considering the language barrier – he wasn't that good of a translator – and the vast differences in our backgrounds.

"That night, countless Haitians gathered around as we settled in, and I understood how creatures in the zoo feel. They were lined up a dozen deep all around the little porch in front of the main building where we sat or prepared our evening meal or readied our tools for the morrow's work. As the sun went down, more and more of them arrived, lining up around us deeper and deeper, but never making a sound. The night was soon as dark as a mine pit, and I had no idea how many were watching, waiting for us to do . . . something. Anything. But eventually, and probably to their disappointment, we went inside and settled in to sleep.

"We quickly settled into a routine that remained mostly unbroken day after day. I was amazed at how small our world became. Petite Source was probably no more than six or eight miles inland as the crow flies from Anse-à-Galets at the sea, but the distance had to have been twice that when traveled by trail to climb into the mountains. By the following daylight, and with a bit of time to look around, I could see the mountain rising to

368

the west of us behind the main house – Morne Petite Source – and that on the opposite side, far away down a long slope to the east and barely visible in the haze, was Anse-à-Galets. As we discovered, beginning in the middle of each night and lasting until mid-morning the next day, a stiff and steady wind would arise from the sea and up along this miles-long slope to our village, often becoming quite cold. La Gonave, in spite of being a Caribbean island, is very much like a desert, with the drastic daily changes in temperature that one finds in such places. We froze at night, and roasted in sunlight.

"Across the road from the main house was a wide field, stripped of vegetation by roaming goats. It was here that the church would be built. Our own church back in England, along with supplying missionaries, had provided funds to construct the new building. Additionally, Jack Hedford had hired local crews to come do much of the actual skilled work, while we provided assistance and more technical skills as necessary. Not long after sunrise of our first full day there, Jack's crew came walking down the road, carrying tools and whistling some local song. I had seen where a number of timbers had been previously brought in and stacked behind one of the side sheds – these would be used for building roof joists. There were also bags of cement to be used in construction of concrete blocks that would form the walls.

"I've since learned that the construction methods used for that church were dodgy at best, and would make an engineer cry. The locals began mixing up the cement with local sand and stones, and then putting the mixture in molds that they'd brought to form the concrete blocks. After just a few minutes, they'd remove a block and leave it to stand, dry, and harden in the sun. Typically, concrete needs a month to reach full strength – but these blocks were used after just a day or two of curing.

"My jobs as an able-bodied nineteen-year-old varied. Mostly I carried things – bags of cement, buckets of water, and finished concrete blocks to the work site, where other locals were mortaring them into place. The original church had been nothing more than a structure of sticks marking the area and providing a bit of shade. They hadn't even used any homemade daub to make it more permanent. The new church was being constructed around it.

"We settled into a routine – making blocks, laying course after course as the walls rose, constructing roof joists for when they'd be needed, and then relaxing in the evenings. Dr. Roberts would see patients at night – mostly children, some with terrible injuries that he couldn't treat, such as open wounds covered with gnats, or one lad who'd burned his knee in a fire. The skin had healed too tight, and he couldn't bend his leg without it splitting open each time. There were many children who showed signs of

369

malnutrition, but their mothers sought medical attention with the faithful hope that the English doctor could do something just by putting his hands upon them.

"I became friends with all the men – Old Able Welsh and my teacher Mr. Birch and Doctor Roberts. The Bills: Bill Brewford – the youngest of them in his early forties – and Bill Brown. Harrison Tipton, an engineer who worked out the best way to build the roof joints, and David Mayer, the father of one of my old school friends who took me under his wing. Perhaps the only one that I didn't get close to was the leader of our little band, Reverend Garrison Anderson, the assistant minister at our church who led these mission trips."

(At the mention of Reverend Anderson, I saw that Holmes showed a flicker of extra interest, perhaps only obvious to me, but he didn't interrupt Enderby's narrative.)

"They were all good men," continued our visitor, "giving of their time and energy to help this little village in the middle of nowhere that no one had ever heard of. You'll never find it in any reference book, and it will never be important for anything, but for a time, it was our entire world.

"The days rolled on as the church grew, and anything that broke the monotony was of great interest. Water was always of great concern. As many of the trees had long-since been cut on La Gonave, it never seemed to rain. Apparently Petite Source was named for a small spring, but I never saw exactly where it was. We had been in our routine for so long that when clouds began to build one afternoon, it seemed to shock us into a new wakeful feeling that we hadn't felt in weeks.

"The wind continued to rise, and the clouds became blacker and blacker. Dr. Roberts was running everywhere, urging everyone to gather whatever containers we could find to catch the coming cloudburst, but actually the locals were already doing so. I worked with Daniel and Marulla to fix a bent gutter that led into the cistern, while others were tying down our supplies from the now gale-like wind. But soon we were forced inside, as the storm began to throw sizzling lightning bolts all around us, one after another, more than we could count. The cracking and deafening thunder from each crash ran together into one long explosive rumble that seemed to last more than an hour. The entire hillside around us seemed to be struck over and over, and we nine huddled in our main building, aware of the sheet metal roof above us that seemed likely to loosen and blow away at any second.

"Eventually the storm passed, and – to our great disappointment – there had been little or no rain at all. Just the terrible electric force from the skies – more destructive than we initially realized.

370

"An hour or so after the storm finished, the last bit of daylight returned, along with great cries and lamentations from someone down the path leading to the village, getting closer with each minute. Daniel stepped that way to converse with some of the locals who were congregated there, whispering, as the wailing voice along the trail came closer. Then he returned to tell us what was happening. During the vicious lightning storm, a boy of eight or so had been killed. Amazingly, he was one of five brothers, and three others had also been killed by lightning in recent months. The boy who had just died had been treated by Dr. Roberts for an infected wound only the night before, and now the last surviving brother, a man of twenty or so, was on his way to confront us, believing that somehow we were cursed, and responsible by our presence for the death of his last brother.

"I noticed that as we heard this story, standing there in the dirt clearing before the main building in the last of the day's light, each of the men in our group seemed to pull in a bit, crossing their arms defensively, and moving a little closer to one another. Before we had a chance to ask further questions, a party of locals came into view along the trail to the south. In front was a tall young man, raising his voice and raving at the heavens. When he saw us, he leaned forward and began to walk faster in our direction. I saw a liquor bottle of some sort in his hand, and he raised it to take a drink as he approached.

"When he was just fifteen or twenty feet from us, lurching our way with mayhem or vengeance on his mind, he was suddenly stopped by the appearance of the matriarch, along with her daughter, Marulla, who both stepped directly into his path. He bobbled to a halt and said something, a sob in his voice that became a snarl while pointing our way with his free hand. I have no idea what he said, but the matriarch raised a heavy arm and slapped him, twisting his head violently sideways. Then she swung her arm again, knocking the bottle from his hand, where it landed to one side and shattered on a stone. She grabbed his collar and shook him, and then slapped him quickly twice more before he cried out and collapsed in a heap at her feet, wailing and shaking his fists at the sky. Some of the men in the group who had been following him stepped forward and dragged him upright, and then pulled him back the way that they had come. But several of them looked back over their shoulders in our direction, and their expressionless and judgmental faces were more terrifying than if they too had been glaring at us with rage.

"'She said that he was embarrassing the village,' explained Daniel. 'She told him that we did not cause the death of his brother, and that to threaten the nine of you – or to curse God as he was also doing – was a sin that she would not tolerate.' He didn't provide any further explanation.

371

"Reverend Anderson tapped Daniel on the arm to join him, and then they walked over to the matriarch and Marulla. As they conversed in low tones, the rest of us, by unspoken agreement, adjourned back to the main building. Surprisingly, there was no conversation, as everyone seemed to be turned inward. I would have expected much more discussion in a frantic manner, such as what would have occurred at school if something like this happened, but these men reacted in a different way. Later, Reverend Anderson joined us and pulled a couple of the older men aside, whispering, but the rest of us weren't included in their counsel, and we drifted to our sleeping spots.

"The next day was subdued, but the work continued as normal. By now the roof joists were in place, and as work continued on the walls and placement of sheet meal on the roof, a number of us gathered rocks which we tossed into the church's interior to serve as a floor. After hundreds – likely thousands – of rocks had been brought in, we set about leveling them, bending and fitting the rocks in such a way that they compacted and didn't roll when walked upon. Perhaps it was because I was so involved in this that I didn't speak to any of the others that day, and didn't know what was going on or being discussed.

"The day progressed as usual, and that night we were preparing our evening meal when the sun began to drop behind the mountain to the rear of our building.

"It was then that we heard the drum.

"We had become so accustomed to the sounds of the village – the wind, the hammering and construction sounds during the day, the conversations and voices of both the locals and the men from England – that anything like this would be unmistakable. It started as a simple steady beat – *Boom Boom Boom* – every few seconds. Everyone within sight, locals and visitors, came to a halt in their tracks and looked upward toward the mountain. Somewhere up there in the blackening shadows, the drummer was maintaining a vigil of sorts, his efforts magnified acoustically by the downward slope that carried the sound directly toward us. At first it was simply unusual – almost too strange to understand, but vastly primitive in a way that sent chills along my spine. I didn't realize what it was – I just knew that it was different. Then Daniel softly explained, '*Vodou*.' There was fear in his voice. "The drum plays for the dead boy – and as a curse.'

"Marulla scolded him, saying something in Creole in a scathing tone that made Daniel wince. Her meaning was clear, but he didn't retract his statement, instead looking at each of us meaningfully, as if willing us to understand him, even if he couldn't explain further.

372

"The drum had started with a steady beat, continuing in this way for an hour or more, as the sun finished its descent and the village darkened. A number of locals, more than usual, gathered at either end of the clearing where the trail vanished in two different directions, but they only talked amongst themselves and came no closer. We went about our usual nightly tasks, and then at some point, the rhythm changed – subtly, but no longer the steady beat that had almost matched a resting heart rate. Now it quickly modified and became more complex – what I demonstrated for you. It took on extra, irregular pulses, seemingly random, but then repeating after a moment, as if there was a longer pattern than we are used to comprehending in Western music. It got under one's skin and could not be ignored.

"Reverend Anderson was in and out. He spent quite a while talking with the matriarch and Marulla, along with Daniel and a couple of the older men in our group. Finally, when the sun was fully set, he returned and gathered us close.

"'There is danger here,' he said. 'We've decided to leave at first light. The native workers can finish what's left of the church without us. There will be a wagon in the morning. Pack only what you need – we'll leave the tools and crates. We'd planned to do so anyway,' he added when Bill Brown started to protest. 'The journey back will go much more quickly, as it's downhill to Anse-à-Galets. With any luck, we'll be back across the bay and in Port-au-Prince by nightfall.'

"The night was long and cold, and the drum never wavered. The complexity of rhythm it had maintained became our only reality. We would have known if it changed – as if someone counted from one to six over and over for many hours, and then suddenly skipped the number four. It seemed that every repetition conjured some evil and terrifying image in my mind – which was certainly the drummer's intent. This was only intensified by the cold wind blowing up the long draw from the sea.

"We agreed that having faith in God to protect us, while of great value, wasn't enough, as God helps those who help themselves. With that in mind, we armed ourselves as best we could with our more dangerous tools and set shifts as guards – but the fact was that none of us slept. All night the drum continued, and that pattern became unforgettable. To this day, as you saw, I can reproduce it.

"Our escape was something of an anti-climax. The matriarch had a wagon waiting for us in the morning. Some of the villagers were there to see us off, and they didn't have the cold antagonistic expressions of those who had been watching us from a distance the night before. They reached out to touch us, whispering prayers and blessings in Creole, their words a mystery as always but their expressions caring. Daniel climbed up to join

373

us, but of Marulla there was no sign. The last I saw of any of the villagers, or the church we'd labored to build, was when our wagon turned on the northern trail, and the matriarch was waving goodbye.

"We crossed from Anse-à-Galets to the main island within a few hours on the same decrepit boat, although I have little memory of it, and then sent word to Jack Helford, who came to escort us back to the capital. We spent several days there sightseeing while our early passage back to England was arranged, and then we said goodbye and sailed for home. The members of the church – and my family – were surprised at our early return, but we reported that the work had gone quickly and we'd finished ahead of schedule. We'd agreed that it would be better not to relate the danger from the drums, as it would worry our families and the church, and future trips might not occur. Instead, we said that since the church was finished, there was no need to stay and keep being a burden on the village in terms of them being displaced or finding us water.

"And so life went on. In a year or so, there was something of a schism in our home church, wherein Reverend Anderson – respected by a great many of the congregation – left to start his own church. I returned to university and my church attendance dwindled and then stopped. Many who had thought I was being called to be a missionary seemed to be disappointed when that didn't turn out to be the case. Over the years, I believe that most of the other eight men who made the trip have died, and I haven't had any contact with them in longer than I can remember."

Chapter III – The Resolution

"Your journal," asked Holmes. "You recorded all of this?"

"I did. I'm able to recall it so vividly now after so many years because I recently re-read it as part of the research for my new novel."

"You say that most of the other men have died," asked Peake. "How do you know?"

Enderby shrugged. "Various ways. I heard long ago by way of my late parents that some of the older men had passed. Over the years, I've seen obituaries in the newspapers."

"So their passings were widely spaced, as far as you know," clarified the consulting spiritualist. "None were recent, or could have been connected with any sort of curse."

"That is my belief. But again, I really know nothing substantial about any of them since our last real contact in the mid-1860's."

"And Reverend Garrison Anderson?" I asked, glancing toward Holmes, who had showed interest when the name was mentioned. He gave a small nod in my direction.

Enderby frowned. "I haven't heard that he's died – but if he's still alive, he must be nearly eighty by now."

"He is," confirmed Holmes, standing and walking to his shelf of scrapbooks, on the wall to the rear of where I was seated. After thumbing through them for a moment, he related, "You are correct. Born in 1825. Associated with various churches from his twenties onward. Widowed in his mid-forties – never remarried. Currently the minister of The Baptist Temple at 14 Shouldham Street since 1876. I've noted that he is something of a king in his own little kingdom."

He closed the book and returned it to its place, and then reached for another. He brought it back with him to his chair and sat, opening the book upon his knees.

"*Vodou*," he said, flipping through the pages and loose sheets tucked between them. "Watson and I have had our share of past encounters with this curious religion. The dockland murders – remember those? The affair at the lodge in Eccles, where we found evidence of a *vodou* sacrifice." He tapped a finger on the book. "I pasted in my notes from Eckermann's invaluable volume. There was the matter of Lady Chatterley's *vodou* dolls, and the matter between Professors Tarrington and Collingwood. There was that confounded affair of that *vodou* woman and the Betrayer Moon – Don't smile, Peake! – and Watson and I won't soon forget Dominic Langley, the sugar merchant's son. There have been several others as well – " He shut the book with a snap. " – but nothing along the lines of what we've heard today." He looked toward Peake. "I'm sure that you have more specialized knowledge on the subject."

The spiritualist investigator nodded. "There have been some instances where *vodou* – or imperfect attempts to copy it – have been noted here in the capital, but for the most part, it hasn't taken much hold in England. It's uniquely Haitian, there's no real Haitian community here. It's a curious mixture of Roman Catholicism and traditional African religions, wherein the African divinities are equated and substituted with Roman Catholic saints.

"Those who practice *vodou* see no contradiction between their religion and the Christian aspects that are infused into it. There are good features to it, in that it can be used to promote healing and cleansing of the spirit. But there is a dark side as well that has gained the most attention. There are those who use it for divination which, as we know from their counterparts here in England, can be used to manipulate and cheat believers. There are the sacrifices of animals to obtain desired outcomes, or to appease the *vodou* saints. There are the curses – such as the *vodou* dolls and fetishes, and also through the use of the drums. And then there are the terrible bogey-man stories of the *vodou zombies* – the reanimated

375

walking dead, similar in some ways to the vampire stories found 'round the world, and particularly in the Eastern European mountains."

"And your personal thoughts about it?" I asked, knowing that Alton Peake was quite willing to expose charlatans, but he also kept an open mind.

"There are more things in Heaven and Earth, Watson," he quoted, "than are dreamt of in our friend's philosophy." He jerked a thumb in Holmes's direction with a smile. "I have *seen* things that defy the dictum that 'No ghosts need apply.'"

"Ha!" said Holmes, rising to his feet. "A discussion for another time." He walked to the shelf and returned the commonplace book to its spot. "Right now we're considering Mr. Enderby's situation. More research is needed, but I have the beginnings of a plan in mind."

"You already seem to have some idea about all this, Mr. Holmes," Enderby replied. "I can't imagine what you've heard in my story that might provide you with an understanding about what's going on."

"I believe you overestimate my grasp of the affair," countered Holmes, "but I do have an intimation where answers can be found, and certain aspects can be examined more closely. In truth, however, the only way to move forward is to catch this *vodou* drummer in the act." He looked at me, and then Peake. "The man will certainly be back tonight. Can you join me in setting a trap?"

Peake said, "Of course," and I added, "I've made arrangements to be free for the rest of the day."

Holmes nodded. "Then we should each pursue our different lines. Peake, can you delve more deeply into this *vodou* business? Clearly in this case it's only a contrived intimidation to obtain the journal, but the method presents certain curious aspects. And Watson – can you accompany Mr. Enderby back to his home in Hampstead and retrieve the journal, and read through it to see why it might be of interest?"

"Certainly."

"Excellent!" He turned to Enderby. "When you sent your wife away, was it obvious to anyone watching the house, or did you do it discreetly?"

"The latter. As nearly as I could arrange it, I've left the house with the impression that she's still there during the day. I have an excellent set of locks on the doors and bars on the windows – the house is rather lonely, after all, and I wanted my wife to feel secure – so anyone trying to get in would find it difficult, and he or she certainly believes in any case that my wife is still in residence."

"And there have been no signs of attempted entry?"

"Not as of this morning."

376

"Good. When you both retrieve the journal, get in and out as quickly and quietly as you can. Our drummer is unlikely to be watching during the day. Leave the impression that your wife is still at home. Then adjourn to The Spaniards Inn and wait until Peake and I join you – around sunset, I think. That should give us time to complete our research and get the pieces in place." He looked at the three of us. "Any questions?"

"Mr. Enderby," I said, shifting forward in my chair, "you indicated that you haven't mentioned plans to use your youthful Haitian experiences in your new novel, but I do recall from your most recent book, *The Regent's Solicitations*, published just a few weeks ago, that there is a minor character, Davison, who references in passing a similar trip to Haiti while in his teens. Knowing that you reuse background characters in following novels as the main protagonists, is this fellow to be the main character in your new book?"

"He is, and bless me, Doctor, and that's very perceptive of you. I'm thrilled to learn that you must have already read the new novel."

I nodded. "I enjoy your books a great deal, and I picked up the new volume at Hatchard's in Piccadilly on publication day."

"Thank you for mentioning that, Watson," interjected Holmes. "That small fact has some bearing on my thinking."

"That this recent interest in the journal only arose when someone saw a mention of Haiti in the new book?" asked Peake.

"Exactly. Are you sure, Mr. Enderby, that no one knows of your plans for the next book and its Haitian theme?"

Enderby sat back and thought for a moment, slowly shaking his head until he suddenly seemed to remember something. "I was at a small gathering at a bookstore in Bloomsbury, answering questions about the new novel, and I told the store owner that I was researching my next book. I explained that in addition to my own journal from when I traveled there in my teens, I might be interested in seeing what they had that was available in terms of a Haitian history volume to supplement my own journal and already-gathered materials. Perhaps someone who was there overheard me mention the journal . . . ."

Holmes nodded. "Quite possibly. Now, if there's nothing else, let us separate to our various tasks. Peake and I will arrive shortly after sunset. Then we'll let this drummer walk into our trap."

We all put on our coats and hats and trooped downstairs together. Outside, Holmes and Peake set off walking toward Marylebone, bent together in conversation, while Enderby and I found a hansom for the long climb to Hampstead.

Having traveled across much of the world in my youth, and a few times to that part of the world, I was full of questions, and Enderby was

377

happy to provide more information about his past journey to the little-known Caribbean island.

"My first full day in Haiti was quite a surprise. Remember, I was just a lad who had barely traveled around the southern parts of England. When we arrived at our destination the night before, it was dark. Only when I awakened could I see just how foreign this land was to my experiences.

"We were up early that first full day for the final push to our destination. As I mentioned, we were to sail fifteen or twenty miles to La Gonave, an island situated in the middle of the bay, which is rather shaped like a fish surrounded by crab claws on that end of the main island of Hispaniola, where Columbus first landed in 1492. Haiti occupies the western side of the island, and the Dominican Republic takes the eastern – and much more prosperous – half. But prosperity isn't safety, as the Dominican Republic was involved in a war just then. Fortunately, it didn't spill over into Haiti, which had its own problems.

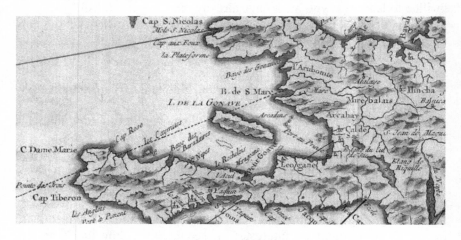

Haiti and La Gonave

"Much of the island, and particularly La Gonave, was already irrevocably damaged then by all of the logging that had been done for decades to build ships. I'm sure that it's only worse now. The climate had changed, leaving it quite barren and brown – not what one would expect to find in a Caribbean island, and quite different from the Dominican Republic not that far to the east. The Haitian people live in incredible poverty, and La Gonave is worse than the rest of the county – not even acknowledged by the official government, and receiving little or no assistance. This was where the missionary, Jack, had asked us to go and serve.

378

"A part of me had wondered about these mission trips that had been supported by our church, and what I'd find when we arrived. There had been some joking during the months of preparation about how we were secretly going to Monte Carlo or some other pleasant spot, but in fact we were visiting a most unpleasant and possibly dangerous place. The eight men, all of whom had businesses or comfortable positions that allowed them to leave the country for several months at a time, were truly dedicated to the work, as I quickly saw, and their willingness to return on multiple occasions spoke well of their character."

He went on to describe the monotony of the days as work continued to build the little church, and also what they did to have a bit of fun.

"One day, David Mayer and I took the afternoon off to climb the mountain behind us, giving us a wonderful overall view of how our village lay in relation to the surrounding countryside. The view down to Anse-à-Galets was much clearer up there as well. On another day, we were running short on water – always a concern, especially as so much was being used to make concrete for the blocks, and also simply for the visiting water-fat Englishmen. We obtained various buckets, pitchers, and gourds, and set off to the north to another village to buy water – much to the displeasure of the matriarch, who felt that such work was beneath us and should be left to the women. (That was according to Daniel, our translator.) We walked through several other villages of equivalent sizes, and then through a market town of twenty or more buildings, all of which were selling vegetables, before finding a house with a cistern that would sell us water. Carrying it back was much worse than you can imagine, especially, as we had wandered so far to find it.

"Occasionally the village was visited by agents of the dictator's secret police. The mood was always subdued during that time, and I was dimly aware that there was a feeling of danger in the air, but nothing ever came of it, and eventually the policemen would wander on, either on foot, or riding on donkeys.

"And still our routine continued. I became strong and brown and slept wonderfully each night. I made friends with many of the laborers, and we tried to communicate – although I suspect that the Creole phrases that they taught me were off-color, for their own amusement. The more I got to know the men from our church, the more I knew them as people. They often surprised me – also occasionally telling humorous stories, or simply sharing aspects of their normal lives that they found frustrating. As a nineteen-year-old, it was a very surprising and important introduction into what it meant to be an adult.

"Things that had bothered me at first – gigantic insects and massive tarantulas hiding under every surface and in each nook and cranny –

379

become nothing more than things to be ignored or brushed aside. I thought of home, realizing that wars could have begun and family members lost and we wouldn't know the difference. The days ran together, and by the time of the storm, and the drumming, I'd lost track of how long we'd been there, and how much longer our journey was intended to continue. Each day was so much like the previous one, and it was a simple life with clear tasks from sunup to sunset, and then deep dreamless sleep."

He then asked me about some of my own experiences, as he'd read my published works and picked up on the hints and allusions to past adventures of my own. The conversation then turned to writing methods, and how he strictly plotted each of his books, with strands stretching forward and backward into his other works, while I recorded actual events, but necessarily changed names and dates on occasion to protect the innocent from needless scrutiny and exposure of their secrets. And so we whiled away the slow journey northwest into the higher elevations above the Thames valley.

We reached Whitestone Pond, and I glanced to my right, along East Heath Road, as I always did when passing this way. I couldn't see Charles Augustus Milverton's old house, but I would never forget that night, and how Holmes and I had kept to the shadows before returning to this intersection, to then make our way more sedately back toward Hampstead village. Then our hansom turned on Spaniards Road alongside the Heath, and our conversation resumed.

We passed the inn and continued around to the northeast. Soon Bishop's Wood stretched away to the north, and not long after, our weary horse turned down the lane indicated by Enderby, bringing us to a most tidy little house tucked in the trees and set well back from the main road.

Asking the cabbie to wait, we walked to the front door, while I looked around, hoping to see if we were being watched. There was no sign of it, as the forest was deep and dark on nearly every side, and I could only trust Holmes's idea that no one would be observing us at this time of day, several hours before the drumming typically began.

We stepped inside, and from the entryway I could see that it was a well-kept abode. Mrs. Enderby had a good sense of what made a nice home, and I knew that my own wife would enjoy my descriptions of it. Alas, I was unable to see very much of it, as Enderby excused himself and went upstairs to retrieve the journal, leaving me alone by the front door. He returned in just a moment, and then we stepped back outside. He locked the door, tested it, and we returned to the cab. Our travel back along Hampstead Lane and then to the Spaniards Inn went quickly and, after Enderby paid the cabbie a sizeable amount and tip, we went inside, finding a quiet corner and ordering both cider and a late but hearty lunch. And

380

there we spent the afternoon and early evening, Enderby making notes on a manuscript that he had also retrieved from his home, while I read the Haitian journal.

I could see very quickly that Enderby's description of his earlier self as "naïve" was accurate – and I wondered if it was still true. Certain things that he had recorded when he was nineteen seemed to leap off the page, and yet he hadn't mentioned them, implying that he hadn't read between the lines in his own journal. Borrowing a sheet of blank paper from the noted author, I made a number of notes to share with Holmes when he and Peake arrived later that evening.

The time passed quickly enough and, after completing my examination of the journal, I shared a long conversation with the innkeeper, an old friend who I had first known in the late eighties when Holmes and I, stopping at the Spaniards for a restorative whisky, had been drawn into the unexpected rescue of the man's daughter, taken as leverage to force him into providing an alibi for a planned jewel theft. He had been grateful ever since, and it was always a pleasure to renew our acquaintance.

Just before sunset, Holmes and Peake arrived, and with them was Inspector Youghal, whom I hadn't seen in several months. Holmes introduced him to Enderby, and while our client repeated his story for the policeman, Holmes, Peake, and I spoke quietly at the bar.

"Only two of the original nine church members to make the trip are still alive," Peak related. "Welsh, Birch, Roberts, and Tipton were all around seventy or older in 1864, and have passed away from natural causes. Brown and Mayer were in their fifties, and died in 1889 and 1893, respectively. Bill Brewford, the youngest of the adults on the trip, was only forty at the time. He died in 1877, having rescued three children from a burning building. While there wasn't time to fully investigate whether there were darker aspects to the deaths, it seems that there was nothing unnatural about any of them – and there were no signs that any type of *vodou* curse was involved."

"And Reverend Anderson," I asked. "The other survivor? Holmes, you had him documented in your scrapbooks for a reason."

"Quite true. He has come to my attention before, although there has never been a way to bring charges against him. The man has had a history of molesting women from the churches where he's been a pastor – although the laws and the circumstances have conspired to allow him to get away with it. I've been keeping track of him for several years, after first becoming aware of him in the mid-nineties by way of a story told to me by a despondent maid who needed my help. I knew that Anderson's day would come, and when I heard his involvement with this affair, I

381

thought that now might be the time. Hearing that he's the only other living member of the expedition besides our client is highly indicative."

"And what you've stated fits with what I read in Enderby's journal," I said softly, going on to explain that Enderby himself didn't seem to realize what he'd innocently observed and recorded so many years earlier. I flipped open the sturdy book and, referring to my notes, showed Holmes page after page of where Enderby had noted that Reverend Anderson appeared to be paying a great deal of unwanted attention to the young lady, Marulla, who had returned to her village to help with the care of the visitors. "All this, plus the many occasions where he documents Anderson's many off-color stories and jokes, paint a vivid picture of the man that is much more rounded in a dark way than the simple mentions of his presence when Enderby told us of the trip."

Holmes nodded. "Excellent, Watson. This explains why the journal has assumed such importance, and augments what facts I was able to discover with my own research."

I nodded toward the inspector across the room. "So Youghal's presence means more than the simple arrest of the harassing drummer."

"Indeed. The case may have international implications. In 1866, a Haitian man in his twenties named Daniel Toussaint arrived in Paris, attempting to find out about a group of Englishmen who had been on La Gonave two years earlier. Soon after they had left Haiti, the body of a young woman, identified as Marulla Laurent, had been found buried under a pile of stones near her village – in what passed for the local cemetery. Due to the remote nature of the area, and the Haitian government's indifference to La Gonave, attempts to obtain some sort of justice went nowhere. Daniel – who was certainly the translator described by Enderby – saved his funds and journeyed to Paris."

"But why didn't he go straight to England?" I asked.

"I would speculate that it was due to Haiti's long-standing relationship with France, from whom they gained their independence nearly one-hundred years ago. Perhaps he felt that France was the place to begin his search, and if he could get the French to take an interest, he'd have more clout when he shifted his efforts to England."

"But how do you know this?" asked Peake. "That's quite a bit of specific information to obtain in one afternoon."

"Watson and I are quite fortunate to know a most notable and gifted French policeman, François le Villard of the *Sûreté*. Over the years, he has become masterfully organized, and my shot in the dark in his direction paid off beyond measure. I had cabled him to ask if he had any records related to possible crimes in Haiti in 1864, and specifically taking place on La Gonave. I was simply hoping for any indication about some incident

382

that might have occurred then to explain what was happening now. I only asked to make sure that I'd looked under every stone, having no hope that anything useful would be uncovered. Luckily le Villard has an encyclopedic knowledge of the Sûreté's unsolved and still-open cases, and he recalled seeing a report from nearly forty years before about Daniel Toussaint's visit and how, when he wasn't satisfied with the indifferent French response to his queries, he'd indicated that he was next sailing for England. Nothing more was ever heard from him, and as relations between England and France were tense then – you will recall that Britain had refused to join the French plan to aid the Confederacy, afraid of assisting the Confederate traitors and angering the legitimate American government, and also England rebuffed Napoleon III's attempt to gain British support when he invaded Mexico to forcibly place his lackey, Maximilian I, on the throne. Thus, there was no follow-up to determine what happened to Daniel Toussaint."

I tapped the journal. "I fear that he came to a bad end."

"Very likely. And perhaps, after all these years, we'll learn what happened to him, and see justice for Marulla Laurent as well."

Holmes spent several minutes intensely reading through various parts of the journal, nodding occasionally and muttering to himself, while Peake related to me some of the additional details regarding the prosaic and uncursed deaths of the Haitian construction party. Then, when Holmes had concluded his research, we rejoined Enderby and Youghal, and Holmes noted that it was now dark enough for Enderby to start for home, as if returning from work on a normal day, and the rest of us to make the short journey to Bishop's Wood, where plans were already in place to capture the mysterious *vodou* drummer.

"Enter the house as normal," advised Holmes, "and then simply go about your business. You will almost certainly hear the drums begin anew. Don't leave the house as you have on previous nights. Instead, when we have the drummer in hand, we'll bring him to you."

"You know who it is, don't you?" asked the author.

"We believe so, and tonight should provide us with the evidence we need to see the end of this business."

Saying goodbye to the innkeeper, Enderby climbed into a nearby hansom cab while the rest of us hailed a growler. After letting Enderby gain a head start, we set out along the same route, and in less than ten minutes, we'd been set afoot a few hundred yards from Enderby's lane. Then, with Holmes leading the way, we entered the woods, stepping carefully through the ancient trees in the last of the dying daylight.

When we'd gone a distance from the road, Holmes drew us aside by a great oak and whispered. "I scouted the woods earlier today and found where the drummer has been conducting his singular performances, and also the route by which he arrives and departs. It was then easy to set various Irregulars in place to catch him. When he begins, we'll interrupt the concert and drive him into our trap. Now, this way." And he turned and led us deeper through the silent forest.

Fortunately for that time of year, sunset was early, and it was a mild night. Holmes placed us behind several trees and indicated a general area toward the south where we should direct our attention. "Be careful when we go forward to capture him," he added. "Don't blunder into the Irregulars' trap."

I raised an eyebrow, which he saw but chose to ignore, my question being just what sort of trap to expect. I knew that he wouldn't say, too interested in providing a surprising performance, in the same way that a magician doesn't reveal quite what to expect until the trick actually occurs. I tried to imagine the Irregulars – that band of urchins who were so at home in the London streets, carrying out tasks as Holmes's agents – out here in the woods, seemingly far out of their element. Yet I knew that they were quite adaptive and clever, and whatever Holmes had asked of them would not be beyond their capabilities.

I have waited in many worse places, and the time passed quickly. It almost surprised me that we hadn't waited longer when the drum began.

At first, from somewhere ahead of us, it was a single beat, repeated as one monotonous tone at the pace of a resting heart. I tried to recognize if there were any added points of emphasis, breaking it into the rhythms recognized in the western world of the 4:4 march or the 3:4 waltz, but there was none of that. I had tried to count – "One – two – three – four" – but soon it became meaningless. The terrible insistence and pondering regularity began to cause an involuntary response – intimations of something older than man and his pitifully arrogant civilizations, built on darker foundations, with no true permanence. And then, when the beat had gone on long enough to cause my own heart to be synchronous with it, a complexity was introduced.

The steady pulse continued, but other flourishes were added – an extra doubling here, and preemptive strike there, sometimes doubled or tripled, but never quite in a way that could be predicted, or perhaps part of a bigger pattern than could be retained and recalled consciously before it began anew. It was the same as had been demonstrated in the sitting room by Enderby and then copied by Holmes – but now, in the dark and suddenly dangerous-feeling woods, it was real, and in my ignorance, somehow I understood.

I could only imagine Holmes and Peake's sharp interest as the complexity of the pattern increased, and I wondered what poor Youghal must be thinking. But I knew that the man was a steady as a rock, and with a rock's imagination as well, so I was certain that he was simply waiting for Holmes's call to action – and when it came, we were ready.

Ahead of us, as the drum continued its assault on our nerves and sensibilities, there was suddenly a high-pitched scream, and then another, followed by a dozen more. Enderby had mentioned nothing like this – surely it was the Irregulars, part of Holmes's plan.

It must have worked, because the drumming stopped. Even as Holmes yelled for us to follow him forward, I heard the sound of scrambling through the brush, and then a cry – from an adult, a man. The screams turned to boys' yells jeering and hollering with joy at the apparent success of their efforts. We entered a clearing just as a number of dark lanterns were opened to reveal a most curious site.

In a great arc on the far side of the clearing was a network of stretched ropes, tied from tree to tree, stretching from the ground to waist-height. Anyone running in that direction in the dark wouldn't have seen them, and would have been blocked from escape, bouncing back before understanding what had happened. On the ground nearby was a man, trapped under a great net, working frantically but uselessly to extricate himself, and hurling ever-stronger curses toward the dozen or so gleeful boys dancing around him. Nearby was a long drum, and as we arrived, one of the lads, taller than the others, leaned forward and stood it upright, giving three taps on the stretched skin top with his thumb. It was clearly the same instrument that had worked so effectively just minutes before – but now it was nothing but a curious artifact, diminished to insignificance.

Holmes and Youghal stepped forward, reaching across the net to lay hands on the trapped man's collar and yank him upright, while Peake congratulated the boys on their fine work. They calmed down to watch as Holmes worked the net from the captured drummer, revealing a heavy-set old man, his white hair wild upon his head, and a snarl of rage twisting his reddish features. He began to curse in a most un-Godly way, and Holmes gave him a shake.

"Not in front of the children."

The boys laughed, and then Holmes handed over the prisoner to the inspector and walked to the tallest lad. He provided words of praise, and then fished a substantial amount of coinage from his pocket, which was transferred to the Irregulars' current leader – an older boy named Creighton Cross. Then, their work done, they began chattering amongst themselves as they drifted away into the trees, back toward the road. In seconds, it was as if they had never been there.

Meanwhile, Youghal, who had cuffed the old man's hands behind him, stated, "You're fair caught, Anderson. Now let's go somewhere and talk about it."

With Holmes leading the way, we soon reached the back of Enderby's house, where we found a note on the back step – a duplicate of the six that had proceeded it. Holmes looked at it and then passed it to Peake and me without comment as we climbed the stairs and knocked on the door.

Inside, it took Enderby several moments to comprehend that we had a prisoner, and he had no initial recognition of the elderly and disheveled disgraced minister. Only when we told him who it was did he begin to see some points of familiarity.

"But why?" he asked the minister, who refused to look at him, instead muttering under his breath and invoking meaningless curses upon all of us.

Holmes then began to explain what he had learned earlier in the day, to Enderby's shocked amazement. When I pulled out the journal, Anderson became quiet, his eyes focused on it like some sort of lizard who is suddenly deathly still before striking. Youghal took a firmer grip on him.

As Holmes spoke, he shifted his attention from Enderby to Anderson. "The journal clearly shows your interest in the girl, as well as her distaste for your unpleasant regard. It's all recorded there, even if Mr. Enderby, at the age of nineteen, naively didn't realize what he was seeing, or if he gave you the benefit of the doubt because of his respect for your position." Holmes glanced at Enderby. "In your colorful recollections, you note that the hillside behind the village was dotted with various graves, randomly located instead of localized in a cemetery. You describe these as cairns, with the bodies covered by local stones, such as the ones you used to line the floor of the new church."

He shifted his attention back to Anderson. "Daniel Toussaint, your interpreter, came to Paris in 1866, two years after your visit. He reported that days after your group departed, the girl was discovered in one of these graves. Wild dogs had dug her up. She was horribly violated, and then whoever killed her had opened an old grave, placed her there, and then restacked the stones. Based on your history, Anderson, can there be any doubt of your responsibility – especially since you were instrumental in getting your group out of the country as soon as possible?"

"Girl?" replied the old man. "She was a tease – flirting with all of us. If there was a murder, it was one of the others – Brown or Tipton or Birch. Or this one!" he snarled, jerking his head toward Enderby. "He talked with her quite a bit, as I recall."

Holmes shook his head. "No. After you left your home this afternoon, you were followed on your various errands before winding up in the woods

386

with your drum." He glanced toward the policeman and then continued. "After you departed, I happened to find myself within your quarters, where I noticed that you also kept a set of extensive and well-hidden journals – going back well past 1864." Youghal pointedly ignored this bit of burglary, and Holmes pulled several little shabby and much-fondled leather books from his coat pocket.

"Men such as yourself," he continued, "need to relive their crimes. You're really quite proud of them – or so one would think, reading your rather prosy descriptions of what you did. You are especially boastful of how you killed the girl on that last night and then – cleverly, in your own opinion – thought of where to hide the body. I'm not sure how you contained yourself on the journey home, so thrilled you seemed to be at getting away with it and then successfully escaping. It almost makes the description of how you killed Daniel Toussaint in 1866, when he came to England to find you, seem dull and rote by comparison."

Anderson began to lunge this way and that, seemingly trying to pull his arms from their sockets as he jerked one and then the other, trying to retrieve the journals from Holmes's firm grasp. Youghal was compelled to restrain him more effectively, leaving the old killer gasping on the floor.

"I'll need to take your journal with me as evidence," explained the inspector to Enderby.

"Of course," eyeing it in my hands with great distaste. "I shan't be needing it back. It's of no use to me now."

I understood that whatever his next book would be, there would be no reference to Haiti.

Garrison Anderson's arrest set off a small hurricane of interest. There were international implications, as France was interested in his capture, and hoped to use the event to gain some goodwill between itself and Haiti, with help from England. Meanwhile, more and more women came forward to indicate that they, too, had been molested by the minister under the guise of "marriage counseling". In several cases, he had then blackmailed them, based on the situations in which they found themselves.

More information was uncovered related to Anderson's activities at the time of the "schism" described by Enderby at his boyhood church, a few years after the trip to Haiti. The principal minister at the time, Reverend Regal Black, had come forward to describe a number of rumors that had divided the church at the time, with many unflinchingly and ignorantly supporting Anderson in the face of certain revelatory accusations. All too often, ignorant fools follow blindly after immoral and evil men.

387

It was unclear what the immediate future held for the disgraced killer between his arrest and the hangman – Would he be held in England, or transported for trial in Haiti as part of some convoluted diplomatic arrangement?

In the end, he cheated all of the different outcomes. One of the women with whom he'd had a relationship, refusing to believe his guilt in the face of overwhelming evidence, managed to visit him in prison, bringing a double-dose of lethal cyanide. The two of them were found not long after her arrival, their limbs twisted in what must have been agony upon the floor, and their lips covered with foam. The woman's husband of thirty-two years was shocked, and he grieved for her terribly. No one was concerned about Anderson's fitting and long-overdue passage into Hell.

Holmes had confirmed that Anderson was visiting the Bloomsbury bookshop on the day Enderby that answered readers' questions, and it was generally felt that this was when he must have heard of Enderby's plan to use the journal for a future book – causing him to fear exposure, and to set in motion the bizarre plan to intimidate the author into giving him the journal. It was also agreed that if much more time had passed without result, Anderson would have killed again.

Before his death, Anderson never provided any information about his crimes, and Daniel Toussaint's body was never recovered.

Peake found a new interest in the practices of *vodou*, which stood him in good stead when he had call to investigate certain matters in the coming years. I maintained a friendship with Enderby, and was later surprised to find a disguised version of myself acting as a character in one of his novels.

And I accidentally learned some years later, without his knowledge that I knew, that Sherlock Holmes had made a sizeable contribution to a Haitian missionary organization in Port-au-Prince to see about making long necessary improvements and restorations at the small church in the village of Petite Source, on the much neglected island of La Gonave.

NOTE

By interesting coincidence, I was also able to make a trip to the small village of Petite Source on La Gonave, in Haiti, when I was nineteen years old in the summer of 1984. Even more coincidental was the fact that I accompanied eight older men from my church who had made the same trip several times before. In fact, my journey mirrored Enderby's pretty-much exactly – without any murders – except that I traveled from eastern Tennessee instead of England.

On our second day in Haiti, we departed the main island from a dock near Port-au-Prince on a small overloaded sailboat with a tree limb for a mast (See Photo 1 – that's me in shorts and T-shirt at the left edge of the stacked boxes). Once on La Gonave, we traveled to a small three-building settlement where we helped to build a church, replacing the existing stick structure (Photo 2, with the home-made days-old cinder blocks going up around the existing stick building). The village really did have a matriarch and her aged-before-his-time husband (with whom I'm posing in Photo 3 in front of the finished church).

The daily work and living conditions in 1984 were just as described in this story. And most interesting of all (and tragic), the lightning strike that killed the young boy – whose three other brothers had also recently been killed by lightning – really occurred, as did the unsettling vodou (voodoo) drums which began playing somewhere above us on the mountainside the next night.

There were no murders, however, and none of the eight men on the trip resemble those described in Watson's narrative – and none of our party were criminals. We didn't pack up and leave the day after the drums played. Instead, we remained until the church was completed, although we did depart a bit earlier than planned because our continued presence was placing a huge water-burden upon the small village.

– DM

The Burglary at Undershaw
by Tim Symonds

The war against the German Kaiser had broken out. I engaged a locum *to run my surgery in Queen Anne Street and offered my services to the Royal Army Medical Corps. Orders arrived. I was to report within the week to a camp on the Western Front, part of the chain of evacuation. These Casualty Clearing Stations were expanding into forward areas, and in some cases could take up to one-thousand patients. Life would become very risky.*

*I boarded a comfortable barouche outside Cox and Company, my bank at Charing Cross, en route to Gray's Inn to discuss my will with solicitors, as it hadn't been updated in quite a while. While most of my possessions would go to my wife, certain objects would go to the 66th (Berkshire) Regiment, some to Scotland Yard's famous "Black Museum", others to our dear former landlady Mrs. Hudson at 221b Baker Street. Particular objects of great sentimental value would go to my old friend Sherlock Holmes. These would include the watch inherited from my brother and the travel-worn and battered tin dispatch-box with "*John H. Watson, MD, Late Indian Army*" painted on the lid.*

A similar box rested on the opposing seat of the carriage which had been taking me hither and thither around London's thoroughfares as I assembled the many medical and personal items, including a number of old documents and souvenirs, that I wished to keep with me at the Front.

I reached across and lifted the lid of the tin box. At the top lay my old water-bottle which had accompanied me at the dreadful Battle of Maiwand, and a pair of brown leather high length field service boots, and also a clipping from a long-ago Sunday newspaper, the ink beginning to fade. The article was accompanied by a press photograph of me emerging from 221b Baker Street, a startled look on my face. Reading it once more, I was transported from the dense traffic and noisome air of Trafalgar Square to an Edwardian idyll, a cricket match in rural Surrey played on the small estate of my sportif literary agent, A.C. Doyle . . . .

The match took place in the summer of 1907, six years into the reign of Edward, the sybarite King of the United Kingdom of Great Britain and Ireland and the British Dominions, and Emperor of India. For some weeks beforehand, Sherlock Holmes had taken up temporary occupation of our old quarters in Baker Street, while working on a most-urgent matter for

391

the Government. Our quondam landlady, the indefatigable Mrs. Hudson, was beside herself with joy to have her old tenant back in the rooms, however temporary. I tried to visit there as often as I could.

The matter reported in the newspaper cutting actually began one Saturday when I stopped by the sitting room for breakfast but Holmes was still abed. I glanced through the windows at the louring clouds, then appreciatively at the crackling fire that dear Mrs. Hudson had constructed like a work of art earlier that morning. I took the morning copy of *The Times* from the breakfast table to a fireside chair. The latest outbreak of Spy Fever was discussed, with rumours of German secret agents under every bed. A new Secret Service Bureau with nineteen military intelligence departments was to be established, particularly concentrating on the activities of the Imperial German Government. The search was on for its first Director.

I turned to *The British Medical Journal*. Correspondence headed, "*Meteorological Conditions And Enteric Fever*" caught my eye. It was a discussion on the dramatic annual reappearance of enteric fever in South Africa during rains which reached maximum strength between November and March. The fever was of particular interest to me. A Jezail bullet struck me on the shoulder at the grievous Battle of Maiwand, shattering the bone and grazing the subclavian artery. This alone might not in itself have been sufficient to lead to a medical discharge on a small wound pension from Army service. Catching enteric fever – the curse of our India possessions – during my recovery at the base hospital at Peshawar was. "*The enteric season in Natal,*" the correspondent wrote, "*as probably in all countries, seems to be due to the pollution of the water supply with infected soil-washings.*"

I was considering composing a letter to *The Journal* supporting the letter-writer's conclusions when I heard Mrs. Hudson's familiar tread mounting the stairs.

I got to my feet and turned to greet her, only to be astounded by her appearance as she stood smiling at me, hand outstretched with the small envelope. Had I not been entirely familiar with her normal appearance and the accent of her social class, I would have sworn our landlady had transmogrified into a rather advanced-in-age American Gibson Girl. She was clad in the ideal walking costume for the wet weather – a short leather-lined wool skirt, a wool jacket, both in greys with a tone of heliotrope in them, and also dark blues (inclining to purple rather than indigo). Her hair was piled high upon her head in the contemporary waterfall-of-curls fashion, topped by a soft woollen rinking cap. Thick-soled walking boots came halfway to the knee to protect her ankles and calves from dampness.

"In case you are wondering, Doctor," she informed me, "I'm setting off now for the United Procession of Women rally in Hyde Park, regardless of – " She pointed at the window. " – the weather. I'll have my ermine hand-muff with me. Keir Hardy and Mrs. Millicent Fawcett are going to speak. It would do you good to attend, Doctor. Men should agree that it isn't right when more than half the adults in your own country don't have the right to vote – and for why? Just because we are women?"

"As a matter of fact, Mrs. Hudson," I replied, "I'm in favour of women getting the vote."

"Then I shall look forward to seeing you at Marble Arch," came the reply.

As Mrs. Hudson left the room, she said, "Don't forget to bring your umbrella! I shall recognise you by it if you get lost in the crowd."

Later, when I was back home, I received a telegram, originating in Hindhead. I stretched towards the mantel for the bamboo paper knife, a souvenir of my former life in the Far East, and slit open the envelope. The telegram was from my long-standing literary agent, Arthur Conan Doyle. He wrote, "*I have challenged J.M. Barrie and the exotically-named Allahakbarries Cricket team to a match against an Authors and Actors team under my captaincy.*" The winning side would take home a silver loving cup. He was an umpire short – Would I volunteer? The other umpire would be the South African, Frank Grey. The telegram continued, "*I realise rugby was your game, but as long as you played cricket at your school – *" (which I had) – he would instruct the players to obey my decisions, however faulty. He had already planned the pitch to suit his own bowling – slows with a puzzling flight – rather than Barrie's left-arm spin. If I had any bias, he added, "*it is to manifest itself in favour of my team*", not Barrie's. Almost as an afterthought he added, "*I told the editor of* Colliers Magazine *he can have 'The Adventure of the Bruce-Partington Plans' (once you've got it to me) if* Colliers *commissions Frederic Dorr Steele for the illustrations. He has agreed. Your remuneration will be substantial.*"

I accepted the invitation to umpire. Two or three days in the short, comfortable Hindhead summer, away from the mud and dung of the Capital's streets would do me a power of good, mentally and physically.

An hour later, I had composed a letter to *The British Medical Journal*. I pointed out that typhoid, otherwise called enteric fever, was mainly caused by *Salmonella enterica serovar Typhi* and, to a lesser extent, by *S. Paratyphi A.*, and that humans are the only reservoir for these organisms, the main sources of transmission being contaminated water, food, and flies. Good sanitation was the answer. I could post it *en route* to Marble

393

Arch. Despite the heavy weather, I would keep my promise to march with Mrs. Hudson and the Suffragists.

The familiar white triumphal Marble Arch came into view as I strode along Oxford Street. To my surprise, there was no large rally anywhere to be seen. Our landlady had failed to tell me that the park at Speaker's Corner was simply the spot to gather like swallows and swifts assembling to migrate southwards, before setting off on the march to the Strand. I turned to make my way back to Baker Street when a burst of raucous laughter drew me towards a considerable throng around a soap-box speaker. In an American accent, he was recounting how he had led a merry life of crime across the Atlantic as a "professional" burglar – now forcibly retired from the fray – who for several years had enjoyed rich pickings among the wealthy houses along a stretch of Long Island shoreline. He was a man of about thirty-five, not tall, athletic-looking, topped by a witty choice of headgear entirely incongruous in the wet and windy weather – a debonair semi-formal summer affair of plaited straw stiffened and sewn in a spiral, the flat crown encircled by a striped grosgrain ribbon. When someone shouted out, "Why did you go into that profession in the first place?" he quoted E. W. Hornung's burglar Raffles: "Why settle down to some humdrum uncongenial billet, when excitement, romance, danger, and a decent living were all going begging together?"

A droll fifteen minutes ensued. He swept off the boater and leapt down among the appreciative crowd, head down, checking the value of the coins being dropped into the collection. I reached into a trouser pocket. Too late I remembered I had only the one coin with me, a half-crown, two-and-a-half times the value of the shilling coin I had decided upon. The American was now in front of me, head down still, looking into his kitty. I dropped the half-crown on top of the assembly of small coins. It contrasted favourably with the ha'pennies, pennies, and the occasional thruppenny bit. The erstwhile burglar's head came up in surprise. For a fraction of a second our eyes met. With a nod of thanks, he moved on.

The next day, I arrived at 221b to find a buff-coloured envelope sealed with red wax. It was from Henry Judson Raymond, addressed to me. It read:

Dear Dr. Watson, or, as the Lakota/Dakota Sioux greeting goes: "Hau",

I was flattered by your presence in my audience at Speaker's Corner yesterday and the substantial coin you placed in my hat to show appreciation. I shall be back on my

394

*soap-box this Sunday around two-thirty, where I shall regale
everyone with a masterpiece of my career in crime, a singular
burglary I carried off at The Hamptons on Long Island last
June, before Pinkertons picked up my scent and obliged me to
escape to your wonderful country or suffer a lengthy term of
imprisonment in the Sing-Sing Correctional Facility. I hope
you will again flatter me with your attendance (and a further
half-crown).*

*Sincerely,
Henry Judson Raymond II*

*P.S. If you do come, this time bring a real half-crown please.
I'm told half the forged coins in your country consist of
Georgian half-crowns. The one you dropped into my hat was
one of them (which I have, however, successfully passed on).*

On Sunday, I decided that I would return to Speaker's Corner. The
United States was an innovative society, exemplified by the famous Singer
Sewing machine, the phonograph, the first flushing toilets, and even safes.
It could be true of burglary. Precisely at two-thirty, the American walked
up to the waiting throng, with me among them. He stepped on to the soap-
box and said, "First, Ladies and Gentlemen, may I extend a welcome to
each and every one of you, and in particular one among you: The right-
hand man of Sherlock Holmes, the world's most famous detective. There
he is! Dr. John H. Watson, take a bow!"

My cheeks flushed with embarrassment. I stepped forward and gave
an encompassing wave and stepped back into anonymity.

At this, Henry Raymond began.

"I intend today to describe the most profitable burglary I ever
undertook, though it was to be my last in the United States, for reasons I
shall explain. It was in June – the eighth of June, as a matter of fact. When
it's summer, the greenery is full and offers valuable cover – laurel hedges
in particular."

He raised a large canvas bag from beside the soap-box.

"I got away with this sailor's kit bag full of gold plate, jewellery,
cash-laden wallets, and a half-dozen gold pocket watches. Back at my
home in Brooklyn, I discovered I also had a silver box containing two
prosthetic glass eyes. These I sent back by mail, a courtesy I now regret
because it led to my downfall."

He related how the owner of a fourteen-bedroom mansion was to hold
a sporting week-end for his wealthy golfing friends and business partners.

Center-shafted Schenectady putters would be made available to all. According to *The East Hampton Meteor*, an excellent time on lawns and links and the well-stocked bar was anticipated. To ensure the safety of the guests' valuables, the article continued, the owner had installed the latest electric burglar alarms, as well as upgrading his main safe to a Chatwood so that the famous lockmakers' craftsmanship would be on display – or rather "not on display", Raymond added, given the deed safe's decorative patterns blended seamlessly with the house's elegant floral designs, making the safe's location invisible to the eye.

He (Raymond) had, he explained, long since completed his apprenticeship on Chatwood's, but he needed someone inside the house well before the eighth to map where the safe was, when and where best to make entry – front door, back doors, windows, an unlatched roof-light – as well as marking out the creaky rungs on the staircases, and which electric bulbs should be partly unscrewed so they wouldn't light up the corridors when he entered during the small hours.

Most cunning of all, the "plant" taken on as temporary live-in member of staff for the gala event had deliberately tripped the newly-installed electric alarms randomly day and night, testing the friendship of staff and neighbourhood to the point the owner felt obliged to de-activate every one of them as faulty before the weekend started. Raymond ended, "However, I made one grievous error. I should have checked the guest list. Turns out one of them was William Pinkerton of the Pinkerton National Detective Agency. I had forgotten to remove my fingerprints from the glass eyes. The whole Agency was put on my track. I was obliged to flee the country of my birth. That, gentleman," he ended, "is why you have the pleasure of my company now – and why I rely entirely on England's generosity!"

At which he swept the boater off his head and jumped down to collect the copper coins, the occasional sixpenny piece, and my now-genuine half-crown.

It was buttercup time at the height of England's *belle époque*. The day came for the country-house cricket match. I took up my position behind the stumps as umpire. My literary agent stood side-by-side with the captain of the opposing team, whose theatre play *Peter Pan, or, The Boy Who Wouldn't Grow Up,* had done wonderfully well a few years earlier. On Doyle's team were two considerable writers of fiction, P.G. Wodehouse and E. W. Hornung, author of 'In the Chains of Crime', which introduced the gentleman-burglar Raffles and his sidekick, Bunny Manders. The hands of the clock just visible on the church moved to within a minute of eleven o'clock. Exactly on the hour, I would signal bowling could commence.

I took a last slow look around the pitch. It was a most attractive sight, one I would recall in exquisite detail eight years later when serving in the mud and slaughter of the Western Front against the Kaiser's Field armies. Barrie won the toss and elected to field. He was waiting impatiently at my side, ready to send his slow lobs down at the opening bat. Ludicrously, he set half-a-dozen slips for his bowling. His smartly pressed flannels were held up by a striped elastic belt with a snake clasp. Almost all the other fielders wore brightly-coloured silk ties around the waist instead of belts. Caps were garishly striped. Several of Barrie's team had donned silk shirts emulating the best batsman of his day, the dazzling Indian cricketer Ranjitsinhji, His Highness the Jam Sahib of Nawanagar. I took a last glance at the church clock and called out "Play!", transferring the first of six farthing coins from my right hand to my left, to be sure I kept the right count of balls per over.

Doyle smacked Barrie's opening delivery for four runs, the hard leather ball rattling against the spokes of a bicycle leaning against the centuries-old oak tree marking the southern boundary. Raucous cheers came from the "pavilion", a former first-class Pullman coach. The cheering grew less when Barrie brought on John Collis Snaith, a dangerous and greatly feared slow-medium left-hand bowler. My Literary Agent's batsmen's wickets began to tumble.

I had returned to London overnight. I had stopped by Baker Street, but Holmes was out. As I was turning to leave, I heard a carriage coming along Baker Street at a fast trot, stopping in front with the wheels scraping along the kerb. Curiously, I stepped across to the open window. Inspector Lestrade of Scotland Yard emerged from the hansom and looked up, giving me a wave. A moment later he bounded up the stairs and came into the sitting room, stating that he'd heard Holmes was temporarily staying in London.

I said, "Inspector, Holmes comes and goes. I'm sorry to say he isn't here."

"No matter, Doctor," Lestrade responded. "I had stopped here first before going on to Queen Anne Street, as it's you I want to speak to. I'm told you attended a cricket match yesterday."

"I did," I replied, surprised. "In Hindhead. I umpired. But why would you know that? And why would you come all the way here from the Yard to ask me about it? Are you a cricketing enthusiast?"

"I am not," came the immediate reply. "Something happened at Sir Arthur's house last night. As you were there all yesterday, I wonder if anything suspicious came to your attention?

"What sort of happening?"

"A most daring and successful burglary. A large haul of his and his guests' valuables from the safe."

"A burglar broke into the safe at Undershaw?" I parroted, staring at Lestrade in disbelief.

"A most daring and successful burglary," he repeated. "Carried out with the greatest professionalism. The miscreant wasn't only a diabolically clever criminal type. He must have emulated the stealthy and acrobatic movements of the cat. If he clambered up a stack pipe, no part of it was pulled from its moorings during the climb or descent. No soil-marks on the walls or roofing, no broken tiles. No footprints on the window-ledges. This was no rag-sorter or sewer worker turned night raider. He slipped away altogether unseen, unreported, uncaptured. If he entered by a skylight carelessly left open, your Literary Agent's insurers may contest whether it could even be deemed a burglary in legal terms. We urgently need an arrest. Did you catch sight of anyone lurking around in a suspicious manner?"

"Other than local villagers passing by, I saw only one non-cricketing person during the whole day, but he wasn't lurking – he was right out in the open, dressed up as a Red Indian doing a rain dance every hour on the hour. When he wasn't yowling and throwing his arms and legs around and passing round the hat for money, he disappeared into a wigwam. The rain dance worked. We abandoned the game in a downpour and declared a draw."

I paused, looking at Lestrade, suddenly realizing something.

"What do you mean 'with the greatest professionalism'?" I asked.

"Whoever it was must have planned it for months. The intruder knew what was what. Unauthorised entry to all the bedrooms would be relatively easy from the surrounding woodland, plus the boudoir and dressing room jewel safes far easier to crack than the Chatwood, but he didn't waste time with them. Sir Arthur asked the guests to place their valuables – watches, jewelled tie-pins, gold cufflinks, wallets – in the main deed safe. The burglar probably knew the doors of the house were unusual in that they open both ways – very useful in the dark. And as far as the stairs are concerned – "

But then a most remarkable thought sprang into my mind.

"Hold on, Lestrade," I interrupted. "Tell me: The light bulbs along the corridors leading to the deed safe – were they – ?"

" – Loosened just enough to stop them lighting up? They were."

"What of the stairs – ?" I prompted.

"Tiny chalk marks on the bannisters indicated which treads creaked."

"The electric burglar alarms?" I asked.

"De-activated by Sir Arthur ahead of the weekend. They'd been clanging off night and day, all of them false alarms waking the household and bringing the police rushing in."

"Inspector!" I exploded. "I believe I know your burglar! There's an American who has a soap-box at Speaker's Corner. He calls himself Henry something Raymond. That's exactly his *modus operandi*! Now that I think about it, there was something familiar about the hat that the Red Indian passed around for coins at Undershaw. It was exactly like the one this Henry Raymond passes around at Speaker's Corner – plaited straw with a flat crown encircled by a green-and-white-striped ribbon."

I proceeded to tell the attentive Lestrade how, some months earlier, I had stayed on in the rain at Speaker's Corner to listen to the "retired" American burglar describing his life of crime in America.

"This Henry Raymond said a burglary he conducted at a wealthy person's house on Long Island also took place in summer – on *June the eighth*! He made a particular point of the detail. He described how the summer greenery of the trees and laurels and stout creepers around the house offered useful cover – and yesterday was also the eighth of June! The burglary in America took place because the chap saw a piece in the Hampton newspapers saying the owner would be holding a weekend of partying and golf for twenty-four important guests. Here in England, Doyle's arrangements were fully described in the local press back in January, including the fact the guests would be comprised of twenty-two players and two umpires. Yesterday's arrangements were almost identical to the Long Island event, except it was cricket rather than golf."

Lestrade said, "If he's our man, that must be how he's organising his burglaries. He avoids meeting his accomplices face-to-face in case he's spotted with them. They would be mingling with the crowd around his soap-box. Through his fabricated stories he gives them instructions – the planned date, a description of which property, the parts each must play – all spelled out as though it was in the past rather than a heist in the offing."

Three hours later, Inspector Lestrade sent me a note, delivered by a Scotland Yard carriage. It read: *"Have enquired of the Long Island Police. I can confirm no such burglary took place in the Hamptons on or anywhere near 8th June that year. I shall personally arrest Raymond the moment he resumes his soap-box oratory at Speaker's Corner."*

Four days later Lestrade sent a further communication: *"Have taken Henry Judson Raymond into custody. The Undershaw haul has been recovered almost intact, and the Red Indian outfit and the wigwam too,*

399

and most significantly the boater which we shall need you to identify. Be ready to take the witness stand at the Old Bailey."

My appearance as a witness for the prosecution at the Old Bailey in Henry Raymond's trial came and went. The description I gave of the boater the Red Indian used to collect donations proved decisive. Raymond was sent down for three years. After the sentence was pronounced, I left the Old Bailey to walk back to Queen Anne Street, reflecting that if through extraordinary self-confidence verging on hubris Henry Raymond hadn't invited me to return to Speaker's Corner that Sunday, he might have got away with the burglary scot-free. Equally, because of Holmes's absences revisiting his old haunts in Southwark or Greenwich, I had come into my own. The case had relied almost entirely on my own powers of observation.

Summer passed to early autumn, a busy period at my surgery. I no longer contemplated on a near-daily basis what a loss to honest society the American had been, given his exceptional ability and charm. I went to a nearby Underground station to buy a newspaper. A *"Late Extra"* piece caught my eye: The Bulgarian Embassy had suffered a break-in overnight. Nothing had been stolen.

The following day was exceptionally hot and humid. I returned to the surgery from a constitutional in the cool of the Regent's Park. A handsome Rolls Royce Silver Ghost was parked a short distance from the entrance. The receptionist had shown a most unexpected visitor into my inspection room rather than the waiting room: Sir Edward Grey, Britain's Foreign Secretary. He was standing by the open window. On shaking hands, he went across to the mantel and stood with his arm stretched along it, looking at me pensively. Then he spoke, but rather than address me customarily as "Dr. Watson", a private citizen, unusually he referred back to my rank at the Battle of Maiwand, nearly thirty years before.

"Surgeon-Major," my visitor commenced, "I am here on the pretence that I'm suffering another bout of quartan fever. In reality, it's because the government believes war against the German Kaiser awaits us just over the horizon. I need you to agree to something which will augment England's safety – one might even say the Empire's safety. In these exceptionally dangerous times, I have given up my weekend of north-country pursuits, my bird watching, fly-fishing, and hill-walking, to come like Muhammad to the Mountain to ask you for the greatest favour you could grant me right now in my task as Foreign Secretary."

His fingers tapped on the mantel.

"Every day, Surgeon-Major," he went on, "I handle questions of war *and* peace . . . the fate of empires. We live in an age of political intrigue,

400

agents provocateurs, foreign anarchists, the many disguises behind which the foreign assassin or terrorist conceals himself. The danger posed by the *femme fatale* and her secret agents – "

"Great God!" I thought. "What could I possibly do of such magnitude to confront all that!"

Sir Edward continued, "What I ask of you will, I regret, inflict pain on your hard-earned reputation and, without doubt on your *amour propre*, though the Home Secretary has agreed it will not lead to your prosecution. For it to work, it must be public – there can be no private arrangements. All must seem legitimate. It concerns the American, Henry Judson Raymond the Second."

"To my prosecution!" I exclaimed. "What about him?" I asked. "Surely he's safely tucked away in Pentonville Prison?"

"He *was* in Pentonville, yes," my visitor returned. "Put there by your testimony at his trial, which is why I am here "Last week we leaned on the Home Secretary to release him quietly and for a specific reason. Now we fear the Home Secretary plans to order his deportation from Britain because his presence is deemed inconsistent with the public welfare. We at the Foreign Office don't want him sent back to America, and I shall tell you why: First-rate burglars are in short supply. Raymond's front-bench burglary skills have already been of the utmost value to us. In the event of war, our Royal Navy is meant to be the primary bulwark against the Imperial German Navy, yet despite the fact the Admiralty's Intelligence Department is its largest Division, it is still lacking in executive authority – lacking in numbers, lacking in brains, and lacking in training. Enemy spies are probing it all the time. Possibly you saw a reference in yesterday's newspapers to a break-in at the Bulgarian Embassy?"

"I did," I replied, "but as I recall, nothing was stolen."

"Something *was* stolen from the Embassy," came the rebuttal, "or rather, stolen *back* by Henry Raymond – a plan drawn up by the Admiralty marked '*Top Secret*'. I hardly need to tell you the designation means any compromise of the document could cause widespread loss of life, or else threaten the security or economic well-being of our country or friendly nations. It gave in exact detail the deployment of the Royal Navy if war breaks out – in particular, how we shall deploy the Grand Fleet against the German High Seas Fleet across the North Sea. In addition, it contained Admiralty Fleet orders and one-hundred photographs documenting alterations and additions to the battleship weapons systems, including the large-calibre guns. The plan was removed from the Royal Navy HQ and passed to the Bulgarians for a very large sum of money by someone in the Naval Department. In turn, the Bulgarians no doubt planned to sell it on to Berlin for a vastly larger sum."

"Why did you need Henry Raymond's services?" I asked. "Surely we have competent burglars of our own?"

"You'd think so, wouldn't you," Sir Edward agreed, "but spy burglary is a very much more delicate and difficult operation than common – or garden – burglary. I asked the Director of Military Operations if he could recommend one of his burglars and I explained why. He told me he had never come across one here who'd be up to an Embassy break-in – and that none of them could have broken into the home of your Literary Agent last June, given the safety measures put in place by Sir Arthur for his guests, even without the alarms. For a small Continental country, the Bulgarians take extraordinary precautions to safeguard their papers. Every window of their London premises is fitted with patent locking devices. Every door has on it a Yale lock and a Chubb mortice lock. Both skylights, even the French windows overlooking the back-garden, have four bolts and Chubb locking devices."

"Sir Edward," I pointed out, "as yet, I have no idea what any of that has to do with me. Why have you chosen to come here? What could you require of me?"

"Because you are the one who can ensure Henry Raymond stays here in England. The matter lies entirely in your hands."

"In my hands?" I repeated.

"Entirely," Sir Edward emphasised. "Specifically, his conviction at the Old Bailey. Henry Raymond's particular skills could prove to be of inestimable value to Great Britain in the years ahead – most of all, his hallmark untraceable methods of breaking in and exiting."

Again I asked, "We're talking about Henry Judson Raymond the Second?"

The Foreign Secretary nodded.

"We are. I should tell you in the utmost confidence that the stolen plan was faked up by the Royal Navy and had no resemblance to the real configuration the Grand Fleet will adopt at the outbreak of a European war, let alone the planned alterations and additions to the weaponry."

"I don't understand," I replied. "If the stolen plan gave inaccurate information on the deployment of our capital ships and the change in their armaments, why did you risk getting Raymond caught breaking into the Bulgarian Embassy to retrieve it?"

"If he'd got caught it could have had an equally convincing outcome. He was told to 'confess' we were his paymasters. We had to get the Bulgarians – and beyond them the Imperial German Navy – to believe His Majesty's Government wanted the plan back at all cost, thereby indicating it must be genuine. Of course, we gave them twenty-four hours to make copies for the Turks and Austro-Hungarians, as well as Berlin, before we sent Raymond in."

I protested, "Sir Edward, that still leaves me entirely mystified as to why you've come to see me – even why you address me as Surgeon-Major. We don't often meet, but you have always called me Dr. Watson."

"I used your former rank," came the reply, "to emphasise how aware I am of your patriotic support for the greatest Empire ever built – for your remarkable services to it. You walk with a slight limp, the effect of a wound from the Battle of Maiwand in gallant defence of the British Raj, the jewel in the Imperial crown."

"And therefore?" I asked.

"I need you to perform one further service to ensure the American remains in England: It may surpass in importance even fighting for your country at the dreadful Battle of Maiwand and suffering such a grievous wound . . . ."

The barouche was bogged down in the maelstrom of traffic in Trafalgar Square. The article I was reading was headed: *Shock Revelation: Sherlock Holmes's Amanuensis Confesses to Falsifying Testimony at the Old Bailey.*

It was from *The News of the World*, the country's highest-selling newspaper, dated late-September 1907. It went on:

> *Famed Consulting Detective Sherlock Holmes's biographer, Dr. John H. Watson, former hero of the Battle of Maiwand against Afghan insurgents, has signed a startling confession to Inspector Lestrade of Scotland Yard. The Good Doctor "made up" the compelling evidence he gave for The Crown during the Old Bailey burglary trial of the American Henry Judson Raymond II, a well-known Speaker's Corner entertainer renowned for his tales of a former life as a burglar on Long Island.*
>
> *Raymond has spent several months in Pentonville Gaol and was liable for deportation to his country of origin upon serving out the three-year sentence. He has been granted immediate release and will be given permission to stay in Britain and receive substantial compensation for wrongful imprisonment.*

403

The Case of the
Missing Minute
by Dan Rowley

Over the years of my association with Sherlock Holmes, there have been a number of cases so sensitive, whether because of the people involved or the issues presented, that my dear friend enjoined me that publication could not take place until a suitable amount of time had passed. The subject of the current tale clearly falls into that category. Holmes required that I not keep it with my other papers, but instead entrust it to a solicitor acquaintance with instructions that it not be opened for at least one-hundred years. Hopefully it will not become lost in the dusty confines of chambers, never to see the light of day.

This story begins in the late fall of 1908. Holmes had long retired to his beekeeping, and I was desultorily maintaining my medical practice and making time for occasionally writing up some of our adventures. It was early one Sunday morning when I received a rather abrupt telegram:

> *Watson:*
>
> *Meet me immediately at Diogenes Club.*
>
> *Mycroft Holmes*

Knowing the peculiarities of Holmes's brother Mycroft, including his disinclination to leave his Club, I wondered what he could want with me that could be so urgent. I hailed a cab at my lodging and directed the driver to the address in Pall Mall. Upon arrival, I asked for Mycroft and was shown to the Stranger's Room, the only location in the Club where conversation was permitted.

As the door opened, I was greeted with, "Watson, so wonderful to see you. It has been too long." Sherlock Holmes never seemed to age, his lean features and piercing gaze the same as always. I cannot say the same for myself and Mycroft, as we both were showing signs of good eating and less, and greyer, hair. Holmes and I clasped hands warmly, quickly giving each other the trivial details of recent events that friends cherish.

Mycroft Holmes nodded at me. "Well, Doctor, you are looking well. Is your recounting of the submarine case ready for publication?" I must have looked a bit startled, as he smiled and continued. "I'm afraid this time there was no deduction required on my part. The editor of *The Strand* is in my debt, so he regularly provides me updates on your writings. I trust you haven't over-dramatized the Bruce-Partington matter, as it was a rather simple affair."

"It will be published in December, and I have been going over the preliminary proof sheets. I haven't yet seen any of the illustrations and am a bit anxious about them."

"Yes, it's unfortunate that Mr. Paget passed away – What, about ten months ago? I hope his successor can live up to the same quality."

Sherlock Holmes smiled. "I believe what Mycroft means is that Paget tended to show him as much slimmer than the facts would warrant."

Mycroft glared at him. "Well, let us get down to business. Doctor, my brother asked that I summon you to assist him. Last night I sent him a telegram similar to the one you received, but with a little more detail."

"Yes, Mycroft, but all you told me last night was that this had something to do with Sir Roger Ormsby. I took the liberty of searching my indices, and there was very little about him, given the type of information I collect. I did see that in his younger days he was a companion to some members of the Royal Family."

Mycroft Holmes cleared his throat. "I believe he was seen at times in the company of one or more of our current monarch's sons some twenty years ago or so. More relevant to our current problem is that he is now a senior member of the Cabinet Secretariat. As such, he has access to quite confidential materials related to Cabinet deliberations. They have been meeting fairly regularly for the past few weeks in preparation for the imminent opening of Parliament. Two days ago, on Friday, Sir Roger was working at his home with his secretary on a draft of a minute of the most recent meetings of the Cabinet."

"What, if you can tell us, did it cover?"

"Normal things like the preparation of the budget for the spring, Irish issues, these demonstrations by suffragettes, and so forth. But the bulk of it relates to foreign affairs. As you may imagine, the recent rising by the Young Turks commencing this past summer, and then Austria-Hungary's annexation of Bosnia and Herzegovina earlier this month, have occupied quite a bit of the Cabinet's attention."

Sherlock Holmes smiled. "I assume there has been more contention in meetings due to the Prime Minister being forced to admit to the Cabinet members of the Radical element of the Liberal Party to maintain his hold on power."

405

"Brother, I don't know if I would so characterize it. Chancellor of the Exchequer Lloyd George and President of the Board of Trade Churchill certainly have their opponents."

I interjected. "Do not some Conservatives call them the 'Terrible Twins', especially given that Churchill switched parties and thus appears to have been rewarded with office?"

Mycroft gave me a cold look. "I am confident the Prime Minister can manage the political situation. To return to our current dilemma: Friday afternoon, Sir Roger finished working on the draft minute, locked it in his safe, and locked the door to the room upon exiting. He then received a notice that the Prime Minister had decided to have a meeting of a smaller group of the Cabinet at Archerfield House, his East Lothian country retreat. Sir Roger was instructed to travel there that evening to staff the meeting Saturday morning. Sir Roger and his secretary then left for East Lothian.

"The meeting concluded in the early afternoon on Saturday, so Sir Roger returned to London on the train, accompanied by the Prime Minister's Private Secretary. The Secretary expressed a desire to review the draft minute, so they proceeded to Sir Roger's home. They unlocked the study and Sir Roger opened the safe, only to discover that the minute was missing."

"Did anyone else have access to the study while Sir Roger was away?"

"That is part of the reason I need you as my eyes and ears, and yes, Sherlock, before you interrupt, I need your mind as well. The Secretary immediately procured a constable to stand guard at the house and then came to see me. He tells me that Sir Roger is the only person who has a key to the study and is the sole possessor of the combination to the safe. You will have to go over there and make such inquiries as you see fit to determine how we can retrieve the draft minute."

"Before that, bear with me so that I may ask a few questions."

"I assumed you would. Yes, I have placed guards watching the house. And I'm sure you're wondering if some foreign agent could have obtained the draft between the time Sir Roger left and returned. Because of the sensitivity of the international situation, everyone wants to discover our Government's plans – France, Russia, Germany, Austria-Hungary, Turkey, the Balkan countries. For the past several weeks we have had all embassies under comprehensive surveillance. We also – and this is highly secret – know every foreign agent under cover in this country and are following them. And before you ask, I'm sure we have them all. Even if we did not, the watch on the embassies and our – *Ahem!* – 'partnership' with the telegraph and cable companies assures that we would know of any transmission. We also are watching all the ports, and the Navy is discreetly patrolling all likely routes out of the country, just in case someone attempts to slip through our net. So far, there isn't a sign that anyone has received a copy of the minute."

"Other than the thief, of course."

"Sherlock, there is no need to state the obvious. I would like you and Watson to go to Sir Roger's home and see what you can learn. There is no need to question the Prime Minister's Secretary, as I have already done that. I have conveyed to you all he knows. If you need any resources, you only need to ask."

"No, Mycroft, I believe I have enough to commence my inquiries. Just provide us with the address, and we will do as you ask." Mycroft Holmes gave him a slip of paper, we said our goodbyes, donned our overcoats and hats, and went out to find a cab. It still was raining fairly heavily, as it had been for the past few days. We finally procured a hansom and were on our way.

Once settled in the cab, Holmes turned to me. "Well, old friend, this matter would seem to have some items of interest."

"Unless a spirit made off with the draft, there must be some logical explanation."

"Yes, we'll need to dig deeper than the bare bones of what Mycroft has provided us. Do you have any suggestions?"

"I suspect we need to better understand the physical layout of the house and determine the whereabouts of the occupants during the relevant period. While I appreciate your brother's confidence in his surveillance, I'm still troubled by the gap between when Sir Roger departed and his return."

"Capital! The absence of recent adventures hasn't dulled your perceptions."

As we were talking, the cab had made its way north of Pall Mall toward Berkeley Square until we came to Charles Street and the address Mycroft Holmes had provided. The Ormsby residence was a stand-alone building nestled between townhouses to one side and some other free standing houses to the other. The house had three stories with gables on the attic. It was made of a ruddy reddish stone with buff trim. An iron fence surrounded it, and there were perfectly manicured shrubs and flower beds on both sides and in the front. A constable stood on guard by the front gate. Holmes and I disembarked from the cab, paid the driver, and went to the front door, which had an impressive family crest. Holmes rang the bell, and the door was answered by a stooped man in his seventies with white hair and dressed in a cutaway coat.

"May I help you?"

407

"Good day. I am Sherlock Holmes, and this is Doctor Watson. I believe Sir Roger is expecting us."

"Yes, sir. Please follow me." The old retainer led us to a drawing room at the front of the house, to the left of the entryway. It was comfortably furnished with sofas and armchairs, with mahogany side tables next to them, all arranged in front of a fireplace where a nice fire was already started. The wainscoting also was of mahogany, and the walls above were adorned with family portraits and historical paintings.

Before I had much time to admire the room, a short, rather thin gentleman in his late fifties bustled into the room. As Holmes was a hawk, he was a sparrow. His forehead was a bit shiny, and his face, with striking blue eyes and a rather large nose, seemed a bit puzzled. One could sense a nervousness, not least shown by his wringing of his hands. "Mr. Holmes, Doctor Watson, thank you for coming. This affair is quite dreadful. I cannot explain it. Please be seated."

Holmes nodded. "We will do what we can, Sir Roger. I know you have already relayed what happened to the authorities, but please indulge me while I ask some questions."

"Proceed as you wish."

"On Friday, you and your secretary were working here at the house?"

"Yes. His name is William Montagu. I have a study upstairs on the first floor directly above this room. If the Cabinet isn't in town on a Friday, I find it convenient to work here at home. I believe you know we were working on a draft of a minute related to this past week's Cabinet deliberations. I understand you have been informed in a general manner that the meetings have related to very sensitive foreign affairs. I would prefer not going into the substance of those deliberations, as they are highly confidential."

"There is no need. We have been acquainted with the contents in a general way. If it is germane to my inquiry, I have means of learning what I need."

Sir Roger shrugged and continued. "When Montagu and I finished the section of the draft on which we were working, we locked it, along with my notes, in the safe inside a folder, after Montagu confirmed we had gathered up all the notes. He then checked the windows in the room and, as we left, I locked the door to the study."

"We'll want you to show us the study, but please continue with your story. Now I understand you received an unexpected summons from the Prime Minister to attend a meeting in East Lothian."

"Yes, He had gone there for the weekend on Thursday. I knew he was troubled by certain of the discussions, and he decided to have a smaller meeting on Saturday morning. Just as I was locking the study door,

George, our butler whom you have met, came to me with the telegram from the Prime Minister. I instructed George to oversee the packing of an overnight bag. We have just retained Stephan as my new valet, and I wanted George to ensure Stephan had properly put everything I required into the valise.

"I went to my bedroom to retrieve the book I'm reading, as I had forgotten to tell George to pack it. I wanted to read on the train. I then went downstairs and left for the station with William.

"We arrived in East Lothian after the evening meal and had a cold snack and some claret. Mr. Asquith is a quite congenial host and made sure we had something to eat. We were joined by one other Cabinet member and chatted briefly."

"Who was that?"

Sir Roger audibly sighed. "Chancellor of the Exchequer Lloyd George. He, along with the War Minister and Foreign Secretary, were there for the meeting."

I asked, "You don't care for him?"

"Personally, he can be quite charming. I really cannot comment on the political situation, as that isn't my place."

Holmes resumed. "So you attended the entire meeting Saturday morning?"

"We started at ten and wound up a little after two. William and I traveled back to the station with the Prime Minister's private secretary. I would have preferred my book as company, but he wanted to discuss the past week's Cabinet meetings with me. As we neared London, he asked if he could see my latest draft of the minute, so we left the station and came back here."

"Was Montagu also with you?"

"Yes, he was. We went straight up to my study. I unlocked the door and went over to open the safe. I was dumbfounded to find the draft minute had disappeared." At this, Sir Roger's nervousness was even more evident.

Holmes sat back and closed his eyes, motionless and seemingly oblivious to our presence. Sir Roger gave me a perplexed look, but I motioned for him to be quiet.

Holmes finally stirred. "Is there anyone in the household who might have a motive to steal the minute?"

Sir Roger squirmed uncomfortably in his chair. "I cannot imagine anyone here who would have the slightest motive."

"Sir, your forbearance is admirable, but we require complete candor as to any possible foreign connections of the members of your household."

After hesitation, Sir Roger, looking at the floor, replied. "Well, Stephan, my new valet, is French. And Paul Henley, my son's friend who

409

has been staying here, is attending school in Berlin. He is quite a Germanophile, but I cannot imagine he or Stephan could be involved in this."

Holmes again sat quietly for a while, clearly in reverie. "Very well. Please take us up to the study." We rose and proceeded up the staircase to the first floor. As Sir Roger had indicated, it was at the front of the house on the left side. Before we entered, Holmes asked, "What other rooms are on this floor?"

"Across from this is my bedroom. My wife's bedroom is behind that, and there is a connecting dressing room and bath between them. On this side of the house, my son Arthur's room is next to the study, and my daughter Isabelle's room is beyond his at the back of the house. When we have guests, they occupy the second floor bedrooms."

"Are there any guests here now?"

"Yes. As I mentioned, Arthur's friend, Paul Henley, has been visiting for about a week. He is conducting some research here in London related to his studies in Berlin. And Montagu has stayed here since we returned Saturday, as the authorities didn't want anyone to leave the premises."

Holmes nodded and proceeded to enter the study. It was a handsome room with dark paneling and built-in bookcases from floor to ceiling, broken only by two windows in the front of the house, two on the side, and the door. The bookcases were full of books and papers, some of which I could see related to parliamentary business. There was a large carved desk with red leather swivel chair by the far wall, the one with no windows or doors. Several chairs were arrayed in front of it. There was a small working table by one of the windows at the front of the house.

Holmes quickly took in the room. "Where were you and Montagu working on Friday?"

"At the table over there by the window. It is more convenient when drafting to work side by side than having him across from me at the desk."

"Now that I see the room layout, describe for me what happened from the moment you began packing up your working materials."

"Montagu gathered up the draft minute and my notes and placed them in a folder, which he handed to me. We went over to the safe there behind the desk. Montagu turned his back while I opened it, so as not to see the combination. Then he handed me the folder, which I placed in the safe. I realized that, because we had been working on the Cabinet meetings from the early part of the week, all of the notes might not be in the folder. Wishing to make sure that everything was secure, I had Montagu go look in my case, but there were no more notes in there, so I locked the safe, Montagu checked the windows to be sure they were locked. Then we took our things and left the room, at which point I locked the door."

410

"And you are the only person who knows the combination to the safe and possesses a key to the door?"

"That is correct. When the safe was installed, I selected the combination. Thus, not even the manufacturer or installer knew it. I have never written it down because it is committed to memory. I have the only key, which is always on my watch chain. At night I lock it in the nightstand in my bedroom and place the key to that under my pillow. When the study requires cleaning, I unlock the door and am present while the maid takes care of it."

"Quite admirable precautions, if I may say so."

"Thank you. My position is quite sensitive, I feel it necessary to be extremely diligent."

"Please also tell us about your return on Saturday."

"As I mentioned, the Prime Minister's Private Secretary decided to accompany me and Montagu back from East Lothian. During the journey, he expressed a desire to look at the draft minute to clarify one or two points. We came straight here from the station, and the three of us came together up to this room. I unlocked the door, then we came over to the safe. I asked both of them to turn away while I turned the combination. When the safe tumblers fell into place, they both turned around. I opened the safe and discovered, to my astonishment, that the folder with the minute was missing. Montagu and I emptied the safe onto my desk. The three of us went through the entire contents, but the folder wasn't there. This is most distressing. I cannot explain what happened, or how the minute came to be missing." Sir Roger's hand-wringing increased at this point, and the expression on his face was manifestly one of concern.

"This has been most helpful," said Holmes. "If we could impose a bit more, we would like to talk to the other people here in the house. We can utilize the drawing room. If acceptable, we can begin with Montagu. Then your wife, son, daughter, and Henley as a group, followed by your butler – alone – and perhaps the other servants. Then I should like to make an inspection of the entire house and grounds."

Sir Roger seemed taken aback but quickly recovered his composure. "Of course. I will give George instructions to bring people to you in that order. But only Montagu is aware of the missing folder. How shall we explain your presence? They will likely recognize you, and I'm at a loss as to what to tell them."

Holmes smiled. "They already know that the police are here. Simply tell them that we are acting on behalf of the Government to assist in its inquiries."

Sir Roger reluctantly replied, "I'm not sure that will do. But I will trust you to ensure they don't discover what has occurred. I will talk to

411

Eleanor before you do and allay her anxiety as best I can. Come, let us return to the drawing room."

Back downstairs, settled in the comfortable furnishings of the drawing room, we were approached by a slim man of average height, in his late thirties with receding sandy hair and myopic eyes peering owlishly at us through thick spectacles.

"Hello, I understand you wanted to see me. Please excuse me if I seem a bit nervous. It isn't often I meet someone as illustrious as Sherlock Holmes. Doctor Watson, I have read every one of your stories and enjoyed them immensely."

Holmes smiled dryly. "Yes. Well, this is unlikely to be as thrilling as one of Watson's tales. We just have a few simple questions. Please make yourself comfortable."

"Thank you, Mister Holmes. Anything I can do to help."

"Please recount for us the events of Friday afternoon until you left the house, and then the return on Saturday. Leave nothing out, however trivial it may seem." Holmes leaned back in his chair and closed his eyes. While he seemed to be distracted, I knew from long experience that he was hearing and analyzing every word, his razor like mind missing nothing.

Montagu's recitation was basically the same as Sir Roger's. At its conclusion, he looked expectantly at Holmes, who opened his eyes and straightened his lanky frame.

"Excellent, Montagu. You have admirable powers of recall. Just a few questions: When you were in the study, were you with Sir Roger the entire time?"

"Yes, sir, I never left the room. We were at the desk side-by-side, until we stopped working."

"And you were with him over by the safe."

"I always turn my back until the tumblers click, and when I turned back, he was just opening the safe. It was the same on Saturday. On Friday, I saw him place the folder in the safe and, after we determined the folder had all the minutes, watched him turn the dial to relock it."

"And the door – you heard the lock engage on Friday and open up on Saturday."

"It is a quite heavy and stout lock, sir. The noise it makes when turned either way is very noticeable and distinctive. I've been through this with Sir Roger on too many occasions to account and am familiar with the lock."

"You're positive that the four windows were firmly locked when you checked them?"

"Quite sure. I tested each one. The windows are rather a tight fit, so it's clear when the lock is engaged because it pulls both the bottom and

412

the sash snug to the window frame. That is especially so when, like on Friday, the weather is inclement with rain and wind lashing against the house."

"We know that Sir Roger had a bag packed. Did you need to fetch a bag for the trip?"

"No. I had planned on a weekend in the country with friends, so brought a bag with me that morning."

"Very good, Montagu. On your way out, please ask George to send in Lady Eleanor and the three younger members of the household who were here after you left."

After his departure, Holmes sat deep in thought, only to arouse himself when the group entered the drawing room. A small, petite woman in her late forties with graying hair and soft features came over to us. "Mr. Holmes, I am Lady Eleanor. I have no idea why you are here, but Roger assures me your presence is necessary. The entire affair is most unsettling, but I must endure it for Roger's sake, as there is clearly something amiss. We will assist you in any way within our powers." I was impressed with this formidable woman. There aren't many who would allow such intrusions without demanding an explanation. Sir Roger was fortunate to have such a life companion. My mind went back to my late wife, Mary, and frankly I couldn't imagine her being so acquiescent. The same was true for my current wife.

She then introduced the other three. Her daughter, Eleanor, was slim and very attractive with the latest hair style and clothing. In her early twenties, she was a younger version of her mother. The son, Arthur, was a bit older and, unlike his father, already starting to put on weight. He had his mother and sister's dark hair and eyes, but I could sense some his father in him as well. Paul Henley was about Arthur's age, but his fading tan and rugged physique showed that, unlike Arthur, he was more an outdoorsman.

After we had all sat down, Holmes began. "Thank you for your time, Lady Eleanor. You have a beautiful home. Quite an exclusive neighborhood."

"I inherited it from my grandfather. We do love it here."

"I take it all four of you were here on Friday when Sir Roger left for East Lothian."

"Yes. We had planned on going for a ride and perhaps tea, but this dreadful rain led us to decide to remain here. In fact, we were having tea in here when Roger came in to tell us he had to leave for East Lothian."

"What did you do after Sir Roger left?"

"Isabelle and I stayed in here. I caught up on my correspondence, and she was reading. Arthur and Paul left the room."

She looked expectantly at her son, who replied, "We went to the billiard room down the hall and played until it was time to dress for dinner. I trounced Paul rather soundly and collected a tidy sum." Henley looked sheepish, as if to suggest he may have allowed his friend to win. I had been inspecting Henley closely due to his German connections, so perhaps his expression had to do with something other than the billiard game.

Holmes turned his attention to Arthur. "And what is your occupation?"

"I am in training at a bank here in London. I should be qualified to be a branch manager in a few months."

"And Henley – what about you?"

"I'm studying the foreign relations of Britain and Germany in the last thirty years, working toward a doctorate in Berlin. I have been here in London to examine the relevant records, and I took the opportunity to see Arthur. Lady Eleanor has been gracious enough to extend her hospitality to me."

"Lady Eleanor, I assume you all had the evening meal together."

"Yes, we had drinks in here at seven, then ate in the dining room, which is next door. After that, we came back in here and visited for a while before Isabelle and I turned in for the night. I believe Arthur and Paul then smoked cigars and had brandy, which is my husband's habit."

Arthur smiled. "Yes, we continued father's tradition. I wouldn't want to let the old boy down."

Holmes again sat for a few minutes. "Lady Eleanor, can you describe for us the events of Saturday before Sir Roger arrived?"

"We had a late breakfast together. Because the rain was continuing, we decided to stay indoors. We all went our separate ways, but met again here at two to play whist, which we did until Roger returned home."

"I apologize for my next question, but the nature of this matter requires that I be as thorough as possible. I understand that there were periods when you all weren't together. It would be tedious to reconstruct what each of you did during those periods, so I will ask a simple question: Did any of you leave the house between the time Sir Roger departed and returned?"

Holmes let his intense gaze light on each of the four, as each said they hadn't left the house. As he sat watching them, Lady Eleanor, who seemed perturbed by the implications of this question, spoke up. "Mr. Holmes, I still don't comprehend what this is all about. At Roger's behest, we will continue to assist you, but I must say, I do not care for your questions."

Isabelle also spoke up. "I agree with Mother. This entire inquisition is becoming unbearable. I intend to speak to Papa about it." Arthur and Henley seemed merely amused by the proceedings.

"I quite understand, Lady Eleanor. We regret having to put all of you out. But as you undoubtedly perceive, this all is in Sir Roger's interest. Is there any other method by which we might ascertain that no one left the house?"

"I believe George can help you with that question. I suggest you talk to him. Otherwise, I would prefer this to be at an end."

"Indeed, I shall. You all may go, but I may have further questions later."

They filed out of the room, leaving us alone. I broke the silence. "Do you actually suspect one of them?"

"It is too soon to tell."

"But what motive could any of them have? This would damage Lady Eleanor's husband's career, possibly ending it in disgrace. Arthur's career also could be damaged indirectly as, given his age, I would assume his rather rapid rise at the bank is due in large part to his father's influence. Isabelle seems to be a sweet innocent, and I cannot imagine her being involved in anything like this. While Henley is studying in Germany, and I imagine that could be some connection, it isn't apparent on the face of it, although I will concede his mannerisms seemed a bit off."

"All astute observations, Watson, even discounting your tendency to romanticize what you see as an innocent maiden." I blushed a bit, as Holmes always had considered me overly susceptible to an attractive woman. He continued. "But deeper forces are at work here. They all seemed a bit uncomfortable – even diffident in the case of the two women – which could be the result either of a guilty conscience, or simply worry over the possible impact of the situation on each of them. One or more of them may have some hidden motive that we cannot as yet discern. And if so, it is highly unlikely they would disclose that to us through interrogation. No, this case will rest on facts."

"So you didn't attempt to reconstruct Friday or Saturday, because none of them would have an ironclad alibi for every minute of the day."

My friend smiled. "This is part of the reason I miss our adventures. You have correctly divined my reasoning. Let us pray that the physical examination will yield results that aren't so ambiguous of interpretation." At this moment, there was a soft knock on the door. At Holmes's behest, George the butler entered the room. Holmes invited him to sit, which he did with great reluctance. I'm sure he didn't think it proper for him to be sitting in the drawing room.

"Now, George, we have a few questions for you. Lady Eleanor suggested you might be able to shed some illumination on whether anyone left the house."

"No one left or entered, sir, from the time Sir Roger departed until he returned."

"Interesting. Please elaborate."

"Well, Sir Roger installed switches on the front and back doors, the only two entrances to the house. I don't understand completely all these new-fangled gadgets, but when either door is opened, a bell rings both in the kitchen and my room. If someone pushes the doorbell at either door, the same thing happens. Stephan, the new valet, is quite unfamiliar as yet with the household routine, and we don't currently have another manservant to help with tasks such as being on duty at the front of the house, serving, and so forth. So when Sir Roger left, I asked Lady Eleanor if it would be acceptable for me to set the alarms so I would know if I needed to come to the front of the house should I chance not to be there. She agreed. The next morning, she informed me that she and her family would remain inside for the day, so I suggested we leave the alarms on so that I might know when Sir Roger returned and could attend to him. And the bells never went off the entire time. All the servants sleep here, either up in the attic or in the basement, which is where Cook and I sleep."

"Could someone have turned off the alarm?"

"No, sir. The switch is in my room, which I keep locked when I'm not present. I have the only key."

"It is my understanding that it is your custom to check all the ground floor windows and doors before you retire to ensure everything is secure."

"That is my instruction from Sir Roger. I did so on Friday evening after everyone retired. Everything was locked as it should be."

"How long have you been with Sir Roger."

"Since he was born. I was his father's valet, and when he was out of the house, it was my pleasure to take Sir Roger to the park."

"Such long-term loyalty is commendable."

"It is my honour and duty, sir. Nothing less."

"Fine. That will be all. May we speak to the other servants?"

"They would be in the kitchen having tea right now. There is Cook, her assistant and two maids, and Stephan." At Holmes's request, he led us back to the kitchen. Holmes questioned the servants and confirmed that no one had left the house, there had been no deliveries on Saturday, and no one had heard the bell other than when Sir Roger returned. I scrutinized Stephan, the French valet, closely, but he seemed unconcerned with Holmes's questions. But then a spy would be trained to so react.

After that, Holmes indicated to George that he and I, with Sir Roger's permission, were going to inspect the premises. Because it was still light outside, Holmes asked George for two mackintoshes to shield us from the ongoing downpour.

416

As we waited for him, I mused, "Well, I don't see that anyone's behavior indicated a single motive among them, but I assume that again we will let the facts decide."

"Again you are correct." He seemed about to say something, but just at that moment George returned with the protective gear and we went outside. Even the heavy rain couldn't hurry Holmes's painstaking inspection. We went around the entire perimeter of the house, with Holmes staring intently at the ground, occasionally raising his eyes to look toward or away from the house. I felt sorry for the four constables stationed on each side, stoically on guard, but must admit I was relieved when he was done so that we could return through the back door and into the kitchen. A short sojourn next to the fire with a hot beverage would have been welcome. Holmes, however, was intent on continuing the search immediately.

We obtained the key to the study from Sir Roger and commenced there. Before entering, Holmes first paced from the study door down the hallway to the door of Arthur's room and peered inside. Returning, he bent over and examined the keyhole in the study door for some time. Upon entering, he paced the perimeter of the room. He then went over to the safe and knelt to look it over. He checked the four windows, then motioned for me to help him roll up the Persian rug, after which he stood looking at the floor. Holmes next spent what seemed to me an inordinate amount of time going over the bookcases and their contents, seemingly handling every item on the shelves. Finally, he went over to the table by the window and sat down there for some time, his eyes roaming over the room.

When he was satisfied, we left the study and slowly walked to Arthur's room. He again paced the perimeter of the room, spending some time looking at the wall adjacent to the study. He then went over to the windows and examined them, even opening one and protruding his head out into the rain, for what purpose I couldn't divine.

He turned to me. "Watson, I'm going to go to the second floor and the attic to have a quick look. I suspect that I have observed the main items of interest on this floor, but it never is a waste of time to be thorough. Surely you're hungry. Why don't you go to the kitchen for something to eat? I'll meet you in the drawing room in a bit."

"Do you want anything, or are you going to follow your normal habit of not eating while in the hunt?"

He smiled. "Some coffee would do nicely, thank you. I can wait until I return downstairs."

I went to the kitchen and was able to obtain some cold meat, cheese, and bread. I asked the cook to brew some fresh coffee and bring it to the drawing room in about thirty minutes.

Holmes came in just as George was bringing the coffee. Holmes thanked him and said, "We should have a visitor soon. When he arrives, please bring him in here and ask Sir Roger to join us."

"Certainly, sir."

I looked quizzically at Holmes. "Before I went upstairs, I went to the front door and motioned for the constable on guard to come to me. I gave him a message to send to Mycroft, asking him to come here. Although he despises weather like this, I'm confident he will join us." I was well aware of the elder Holmes's predilection for not venturing out, but when occasions warranted, he would do so. He had even come to our lodgings in Baker Street when he needed Holmes's assistance.

"Have you solved this then? It is quite beyond me how those papers could have left the study."

"I believe I have."

At that moment, Mycroft Holmes, somewhat disgruntled, appeared at the doorway. "Sherlock, I trust my sodden journey was worth the exertion."

"It will be rewarded as soon as Sir Roger joins us." Shortly he also entered the room, and the four of us settled in front of the fire. Sherlock Holmes began.

"The most interesting aspect of this case was how the draft minute was removed from the study."

Mycroft Holmes interrupted. "Of most interest to me is where the draft is and how to retrieve it."

"Mycroft, once we understand how it was removed, retrieval is quite simple. Allow me to continue. Watson and I made a careful inspection of the premises to ascertain the facts. My first thought was that, despite Sir Roger's assurances, there was a duplicate key to the study. But when he loaned it to us, there was no trace of wax or any other substance on it. The deep grooves in the key would have contained some evidence of copying, but there was none. If the culprit had used some chemical in which to soak the key to remove such traces, that likely would have removed also the patina of age on the key, but again it didn't appear to be altered in that manner.

"I easily determined that no one had tampered with the door into the study. Any such attempt inevitably leaves scratches or other marks. As to the safe itself, there also was no evidence of an attempt to open it without the combination. Any attempt to open it by guessing the combination would be impractical, and there would have been evidence of a physical attempt, but there wasn't.

"The windows in the study were solidly locked with no sign of interference. Watson and I pulled up the rug to ensure the floor is solid,

418

which it is. As you can see by looking up, the ceiling in this room hasn't a seam in it, which confirms the solidity of the floor above us. I also looked behind all the furniture, made sure that the bookcases were immovable, and that none of the books concealed a hidden mechanism that allowed the bookcase to swing out as a hidden door.

"I paced off the dimensions of both the study, the hall, and the bedroom next door. Those measurements match exactly the thickness of the walls, so that there could be no passageway through which anyone could enter the study. In Arthur's bedroom, the wall adjacent to the study is solid. I looked outside the window in his room. There is no ledge on which someone could have crawled over to the study. There also is no sign on the walls or roof that anyone used a grappling or other hook to swing.

"When I went to the attic, I ascertained there is no egress to the roof. Indeed, the windows are painted shut and no one could have let themselves down a rope to outside the study. Similarly, my examination of the grounds outside showed that no tree is close enough to the study windows to allow access. Moreover, because of the rain, all the surrounding ground is soggy and shows no signs of a ladder being propped against the house or of anyone walking on the grass or flower beds."

"Holmes," I said, "I don't quite see where you are headed. You seem to be proving that no one could have done this."

"Watson, you actually provided one essential clue."

"What was that?" I glanced at Mycroft Holmes and realized he had a knowing look on his face. He clearly had realized what his brother had concluded, and may have suspected it long ago.

"I will come to that in a moment. First, let us recall that, due to the door alarms energized by the butler, we can be fairly confident no one entered or left the house after Sir Roger and Montagu departed on Friday. That strongly suggests the culprit is someone in the house."

"Preposterous. Why would someone in my family circle wish to do such a thing?"

"Quite correct, Sir Roger. That is where Watson's insight comes in play. He astutely observed that none of your family would have the requisite motive – to the contrary, the theft of the draft minute is distinctly against their individual and collective interests. Likewise, after questioning your servants, I could detect no motive or prevarication on their part. George is devoted to you, so is like your family in that respect. The others were utterly guileless when I questioned them. While Henley's manner is a bit odd, I put it down to his youth and callowness. I also don't believe his interest in German diplomatic history translates into a motive – he seems a typical naïve student.

419

"The most logical conclusion is that *you*, Sir Roger, are the thief. Before you deny it, allow me to explain how the facts condemn you. Your obvious nervousness has one of two explanations. Either it's due to your distress over the theft, or because you are concerned you will be exposed as the culprit. The latter is clearly the case.

"Based on the facts you and Montagu provided, he had no opportunity to take the folder. After you and he packed up your things, you had possession of the folder, you placed it in the safe, and he never touched it or was near enough to the safe. I suspect you removed the folder when you sent him over to the worktable to look for notes you undoubtedly knew weren't there. You shielded the open safe with your body and then slipped the folder under your jacket.

"What was unusual about this case is that, in the normal situation where it appears that a crime wasn't possible, the perpetrator intended it to appear so. At first, that's what I thought might be the case. The solution became clear once I realized that this aspect of the matter was quite by accident. In other words, you became ensnared in a web of accidents not of your own devising and which you had never intended.

"After you locked the door to the study, that's when your plans began to go awry. You unexpectedly received the summons to attend the Prime Minister. You then used the excuse of retrieving the book to leave Montagu in the hall and enter your bedroom, where you secreted the folder."

"Sherlock, you seem fairly certain on that point."

"Yes, Mycroft. While I was searching the house, I sent Watson to have a repast. As you know, he is at times too honest to dissemble, so I needed a few minutes alone. I trust you will forgive me, dear friend. I used the opportunity to enter Sir Roger's bedroom, where I found the folder locked in in his nightstand. It was child's play to open the lock." With a flourish, Holmes reached into his pocket and produced a folded sheaf of papers. Sir Roger had turned ashen and was staring at the floor.

"The remainder of the events are fairly straightforward. You had another unforeseen problem when the Prime Minister's Secretary insisted on accompanying you back here. I assume you had taken the paper and planned to do something with it on Saturday, never anticipating the trip to East Lothian on Friday or the discovery of its disappearance on Saturday evening."

Sir Roger's voice weakly replied. "Yes. I was to turn over the papers over the weekend. I took them out on Friday because I didn't want anyone in the house accidentally seeing me entering the study to remove them. The person to whom I was to give them was going to photograph them and return them to me, at which point I could simply take them to work on Monday."

"As I surmised. I also was taken aback by your craven attempt to misdirect blame onto Stephan or Henley. I would have expected more from someone of your stature."

"I am truly ashamed of that. I have no excuse, other than my despair when you arrived here. I realized it was unlikely I could deceive you, but I felt I had to make the attempt. You see, I was trapped and saw no other way out."

"That confirms what I had concluded. My further deduction is that you are being blackmailed into providing the minute, most likely based on your involvement with members of the Royal Family in your youth. I'm aware, although Mycroft may deny it, of rumours that certain scandals concerning the eldest son of our current King were suppressed by the Government. Although the Prince has passed away, any such revelation would end your career, and perhaps those of others."

"You are correct. I was a foolish young man. There are a few letters and at least one photograph which the scoundrels are to exchange for the draft when I deliver it to them.

"It may not be too late to rectify the situation. What arrangements has the blackmailer made for the handover?"

"When I had secured the minute, I was to close one shutter in the front window of my study. The blackmailer would ride by every morning at eight in a cab. Then I would go for a walk, meet him in nearby Berkeley Square, make the exchange, and come back here. A messenger would return the draft in a few hours so that no one would be the wiser."

"Splendid. We shall carry out that exact plan in the morning. Mycroft, please withdraw all the constables. Watson and I will spend the night here and leave at dawn for the Square. I will speak to George about a possible disguise for myself. Sir Roger, please provide Watson with a pistol, as I'm sure he didn't bring his service revolver."

"What am I to tell the blackmailer if he saw the constables this morning?"

"Simply explain there was a bomb threat to certain members of the Cabinet administration, and that the perpetrators – radical Irish – were captured late Sunday evening."

Mycroft turned to our host. "Sir Roger, I assume we can rely on your cooperation. Only the four of us need to know about this. It is in the interest of His Majesty's Government that neither the reason for your blackmail, nor the attempt to purloin the minute, become public." Sir Roger bleakly nodded his assent. He had the aspect of a condemned man, even though the Holmes brothers were offering him a form of salvation. He likely felt the humiliation of even the three of us knowing of his secret and his less-than-gentlemanly actions.

"I assumed you would feel that way, Mycroft. Come, Watson, let us prepare and get some rest."

At dawn the next morning, we slipped out of the house and made our way to Berkeley Square. Holmes was dressed as an elderly gentleman, and he explained that he would hobble along with the aid of his walking stick. At about nine, we both sat on benches near the west end of the Square, which is where Sir Roger told us the meeting was to take place. I hid behind a newspaper, while Holmes busied himself with feeding pigeons.

A little after nine-thirty, Sir Roger entered the Square and stood nervously looking about. Holmes slowly rose from his bench and started tottering toward Sir Roger. At that moment, a short man dressed in a suit with vest and striped trousers approached Sir Roger. Just as the two began exchanging packets, Sir Roger's containing sheets of blank paper, Holmes swiftly ceased his charade and darted toward the stranger. The man was startled and looked ready to run, but Holmes tripped him with his stick, while I hurried over to cover him with the pistol.

"What is the meaning of this?" he demanded in a polished English accent.

"Your game is up. A member of the Home Office will be here in a moment to escort you away. Sir Roger, please confirm the packet he gave you has the materials we want."

Sir Roger blushed as he went through the packet containing several letters and a photograph. He nodded. "It does. Thank you so much."

"There is no need for that. Please go home and resume your normal routine. We will watch this blackguard."

After the Home Office man removed the blackmailer, Holmes and I repaired to a nearby café for a late breakfast. While enjoying some excellent coffee, I asked, "There is one thing you didn't explain. Who was behind all this? Which one of the foreign nations your brother mentioned arranged the blackmail attempt?"

Holmes smiled. "I'm a bit suspicious of Mycroft's explanation. The fact that his agents didn't detect any relevant activity was suggestive, so I took the liberty of reading the minute when I uncovered it. While it did contain material on foreign affairs, there was a far more contentious subject of debate: Chancellor Lloyd George, supported by his ally Churchill, plans on introducing a budget in the spring that he refers to as the People's Budget. It would impose very high taxes on the wealthy to fund certain social programs that the Radicals favor, also thereby redistributing wealth."

"But that would never get through the House of Lords."

"The minute reveals the answer to that objection. Lloyd George and Churchill are pressing the Prime Minister to threaten the creation of enough additional Peers in the House of Lords to obtain passage. The King would either have to give in and create the additional peers, or refuse, which would allow the Lords to block the budget and override the House of Commons' traditional authority over monetary matters. In either event, there would be a showdown between the two Houses and the Monarch, a potentially untenable constitutional situation. Given the explosive nature of this proposal, I suspect that the people behind the blackmailers were political opponents of the Radicals, not foreign agents. It is entirely a domestic political matter. The cultured accent of the man we captured buttresses that conclusion."

"That is extraordinary. Do you think your brother knew all this?"

"I'm sure he would claim he did, but with Mycroft, one never knows."

The Peacock Arrow
by Chris Chan

Sherlock Holmes was a man who enjoyed being active, even after he retired to Sussex. He did, however, take on the occasional case when very influential people made a very polite request. It was therefore particularly frustrating to him when, as he was enjoy a brisk stroll in a marshy corner of a client's country estate on a beautiful late autumn day, his left foot became caught in a small but deceptively deep patch of mud. His leg sank into the mud up to a third of the way up his calf, and when he attempted to extract his foot, he inadvertently twisted his ankle. The damage to his body was not serious, though the harm to his trousers took his housekeeper a full four hours to repair when she finally had a chance to look at them several days later. I advised Holmes to take a full week to recuperate, and when he argued that a mere fifteen minutes of rest would be sufficient to bring him back to full fettle, the pain caused from standing was enough to convince him, albeit very reluctantly, that my recommendation was indeed a sound one.

Our host very generously set Holmes up in a small but comfortable cottage on the edge of the estate, where there were no stairs to aggravate him. I provided Holmes with a few books and a couple of puzzle boxes from our host's collection in order to amuse him, but these only served to distract him for a day. Just over forty-eight hours after his injury, Holmes was tired of reading and the puzzle boxes were fully disassembled. His restlessness was obvious, and his temper was becoming increasingly evident in his voice.

It was therefore a great relief when we received a visitor late that evening – Mr. Elmer Albron, who lived on a small estate bordering our host's. After the standard introductions, a clearly flustered Mr. Albron sat down in a chair across from Holmes and began to tell his story. He passed a hand through his sparse grey hair and sighed.

"Mr. Holmes, my great-uncle, Silas Albron, is dead."

"How did he die?"

"He was shot in the chest with an arrow adorned with peacock feathers."

"A very distinctive weapon," Holmes noted.

"Yes. Great-Uncle Silas joined us for lunch today, and my cousin Ives picked him up this morning from his home about seven miles away. He returned him to his home immediately after the meal had ended. Ives has a very fine carriage with reliable horses, and Great-Uncle Silas was able to travel in it relatively comfortably. Shortly after Ives returned home, my wife Emmeline suggested that we engage in a friendly competition of her favorite pastime: Archery.

"Now, it's necessary to describe the area before I proceed. Off to the side of the house, we keep a set of four archery targets in a row at the base of a large, artificially made berm. Each target is two feet in diameter, and the berm, which is made of soil and stone and is now covered in thick grass, reaches fourteen feet above ground level. It's meant to be a protective measure, you see. If a shot goes above the target, the arrow will stick in the berm, where it will be easily retrieved, Also, the berm prevents a stray arrow from soaring elsewhere and potentially hitting something or someone it shouldn't. At least, that how it's supposed to work."

"Are you saying someone was injured?" Holmes asked.

"Someone was killed, Mr. Holmes, but it's impossible. If I may please continue, I'm sure I'll be able to address any questions you may have."

With a little nod, Holmes indicated that it was fine for our guest to proceed.

"The three of us gathered our archery equipment. We all have our own distinctive arrows. Mine are fletched with red-and-yellow feathers. Ives' have jet-black feathers, and Emmeline's are fletched with portions of peacock feathers – not the entire feather, as that wouldn't be aerodynamic – but pieces of the iridescent blue and green portions of the feathers that shimmer and shine in the light, looking almost like gemstones. They were a present I gave her last year for her twenty-fifth birthday. She's very fond of them.

"We shot at the targets for about fifteen minutes, and then, when it was Emmeline's turn to take a shot, Ives pointed at a tree to our left, asking me if he was seeing things, because he thought there was an eagle sitting on a branch. Well, I looked and saw nothing remotely resembling an eagle and told him so. Then I heard Emmeline scream, and turned back towards her just a second later. She told me that she'd felt a sharp pain in her arm, and it caused her to move her arm just as she was releasing the arrow, causing it to fly up into the air at a far steeper angle than is typical, sailing over the berm. That was doubly surprising to me, as Emmeline is very careful, and I've never known her to shoot a wild arrow before today. She told me that she'd been stung by a bee or a wasp, or something like that, and it had made her arm jump."

"Is this connected to your great-uncle's death somehow?"

"I'm afraid so. You see, we went to look for the missing arrow. I don't believe I made this explicitly clear, but these are custom-made, and cost a pretty penny, I can tell you. I didn't want to see one of them lost."

"How many arrows are in the set?" Holmes asked.

"There are twelve in the quiver," our guest explained. "We searched and searched for half-an-hour, but the arrow was nowhere to be found."

"Could it have hit some unfortunate animal, I wondered, who was only slightly wounded, and then it ran away, carrying the arrow along with it in its body?"

Mr. Albron looked over at me with a trace of surprise in his face, as if he had forgotten that I was there, and he didn't care much for my interruption. "Unlikely. There was no trace of blood and no animal footprints. And we heard no sound of an animal in pain, either. In any event, the woods are some distance away, so there would have been no place for this hypothetical injured animal to run to and hide."

"And you found no hole in the ground where the arrow might have lodged in the soil, only to be removed by someone or something later?"

"Nothing of the kind, and despite the velocity of the arrow, it would have been impossible for it to have been driven completely into the soil, leaving no sign of its presence. In any case, we soon learned what had happened to the arrow, but how it managed to land where it did is absolutely impossible."

"What happened?"

"Just as we were getting frustrated in our search, my butler arrived with a note that had arrived by messenger. It was from my great-uncle, telling us that he believed he was in danger, and begging us to come to him immediately."

"Did he specify the source of the danger?"

"No, he did not. Still, my great-uncle has never asked me for any help in the past, and I was worried, and so were my wife and my cousin. He lives alone, without servants, in a small cottage. We all climbed into my cousin's carriage and we made our way to my great-uncle's home in record time. His door was locked, and he didn't answer to my knock. He'd given me a key a while ago, but when I looked on my key ring, I couldn't find it.

"My cousin took a walk around the cottage to examine the rear window. I should be more specific: It isn't a large pane of glass, just a small panel, and it had a small hole broken through the middle of it, only a few inches in diameter. Ives peered through the hole and gasped. He said our great-uncle was lying on the floor. We weren't quite sure what to do at first, and then Ives used the silver handle of his umbrella to smash the glass in a window next to the front door in order to let us inside the house.

426

We found my great-uncle on the floor of his sitting room, on his back in front of his chair. One of my wife's peacock arrows was sticking in his chest."

"You called the police, of course."

"Yes, and it wasn't very pleasant, I can assure you of that. The inspector – or whatever his title was. I can't remember for certain – he seemed certain than my wife's arrow – the one that went wild – must have travelled across the countryside, smashed through the window of my great-uncle's cottage, and struck him, killing him instantly."

Holmes stared at our guest for several seconds before replying. "Ridiculous!" he finally said.

"That's what I told the inspector! There is no way that an arrow could travel several miles, all the way to my great-uncle's cottage! It is true that our archery field requires the shooters to fire in the general direction of my late great-uncle's home, but to imagine that an arrow could be fired so far, without striking anything else in its path first . . . ."

"Not only that," Holmes added, "but the odds of it just happening to strike a window and still have the velocity and accuracy to break through and strike a man directly in the heart are astronomical. If it were not deliberately aimed from a relatively short distance, the odds of such an event happening are well-nigh impossible. I must say, I am highly unimpressed with the investigative abilities of this inspector."

"As am I, Mr. Holmes. He told me that he recognized that this was an accident, and that my wife wasn't responsible for the stray shot, but he would see us at the Coroner's Inquest, where an official decision would be reached in due course."

"Just how did this inspector think that the arrow reached your great-uncle's house? In the Middle Ages, the best military bows are estimated to have been able to propel an arrow no more than about three-hundred-fifty yards. Even if we treble, or even quadruple that number, it doesn't come close to the seven miles the arrow would have needed to cover in order to reach your great-uncle's home."

"The inspector suggested that the arrow was caught in a powerful gust of wind."

"Do you recall feeling any powerful gales at the time of your archery game?"

"I do not. If there had been any significant winds, we probably wouldn't have fired our bows in the first place."

Holmes nodded. "Even if an arrow had been caught in the strongest possible wind, it almost certainly would not have travelled straight and true. It would have rotated, and if by some meteorological miracle it had managed to travel over six miles more than it could have normally, it's far

427

more likely the window would have been hit by the feathered shaft of the arrow rather than the deadly point."

"And once again, there was no wind!"

"So what ideas, if any, do you have about how the arrow might have travelled as far as it did?"

"I can only imagine that there was some sort of twist of fate. Perhaps someone was riding past in a carriage, or perhaps a bicycle, too far away for us to see or hear, but close enough for a falling arrow to strike as it fell in a parabola. Maybe it landed on the roof of a carriage or lodged in a rucksack strapped to the back of the bicycle. Then the owner of the vehicle discovered the arrow sometime later, and decided to use it against my great-uncle. That person took a bow of his own and fired it through the window."

Holmes managed to keep his face impassive. "Did your great-uncle have many enemies?"

"Unfortunately, yes. He was always quarreling with neighbors about their property lines."

"Who profits by his death?"

"Ives gets fifty pounds and a gold watch. I inherit everything else."

"Are you his only living relatives?"

"Yes."

"Please excuse me for saying this, but that seems like a very unfair division."

"Yes. I suppose it's because I'm so much older than Ives, and I'm in charge of the family estate. The inheritance will keep everything running nicely for years to come."

"I see. Please excuse me for asking, but would you have any trouble funding the needs of the estate without this inheritance?"

"Oh no, certainly not. Like most people with large land holdings, I've had to tighten my belt here and there, but the income from the farmland and the revenue from my investments is enough to handle the general costs. But the inheritance will help pay for some additional improvements that will reap deeper dividends down the line. Properly handled, the inheritance will help assure the long-term stability of my estate for decades to come."

"I see. How is your wife handling this situation?"

"I'd say she's perplexed rather than worried. She knows that no one can possibly fault her, because there's no way her arrow could have made that seven-mile journey. I don't believe she thinks she's in any danger whatsoever of legal repercussions, but still, she can't figure how that arrow made its way to my poor great-uncle. It couldn't have happened! But it did."

428

Holmes said nothing in reply. He stared up at a corner of the ceiling for a while, and it wasn't until a few minutes later that he responded to my questioning.

"My apologies, Watson. I was reflecting on the nature of this problem."

"Do you know what happened?" Mr. Albron asked. "I realize that you can't go out and investigate the scene right now, due to your injury."

"Even though I often prefer to view an area with my own eyes, I don't believe that this is necessary in this case."

"Then you've solved it?" I tried to keep the amazement out of my voice.

"That remains to be seen. At the moment, all I have is a theory – a theory that, while it explains everything, isn't sufficiently supported by evidence at present. It's possible that just a little bit of investigating will produce a clue that completely disrupts the ideas that are currently circulating in my mind. There is a very real danger to theorizing without proof. I may know the truth behind what happened to your great-uncle, or I may have built a castle in the air. Please, I need you to answer some more questions."

"Of course. What do you wish to know?"

"Can you describe the note?" Holmes asked.

"I just told you what it said. It was addressed to me: *'Dear Elmer – I'm in danger. Come immediately.'* It was signed *'Uncle Silas'.*"

After a very long sigh, Holmes continued. "I meant, could you please describe the stationery? What color was the ink?"

This question seemed to confuse Elmer. "I can't remember. But I have the letter here, if you'd to see it."

"I would!" Holmes snapped. After Elmer silently withdrew the letter from his pocket, Holmes snatched it from him and looked over it. "Hmm! A plain white card, the kind that's sold in any stationery shop. Ordinary black ink. Is this how your great-uncle normally sent notes?"

"I don't know. He's never sent me a note before, as far as I can remember."

Holmes gave a little nod. "So you wouldn't recognize his penmanship, either?"

"No."

"This is very good handwriting," Holmes mused. "Nice and neat."

I felt the need to reenter the conversation. "Are you saying that his great-uncle didn't write this note?"

"I find that highly unlikely," he replied. "Mr. Albron, did you ever wonder why your great-uncle supposedly sent a note to you, instead of summoning the police? Surely there was someone closer – physically, I

429

mean – who could have helped him? How did he get the note to someone? Did he have a usual person that he used to send messages?"

"I doubt it, Mr. Holmes. My great-uncle rarely felt the need to send notes by messenger. In fact, I actually can't think of a single instance where he hired someone to a deliver a message immediately. The post was always adequate for him. There's a box quite close to his house. He'd deposit his letters there himself."

"Your great-uncle apparently was a wealthy man – yet he lived in a very small house and had no servants."

"He was a miser. He didn't like spending a penny more than absolutely necessary. He had a charwoman come in frequently to clean and take care of his basic chores, including a little light cooking. He had a valet until a few months ago, when they quarreled – I don't know why – and my great-uncle fired him and never bothered to hire someone else. He didn't get along with most people, aside from family members."

"And your great-uncle had no other means of travelling to and from home?"

"No. He didn't keep horses."

"I wonder, if he was in fear for his safety, why he didn't travel with the messenger?" I mused. "Perhaps the messenger travelled by bicycle."

"Was your butler able to identify the person who delivered the note?" Holmes asked, not bothering to address my comment.

"Apparently not. It was delivered by a young man in shabby clothes with a cap pulled down over his eyes. The messenger looked downwards as he handed over the letter, and as soon as it touched my butler's hand, he turned around and ran away without a word. This struck him as being very unusual, as most boys who stop by on any sort of business stick out their hands, hoping for some sort of gratuity."

"Does your butler oblige?" I asked.

"He keeps a few farthings in his waistcoat pocket if he feels the situation calls for such a payment."

"And this messenger was unfamiliar to him?"

"Yes. Normally the young people who stop by the house for various jobs and errands are quite eager to collect their farthings. Perhaps this fellow was too shy to ask for a gratuity."

"No, I don't think that was the reason why he didn't wait for a coin," Holmes remarked. "I believe that he was given strict instructions to deliver the message and go as soon as possible."

"But why would my great-uncle tell him to act in such a manner?"

"Your great-uncle never spoke to the messenger. Your great-uncle never sent that message. It was sent to you, sir, purely to get you to travel

430

to your great-uncle's home and discover the body. It was all part of a clumsy illusion that the killer desired to create."

"But why? What was the purpose of all of this?"

"I believe this was an imaginative plan that was a bit too far-fetched to be truly convincing. The party responsible for the crime wished to create an impossible circumstance, which would lead the authorities to conclude that it only could have happened through a fluke – an impossible twist of fate."

"So what do think happened, Mr. Holmes?"

"Sir, I am currently confined to a chair. It's possible that my time stuck in the same spot has affected by deductive skills for the worse. I may be subject to a flight of fancy that would only serve to tarnish my reputation. Please do me the courtesy of allowing me to protect my own public image."

Mr. Albron started tugging at his lapels. "I understand, Mr. Holmes, but I would really like to know what you're thinking."

"I must beg your indulgence. If you'll please be so kind as to leave me to write some messages, I'll have Watson send them to some of my agents who will do a bit of digging and report back to me. If all goes well, I should have an answer for you by tomorrow morning, or possibly after dinner tonight."

Mr. Albron begged Holmes to explain his thoughts in more detail, but my friend held firm, and Mr. Albron was eventually compelled to leave, muttering something I couldn't understand as he stormed out the door.

"He isn't pleased with you."

"I dare say he'll be downright furious with me by the time this case is settled. I rather think that I stand little chance of getting a fee from him. Perhaps I should ask for payment before I tell him my conclusions. Well, the financial side of this business was never my strongest suit. Please hand me a few sheets of paper, a pen, and some ink."

I obeyed and he hurriedly scribbled out three notes. "Please go to the nearest telegraph office and send these out for me. You will recognize some of these names. They are individuals in the area who I believe to be skilled information-gatherers. Hopefully we'll get a response from them as soon as possible."

"Will you be all right on your own?"

"I am not a child, but thank you for your concern, totally unnecessary though it may be."

On my way to the telegraph office, I read the notes and felt my eyebrows arching. I found myself hoping that Holmes's suspicions were incorrect, though deep in my heart I believed that he was completely right. It was only a twenty-minute walk there, and I was back forty-five minutes

431

after leaving. Holmes was dozing when I returned, and I managed to suppress my impatience and waited for him to awaken before I questioned him.

Finally, he opened his eyes and checked his watch. "Hmm! Living as an invalid has sapped my stamina. If my leg doesn't heal itself soon, I will find myself napping away the lion's share of the day, sitting by the fire with a blanket over my legs. I fear that I am slipping into my dotage, Watson."

"That day is a long way off. Would you care to talk about your theories on this case, please?"

"Of course, my dear fellow. But first, I would like to hear your ideas on what happened."

"My first thought is that there must have been some sort of duplicate arrow. Someone made an identical peacock-feather arrow, brought to the great-uncle's house, and fired it through the window."

"And what happened to Mrs. Albron's arrow? How did it disappear so completely and at exactly that time?"

I had no answer to those questions, and after a few moments of desperately trying to come up with a solution, I admitted that I couldn't explain those points. For his part, Holmes displayed no condescension to me for my failure.

"The existence of a duplicate arrow – a *thirteenth* arrow, if you will – is a possibility. The question, however, is *Why?* Why would somebody create a distinctive weapon with a link to a woman who couldn't possibly have killed a man with it? Why go through the time and trouble of creating an impossible crime? Why try to implicate someone with a perfect alibi?"

"Could it have been pure serendipity? The arrow really did lodge itself in some moving vehicle, or got caught in some powerful gust of wind, and it really did get transported a substantial distance? And then the killer found it, possibly recognized it, and thought to commit a murder with it? Is that possible?"

"Watson, I am not trained in statistical analysis, but it is my belief that the odds of that happening are so small that one would have a better chances of casting a line into the sea and managing to hook one particular fish that had been marked earlier."

"Then what happened?"

"The arrow didn't fly seven miles, smash through the window, and strike the victim dead. That is an improbability so infinitesimal as to be ludicrous. It is also ridiculous to assume that someone found this particular weapon and decided to use it at that moment. This is a distraction, Watson. This entire pantomime was meant to mask a simple crime with confusion over an impossibility."

"Then what was the point of it all? Was it simply a farce to confuse us?"

"Precisely. You have identified the issue exactly. This was all smoke and mirrors. Force everybody to ponder the impossible, and it distracts everybody from what really happened. This was a simple murder. Who benefits?"

"Mr. Elmer Albron. He receives the lion's share of the inheritance. But he had no opportunity to kill his great-uncle as far as I can tell. His cousin took Great-uncle Silas home, and when Elmer Albron later arrived at Silas' house, he was always with his wife and his cousin. I don't believe that he had a chance to commit the crime."

"Nor do I. In any case, though I put little stock in expressions of emotion, I found Elmer Albron to be, though not a brilliant intellect, an honest and genuinely perplexed man. I don't believe that he has the death of his great-uncle on his conscience. He is an unimaginative man, but not a killer."

"Then what does all of this mean?"

"Hand me my pipe, please." I acquiesced to his request, and provided him with his smoking materials. A few moments later, after he had filled and lit his pipe, he said, "There's a passage in one of the books you gave me to read, Watson – Mr. G.K. Chesterton's new book of essays, *Alarms and Discursions*. In it, he writes, '*In a very old ninth-century illumination which I have seen, depicting the war of the rebel angels in Heaven, Satan is represented as distributing to his followers peacock feathers – the symbols of an evil pride. Satan also distributed peacock feathers to his followers on Mafeking Night . . . .*'" His voice trailed off and he began to direct his focus back to his pipe.

I prompted him to pay attention to me again, and he casually returned to discussing the passage. "Years ago, in the early days of our acquaintance, when you compiled that notable little list of which topics I was familiar which and which subjects of which I was willfully ignorant, you neglected to include art and art history in your analysis. I do not claim to have an expert's knowledge of the Great Masters, but as you know, I have a prominent artist in my family, and in connection to my study of the family legacy, I have picked up a little bit of information on some of the more obscure artworks of our continent's history. I believe I'm familiar with the ninth-century illumination that Mr. Chesterton mentions. In it, the forces of darkness are armed with arrows fletched with peacock feathers, retaining their length to such an extent that it would be impossible for the arrows to fly any distance accurately. In contrast, the forces of light wield plain but practical spears, which are far more effective weapons in battle.

It shows the vanity and futility of evil. The wicked may be gaudier and garner more attention, but the virtuous get the job done."

"I thought that the peacock feathers in the arrows used here had been trimmed to fly effectively?"

"They were. You miss my point, Watson. The peacock feather arrows in this case are all a distraction, but they are symbolic of the foolish pride of two wicked people."

"To whom are you referring?"

He shrugged. "Why, Cousin Ives and Mrs. Emmeline Albron, of course. They were in it together. You may have gathered from snippets of our recent conversation that both of them are far younger than Elmer Albron. I dare say that when the two of them were in repeated close proximity, the old, old story played out as it has many times in the past."

"Holmes!" I felt a wave of shock pass through me, even though past experience has taught me that my friend is usually correct in making statements like this. I knew that Holmes suspected adultery due to the fact that he had asked one of his agents to make inquiries at local hotels and inns, but the fact that he was making this statement before receiving confirmation rankled me somewhat, and I felt obliged to defend two people who I had never met. "You cannot possibly make a statement like that without evidence. You've never even met Mrs. Albron or Elmer Albron's cousin."

"No, I have not, but I have seen Elmer Albron's suit, and I notice that it has some loose threads and a few tiny holes here and there. Certainly his valet is no prize, but no loving wife would let this pass. Do you remember my comments on the shabby state of a gentleman's lost hat in that Christmas time case you referred to as "The Blue Carbuncle?"

"I do, but to make such an allegation based on the flimsiest of assumptions – "

"I should add that I have read the local newspapers, and both Cousin Ives and Mrs. Emmeline Albron have appeared in recent additions. Both are young and attractive. Elmer Albron is in late middle-age, and physically – if you will permit a bluntness that verges on cruelty – there is nothing in his face or physique that would ensnare a pretty woman who could be his daughter. He may be a decent man, but from our conversation I can safely say that he isn't a man of particular charm or intelligence."

"Holmes, your recovery as made you irritable and uncharitable."

"Perhaps, but not dishonest, my dear fellow."

"It's lucky that no one else is here. You might be the subject of a terrible lawsuit."

"I've been in that position several times before. Every time I was in the right, though it was sometimes challenging to prove. Fortunately, my brother was able to pull some strings and the cases never came to court."

"I know better than to challenge your assertions, but didn't you just say that you were waiting for more evidence?"

"Of course. Even though I'm quite certain of my conclusions, I know better than to announce an allegation of this magnitude before I have the sort of evidence that would convince someone like you. In any case, it stands to reason. The two of them *must* have committed the crime together, and if they would do something so horrific together, it is a logical certainty that they are romantically involved."

"Would you care to tell me why you think they committed the crime together?"

"How else could it have been done? First, the arrow could not have been fired from several miles away. It simply isn't possible. No gust of wind, no bird of prey with the ability to grab the arrow. The odds of an enemy coming across the weapon somewhere . . . Ridiculous. Absolutely not. I put no credence in any of the aforementioned theories. No, that arrow was carried there all the way by the killer: Cousin Ives."

"But that's impossible!" I declared. "He didn't have the opportunity to kill Great-Uncle Silas. The Albrons were watching him when he came there after they got the note."

"What do you think I'm suggesting?"

"Don't you think he found the misfired arrow, tucked it under his jacket or something, and then brought it with him up to the house and then shot or maybe stabbed Great-Uncle Silas with it?"

"You have the right idea, but no. He didn't kill Great-Uncle Silas then. He did it when he drove him the first time. I don't know if he had a bow hidden in his carriage or if he stabbed him using the arrow as a dagger, though I suspect the latter, and he smashed the window to make it look like the arrow came in from outside."

"But the arrow – it wasn't fired until much later."

"That was what you were made to think. Did anybody count the arrows in the quiver beforehand? I believe that if they had, there would only have been eleven. Ives had the arrow hidden away in the carriage on the way back to his aged relative's house. He committed the murder as previously described, smashed the window pane with the same umbrella handle that he used later to break into the front and then went back, having left a note with someone he recruited to deliver it. I don't know if the note was given to the messenger that day or sometime earlier, but that's irrelevant."

"But the vanished arrow?"

435

"Never fired. Remember our guest's description of the event: He believed he turned his head a little too late. He never actually saw it fired. In reality, it was never fired. His wife pretended she'd shot the arrow over the hill, and the three of them searched for an arrow that wasn't there. The note arrived, they discovered the body, and they discovered the impossible crime."

"It makes sense when you say it, but will you ever be able to prove it?"

"I dare say proof of the affair will be found soon enough, and everything will follow from there."

"But why go through this entire rigmarole?"

"I doubt they had any idea how to make it look like a natural death, and when a wealthy man dies after seemingly perfect murder, or even a simple accident, it's always heavily scrutinized. But an 'impossible' accident? When people can't explain something, especially people who are supposed to be in positions of authority, they don't like not having the answers. If they're embarrassed by their ignorance, they move on, using the most convenient excuse to keep everything quiet."

"And the motive was money? But the inheritance goes to Elmer Albron. Are they planning to kill him as well?"

"It's possible, though perhaps not necessary. Mr. Albron doesn't strike me as being terribly observant, and he seems devoted to his wife. With all of that extra money, he's likely to be quite generous to her. Having ready access to his money is as good as having that money themselves. A few more luxuries for them, and they continue to carry on their affair under Mr. Albron's nose."

Holmes was correct, and the investigations of his agents soon proved all of his theories. Cousin Ives proved to be surprisingly fragile under questioning, and a full confession followed quickly. Our guest was never officially a client, and he was so upset over his wife's infidelity and arrest that he never offered to pay Holmes for his time and ingenuity.

Holmes was too happy to be walking around again to complain.

The Spy on the Western Front
by Tim Symonds

Some of Dr. John H. Watson's
Recollections from The Great War

During the years Dr. John H. Watson shared lodgings with Sherlock Holmes at 221b, Baker Street, his battle-hardened medical skills honed as an Assistant Surgeon in the Indian Army tended to take second place to the forensics of the crime scene at which Holmes excelled – tobacco ashes, brownish stains (Blood? Mud?), hair, finger-marks, palm prints, tattoo marks, tyre tracks and footwear evidence, glass fragments, fibres, soil, vegetation. Watson returned to the medical world in 1902 upon his marriage, while Sherlock Holmes retired to a bee-farm in the Sussex South Downs in late 1903.

In 1914, the First World War broke out. Watson engaged a locum to run his medical practice in Queen Anne Street in London's fashionable "Doctors' Quarter" and joined the Royal Army Medical Corps, involving himself in a number of activities, including service on the Western Front. After some time there, Watson decided it was time to visit his old friend and former Comrade-in-Arms, Sherlock Holmes . . . .

Chapter I: I Plan a Brief Trip Back to England to Visit Holmes

My diary recorded:

> *January 1ˢᵗ, 1917. Another New Year's Day. Am still on the Western Front. The terrible war against the Kaiser's land forces, the* Deutsches Heer, *is at a stalemate. The winter weather is poisonous as usual, deep slush and a biting N.E. wind. It blew and raged all New Year's Eve, leaving behind deep snow this morning.*

The moment in August 1914 that Prime Minister Asquith took Great Britain and the British Empire to the war with the German Kaiser, I joined the Royal Army Medical Corps. Now, two years later, I was based at a Casualty Clearing Station at Lapugnoy, on the Front, part of the chain of evacuation for badly-wounded soldiers. The enemy's losses through the previous year had been immense. As a response, the Germans spent the winter building the *Siegfriedstellung*, a set of highly-defensible underground fortresses which we immediately dubbed "The Hindenburg Line". With tactical dispersal, reverse-slope positions, defence in depth, and camouflage, German infantry could be conserved, while at the same time the new Prime Minister, David Lloyd George, and his War Cabinet were coming under extreme pressure from Press and public to "*do something*". It was an unhappy position for the Cabinet and the Military High Command to be in.

In the evenings, by lamplight, I recorded my daily routine in a set of diaries:

> *We all eat whatever comes, whether cold or hot, raw or cooked, nice or nasty, and do very well on it. The kitchen range is made of petrol tins, cement, and draughts. Today the Quarter-Master paddled me round all his soak-pits, incinerators, thresh disinfectors, ablution huts, bath huts, laundry etc., etc. They are primitive but clever. Another night of continual din. We are bombarding them harder than ever. We took in another convoy.*
>
> *I've already had to begin writing the Break-the-News letters to the wives and mothers. So many are dying I shan't possibly be able to write to all their mothers, and some have no trace of next of kin. Stretcher-bearers are the unsung heroes. Under normal circumstances, two bearers are sufficient to retrieve a wounded man from the battlefield, but in the appalling mud and shell-holes of the Front, four are needed to lift the stretcher, and ten to carry it more than a short distance. The walking-cases came in lorries today, the lying-cases in electric-lighted Motor Ambulances.*

Even at the start of 1917, there was no certainty England would defeat the *Westheer*, the German forces opposing us across No-Man's Land. It was true that the British Grand Fleet with its more than one-hundred-sixty ships of all sizes, including the *King George V, Thunderer, Monarch,* and *Conqueror*, had kept the vaunted German Imperial Navy blockaded in harbour for much of the war so far, despite the Hun's technological advantages such as better shells and propellant. On land, not a day went by when we didn't anticipate some sort of lightning strike across the Hindenburg Line by the enemy's Generals such as Erich Ludendorff, mastermind of victories over us at Liège and Tannenberg at the start of hostilities. The fate of both the German Empire and the British Empire would depend a very great deal on the spring push which rumour had it our High Command planned to launch near Arras, aiming to break through the Hindenburg Line and race towards the Rhine.

I looked out at the sky over the bleak Pas de Calais landscape. The rain was still falling but the clouds were dissipating. Depressed by the foul weather, I felt a sudden urge to visit Sherlock Holmes, combined with nostalgia for the England *Profonde* exemplified by the Sussex South Downs where he had retired before the war. My return trips over the previous two years had taken me to London to check on my surgery, with little time to visit Holmes.

No further transports were scheduled to bring in a new batch of wounded and shell-shocked soldiery for the following week. I pushed myself up from the canvas stool and reached for my rainwear. I would go to the Station Commander and ask for a few days' leave. He granted my request after I gave my word that only my accidental death would serve as an excuse not to be back as promised. "Things are afoot," the Station Commander advised. I had already gathered this. Bridges were being strengthened. There had been an increase in constructing further dormitories for the wounded. Added to this, an advance party of surgeons of the Canadian Army Medical Corps was in residence, instructing my medical team on transfusions, knowledge gained from doctors in the United States. Transfusions were becoming increasingly frequent, particularly as part of pre-operative preparation in cases of wound shock and haemorrhage.

I cabled Holmes:

> *Have immediate chance of a few days leave (STOP) Would enjoy catching up. (STOP) – Watson*

At midday the reply came:

> *Suggest you make every effort to arrive in Eastbourne on the train from London in three days' time (STOP) Am temporarily back in Sussex. Will explain when we meet at the station. (STOP) - Holmes*

I returned to the wooden hut which acted as my surgery. A knock on the door was followed by the entry of my Staff Nurse, Blanche Barwell. She wore the white uniform of a Voluntary Aid Detachment with blue active-service stripes on her sleeve. I spoke of her as "my right-hand man". She had become skilled enough to carry out minor surgery when patients were rushed in from the battlefield in my absence. She had become so invaluable over the past year that I planned to put her name forward for the Distinguished Conduct Medal for Gallantry in the field.

Nurse Barwell had heard I was to leave for the Home Front the following day. "Before you leave, Doctor," she said with a slight Scottish accent, "will you order a further supply of chlorodyne," she requested. I was familiar with the patent medicine from my Indian Army days, a mixture of laudanum, tincture of cannabis, and chloroform. It readily lived up to its claims of relieving pain.

Beyond the physical needs of the wounded was the fact that war neuroses accounted for one-seventh of all soldiers discharged for disabilities. Symptoms included fatigue, tremor, confusion, nightmares, and impaired sight and hearing. Soon after her arrival at the Station some fifteen months earlier, Nurse Barwell had taken a deep liking to one of the stretcher-bearers before he was executed a week later in a classical Candide style – "*pour encourager les autres*" – after sentencing by the seven commissioned officers on the Court Martial Board. Following this tragic event, even in deepest winter, she went out of the camp on a lonely journey to the isolated burial area, taking any flowers she could get hold of to place on the spot she believed the young man's corpse lay.

Chapter II: I Arrive at Holmes's Bee Farm and Meet Unexpected Guests

Dawn. It was time to set off for England and the Sussex South Downs. I looked forward to a stay of three or four days on Holmes's tranquil bee farm, away from the ceaseless roar of armaments and military traffic, disease and death, the Maconochie stew of beef and vegetables in congealed animal fat. My first cup of tea of the day had been accompanied by a distant volley of rifle fire, followed by a further volley a minute or so later. Two more victims of shell-shock were meeting their Maker, dispatched as cowards and deserters.

The ferry from the Hook of Holland took me across the Channel. Holmes was waiting at the Eastbourne Station. He came forward, a hand held up in greeting. Years of damp, cold winters on the South Downs had had an effect on the shoulders and knees. He greeted me almost casually with "Good to see you, Watson," as if months had been just weeks.

"And to see you too," I replied in the same vein.

"There are two passengers in the car taking us to the farm," he continued. "One of them responds to the epithet '*K*'."

"Just the letter?" I questioned.

Holmes nodded, leading me out of the station. He pointed towards a most-wonderful automobile, a Rolls Royce Open tourer. The hood was ivory, the upholstery dark red hide.

"'K', for his family name Kell. Major General Sir Vernon George Waldegrave Kell. Only son of Major Waldegrave Charles Vernon Kell and his Polish wife, Georgiana Augusta Konarska."

"Should I know who he is?" I asked.

"No. He's Founder and Director of the British Security Service, otherwise known as MI5. His counter-espionage department – with my small help, I might mention – has had considerable success bringing German agents to trial, including Carl Hans Lody, who operated under the alias of Charles A. Inglis."

I recalled Lody's capture, though I had not gleaned from the newspapers that Holmes had been involved. For years in the run-up to the war, the German toured Britain gathering military intelligence. He was found guilty of war treason and, in November 1914, and he met the fate of enemy spies in wartime: Killed by firing squad at The Tower of London, the first person to be executed at the Tower for one-hundred-and-fifty years.

"And your other guest?" I asked.

The chauffeur saw us approaching and jumped out to take my case.

"David Lloyd George, the Prime Minister," Holmes said. "You've invited yourself over from France at a very opportune moment, my old friend."

I was tucked in the back seat of the Tourer between K and the Prime Minister. K said nothing during the ride to Holmes's farm. The PM paid close attention to my account of life at the Casualty Clearing Station. He made no comment when I mentioned something seemed to be hotting up, given the recent addition of several hundred beds, with an overall capacity to receive some thousand wounded. He picked up quickly when I mentioned how so many men were coming to the Station with "the thousand-yard stare", an unfocused, despondent, and weary gaze, a frequent manifestation of shell-shock. Repeated savage engagements with the enemy left them dazed and unresponsive, refusing any longer to obey orders.

I told him the story of the hapless stretcher-bearer. For two years, the man had clambered down labyrinthine trenches, side-stepping scattered body parts. He would run over enfiladed fields to answer shrieks from No-Man's Land. I pointed out the Boche were known to booby trap British corpses found in there, which they then left out in the open to explode when picked up by our stretcher-bearers. I told the Prime Minister these men were the unsung heroes of the fighting, not villains of the piece. None of them deserved to be executed at dawn and buried in desolate patches of unconsecrated foreign ground.

Twenty minutes later the Rolls Royce came to a halt in the farm's spacious yard. As we got out of the Tourer, the Prime Minister said, "Doctor, if you can identify where that stretcher-bearer is buried, we should bring him home for a decent burial."

A biting wind was blowing from the northeast and we hurried into the house.

The small talk ended the moment we were seated in the lounge with a lively fire in the grate and a pot of tea at each elbow. I recognised the Persian slipper in which Holmes kept his tobacco during our days at 221b. He proceeded to press tobacco into the bowl of his favourite briar. The Prime Minister went across to the fireside.

"Dr. Watson, you may wonder why I am here – " He gestured, " – along with Major-General Kell. It is at the behest of His Majesty the King. He has authorised me to pin a medal on your friend, Mr. Holmes, in his own home. Thanks to Holmes, we think we've cleared much of the Kingdom of German spies – ten so far in Liverpool, five in Manchester, eight in Southampton. We calculated there were at least one-hundred-twenty spies sent here from the Fatherland. We have caught sixty-five. No remaining agent is able to pass on potentially crucial intelligence. The few who remain content themselves with reading the newspapers and making up matters to send to Berlin, stories without a morsel of truth in them. Some appear to be sent by 'reconnaissance agents' on neutral shipping, able to report only what they could observe when calling at British ports.

"But suddenly, a few months ago, something changed. It's as though eight or ten first-rate German spies have got to work where you are, on the Western Front, specialising in military intelligence – information on how our Generals are planning to break through the German lines, where the main thrust will be – what armaments we're bringing to bear. Even where we'll be making inconsequential diversionary moves – for example planning to take a strategically-placed farmhouse. It's bewildering. Everyone is asking: Where are these spies located? Are they around me in Parliament? Or in the War Office? In MI5? Are they German nationals – or British traitors doing it for large sums of money? No one knows."

With that he put a hand in his pocket and said, "It's time we held the ceremony. Come stand here, Mr. Holmes."

I stood up quickly and shook Holmes's hand.

442

The Prime Minister pinned the newly-inaugurated Order of the British Empire to his lapel. On cue, celebratory drinks were brought in by Holmes's housekeeper.

A few moments later, the Prime Minister invited Major-General Kell to take the floor. Kell began, "The Director of Military Operations is convinced that Berlin's principal espionage ring has exited Britain *in toto* to one of the Dutch-speaking provinces of Flanders – in fact remarkably close to you, Dr. Watson. I should therefore add to the Prime Minister's remarks that we at MI5 are handing the baton to Mansfield Cumming at MI 1(c) to continue the search away from the Home Islands. The name of the Kaiser's master spy in charge of that particular ring will be rather familiar to you and Mr. Holmes here. More on him shortly. It's interesting that you commented on certain preparations being made at your Clearing Station. You will not by any means be the only person noting 'goings-on' in the Arras region, goings-on implying – correctly – that the War Office plans a major push against the enemy as soon as the last of the snow has melted.

"I can tell you in the utmost confidence that the High Command will be ready to start a second Battle of Arras in a few weeks' time if the Prime Minister gives the go-ahead. The first two actions, the battle for Vimy and the simultaneous opening battle of the Scarpe, will take place as early in April as possible. It's especially vital that a spy sweep is made of every part of the Arras region under our control over the next few weeks. The German spy I mentioned is Von Bork. He may well have infiltrated his men into positions among our forward operating bases or the Army Service Corps, possibly even specific Casualty Clearing Stations, from where they can garner military information of the greatest value. In possession of up-to-date information, the Germans could bring the Offensive to a stand-still from Day One. Our casualties could be high, the loss of war *matériel* tremendous. Rather than bring the fighting to a speedy end, Arras could cause the war to drag on for several more years yet."

At this, Kell pinned a large map on the sitting room wall with Arras at its centre.

"Doctor," he recommenced, "it was Mr. Holmes who suggested that the Prime Minister and I come down today. He told us you would be taking a few days' leave at the same time. For the last year, our agents in Northern France and Belgium have been watching a German masquerading as a businessman in the Dutch-speaking region of Flanders. As I say, we have every reason to believe that he is Von Bork, up to his old tricks again. We at MI5 in particular remember with gratitude how you and Mr. Holmes

443

tracked down Von Bork three years ago, the most accomplished German spy ever to be caught red-handed in England."

Yes, I reflected. Von Bork was a man who could hardly be matched among all the devoted agents of the Kaiser. The very mention of his name brought back in detail the last words that we'd had with this Napoleon of Spies after we entrapped him during the fateful month of August 1914. Coincidentally *The Strand Magazine* planned to publish the adventure in a few months' time. In it, I had described the conversation we'd had with our unhappy captive.

> *"I suppose you realise, Mr. Sherlock Holmes," said Von Bork, "that if your government bears you out in this treatment it becomes an act of war."*
>
> *"What about your government and all this treatment?" said Holmes, tapping the valise.*
>
> *"You are a private individual. You have no warrant for my arrest. The whole proceeding is absolutely illegal and outrageous."*
>
> *"Absolutely," said Holmes.*
>
> *"Kidnapping a German subject."*
>
> *"And stealing his private papers," Holmes agreed.*
>
> I had continued: *It had been no easy task to move Von Bork, for he was a strong and a desperate man. Holding either arm, we walked him very slowly down the garden. After a short, final struggle we hoisted him, bound hand and foot, into the spare seat of our little car. His precious valise holding the evidence against him was wedged in beside him.*

Yet here was Kell locating him on the Continent, back at his old tricks.

"But surely – ?" I blurted out.

" – But surely he's incarcerated in one of our most secure prisons, you are about to say?" the Prime Minister intervened.

"I'm afraid he isn't, Doctor," Kell explained. "The war between Germany and Britain had yet to be declared, if you remember. Berlin made the strongest representation. We had to let him go just before war broke out."

"And now you say he's in Flanders?" I asked. "What makes you think he has his spies in place on the Western Front?"

Kell answered, "Because just as the PM says – suddenly, a few months ago, matters changed. I'll show you."

The staff in his hand began to do a *rat-tat-tat* on the map.

444

"The detail for a second Arras Offensive was completed last year. It involved infantry, cavalry, artillery, and aircraft. It mapped exactly where our Generals planned to break through the German lines, the type of armour we would assemble, the timing, and even where the cavalry would make diversionary moves – planning to take a certain German-held hill. We have reason to believe every detail of that plan was passed to the enemy. We cannot otherwise explain why they made adjustments entirely commensurate with confronting us with maximum force at every point, including laying mine-fields across our path. It was utterly bewildering.

"Thanks to Mr. Holmes, we thought we'd cleared all the spies out. There's no possible explanation other than some are tucked in somewhere among the British Expeditionary Force stretched along the Hindenburg Line. Our original plan had to be abandoned. A new one is in preparation, but there's the rub: We must presume those half-dozen or so enemy spies are still inside the Expeditionary Force and able to get word of any changes through to Von Bork. As yet, we haven't the faintest idea how they transmit their information. Dr. Watson, you may remember some weeks ago a small squad led by a senior officer made a thorough inspection of your station, ostensibly to report on fire hazards. Among them were three members of the Signal Service searching for small transmitters. They found nothing."

Kell continued, "I asked the Prime Minister to let me hand the matter over to one particular person to be attached to MI 1(c) with the sole aim of winkling out these fiendishly clever agents. And the PM agreed."

Curious, I asked, "Who might that particular person be?"

With a chuckle, once more the Prime Minister intervened.

"K wouldn't even disclose the man's name to me!"

Kell shook his head.

"As the Prime Minister says, I'm unwilling to disclose his name to anyone. Even to you, Dr. Watson."

The extraordinary session with the Prime Minister and K wrapped up. The chauffeur had spent his time with buckets of water and a chamois cloth. The gleaming Rolls Royce Tourer departed for London. Holmes and I returned to the veranda. Holmes fetched his old and blackened clay pipe to try the two-hundred-fifty grammes of Chacom tobacco I had brought with me. I marvelled openly that the Prime Minister of Great Britain and Ireland would take time away from Downing Street and Parliament to confer with Holmes at such an isolated abode.

"And not for the first time, Watson," Holmes replied, puffing hard. "I marvel at it myself. It was Lloyd George himself who pressed me to return to my profession. The fact is, things are going wrong again. There is

445

evidence of some strong and secret central force led by Von Bork embedded amongst our units on the Front Line."

"Holmes," I interjected, "if you aren't already this new spymaster – this attaché – why not come to my Station and work out who's doing the spying? I can think of no one in this world more qualified than you to discover the wretches passing secrets to Von Bork."

With a rather curious smile he replied, "I must refuse, Watson. As Kell said, there is someone about to do that, of a mental capacity even beyond mine. Now, let us forget all about the war. I shall take you up to a hive of *Apis mellifera ligustica*. They will entertain us with a figure-eight dance I've been studying. I'm certain it's a code for the direction and distance of a resource the dancing bee wants to communicate."

Chapter III: I Discover the Identity of the Special Attaché

I was back in France. A military vehicle came to a sliding halt in the mud outside my marquee. It was about an hour after sunset, often the time the Station Commanding officer made his rounds. I looked up. Instead of the Colonel, seated in the passenger seat, lifting a podgy hand in salutation, was almost the last person I would have expected to see on the Western Front: The corpulent figure of Mycroft Holmes, Sherlock Holmes's older brother. I could think only of the words I scribbled immediately after our first encounter, that "*he was heavily built and massive, that there was a suggestion of uncouth physical inertia in the figure, but above this unwieldy frame perched a head so masterful in its brow, so alert in its steel-grey, deep-set eyes, so firm in its lips, and so subtle in its play of expression, that after the first glance one forgot the gross body and remembered only the dominant mind.*"

Mycroft Holmes lowered his great bulk carefully to the ground, waving his driver away.

"How are you, Doctor?" he asked.

"Utterly astonished at your presence," I replied, "but delighted – and curious to know why you are here."

"You were not apprised by Kell then?" he asked, smiling.

"You mean that *you* are the MI 1(c) – ?" I began.

"Later," Mycroft interrupted. "Tell me – where's your Staff Nurse, Blanche Barwell?"

Mystified by this unexpected turn of the conversation, I replied simply, "She should be back any minute."

Mycroft continued, "From doing what?"

I frowned. I wondered how Mycroft knew of my Staff Nurse by name and rank. Now there was this persistent line of questioning.

446

"Does it matter what she's up to, Mycroft? If it doesn't, then I'd rather not say."

"It might matter, yes," came the reply.

I looked at him for a moment.

"My dear Doctor," Mycroft said, smiling. "I understand your reticence, but I must insist."

"Against the Commanding Officer's orders, she takes flowers to put on the grave of a stretcher-bearer whose corpse lies in unhallowed ground a half-mile from here."

Any such activity as taking flowers to the grave-site of the executed men was strictly forbidden on the grounds such men had been found guilty of desertion of duty and deserved no compassion. When the stretcher-bearer was under her care, Nurse Barwell had wanted more time to bring him back to normalcy from a severe case of war neurosis, but her request was refused. The man had reached the end of his tether after three years at the Front, stretchering on frozen slimy duckboards under heavy shelling.

The men he carried had suffered terrible injuries, some sobbing with pain, with half their faces shot away, or where shrapnel had eviscerated them, the intestines spilling off the side of the stretcher and having to be scooped back on to the wounded men's chests. Finally he had refused to carry out any more orders. Nurse Barwell had taken to visiting the site alone, at night, putting posies on differing mounds each time in the hope that one of the anonymous graves would be that of the stretcher-bearer. The entire grave-site had gained a reputation of being haunted and was given a wide berth – mysterious posies of flowers appearing out of nowhere, described by one panicked night-time passer-by as "glowing in the dark" and "floating in the air a foot above the grave".

"And the flowers she took today?" Mycroft continued.

"Calla lilies. She says they represent the soul of the deceased returning to a place of peace."

"Calla lilies?" Mycroft exclaimed. "It's mid-winter. Where did she get them? It's months before they bloom."

"She made them out of silk," I replied. "She cuts the petals to size, dyes them, and moulds them into shape."

"I would like to see these lilies," Mycroft continued. In a lower voice he added, "Can you take me there, Doctor, by a route which will avoid encountering Nurse Barlow?"

We equipped ourselves with a dark lantern each and set off. At my companion's slow pace, our roundabout circuit it took some twenty-five minutes to get to the dismal patch of ground containing the unmarked graves of thirty or so men. From a hundred yards off we could see the white of the silk lilies. A magpie perched on a shattered stump of a tree,

447

as though waiting for us. My Staff Nurse had taken to bringing it bread. She thought it had been the pet of one of the forcibly departed. I readily understood why the site would spook the superstitious. Soon it would be different. When spring came, cowslips and anemones and snowdrops would push up among the anonymous grave mounds.

For a moment Mycroft stood looking down at the lilies. He pointed to the northeast.

"How far are we from Dutch-speaking Flanders? From Courtrai, for example?"

"A risky fifty miles of open ground," I replied. "Why do you ask?"

"That's where we believe Von Bork is holed up these days."

I paused.

"Mycroft," I recommenced. "I realise you really must be the chap co-opted to winkle out the half-dozen traitors in the Expeditionary Force, so I'm assuming this is far from just a friendly social call, however welcome that would be. Surely you aren't thinking that I have anything to do with passing information to Von Bork?"

"Not purposely, Doctor, no. MI5 and MI 1(c) may be convinced there are a half-dozen or so enemy spies in the Expeditionary Force, such is the quantity and value of the intelligence being passed to the Germans – trains, frequencies and lengths, types of rolling stock, fodder stores being replenished, ammunition dumps filling up, new soldiers getting 'lost', field engineering works, strengthening of roads and bridges. I have concluded there are nowhere near so many."

"Then how many?" I asked.

"Just one well-placed person."

"Do you have you any idea who he is?" I asked.

"It's not a *he*."

"Not a he!" I exclaimed, startled.

"It's your Staff Nurse – Blanche Barwell."

I stared at him in amazement.

"Mycroft, are you utterly – ?" I stammered, shocked beyond measure. Then, "That's preposterous. She's been my principal aide for nearly a year. I would trust her with my – "

"It's been during that time so much of our plans have found their way into enemy hands," Mycroft interrupted. "The reason our Generals were forced to rethink the pending Offensive and call it off before it even began."

"What makes you think anyone at this Station – let alone my nurse – has got anything to do with it in the first place?" I asked.

"Sherlock spotted the connection," Mycroft replied. "He made a brilliant observation. Kell was rapping his baton on the map at the farm.

448

Each rap fell where information of real value had found its way to the German commander on the other side of the Hindenburg Line. Sherlock noted the several points where the baton landed. The locations were so disparate it was understandable why Kell came to his conclusion – that at least half-a-dozen spies were at work."

"Whereas?" I asked.

"My brother worked out that those locations had been the site of intense offensives, often involving days of heavy barrages between the two sides. And that meant a potential large inflow of officers and other ranks into your Clearing Station, many suffering from shell-shock. In effect, your Station is a bullseye on a dart-board stretching miles in every direction, covering every tap of the baton on that map. And who took a great interest in these shell-shocked arrivals, as you've described?"

"My Staff Nurse," I agreed. "But evidence? Your brother always says, 'It is a capital mistake to theorise before you have all the evidence. It biases the judgment.'"

Mycroft replied, "On the other hand, how often have we heard Sherlock say that 'when you have eliminated the impossible, whatever remains, however improbable, must be the truth'?"

After a short pause, Mycroft asked, "You say she regularly brings flowers to this spot. Is that right?"

"About every fortnight," I replied, trying to stifle my unease. "So?"

"And she brought these this afternoon?"

"She did," I replied.

"Pick them up."

I lifted the flowers off the grave mound.

"See if anything's hidden in them," Mycroft ordered.

Tucked among them was a tightly-rolled scroll.

"Open it," Mycroft continued, "and read it."

In Nurse Barwell's familiar handwriting it said:

> *First action will start at the Rue d'Achicourt, but not before April 19. The British Third Division will take over the front immediately south of the Arras-Cambrai Road. The Artillery Brigade has had two days preparation with 4.5 Howitzers firing gas shells.*

My heart sank. Any thought the information being passed to Von Bork was relatively inconsequential – food supplies, soldiers repatriated and so on – quickly evaporated. Instead, she was giving the enemy our entire order of battle.

My throat was getting dry.

On the night preceding the attack, [the writing continued] *the Artillery Brigade will fire two-hundred rounds per gun of gas shell at German batteries. During the same night, they will carry equipment, apparatus, and supplies up to the front line: Bombs and ammunition, ladders for springing up from the trenches when they advance. There will be a creeping barrage, lifting the gun sights two-hundred yards every eight minutes. A single Canadian division will start on the same day (April 19) by launching an attack at Vimy Ridge.*

Mycroft was observing me closely. He pointed at the scroll.

"Doctor, can you conceive of anything more valuable to the Boche? Your Staff Nurse has been perfectly placed to listen in on every conversation in the Station, including yours with the Royal Engineers and men of the Army Service Corps. She's been gleaning important information straight from several Fronts – from shell-shocked officers only hours from leaving their forward postings, men whose mental anxieties could lead to a dangerous loosening of the tongue."

He gestured at the lilies.

"Now roll the message up and put it back among the flowers. It's vital that Von Bork doesn't discover his best spy has been uncovered. I shall inform the High Command. It'll be up to them to adjust to the situation. I can assure you, it'll be the very last information Nurse Barwell will ever transmit to the enemy."

On the trek back to the Station, I said, "Mycroft, one day when all this is settled and our real lives recommence, I would like to publish this strange case, so let me get the facts straight. In the utmost secrecy, the British High Command spent months last year planning a coordinated Front-wide offensive against the Hun, a second battle of Arras designed to make the final break-through to victory, and you personally knew my Staff Nurse was handing over information to Von Bork?"

"Yes, Doctor," my companion affirmed.

"The information she passed about the planned Offensive – was it accurate?"

"Accurate and detailed."

My face flushed.

"Mycroft – what now?"

"You and I have caught her *in flagrante*. As we speak, she's being given twenty-five minutes to pack her belongings."

"And then?"

450

"We shall offer her the option – commit suicide or face a court-martial. Von Bork will have supplied her with a death-pill for this contingency. On our part we'll hush it up. Revealing the truth would cause Britain's nursing services very considerable embarrassment. If it makes you feel better, I expect we can lean on the Red Cross to award her a posthumous Florence Nightingale Medal for significant services rendered at the Front."

"And if she refuses to take her own life?" I asked, astounded at Mycroft's perfunctory tone.

"Firing squad at dawn."

I pointed back to where the lilies lay.

"Then her corpse bundled into an unmarked grave in a patch of land as desolate as that?" I asked.

"Yes. Possibly that very patch."

After a momentary silence, Mycroft came to a halt.

"I understand how distasteful this messy business is, Doctor, and how callous I must seem to you, but I think you'll agree we're fighting a war for good against evil, for the survival of England and her Empire. For an enlightened civilisation against Hunnish barbarism. Measured against all that, the execution of one traitorous young woman is – to be frank – of small account."

On my return to my desk at the surgery, I found a scribbled note. My Staff Nurse had been asked to pack her possessions and go with an escort to an unknown destination. She wished me well.

A post-script reminded me to order more Chlorodyne.

During the weeks which followed, I was puzzled by the nature of our High Command's preparations for the Offensive. I could discern no abrupt change of strategy being made as a consequence of leaving Blanche Barwell's scroll in the lilies, only a perceptible acceleration which meant we would be ready somewhat ahead of the April 19th date she had disclosed to Von Bork. The acceleration had extremely favourable consequences when hostilities commenced. Ten days earlier than the date transmitted to the enemy, the roar of artillery so deafening it was heard as far away as Dover. When the barrage announced the start of battle, the German commanders were still in the process of getting the Front Line in a state of readiness for April 19th, not April 9th, and doing so as circumspectly (and therefore slowly) as possible to avoid our aerial reconnaissance.

The scroll which reached Von Bork's hands proved deceptive in other vital respects. It said the creeping barrage would mean lifting the gun sights two-hundred yards every eight minutes. Instead, on the opening day,

451

our artillery sights were lifted one-hundred yards every minute, catching the enemy on open ground as they made a tactical retreat to emplacements only half-readied further back.

The capture of Vimy Ridge formed one of the major British objectives of the battle. So long as it was held by the Germans, the British lines of communication were under constant observation. The enemy machine-gun units on the Ridge had readied themselves for an attack by a single Canadian Division. In fact the attack comprised four Canadian Divisions, and the strategic ridge was taken with relative ease. The scroll told Von Bork our Artillery Brigade would have had just two days' preparation with 4.5 Howitzers firing gas shells, giving the impression we were short of this ammunition and insufficiently practiced in delivery of the shell to the targets. The reality was the Brigade had had two weeks' preparation and stock-piled all the shells they needed. Blanche Barwell's message had said that on eve of the main attack, our side would open up with two-hundred rounds-per-gun of gas shell aimed at German batteries. Instead it was five-hundred rounds-per-gun of gas shell.

A week into the Offensive, a second-lieutenant from the Army Service Corps taking shelter in my office from a rainstorm left a soggy copy of *The Times* behind. Automatically I turned to the Obituaries pages. Some way down the long list I read *"Miss Blanche Barwell, 1915 Star. Royal Red Cross and Bar. Voluntary Aid Detachment. Aboard Ferry sunk by enemy action mid-Channel."*

I cut out the obituary and put it in a drawer.

I managed to discover the stretcher-bearer's burial site. Bringing up his body was a further traumatic experience for the exhumation party. They were bitterly aware that shell-shocked officers were sent to 7 General Hospital at St. Omer and onwards to England for further treatment and reassignment far from the Front. Other Ranks who suffered from shell-shock were convicted of cowardice and shot.

At the instance of the Prime Minister, the stretcher-bearer's remains were shipped back to Burwash, the village of the dead man's birth, the home of Rudyard Kipling who, two years before, had composed the poem "My Boy Jack". The stretcher-bearer's pathetic assembly of personal possessions were exhumed with him, including a diary he kept, titled *A Voice from the Trenches*.

Chapter IV: I Return To England

The was early January 1919. The German Kaiser had abdicated and fled into exile in Holland. My wife and I had celebrated my first Christmas

452

in "Blighty" in four years, following an honourable discharge from the Army. I would need to rebuild my medical practice. I was determined to make it a focal point for distressed former combatants. I placed an advertisement in *The Evening Chronicle* for a nurse with experience of antibiotics and antiseptics and some complex surgical and anaesthesia techniques, ideally *"with experience of patients physically or mentally damaged by the late war"*. The receptionist took it upon herself to conduct the first job interviews, to bring the numbers down to the most promising three or four applicants. She especially commended one, a Sylvia Craig, a nurse with considerable experience of treating wounded soldiers at the Front.

"Ask Miss Craig to come to my office after morning surgery tomorrow," I ordered. I wondered if she might have known Blanche Barwell.

At mid-day on the morrow, Silvia Craig was led to my office. I heard the receptionist open the door just as I was coming to the end of writing down my diagnosis (*"Wart-like patches around skin folds indicating secondary syphilis."*) on the medical records of the Earl of C---------, the last patient of the morning. I could hear the arrival's quiet breathing as she stood waiting.

I rose to greet her. I was still half-way to my feet when I was hit by a shock so extreme I had to clutch at the edge of my desk to avoid crashing to the floor in a faint. I recognised at once the face with the large sympathetic blue eyes so like my late wife Mary's, and the sweet and amiable expression of my current wife. Standing before me was Blanche Barwell, my former Staff Nurse who had been executed for treasonably *"adhering to the King's enemies outside the realm"*. Only once before had I experienced such an extreme reaction when confronted with what seemed to be an apparition standing in front of me. That was when my friend Sherlock Holmes returned from the dead twenty-five years earlier, after I had suffered three painful years believing he had died at the Reichenbach Falls in the Swiss Alps, locked in a final struggle with the Napoleon of Crime, Professor James Moriarty – the case I published under the title "The Final Problem".

"Miss Barwell!" I stammered. "Can this be you? You are . . . How? You're – "

"Dead?" the apparition laughed. She continued in her melodic Scottish lilt, "If so, Dr. Watson, my spirit is here very much in search of a cup of tea, followed by gainful employment."

I managed to walk rather unsteadily to the door to order a pot of tea for two and a plate of Garibaldi biscuits.

Once re-seated, I reached into a drawer for a brandy-flask.

453

"Miss Barwell – or Miss Craig – " I said, "while I recover my equilibrium, please take a seat and explain everything. You were removed from the Station by military guards. Word came back you'd been shot at dawn for treason, a sentence with which – with great reluctance – I concurred. Next I came across a puzzling obituary *The Times*. Yet here you are!"

"Before I start," she said, "there's something I want to show you."

She reached into her handbag and held up a small, elegant box, opening it to reveal the Distinguished Conduct Medal for Gallantry in the Field.

"His Majesty the King presented it to me at Buckingham Palace this morning. Mycroft Holmes knew you had recommended me for it – before you discovered the scroll in the lilies, of course! Now," she continued, "to start at the very beginning. I finished my training in 1915 and was wondering how to use it when I chanced across a copy of *The War Illustrated*. It featured a Russian nurse on the Eastern Front called Mira Miksailovitch Ivanoff, who rallied a group of soldiers so splendidly they fought off a German attack. Unfortunately, she was killed at the moment of victory. I knew at once I wanted to do something just as spectacular, even if it meant I too ended up dead, but what or how I had no idea. I learnt that Craiglockhart War Hospital up in Edinburgh was to open psychiatric wards to care for officers suffering from the psychological effects of battle. I applied for a post and they accepted me.

"Just after the Second Battle of Ypres, Mycroft Holmes came to my ward with General Sir Douglas Haig to talk to British soldiers recuperating from being gassed by the Germans. Mr. Holmes took me to one side. He told me that General Haig had just taken command of the British Expeditionary Force and was charged with unlocking the stalemate along the Western Front. I told him on my mother's side there was a Captain in the Peninsular War under Sir John Moore at Carrión in 1808. I said I was ready to do absolutely anything to bring the war to an end. By that time, all thoughts of the conflict being over by the first Christmas had long since been seen as the chimera it always was. 'Absolutely anything, you say?' he asked, giving me a hard stare. 'Absolutely anything!' I repeated. 'Even going to the Western Front?' he asked. "Even," I replied, thinking of Mira Miksailovitch Ivanoff.

"On duty not long afterwards, I received a summons to the Matron's office. She said she had been very pleased with my work, but 'someone high up' had asked for me to be transferred to St. Bart's, Rochester, for further training in neurasthenia. I'd hardly learnt my way around my new hospital when I received an order to report to the Matron's office – 'at once'. I assumed I was to be complimented on my work with shell-shocked soldiers.

"When I went into her office, Matron was reading or re-reading a communication on the desk in front of her. Next to it was an official-looking package. Her expression was grim. She didn't look up for quite some time. Then she told me the letter was from the War Office. It said information of a disturbing nature had been sent to General Haig's office, stating that while at the hospital in Edinburgh I had become known for my 'extreme sympathy' for the enemy, accusing me of saying things like, 'Well, one can easily understand why the Germans are using gas against us. We started it in the first place, and shouldn't have.' I told her I couldn't possibly have said that. I'd been treating our own soldiers from Ypres since April 1915, because that's when the first use of chlorine took place – and it was by the Germans, not us. But she refused to listen. She waved the communication at me and said, "They are considering putting you before a drumhead court-martial, but because of your youthful naivety and your excellent clinical work with the neurasthenic patients, they're prepared to give you one final chance to redeem yourself. You'll find out what that is when you open this package. Now, go to your quarters and pack your things and be sure to quit my hospital today."

Sylvia Craig was silent for a moment. In a low voice she said, "It was very alarming. I couldn't see what choice I had except to go along with this bizarre order. I opened the package the minute I got home. It contained a *laissez-passer* in English and French in the name of *Blanche Barwell*. As you now know from my reply to your advertisement, my real name is Sylvia Craig. Once I had read the accompanying documents, I was to destroy them and adapt as quickly as possible to my new name. I was to go to a certain address in Whitehall, where I would sign the Official Secrets Act. Then I was to await instructions from Mycroft Holmes. Even mentioning his name to anyone would be considered treasonous. It was becoming terribly exciting."

"You had no idea what was expected of you?" I asked.

"None at all," she agreed, "though later a passing remark Mycroft Holmes had made when we first met came back into my mind: That in modern warfare, military intelligence misleading the enemy was of greater value to our war effort than an extra ten Divisions. Mr. Holmes found it a simple matter to get news of my so-called traitorous sympathies for Germany to Von Bork. I know you and Mr. Sherlock Holmes captured the German spy just before the war started, but you may not know it was Mycroft Holmes who insisted on getting Von Bork released from gaol and sent back to Germany, deliberately to keep tabs on his activities once the war began."

455

She laughed.

"The rest you know. I became a Staff Nurse at your Clearing Station at Lapugnoy."

"And passed on messages in the bunches of flowers you took to the stretcher-bearer's grave-site – information I now assume was concocted by Mycroft."

"As you say. I felt the stretcher-bearer would forgive me for visiting him when I had messages for the enemy. It was the perfect place for Von Bork's people to come at night to collect them. I had good reason to leave bouquets of flowers, despite the Commanding Officer's strict rules against any such signs of sympathy. I'd been deeply upset when the stretcher-bearer was executed. I tried to get the court-martial board to understand such men at the front line have a given stock of courage – a finite stock which is never replenished in rest periods between battles."

I shook my head in admiration.

"So the half-dozen devilishly cunning German spies scattered hither and thither throughout the British Expeditionary Force, spies who had so bedevilled Kell at MI5 and Cumming at MI 1(c) . . . those were just you, acting on Mycroft's instructions."

"That's right."

"So your first assignment – was it Mycroft and Mycroft alone who ordered you to reveal the first plan for a Second Battle of Arras to Von Bork, resulting in a complete revamping of our preparations?"

"It was."

"But why did your information need to be so accurate?"

"That was essential. Mycroft Holmes was setting up Humpty-Dumpty – the Kaiser's men – for a great fall. The Prime Minister had tasked him to set the scene for a final break-through at a second battle at Arras. You'll recall the first battle of Arras at the start of the war. Both sides tried to outflank the other's trenches in the race to the North Sea coast. Neither succeeded, a debacle which led to the long period of stalemate."

"Which is why you arrived out of the blue at my marquee at the Station."

"That was why I arrived at that particular CCS, because of its proximity to Arras, yes. None of it would have worked if we failed to convince Von Bork I was prepared to be a traitor to my country. Before Mr. Holmes arranged for me to come to your Clearance Station, he had to make sure Von Bork thought I was deeply embittered from the treatment I received from St. Bart's, Rochester, and the War Office. Von Bork seized the opportunity. When he forwarded my first communication on to General von Falkenhausen's 6th Army, they were probably wary, until the

456

German Rumpler and Albatross reconnaissance planes with their Görz and ICA cameras soon confirmed the accuracy of important parts of my information. My credentials were established."

Again a merry laugh.

"As it was, the first message very nearly wrecked the whole ruse. I wrote it on stationery supplied to me by Mr. Holmes. We missed the fact each page was water marked. Such paper was incredibly restricted to officialdom. There was no way an ordinary nurse could have obtained it."

"Did Kell at MI5 know about Mycroft's gambit, to reveal the earlier battle-plan in its entirety to the enemy, solely with the aim of establishing your *bona fides*?"

"No. The Prime Minister and Mr. Holmes kept him in the dark until it was all over."

I asked, "Given Mycroft could make such mistakes as giving you watermarked writing paper, why did he eschew help from MI 1(c)?"

"An unhealthy rivalry was raging between the War Office and our French and Belgian Allies. It had led to denunciations, even buying up of other services' agents. Mr. Holmes thought they were a very leaky ship. The only person other than me who knew about his ruse was Lloyd George. The Prime Minister had to agree to taking such an immense risk to convince Berlin I was genuine. Once we achieved that, we could set up Mr. Holmes's plan – at the most strategic moment to place misleading information in the flowers which would be accepted as gospel by the Kaiser's *Großer Generalstab* – the Great General Staff."

I said, "What I haven't yet understood is why Mycroft took me to the bouquet of lilies and allowed me to discover the scroll."

"As soon as the Second Battle of Arras commenced, Von Bork would realise we had fooled him. The gain in terrain by our forces in the first two days alone was greater than in any previous battle of the war, far greater than the Somme offensives. I had served my purpose. I had to be removed very quickly from Lapugnoy. My life within such easy striking distance from Von Bork's headquarters in Belgium would be very much in peril. My obituary was the final stage in Mr. Holmes's plan – to avoid being tracked down and assassinated by a vengeful Von Bork, Blanche Barwell was to disappear from the face of the Earth."

"Not even getting a fake burial," I added.

"Not even."

I sat back, wonderstruck at the story. It cleared up why "Blanche Barwell" had handwritten the information to Von Bork. At the time, it seemed a dangerous oversight for someone spying for the enemy. Mycroft must have decided it would look the more convincing than some such device as letters cut one by one from a newspaper. If separately MI 1(c) came across the scrolls before Von Bork's people could retrieve them, or burgled them from his offices, Mycroft could step in and vouch for her loyalty to King and Country.

I adopted a rueful expression. At every point along the way, from my visit to Sherlock Holmes's farm where I met K and the Prime Minister, to my relationship with my Staff Nurse, to my stroll to the lilies with Mycroft, I had been as misinformed and hoodwinked as if I had been Von Bork himself. Even Holmes had been forced to deceive me, to ensure I could at no point inadvertently give aid and comfort to the enemy or – most of all – reveal Mycroft's seminal role in this gigantic *coup de théâtre*. Now I could see what Sherlock Holmes had meant at the time of the case of the Bruce-Partington Plans when he told me, "*You are right in thinking that Mycroft is under the British government. You would also be right in a sense if you said that occasionally he is the British government.*"

I asked, "Do we have any idea what happened to Von Bork when the German High Command realised they'd been fooled?"

"No, but it wouldn't have been good. Once the Offensive got underway, Mycroft Holmes spread the rumour that Von Bork had gained his release from a British gaol only after agreeing to become a double-agent in the event of war breaking out. It wasn't true, but given the misinformation hidden in the lilies which Von Bork passed on to the German military, it would have sounded entirely plausible."

I stood up and pointed to the coat rack.

"At the favourable conclusion of yet another of our cases, Sherlock Holmes always said, 'Something nutritious at Simpson's would not be out of place.' Miss Craig, may I continue with this tradition by inviting you to Simpson's-in-the-Strand for a good lunch?"

As we stepped outside into bright sunshine, I said, "I have a favour to ask. We have come through extraordinary times together. Might you allow me to continue calling you Blanche – at least for today?"

Epilogue

Three years passed before I received permission in writing from Mansfield Cumming at MI6 to put pen to paper and record these events. I went to my bank at Charing Cross and retrieved the travel-worn and battered tin despatch-box with "*John H. Watson, M.D., Late Indian Army*" painted upon the lid. It was crammed with notes of many hundreds of cases to which I have never alluded. On the top lay the sealed envelope containing the pages of notes I'd made at the Casualty Clearing Station at Lapugnoy.

I picked up my pen and began to write . . . .

January 1ˢᵗ, 1917: Another New Year's Day. Am still on the Western Front. The terrible war against the Kaiser's land forces, the Deutsches Heer, *is at a stalemate. The winter weather is poisonous as usual, deep slush and a biting N.E. wind. It blew and raged all New Year's Eve, leaving behind deep snow this morning.*

NOTES

1. "*K*": The real Vernon George Waldegrave Kell was the only son of Major Waldegrave Charles Vernon Kell and his Polish wife, Georgiana Augusta Konarska. His aptitude for languages led to thoughts of a diplomatic career but instead he decided to become a soldier and entered the Royal Military College at Sandhurst in 1892. As MI5's leader, he proved supremely diligent, and by 1917, the organisation's registry contained almost forty-thousand files and one-million cross-indexed cards.

2. Voluntary Aid Detachment (*V.A.D.*): Because the British Army was so resolutely opposed to female military nurses except the Queen Alexandra's Imperial Military Nursing Service (QAIMNS), early volunteers from Britain were obliged to serve instead with the French and Belgian forces. V.A.D Staff Nurse "Blanche Barwell" was lucky to find herself with Dr. Watson, who clearly advanced her medical and surgical skills. In real life, the pacifist, feminist writer Vera Brittain, became a V.A.D. on the Western Front in the First World War. In her autobiography *Testament of Youth* (1933), she wrote coruscatingly about the way *V.A.D.*'s were undervalued and insolently treated.

3. MI5 and MI6: The two British organisations were established in 1909 as the Secret Service Bureau. They are often confused with each other but have distinct areas of operation.

   Military Intelligence Section 5 concerns itself largely with internal threats to the United Kingdom. At any time, several hundred staff work on secondment or attachment from other government departments and agencies. Roles include investigations, technology, surveillance, communications, information, and protective security.

   Military Intelligence Section 6 carries out operations against persons outside the British Isles. It had existed in various forms since the establishment of a secret service in 1569 by Sir Francis Walsingham, who became secretary of state to Queen Elizabeth I. In World War I, MI6 recruited authors such as W. Somerset Maugham as an asset in Switzerland.

4. RAMC: At the outbreak of war in 1914 the majority of transport was horse-drawn. Organisation for casualty evacuation was based on a "chain of evacuation". The sick and wounded were moved backwards by a series of posts: The regimental aid post, the collecting post, the advanced and main dressing station, the Casualty Clearing Station (CCS) and finally the general hospital, either in France or via hospital ship to England. At an early stage in the war, the Casualty Clearing Stations were expanded into forward areas and in some cases could take up to one-thousand patients.
   See *http://www.ramc-ww1.com/chain_of_evacuation.php*

4: Shell Shock (or Shellshock) was the name given to the psychological breakdown encompassing an array of disorders following horrific experience in the trenches – hysterical paralysis, blindness and mutism, insomnia and nightmares, anxiety, amnesia, and psychosis. Initially it was thought to be the result of proximity to a shell explosion and the subsequent

460

forces of compression and decompression causing microscopic cerebral haemorrhages. This was soon superseded by the psychiatric theory of extreme emotional disturbance and psychic repression of traumatic experience.

Craiglockhart War Hospital opened in 1916 as a military psychiatric hospital to care for officers suffering from the psychological effects of the Great War, such as neurasthenia, but many physicians and large parts of the Military refused to recognise the disorder's existence, believing shell-shocked soldiers to be "lead swingers" and malingerers. For an excellent paper on this complex affliction see *Battle for the Mind: World War I and the Birth of Military Psychiatry* by Professors Edgar Jones and Simon Wessley.
https://pubmed.ncbi.nlm.nih.gov/25441201/

5: The Second Battle of Arras: This major battle took place from 9 April to 16 May, 1917. There had been many delays. The Germans, suspecting an attack at some point, had shortened their lines to the strong *Siegfriedstellung* ("The Hindenburg Line"). The weather was frequently heavy with rain and at times snowstorms. The British offensive was initially very effective but suffered higher casualties than the Germans, nearly 160,000 British compared to an estimated 125,000 German. The British Artillery support was more effective at Arras than at the battles on the Somme, thanks in part to improvements in training and scheduling. The preliminary bombardment at the Battle of Arras saw German positions pulverised by more than 2.5-million shells, about one-million more than at the Somme. When the British troops attacked, they were supported by a creeping barrage. A combination of such tactics was used by the British to great effect – including careful rehearsal of the assault, and digging tunnels to bring the troops forward. A major success was the attack launched by the Canadian Corps at Vimy Ridge. For further insight into the Arras Offensive see the Imperial War Museum link at:
https://www.iwm.org.uk/history/voices-of-the-first-world-war-arras-and-vimy

6. Maconochie beef and vegetable stew had a dubious reputation in World War I. The cans proclaimed the contents contained the *"finest beef"*, potatoes, haricot beans, carrots, and onions, but one account from the receiving end described it as *"a tinned ration consisting of sliced vegetables, chiefly turnips and carrots, in a deal of thin soup or gravy."* The account claimed, *"Warmed in the tin, Maconochie's was edible. Cold it was a man-killer."*

7. *A Voice from the Trenches 1914-1918: From the Diaries and Sketchbooks of Bernard Eyre Walker (RAMC).* Edited by Sara Woodall. I adapted descriptive passages from this remarkable voice for Dr. Watson's Western Front diaries. For example:

> *Stretcher-bearers are the unsung heroes. Under normal circumstances, two bearers are sufficient to retrieve a wounded man from the battlefield but in the appalling mud and shell-holes of the Front, four are needed to lift the stretcher and ten to carry it more*

461

than a short distance. The walking-cases came in lorries today, the lying-cases in electric-lighted Motor Ambulances.

A Voice from the Trenches is a rare account of life on the Western Front in the Great War by the artist Bernard Eyre Walker, a stretcher-bearer with the 81st Field Ambulance and 133rd Field Ambulance. The diaries were lost by Walker, but by amazing luck found by a German, who passed them to the "Toc H", an international Christian movement, who later tracked Walker to Cumbria, where he was painting the peaceful hills.

8.   "My Boy Jack": Rudyard Kipling never wrote directly about the loss of his son, John, and he never called him "Jack", but his poem "My Boy Jack" is clearly a thinly disguised cry of mourning and regret and also the importance of sacrifice. John Kipling was killed on the Western Front in September 1915. He had only been in France for three weeks, and because of his very poor eyesight, he had initially been rejected by the army. It was only through the advocacy of his influential and famous father that he was subsequently accepted into the Irish Guards regiment.

The verses go:

"Have you news of my boy Jack?"
Not this tide.
"When d'you think that he'll come back?"
Not with this wind blowing, and this tide.

"Has any one else had word of him?"
Not this tide.
For what is sunk will hardly swim,
Not with this wind blowing, and this tide.

"Oh, dear, what comfort can I find?"
None this tide,
Nor any tide,
Except he did not shame his kind—
Not even with that wind blowing, and that tide.

Then hold your head up all the more,
This tide,
And every tide;
Because he was the son you bore,
And gave to that wind blowing and that tide!

About the Contributors

The following contributors appear in this volume:
The MX Book of New Sherlock Holmes Stories
Part XXXVI – "However Improbable . . . ." (1897-1919)

Brian Belanger, PSI, is a publisher, illustrator, graphic designer, editor, and author. In 2015, he co-founded Belanger Books publishing company along with his brother, author Derrick Belanger. His illustrations have appeared in *The Essential Sherlock Holmes* and *Sherlock Holmes: A Three-Pipe Christmas*, and in children's books such as *The MacDougall Twins with Sherlock Holmes* series, *Dragonella*, and *Scones and Bones on Baker Street*. Brian has published a number of Sherlock Holmes anthologies and novels through Belanger Books, as well as new editions of August Derleth's classic Solar Pons mysteries. Brian continues to design all of the covers for Belanger Books, and since 2016 he has designed the majority of book covers for MX Publishing. In 2019, Brian received his investiture in the PSI as "Sir Ronald Duveen." More recently, he illustrated a comic book featuring the band The Moonlight Initiative, created the logo for the Arthur Conan Doyle Society and designed *The Great Game of Sherlock Holmes* card game. Find him online at:
www.belangerbooks.com and
www.redbubble.com/people/zhahadun and
zhahadun.wixsite.com/221b

Josh Cerefice has followed the exploits of a certain pipe-smoking sleuth ever since his grandmother bought him *The Complete Sherlock Holmes* collection for his twenty-first birthday, and he has devotedly accompanied the Great Detective on his adventures ever since. When he's not reading about spectral hellhounds haunting the Devonshire moors, or the Machiavellian machinations of Professor Moriarty, you can find him putting pen to paper and challenging Holmes with new mysteries to solve in his own stories.

Chris Chan is a writer, educator, and historian. He works as a researcher and "International Goodwill Ambassador" for Agatha Christie Ltd. His true crime articles, reviews, and short fiction have appeared (or will soon appear) in *The Strand*, *The Wisconsin Magazine of History*, *Mystery Weekly*, *Gilbert!*, *Nerd HQ*, Akashic Books' *Mondays are Murder* web series, *The Baker Street Journal*, *The MX Book of New Sherlock Holmes Stories*, *Masthead: The Best New England Crime Stories*, *Sherlock Holmes Mystery Magazine*, and multiple Belanger Books anthologies. He is the creator of the Funderburke mysteries, a series featuring a private investigator who works for a school and helps students during times of crisis. The Funderburke short story "The Six-Year-Old Serial Killer" was nominated for a Derringer Award. His first book, *Sherlock & Irene: The Secret Truth Behind "A Scandal in Bohemia"*, was published in 2020 by MX Publishing. His second book, *Murder Most Grotesque: The Comedic Crime Fiction of Joyce Porter* will be released by Level Best Books in 2021, and his first novel, *Sherlock's Secretary*, was published by MX Publishing in 2021. *Murder Most Grotesque* was nominated for the Agatha and Silver Falchion Awards for Nonfiction Writing, and *Sherlock's Secretary* was nominated for the Silver Falchion for Best Comedy. He is also the author of the anthology of Sherlock Holmes stories *Of Course He Pushed Him*.

Leslie Charteris was born in Singapore on May 12th, 1907. With his mother and brother, he moved to England in 1919 and attended Rossall School in Lancashire before moving on to Cambridge University to study law. His studies there came to a halt when a publisher accepted his first novel. His third one, entitled *Meet the Tiger*, was written when he was twenty years old and published in September 1928. It introduced the world to Simon Templar, *aka* The Saint. He continued to write about The Saint until 1983 when the last book, *Salvage for The Saint*, was published. The books, which have been translated into over thirty languages, number nearly a hundred and have sold over forty-million copies around the world. They've inspired, to date, fifteen feature films, three television series, ten radio series, and a comic strip that was written by Charteris and syndicated around the world for over a decade. He enjoyed travelling, but settled for long periods in Hollywood, Florida, and finally in Surrey, England. He was awarded the Cartier Diamond Dagger by the *Crime Writers' Association* in 1992, in recognition of a lifetime of achievement. He died the following year.

Ian Dickerson was just nine years old when he discovered The Saint. Shortly after that, he discovered Sherlock Holmes. The Saint won, for a while anyway. He struck up a friendship with The Saint's creator, Leslie Charteris, and his family. With their permission, he spent six weeks studying the Leslie Charteris collection at Boston University and went on to write, direct, and produce documentaries on the making of *The Saint* and *Return of The Saint*, which have been released on DVD. He oversaw the recent reprints of almost fifty of the original Saint books in both the US and UK, and was a co-producer on the 2017 TV movie of *The Saint*. When he discovered that Charteris had written Sherlock Holmes stories as well – well, there was the excuse he needed to revisit The Canon. He's consequently written and edited three books on Holmes' radio adventures. For the sake of what little sanity he has, Ian has also written about a wide range of subjects, none of which come with a halo, including talking mashed potatoes, Lord Grade, and satellite links. Ian lives in Hampshire with his wife and two children. And an awful lot of books by Leslie Charteris. Not quite so many by Conan Doyle, though.

Sir Arthur Conan Doyle (1859-1930) *Holmes Chronicler Emeritus*. If not for him, this anthology would not exist. Author, physician, patriot, sportsman, spiritualist, husband and father, and advocate for the oppressed. He is remembered and honored for the purposes of this collection by being the man who introduced Sherlock Holmes to the world. Through fifty-six Holmes short stories, four novels, and additional Apocryphal entries, Doyle revolutionized mystery stories and also greatly influenced and improved police forensic methods and techniques for the betterment of all. *Steel True Blade Straight*.

Steve Emecz's main field is technology, in which he has been working for about twenty-five years. Steve is a regular speaker at trade shows and his tech career has taken him to more than fifty countries – so he's no stranger to planes and airports. In 2008, MX published its first Sherlock Holmes book, and MX has gone on to become the largest specialist Holmes publisher in the world with over 500 books. MX is a social enterprise and supports three main causes. The first is Happy Life, a children's rescue project in Nairobi, Kenya, where he and his wife, Sharon, spend every Christmas at the rescue centre in Kasarani. They have written two editions of a short book about the project, *The Happy Life Story*. The second is Undershaw, Sir Arthur Conan Doyle's former home, which is a school for children with learning disabilities for which Steve is a patron. Steve has been a mentor for the World Food Programme for several years, and was part of the Nobel Peace Prize winning team in 2020.

466

John Farrell Jr. was born and raised in San Pedro, California. He became interested in Sherlock Holmes in the late 1960's. He joined *The Non-Canonical Calabashes* (A Sherlock Holmes scion Society) where he met and became friends with another Sherlockian, Sean Wright. He collaborated with Mr. Wright on *The Sherlock Holmes Cookbook*. Later he was a member of *The Goose Club of the Alpha Inn*. He submitted articles to *The Baker Street Journal*. *The Baker Street Irregulars* awarded him the title The Tiger of San Pedro in 1981. He was proud to include "*BSI*" after his name. John made his living as a classical music and play reviewer for multiple newspapers in the Los Angeles area. He passed away in 2015 while he was writing a review. He left behind his family and many friends. He has been accurately described by those that knew him as larger than life.

Mark A. Gagen BSI is co-founder of Wessex Press, sponsor of the popular *From Gillette to Brett* conferences, and publisher of *The Sherlock Holmes Reference Library* and many other fine Sherlockian titles. A life-long Holmes enthusiast, he is a member of *The Baker Street Irregulars* and *The Illustrious Clients of Indianapolis*. A graphic artist by profession, his work is often seen on the covers of *The Baker Street Journal* and various BSI books.

Hal Glatzer is the author of the Katy Green mystery series set in musical milieux just before World War II. He has written and produced audio/radio mystery plays, including the all-alliterative adventures of Mark Markheim, the Hollywood hawkshaw. He scripted and produced the Charlie Chan mystery *The House Without a Key* on stage, and he adapted "The Adventure of the Devil's Foot" into a stage and video play called *Sherlock Holmes and the Volcano Horror*. In 2022, after many years on the Big Island of Hawaii, he returned to live on his native island – Manhattan. See more at: *www.halglatzer.com*

Denis Green was born in London, England in April 1905. He grew up mostly in London's Savoy Theatre where his father, Richard Green, was a principal in many Gilbert and Sullivan productions, A Flying Officer with RAF until 1924, he then spent four years managing a tea estate in North India before making his stage debut in *Hamlet* with Leslie Howard in 1928. He made his first visit to America in 1931 and established a respectable stage career before appearing in films – including minor roles in the first two Rathbone and Bruce Holmes films – and developing a career in front of and behind the microphone during the golden age of radio. Green and Leslie Charteris met in 1938 and struck up a lifelong friendship. Always busy, be it on stage, radio, film or television, Green passed away at the age of fifty in New York.

John Atkinson Grimshaw (1836-1893) was born in Leeds, England. His amazing paintings, usually featuring twilight or night scenes illuminated by gas-lamps or moonlight, are easily recognizable, and are often used on the covers of books about The Great Detective to set the mood, as shadowy figures move in the distance through misty mysterious settings and over rain-slicked streets.

Arthur Hall was born in Aston, Birmingham, UK, in 1944. He discovered his interest in writing during his schooldays, along with a love of fictional adventure and suspense. His first novel, *Sole Contact*, was an espionage story about an ultra-secret government department known as "Sector Three", and was followed, to date, by three sequels. Other works include seven Sherlock Holmes novels, *The Demon of the Dusk*, *The One Hundred Percent Society*, *The Secret Assassin*, *The Phantom Killer*, *In Pursuit of the Dead*, *The Justice Master*, and *The Experience Club* as well as three collections of Holmes *Further Little-Known Cases of Sherlock* Holmes, *Tales from the Annals of Sherlock* Holmes, and

467

The Additional Investigations of Sherlock Holmes. He has also written other short stories and a modern detective novel. He lives in the West Midlands, United Kingdom.

In the year 1998 **Craig Janacek** took his degree of Doctor of Medicine at Vanderbilt University, and proceeded to Stanford to go through the training prescribed for pediatricians in practice. Having completed his studies there, he was duly attached to the University of California, San Francisco as Associate Professor. The author of over seventy medical monographs upon a variety of obscure lesions, his travel-worn and battered tin dispatch-box is crammed with papers, nearly all of which are records of his fictional works. To date, these have been published solely in electronic format, including two non-Holmes novels (*The Oxford Deception* and *The Anger of Achilles Peterson*), the trio of holiday adventures collected as *The Midwinter Mysteries of Sherlock Holmes*, the Holmes story collections *The First of Criminals, The Assassination of Sherlock Holmes, The Treasury of Sherlock Holmes, Light in the Darkness, The Gathering Gloom, The Travels of Sherlock Holmes*, and the Watsonian novels *The Isle of Devils* and *The Gate of Gold*. Craig Janacek is a *nom de plume*.

Roger Johnson, BSI, ASH, PSI, etc, is a member of more Holmesian societies than he can remember, thanks to his (so far) 16 years as editor of *The Sherlock Holmes Journal*, and thirty-two years as editor of *The District Messenger*. The latter, the newsletter of *The Sherlock Holmes Society of London*, is now in the safe hands of Jean Upton, with whom he collaborated on the well-received book, *The Sherlock Holmes Miscellany*. Roger is resigned to the fact that he will never match the Duke of Holdernesse, whose name was followed by "*half the alphabet*".

Amanda Knight was born and grew up in Sydney Australia. At the age of nineteen, she decided to travel and spent a wonderful time in the UK in the 1980's. Travelling through Scotland and Wales, as well as living and working in England for an extended period, and working in pubs, which is almost obligatory if you are an Australian in the UK. As a long-time fan of Sherlock Holmes, she spent many a pleasant hour investigating many of the places mentioned by Conan Doyle in the Sherlock Holmes stories. Amanda still lives in Australia and is enjoying the invigorating mountain air where she now resides. Amanda is the author of *The Unexpected Adventures of Sherlock Holmes* (2004)

David L. Leal PhD is Professor of Government and Mexican American Studies at the University of Texas at Austin. He is also an Associate Member of Nuffield College at the University of Oxford and a Senior Fellow of the Hoover Institution at Stanford University. His research interests include the political implications of demographic change in the United States, and he has published dozens of academic journal articles and edited nine books on these and other topics. He has taught classes on Immigration Politics, Latino Politics, Politics and Religion, Mexican American Public Policy Studies, and Introduction to American Government. In the spring of 2019, he taught British Politics and Government, which had the good fortune (if that is the right word) of taking place parallel with so many Brexit developments. He is also the author of three articles in *The Baker Street Journal* as well as letters to the editor of the *TLS: The Times Literary Supplement, Sherlock Holmes Journal*, and *The Baker Street Journal*. As a member of the British Studies Program at UT-Austin, he has given several talks on Sherlockian and Wodehousian topics. He most recently wrote a chapter, "Arthur Conan Doyle and Spiritualism," for the program's latest book in its *Adventures with Britannia* series (Harry Ransom Center/IB Tauris/Bloomsbury). He is the founder and Warden of "MA, PhD, Etc," the BSI professional scion society for higher education, and he is a member of *The Fourth*

Garrideb, The Sherlock Holmes Society of London, The Clients of Adrian Mulliner, and *His Last Bow (Tie).*

David Marcum plays *The Game* with deadly seriousness. He first discovered Sherlock Holmes in 1975 at the age of ten, and since that time, he has collected, read, and chronologicized literally thousands of traditional Holmes pastiches in the form of novels, short stories, radio and television episodes, movies and scripts, comics, fan-fiction, and unpublished manuscripts. He is the author of over one-hundred Sherlockian pastiches, some published in anthologies and magazines such as *The Strand*, and others collected in his own books, *The Papers of Sherlock Holmes, Sherlock Holmes and A Quantity of Debt, Sherlock Holmes – Tangled Skeins, Sherlock Holmes and The Eye of Heka*, and *The Collected Papers of Sherlock Holmes*. He has edited over sixty books, including several dozen traditional Sherlockian anthologies, such as the ongoing series *The MX Book of New Sherlock Holmes Stories*, which he created in 2015. This collection is now at thirty-six volumes, with more in preparation. He was responsible for bringing back August Derleth's Solar Pons for a new generation with his collection of authorized Pons stories, *The Papers of Solar Pons*. His new collection, *The Further Papers of Solar Pons*, will be published in 2022/. Pons's return was further assisted by his editing of the reissued authorized versions of the original Pons books, and then several volumes of new Pons adventures. He has done the same for the adventures of Dr. Thorndyke, and has plans for similar projects in the future. He has contributed numerous essays to various publications, and is a member of a number of Sherlockian groups and Scions, as well as The Mystery Writers of America. His irregular Sherlockian blog, *A Seventeen Step Program*, addresses various topics related to his favorite book friends (as his son used to call them when he was small), and can be found at *http://17stepprogram.blogspot.com/* He is a licensed Civil Engineer, living in Tennessee with his wife and son. Since the age of nineteen, he has worn a deerstalker as his regular-and-only hat. In 2013, he and his deerstalker were finally able make his first trip-of-a-lifetime Holmes Pilgrimage to England, with return Pilgrimages in 2015 and 2016, where you may have spotted him. If you ever run into him and his deerstalker out and about, feel free to say hello!

Sidney Paget (1860-1908), a few of whose illustrations are used within this anthology, was born in London, and like his two older brothers, became a famed illustrator and painter. He completed over three-hundred-and-fifty drawings for the Sherlock Holmes stories that were first published in *The Strand* magazine, defining Holmes's image forever after in the public mind.

Tracy J. Revels, a Sherlockian from the age of eleven, is a professor of history at Wofford College in Spartanburg, South Carolina. She is a member of *The Survivors of the Gloria Scott* and *The Studious Scarlets Society*, and is a past recipient of the Beacon Society Award. Almost every semester, she teaches a class that covers The Canon, either to college students or to senior citizens. She is also the author of three supernatural Sherlockian pastiches with MX (*Shadowfall, Shadowblood,* and *Shadowwraith*), and a regular contributor to her scion's newsletter. She also has some notoriety as an author of very silly skits: For proof, see "The Adventure of the Adversarial Adventuress" and "Occupy Baker Street" on YouTube. When not studying Sherlock, she can be found researching the history of her native state, and has written books on Florida in the Civil War and on the development of Florida's tourism industry.

Nicholas Rowe was born in Edinburgh Scotland and attended Eton before receiving a Bachelor of Arts degree from the University of Bristol. He has performed in a many films, television shows, and theatrical productions. In 1985, he was Sherlock Holmes in *Young Sherlock Holmes*, and he also appeared as the "Matinee Holmes" in 2015's *Mr. Holmes.*

Dan Rowley practiced law for over forty years in private practice and with a large international corporation. He is retired and lives in Erie, Pennsylvania, with his wife Judy, who puts her artistic eye to his transcription of Watson's manuscripts. He inherited his writing ability and creativity from his children, Jim and Katy, and his love of mysteries from his parents, Jim and Ruth.

Alisha Shea has resided near Saint Louis, Missouri for over thirty years. The eldest of six children, she found reading to be a genuine escape from the chaotic drudgery of life. She grew to love not only Sherlock Holmes, but the time period from which he emerged. In her spare time, she indulges in creating music via piano, violin, and Native American flute. Sometimes she thinks she might even be getting good at it. She also produces a wide variety of fiber arts which are typically given away or auctioned off for various fundraisers.

Liese Sherwood-Fabre knew she was destined to write when she got an A+ in the second grade for her story about Dick, Jane, and Sally's ruined picnic. After obtaining her PhD, she joined the federal government and worked and lived internationally for more than fifteen years. Returning to the states, she seriously pursued her writing career, garnering such awards as a finalist in the Romance Writers of America's Golden Heart contest and a Pushcart Prize nomination. A recognized Sherlockian scholar, her essays have appeared in newsletters, *The Baker Street Journal*, and *Canadian Holmes*. She has recently turned to a childhood passion: Sherlock Holmes. *The Adventure of the Murdered Midwife*, the first book in *The Early Case Files of Sherlock Holmes* series, was the CIBA Mystery and Mayhem 2020 first-place winner. *Publishers Weekly* has described her fourth book in the series, *The Adventure of the Purloined Portrait*, as "*a truly unique, atmospheric tale that is Sherlockian through and through.*" More about her writing can be found at *www.liesesherwoodfabre.com.*

Tim Symonds was born in London. He grew up in the rural English counties of Somerset and Dorset, and the British Crown Dependency of Guernsey. After several years travelling widely, including farming on the slopes of Mt. Kenya in East Africa and working on the Zambezi River in Central Africa, he emigrated to Canada and the United States. He studied at the Georg-August University (Göttingen) in Germany, and the University of California, Los Angeles, graduating *cum laude* and Phi Beta Kappa. He is a Fellow of the Royal Geographical Society and a Member of The Society of Authors. His detective novels include *Sherlock Holmes And The Dead Boer At Scotney Castle*, *Sherlock Holmes And The Mystery Of Einstein's Daughter*, *Sherlock Holmes And The Case Of The Bulgarian Codex*, *Sherlock Holmes And The Sword Of Osman*, *Sherlock Holmes And The Nine-Dragon Sigil*, six Holmes and Watson short stories under the title *A Most Diabolical Plot*, and his novella *Sherlock Holmes and the Strange Death of Brigadier-General Delves*.

William Todd has been a Holmes fan his entire life, and credits *The Hound of the Baskervilles* as the impetus for his love of both reading and writing. He began to delve into fan fiction a few years ago when he decided to take a break from writing his usual Victorian/Gothic horror stories. He was surprised how well-received they were, and has tried to put out a couple of Holmes stories a year since then. When not writing, Mr. Todd is a pathology supervisor at a local hospital in Northwestern Pennsylvania. He is the husband of a terrific lady and father to two great kids, one with special needs, so the benefactor of these anthologies is close to his heart.

Margaret Walsh was born Auckland, New Zealand and now lives in Melbourne, Australia. She is the author of *Sherlock Holmes and the Molly-Boy Murders*, *Sherlock Holmes and the Case of the Perplexed Politician*, and *Sherlock Holmes and the Case of the London Dock Deaths*, all published by MX Publishing. Margaret has been a devotee of Sherlock Holmes since childhood and has had several Holmesian related essays printed in anthologies, and is a member of the online society *Doyle's Rotary Coffin*. She has an ongoing love affair with the city of London. When she's not working or planning trips to London, Margaret can be found frequenting the many and varied bookshops of Melbourne.

Emma West joined Undershaw in April 2021 as the Director of Education with a brief to ensure that qualifications formed the bedrock of our provision, whilst facilitating a positive balance between academia, pastoral care, and well-being. She quickly took on the role of Acting Headteacher from early summer 2021. Under her leadership, Undershaw has embraced its new name, new vision, and consequently we have seen an exponential increase in demand for places. There is a buzz in the air as we invite prospective students and families through the doors. Emma has overseen a strategic review, re-cemented relationships with Local Authorities, and positioned Undershaw at the helm of SEND education in Surrey and beyond. Undershaw has a wide appeal: Our students present to us with mild to moderate learning needs and therefore may have some very recent memories of poor experiences in their previous schools. Emma's background as a senior leader within the independent school sector has meant she is well-versed in brokering relationships between the key stakeholders, our many interdependences, local businesses, families, and staff, and all this whilst ensuring Undershaw remains relentlessly child-centric in its approach. Emma's energetic smile and boundless enthusiasm for Undershaw is inspiring.

The following contributors appear
in the companion volumes:

The MX Book of New Sherlock Holmes Stories
Part XXXIV – "However Improbable . . . ." (1878-1888)
Part XXXV – "However Improbable . . . ." (1889-1896)

Tim Newton Anderson is a former senior daily newspaper journalist and PR manager who has recently started writing fiction. In the past six months, he has placed fourteen stories in publications including *Parsec Magazine*, *Tales of the Shadowmen*, *SF Writers Guild*, *Zoetic Press*, *Dark Lane Books*, *Dark Horses Magazine*, *Emanations*, and *Planet Bizarro*.

Donald Baxter has practiced medicine for over forty years. He resides in Erie, Pennsylvania with his wife and their dog. His family and his friends are for the most part lawyers who have given him the ability to make stuff up, just as they do.

Thomas A. Burns Jr. writes *The Natalie McMasters Mysteries* from the small town of Wendell, North Carolina, where he lives with his wife and son, four cats, and a Cardigan Welsh Corgi. He was born and grew up in New Jersey, attended Xavier High School in Manhattan, earned B.S degrees in Zoology and Microbiology at Michigan State University, and a M.S. in Microbiology at North Carolina State University. As a kid, Tom started reading mysteries with The Hardy Boys, Ken Holt, and Rick Brant, then graduated to the classic stories by authors such as A. Conan Doyle, Dorothy Sayers, John Dickson Carr, Erle Stanley Gardner, and Rex Stout, to name a few. Tom has written fiction as a hobby all of his life, starting with *The Man from U.N.C.L.E.* stories in marble-backed copybooks in grade school. He built a career as technical, science, and medical writer and editor for nearly thirty years in industry and government. Now that he's a full-time novelist, he's excited to publish his own mystery series, as well as to write stories about his second most favorite detective, Sherlock Holmes. His Holmes story, "The Camberwell Poisoner", appeared in the March-June 2021 issue of *The Strand Magazine*. Tom has also written a Lovecraftian horror novel, *The Legacy of the Unborn*, under the pen name of Silas K. Henderson – a sequel to H.P. Lovecraft's masterpiece *At the Mountains of Madness*. His Natalie McMasters novel *Killers!* won the Killer Nashville Silver Falchion Award for Best Book of 2021.

Josh Cerefice *also has a story in Part XXXV.*

Leslie Charteris *also has a story in Part XXXIV.*

Martin Daley was born in Carlisle, Cumbria in 1964. He cites Doyle's Holmes and Watson as his favourite literary characters, who continue to inspire his own detective writing. His fiction and non-fiction books include a Holmes pastiche set predominantly in his home city in 1903. In the adventure, he introduced his own detective, Inspector Cornelius Armstrong, who has subsequently had some of his own cases published by MX Publishing. For more information visit *www.martindaley.co.uk*

The Davies Brothers are Brett and Nicholas Davies, twin brothers who share a love of books, films, history, and the Wales football team. Brett lived in four different countries before settling in Japan, where he teaches English and Film Studies at a university in Tokyo. He also writes for screen and stage, as well as articles for a variety of publications on cinema, sports, and travel. Nicholas is a freelance writer and PhD researcher based in Cardiff. He previously worked for the Arts Council of Wales, focusing on theatre and drama. He now writes for stage and screen, as well as articles for arts and football magazines. They are the authors of the novels *Hudson James and the Baker Street Legacy* (based upon an ancient puzzle set by Sherlock Holmes himself!) and *The Phoenix Code*. They also serve as the "literary agents" for Dr Watson's newly uncovered adventures, *Sherlock Holmes: The Centurion Papers*.

Ian Dickerson *also has a foreword s in Part XXXIV.*

Alan Dimes was born in North-West London and graduated from Sussex University with a BA in English Literature. He has spent most of his working life teaching English. Living in the Czech Republic since 2003, he is now semi-retired and divides his time between Prague and his country cottage. He has also written some fifty stories of horror and fantasy and thirty stories about his husband-and-wife detectives, Peter and Deirdre Creighton, set in the 1930's.

Anna Elliott is an author of historical fiction and fantasy. Her first series, *The Twilight of Avalon* trilogy, is a retelling of the Trystan and Isolde legend. She wrote her second series, *The Pride and Prejudice Chronicles*, chiefly to satisfy her own curiosity about what might have happened to Elizabeth Bennet, Mr. Darcy, and all the other wonderful cast of characters after the official end of Jane Austen's classic work. She enjoys stories about strong women, and loves exploring the multitude of ways women can find their unique strengths. She was delighted to lend a hand with the "Sherlock and Lucy" series, and this story, firstly because she loves Sherlock Holmes as much as her father, co-author Charles Veley, does, and second because it almost never happens that someone with a dilemma shouts, "Quick, we need an author of historical fiction!" Anna lives in the Washington, D.C .area with her husband and three children.

Matthew J. Elliott is the author of *Big Trouble in Mother Russia* (2016), the official sequel to the cult movie *Big Trouble in Little China*, *Lost in Time and Space: An Unofficial Guide to the Uncharted Journeys of Doctor Who* (2014), *Sherlock Holmes on the Air* (2012), *Sherlock Holmes in Pursuit* (2013), *The Immortals: An Unauthorized Guide to* Sherlock *and* Elementary (2013), and *The Throne Eternal* (2014). His articles, fiction, and reviews have appeared in the magazines *Scarlet Street*, *Total DVD*, *SHERLOCK*, and *Sherlock Holmes Mystery Magazine*, and the collections *The Game's Afoot*, *Curious Incidents 2*, *Gaslight Grimoire*, *The Mammoth Book of Best British Crime 8*, and *The MX Book of New Sherlock Holmes Stories – Part III: 1896-1929*. He has scripted over 260 radio plays, including episodes of *Doctor Who*, *The Further Adventures of Sherlock Holmes*, *The Twilight Zone*, *The New Adventures of Mickey Spillane's Mike Hammer*, *Fangoria's Dreadtime Stories*, and award-winning adaptations of *The Hound of the Baskervilles* and *The War of the Worlds*. He is the only radio dramatist to adapt all sixty original stories from The Canon for the series *The Classic Adventures of Sherlock Holmes*. Matthew is a writer and performer on *RiffTrax.com*, the online comedy experience from the creators of cult sci-fi TV series *Mystery Science Theater 3000* (*MST3K* to the initiated). He's also written a few comic books.

James Gelter is a director and playwright living in Brattleboro, VT. His produced written works for the stage include adaptations of *Frankenstein* and *A Christmas Carol*, several children's plays for the New England Youth Theatre, as well as seven outdoor plays co-written with his wife, Jessica, in their *Forest of Mystery* series. In 2018, he founded The Baker Street Readers, a group of performers that present dramatic readings of Arthur Conan Doyle's original Canon of Sherlock Holmes stories, featuring Gelter as Holmes, his longtime collaborator Tony Grobe as Dr. Watson, and a rotating list of guests. When the COVID-19 pandemic stopped their live performances, Gelter transformed the show into The Baker Street Readers Podcast. Some episodes are available for free on Apple Podcasts and Stitcher, with many more available to patrons at *patreon.com/bakerstreetreaders*.

Paul D. Gilbert was born in 1954 and has lived in and around London all of his life. His wife Jackie is a Holmes expert who keeps him on the straight and narrow! He has two sons, one of whom now lives in Spain. His interests include literature, ancient history, all religions, most sports, and movies. He is currently employed full-time as a funeral director. His books so far include *The Lost Files of Sherlock Holmes* (2007), *The Chronicles of Sherlock Holmes* (2008), *Sherlock Holmes and the Giant Rat of Sumatra* (2010), *The Annals of Sherlock Holmes* (2012), *Sherlock Holmes and the Unholy Trinity* (2015), *Sherlock Holmes: The Four Handed Game* (2017), *The Illumination of Sherlock Holmes* (2019), and *The Treasure of the Poison King* (2021).

Denis Green *also has a story in Part XXXIV.*

Arthur Hall *also has stories in Parts XXXIV and XXXV*

Stephen Herczeg is an IT Geek, writer, actor, and film-maker based in Canberra Australia. He has been writing for over twenty years and has completed a couple of dodgy novels, sixteen feature-length screenplays, and numerous short stories and scripts. Stephen was very successful in 2017's International Horror Hotel screenplay competition, with his scripts *TITAN* winning the Sci-Fi category and *Dark are the Woods* placing second in the horror category. His two-volume short story collection, *The Curious Cases of Sherlock Holmes*, was published in 2021. His work has featured in *Sproutlings – A Compendium of Little Fictions* from Hunter Anthologies, the *Hells Bells* Christmas horror anthology published by the Australasian Horror Writers Association, and the *Below the Stairs*, *Trickster's Treats*, *Shades of Santa*, *Behind the Mask*, and *Beyond the Infinite* anthologies from *OzHorror.Con*, *The Body Horror Book*, *Anemone Enemy*, and *Petrified Punks* from Oscillate Wildly Press, and *Sherlock Holmes In the Realms of H.G. Wells* and *Sherlock Holmes: Adventures Beyond the Canon* from Belanger Books.

Paul Hiscock is an author of crime, fantasy, horror, and science fiction tales. His short stories have appeared in a variety of anthologies, and include a seventeenth-century whodunnit, a science fiction western, a clockpunk fairytale, and numerous Sherlock Holmes pastiches. He lives with his family in Kent (England) and spends his days taking care of his two children. He mainly does his writing in coffee shops with members of the local NaNoWriMo group, or in the middle of the night when his family has gone to sleep. Consequently, his stories tend to be fuelled by large amounts of black coffee. You can find out more about Paul's writing at *www.detectivesanddragons.uk*.

Anisha Jagdeep is a 21-year-old senior at Rutgers University, currently pursuing a degree in Computer Engineering. With her twin sister, Ankita, a fellow Sherlock Holmes enthusiast, she enjoys watching classic films and writing short stories inspired by notable short story writers such as Dame Agatha Christie, John Kendrick Bangs, O. Henry, and Saki. They are also students of Indian classical music and dance. Anisha expresses her gratitude to Sir Arthur Conan Doyle for his unparalleled contributions to mystery literature with his exceptional characters, Sherlock Holmes and Dr. Watson.

Christopher James was born in 1975 in Paisley, Scotland. Educated at Newcastle and UEA, he was a winner of the UK's National Poetry Competition in 2008. He has written three full length Sherlock Holmes novels, *The Adventure of the Ruby Elephant*, *The Jeweller of Florence*, and *The Adventure of the Beer Barons*, all published by MX.

Naching T. Kassa is a wife, mother, and writer. She's created short stories, novellas, poems, and co-created three children. She resides in Eastern Washington State with her husband, Dan Kassa. Naching is a member of *The Horror Writers Association*, *Mystery Writers of America*, *The Sound of the Baskervilles*, *The ACD Society*, *The Crew of the Barque Lone Star*, and *The Sherlock Holmes Society of London*. She's also an assistant and staff writer for Still Water Bay at Crystal Lake Publishing. You can find her work on Amazon. *https://www.amazon.com/Naching-T-Kassa/e/B005ZGHTI0*

Susan Knight's newest novel, *Mrs. Hudson goes to Paris*, from MX publishing, is the latest in a series which began with her collection of stories, *Mrs. Hudson Investigates* (2019) and the novel *Mrs. Hudson goes to Ireland* (2020). She has contributed to several of the MX anthologies of new Sherlock Holmes short stories and enjoys writing as Dr. Watson as much as she does Mrs. Hudson. Susan is the author of two other non-Sherlockian story collections, as well as three novels, a book of non-fiction, and several plays, and has won several prizes for her writing. Mrs. Hudson's next adventure, still evolving, will take her to Kent, the Garden of England, where she is hoping for some peace and quiet. In vain, alas. Susan lives in Dublin.

Gordon Linzner is founder and former editor of *Space and Time Magazine*, and author of three published novels and dozens of short stories in *F&SF*, *Twilight Zone*, *Sherlock*

Holmes Mystery Magazine, and numerous other magazines and anthologies, including *Baker Street Irregulars II*, *Across the Universe*, and *Strange Lands*. He is a member of *HWA* and a lifetime member of *SFWA*.

David Marcum *also has stories in Parts XXXIV and XXXV.*

John McNabb is a Welshman and an archaeologist, and a proud member of *The Sherlock Holmes Society of London*. He has published academic analysis of aspects of Conan Doyle's work, as well as its broader context. Mac also has a long-standing interest in Victorian and Edwardian scientific romances and the portrayal of human origins in early science fiction.

Mark Mower is a long-standing member of the *Crime Writers' Association*, *The Sherlock Holmes Society of London,* and *The Solar Pons Society of London*. To date, he has written 33 Sherlock Holmes stories, and his pastiche collections include *Sherlock Holmes: The Baker Street Case-Files*, *Sherlock Holmes: The Baker Street Legacy*, and *Sherlock Holmes: The Baker Street Archive* (all with MX Publishing). His non-fiction works include the best-selling book *Zeppelin Over Suffolk: The Final Raid of the L48* (Pen & Sword Books). Alongside his writing, Mark maintains a sizeable collection of pastiches, and never tires of discovering new stories about Sherlock Holmes and Dr. Watson.

Will Murray has built a career on writing classic pulp characters, ranging from Tarzan of the Apes to Doc Savage. He has penned several milestone crossover novels in his acclaimed Wild Adventures series. *Skull Island* pitted Doc Savage against King Kong, which was followed by *King Kong Vs. Tarzan*. *Tarzan, Conqueror of Mars* costarred John Carter of Mars. His 2015 Doc Savage novel, *The Sinister Shadow*, revived the famous radio and pulp mystery man. Murray reunited them for *Empire of Doom*. His first Spider novel, *The Doom Legion*, revived that infamous crime buster, as well as James Christopher, AKA Operator 5, and the renowned G-8. His second *Spider, Fury in Steel*, guest-stars the FBI's Suicide Squad. Ten of his Sherlock Holmes short stories have been collected as *The Wild Adventures of Sherlock Holmes*. He is the author of the non-fiction book, *Master of Mystery: The Rise of The Shadow*. For Marvel Comics, Murray created the Unbeatable Squirrel Girl. Website: *www.adventuresinbronze.com*

Tracy J. Revels *also has stories in Parts XXXIV and XXXV.*

Roger Riccard's family history has Scottish roots, which trace his lineage back to Highland Scotland. This British Isles ancestry encouraged his interest in the writings of Sir Arthur Conan Doyle at an early age. He has authored the novels, *Sherlock Holmes & The Case of the Poisoned Lilly*, and *Sherlock Holmes & The Case of the Twain Papers*. In addition he has produced several short stories in *Sherlock Holmes Adventures for the Twelve Days of Christmas* and the series *A Sherlock Holmes Alphabet of Cases*. A new series will begin publishing in the Autumn of 2022, and his has another novel in the works. All of his books have been published by Baker Street Studios. His Bachelor of Arts Degrees in both Journalism and History from California State University, Northridge, have proven valuable to his writing historical fiction, as well as the encouragement of his wife/editor/inspiration and Sherlock Holmes fan, Rosilyn. She passed in 2021, and it is in her memory that he continues to contribute to the legacy of the "*man who never lived and will never die*".

Dan Rowley *also has stories in Parts XXXIV and XXXV.*

Jane Rubino is the author of *A Jersey Shore* mystery series, featuring a Jane Austen-loving amateur sleuth and a Sherlock Holmes-quoting detective, *Knight Errant*, *Lady Vernon and Her Daughter*, (a novel-length adaptation of Jane Austen's novella *Lady Susan*, co-authored with her daughter Caitlen Rubino-Bradway, *What Would Austen Do?*, also co-authored with her daughter, a short story in the anthology *Jane Austen Made Me Do It*, *The Rucastles' Pawn*, *The Copper Beeches from Violet Turner's POV*, and, of course, there's the Sherlockian novel in the drawer – who doesn't have one? Jane lives on a barrier island at the New Jersey shore.

Geri Schear is a novelist and short story writer. Her work has been published in literary journals in the U.S. and Ireland. Her first novel, *A Biased Judgement: The Diaries of Sherlock Holmes 1897* was released to critical acclaim in 2014. The sequel, *Sherlock Holmes and the Other Woman* was published in 2015, and *Return to Reichenbach* in 2016. She lives in Kells, Ireland.

Robert V. Stapleton was born in Leeds, England, and served as a full-time Anglican clergyman for forty years, specialising in Rural Ministry. He is now retired, and lives with his wife in North Yorkshire. This is the area of the country made famous by the writings of James Herriot, and television's *The Yorkshire Vet*, to name just a few. Amongst other things, he is a member of the local creative writing group, Thirsk Write Now (TWN), and regularly produces material for them. He has had more than fifty stories published, of various lengths and in a number of different places. He has also written a number of stories for *The MX Book of New Sherlock Holmes Stories*, and several published by Belanger Books. Several of these Sherlock Holmes pastiches have now been brought together and published in a single volume by MX Publishing, under the title of *Sherlock Holmes: A Yorkshireman in Baker Street*. Many of these stories have been set during the Edwardian period, or more broadly between the years 1880 and 1920. His interest in this period of history began at school in the 1960's when he met people who had lived during those years and heard their stories. He also found echoes of those times in literature, architecture, music, and even the coins in his pocket. The Edwardian period was a time of exploration, invention, and high adventure – rich material for thriller writers.

Award winning poet and author **Joseph W. Svec III** enjoys writing, poetry, and stories, and creating new adventures for Holmes and Watson that take them into the worlds of famous literary authors and scientists. His *Missing Authors* trilogy introduced Holmes to Lewis Carroll, Jules Verne, H.G. Wells, and Alfred Lord Tennyson, as well as many of their characters. His transitional story *Sherlock Holmes and the Mystery of the First Unicorn* involved several historical figures, besides a Unicorn or two. He has also written the rhymed and metered Sherlock Holmes Christmas adventure, *The Night Before Christmas in 221b*, sure to be a delight for Sherlock Holmes enthusiasts of all ages. Joseph won the Amador Arts Council 2021 Original Poetry Contest, with his Rhymed and metered story poem, "The Homecoming". Joseph has presented a literary paper on Sherlock Holmes/Alice in Wonderland crossover literature to the Lewis Carroll Society of North America, as well as given several presentations to the Amador County Holmes Hounds, Sherlockian Society. He is currently working on his first book in the *Missing Scientist Trilogy*, *Sherlock Holmes and the Adventure of the Demonstrative Dinosaur*, in which Sherlock meets Professor George Edward Challenger. Joseph has Masters Degrees in Systems Engineering and Human Organization Management, and has written numerous technical papers on Aerospace Testing. In addition to writing, Joseph enjoys creating miniature dioramas based on music, literature, and history from many different eras. His dioramas have been featured in magazine articles and many different blogs, including the North American Jules Verne society newsletter. He currently has 57 dioramas set up in his display area, and has written a reference book on toy castles and knights from around the world. An avid tea enthusiast, his tea cabinet contains over 500 different varieties, and he delights in sharing afternoon tea with his childhood sweetheart and wonderful wife, who has inspired and coauthored several books with him.

Kevin P. Thornton was shortlisted six times for the Crime Writers of Canada best unpublished novel. He never won – they are all still unpublished, and now he writes short stories. He lives in Canada, north enough that ringing Santa Claus is a local call and winter is a way of life. This is his twelfth short story in *The MX Book of New Sherlock Holmes Stories*. By the time you next hear from him, he hopes to have written his thirteenth.

DJ Tyrer dwells on the northern shore of the Thames estuary, close to the world's longest pleasure pier in the decaying seaside resort of Southend-on-Sea, and is the person behind Atlantean Publishing. They studied history at the University of Wales at Aberystwyth and have worked in the fields of education and public relations. Their fiction featuring Sherlock Holmes has appeared in volumes from MX Publishing and Belanger Books, and in an issue of *Awesome Tales*, and they have a forthcoming story in *Sherlock Holmes Mystery Magazine*. DJ's non-Sherlockian mysteries have appeared in anthologies such as *Mardi Gras Mysteries* (Mystery and Horror LLC) and *The Trench Coat Chronicles* (Celestial Echo Press).
DJ Tyrer's website is at *https://djtyrer.blogspot.co.uk/*
DJ's Facebook page is at *https://www.facebook.com/DJTyrerwriter/*
The Atlantean Publishing website is at *https://atlanteanpublishing.wordpress.com/*

Charles Veley has loved Sherlock Holmes since boyhood. As a father, he read the entire Canon to his then-ten-year-old daughter at evening story time. Now, this very same daughter, grown up to become acclaimed historical novelist Anna Elliott, has worked with him to develop new adventures in the *Sherlock Holmes and Lucy James Mystery Series*. Charles is also a fan of Gilbert & Sullivan, and wrote *The Pirates of Finance*, a new musical in the G&S tradition that won an award at the New York Musical Theatre Festival in 2013. Other than the Sherlock and Lucy series, all of the books on his Amazon Author Page were written when he was a full-time author during the late Seventies and early Eighties. He currently works for United Technologies Corporation, where his main focus is on creating sustainability and value for the company's large real estate development projects.

Margaret Walsh *also has stories in Part XXXV.*

I.A. Watson, great-grand-nephew of Dr. John H. Watson, has been intrigued by the notorious "black sheep" of the family since childhood, and was fascinated to inherit from his grandmother a number of unedited manuscripts removed circa 1956 from a rather larger collection reposing at Lloyds Bank Ltd (which acquired Cox & Co Bank in 1923). Upon discovering the published corpus of accounts regarding the detective Sherlock Holmes from which a censorious upbringing had shielded him, he felt obliged to allow an interested public access to these additional memoranda, and is gradually undertaking the task of transcribing them for admirers of Mr. Holmes and Dr. Watson's works. In the meantime, I.A. Watson continues to pen other books, the latest of which is *The Incunabulum of Sherlock Holmes*. A full list of his seventy or so published works are available at: *http://www.chillwater.org.uk/writing/iawatsonhome.htm*

Marcia Wilson is a freelance researcher and illustrator who likes to work in a style compatible for the color blind and visually impaired. She is Canon-centric, and her first MX offering, *You Buy Bones*, uses the point-of-view of Scotland Yard to show the unique talents of Dr. Watson. This continued with the publication of *Test of the Professionals: The Adventure of the Flying Blue Pidgeon* and *The Peaceful Night Poisonings*. She can be contacted at: *gravelgirty.deviantart.com*

DeForeest Wright III has a day job as a baker for Ralphs grocery stores. It helps support his love for books. A long-time lover of literature, especially of the Sherlock Holmes tales, he spends his time away from the oven hunched over novels, poetry, anthologies, or any tome on philosophy, mathematics, science, or martial arts he can find, sipping an espresso if one is to hand. He writes prose and poetry in his off hours and currently hosts "The Sunless Sea Open-Mic: Spoken Word and Poetry Show" at the Unurban Coffee House in Santa Monica. He was glad to team up writing with his father.

Sean Wright makes his home in Santa Clarita, a charming city at the entrance of the high desert in Southern California. For sixteen years, features and articles under his byline appeared in *The Tidings* – now *The Angelus News*, publications of the Roman Catholic Archdiocese of Los Angeles. Continuing his education in 2007, Mr. Wright graduated from Grand Canyon University, attaining a Bachelor of Arts degree in Christian Studies with a *summa cum laude*. He then attained a Master of Arts degree, also in Christian Studies. Once active in the entertainment industry, and in an abortive attempt to revive dramatic radio in 1976 with his beloved mentor, the late Daws Butler, directing, Mr. Wright co-produced and wrote the syndicated *New Radio Adventures of Sherlock Holmes*, starring the late Edward Mulhare as the Great Detective. Mr. Wright has written for several television quiz shows and remains proud of his work for *The Quiz Kid's Challenge* and the popular TV quiz show *Jeopardy!* for which the Academy of Television Arts and Sciences honored him in 1985 with an Emmy nomination in the field of writing. Honored with membership in The Baker Street Irregulars as "The Manor House Case" after founding The Non-Canonical Calabashes, the Sherlock Holmes Society of Los Angeles in 1970, Mr. Wright has written for *The Baker Street Journal* and *Mystery Magazine*. Since 1971, he has conducted lectures on Sherlock Holmes's influence on literature and cinema for libraries, colleges, and private organizations, including MENSA. Mr. Wright's whimsical *Sherlock Holmes Cookbook* (Drake), created with John Farrell, BSI, was published in 1976, and a mystery novel, *Enter the Lion: a Posthumous Memoir of Mycroft Holmes* (Hawthorne), "edited" with Michael Hodel, BSI, followed in 1979. As director general of The Plot Thickens Mystery Company, Mr .Wright originated hosting "mystery parties" in homes, restaurants, and offices, as well as producing and directing the very first "Mystery Train" tours on Amtrak, beginning in 1982.

The MX Book of New Sherlock Holmes Stories
Edited by David Marcum
(MX Publishing, 2015-   )

"This is the finest volume of Sherlockian fiction I have ever read, and I have read, literally, thousands." – Philip K. Jones

"Beyond Impressive . . . This is a splendid venture for a great cause!
– Roger Johnson, Editor, *The Sherlock Holmes Journal,*
The Sherlock Holmes Society of London

Part I: 1881-1889
Part II: 1890-1895
Part III: 1896-1929
Part IV: 2016 Annual
Part V: Christmas Adventures
Part VI: 2017 Annual
Part VII: Eliminate the Impossible (1880-1891)
Part VIII – Eliminate the Impossible (1892-1905)
Part IX – 2018 Annual (1879-1895)
Part X – 2018 Annual (1896-1916)
Part XI – Some Untold Cases (1880-1891)
Part XII – Some Untold Cases (1894-1902)
Part XIII – 2019 Annual (1881-1890)
Part XIV – 2019 Annual (1891-1897)
Part XV – 2019 Annual (1898-1917)
Part XVI – Whatever Remains . . . Must be the Truth (1881-1890)
Part XVII – Whatever Remains . . . Must be the Truth (1891-1898)
Part XVIII – Whatever Remains . . . Must be the Truth (1898-1925)
Part XIX – 2020 Annual (1882-1890)
Part XX – 2020 Annual (1891-1897)
Part XXI – 2020 Annual (1898-1923)
Part XXII – Some More Untold Cases (1877-1887)
Part XXIII – Some More Untold Cases (1888-1894)
Part XXIV – Some More Untold Cases (1895-1903)
Part XXV – 2021 Annual (1881-1888)
Part XXVI – 2021 Annual (1889-1897)
Part XXVII – 2021 Annual (1898-1928)
Part XXVIII – More Christmas Adventures (1869-1888)
Part XXIX – More Christmas Adventures (1889-1896)
Part XXX – More Christmas Adventures (1897-1928)
Part XXXI – 2022 Annual Part (1875-1887)
XXXII – 2022 Annual (1888-1895)
Part XXXIII – 2022 Annual (1896-1919)
Part XXXIV "However Improbable . . . ." (1878-1888)
Part XXXV "However Improbable . . . ." (1889-1896)
Part XXXVI "However Improbable . . . ." (1897-1919)

In Preparation
Part XXXVI (and XXXVIII and XXXIX???) – 2023 Annual

. . . and more to come!

The MX Book of New Sherlock Holmes Stories
Edited by David Marcum
(MX Publishing, 2015-   )

Publishers Weekly says:

Part VI: *The traditional pastiche is alive and well . . . .*

Part VII: *Sherlockians eager for faithful-to-the-canon plots and characters will be delighted.*

Part VIII: *The imagination of the contributors in coming up with variations on the volume's theme is matched by their ingenious resolutions.*

Part IX: *The 18 stories . . . will satisfy fans of Conan Doyle's originals. Sherlockians will rejoice that more volumes are on the way.*

Part X: *. . . new Sherlock Holmes adventures of consistently high quality.*

Part XI: *. . . an essential volume for Sherlock Holmes fans.*

Part XII: *. . . continues to amaze with the number of high-quality pastiches.*

Part XIII: *. . . Amazingly, Marcum has found 22 superb pastiches . . . This is more catnip for fans of stories faithful to Conan Doyle's original*

Part XIV: *. . . this standout anthology of 21 short stories written in the spirit of Conan Doyle's originals.*

Part XV: *Stories pitting Sherlock Holmes against seemingly supernatural phenomena highlight Marcum's 15th anthology of superior short pastiches.*

Part XVI: *Marcum has once again done fans of Conan Doyle's originals a service.*

Part XVII: *This is yet another impressive array of new but traditional Holmes stories.*

Part XVIII: *Sherlockians will again be grateful to Marcum and MX for high-quality new Holmes tales.*

Part XIX: *Inventive plots and intriguing explorations of aspects of Dr. Watson's life and beliefs lift the 24 pastiches in Marcum's impressive 19th Sherlock Holmes anthology*

Part XX: *Marcum's reserve of high-quality new Holmes exploits seems endless.*

Part XXI: *This is another must-have for Sherlockians.*

Part XXII: *Marcum's superlative 22nd Sherlock Holmes pastiche anthology features 21 short stories that successfully emulate the spirit of Conan Doyle's originals while expanding on the canon's tantalizing references to mysteries Dr. Watson never got around to chronicling.*

Part XXIII: *Marcum's well of talented authors able to mimic the feel of The Canon seems bottomless.*

Part XXIV: *Marcum's expertise at selecting high-quality pastiches remains impressive.*

Part XXVIII: *All entries adhere to the spirit, language, and characterizations of Conan Doyle's originals, evincing the deep pool of talent Marcum has access to. Against the odds, this series remains strong, hundreds of stories in.*

Part XXXI: *. . . yet another stellar anthology of 21 short pastiches that effectively mimic the originals . . . Marcum's diligent searches for high-quality stories has again paid off for Sherlockians.*

The MX Book of New Sherlock Holmes Stories
Edited by David Marcum
(MX Publishing, 2015-)

483